The RAIN CROW

The RAIN CROW

Sometimes spies wear crinolines.

Julie Weathers

Heart Ally Books, LLC
Camano Island, Washington

The Rain Crow

Cover design: Deranged Doctor Designs

Published by:

Heart Ally Books, LLC
heartallybooks.com
26910 92nd Ave NW C5-406
Stanwood, WA 98292

Published on Camano Island, WA, USA

ISBN-13: 978-1-63107-075-4 (paperback)

ISBN-13: 978-1-63107-076-1 (epub)

LCCN: 2025926760

10 9 8 7 6 5 4 3 2 1

Dedication

I've thought about this a lot but now that the time has come, I have no witty comment to make here. They say that children step on your toes when they are young and your heart when they are older and I believe that to be true.

My two older boys, Brandon and Cody, competed in rodeo and I came to know a lot of emergency staff well. I breathed a heartfelt prayer when the youngest, Will, wasn't interested in rodeo. At last, one I didn't need to worry about all the time. He joined the National Guard and went to Iraq straight out of high school.

I cherish their grit and humor. They are my reason for living and a blessing untold.

Thank you, boys. This book is for you.

Love,
Mom

Chapter One

Mother's rapier elbow jabbed me in the ribs so sharply my breath caught. "Lorena Dobbs McKenzie," she snapped, "stop glaring at that girl right now and act pretty."

At that moment, "that girl"—my nemesis—swiveled her perfectly coiffed head and flashed that cloying smile with her wide white teeth that always reminded me of freshly limed planks, while her claws tightened possessively on Joseph Sullivan's arm. Mother caught the exchange and huffed like a small dragon. "You rise up, young lady. You're a McKenzie, and this is our night."

Our night.

How could I? That scheming Jezebel, with her crooked nose and braying laugh, had stolen my happiness—my everything. If she were beautiful, I could understand it, but she was anything but.

Mother had kept me busy all day festooning the hall with pine boughs and small floral bouquets or bunches of grapes tied with colorful ribbons at the apexes. While it was a customary decoration, I didn't usually spend the entire day gathering pines, flowers, and scuppernongs for it. "You're not going to sit in your room mooning about that boy when there is work to be done," she fumed when I complained. "Your eyes will be swollen shut from crying, and I won't have you looking less than perfect tonight, young lady. Bear up. You're a McKenzie," she repeated, "not some wilting violet."

I rallied before she could assault my ribs again, glanced at the offending pair, and then pulled my shoulders back, like a dragoon marching to war. Mother was right. This was our night, and I wouldn't let that weasel Joseph Sullivan ruin it. Nor his harpy.

The Pines Fall Production Horse Sale was one of the premier events in Charleston, South Carolina, every year, with a grand ball preceding the sale. Everyone who was anyone attended the ball the night before, socialites anticipating it as much as horse enthusiasts did the sale. Even more so than the ball, our annual fall sale was an elite event, and we limited the sale to a total of 150 horses to keep quality high. With catalogues in hand, two men from New York and some from Georgia—trusted breeders and sellers we had invited to consign—gathered, earnestly discussing pedigrees, prospective purchases, and prices. Distressed dance partners would soon drag them away, but they would drift back together like iron filings to a magnet. People valued fine horses, but balls were as common as dust.

Though I was only sixteen, I had helped with the horses and our breeding program for as long as I could remember. Papa and I studied bloodlines like treasure maps for perfect crosses to result in horses with the ideal conformation, speed, stamina, and temperament, and we were largely successful in our breeding theories. It was a great source of pride for my father that my ability to remember things in complete detail after one reading meant I could reel off any pedigree in perfect order.

While Papa and I studied horses thoroughly, Mother studied bank accounts, properties, and family histories equally minutely. Looks, personalities, and the occasional blackguard were minor attributes to her. Money and social standing excused a considerable many shortcomings.

My mother believed that memorizing horse pedigrees was a waste of intelligence, when I should have been concentrating on assisting her in preparing her annual presale party. She insisted on making the ball the season's social highlight. Not only was it a grand party, but it also provided her with the chance to introduce me to the most eligible young men in the South. If I would not marry well in the North, and my father assured her I wouldn't, I would marry the best in the South. Not while he drew breath would he permit a Yankee to claim my hand, he declared in one such debate. She replied she might arrange that if he didn't see reason, swore she wasn't speaking to him, and stormed off to her room to sulk. He danced on the veranda later and shouted up toward her window, "Ye speakin' tae me yet, then?"

Whiskey may have been involved.

Tonight, she wore a bespoke aubergine gown with an extravagant amethyst and pearl necklace adorning her enviable bosom. Two maids and substantial lacing in her corset helped her draw in her naturally small waist, slender even after six pregnancies. Aunt Gertie, whose first words upon arrival were a reprimand about freckles and an order to fetch lemon juice, had brought me a gown from Washington, as I was expected to follow in Mother's wake as one of Charleston's social queens and fashion icons.

"Fresh from Paris," she said, pulling it from the box. "That emerald color is the perfect complement to your complexion. And who doesn't look beautiful in satin? I already had it altered. Let's hope you haven't grown much."

I looked at Mother, who scrutinized every detail. The corsage had dropped, puffed sleeves and was rounded at the waist to mimic the intertwining serpentine bands of the same fabric that bordered the skirt hem. "I love it," I said, hoping Mother would approve.

"I do, too," she said, and they promptly plotted how to dress my hair to make me so gorgeous Joseph would regret the foul betrayal of sending me a message the week before, saying he would be taking someone else to the ball.

"She's the image of her father," Mother pronounced almost as an indictment.

"She has your lovely storm-gray eyes," Gertie offered.

"But everything else about her is pure Kieran. She even has that choirboy-gone-rogue look half the time. I think it's that crooked smile."

Guilty. I vowed to work on that, as rogue choirboy looks were not in fashion for young ladies.

"*His* oval face, arched brows—"

Gertie peered at me. "Her face is round, don't you think?"

"No, oval. Definitely oval. That generous mouth and turned-up nose. Kieran's. Red hair."

"Yes, red hair," Gertie agreed.

"Chestnut, I think," I interjected, uncomfortable with this odd dissection of my looks.

Papa made the mistake of coming by as they were curling, conversing, and debating my hair color, so he was asked.

He gauged me momentarily, as if sizing up a new acquisition, and shrugged. "Blood bay. Aye, definitely blood bay."

Mother gasped. "Did you just compare our daughter to a horse? Get out!"

He always knew exactly the right thing to say to get banished from a conversation he had no interest in.

I took the opportunity to escape, but my maid Annie found me moping in my room and bustled about finishing my hair and getting me dressed. I put my foot down when she tried cinching me in as they had Mother. We were setting an unusually fine array of food for the ball, and I intended to indulge. If Joseph were not to be mine, the food would be. I would eat, force a smile, make the obligatory rounds, and be charming, then disappear as quickly as possible. I had no intention of watching someone toss her false golden curls hither and thither as she beamed at Joseph and smirked at me.

After the grand march that night, Mother came to me, laid a lace-gloved hand on my arm, and nodded across the room. "Lorena, do you see that young man over there with the lady in the blue plaid gown? His family goes back to Plymouth. Revolutionary War heroes. Five bankers, two senators, and one governor in the family tree. Plus, that boy's father is one of the wealthiest planters in North Carolina. You could do far worse."

I peered to where she indicated. "The dark-headed boy picking his nose?"

"Yes, well, they grow out of that. Usually."

I quickly dismissed him as well as Mother's next conversation. I could not tolerate hours of incessant plotting and matchmaking tonight and began looking for a convenient place to swoon. Papa might send me away to fetch horse papers he didn't need, and I wouldn't return. Looking around, I spied him standing near the entrance with Mr. Callahan, an old friend and frequent buyer from Virginia. Next to Mr. Callahan was a striking young man in a gray Virginia Military Institute uniform with three rows of brass buttons marching up his chest. My breath caught at the sheer beauty of him, if a man might be called such. With his long legs, he was taller than Papa by far, but then Papa was short and stocky, broad-shouldered and built to fight men and life. The young cadet had gleaming hair the color of deep, rich honey, oddly marbled with darker streaks. His trim sideburns, however, were auburn. He smiled, visited easily with the men around him, and laughed often. His uniform tunic stretched tightly across a broad chest, and a golden sash cinched in his trim waist. I exhaled pure admiration and, for a moment, forgot I was hurt and mad and…well, anything.

Mother nudged me. "For pity's sake, Lorena. Stop staring. There's no future in a military man. Look at poor Mary. Colonel Lee is never at Arlington when she needs him."

Papa glanced at us, caught me watching, and winked. Then he strolled over to us with Mr. Callahan and the young cadet. He handed Mother one of the bouquets he'd purloined from the evergreen swags and kissed her fondly on the cheek.

Papa stepped aside and introduced the young man, who was Mr. Callahan's nephew. To my surprise, Cadet Baron Patrick Callahan bowed deeply, took my hand, and kissed it but did not release it immediately. Looking into my eyes as if he were plumbing my soul, and maybe he was, he smiled. "I'm pleased to meet you, Miss McKenzie. I understand I'm to be your escort for the evening," there was a pause, "and perhaps forever."

I returned the smile, looking into eyes so blue they could pierce your spine and unmoor your heart with surgical precision. Mine was certainly unleashed.

My astonished mother gaped between me, Cadet Callahan, and my father, who simply sipped his whiskey. Finally, she blurted out, "Kieran! This young man has just claimed our daughter!"

"Aye," he said, "I recognize the look."

She threw her hands into the air in exasperation. "Aren't you going to do something?"

He judged the two of us, but I was too busy trying to still my heart fluttering about like a tethered moth to pay much attention to either of my parents, nor care that Mother's matchmaking efforts were being razed and salted as completely as Troy. "What would ye like me do, Bert? Give him permission or challenge him a duel?"

"For pity's sake. Are you drunk?" Luckily, Mother wasn't in the habit of carrying deadly weapons, or she might have dispatched him then and there.

"Not just yet, me dear."

Several people around us turned to stare at Mother's outburst and watched her storm away, shimmering purple silk swaying in her wake. I was accustomed to them and paid her little mind.

"Would you care to dance?" Cadet Callahan asked nonchalantly.

"My first dance always goes to my father," I replied regretfully. "Perhaps another?"

"Mr. Callahan, would ye mind terribly?" Papa replied. "I should go settle me wife's ruffled feathers."

If Papa spent all his time soothing Mother's ruffled feathers, she would have none left to soothe, and he would never get anything done, but I let the lie pass. Papa winked at me and leaned over to whisper. "I told ye, I'd find someone tae dry those salt tears."

"If I may," Callahan said, offering a charming smile and bow.

"I believe I would," I said, and held up my hand. His fingers closed around mine and he led me to the floor for a lively schottische. It was with some regret he surrendered me to my next dance partner, but not before he requested my dance card.

"People will talk if I dance with you a second time," I said, handing him the card and pencil.

He glanced over it and signed his name. "Do you care if people talk?"

I had seen some of the looks he was getting. People were going to be talking anyway. "Not in the least."

He handed the card back to me. "Excellent."

During intermission, young Callahan swooped in and handed me a bouquet that was actually two twined together. He took me to the refreshment tables, insisting I try this delicacy or that and loaded my plate as if I had never seen any of this food. Mother was aghast when she saw the plate. "Surely you aren't going to eat all that!"

"She's merely holding it for me, Mrs. McKenzie," Callahan answered. We escaped, giggling, to a bench in the garden to enjoy our feast and visit.

He asked me about my hobbies, and I listed the musical instruments I played. He was delighted.

"My mother plays piano and guitar," he said. "Well, everyone plays something, really. When my grandmother and her four sisters get together, it's a lively little band."

"Five sisters. That must be amazing. I always wanted a large family."

"Yes," he replied, fondness washing over his features. "They're the oldest and the toughest, I think. I don't tell their brothers that, but they probably know. I think you'd like the Callahan crew." He smiled at me again, his dimples deepening.

I nibbled on another champagne cracker, considering this. A faint blush warmed my cheeks, I was sure. He was already imagining me meeting his family, and I didn't mind.

He glanced toward the dance floor, where the band was returning. "And, in case your mother spirits you away before I can say good night—" he pulled a knife from his pocket.

"What are you doing?" I asked, alarmed.

"Giving you something to remember me by."

"You already gave me these flowers," I protested.

"Flowers are fleeting."

With a swift motion, he cut a brass button from his uniform and placed it in my hand.

"You shouldn't have cut it from the chest where everyone will notice."

"It was the one over my heart," he said, taking my hand. "I believe the next waltz is mine?"

I stared at the bare spot on his chest. His heart may have been bared, but mine was pierced—and tumbling.

Toward the end of the ball, the young man pledged for the German Waltz came up to me with Cadet Callahan in tow. He apologized profusely and said he wasn't feeling very well. Would I mind terribly if his new friend danced with me? I hoped he felt better soon and accepted, even though I had already danced twice with Callahan. Once was Papa's dance, and once was Cadet Callahan's properly, but I had noticed people whispering about me dancing with the same boy again.

Three times would be a true scandal.

Joseph glared my way and started over, but she of the donkey bray laugh jerked him back with a vulture grip. I tried to think of what I had ever liked about Joseph.

His horse, I think.

During the dance, Callahan confessed George wasn't sick. He had bribed him to give up the dance. Not that I was unhappy to be dancing with the young cadet again, but I was a bit galled that George had passed me off so willingly.

"Believe me, there was no willingness at all," Callahan assured me. "The hardest part of the adventure was finding anyone disposed to forfeit a dance with you. You had saved the first dance for your father, which he gave to me, but I glanced at the other names when I penciled in my name for a later dance. Then I set about doing some horse-trading to get someone to give up a dance. This was the result of three trades, Miss McKenzie."

I was even more impressed. "Are you always so bold?"

"Venus favors the bold."

Indeed, she does . . . and so did I.

That night, I wrote in my journal that it was the best day of my life and that I would not marry the dark-haired boy, even if he stopped picking his nose. I did not mention who I hoped to marry, as that could bring misfortune, but before I went to bed I woke Annie up to make a wish with me.

"What wish?" she asked groggily, rubbing her eyes with delicate brown hands.

"I can't tell you; just spit in your hand and take mine."

We spit in our hands, and I dropped the brass button Baron had cut from his tunic into my palm. With wet palms clasped firmly over it to bind it, I made my wish, thanked Annie, and went back to my room, where I added the button to my wish box.

Chapter Two

Two years later, I was the hostess of the McKenzie Sale and Ball since Papa had finally returned Mother to her natural nesting grounds, as he called Baltimore, with a generous divorce settlement. I didn't mind that, but it annoyed me that she had abandoned his name that afforded her largess. Everyone complimented me profusely on the décor, though it was the same as every other year.

The previous year, Baron had successfully secured leave to attend the ball and sale, bringing along his highly popular academy friends. I had saved each stolen bouquet he gave me and made a potpourri from the dried petals. In a separate bowl were petals from other flowers he gave me when I attended dances at the Institute, or he simply visited when he could, as I had taken up residence at our Rosemount farm in Virginia in recent years and started a boarding school for young ladies there, making it easier for us to visit. We had written enough letters to fell a small forest, worn out boxes of horseshoes riding to visit each other, and still it was never enough. Whether it was a dance, a picnic, a peaceful stroll, a drama, a Sunday meal, a card game, or a journey across the countryside, it remained insufficient. We didn't require elaborate entertainment when we were together.

He sat for a portrait before he left for Texas, but oh, how I wished he were home to hold me again and stroll innocently behind the lilacs to steal a kiss…or ten. His letters always stirred my heart but never eased my longing to be with him. Even now when I closed my eyes, I could smell him; my fingers traced along his arms, his chest. In my mind, I felt his breath on my neck. My eyes fluttered open again, and a sigh so heavy escaped that the couple strolling by looked askance at me.

Enough mooning. I lowered my head and waved my fan lazily to hide my feelings until I could regain the rudder of my emotional wreck of a life.

This year, I was deluged with offerings of bouquets and bunches of grapes since Baron could not attend due to duty chasing Comanche in the wilds of west Texas. There was no formal agreement between us, as Baron wanted to wait until he was promoted, but the understanding was there. Papa didn't care about rank. Baron had become a devoted son to him. It didn't stop other men from hoping his absence gave them an opening, however. Being the hostess, I tried to be gracious without offering encouragement, but it was a difficult line to walk. The latest gift lay in my lap, where I fingered the pale pink ribbons trailing from the stems. It would not be joining any saved bouquets and potpourris later.

Since I was a little girl, I had always reserved my first dance for Papa, but Mr. Callahan persuaded me to give him Papa's dance this year, along with possibly his missing nephew's dance later. I would have left my dance card empty to remain at Papa's side, but he insisted I enjoy the ball and do my duty.

It was nigh impossible even to pretend to enjoy the ball, considering the circumstances, but I was a McKenzie, and people depended on me. Normally, Papa was fit as a butcher's dog. Tonight, he was positively phthisic. The glass in his shaking hand trembled so I feared he would soon be awash in whiskey. His pale face, drawn and slicked with sweat, only accentuated the dark circles under his eyes.

When I wasn't accepting bouquets from hopeful young men, people offered me condolences over the divorce as if one of my parents had died, and in the next breath, Widow This or That assured me they were there if ever I or Papa needed anything, anything at all; they were there for us. Papa was still handsome but, most of all, propertied and, therefore, a catch. Divorce was the greatest of scandals, but they could overlook that fact since Mother was a Yankee and probably a Lincolnite.

Many an offer was made to bring out chicken soup or some salve or another to help with Papa's cold.

"Kieran doesn't look good at all," Mr. Callahan said after our second dance. He wasn't wrong; Papa was fading and listed severely against a marble column at the ballroom entrance. Not all of it from the whiskey, I feared.

"We had a pen of yearlings break out of their pasture in that storm a few nights ago, and he insisted on going to help find them," I replied. "His mare, Dorcha, took the bit as she does and was flying when she stepped wrong and broke her leg. Papa sat with her in the deluge, holding her for half the night before he finally put her down and then walked home. He's got a terrible cold. The doctor advised him to remain in bed, but he was determined to attend the ball and sale."

Mr. Callahan was a horseman; he understood why Papa had done what he did but still shook his head. "I'll ask him to show me some horse papers to get him out of here and pour him in bed."

I whispered a prayer of gratitude. "Thank you. He keeps refusing my efforts to get him to leave. I think he feels he needs to support me."

"I'll fix him a hot toddy. Whiskey, lemon, and honey. That will break that cough."

"I think he's got the whiskey part taken care of. We just need to get the lemon and honey down him."

"Don't worry, girl, I have you." He hugged me tightly and headed toward Papa with a hearty greeting. Wrapping his arm around Papa's shoulders, he herded him out of the ballroom.

❧

Against my better judgment, I wired Mother and Gertie and told them Papa was sick. Mother responded she would come as soon as she could, but she had garden club business to deal with first. Gertie replied, "I'm on my way."

Baron was still chasing Indians, but they promised to get word to him as soon as he returned to civilization. I heard Mother's voice in my head mocking me, "For pity's sake, Lorena. Stop staring. There's no future in a military man. Look at poor Mary. Colonel Lee is never at Arlington when she needs him." Oddly enough, Baron was in west Texas with Colonel Lee at that moment. I wondered if Mary needed him also and set the frustration aside. I had to shore up for Papa's sake.

Pneumonia, the doctor said.

I'd been by his side for much of the three-day sale, and afterwards, when Hope turned her cheery face away. I barely took time to wash and change clothes and ate only when Della forced me to choke something down. I would have lived on tea had she not been such a harpy.

"Yes, Papa. The sale went well. Prices were up this year." I smiled faintly at him, though my heart shredded with the effort. He asked the same thing each time he roused.

"Aye, were they then?" He settled back in his sweat-soaked pillows, staring at the ceiling as if trying to remember. His dewed brow furrowed. "And Dorcha? How is she?"

"Rest now. You need to save your strength. I'll get you some fresh pillows."

Each time he settled, I offered a prayer of thanks and felt the tension flood away. I wiped his face again with cooled cloths. Then I'd change his soaked bedclothes and wash his body with vinegar to relieve the furnace raging within. Had it been winter, I would have tossed him into the nearest snowbank. Just one more day, I told myself, and the fever would break. He would cross that hill.

In between the ravings and the troubled sleep, he awakened and gazed at me. He squeezed my hand weakly and told me over and over how much he loved me. Then he talked to my dead brother James, and I wept. He was shuffling across the veil between life and death, but I wasn't ready to let him go.

Gertie arrived and rushed upstairs without stopping to catch her breath or brush the train soot from her clothes.

"Now you listen here right now, Kieran McKenzie. You promised me a drink of that damned whiskey you were bragging about." She leaned over and kissed him. "Besides," she said softly, "you never finished telling me the story about the time Poe drank brandy with you and told you of that letter he wrote to Dickens."

His eyes fluttered, and he smiled at her. "Me darlin' Gertie."

"Yes. Now you quit lying around. You also owe me a dance." She kissed him and held him close, but tears flowed down her cheeks.

We stayed with him all that day and the next. He spent more and more of his time with James. His breath labored so, it hurt me to watch him struggle, but I couldn't release him. Miracles happen, and I was holding for one though Hope had nearly forsaken me.

I wanted to send Father Bellini away, but I could not in good conscience, and I allowed him to administer last rites. He stayed with us those final hours and continued to pray and offer what comfort he could. I nodded but could not answer. Papa was my rock and my heart. Then, the priest asked us to tell stories about Papa, trying to take our mind off what was surely coming as Hope slipped quietly away.

Gertie continued to remind Papa of unfulfilled promises. I begged him to live and told him I couldn't go on without him. Then I reminded him of the stories he had promised to tell my children. When I ran out of ideas to lure him back from the brink, I asked him which stallion I should breed Maddie to next year. I cried a million useless tears and then chastised myself for being weak when I was telling him to be strong. When my pleadings to him fell on deaf ears, I dropped to my knees and beseeched God. I bargained with Him. I begged Him. I quoted the Bible's promises of miracles and healing to Him.

Those pleadings also fell on deaf ears.

In the end, I told Him I hated Him.

Chapter Three

I was still at his side, holding his hand and sobbing uncontrollably when Gertie gently drew me up. "Come, child, let's get some tea and decide what must be done first."

Father Bellini had departed to prepare the way for what must come. He begged me to bury Papa in the church cemetery, but I declined. We would hold his mass and service there, but the Rite of Committal would be at The Pines with his babies.

Della had the tea kettle on, cups set out, and lengths of crepe on the table tied into bows. Everyone in the kitchen was sniffling and wiping noses. She put her hands on slim hips with authority and shooed two of the girls out, who kept wailing in sorrow. "Out with that caterwauling. Miss Lorena don't need that now."

I didn't, but how I wished I could howl and caterwaul myself. I would have wailed to the moon like a forlorn wolf without apology if not for the many things waiting to be done, and I had only a vague clue where to start.

Gertie set a cup of chamomile tea before me. "Della boiled sugar water that should be cool now. The girls cut crepe for bows and gathered flowers for the bees. Do you want me to go tell them your father is gone?"

I looked up as if waking from a daze. "No, that's my job. The clocks have been stopped and mirrors covered?"

She looked to Della, who pointed to the clock on the wall stopped at 3:17. The family portrait that hung in the hallway had already been turned to face the wall. "Let me drink this tea, then I'll go visit the bees." Then looking at the covered mirror, it occurred to me. "I'm surprised we had any crepe."

"Bad luck to keep any from deaths, but I always keep a bit for emergencies," Della said. I should have known she would have taken care of all these things. She was the heart of the McKenzie house.

Gertie reached over to hold my hand, rubbing it softly with her thumb. "I'm so sorry, darling. We all loved him. Someone's already been sent to town for fresh crepe."

I sniffled and nodded, tried to respond, but the words crawled up my throat, wadded into a ball, and threatened to choke me. I could barely swallow past them. Unable to bear more sympathetic looks, I gathered up the basket with the bee supplies and put on a bonnet.

Normally, I looked forward to tarrying in the bee grove, but I trudged out there today with heavy feet and a heavier heart. Once there, I set out a saucer on the first hive and filled it with sugar water, set out one of the small flower bouquets, and put a black crepe bow on the hive. Then I stepped behind it, knocked softly three times, and inhaled deeply.

"Dear little bees," I said, choking out the words. "Your master is dead, but please don't go. I'm your new mistress in weal and woe." This I repeated until all the bees had been informed. With my task done, I sat down on the bench beneath the great pine tree towering over the bee grove. He arranged the hives in a semicircle around the grove so they could get sunlight in the morning and shade in the afternoon. The log gum hives made from hollowed logs with tops on them had gradually been replaced with Langstroth box hives with their movable frames inside until only two log hives remained for sentimental reasons. He had planned on replacing those two relics also, as harvesting them upset the bees too much. Papa always worried about their happiness. He was convinced they were God's little messengers. What message did they bear today, I wondered.

Papa used to bring me out here to talk to the bees and tell them stories. Sometimes he'd bring his concertina and play for them. Sometimes we'd simply enjoy the bees and butterflies. At times I think he enjoyed this place particularly because Mother avoided it like the depths of hell for fear of the bees.

I hadn't realized it before, but my attire had gradually darkened until the deep charcoal dress I wore today was almost a once-black faded to dingy nothingness. I also felt faded to nothing. My pale hands resting in my lap seemed even paler, almost deathlike. A tear fell. "Oh, my dear bees. What a bitter bale I have visited upon you. Forgive me this dread duty." As pleasant as the bee grove was, I could not remain with them and rose to leave. I was the mistress now.

Word spread quickly through the farm of Papa's passing, and bits of black already fluttered from doors. Keening cries echoed across The Pines as if the farm itself was mired in heartrending grief. I set the bee basket on the veranda and trudged in with scattered thoughts of what needed to be done. My bonnet dropped from my fingers. My mouth dropped open. My heart dropped to the very pits of my stomach. There on the table lay Papa with a towel across his loins and Gertie gently combing his freshly washed hair. I knew this because I smelled the bay rum shampoo he used.

"Lorena," Gertie said, looking up in surprise as she readjusted the towel. "I'm sorry. We didn't expect you back so soon. I thought we'd be finished before you returned. We just need to shave him and trim his nails. We'll finish dressing him as soon as you choose a suit." Della looked up from scooping freshly shorn hair from the table and went over to toss it in the fire. Never leave hair or nail clippings around for others to do mischief, she always warned, but I would gather a lock of his hair for my locket.

I was still clutching the doorjamb to keep from collapsing. "I'll shave him. I did it when he broke his arm."

"There's no need for you to do that, girl," Della said. "No sense both of us upsetting him. He hated getting his hair cut out of the new moon."

"I want to, and I'm sure he won't mind. He'd want to be dressed in his brown tweed suit."

I lathered his soap and stropped the razor, then stretched his cheek with trembling fingers and wept afresh. The beard and mustache I would trim neatly with scissors. I had to stop several times because my eyes were so blurred, but I declined the offered help.

Though I'd wiped my hands after applying pomade to him, I still smelled the bergamot cloud about me as I came down the stairs with his funerary clothes. My mind must have wandered because I hadn't heard a carriage drive up. I had just reached the landing when Mother burst through the doors in a flurry of feathers and fuss. She kissed me on the cheek and looked around. "Well, what has your father got himself into now? Kieran! Where are you?"

I stared at her, aghast. "Mother, what are you doing?"

The driver stood behind her, burdened with baggage that crashed to the ground. His mouth and eyes were agape with shock.

"Do be careful," Mother snapped.

I pulled money from the drawer in the hallway and paid the driver. "Is that all her bags?"

"No, ma'am. Two more. I'll get them."

The driver, who undoubtedly knew Papa was dead as word would have spread like wildfire, apologized, thanked me profusely, and fled.

"Why didn't you have someone in town to meet me?" Mother demanded. "And what is all that infernal hammering?"

"I didn't know you were coming," I said. "I got a telegram that you were busy with the garden club and would come later."

"I sent another telegram. Have you not been into town to fetch mail?" She was pulling pins out of her hat and looking around the house at the gathering servants streaming in to gawk at her. Gertie stood at the end of the hall, glaring death and destruction her way.

"We've been rather busy, Mother," I replied and turned away before I broke down again.

"What did your father do?"

Gertie took the clothes from me and put her arm around me. "He died, Bertha. That hammering is the men opening the death's door to take him out. Please do sit down in the withdrawing room and hush."

I left, unable to deal with anything larger than a mosquito, and retired for the night.

Chapter Four

Sean Finnegan approached me the next morning about holding a wake. Despite my misgivings, I knew Papa's friends would expect it, as he had attended every wake held for every friend at Finnegan's Harp and Fiddle, his favorite watering hole. They lost Paddy O'Malley's body last year while taking him on a last tour during the wake. His body was found the next morning in front of the newspaper office, much to Mrs. O'Malley's horror.

I agreed but said they'd have to make do with a painting of Papa, and I expected it to return in good condition.

"Why in heaven's name would you agree to those hooligans?" Mother protested.

"Because Papa was the head hooligan," I replied peevishly. I wouldn't have said that in public as I was already concerned about his reputation, but she couldn't even be bothered to arrive before he died, and now she was trying to dictate his arrangements?

Gertie had united with Father Bellini and the funeral home to pave the way for me in most of the arrangements. All I had to do was choose this or that. The funeral home sent out samplings of funeral biscuits and wrappers. We sampled them all and chose our favorite, and after minor alterations, the wrapper was approved. When it became clear he would not survive, Gertie, bless her, had already written the obituary and handed it to me for inspection at breakfast. After making a few minor adjustments, we sent the obituary to the newspaper, approved the funeral invitations, and compiled a list of formal invitees, though it was a public funeral and mass. The committal rites at The Pines would be for McKenzie people.

The house was appropriately swaddled in crepe. Mother deployed to town to shop for dresses as I didn't care whether I wore bombazine or sackcloth. After a successful campaign, Mother returned with dresses, hats, veils, jet jewelry, and various other items. I was surprised there was room for her in the carriage.

"Are you ready?" Gertie asked.

I nodded. I was worn thin as Pilate's patience after sitting with Papa and welcomed the suggestion we lodge in town after the mass; the funeral would be held the next day, and then the committal rites and interment at The Pines. Thankfully, Father Bellini didn't draw attention to where we sat secluded during mass. I could not deal with well-meaning but unwelcome throngs of carrion birds descending upon us.

Mother and Gertie dressed my hair the next day after I fumbled and stopped, stared at the mirror, forgot what I was doing, and then broke out in hopeless tears once more. Mother handed me a linen handkerchief so indelicate it might have been wagon tarping that I had embroidered with my monogram when I was first learning. I had forgotten that I still had it tucked away in my handkerchief drawer, and I was a bit perturbed to find Mother rummaging through my things. The coarse cloth was the only thing that withstood my merciless needle mauling. "Really, Mother?"

"That elegant silk handkerchief in your bag will be sodden before you alight from the carriage. Just take it. No one is going to count your stitches."

I wasn't in the mood to argue with her and crammed it in my reticule.

They had offered us the small room off the main chapel where we had hidden during the mass, but I chose to sit in the front pew to spend as much time as possible with Papa. I sat down, thoroughly spent already, veils covering my tear-swollen face. Mother sat on one side, and Gertie on the other, propping me up. I blew my nose again, not caring that it was unladylike, and tore my gaze from the casket and focused on the knots of flowers mounded about the church. Then, I leaned closer and stared in amazement at a dollhouse nestled between two bouquets. There was another. And a train set. An entire toy store was arranged along the altar. Though I had given permission for Sean and the Harp and Fiddle crew to hold a wake, I hadn't intended the formal service to be turned into a joke. I had specifically asked Father Bellini to please make people think of Papa as something besides that crazy Irishman. Gertie saw what I was looking at and grabbed my arm before I stood. "Calm, Lorena. I'm sure there's a reason."

"Lorena, sit!" Mother ordered.

Father Bellini touted Papa's success as a businessman, discussed our wonderful horses, and even how he sat with Dorcha. There were a few sniffles at that. He held up a carved wooden horse with a real mane and tail and a twin to the one my little brother James had. "You may have noticed some toys, train sets, chess sets, toy soldiers, a well-worn velvet tiger, and dollhouses—oh, the dollhouses," he said. "Every year the orphanage promised the best boy and girl a special gift for Christmas. Each year, the girls requested the same thing, these wonderful dollhouses. The boys wanted various treasures."

I looked closer at one of the dollhouses. It was almost identical to mine.

"During my visit with the McKenzies to gather information about Kieran's life, I discovered that they were unaware of his whereabouts every Christmas Eve. They thought he was going to party with his friends at the Harp and Fiddle."

There was a small cheer at the back of the church.

"He visited the orphanage to assist in organizing a celebration for the children and staff. Many of the toys were handmade by McKenzie people, including these wonderful dollhouses and horses. He brought in stockings, sweaters, mittens, new shoes, and small treats such as fruit, nuts, and candies. His friends at the Harp and Fiddle, along with many other businesses and planters, generously donated more clothes. Even as the number of orphans grew to hundreds, he never faltered." Another small cheer and clapping from others now. I'd never heard applause at a funeral before, but this was Kieran McKenzie's final goodbye. "This was important to him that every child be remembered and have warm clothes," the priest continued, "because he grew up without family, too."

I never knew about the orphan parties. He always had a soft spot for the lost and forgotten things of the world and would drag them home even when I knew we were on precarious financial footing, though my parents always tried to hide such things from us.

"Miss McKenzie was concerned that people would only recall his eccentricities, but he was so much more." Father Bellini looked at me then. "Kieran Aiden McKenzie was not a saint. He knew his faults."

I remembered Papa telling me he always took a flask of whiskey with him to confession and offered the priest a drink to prepare himself. "Right, then. Ye bring a sack lunch?" Then he'd readily confess he beat this fellow or that fellow, but they deserved it, didn't they?

"Kieran was a good man," he continued. "He came up hard. At the age of five, he was sent to live with his aunt in New York, and after his aunt's widowhood, he was sold into indenture, which deepened his understanding of hardship. He ran away at age eight when his master nearly whipped him to death for something he didn't do. He crawled away and vowed to come back and kill the man. Then one day a man found him shivering, covered in rags and newspapers, nearly dead from starvation, cold, and fever. 'Bless my soul,' he said. 'Someone threw away a perfectly good newspaper here and a little boy to boot. Now who would go and do such a thing?'

"Kieran learned forgiveness through the kindness of a man who took him in and taught him what he needed to succeed. Oh, what a success he was!

"For all that he accomplished, he always felt the greatest pride in his daughter, Lorena Dobbs McKenzie. She may feel his mortal loss here, but think how overjoyed he is to see James and those babies who went before him. How he must be rejoicing to see the face of God."

I had heard that so many times in the past few days I wanted to scream. He was no longer in pain. He would never know the pain of growing old. He was with James and his babies. How happy he must be! My fists balled up in fury as Father Bellini droned on about how fortunate Papa was. I didn't want him looking at the face of God. I wanted him holding me.

At some point I realized he had stopped talking and we were supposed to stand and sing. Mother nudged my elbow and whispered, horrified, "My stars, Lorena. What have you done?"

She was staring at my lap, where a nest of white shreds lay, the remnants of my handkerchief. I had torn it to bits until the only thing that remained was the LDM of the monogram. My breath hitched. That's exactly what I was, adrift in the shreds of my life. All my mooring was torn asunder, and I was left totally alone.

She scooped the scraps off the Parramatta skirt and into her reticule before anyone noticed I had gone mad.

I mouthed the words of the familiar songs and allowed myself to be led away to stand in line, numbly thank people for attending, and pass out the funeral biscuits and little fruitcakes to the guests. Father Bellini, at last, swooped in and insisted we must go for the commitment rites, and the Ladies' Aide would finish. I would double whatever fee was normal.

With the formal service done, we loaded into carriages and followed the hearse back to the farm for the internment.

The McKenzie people were waiting in their Sunday finest to welcome Marse Mac back home. They had helped sit vigil with us. The Roby Brothers had insisted on making a casket of pine and live oak from The Pines, and it was as beautiful as anything in the catalogue Mr. Emmerson's Funeral Parlor had offered. In the McKenzie cemetery, so many bouquets waited that I wondered if any flowers were left on the farm.

After Father Bellini read the commitment, they filed by solemnly, many openly weeping, often saying final goodbyes or speaking to him, and brought gifts to place in the casket with him and tucked them in carefully as they passed.

Horrified at the grave offerings, Mother started to protest. I told her to hush. These were Papa's people.

"Lorena, this isn't dignified at all," Mother whispered angrily. "Put a stop to this now."

"I most certainly will not, nor will you," I replied so forcefully her lips drew into a censorious tight line but stopped moving. Della was one of the last to stop at the casket and leaned down to kiss his forehead and whispered something to him, then slipped something wrapped in a handkerchief in his pocket.

I placed his favorite book of poetry in last with a message to him inscribed on the fly page. I saw naught but a sea of grief surrounding me and tried to be strong for them, but I felt as if I were drifting further and further from shore and would soon be lost myself.

"What did you put in his pocket?" I asked Della.

"Some fried chicken. Your daddy loved my chicken."

I glanced over at Mother to see if she had heard. "Well, don't let Mother know. She'll be spitting and fuming."

Della looked at me indignantly. "Course not. That chicken Mr. Mac's. She can get her own."

I surveyed Papa's treasures. Hand-carved horses, pretty rocks, coins, fishing lures, flowers, some knitted socks, a riding crop, Dorcha's bridle, various things made of plaited horsehair, several notes. He was going into heaven a rich man indeed. I patted his cheek, leaned over and kissed him, and nodded for them to close the casket.

The next day, Mother insisted I come back to Baltimore with her and Gertie.

I refused, totally unprepared to spend another moment with her. Though she had been helpful during the arrangements, her overbearing ways were already creeping back in, and I needed to be away from her. "I'm going to make sure things are in order here, and then I need to check on the school and go to Richmond to talk to Papa's lawyers and the bankers, I suppose."

She waved a hand in dismissal. "I'll send my attorney to deal with those unsavory details. Come to Baltimore and relax."

"I need to see my girls, Mother."

"You're going to divide your time between The Pines and Rosemount in Virginia, and in your spare time take care of that boarding school with three dozen young ladies. What a remarkable young woman you are. If you had a man here you could depend on…" She looked under the pillows on the settee and in a chair. "Where is Mr. Callahan when you need him, by the way?"

I noticed that when Baron was out of favor, he became Mr. Callahan. He was often Mr. Callahan with her. "You know very well he's in Texas."

"Exactly. Remember the time Colonel Lee was off playing soldier somewhere and Mary almost died after that child was born? She telegraphed he must come home, and he responded he had duties. Then what happened?" She almost crowed this. "Colonel Lee had been so aghast at his wife's condition when he did return that he took a long leave of absence from the military. That's how it will go with you and Mr. Callahan. He'll never be here when you need him. Mark my words, Missy."

"Bert, this isn't the time to be harassing the girl," Aunt Gertie hugged me. "You know you're welcome to come visit when you're ready." Then, turning to Mother, "Ready your things. We need to go."

"I'll have Della pack some food to take with you that won't spoil," I said.

I returned from the kitchen with the basket to find two of the house servants dragging Papa's trunk down the steps. *Thunk. Thunk. Thunk.*

What are they doing? Even more important, why?

Gideon was barely holding on in the back while Jackson tried to lift the front end up with little success. In astonished silence I watched, wondering who or what would come tumbling down the steps first.

It was the trunk.

Gideon, who was older than sin and had no business trying to move anything heavier than a serving tray, let alone that heavy steamer trunk, lost his footing and plopped down, tearing Jackson's grip loose. The trunk careened down the marble stairs like a green leather sleigh hurtling down a steep, snowy hill. It slid across the floor until the crumpling rug proved too much for it. Jackson stood there on stork legs, hopping back and forth, eyes wide as windows and waving his arms about like a rooster. Had Mother picked the two oldest servants in the house because she thought they were the only ones insane enough to do what she told them?

"Gideon, are you all right? What on earth are you doing?" I should have known better than to ask. The empress stood near her pile of luggage, overseeing the operation. Mother had shifted into full overseer mode again.

"Miz Bertha said pack up your daddy's suits," Gideon said, hobbling down the stairs and rubbing his backside. My maids Annie and Rachel followed him, loaded with more suits.

I couldn't believe she was stealing his suits and him barely in the ground. "You can just pack them all right back up to his room. They're not leaving this house." The girls turned and scampered back up the stairs like squirrels.

"Now you see here, Lorena," Mother said in her best little-lady-you-better-listen-up voice and pointed to them. "You bring those suits right back down here."

I spun to face them as they danced in indecision. "You better not! I'm the mistress of The Pines now." It was bad enough Mother had left Papa; he was probably grateful, but if she didn't even want Papa's name, she didn't need his suits.

"Stop being such an ungrateful, miserly whelp," Mother snapped. "These suits can go to the Ladies' Aide there, where they will help poor, destitute men."

There was the guilt, but I was mostly immune after years of it. "No."

"Oh, dear heavens. Someone help me to the parlor." She whipped out her fan and waved it about as if directing an orchestra. Everyone looked at each other, unsure what to do, until Gideon stepped forward to hold her arm.

"Moses, Mary, and Joseph, Mother. Please don't faint on that frail old man. You'll break something." Not that I cared if *she* broke something in one of her performances, but I did care about Gideon. Once settled on the fainting couch, she drew in a heavy breath, as if it might be her last. I should be so lucky.

"Dear Lord," she began dramatically, "forgive me for bringing this selfish child into the world." Her arm flew into the air like Moses parting the sea. "Then he said to them, 'Watch out! Be on your guard against all kinds of greed; life does not consist in an abundance of possessions.' Luke 12:15."

"You only want Papa's suits so everyone will swoon over how generous you are to donate Beason and Switzers to the poor. He earned them in South Carolina, and here they shall stay."

"He coveteth greedily all the day long: but the righteous giveth and spareth not. Proverbs 21:26."

It was remarkable how she could call up biblical verses to suit on command, but we had been at this a long time. "And Baltimore, the glory of kingdoms, the beauty of the Baltimorian's excellency, shall be as when God overthrew Sodom and Gomorrah. Isaiah 13:19."

"That's Babylon, not Baltimore, Lorena. Stop being a heathen."

"I'm sorry. I always get them confused."

"I refuse to speak to you. Wallow in your greed. I'm going home."

After the door slammed and the hoofbeats faded, I stood in the great hall, alone for long minutes. "I'm the mistress of The Pines now," I whispered. Then I sank with my sundered soul into a forlorn puddle and wept.

Chapter Five

My hair was pinned up neatly off my neck as might befit a woman bound for execution. I wasn't. *Bankers can't kill me. They can only steal my property, though for a woman of the land, that would be as good as death.*

"I picked this growler out for you special," Darcy, the hotel stableman, had said when he helped me into the carriage at the hotel. "They're newly upholstered seats, and I know how you like that smell." He looked out for me, just as he carefully guarded my Charlemagne. Our bond had quickly formed over the horse.

He knew about my fondness for the smell because I'd planted my nose to a side of new leather in the stables yesterday. I sucked up every morsel of scent like most women draw in a heady bouquet of roses. A horsewoman appreciates the simple things in life: fresh hay, horse sweat, leather.

Horsewoman. But for how long?

I'd been able to forestall the Virginia bankers from foreclosing, but the South Carolina money counters wanted the successful, if indebted, horse farm and didn't care that I helped build it. I was a woman. Worse, I was young. Worst of all, I was single.

They knew almost before I did when my manager quit to join the newly formed Confederate army. It had taken everything my Richmond lawyers could do to convince them to grant me the upcoming appointment. I exhaled heavily thinking about it. Had I been a dragon, I'm sure it would have been pure fire.

Now, Lorena girl, don't get yer Irish up, my father's voice echoed in my mind. That admonition had normally been followed by him getting *his* Irish up to do my battles. He wasn't here, though, and this battle was mine. Clutching my crucifix with the one-armed Jesus, I bowed my head to pray yet again. Was God tired of hearing from me?

If God was speaking to me, I couldn't hear Him. There was simply the hollow clop clop clop of steady hoofbeats mingled with the jingling harness, carriage squeaks, and the signature growling of the steel-rimmed wheels on the cobblestone streets drowning out anything else. I gave up trying to pray and asked for a word of wisdom from Papa.

In me name shall they cast out devils.

I sighed. *Really, Papa? That's the best you can do?*

Since Papa offered no help, I stood on my standard prayer for protection. *For Thou, LORD, wilt bless the righteous; with favour wilt Thou compass him as with a shield.*

We at last lurched to a stop in front of the Union Bank. Would they change their name if this unpleasantness with the north continued? Darcy hopped down, setting the carriage into a gentle rock. My Richmond attorney had grilled me on the legal papers until I dreamed clauses and addenda. Papa's new Charleston attorney agreed to meet me at the bank in case I needed him. There was nothing else I could do. Sometimes you just have to fight the battle and see which way it goes.

The door swung open, flooding the interior with Charleston sunshine, which rivaled Darcy's smile in brilliance. "We're here, Miss McKenzie." I leaned out, putting my hands on his slim shoulders so he could clasp my elbows and guide me down.

Taking a deep breath, or at least as deep as my tightly cinched corset would allow, I prepared myself for the task ahead. My darling maid Annie was adamant a tiny waist was the key to success today. Although I wasn't normally concerned about a tiny waist, I did fear I might sag in the presence of the enemy and allowed her to have her way with the laces. We'd have words later if I fainted from lack of air.

"Don't fret so, Miss McKenzie. These are fine men."

Such praise for moneylenders. I tore my eyes away from the four massive Corinthian columns that graced the bank's entrance. "Do you think so? Papa always said bankers are the spawn of the devil."

"We're not allowed to speak ill of customers," he whispered conspiratorially, "but your Papa was right. Though *these* are the best devil spawns Charleston has to offer, *you're* a child of God." He nodded toward my crucifix and handed me the leather binder I'd placed by the door. "You'll be fine. Send a runner to the hotel and I'll be back to get you."

"Thank you, Darcy."

He leapt to the carriage seat, light as a sprite. His unruly shock of strawberry blond hair waving in the breeze made me think he'd recently turned from fiery *daoine maithe* to human for some puckish mission. Though he vowed he was twenty, he was smaller than me and looked fourteen, reinforcing the fae impression.

"*Ádh mór ort!*" he called out.

Good luck to me, indeed.

Inside the bank, lining the mahogany walls of the reception area, portraits of men scowled at me from gilded frames. Wrought iron railing rivaling anything in the French Quarter fenced wide, curved Carrara marble stairs sweeping up from the lobby's mosaicked floor. Three stories of offices rose on either side with people looking out from the mezzanines over the lobby. More marble columns supporting the roof completed the temple effect. An epic mural with Greek deities looking on or aiding their champions in battle covered the vaulted bank ceiling. That the gods of commerce resided within was without doubt and here I stood a mere supplicant.

A respectable middle-aged woman in a cropped bolero jacket looked up from her paperwork with a practiced but pleasant smile. "May I help you?"

Ah, smiles were allowed. "I'm Lorena McKenzie. I have an appointment with Mr. Mondovi."

"Oh, yes, you're from Richmond, aren't you? He's in a meeting, but I'll tell him you're here. He's expecting you."

"Winchester, actually," I said as she retreated up the stairs.

"He said he'd be right with you," she puffed breathlessly upon her return. "I'm Mrs. Whimple, his assistant." She set a tea tray on the corner of her desk in a clear invitation to join her while she continued her assistantly duties.

"Thank you. I confess I'm a bit nervous."

Shooing my concerns away with a wave of her file, she reassured me. "No need to be." She prattled on about local events and questioned me nigh to the point of interrogation about everything but the weather. "You must be so busy. Mr. Mondovi mentioned you had a boarding school on your farm in Virginia also." And on she went while I wondered why Mondovi had been discussing my school at all.

Yes, I had a boarding school. Yes, I loved teaching a variety of subjects beyond watercolor and embroidery. Persy and Lucy were my favorite students because they were my problem children and had been expelled from so many other schools. Yes, the horses. Girls love horses.

"You simply must keep that marvelous school open!"

Nervously fingering the binder in my lap, I thought about the unsettling rumors about Mr. Mahler, and wanted to know more, since the bank had assigned him to represent my legal interests. "Will Mr. Mahler be here? I heard he was injured in an accident."

Her fingers darted anxiously to the amethyst brooch at her throat as if she were pressing a button to release words suddenly caught in her throat. "Oh, it was no accident. Mr. Beddow hit him quite deliberately."

I *hadn't* heard this. "My word. What happened?"

She cast a furtive glance around and leaned closer. "Mr. Mahler and Mr. Beddow are members of the Charleston Gentlemen's Debate Club. In February, things got heated and Mr. Beddow bested Mr. Mahler handily, making him look like a buffoon. Mr. Mahler hit him when he wasn't looking." She threw her fist to emphasize the punch. "Beddow picked himself up, 'Mahler the Brawler, eh?' Then he broke Mr. Mahler's nose. Splat!" She went from subdued whispering to throwing and dodging blows. "He's a lawyer now, but he was a decorated cavalry officer, you know, so he's not going to tolerate Mr. Mahler's cowardly attack. They finally separated them, but Mr. Mahler was thrashed soundly.

"Then Mr. Beddow said, 'If this is your level of competence in all areas, it's no wonder your wife left you for Dolan.' The entire debate club jumped in then and the police had to quell it. It was a real dustup. The Ladies' Club was serving refreshments. At first, we tried to pull the men apart before some of us, uh, got into it."

At this point, I was laughing. Loudly.

"It rated *two* columns in the society page." She held up two fingers to stress the importance. "Needless to say, Mr. Mahler despises Mr. Beddow now. No doubt he'd challenge him to a duel if he weren't such a coward."

"Oh, my. That serious?" She'd filled in details I didn't know and confirmed what I'd already heard. "It doesn't sound like a very civilized debate club."

She shrugged. "It usually doesn't come to fisticuffs and broken noses."

A young spit-polished cavalry captain came in and sat nearby but declined help. Mrs. Whimple went back to prattling, now about the garden club.

I glanced apprehensively at my watch. "Is Mr. Mondovi usually this late?"

She frowned at the clock above the teller cages. "Hmm, how odd. No, he's the height of punctuality."

Mondovi was twisting me in the wind.

"Mrs. Mahler was president of our garden club. She adored roses. Mr. Dolan–" she looked around and continued with lowered voice, "you know the one Mrs. Mahler ran away with, was a visiting botanist with the university. He used to speak at our garden club. That man was fascinating and so handsome." She fanned herself with a file and closed her eyes in a picture of bliss.

I leaned forward, intrigued.

"He doubled our membership. We so hated losing him, and Mrs. Mahler, of course. And those roses. Those poor, dear roses."

"What happened to the roses?"

"Mr. Mahler massacred them," she exclaimed. Her voice had returned to normal after the first whispered lines, but now was quite animated as she waved her pencil around like a weapon. "He charged out of the house one afternoon with his grandfather's sword in one hand and Mrs. Mahler's lovely brass garden syringe in the other. Beheaded buds, shredded leaves, chunks of canes sailed through the air while he cursed her name to heaven and hell alike. He sliced with one hand and pummeled with the other until there wasn't a rose left; then he attacked the rest of the garden. Then," she said, still horrified, "he grabbed a spade, dug up what was left, and tossed the mangled roots into the street.

"I managed to save some, but the poor darlings aren't doing well. I expect they're in shock. 'Out damned rot!' he screamed and cursed her name again. 'Love-Lies-Bleeding! How's that for Love-Lies-Bleeding?' and red blooms writhed through the air. It truly was a massacre. No other word describes it. As if that weren't enough, he threw her garden syringe to the ground and stomped it flat as a fritter; the one she ordered from England. He jumped up and down, screeching her name, and calling her a Jezebel and Beelzebub and nine orders of demons. The lovely little rosewood handle popped off and bounced across the street like a head from a guillotine. *Plink. Plink. Plink.* I wept for weeks. The most beautiful garden in Charleston gone. Poof."

Mrs. Whimple, on the verge of tears, collapsed onto her little wheeled chair.

"Mrs. Whimple, are you all right?"

"Yes, dear. I get emotional sometimes. Forgive me," she said with a little sniff and rolled away to finish her work.

I sat in shocked astonishment, the massacre replaying in my mind, right down to the forlorn wooden head bouncing across the cobblestone street. "Is Mr. Mahler better?"

"His brother took him to a, uh, spa to recuperate," she said with another sniffle. "Aside from a twitch in his left eye if he gets upset or nervous, he's fine I suppose. Mr. Whimple says it's raised havoc with his poker game. The eye spasms madly when he gets a bad hand. He may need to play dice or something. He still has his racehorses. I suppose they don't care about the nervous winking."

Moses, Mary, and Joseph. Mahler the Mad is supposed to represent me?

Proper Mrs. Whimple leaned back in her chair, exhausted from the animated recounting of the war of the roses and Mr. Mahler's portrayal of Robespierre. Her pale gray bolero jacket skewed off her left shoulder from brandishing the pencil sword. She tugged the jacket back into place with a sigh and caught me staring at her hair. I looked away, embarrassed at my rudeness, but I'd never seen hair do such a perfect imitation of wings sprouting from a person's head. The white streaks at her temples particularly made it look like a dove about to take flight.

"Tarnation," she mumbled, feeling the hair. It was quickly subdued with pomade from her desk. "Your father had racehorses, didn't he? I heard Mr. Mondovi discussing them."

"Yes." I had to look away to hide my irritation. *Why would Mondovi discuss our horses AND my school?* "There's certainly a lot of brass here," I said, quickly changing the subject.

"Hmmm?" She looked away from the small mirror and around. "Yes, two ladies do nothing but polish brass."

My mind still mulled the massacre scene when Frank Schoenberger, my new farm manager, came in.

"This is my farm manager; my previous one having quit to join the army." I said. "I thought it might help if Mr. Mondovi could see I already have another, extremely qualified man."

"I'm sure that's a good idea," she said, picking up a new ledger.

"Miss Mac," he said and tipped his hat before hobbling over to sit next to the captain.

His cleaned, well-pressed suit was neither new nor the latest cut. He was a practical, down-to-earth German with a good head for farming and a natural way with horses. A badly healed broken leg left him with a permanent limp that made him unfit for the military, but he'd impressed me immediately with his ideas for improving The Pines. That made him perfect for me. If Mr. Mondovi had doubts about my abilities, and I'd been warned he would, Frank should ease them.

"Mrs. Whimple," a man leaning heavily on the third-floor railing boomed, "bring Miss McKenzie to the main conference room."

The captain opened the door for another man coming in who was juggling papers and a satchel. The newcomer took off his top hat and grinned like a choir boy with mayhem in mind and a frog in his pocket. "Hello, Mrs. Whimple."

"M-Mr. Beddow. What are you doing?" she stammered.

"I'm here to meet a client."

"Well—have a seat," she said, completely flummoxed.

The two sat next to Frank, who smiled reassuringly at me as a parent might to a nervous child at a recital. I'd done all I could do to prepare, and I had to trust.

Not my will but Thine, I reminded myself and followed Mrs. Whimple with a faint and fugitive hope.

Chapter Six

Inside the conference room, Mrs. Whimple introduced me to Messrs. Mondovi, Ellis, Catton, and the infamous Mahler, who lined up along the conference table like birds on a wire. Mondovi pointed to a chair opposite him.

Mr. Mahler reminded me of the Poe portrait in our library, except his hair was lighter and more disheveled. He'd buried his head in his hands twice since I entered the room, rumpling his hair with fidgety fingers. His eyes were large and dark, and darted about nervously.

The other men were mostly unremarkable aside from exuding wealth and power in posture and appearance. Only Mondovi stood out, and that because his funeral director looks in his undertaker-black suit and exaggerated white side whiskers flowing down his jowls.

I wondered if I should have worn a more businesslike top hat instead of the velvet empress hat with its black ostrich feathers, then laughed inwardly at the idea that a hat might make a difference.

Mr. Mondovi proceeded to explain how the bank operated. Each man in turn added to the lecture. They professed to be looking out for my father's—and therefore my interests—but there was no mention of how they might help me and only what they expected of me. Sitting quietly with my hands folded, I listened to lessons on banking, the economy, and how women lack the necessary skills to manage business.

Calm.

"I took out a loan for my boarding school, and it's prospering," I said when I could finally break into the screed.

They laughed as if on cue. "That loan was on your daddy's good name," assured Mr. Catton. "There's a great deal of difference between operating a boarding school in your home and overseeing a plantation. Those aren't sterling references. The bank isn't heartless, however. We'll manage your properties until our debt is paid, for a small management fee. You'll be placed on a budget. It won't allow for extravagant jewelry, but you can live comfortably." He said this, gesturing toward my crucifix.

The crucifix *was* exquisitely wrought with tiny glittering garnets and seed pearls in an intricate setting. The Irish rival the Greeks in their penchant for tragedy, but they also look for luck and joy around every corner. So it was with my one-armed Jesus. Grandmamma insisted it was a reminder I was to be the left arm of God, and the crucifix would bring me great luck. In truth, the defective Jesus that was about to be scrapped was all she could afford. Nevertheless, I treasured it more than perfection.

Breathe.

Sunlight glared intensely through the leaded glass windows behind the men, yet they made no attempt to close the shutters or drapes. My hand wrapped around the crucifix as if to protect it. Struggling to form measured words, I said, "This was a gift from my grandmother. Mr. Schoenberger can explain his plans for The Pines if you'll but speak to him."

Mr. Mahler harumphed and looked at his watch. "I've never met a woman who didn't need a strict budget and a firm hand. I doubt we need to discuss your grand schemes when what's required is a business plan. Your father owes $78,000 that's due in two weeks."

"$78,849.32," Mr. Catton corrected primly. "That's a sizable amount of money, Miss McKenzie. I doubt you have any concept."

I made a show of leafing through the papers in the binder and reminded myself it wouldn't be ladylike to launch myself over the table to throttle them. Looking up from the papers and into Mahler's eyes, I asked, "What do you propose I do while the bank manages my properties? Tend my rose gardens?"

To mask my malice, I went back to sorting papers. *I know you have a plan, Lord. Not my will, but Thine.*

Heads swiveled in dismay to stare at Mahler, who was making an odd, strangling noise. Mr. Catton swiftly changed course. "Of course, if you were to marry someone suitable to manage your properties, that might suffice."

My eyes snapped open in shock. *Now Lord, we both know it isn't Your will that I marry a perfect stranger.* "I *won't* be marrying someone to save my property but lose my freedom," I said, leveling a granite gaze on him. "I'll sell some land, and the army will buy horses to pay the debt."

Mondovi guffawed. "My dear. General Beauregard speak to you? Even if he did, those horses won't bring nearly enough to satisfy your debts. Mr. Mahler said he'd buy some of your stallions and a few select mares, but generously, that would be a few thousand at most. I'd take a young stallion named Charlemagne for, say, $400?" He laughed again. "General Beauregard to the rescue. Do you know how busy he is?" The other men tittered like a society of old ladies.

Smoothing my skirts, I stood and stalked to the door. The time for negotiating with fools was done. Leaning at Mondovi's rail, I motioned to Frank to bring everyone. Back at the table, I laid out the papers and waited for them.

"What's this?" Mondovi blustered when they appeared, half rising in his chair. "This is a private meeting. What's the meaning of this?"

"Mr. Beddow is here to represent my interests," I responded. "Mr. Mahler's services are not required, since I don't need a pettifogger only concerned about my horses and your bank."

Mahler's left eye twitched madly. His face turned a vivid mulberry that nearly matched the lush draperies they'd now drawn across the tightly shuttered windows. Was the shuttering to save Mahler or me from defenestration?

"This is Mr. Schoenberger, the man you refused to hear," I continued. "But now you'll hear from him and Captain…?"

"Decker, ma'am."

"Captain Decker is an aide to G.T., uh…I mean General Beauregard." There was a visible blanching across the table. "Yes, he'll talk to me. I've known his family for many years. My cousin and he are neighbors in Louisiana, and we visit often. He assures me either the army or individual soldiers will buy every horse I'll sell and at fair prices." I looked at Catton and Mahler. "The stallions aren't for sale to you. Most especially Charlemagne. I'm giving him away."

"Now see here!" Mondovi exploded. "You can't give away bank property. Do you know how valuable that horse is?"

My brow lifted. "The going price of a prime mule, according to you. Charlie—Charlemagne—is my personal horse. My father gave him to me for my birthday, and I only send him here to stand at stud. Lexington stallions are quite in demand, as I'm sure you know. What I do with him is my business. Anyone who doesn't know his value has no business owning him. Unless, of course, you're trying to cheat me?"

"How dare you," exclaimed Mahler.

"How dare I, indeed." I cast a louring look over the lot of them, no longer caring if they caught the fire in my eye. "How dare I understand the note is on the land. How dare I understand the note is not on my horses. How dare I understand you're trying to steal my horses and think I don't understand how much they're worth? And how dare *you* even suggest you might deal with me if I marry someone of your choice as if I were chattel to be bargained away."

Mr. Beddow furiously scribbled notes during this. "When do you want this sale, Miss McKenzie?"

"Post notices for Thursday, Friday, and Saturday next. I have a list of breeders you can telegraph."

He did some calculations. "April fourth, fifth, and sixth?"

"Yes, dinner served and church service on Sunday morning to any who wish to attend." The burgoo would be available all day, but we typically broke midday meal to eat and regroup.

Mr. Catton pulled Mahler, who was now visibly shaking, from his chair and led him away. Shortly before they reached the door, Mahler lunged, trapping me against the table. Captain Decker hit him once, dropping him to the floor in an inglorious heap. The others leaned over the table, peering in astonishment. "Did you have to mention rose gardens?" Mondovi muttered.

Catton and Ellis dragged Mahler's unconscious form out the door. With a fleeting glance to make sure no more attacks were forthcoming, I took a deep breath and settled into my chair. "Where were we?" I tried to gather my thoughts, but they had scattered like a covey of quail. "The sale. Mr. Schoenberger, no one from the bank or their representatives may buy my horses. Not only that, if any of these men set foot on my property, I want them arrested for trespassing or shot, at your pleasure."

"Yes, ma'am," Frank replied, a small, satisfied smile on his lips as if imagining shooting one of them at that very moment.

"That would be murder!" Mondovi cried.

"The last time we dealt with horse thieves, the sheriff told us it would save trouble if we shot them. You just revealed your intention to steal my horses. Please, come calling at your own peril."

Then, looking directly at Mr. Mondovi, who was mopping his forehead with a handkerchief, I smiled. It was a small, reptilian smile much as a snake might give while eyeing its dinner. One of the bankers squeaked. I didn't know which one and didn't care because I was about to eat them all alive with a side of grits.

"You remember Mr. Schoenberger? You foreclosed on his farm when he broke his leg, and the crops flooded three years ago."

The reassembled bankers, minus Mahler, mumbled amongst themselves, unsure what to do with one small recalcitrant woman.

"I believe that concludes our business, gentlemen," I said, rising.

"You don't want to deal with these people?" Beddow said, looking at me with a feigned innocence that only further fueled the flames.

"I'll see to it not another bank does business with you," Mondovi shouted.

"That reminds me," I said, drawing on my gloves with the air of a pugilist. "I'm closing my account."

"Do you realize what you've done, you foolish woman?" Mondovi slammed his fist on the table.

Decker offered his arm. "I believe she's just outflanked you, gentlemen. And quite masterfully."

Chapter Seven

Though I kept my chin up and my back straight, I wanted nothing more than to melt into a puddle like ice cream on a hot July afternoon. I couldn't let them see me waver, however, and marched purposefully toward the stairs. Sensing I was on the brink of collapse, Captain Decker whispered, "Lean on me if you must. I'll make a show of being annoyingly gallant and shield you."

A bank runner flying around us nearly knocked us down at the landing. "Is Mondovi warning the other banks about me?" I said with considerable dismay.

"Don't worry," Beddow said. "I already made the rounds and have a list of banks who'd love to poke Mondovi with a sharp stick. Once we finish here, we'll discuss our options at Mrs. Clemson's."

"I need to speak to General Beauregard if everything's in hand," Decker said.

"Oh!" I stopped dead. "Our blacksmith quit, and Mother took Castor, my other farrier. We can't trim the horses."

Decker chuckled. "We have a few in the army. I'll ask to borrow them. The general will afford you every assistance, I'm sure, given my instructions."

Curious, I cast a sidelong glance at him. "And what was that?"

"Take care of my girl and don't let anyone run over her, though God help the man who tries."

I snorted. "He gives me too much credit."

Tellers trapped behind burnished brass bars set in ornate mahogany fretwork beamed at our approach. The female clerk with the perpetual smile lost her bearings when I told her I wanted to close my account. She stuttered and stammered and finally fled to the floor manager, who hurried to assure me that I didn't want to close my account with the most venerable bank in South Carolina. I assured him I did. Mr. Beddow also assured him I did, and I wanted it closed immediately unless they wanted legal and publicity problems.

"Of course," he snipped. "Mr. Mondovi must approve a transaction this large."

Mondovi's shouts at the manager echoed through the grand vault, and then he faced the balustrade, leaning heavily on it with fists clenched about the rail. With one final withering glare at me, he spun around and vanished. The manager returned shortly with the bank draft in his trembling hand. "I assume this is acceptable?" he said, shoving the hapless teller out of his way.

Unsurprisingly, the writing was large and angry, but there would be no mistaking the numbers even with the splotches and droplets. Five thousand two hundred twenty-nine dollars and ninety-eight cents. While not a small amount, it was a pittance compared to what I owed. "Yes, and you should apologize to this young lady. It's not her fault your employer is an ass." She was the only female teller, and life was surely hard enough without his abuse on my account.

Mrs. Whimple looked up from her ledger when we neared her desk. Her burgeoning smile froze upon seeing my grim countenance. "How did your meeting go?"

"Not well, I'm afraid."

She cleaned her pen and laid it aside. "I'm sorry."

I rolled my head back to ease my stiff neck, catching sight of the ceiling as I did. "Out of curiosity, are the board members in the mural?"

She gazed up, surprised. "Yes. They wanted to be the gods." She lowered her voice and twittered nervously. "The painter wanted to put me in, saying I was the true power here. I refused.

It's proper for men because they *do* have power after all, but it would be overweening for a simple woman. Don't you agree? He inserted my pug instead. Gellie hates Mr. Mondovi and bites him every time she sees him, so she's tugging at Zeus's robe. Mr. Mondovi is Zeus." She pointed to a portion of the scene where the father of the immortals directed the battle. It wasn't easy to see, but there was a small brown figure at his hem.

"The painter's right," I said. "Stop discounting your value."

She looked at Mr. Beddow and then me, boring into us with large, brown, serious eyes. "I like to walk Gellie along Fifth Street." The smile reappeared like a ray of sun popping out from behind a rain cloud. "Have a good day."

I was anxious to get the draft safely deposited, but my legs were jelly by the time the tinkling brass doorbell announced our departure. "Coffee," I implored.

"Will y'all be all right?" Captain Decker asked.

"We'll be fine," Beddow replied. "I brought my carriage, but I can hail a cab for propriety's sake."

I removed the draft from my purse and tucked it into the inner pocket under my skirt next to my baby dragoon. "I've no intention of waiting for a cab. If someone dares mention I'm inappropriate, I swan I'll shoot them. Then I'll not only be inappropriate but also a murderess."

The men laughed. "While I believe I could get you off on an insanity plea after dealing with those men, let's not test the theory," Beddow said.

"Good, I'm in no mood to suffer fools further today."

"Is there anything else you want me to do, Miss Mac?" Frank asked.

"Yes, start gathering horses and get them sorted. Even mares and foals." By our normal fall sale, we had foals weaned and ready to go. Now we'd have to sell pairs if buyers were interested. "Everything is up except the stallions, but I suppose if someone offers a ridiculous amount, they go also. Put the pensioners out of the way." As much as I needed money, I wasn't selling old horses we'd retired from racing or breeding. "Make a list of supplies and ask the girls what they need to feed the buyers. Send in the list of past buyers and breeders so I can contact them. Get the men and boys started tying halters and leads. I'll send more rope." We usually sold horses with leather halters in our fall sale, but there wasn't time now. Rope halters would do. I swiveled my attention to Decker. "Two days will be sufficient to gather men?"

"Yes, I wish I could promise them sooner, but I'll have to scour units to find the farriers and horsemen I want. Once found, we'll make up for lost time."

"That's fine. I still need to take care of other business and gather shoeing material, et cetera."

Decker promised to contact me soon and departed.

Mr. Beddow helped me into his carriage, a smart Spider Phaeton with a team of matched black geldings. "It's less roomy than a cab, but we can go wherever we wish."

Settling in, I laid the binder across my lap and breathed a sigh of relief that my first trial was over. "It's perfect. Beautiful, in fact."

"Hmm, yes. My wife wasn't so impressed with my showy new ride, and we have to use the other carriage for the family, but I like it. I bought the horses off the track, and they're turning into darned fine trotters. They can fair outrun about anything in the city. Not that I care for such things." From his mischievous grin, I imagined he wasted no opportunity trying out his darned fine trotters against anyone foolish enough to match him.

"Of course not," I responded with a knowing smile. I liked this man. He had starch. "Do you find it odd Mrs. Whimple mentioned she liked walking on Fifth Street?"

He smooched the horses into a brisk walk. "Exceeding. And that stern look wasn't her at all. Fifth Street niggles at my brain. I'll check my notes at Mrs. Clemson's."

Now that my mind wasn't on praying, plotting, and fretting, I basked in the beauty that was Charleston. It was as if the ladies had declared to their men, "We will allow you to assume power if you surround us with majesty." The finest architecture show-cased both homes and businesses. Tousle-headed palms stood at attention. Crepe myrtles promised a spectacular display when they bloomed, and I was sorry I might miss it. "The flowers look like they're trying to compete with the ladies crowding the sidewalks," I said.

Beddow followed my gaze to a gaggle of women passing a pale terracotta-colored building. Under the veranda, baskets spilling mounds of brilliant flowers swayed gently in the breeze. "Yes, the ladies are giving Mother Nature a run for her money, but she's been at this longer. I believe she'll win. That building ahead sets Mahler to ranting. He can't stand the uncivilized way they mixed pink, blue, and yellow flowers together in the same baskets. I kind of like it. It looks like vomited rainbows."

Leave it to a man to describe such loveliness as vomited rainbows, but I agreed and decided to plant some similarly.

Since the street was full, we parked in an alley, and he hooked one of the horses to a tether weight. Mrs. Clemson's was identical to many small eateries run by aging widows. It was clean, filled with customers, small round tables, and one small round proprietor. The walls, like the rooms, were filled. Photographs of locals and family members, I assumed, peered down upon the diners. Many new ones of men in uniform looked grim and ready to do their worst.

Beddow doctored his coffee until it resembled tan cream. "Yes!" he exclaimed in eureka fashion at the perfect sugary concoction, "I have it figured out. Grand National Bank of Charleston is on Fifth. It's on my list. I didn't have time to shop rates with him, but I did the others."

"It's interesting she'd reference it, if that's what she was doing."

"Isn't it?"

I lifted my undiluted coffee to my lips and held the cup there, inhaling the strong, earthy scent. It was like sugar browning on a stove stoked with cherry wood and swept me away in steamy clouds of delight. My eyes opened to see Beddow smiling, utterly amused. "Mrs. Clemson serves the best coffee in town as well as a credible variety of teas."

"How would you know? You've doctored yours until it's nigh on a syrup."

"I've been sick and need to settle my stomach. Your father hired me for another matter, but when you wired me about possible business with Mahler—" He wriggled his brows. "I'd have paid to see that show, though my family would appreciate a roof over their heads."

I set the cup down, chagrined that I'd chided him. "I'm sorry. You shouldn't have come if you're ill."

He waved a hand. "I'd have been there if they had to carry me in on my deathbed, and I believed they might for a while. Someone sent me a gift basket a few weeks ago, and I foolishly gobbled it down thinking it was from a client. It wasn't, and the food was, shall we say—tainted."

"You never found out who sent it?"

"I have an idea. He's a vindictive little rat."

"Yes, but if you're ill—"

"Don't give it another thought. You don't always get what you want in life, and you can't always win no matter how hard you try, but I will do all I can to help you win this fight."

We were convinced Mrs. Whimple had directed us to the bank on Fifth Street, but he suggested saving them until last to compare offers. The cheque in my pocket made me nervous, and I was anxious to get the banking business settled, so we didn't tarry. Since Mr. Beddow insisted on paying for coffee, I replaced my coin purse in my reticule and hitched the velvet cords around my wrist.

He held out his arm to me to help me into the coach, and I had no more than started to lift my foot to the step when a gun smashed across his head. The sound was sickeningly solid, like wood cracking, followed by an escaping sigh as Beddow slumped to the ground. I screamed and spun to face the attacker, who grabbed my purse.

"Let go!" I jerked my arm back, but he had a firm hold. With it looped around my wrist, it was a desperate tug-of-war.

"Turn loose before I shoot you!"

"I can't, you idiot," I gasped. "It's knotted around my wrist."

My wrist burned from the cords digging into the flesh. He shoved the gun in his waistband and rummaged in his pocket. I fumbled to get my free hand inside my skirt to the pocket with my gun while kicking and stomping on his foot like a bad-tempered mule. Beddow stirred, but I knew he'd be no help.

"Stop it, or by God, I'll shoot you here and now!" he yelled. A few people peered down the alley at the commotion. I screamed for help to no avail. He flashed a knife in his other hand and cut the purse strings. "I warned you," he growled, and snatching the gun back out, shot.

The gun belched flame inches away from my face and sent a bullet whizzing through my hat. I had my gun out now and fired at his rapidly fleeing backside. He turned and fired again, sending a trail of fire across my arm. "Ouch! Damn it, that hurts."

My first shot missed, likely due to me jerking when he shot me. Ignoring the pain, I leveled my gun, determined not to miss. *Slow down and aim.* The second shot hit him in the thigh, dropping him. I ran to where he lay and stooped to retrieve his gun and my purse. Seeing as not a one had come to our aid, I glowered at the gathering crowd.

"Not only am I taking back my purse, but I'll have twenty dollars to replace my new hat and this dress you shot a hole in."

"What?" He rolled on the ground, groaning and clutching his leg. "You're crazy. You're robbing me? You tried to murder me!"

"I can arrange that." I leveled my gun at him. "This is a six shot. You know how excitable women are."

He looked around at the crowd, eyes popped wide. "Do you hear her? She confessed. She's planning on killing me. She's insane. Someone help me."

"He's killed Mr. Beddow." To show him how overwrought I was, I yowled and pointed to the alley. "You murderer!" I waved the guns wildly, sending bystanders ducking and running.

"Christ almighty." He threw a wad of cash at me. I counted out twenty dollars and dropped the rest in front of him and the newly arrived police officer. "Arrest her," the robber demanded. "She tried to kill me. She robbed me. I have witnesses."

The confused officer stared at me in disbelief. "Did you shoot this man?"

"Yes, sir. He robbed me and killed Mr. Beddow." I sniffed. "He tried to kill me, but I defended myself."

"Beddow? The lawyer?"

I pointed to the alley where Beddow lay unconscious.

"I didn't kill any lawyer. I crac—"

"See?" The crowd, deeming it safe with a police officer in charge, drifted back to hear the details. I waved a gun at the crowd. "And nary a one of these brave citizens would help."

"She shot me," the robber moaned.

The officer reached out gingerly. "Let me hold the guns. Someone look for Mr. Beddow."

"No need," Beddow rasped from behind us. "I'm alive. No thanks to that scapegrace."

I dashed to him, clutching my hat with one hand and lifting my skirts with the other. "Mr. Beddow, are you all right?" He was ghost pale with blood running down the side of his head and soaking his collar as if someone had tried to cut his throat. My stays were so tight I was near to collapse myself when I reached him.

He leaned on the corner of the building, tenderly feeling a knot on his head. Bloody as it was, his skull appeared intact. I pulled my handkerchief out of my mangled purse and dabbed at the laceration. "It's not bad, but you need stitches," I gasped breathlessly.

"Later. We need to finish before something else happens."

The officer peered across my shoulder, looking at the wound. "Can you tell me what happened?"

Beddow took the cloth and pressed it to his head. "Let me sit down." He hove away from the building and lurched to the edge of the sidewalk, holding tightly to my proffered arm. There, he sank unsteadily to the curb and bent forward, head in his hands. "I was helping Miss McKenzie into the carriage when that blackguard accosted us. He hit me with his gun. I tried to help her but passed out.

"So, you didn't see him rob her?"

"I saw him pulling on her purse."

The officer turned to me. "Miss McKenzie. You tried to shoot a man in the back. It's by the grace of God you didn't murder him."

"I most certainly did not!"

"You deny you shot him?"

"Not at all." I took my hat off to inspect the damage. "I'm denying I tried to shoot him in the back. I was aiming for parts lower. It's to my everlasting shame that my aim was off that far. I'm not in the habit of shooting into the brown. I always hit my target."

"You were trying to shoot him in the—"

"The hindquarters. Correct."

"You could have killed him."

I stuck my finger through the hole in my hat. "He tried to shoot me in the face. What would that have done to me?"

Beddow waved his hand. "Officer. It's obvious the man robbed Miss McKenzie and tried to kill her. He nearly killed me. Why are you questioning *her* so?"

"She threatened him. She robbed him. It's possible she's a bit…dizzy."

"Arrest him," Beddow said. "We'll give you statements later."

"I'll expect you both in the office."

"I require my gun, officer. It's the baby dragoon, and I didn't rob him. I only demanded reparations for the damage he caused." I pulled the sleeve tight around my arm where he shot through the upper sleeve, leaving a ragged trail. "He's ruined both hat and dress, and I deserve compensation." I examined my arm where the bullet had grazed me and held up my bloody hand. "The skin will grow back. I won't charge him for that, though I should. He's marred my perfect arm. What will polite society say about a woman with bullet scars?"

"Probably less than what they'd say about one shooting a man. Regardless, here's your gun. Perhaps you could let Mr. Beddow hold it for you?"

"Phfft. What good would that do? I'm sure he's seeing double."

I insisted on putting off the banking business. Beddow was more insistent, and we continued.

"Then let's at least go to Grand National first since Mrs. Whimple hinted at it."

"We can do that. That was quite a performance," he said after we were safely back in the carriage.

"Thank you. A bit dramatic, but I had to convince the miscreant I was verging on madness so he'd pay me. This is a new outfit, darn it."

He chuckled. "I'm sure everyone is convinced."

Mr. Owens at Grand National demanded to hear all the details of our adventure while his secretary tended to Mr. Beddow. He was nearly rolling on the floor with laughter at the recounting of the banking business and demanded Beddow repeat a few parts.

"I quite adore you, Miss McKenzie," he said wheezing. "Please," he tried to catch his breath. "Tell your manager not to shoot me should I appear at the sale. Not all bankers are blackhearts."

Mr. Beddow, who had recovered some of his color with tender ministrations and some hot tea, beamed at Mr. Owens with great pride like a boy who had just presented the greatest jumping frog in the county. "I knew you'd like her. I wish you'd seen her cut Mondovi to ribbons. Then they suggested they might work with her if she married properly."

Mr. Owens leaned back in his chair and slapped his hands on the arms. "I wish I had," he said and burst out laughing. "I'm sure Mondovi had some weaselly sycophant on a string for you," he said when he got control. He happily offered better terms than the other banks had offered Mr. Beddow the day before and introduced me to his agricultural manager, Mr. Updike, who listened with interest to my plans for the operation. Finally, someone with expertise to work with me instead of telling me what I was going to do. I was happy to open an account in his bank.

"I've been to The Pines many times as a hunting guest and love that farm dearly," he said with some fondness. "Union Bank was the first bank willing to take a chance on him, and he remained loyal to them, though we were fast friends. I'm honored to be your advocate."

This understanding cemented my confidence in our decision, but what a shame Papa's loyalty should be repaid so. Owens agreed my neighbor Mr. Woodman, who had been trying to buy adjoining acreage for years, would be the ideal prospect to buy the land I intended to sell.

"Mr. Owens," I said. "I noticed the gilt lettering below your name on the transom. *Respice post te, hominem memento te.* Is that not a bit odd for a man such as yourself?"

He rocked in his chair. "On the contrary. 'Look behind you, remember you are a man' is the perfect motto for any man who wields power. So thought the Roman conquerors. Men of power particularly should be reminded to be humble. It's why I keep my office on the ground floor. I started out in the basement mailroom. Every man should remember where he came from. Your father did."

Mr. Owens kindly called a young man in to drive Mr. Beddow to the doctor and summoned me a cab so I might return to my hotel. Even though I'd put up as brave a front as I could muster, I felt like a balloon that had lost all its air—not in a sudden whoosh—but slowly, until a person looks at the end of their string and notices a sad little scrap of a thing dragging on the ground instead of bobbing along. If Old Nick himself came calling for my soul, I wasn't sure I could give him much of a battle.

But hadn't I already faced off with him earlier?

Chapter Eight

I threaded my way through the crowded hotel lobby, ignoring calls as if I'd been struck deaf, and whisked up the stairs to my room. Annie, bless her, immediately saw how frazzled I was and sent for some soup, as I hadn't eaten, and the doctor to dress my arm, though I demanded she wrap it herself. I only imagined I was her master. As soon as the doctor departed, she poured the pain killer down me, peeled me out of my clothes, and put me to bed.

"Miss Mac, Mrs. Whimple says she must see you." She shook me to emphasize her words.

I blinked awake, staring into her wide, hazel eyes. "Mrs. Whimple?" As if in answer, a soft, but insistent rap sounded at the door. "What time is it?"

"Almost supper time."

There was another persistent knock. "Show her in." I wriggled my feet into slippers and pulled on my cotton wrapper.

Mrs. Whimple glanced down the hall furtively and slipped inside. "Miss McKenzie, forgive me, but I simply must talk to you." Her hands clutched the handles of the small carpetbag in front of her so tightly her knuckles matched her pristine white blouse.

"Come in." I motioned to a small table near the window opening onto the balcony.

She hurried to the table but pulled her seat away from the open window. There was a small swoosh when she sank into the chair, and her skirt fluttered out about her.

"It's bright in here," I said and pulled the drapes. It really wasn't as it was nearing sunset, but she seemed to be afraid of the window.

With the drapes securely drawn, she scooted closer to the table and set her bag on top of it. "I asked Mr. Whimple to meet me here for supper, so I can't tarry, but I had to warn you." Her eyes darted to Annie, who regarded the distraught woman suspiciously. "I must be discreet."

Annie took her cue and excused herself to fetch tea.

"First, I must apologize," Mrs. Whimple said breathlessly, spilling the words out quickly, accompanied by fluttering little hummingbird hand movements. "I asked a great many questions about you earlier. I'm sure you thought I was a Nosy Nancy, but I had to know how serious you were before I—" she paused, searching for the right words, "committed myself, as it were. Many women don't have a mind for business. It's plain you do, and you care about your properties and people."

I had been curious about all the questions regarding me and my school. The farm.

"Rosetta Mahler was brilliant and highly educated, a passionate teacher before Mahler ruined her. I watched her go from a vibrant young woman to a meek little mouse. He made her stop her nature hikes and classes for young ladies." She twisted her hands in agitation. "You don't know what he did to her."

It made me loathe Mahler even more as I understood the joy of traipsing outdoors with my girls.

"When Dolan showed up, it was like a spark rekindled." As she spoke of Mrs. Mahler's spark, one also flamed in the woman before me. "What she ever saw in Mahler…but she's safe now. However, we need to protect you. You'll be fine if we get you out of this financial mess. Just promise me you'll keep your school going."

"I have no plans to close it."

"Mondovi is setting a trap," she said this calmly, but her gaze and voice dropped with the words. "Your neighbor, Mr. Woodman, is our client also. They know that's who you'll approach to sell land. They'll assure him he has the loan but decline him when it's too late to go elsewhere. You won't raise enough money from the sale, and they'll foreclose."

I sat stone still, too astounded to respond or even breathe.

She pulled an assortment of newspaper-wrapped objects from the bag and an amethyst pin from her hat and laid them on the table. With trembling fingers, she unwrapped a perfume decanter, a bud vase, and an apothecary bottle. Sunlight slicing through the drapes cast rich purple shadows on the white linen cloth under the glass. "These are for you," she said. "I keep amethyst glass in every window of my home and over every doorway. Amethyst and amethyst glass protect a person from danger and a home from thieves. Keep one of these pieces in your room, take one to The Pines, and then home with you to Rosemount. Keep the hatpin with you, but maybe in your reticule so no one recognizes it. I can't let anyone know I helped you. Buy more amethyst when you can, as much as you can."

Was there enough amethyst in Charleston to fend them off? Absently, I traced the outline of one of the shadows. "I can't believe they'd do this."

She huffed her disdain. "These are dangerous men and not to be trifled with. You did more than trifle, and they won't take the insult lightly. Especially from a woman, and a young one to boot. No, they're going to teach you a lesson. They intend to destroy you. There won't be enough left of you to rise from the dust when they get through."

I had left the bank feeling drained but victorious as Nelson at the Nile. Now I wondered if I wasn't facing Tenerife and might not lose more than my arm and honor, but I'd never failed at anything I ever truly desired. This would be no different. I wouldn't let them win.

Drawing myself up for battle, I replied, "I may surprise them."

She shook her head as if she felt sorry for me. "I hope so. I send as many people as I can to Mr. Owens, but I can't do too much, or they'd find I'm working against them. It breaks my heart when I can't warn someone, but I must be careful. Mr. Whimple is their chief accountant, and the old fool insisted on borrowing money to expand our house as befits our social status. Who does he think we are? They just want people obligated to them. I don't even like entertaining. Mondovi calls me Lavender Lou because I wear so much amethyst. I'd encase myself in it if I could to ward his evil."

Any further comment was interrupted by Annie's return. "I wanted to bring these pieces by you asked for," Mrs. Whimple said with a faint and forced smile.

Annie poured tea and looked to me wordlessly for further instructions. I inclined my head toward the door between our rooms, and she disappeared silently. Mrs. Whimple made small talk and sipped her tea, declining to say more about Mondovi even with Annie gone. "I must go. Mr. Whimple will be here soon to take me to supper. Good luck with your sale."

I tied the drapes back to let the fading sunshine flood in, hoping to dispel the shadow of treachery. When I opened the door between our rooms, Annie sat near the window hemming a dress. "Do you need me, Miss?"

"Not unless you want to join me for tea." I didn't feel like talking, but neither did I particularly want to be alone. She sensed my mood, and we sat quietly watching the sun set like two old cats with nary a bird nor mouse to be bothered with. The silence was broken only by the clink of cup on saucer or a muffled shout in the street below, and that suited me admirably as I muddled through my options. It was like one of those Chinese puzzle boxes Papa used to bring me, but now it seemed each time I solved a drawer, something terrible was going to pop out.

I'd have to warn Mr. Woodman, but we couldn't be obvious for fear of exposing Mrs. Whimple.

"Oh," she said. "I forgot. You have a letter from Marse Baron."

I carefully unsealed the cover and lifted the paper to smell it, anxious for the scent of Baron, then scanned the words.

March 23, 1861
Alexandria, Virginia

Beloved Baroness,

I trust you are well and your banking business goes satisfactorily. Please do write and tell me the results and when you'll be returning. I'm staying at the Green Hotel and will be for a while. I travelled to Washington and now Alexandria though I may be moving to Richmond soon. I intended to pay respects to Col Lee, who has returned to Arlington before reporting to our unit, and ask his advice on how I should proceed but had not the chance. As soon as I had stowed my gear, a smart major from Massachusetts confronted me and demanded to know where my loyalties lie. I was surrounded by friends when he approached, so he turned on them also as they were mostly southern.

"Well?" he demanded. "Who are you loyal to?"

"What do you mean?"

"Follow me to the commander's office."

We were taken aback but did. I'm sure he just meant for me to come, but the whole crew did. He looked like the fox who had gone looking for a hen and caught the whole flock when we walked in. "I require an answer," he demanded. "Where do your loyalties lie?"

"In regards to what?"

He looked at me as if I were addled. "In the coming conflict. I believe I'd like you to sign an oath of allegiance to the president and the United States of America. I don't trust you one bit, sir."

He shoved a paper he'd already prepared across a desk at me.

"You want me to swear I will take up arms against my home state?"

"I want you to state you will take up arms against all enemies of the United States of America, including those who may soon be in rebellion."

"No, sir. I, by God, will not do that."

"Then you are a coward and a traitor."

Ice descended upon the room. "No one calls me a coward, sir." I pulled the paper to me and he smiled as if he had cut a fat hog. I turned the paper over and scribbled out my resignation on it and handed it to him. "Is that sufficient for my needs?"

"If you are resigning your commission." My men stepped forward and added their names asking if they were also resigned and he accepted them saying, "Good, the army is better off without cowards and turncoats."

"I am out of the army?" I repeated.

"You are and damned good riddance, too. I'll be happy not to have to listen to any more of that southern drawl no one can understand." I laughed at that, as he is from Bahston and who can understand those fellows?

By now, a crowd had gathered, and tempers were flaring. I turned to my men. "You heard this blackguard call me a coward?" I asked. They affirmed they had. Then I proceeded to beat the tar out of him. My men at first told the other soldiers to stay out of it as they had no hound in the hunt, but it wasn't long before we had an Irish dance going and everyone was involved.

We spent two days in jail, but the judge agreed that the major provoked the attack by calling me a coward and released us. The major was unavailable for comment as he is still in the infirmary with a broken jaw and sundry other problems, but I am not one of them.

I know you are thinking I'm free to come to you, and if you were in love with a sane man, I would be. However, the longer I sat in jail, the more I stewed, and as soon as we were set free, we joined up with the first militia we could find with the agreement we would be released to join Col Lee if he comes over. There is still some debate over who has command of me as I have experience and seem to be in demand. Two unit commanders will have a horse race this afternoon to settle the issue. In the meantime, I am busy training green troops and will not be released on furlough.

Please forgive me. Had I spent more time dreaming and thinking of you, which I did plenty of, but not enough apparently, I would have waited to join a new unit and winged my way south like a wild goose. I wish I had stayed in Charleston and let them charge me with desertion or attempted to gain an extension but spit in one hand and wish in the other.

Were I there, I would lay my lips on yours and drink your soul.

Hurry home, please. I so long to see you.

Find enclosed a book of poetry to pass your time and some headache powders because you will need them to deal with me.

All my everlasting love,
Captain Baron Patrick Callahan, CSA

My heart skipped at the thought. I had carefully hidden my pauper status from him for a reason. He would insist on getting involved with my bankers, though maybe they could use a little Irish dance themselves. Then he would get his family involved and put them in massive debt to save me. Though I desired nothing more than to marry him, I couldn't saddle him with my debts and responsibilities, nor would I burden him with the worry. He had enough to think about.

A knock at the door cut off my meanderings. It was a hotel clerk with a message. Would I join Captain Decker for supper at 6:30 to discuss business? Of course, I couldn't decline.

Annie cast a skeptical look my way. "Looking like that? I don't have time to get you done up. What you need is a day to rest."

"I've no time to waste on flitter and fluff," I said to Annie, who was buried in the armoire and indecision. "Something simple with my hair and dress. Maybe the black muslin."

She pulled me to the dressing table, clucking and rolling her eyes in disapproval. "Missy, I have a reputation to uphold. You not going to spoil it by going out looking like a frumpity old maid. White poplin with blue rosebuds or the emerald stripe?"

"White? Why did you pack that?"

"In case you dined with a handsome officer. Besides, blue for your eyes."

"My eyes are gray. Regardless, no white with those sheer sleeves. I don't want to explain the bandage on my arm and I'm still in half mourning. The gray will do."

"Purple bombazine I think."

It did no good to rant about her manipulating my life and fashion, so I sank into sullen silence and let her arrange my hair and stuff me into a fitted dress. Annie, who had a remarkable eye for style, had copied the design from a French newspaper, and I learned long ago not to argue with her.

"The amethyst necklace and earbobs," she said, pulling a few pieces out of my jewel box. "And the pearl tucking combs."

"No, more. It's just supper!"

"It's never *just* supper," she said, straightening the bodice. "You in Charleston, the center of the world. Powerful people everywhere, and it'd do you good to be noticed, Missy. Maybe that French actor might help you get what you want."

"Really? And he's Belgian."

She twirled dramatically, her dress flaring out around her petite form. "*Oui.*"

"Do *you* like him?" I asked as she finished pinning my hair. I had seen him watching her before, not surprisingly. Annie was a strikingly beautiful mulatto like her mother. Exotic, moss green cat eyes and delicate features.

"Phfft. That tomcat? I don't want him. He's worse than a little Shanghai rooster trying to court any hen that gets close. Married, single, young, old. He don't care. How many French-speaking babies gonna pop up here next winter?"

"I don't think it works that way."

"Hmph." She readjusted the combs and smoothed on more pomade.

"What *do* you want? More than anything in the world?"

"I want you to sit straight so you don't wrinkle that dress. Then I want a little dress shop in Richmond or Charleston, so I can dress all the fine ladies when this mess is done. You can help me get that."

I laughed. "As long as you remember I was your first customer and don't push me to the bottom of the list. We'll be partners."

"Never would I forget you. Now go."

Captain Decker, resplendent in his deep blue uniform with golden braid and sash, waited at the foot of the stairs for me with four equally turned-out officers. His dark blond walrus mustache that flowed down to his jaw had been neatly trimmed since our earlier meeting.

Annie, refusing to spoil the line of her dress, sewed no slits in the skirt for my pockets, and so I was reduced to one gun in my purse for protection. One gun, a secreted amethyst hatpin, and a cadre of armed men.

"Captain Decker." I greeted and descended the wide white marble stairs in a cloud of aubergine. Decker stepped away from the Corinthian column he'd been leaning on and held out his hand. The other men also looked up, frank appreciation plain on their faces. Annie had worked her magic, bless her. I adjusted the crooked smile Mother hated. Crooked smiles were not becoming to young ladies, after all, as they are much too close to smirks.

Decker no sooner made introductions and claimed my arm than I was waylaid by Miss Jenny Nightingale and company, who rushed up to me breathlessly. (She had changed her name to honor Jenny Lind, the Swedish nightingale, she explained on our first meeting.) "Miss McKenzie, will Mr. de Wilde be joining your party? I've attempted several times to get an audition with his troupe. I know if he could but hear me sing, he would be enraptured and hire me."

"I've dined with him a few times by chance, but I have no plans today, Miss Nightingale."

"Oh," she looked crestfallen. "I shall try again another day. Thank you."

Decker got right to business as soon as we were seated. "How many horses do you have, Miss McKenzie?"

"Broke to ride?"

"No, we can train them. No bred mares for the army, but some will buy private breeding stock. I'm buying some to send home."

"Are you selling them all?" Lieutenant Stone asked.

Mr. de Wilde strolled in with his company, diverting my attention. He flashed his best actor smile at me, as did Miss Lily Atteberry, the English actress and singer who graced his arm and the stage with him in their current production of *Our American Cousin*. De Wilde swept an approving glance over the assembled officers and nodded as if he thought I was holding court. In the distance I heard a plaintive female voice calling his name, but the stewards were good at guarding their renowned diners from unwanted attention, and the cries faded.

I wrangled myself back to Stone's question. We'd worked so hard to build this herd. Everything should sell, but if it did, I was out of the horse business, and how would I build another herd?

"We should have at least 210 horses for sale, including mares and foals, so there will be something for everyone. I'm holding a few personal horses back, but all are for sale unless they don't sell well. I'm not giving them away."

"I've been authorized to bring as many men as required," Decker said. "Plus, there are several who will buy to send home or for personal use. We can get them cleaned and shod, or at least trimmed. Broodmares won't need shod, of course. Artillery crews are busy swapping cannon fire with Sumter to train green crews, but cavalry can be spared."

"Yes," I replied, "it's a bit hard to miss the daily barrage. I wake up each morning thinking we are under the direst thunderstorm and then remember, 'Oh, no, 'tis just the war.'"

There was a smattering of laughter.

We discussed the sale and preparations until I feared my brain would erupt in numbers and excused myself.

Annie sensed my fatigue as soon as I shut the door and helped me into a comfortable wrapper. "You get your business taken care of?"

"I don't know that it will ever be done," I replied. "It must, of course. The clock tick-tocks whether I'm ready or not."

After such an exhausting day, I looked forward to a bath and leisurely inhaled scented powders, going from one to another like a lazy bumblebee on a summer day. With bath finished and freshly powdered, I was Botticelli's Venus, newly risen.

"I'd open the balcony door, but it's still noisy," Annie said. "These people don't ever sleep."

She was right. There was a nervous energy in the city between the legislature hammering out new business and armies forming and re-forming. Troops marched through the streets. Riders raced to and fro with urgent messages, and carriages hurried up the streets and back down again. Graybeards who hadn't worn a uniform since their youth dug them out of trunks or had new ones made (usually with ranks they attained only in their dreams) and marched around to keep Negroes from imagined riots. West Pointers who earned every stripe refused to answer storekeepers who'd never seen formation, let alone action. Fights broke out regularly. Charleston, Chaos was her name.

As the pins came out of my hair, so did the tightness in my neck and shoulders ease. I unbound one braid, combing my fingers carelessly through the strands. Annie finished the nightly brushing ritual, pomaded the ends with gentle hands, and retired.

It was so warm I pondered raising the window more in hopes of catching a breeze before I settled in with my poetry.

As if in answer, the drapes stirred...but not from a draft. I stared in horrified fascination and fumbled for the gun on the table next to me, knocking the book and holy water to the floor. My room was three stories up, and someone was eeling their way through my window. A porkpie hat rose, revealing the startled face of my favorite fae, Darcy Hawkins, who stared at the muzzle of my dragoon. "Could you raise the window a bit, Miss? And not shoot me, please."

"Oh…yes." I shoved the gun in my wrapper pocket and rushed toward him. With Darcy wedged in the window, the pins locking it in place were firmly stuck. I tugged them free with some effort and jerked the sash up, whereupon Darcy tumbled to the floor at my feet with a solid thump. Annie dashed into the room, stick in one hand and her Deringer in the other. She looked from one to the other of us, ribbons on her nightcap whisking about like a nervous cat's tail. "Miss Mac? Do you want this fella in your room?"

"It's fine, Annie. I know him."

"Yes, but do you want to know him here?"

"I'll let you know if I need help."

"Your hair's all undone. You know that ain't proper," she complained on her retreat.

Leave it to Annie to worry about my unbound hair. I drew the drapes shut and turned to my intruder. "Why are you slithering into my room?"

"I have a message. I tried to catch you earlier, but you left abruptly while I was taking…stepped away. I can't be seen coming to your room." He shrugged as if that made perfect sense and moved away from the window.

I put on my shawl, making things more acceptable, and motioned him toward the chair opposite me. "You couldn't leave it with the desk clerk?"

"Miss McKenzie, if you want everyone to know what's in a message, give it to a desk clerk. If I want someone watched, I pay one of them five dollars, and I'll know every move the person makes, every message they receive, every bite they eat, every dollar they spend, and who they spend it on. There's so much information changing hands, there won't be a boy with shoe leather left by the end of the month."

"Why?"

"Do you think Belgian actors and English songbirds are here because Charleston is the newest cultural center? No. More than the North craves the goods the South produces. The whole world is interested in our little dispute." He pulled an envelope from inside his shirt. "I was to deliver this discreetly."

I remained suspicious and not a little irked at his unconventional entrance but recognized who it was from instantly, though there was no name on the cover aside from mine. "Why would General Beauregard send me a private message?"

"I'm only the messenger."

"You're Beauregard's man?"

"Not all soldiers wear uniforms, ma'am. Some of us serve better in the shadows."

I quickly read the short note.

Important information about your father and other matters.

With little explanation beyond that, he simply asked to meet me at an abandoned cabin a few miles out of town in the morning and gave a small sketch of the location. I knew where it was, but why the secrecy? "Do you know what this is about?"

"I have an idea."

"But you won't divulge it?"

"That's not my place. My nonsense chatter convinces all I'm a fool to be ignored." He grinned mischievously. How many people made the mistake of discounting him?

"Tell him yes."

How could I resist? *I must meet with you in private to discuss urgent matters.*

G.T. could meet with me at any time he chose and even in a private room or office if need be, though it might set tongues to wagging as I had no chaperone. This was different. Not only private, but somewhere no one would see the meeting take place. If I weren't so familiar with his handwriting and knew for certain the note was from him, I would have declined the clandestine rendezvous. I looked at the note again and was surprised at my trembling fingers.

Even with the heavy drapes drawn, we could hear the usual comings and goings of after-hours Charleston. Wagons rumbled by. Someone called out to a friend. Laughter. It grew quieter as the hour deepened, but never quiet.

"I best be going," Darcy said, looking at his pocket watch. "Time for Hatch to make his rounds, and he don't like me anyway. I'd as soon not be on the other end of his club again."

"Surely you're not going out the window!" My curiosity about how he'd gotten to my window in the first place had been pushed aside with the other mystery, but now I wondered anew.

"Have to, ma'am. Can't risk being seen coming out of your room or even inside the hotel." He peered out the window. "Maybe get a room closer to the ground for next time, though."

"Next time?"

Chapter Nine

A gentleman would never have asked a lady to meet him alone at an abandoned cabin. Yet there the note lay in my inner pocket. *Dear Miss Lorena McKenzie*, it began in the bold, elegant script of an educated man. A lady would never have agreed, but how could I deny the hero of Charleston?

Mild weather had lured woodland flowers out in bright splotches against the blackened forest floor of an autumn fire. This bleak morning, however, the frigid air whispered winter with no thought to the promise of spring. It had rained through the night and earlier in the morning but was clear when I left Charleston. Charcoal clouds unraveling across a tenebrous sky threatened another deluge at any moment, and though I'd worn my woolen riding habit, it would be faint protection. The Deringer secreted inside my cloak offered a different kind of protection, and it was probably inadequate also.

I let Charlie pick his way through the debris of the fire, trusting the horse to find a safe path. To my right an ancient pine had toppled during the blaze to land in the crown of an equally senior tree. A chipmunk scampered up the charred incline of the leaning trunk, chattering disapproval at me. He wanted me gone no more than I wanted to be gone. The gnawed bones of a deer trapped under a blackened log were a stark reminder of danger. As if I needed any.

A vague note from G.T. and I left willingly with my only explanation to Annie: a morning ride.

Charlie perked his ears and looked to the right. A man? No, surely it was the swirling fog. The woods hereabouts were rumored to be haunted. I'd heard all the stories. Indian spirits who refused to leave their ancestral lands even in death. A mother searching for her lost children. Massacred settlers. A little girl crying and even a baying hound with glowing red eyes. I drew my cloak closer, leaned low over his neck, and nudged the horse, wanting to burst into a gallop but knowing the overgrown trail was too treacherous for speed. Nevertheless, he dropped his head to nose out the uneven path and quickened his pace.

Lightning split the darkening sky, revealing the shape of a hunched-over man darting between the trees, greatcoat flowing behind him, wraithlike. My heart tripped. Had the robber's friends followed me? I touched the gun for reassurance.

Smoke, piney and fresh, mixed with the moldering scent of decay and charred wood. Rain crows called to their mates with a knocking chant before dropping to their doleful *kows*. A faint golden glow reflected off the fog, and the cabin emerged out of the mists just as the heavens opened.

Thank you, Lord.

Charlie trotted steadily in the downpour, alert, his ears swiveling back and forth. He smelled horses and nickered a greeting. If he had a fault, it was his desire to converse with other horses as soon as he came in range of them. The stout blue roan horse with three white stockings and a broad, bald face tied to the side of the cabin merely watched and made no reply. The bay beside him, however, eagerly answered. Greased paper windows glowed a welcoming shade of amber. A sadly sagging porch partially obstructed the person leaning in the open doorway. He ducked under the eave and ran out in the deluge to meet me.

A familiar face peered up at me. "Miss McKenzie."

My fears evaporated in faintly frenetic laughter. "Darcy! What are you doing here?"

"It's my day off," he replied as easily as if we'd met on the street. "I was asked to help."

Lifting my leg over the pommel, I leaned into his arms, hoping his slight frame could bear my weight so we wouldn't both land in the mud. He wavered not a bit, swung me to the sodden ground with ease, and took the reins from me. I lifted my skirts, but the extended lengths trailed behind, with the leather binding soaking water like a sponge, until I felt I was dragging an anchor. Under the protection of the porch, we shook off the rain and laughed about our ungainly race. What else could a pair of drowned rats do?

"Do you receive many young ladies out here?" I said breathlessly.

"Can't say as we do. It appears we've dropped off the social pages this season. Go on in, ma'am. I'll put the horses up."

I grasped his arm, feeling foolish for bringing it up now, but I had to. "Wait, you should know I think I saw a man shadowing me along the trail. Perhaps it was my imagination, but it looked like a man in a greatcoat."

"He was one of the captain's men set to watch for you and make sure you weren't followed. You're safe." He swung the door open for me and dashed back into the raging storm, where he had looped Charlie's reins around a hitching post and gathered the others.

Fear faded, and I stepped into the cheerily lit room. I expected the musty smell of rodents who take up residence as soon as humans leave, but instead there was fresh-cut pine wood, rum, tobacco, smoke, linseed oil, and the faint notes of a cologne I didn't recognize but instantly liked. It belonged to a man in a sharp Union uniform and greatcoat bent over a fire in the rough stone fireplace. A sodden black Hardee hat lay as if exhausted on the table. Most of the Confederate army who had resigned were still in Federal uniforms, but it put me on edge. His boots were tall and black, caked in drying mud and spurred. A cavalryman. More than that I could not tell.

The interior of the cabin belied its ramshackle exterior. The greased paper windows were tight and new. The puncheon floors, though worn, were swept and clean. A new corn shuck mop rested beside the door. New quilts covered the cots in the corners. A sheet draped across a door I assumed led to a bedroom or maybe a pantry.

Violets overflowed a clouded jar half filled with water in the middle of the table. "What beautiful flowers," I said, fumbling for something to break the silence.

"I picked them earlier but beg forgiveness," said the man turning from the fire he'd been tending. "I should have been building a fire instead. Thank you for coming. Major Fox at your service."

I nodded stiffly. "I don't understand. I was supposed to meet…someone else."

He pointed to a chair near the hearth and scooted it nearer the fire. "You're chilled. Please accept our apologies for drawing you out in this weather. We didn't anticipate it turning so cold. Or wet. The others will be here shortly, and I'll explain all."

The face was remarkably ordinary, neither handsome nor homely, but given to good humor as evidenced by the deep smile lines for his age, which I guessed to be late thirties. He also spent a lot of time deep in study with brows drawn together from the elevens between his eyes, which were large and gray and intently watching me.

What he determined, I know not, but I beheld a bird of prey behind the charming smile. I could well imagine ice-gray eyes counting a mouse's whiskers at a hundred yards and measuring its remaining breaths. Those piercing eyes would assess a situation, taking in every detail, and formulate an attack with methodical grace and speed. This was a man accustomed to action. He slid the greatcoat off and hung it over another chair to dry. His damp, dark hair tended to curl in the weather. I sympathized with him and knew my own hair must look a fright. Though it was not unattractive, it vexed him to no end as he pushed a wayward strand out of his eyes.

Lightning and thunder warred with each other in increasing rage. I wondered if the shake roof would long withstand the onslaught of pelting rain that struck like stones. "Thank you," I said, maintaining my composure but wishing G.T. would hurry. "It's a day fit for naught but ducks or the devil." I pulled the pins out of my top hat and squeezed some of the excess water out of the veils onto the hearth. Hopefully it wasn't ruined, but the poor peacock feather spray was well and truly drowned.

He helped me take my cloak off and spread it across the back of the cane chair, which creaked in protest when I sat. Pulling my skirts back modestly to expose my frozen toes to the heat made a great difference in comfort, and I could almost hear them whisper, "Thank you." The skirt hem had sopped water at least a foot up and lay heavy on the floor and my feet. I gave up fidgeting with my soaked gloves and drew them off to lay them across my knees.

"They should be here soon," he said and ran his fingers absently through his hair in some attempt to tame it.

Nodding, I resumed taking in my surroundings and studying Fox. Papa had trained me to observe and record people after an incident in New York with ruffians robbing Mother and me. Now it was a habit.

He glanced over at me as if aware of being watched. "You're attentive."

"Forgive me. Your face intrigues me. I thought to sketch it later." It was the best excuse I could think of.

"Oh, that could be…hazardous for me if the wrong people knew I was here. I prefer my neck unstretched." He said this, extending his neck upwards and chuckling.

Why would anyone wish to hang him, and had I unwittingly been lured into an ambush myself? The image of the trapped deer flashed through my mind. Now wary, I mentally reviewed the contents of the note, innocent as it seemed. On the pretense of warming my hands, I slipped one inside my pocket and withdrew the note.

Fortuitously, Darcy slipped in the door, slapping the rain from his hat. "Horses taken care of. How is our little rain crow? Is she warmed up yet?"

I leaned forward and dropped the envelope into the fire, but the creaking chair betrayed my movement.

"Thank—" Fox caught my startled eye and grinned. "Clever. I might have missed that if your chair hadn't told on you. G.T. will be disappointed you disposed of him so easily."

The color rose in my cheeks. *G.T. Only people close to G.T. called him that now. Even I had stopped for propriety's sake as he had dropped the Gustave Toutant from his signature and greetings.* "So, you do know—oh, dear. My woman's mind creating skullduggery. And, yes, I am warming."

Fox laughed. "Do I know the general? Yes."

Darcy wiped his feet on the tattered rag rug and looked between us. "Is he up to shenanigans?"

"The fault's all mine. That roan outside was exquisite. Is she yours?" It was a clumsy attempt to change the subject.

"Fie, I wish. That's Fox's Grey Sadie."

"I see you know Mr. Hawkins," Fox said.

The sound of boots clattering across the porch interrupted the questions brewing. Two men came through the door, their hats pulled low and collars high. One remained outside on watch, with the edge of his hat silhouetted against the window. The newcomers shook the rain off, sending droplets through the air like wet hounds, and stomped the mud from their boots. They then melted silently into the shadows and threw quilts from the cots over their shoulders. Had my life depended on it, I couldn't have given any description of them save wet.

Fox retreated to the corner to talk to them. One or another glanced over at me from time to time, but I saw only vague outlines and heard not a word of the conversation. Presently, they pulled their hats back down over their faces again and left as mysteriously as they had arrived.

Darcy slipped out the door to replace the guard outside. This man also kept his hat pulled low and his face hidden as he passed by me and into the back room. He came out in dry clothes and oft-darned stockings that were as colorful as the patchwork quilt he cocooned in.

"As we feared might happen, G.T. has been detained in meetings," Fox said.

"Then I have no reason to stay," I said and tried to draw my sodden gloves on.

"Miss McKenzie, hold a moment." He shot me an astounded look, clearly asking if I'd taken leave of my senses, then pulled some letters from the inside pocket of his jacket and handed me one.

I recognized the familiar script and read the letter. Fox kept his gaze on me, studying my reaction. I read it again, occasionally glancing up at Fox. I wasn't sure what I expected an intelligence officer to look like. My father had been a voracious collector and reader. Though he preferred I read the classics and poetry, he denied me nothing in his library, and I had read James Fenimore Cooper's *The Spy* and *The Bravo* many times, but those were stories, adventures. Now I sat before one of these conspirators? G.T. had very elegantly introduced me to his agent as if he were setting me before a favored cousin and would I be so kind as to offer him hospitality? "Is this true?"

"Yes, ma'am. I'm General Beauregard's spymaster. He wanted this meeting to introduce me and my mission in person. He's a great military tactician, but we'll need information desperately if we're to win this war, and there will be one." Fox said this as if beginning a lecture.

I didn't want to argue with him, but surely, he was wrong. "From the newspapers, Congress thinks the states will return, and only South Carolina may sulk for a bit."

He snorted in derision. "Yes, even now Governor Pickens's envoy is in Washington negotiating an agreement about what South Carolina owes the federals for taxes, Federal properties, et cetera, in good faith." He huffed his derision at that. "While Lincoln's people assure them all is well and distract them with inventories and numbers, a convoy of his warships, full to the gunnels with troops and supplies, steam toward us as we speak."

Was the entirety of mankind a den of vipers? Bankers and politicians alike, nothing but deception and lies. I mulled this over. Enough tidbits dropped during indiscreet dinner conversations to support what he said, but outright trickery?

A log popped like gunfire, collapsing into the fire and sending a shower of sparks onto the flagstone hearth. He prodded the remaining logs with a poker and added another. I leaned away and closer to the table, where I pulled a flower from the vase. Regardless of the water, it looked as wilted as I felt. "I don't know what I have to do with this," I said, twirling the drooping bloom in my fingers.

Fox handed me another envelope. On the outside of one was my name in G.T.'s flourishing script. It was a more in-depth introduction to Fox, an explanation, if vague, of his mission to gather intelligence and supplies that might soon be considered contraband, and an invitation to join Fox's circle. How unerringly polite. He might just as well have said, *You've been invited to join the grand ball, mademoiselle—one that could get you hanged.*

I sat with the letter open before me, stunned that he would consider me for this. In my lap lay my gloves I'd folded over and over into a stiff little cord as tight as my stomach. I unrolled them and tried to smooth them, wishing I could ease my nerves as easily. My head spun until I thought I might pass out. I couldn't even form a coherent thought, let alone an effective argument. "Might I have some of that brandy?" I asked quietly, almost a whisper, motioning to the bottle on the mantle.

"Pardon. Where are my manners?" Fox answered.

He polished a glass with his handkerchief before pouring a generous portion and setting it before me gracefully as if we were in a Charleston mansion withdrawing room. A tin cup received another measure, but he only sipped it before passing it to his man.

"That's good brandy." It warmed its way down my throat and into my knotted stomach. "Between dealing with bankers and this, I may become a drinking woman before it's all over."

"I hope not. G.T. would be most unhappy with me if I led to your downfall. He's already threatened me with the wrath of God if I get you hurt."

Lightning lit the sky, turning the windows bright gold. Thunder rattled the cabin moments later, shaking dust from the rafters. I hurriedly put my hand over my glass.

Fox looked up. "Something like that."

"G.T.'s a bit protective," I said. "Why did you wait to give me the other letter?"

"Because if you had recoiled at the idea of who I was from his introduction, brief as it was, I wouldn't proceed. Some people think information officers, spies if you will, are the spawn of Satan."

"I'm not convinced of that quite yet."

"Beauregard wanted to be here to fully explain this to you. He told me how much The Pines means to you, but in the end, this is my spy ring. My responsibility. Your father also knew that if war comes, there won't be a safe place in the south. Not here and certainly not in Virginia, which will be hotly contested." Fox took on a decidedly fatherly expression when he sat opposite me. "I'd rather have taken a whipping than come here today." He said this as if he were about to tell me he'd just shot my favorite dog.

"Why?"

"Because I've already inquired about you. It's what I do. You're in dire straits financially. I know you have a buyer for Rosemount should you need it to save The Pines. That's your backup plan. I'm going to ask you not to do that. I need you in my spy ring, and I need you in Virginia."

It might take more than one glass of brandy. I swallowed more fortitude and turned back to fiddling with the gloves in my lap. "If the South has been so preparing, it stands to reason so has the North. How are you conducting such an operation? Aren't Southern people suspect?"

"Not to my knowledge, and I have deep sources." He stood and began to pace, his hands clasped behind his back. "Old Fuss and Feathers General Scott frantically woos Southern officers to remain. I can't imagine Lincoln will keep him as head of the army if war proceeds. He's nearly eighty years old and all but bedridden. Still, he's a war hero, and men respect him. Some will be swayed, but he's like a love-struck suitor promising the moon when he has but a dollar to offer. We're guaranteed if war comes, Southerners won't be compelled to fight against the South. He'll assign us elsewhere. He assures us it's a passing squall. His aides protest these promises, saying we must do our duty wherever it is. I'll stay until it gets too hot. Scott's optimism gives me cover, and I'm ever vigilant."

He stopped pacing. His shoulders rose and then fell, expelling a heavy huff. "We may not depend on the words of desperate, octogenarian generals or lying politicians. The storm is coming. Your father knew this. G.T. knows this better than any and yet, like Cassandra, few listen to him. If war comes, it will be long, it will be hard-fought, and it will be bloody. The only way to save the South is to end it quickly. The only way to do that is with vastly superior intelligence."

"My father discussed this with G.T.?" He wasn't shy about discussing politics with me, but he had never indicated an opinion on the coming war or perhaps offering Rosemount to the effort. My father was my rock. Even in death, he'd been something I might count on. What would he do? How would he have protected me? Was it all a lie? Was he willing to put us all in danger? I was surprised at the level of anger at the thought. My mooring had been cut, and I was adrift.

Fox looked around, surprise plain on his face. "Of course. He believed ending the war early was the best way to protect you. He could send you to Charleston, but the Lincolnites blame the fire eaters who had urged secession for this—" he waved his hand in the air, "confrontation. Many think they'll make an example of South Carolina and bring the rest of the states to heel. Cut off the head of the viper if you will. Winchester, and therefore Rosemount, will be a hotly contested area for both armies if this drags on. His two options were to send you north to Baltimore and safety or do all he could to help end the war quickly. Sending you north wasn't in his vocabulary."

"It wouldn't be." Nor was it an option for me. I could tolerate my mother only in small doses.

If war came, it would be fought in our homeland, in our homes. It was our gardens that would sprout gravestones instead of cabbages. I tried to envision Rosemount and The Pines as battlegrounds and recoiled at the horror as soon as my mind touched it. "I don't see how a woman can be of any service to you and why you're approaching me in this—" I didn't even know what to call it. I couldn't bring myself to admit we were at war. Not yet.

"Women have a great advantage. No one suspects them, especially a Southern woman. They are too genteel. Plus, if you'll forgive me, men are particularly susceptible to a beautiful woman. Sometimes spies wear crinolines."

I shifted in my chair uncomfortably.

Noting my discomfiture, he shifted his assault to another flank. "I wouldn't put you in more danger than necessary. My men will offer protection as they can, and I will have people watching after you while you are north, but you may need to depend on your wits. I believe you've a stout heart; else you wouldn't come here alone. G.T. felt you were right for the job, and I trust his judgment. We need you and Rosemount in my circle."

"I—I just can't consider it. Not yet. My girls would be in danger. I have to believe we won't come to war."

He ran his hand through his hair in frustration. I could tell it was taking everything in him to keep from calling me a fool, and maybe I was. "War is coming, Miss McKenzie, but I won't press you. For the love of all that is holy, though, please keep Rosemount. Should you change your mind later, you'll need to be in Virginia to slip across the border to collect information and contraband. You would be of little use in Charleston."

"I'm sure it won't come to that. I hope to save The Pines without sacrificing Rosemount, and the union will be preserved, I believe." Bold words on my part, but I was sure of neither.

Chapter Ten

Once the proposition had been laid out and he had pressed the importance, there was little more to discuss without revealing more than was prudent, given my indecision. Fox told me more about G.T. and my father's friendship that I was unaware of. Little was mentioned about how he knew them, however. He discussed DC social life and the latest gossip. He knew my aunt and uncle well. I knew all the people he mentioned, and he soon had me laughing with stories and impersonations of various people. Another glass of brandy.

"Major Fox, I think you're trying to charm your way into my good graces," I said, accepting the brandy.

He smiled and shrugged somewhat ruefully. "Guilty. Is it working?"

I studied him more closely than I had before. This was a man who bore careful watching, but I couldn't help liking him. "A little."

"Then there is hope," he said and touched his tin cup that he had collected and refilled my glass.

"There is always Hope. She is the last to flee."

The storm, violent as it was, at last passed with no damage. I was like the girl who'd spent the night dancing with fairies and wanted a petal from a dress or an acorn cap to prove she wasn't mad and soaked old newspapers in water to wrap my flowers. And yet, what I had been asked to consider was mad. Could I really join Fox's spy ring and deliver information and contraband? Offer Rosemount as a way station? No, folly. Of course, I couldn't.

The men who had delivered the message earlier had waited in the barn while we negotiated but joined us now as escorts. There wasn't a scrub horse in the bunch. The horses were running stock with enough bone to stand hard use. They were horses with a single purpose: Don't get caught.

Darcy returned Charlie to me, but it was Fox who helped me mount. "Will you at least think on it?" he asked, still holding my hand and looking up at me.

"I will." It was the only assurance I could give.

"I'll be in contact with you when the time is right."

I couldn't help feeling I had made a deal with the devil who would appear one day to collect his due.

The others fell away closer to town, but Darcy accompanied me into Charleston with small talk about his family and girlfriend, his hopes to become a teacher one day, and his love of the mountains. What would happen to his beloved Georgia valley in the coming war? Who would care for his family and girlfriend in the coming war? Each thought was followed by the whisper of war.

I had begged a few biscuit and ham sandwiches before I rode out this morning, but that was long ago, and I now only longed for a hot bath and a quiet meal in my room. As ever, the hotel lobby was filled with milling people when I stepped through the wide double doors especially built for ladies and their fashionable hooped skirts. My bedraggled and still sodden affair might have slipped through a mouse hole. I kept my head down to avoid being recognized and drawn into unwanted conversation but was outmaneuvered by General Beauregard, who stepped gracefully in front of me as if he were at a dance.

"Miss McKenzie," he said, bowing and tipping his hat to me.

"Good afternoon, sir. How are you?" I replied, trying to signal I needed to flee.

"Very well, mademoiselle. You'll be joining our table?"

"Unfortunately, I'm soaked from my ride."

The corner of his mouth twitched down in a fleeting grimace. "I'm sure no one minds waiting for you to change."

Beauregard, a career soldier who'd been classically educated before entering West Point, suffered fools no better than I did and probably resented the interruption to his business. Even if I hadn't known him, it was easy to guess him a Creole. He bore that dark, exotic look that set them apart. His large, brown eyes under finely arched brows would have been devastating on a woman, expressive, deep, and doleful above high, fine cheekbones.

He slipped into Creole French and asked me how my cousin Isabella and her children were and gave me the latest news about Baton Rouge.

"I regret I was unable to meet you," he said, apologizing again. "Please, change out of your wet clothes."

Thus resigned to another hectic meal, I hurried to my room. Annie would be horrified at my hair that was askew with wayward curls escaping the braid and net as it always did when it got damp. With luck, she'd be gone.

"Miss Mac! Your hair!" met me as soon as I poked my head in the door.

Luck was ever a stranger. "Annie, G.T. and half his staff are waiting. Help me get into something dry, please. There's no time to fool with my hair. Besides, I think Spaniel curls are popular again."

"Is that what you call that disaster?"

I was ready within minutes, and Annie even managed to change the ribbon on freshly sleeked hair before I bolted away. Matching hair ribbons being of utmost importance.

"Forgive me," I said, arriving breathless. G.T. introduced me to his officers, and we proceeded to the dining room, where a long table was already half seated with chattering people. I looked about the crowded room at various officers, ladies, men of power, actors, and celebrities. All pawns in a giant game of chess. Not surprisingly, a large round table near the door was filled with young ladies who were fans of Miss Nightingale. They obligingly dropped handkerchiefs for interesting male prospects to fetch for them and tried to draw them into grateful conversation.

G.T. took his place beside me, but there was a brief scuffle between two of his officers, with one tripping over another, before they settled on the other side. Opposite me, Miss Nightingale and her brother Budge Gundy were already seated. I had hoped to escape them, but luck still fled from me. She was aghast at my hearty order and reminded me ladies eat like sparrows. Her brother disagreed and appreciated women with a good appetite.

"I tell you," an elderly lady proclaimed, "none of us will survive. The Yankees will descend from the North, and the Negroes will rise from behind and murder us in our sleep." A servant lifted her glass to fill it with water, his ebony face stone still. It astounded me when people relegated servants to the same stock as furniture. If I desired to be a spy, which I didn't, I reminded myself, I'd be a politician or general's housemaid and thus become invisible. They'd spill their innermost secrets in front of me with catastrophic results.

On the conversations droned. Was it too early for wine? An excellent first course of hot and cold hors d'oeuvres poured out of the kitchen. I was partial to Charleston's oysters and sated my appetite while I could.

I inhaled the green turtle soup when it was served and tried to ignore the new debate. "Tell me it isn't so!" the woman declared. "That Negro Washington already tried to raise a rebellion, and Esquires Shannon and William nearly rushed to their deaths in a duel over the wretch. Between the Negroes and the Yankees, we're doomed, I tell you!"

"Nonsense, my dear," her husband replied. "Our boys will send them packing back to Washington in ten days. They'll howl for peace, isn't that right, General?"

"You are a fool, sir," G.T. said in between bites and set his spoon down, then carefully wiped his mustache. "Lincoln will not allow his cash cow to go without a fight. The fight will be long and bloody, and before it's over, there is not a one of you who will not wail over the coffins of the boys you so gleefully send to war with balls and banquets today. Fools, the lot of you. If you had any sense, you'd be spending every dime on rifles and ammunition, not parties and silk ballgowns."

He leaned over to me and smiled conspiratorially, "Except you, *ma pet*, you will need beautiful gowns for the work ahead."

I stared at him like a stunned dove. Did he believe I had accepted Fox's offer?

The remainder of the table looked at each other in sheer shock as if they had just been dipped in ice water. At last, the woman broke the spell and laughed. "Oh, General. You are so funny. Keit said just last night—" and she started droning with one of his fire-eating speeches.

Dear heavens, a bit of peace. "Have you tried the soup?" I asked, breaking out of my own shock.

She stared at me as if I'd asked her to dance a highland fling. "Not yet," she replied peevishly. "I've been conversing."

"How about you stop conversing and eat, darling?" her husband said with an indulgent but firm look. He gave me the slightest wink and returned to his soup. She might have no shortage of words for him later, but for now she was quiet. Praise the Lord.

I remained quiet throughout the various debates but continued to eat everything put in front of me with the greatest pleasure, proving, I suppose, I was no lady. I couldn't resist ordering the lemon cake and raspberry sauce, however, as both were favorites and together promised to be divine. I had just bailed into it when someone sat down at the piano, and Miss Nightingale stood up from the table and glided to the center of the room, her eyes locked on Mr. de Wilde and his table. The Nightingale flock swiveled their long, thin necks like a flamboyance of flamingoes to better watch the coming show.

Please, Lord, no. I was already ill and on the verge of fading and clutched at the table to keep upright. I simply couldn't tolerate an impromptu concert. G.T. cocked an eyebrow at me.

Lieutenant Stone coughed nervously. If I aimed right, I could faint into his side. I scooted my chair back a bit more lest I collapse into the remnants of the cake's raspberry sauce. He matched my action and leaned back in his chair, giving me a straight shot to his chest or possibly blocking my exit if I decided to run. You never know how a disaster will unfold.

"This is for my dear friend Lorena, who encouraged me to be brave," and she smiled at me, then swiveled back to de Wilde to make sure he didn't escape. She was not only using one of the most popular songs of the age but blaming me for the atrocity she was about to commit! Without warning, she opened her mouth as if to scream, and out came something akin to a banshee's wail. "The years creep slowly by, Lorena. Snow is on the grass again." Behind me, a servant dropped a dish. I stared at Miss Nightingale flailing her arms about like a demented windmill as she sang. I imagine I looked horrified, because I truly was. How could this get any worse? I reminded myself too late never to ask that question of the universe because it will surely answer. And it did. The Nightingale fan club stood to join her in serenading the last two lines of the first verse. The first verse? Moses. There were five more to go. The flock sat, atwitter with delight at their performance, and she launched into the second verse. Lieutenant Stone nudged me with his elbow. I, being a coward to my marrow about some things, accepted the offer to retreat. I sighed and pitched away so quickly he scrambled to catch me. "Bravo!" cried someone from the fan club. "She's swooned with joy. Sing on, my dove, sing on." Stone pulled me from my chair and into his lap. I dared not open my eyes, but I heard the elderly woman demand he unhand me. The lieutenant stood, along with the rest of the soldiers, judging from the sound of scraping chairs. "And what would you like me to do with her? Drop her to the floor? We'll take her to her room and call for the doctor."

Please, Lord, no.

"I mightn't have stuffed you with so much food if I'd known I was going to carry you three flights of stairs," he whispered.

The others in my escort chuckled while I could only squinch a jaundiced eye at him and pinch his arm.

"Ouch."

"You should let me walk," I whispered.

"Nonsense. When is the next time I'll get to carry a young lady around?"

"Stone wouldn't put you down if his legs were breaking," came from beside me. "He knows one of us would rescue you. He's greedy like that."

"I am. Should have been faster, boys."

"You stomped on my foot, or I'd have been sitting beside her."

"That's why I stomped on your foot, Henry."

I'd objected to his chivalry at first, and Stone was puffing a bit when he reached my room, but I was thankful he carried me. My throat and face tightened uncomfortably, and there was an odd twitchiness throughout my body as if I couldn't be still.

"Set me down," I rasped. "Annie, get me out of these clothes!" The men stared at my outburst. "I'm sorry. I feel like I've been eating ground silver." There was no other way to describe the metallic taste in my mouth.

Henry's eyes flew open in alarm. "I'll find that doctor."

"Annie, get your mistress comfortable," Beauregard said. "We'll wait outside."

She nearly tore my clothes off as soon as they left. For once there were no reproaches about propriety. "Stop clenching your toes. You'll get cramps."

"I can't!"

Dressed in a gown and wrapper, I pondered my malady. It wasn't food poisoning. That began with a heaviness in the stomach followed by violent heaving. Annie ushered G.T. back into my room, where we awaited the doctor. He'd dismissed the rest of his men. "G.T.," I greeted with a painful smile. My constricted face would allow no more.

He looked at me, horrified. "*Ma chère petite amie.* What's wrong with you?"

"I don't know." I prowled the room nervously, unable to sit for more than a moment, and might climb the walls in madness shortly. At last I was forced to the bed and covered. My legs drew up painfully, jerking in uncontrollable little spasms. Like a dead hen's claws, my toes curled up, and I could do naught to straighten them.

Dear Lord, what is happening to me?

The room was no doubt sweltering, but my teeth chattered as if I were freezing. He called for more blankets and covered me tenderly. My back arched, making me look like a fish out of water, I was sure, but there was nothing I could do but lie and flop and pray. I closed my eyes and wished for a dark cave or a grave.

"Get back." I recognized the hotel doctor's voice through my swaddling.

Did he have to clink that spoon so loudly as he mixed his potion?

"Drink this."

"What's wrong with her?" G.T. demanded.

"Strychnine poisoning. Billy, her server, has the same symptoms. That's why it took me so long to get here. He ate the rest of that cake and was afraid of getting in trouble. I finally dragged out of him what he'd been eating and where he got it. I didn't believe her malady was serious until I realized it was Miss McKenzie's cake and connected the two. I apologize." He studied me as I forced the medicine down. "All of it. It's an experimental drug mixed with bromide of potassium. Another dose in about thirty minutes. You may have a headache or stiffness tomorrow, but I think you'll be all right. I told them to be more careful in the kitchen with that rat poison. Not enough to kill you, I'm sure, but it might have put you down for a few days."

"I'm about to come out of my skin; must I stay in bed?"

"I don't wonder. University students use strychnine in small doses to excite their senses when they're studying for examinations. You're overcharged. Like too much electricity through a wire. Send for me if something happens."

He left the glass with the second dose and departed to check on Billy. Annie went to fetch tea, it being the great healer.

G.T. stared out my window, his jaws clenching in fury. The sunlight streaming in glinted off his golden epaulets, made brighter by contrast with the dark uniform. At his slim waist, a polished black belt cinched in the gold sash. Gold sashes seemed the only uniform standard, as some wore Federal blue, some black, some gray, and various shades in between. He was in full dress uniform, meaning the earlier meeting was undoubtedly with politicians who loved the pomp. It was surprising to notice everything in minute detail. If this was a side effect of the poison, I'd be amazed if it weren't abused.

"I hoped to be able to visit with you, but the…entertainment interrupted my planned after-dinner conversation. And now this awful—" He waved his hand in the air, his features darkening like one of those bayou storms that blow in from the gulf, where you batten the shutters and wait for it to roll over. "I swear if I ever find out who did this!"

"There's nothing you can do, and you have greater things to worry about."

He came back over to me and squeezed my hand. "I wanted to express again my great appreciation for your cousin's kindness to Mrs. B. in my absence. As to the other matter, pray about it. I'm sure Major Fox presented his case. I need you and Rosemount and wouldn't ask if I didn't. You won't be allowed to remain neutral, and ending this quickly is the best way to protect the little girls and everything you hold dear. You must realize this, but we'll talk more when you feel better."

He kissed me on the cheek and promised a letter as soon as he was able. Annie arrived as he was leaving.

"Mr. Beddow's waiting in the lobby for your appointment."

Would this day never end? I'd forgotten about the police statement. "I simply can't today."

"Do you want to talk to him or send him away? When I say talk, I mean for a minute. You going to bed, Missy."

"Tell him I'll meet him in the morning and apologize for my rudeness."

She rolled her eyes. "Yes, because you planned on being poisoned."

Chapter Eleven

Doctor Bartholomew ordered me to stay in my room the next morning, though I awoke with no ill effects. Under no circumstances was I to leave my room.

"I have a horse sale, and I need to give a statement to the police," I further protested. Unstated, I also intended to put wheels in motion to deliver a clear message to my attacker and his partner.

He tapped my shoulder with a long, bony finger, shushing me so he could listen to my heart. His cinnamon goatee, mostly faded to white, worked itself about, reminding me of a cow chewing its cud. At last, the contemplative teeth grinding stopped, and he wrapped his stethoscope. "I'll be back to check on you." His fingers ran through the shock of cotton-white hair. "Rest. Read a nice book."

I had other plans.

As soon as he left, I dressed and put the final touches on my strategy. Pulling the small penknife from my purse, I scraped gray dust from a pastel stick in my artist kit and smudged it under my eyes. Annie, who took great joy in my perfect complexion as if it were something directly attributable to her efforts, gasped and plummeted into a nearby chair.

"You lost you mind?"

I followed that with dark blue deftly applied with a small watercolor brush, fading to lavender. Satisfied that I looked properly ill, I powdered my face liberally as if trying to cover the ghastly dark circles under my eyes.

"I'll fetch the doctor. That poison setting in you brain."

"You'll do no such thing. Do I look sick?"

"You look like a consumption patient bout to hack her last bit of life out."

"Perfect."

Dressed in black, I was a perfect figure of wretchedness. Poe, being so enamored of tragically dying young women and all, would have loved me. A pity we hadn't met. I put the modest black veil over my face and left, hoping Mr. Shroeder was on duty at the front desk today as he was kindly disposed toward me. The light veil was enough to appear concealing, but not enough to hide my deathbed eyes. Faint twinges of guilt faded when I remembered being poisoned.

I hurried down the carpeted hallway but slowed at the top of the stairs to appear convincingly frail. Clutching the mahogany rail, I crept slowly down like a dowager on her last leg, each step clicking hollowly on the marble treads.

At the desk, I clasped the edge of the counter as if I might topple at any moment. "Is the manager about?" I inquired meekly.

"Yes, but I think he's busy," replied the clerk, looking around from sorting mail into wooden pigeonholes.

Lifting the veil, I set it over my hat with trembling fingers. "I must speak to him. It's important." My voice quavered, dying quail weak and pitiful. "Please."

He gasped at my appearance and hurried away, not wanting to deal with me at all.

I traced the gray veins in the marble countertop as I waited until someone grasped me by the hand. "*Mon Dieu!* My dear little dove, what has happened to you? You look like death!" *Monsieur* de Wilde pulled me to him and patted my shoulder. Moses, I didn't need the actor and his entourage in this. "My dear, there, there. Do not cry." He whipped out his handkerchief and rubbed at my cheek, though I wasn't close to crying, and managed to jab me in the eye as he was doing so. I caught his warning glance and didn't recoil. Miss Atterbury's hands shot to her mouth in horror at my appearance, adding to the growing drama.

Due to the poke in the eye, I *was* crying and dabbed at the tears.

Blowing in like a winter squall, Mr. Humphreys plopped his hands on the counter. "What's this all about?" he demanded.

Drat. I'd have to work on him. He was something of a hard case and always shouting at people and complaining. He was on duty when I first checked in and at first denied me a room because I was too young and unchaperoned. He was northern and new, had little patience for women, and none for me. Out of patience with his bumptious attitude, I finally drew myself up and introduced myself properly and reminded him that the McKenzies had recommended the Charleston for our out-of-town buyers and booked blocks of rooms ourselves. The hotel was nearly booked full the week of the sale thanks to us, but I would be happy to steer my business elsewhere.

He found me a room.

Interrupting his impatient drumming fingers, I said, "We should discuss this privately in your office."

"Most certainly not. Guests aren't allowed in the office."

"Let me call my physician," Miss Atterbury exclaimed.

"No, I'll be fine," I said feebly and held de Wilde's arm for support. "I just need to discuss some business and sit down before I faint."

De Wilde turned to the songstress and the rest of the group, who milled about in consternation. "Please, go to the dining room. I'll join you directly." He glared at Humphreys. "Can you not see how distraught the lady is?"

"I don't care. She isn't coming behind the desk."

"Fine," I replied, raising my voice, "Then we'll discuss it out here in front of God and everyone how your hotel poisoned me with your lemon cake, and it's but by the grace of God and my not finishing it I didn't die. I can see the headlines. 'Orphan Girl Staying at The Charleston Murdered by Staff.'"

"The editors of all the newspapers here and in many other cities are very good friends of mine," the actor said with a charming smile. "Not to mention the many editor fans of Miss Atterbury, who was so concerned." His unutterably handsome features took on the innocence of a child. "I'm sure you don't want that."

Humphreys looked around quickly to see if anyone heard me and ushered me around the desk. "Come along." He glared at de Wilde. "Do you have business with her?"

"Why, yes, I do. I don't trust you. You might take advantage of the young lady or perhaps murder her more permanently this time."

Humphreys sputtered but allowed him to follow us into his office.

"Now," I said after Humphreys begrudgingly offered me a chair, "I require you to make another lemon cake with raspberry sauce. The same one that was used to poison me."

"No, ma'am. We'll not be doing that. It's been taken off the menu."

"I need two servings in pastry boxes for Monday, April 8th, in the morning."

"I can't imagine why anyone would want you gone," he muttered.

"Careful, Mr. Humphreys. Should I become ill again while I'm here, I'll make sure the sordid story appears in every major newspaper in the country. Mary Chesnut will hear of it, and you know how she is. That gossip will have it spread far and wide across the South by nightfall." Mrs. Chesnut was well known in Charleston society for her wealth, her beauty, and her endless and often malicious quidnunc ways. I put a hand to my chest to emphasize my distress. "Plus, my uncle's one of Lincoln's men. He wouldn't take kindly to harm befalling me."

Humphreys tugged at his collar. "I meant no offense. Trust me, your food will be most carefully guarded. I've already thoroughly chastised my staff."

De Wilde offered me his arm as we departed the very agitated manager. "Do you play poker, mademoiselle?"

"I used to play with my father and some of his friends. My mother put a stop to most of that when she came home early once and found her fifteen-year-old daughter drinking whiskey and smoking cigars with the men while we played cards. She thought it would ruin my chances of a decent match if anyone found out and threatened to send me to a finishing school in Europe. I don't think the men cared, but the mothers would have been horrified at the prospects of a cigar-smoking, poker-playing daughter-in-law."

He laughed. "Some women have no sense of humor. You should play poker more often. Also, the next time you decide to smudge your eyes, be careful of loose powder. You had blue dust on your cheek I was obliged to clean before someone noticed. If you'll come by the theater, I'll show you some makeup tricks."

"I don't think I—"

"Miss McKenzie!" There was no mistaking Dr. Bartholomew's enraged bellow from across the lobby. "I told you to rest."

My heart went tumbling down a steep slope. I flipped the veil down and ducked my head. "I can't let him see me like this."

"I will save you. I have laryngitis," he croaked convincingly.

De Wilde intercepted him, and I escaped without reservation or honor, doubly in debt to the actor.

Chapter Twelve

Annie looked up from the dress she was mending when I dashed in the door. "That didn't take long."

"The doctor caught me." I rushed over to wash my face in case he followed me. Having seen me less than two hours ago, he certainly wouldn't fall for the ruse. I examined my face quickly in my looking glass to make sure all traces of the shadows were gone.

Further discussion was cut off by a knock on the door that sent my heart tumbling. "Blast. He's here."

Annie opened the door when I signalled. "Sir?"

"Is Miss McKenzie available?" Mr. Beddow asked. "They said at the desk she was indisposed."

I peered around Annie. "I've been confined to rooms."

He hesitated, frowning. "Contagious? I have a wife and babies."

"Poisoned. The doctor insists I stay in."

Anger quickly chased the initial shock. "Poisoned! The hell?" He stepped inside and slammed the door. "Pardon my language. What happened?"

We sat at the table near the window, and I related the story. He stopped me at various points, questioning me to pull out details. At the end, he sighed and rocked back in his chair, lacing his hands behind his head. "I have a good idea of who's behind it, seeing as I was poisoned also."

"Mahler."

"Mhmm. I told you he was a cowardly, vindictive little rat, but I never expected this."

In the back of my mind, I wondered if it might have something to do with my meeting with Fox but dismissed it.

Annie disappeared and returned presently with blueberry and mint scones and a pot of coffee, as I hadn't had breakfast yet, and she was ever a gracious hostess.

"My stars, these are good." I sighed in deep contentment. Annie shook her head at my scone ecstasy and parked nearby to protect my honor, which had curiously been safe enough while she was gone.

Mr. Beddow nodded, licked the crumbs from his fingers, and reached eagerly for another. "We were supposed to go to the police today," he said between bites. "And now, I find you've been poisoned."

"The doctor won't let me leave."

"It doesn't matter. I went earlier to give my statement and to make arrangements for yours. They said it wasn't necessary, so I pressed them. The culprit hanged himself, they claim."

"What!"

He snorted. "Yes. I said since I was there, I'd like to talk to another of my clients and save a trip. It was a lie, but I'd seen the man arrested a few days ago, so I got back to the cells. With great difficulty and promises to represent a couple of them pro bono, I convinced some prisoners to talk. Rascal Michener, the man who robbed you, kept yelling he wanted an attorney. Said he wasn't going down for those yellow dogs because they had money. Sometime after midnight they put him in a private cell. The jailer said he committed suicide this morning, but my fellows said he got quiet right after they took him away."

"Who do you think was behind it?" I said softly as if someone might be behind me.

"I'm sure your bankers were involved. People seem to die mysteriously or disappear to the bank's great advantage. Had

Rascal gotten away with your cheque, Mondovi wouldn't have replaced it before the note was due. Another nail in your coffin."

"What should I do?"

"Exactly what you're doing. Play your hand out. I'm certain that caitiff Mahler is behind the poisonings, but he'll get his comeuppance. Rosetta Mahler is Senator Gibbon's daughter, and she's home suing for divorce. Gibbon is fiercely protective of his daughters. As to the others, God has a way of dealing with people." He snagged another scone and more coffee.

We discussed necessary legal arrangements, and Annie sent him off with the rest of my breakfast scones. Bless her heart.

Gatekeeper Annie turned away all invitations after I returned to the room, saying I was indisposed. Later, she went to fetch hot chocolate and the mail.

"Here's a note from your cousin Carl," she said and handed me a sealed envelope with an unfamiliar, and very bold, man's handwriting on it.

Confusion, suspicion, and irritation assaulted me all at once. "I don't have a cousin Carl."

Chapter Thirteen

I had slept fitfully, dreaming of hanged men and Mr. Mahler falling backwards into a bog. Frantic to help, I raced about searching for a stick to rescue him. He cursed me as he had his wife even as he sank. Just as I extended a branch to him, it all changed. I took his place and floated in the mire instead. My skirts and unbound hair billowed about me in the bistre waters. I gave one terrified scream for help. Then, gasping for air, eyes wide and terrified, I began to sink. My face disappeared under thousands of round, golden leaves. Fingers stretched heavenward, relaxed, and vanished at last beneath the waters also. The leaves swirled in, leaving no trace I'd ever been there.

I awoke to a bed so sweat-soaked I might have poured a pitcher of water in it and threw the covers back, heaving and coughing and swiping away tears. Annie, ever a light sleeper, padded into my room. "What you doing up in the middle of the night?"

"I had a nightmare." I paused, trembling all over. "I dreamt I was drowning in leaves like gold coins."

She patted my head. "No wonder with all the worries you got. That hair's sopping wet. Let's see about getting a bath. Won't do for you to go out like that. Maybe they have some ginger cookies."

Where did Annie come up with these outlandish thoughts? "I doubt they have ginger cookies."

She threw on a dress and hurried out the door, still in her nightcap. I didn't particularly want anything except sleep, but it was nearly dawn, and another long day loomed ahead.

"Hot ginger cookies and tea, Miss Mac," Annie announced cheerfully upon her return. "Another note from your cousin. You ever read the other one?

I hadn't, thinking it was from some fortune hunter. Would they be interested if they knew my property came with choking debt? I ate one of the ginger cookies and cast a withering look at Annie. "This tastes remarkably like ours. You know, that receipt we don't share with anyone?"

"Does it?"

I ate another one. "Yes, it does."

"Imagine that." She handed me the notes from Cousin Carl.

Cousin Lorena

> *Uncle Beddow asked me to contact you.*
> *Might we have breakfast?*

Cousin Carl

What was he up to now? I opened the second one.

Cousin Lorena

> *I understand you enjoy Mrs. Clemson's. Perhaps I can meet you at 8:00 for breakfast?*

Cousin Carl

"Bath's ready," Annie chirped as if I had forgotten about her transgression of the cookie receipt, then cracked eggs into a bowl and whisked in some brandy for a hair shampoo. "Let's wash your hair."

I had misgivings about my hair as it took forever to dry, but Annie was right. It was soaked with sweat. The hot bath soothed my fears of the night, but I couldn't erase the sight of Mahler's face nor mine in the mire.

"Come," Annie said, bundling me in a blanket, "let's go out on the balcony. Maybe we can catch a breeze."

Dawn was breaking, but it was still chilly, and I pulled the blanket tighter. Charleston wasn't awake yet, but the smell of fresh-baked bread and hot lard already heating in vendor stalls to cook street food combined with the salt air, ever-present fish, and moldering seaweed filled the air. Fully cocooned, I sat near the railing and relaxed under her tender ministrations. She combed through my hair and hummed a sad song. Switching to the boar's hair brush, she lifted the hair and let it drop in the faint breeze. The stiff bristles massaged my scalp each time she drew the brush over my head and through the length. It was so relaxing I might have gone back to sleep if I hadn't been singing along with her. She stopped mid-stroke. "What you looking at?"

I followed her glare down to a man across the street who leaned against a building, gazing up at our balcony.

"Aglaope, of the lambent voice, I believe," he replied and drew on his cigar, unperturbed that he'd been caught spying. A faint, amused smile revealed itself in the brightening glow.

"Hmph, siren, indeed," I muttered.

We returned to the room and closed the door. Annie peered out once more before pulling the drapes. "He's gone."

By the time I dressed, finished correspondence, and argued with Annie about the amethyst jewelry, it was time to go. The black Parramatta silk dress matched my morose feelings.

It was nearly 8:00, and me with no idea how to find Cousin Carl. Was I to meet him at Mrs. Clemson's? The note gave no instructions. I descended into the early morning mass of people eddying around in the hotel lobby but saw no one who seemed to be looking for someone particularly.

Before I could push my way to the desk to order a carriage, a fashionable older lady approached and put her hand on my arm. "Hello, my dear," she greeted. "My name is Mrs. Pelton. We've noticed you dining with General Beauregard a few times. Are you related to him?" Mrs. Pelton nudged her charming, and eligible, I assumed, son forward. Her handsome husband stepped out from behind her, appraising me familiarly.

I curtseyed and looked up shyly at the son. "I'm but a poor orphan girl come to Charleston to find a man."

Mr. Pelton pressed forward. Surely, they had room for another housemaid. "James Pelton," replied Pelton the Younger, eagerly surging ahead of his father. His mother clutched his arm and dragged him away from me as if I had the plague, ignoring the plaintive looks back and protestations. "My condolences," he called over his retreating shoulder.

"Will I do?" inquired a vaguely familiar voice behind me.

I choked on my laughter and spun about. "Excuse me?"

"You said you're looking for a man."

"I didn't mean it. I—" I certainly wasn't looking for *this* man! There before me was a perfectly lovely new black frock coat over a subtle gray satin vest and a cleverly arranged burgundy silk cravat. The immaculately tailored trousers cuffed precisely over freshly polished boots. Inside, what might have been an advertisement for fine gentleman's wear, someone had stuffed a bull. Appropriately enough, crowning it all was a John Bull top hat.

He adjusted his already faultless handkerchief in his pocket while I sputtered a bit more and prepared to flee. He extended an envelope and smirked the tiniest bit. "A note from Uncle Beddow."

> *This is the man I've hired to watch over you.*
> *Please go with him to Mrs. Clemson's.*
>
> *Paul Beddow*

"...Cousin Carl."

He offered his arm. "Yes, I'm sorry to hear about you becoming a poor orphan," he said, feigning a look of sadness. "Shall we go?"

"Thank you," I replied icily. "You were watching me earlier."

"It's what I do. Lovely song."

"Hmph."

At Mrs. Clemson's, Beddow waved us over to a patio table where we placed our orders. "I see you've met Carl," he said without further introduction.

"I'm not sure a bodyguard is necessary."

Carl cast a sidling glance at me. "You've been robbed, shot, and poisoned in the last couple of days. What requirement do you need?"

"I—you'll add his fee to my bill?"

"Yes, but I still have money from your father's retainer. Carl's unknown here and good at what he does."

"Which is?

Carl replied blandly as if discussing flannel cakes. "Kill people, among other things, but mostly, I keep people safe."

I had no doubt he could do either or both. He walked with the rolling gait of a sailor, but I had the impression he'd been landbound for some time. His nose had been broken more than once and set poorly, giving his face a craggy don't-mess-with-me look.

"And are you good at what you do?"

"I haven't lost anyone yet."

Beddow waited to continue business until the waitress finished delivering our food. "Our appointment to discuss the land sale with Mr. Woodman is canceled."

I looked over to the basket of geraniums swaying in the breeze, searching for something to focus on. This only meant bad news. "Why?"

"I met with the Woodmans in my office yesterday to determine which acreage they wanted and negotiate the best price according to the land office appraisals."

Carl said nothing through all this but watched me attentively. I cut my food into small, deliberate bites. What I wanted to do was fly into a rage and stab the table repeatedly while imagining it was Mondovi.

"Mr. Woodman pushed for the border land, but Mrs. Woodman would have none of it. He insisted they at least needed the hay meadows until she pulled him out of my office. I may have overheard the argument." He cupped his hand to his ear and leaned sideways as if listening. "She's terrified Mondovi will make life so hard on them they'll lose everything. He said they'd take their business elsewhere, but she's not willing to chance it. Then she threatened to leave him and take the children if he proceeded. He came in and apologized, saying he'd misfigured and they were overextended. Mondovi got to Mrs. Woodman."

"I see," I said, swallowing hard. I'd never raise enough money from the sale of the horses alone.

"Didn't you say you had a buyer for Rosemount?"

I viciously carved a square of ham. "Yes, but circumstances have changed. That may not be possible." I hadn't given Fox an answer, but the decision would be forced on me soon. My head felt like it was going to explode.

Carl's right eyebrow, or what was left of it, went up. It had been intersected at some point, leaving a broad white scar.

"Then you have a decision," said Beddow. "While I was poking around at the land office, the clerk told me Mr. Owens was pulling legals on The Pines."

I almost laughed in hysteria. What else could happen? "Maybe he coerced Mrs. Woodman."

"It's possible, but I think she's genuinely afraid of Mondovi. Take care of your sale. I'll look for a buyer, of course, but on such short notice…." He shrugged. "I'll try to find out why Owens is snooping around about The Pines."

Was it possible there was something wrong with the deeds? I set my silverware across my plate, no longer hungry, and glanced at my pocket watch. "I need to meet Captain Decker and finish arrangements. I'm already a day behind due to that poisoning mess. I won't be back until Sunday night before the bank meeting."

Carl hurried to finish his breakfast and drained the last of his coffee. "Whither thou goest, there also wilt I go," he said, wiping his mouth.

"Come along, Ruth."

Chapter Fourteen

Baron had been in jail before. For fighting mostly. A few times for being drunk. Once for illegal dueling, as they'd misjudged which county they were in. Once as a result of a dare for stealing a pair of Mrs. Abner's drawers off her laundry line and putting them on a donkey. His father thought it didn't do the boys any harm to cool their heels in jail now and again, much to his mother's everlasting shame.

He'd never been in jail for anything that might get him hanged before. This particular morning, he sat on the cot with his back braced against the corner of the cell, wrapped in a thin blanket. Maybe the brick wall would warm up with the sunrise. His knees were drawn up to his chest for warmth. It had been an uncommonly cold night, and the army wasn't concerned about the comforts of drunks, murderers, and deserters. It was only because he hadn't had time to buy a bottle of whiskey and make it to Charleston that he wasn't either of the first two. He was certainly guilty of desertion.

Normally, he enjoyed sunrises and might have this one if the window weren't open to the elements and therefore the cold. As it were, it merely cast a pale square of light on the cell floor with no hint of warmth, as if the sun were too tired to care. He understood.

The cell door opened, and in strode Major Burns, already spit-polished, neatly shaved, and bay-rummed. He'd had bacon for breakfast. Baron could smell it. It smelled a lot better than the sweat and vomit-stained mattress and certainly better than the piss bucket in the corner he desperately needed to use. Would they feed him before they shot him? He hoped so, and not that damned porridge either. He ought to get up and salute, but he was too cold and too stiff and just too tired to give a damn.

"Captain. What were you thinking?" Burns locked his hands behind his back and rocked on the balls of his feet like he did when he was addressing someone like an errant schoolboy caught with a frog in his pocket. Baron wished he had a frog in his pocket now. He was starving, as they hadn't fed him last night.

"I was thinking I was going to go to Charleston and kill some lowlife son-of-a-bitch. Two, actually."

"Any particular ones? I'm guessing you have a reason for this sudden desire to commit murder."

Baron pulled the telegram from his breast pocket and handed it to him. The major read it, his brows wavering between furrowed and shooting up. "Who is Lorena?"

"My fiancée. Almost."

"And why would someone poison her?"

"Because that—you see that F with a box around it? That stands for Beauregard's spymaster. Because that bastard had a clandestine meeting with her to recruit her into his spy ring, and apparently someone found out about it and poisoned her. I planned on killing both of them. The spymaster and the poisoner."

"You're sure they're connected? It doesn't say so in the telegram."

The blanket dropped from around his shoulders when he leaned forward and swung his feet off the cot. "That's a mighty strange coincidence, don't you think?" He huffed his disdain. "She has a meeting and gets poisoned right afterward. She got robbed and shot, and now this? She needs protection, and I needed to be there."

The major scanned the letter again. "Can you trust the person who sent this to you?"

"Darcy's my cousin. We were raised together after his folks died, and he's been keeping an eye on her. Plus, he's close to other people who know what's going on."

"How did you plan to find the poisoner?"

"I figured I'd knock heads together in that kitchen until someone talked."

Burns rolled his eyes. "Yes, that's a sound plan." He folded the telegram and rocked back and forth some more. "You should be thankful Billings clubbed you over the head as you were getting on that train. As it is, you didn't really desert, and the colonel is fond of you. You're normally more levelheaded than this. You need to get control of your emotions and exercise a little more wisdom before you get yourself killed. You won't do her any good dead."

"Not even the gods are wise when they're in love," Baron muttered around the lump in his throat that was soon to be stretched. There was a squeak of steel slats as he shifted to stand up. It was sunrise and time. He paused, cocking his head to the side. "Wait, you're saying I'm not going to be hanged?"

"Not today. But try this again, and I assure you, you'll be riding your coffin at sunrise instead of that ugly mare of yours. Now get out of here. Billings is waiting outside with her. And Jackson will look for you at Easter service Sunday, I expect." He handed the telegram back and walked away with one more warning glance.

"Yes, sir. Thank you."

Billings sat outside grinning at him. "How's the head?"

Baron rubbed it, reminded of it now where Billings had bludgeoned him with his pistol. "Sore, damn it. Thank you."

"Anytime, Cap'n. We got a scout to go on."

"Do I have time to eat? I'm starving."

"I grabbed you some bacon sandwiches."

"Good man. But don't club me again."

Billings bit off some tobacco and stuffed the rest back in his pocket. "Don't go crazy again."

Chapter Fifteen

arl had waited in the lobby while I returned to the room to change into a riding habit. Annie insisted on rearranging my hair to suit my top hat and fussed about the peacock feathers I gave Fox's men. That fashion faux pas segued into some magnificent fabric she found. "We could make something to catch every man's breath in ten counties, Missy."

"Only one man I want to make breathless, but buy it if you like and whatever else that catches your fancy. We won't be back for a while." I instantly regretted giving Annie carte blanche in fabric stores, but when would she have the chance to shop unfettered again? Plus, if I went along with Fox's plan, I'd need new clothes. Mother would doubtless drag me to every social event available to introduce me to the most eligible bachelors in the north. Maybe even some who weren't eligible; sweethearts could be dealt with later. Thank God she'd been born a woman. She'd be a formidable general. "Stock up on needles and sundries. Get those things I asked for and bring them out to The Pines. Someone will be in later to get you."

Content as a cat in a creamery, she began to hum.

"Annie, within reason. You do know what reason is, don't you?"

"Of course, Miss Mac." Her voice rang with astonishment as if the idea of going hog wild had never occurred to her, though it was probably what she dreamed of every night.

The agriculture manager, Mr. Updike from Grand National, was going with us to look at ledgers, examine the farm, and make suggestions on a business plan. Perhaps fresh eyes could see a way to maximize the sale or suggest another buyer for some of the land.

He had huffed in irritation when I asked to meet him after my breakfast meeting. I had missed Good Friday services and hoped God would forgive me for not formally observing such a solemn day of mourning.

Something else to worry about. My hand went to the one-armed crucifix. *Sorry, God.*

Though I needed his favor, I didn't much care if I inconvenienced Updike. Decker had sent most of his men to The Pines previously along with the wagon of Frank's requested supplies. He gallantly offered to take a carriage today, but Charlie was in town, and I much preferred riding. Although he looked like he'd been sucking lemons, Mr. Updike looked perfectly at home on a fine hunter as they waited for me. Thus, we set out with my escort and amethyst and every prayer I could lay hold of for a successful sale and protection over The Pines. No matter how hard I prayed, I couldn't restore peace to my heart. A cloud of doom had taken hold of me, and it was only through concentrated effort that the men drew my mind to other things at last, and the journey passed somewhat tolerably.

Papa, ever the artist at heart, had kept the land on either side of the entry pastoral with clumps of trees here and there to shade the horses. A bold baby with three stockings raced by with his concerned, nickering mama trotting after him, head up, ears pricked. That started a miniature stampede with a host of youngsters racing down the whitewashed fences, tails in the air, spindly legs flying. I always marveled that their legs, all akimbo, never got tangled in these mad dashes, but they were born to run and did. Mothers too old for this nonsense mostly went back to grazing while a few young mares kept a nervous eye on their babies or ran with them.

The main horse operation was at The Pines, and even with the school, I found excuses to come as often as possible for foaling and brought the girls down for extended stays. We spent untold hours in the pastures sketching and painting both horses and plants. They helped gentle the babies, and many a tear was shed when we returned to Virginia. I pictured the pastures bare or plowed under but pushed it out of my mind.

The side road to the farm was wide enough for two wagons to drive comfortably side by side. On each edge of the road stood two imposing columns with brick walls fanning away, and on these was *The Pines* in ornate black metal letters. All the masonry was the well-known McKenzie brick kilned on the plantation. Under the brick arch were wrought iron gates with metallic pine trees arrayed across them. The copper and bronze pine trees mellowed to a pleasant verdigris and brown against the black bars. The entryway was Papa's last major improvement to the plantation. It was his signature and his *finis*.

There was a mixture of pride and sadness at the sight. Overall, it was the abiding satisfaction of being home, like someone laying a comforting blanket over me on a chill winter night. The Pines would always be my first love. Spanish moss waved a lazy greeting from the live oaks lining the lane leading to the manor house, and inside the pristine fences, more horses raised their heads from verdant pastures to watch with passing interest.

Once arrived, we walked back toward the barn discussing sale arrangements. Frank had the horses gathered besides mares, and they were well on the way to being prepared aside from trimming and shoeing. Decker's men were working on that and would hopefully finish before the sale. The extra men he'd sent would help.

With the introductions finished, Frank took me aside. "Maddie foaled."

Maddie was my first "big girl" horse, and this would be her last foal. "Colt or filly?"

"Big, long-legged filly like her mama."

"Good, this is her last. I was hoping for a filly."

"Miss McKenzie," Mr. Updike reminded me with some irritation that I was delaying his carefully planned day with chatter.

"Yes, sir. Just let me change out of this habit. Frank, can you show Mr. Updike to the library? The papers are laid out?"

"Yes, ma'am. It's ready."

"I won't be but a minute," I said cheerily. I wasn't one to dawdle over frippery, but I simply wasn't going to ruin my habit with ink stains. Plus, while the heavy wool made it ideal for cross-country riding where brambles might shred a lesser fabric, it was insufferable indoors.

This room wasn't as large or elegant as my room at Rosemount, but it was comforting with its rose and green walls. I caressed the velvet window seat, longing to curl up like a cat.

Enough woolgathering. You have work to do!

"The short-sleeved yellow muslin. I can clean ink off skin, not fabric."

Rachel raised an eyebrow but said nothing about my abrupt shift from mourning colors and fussed instead about my corset laces. "Need to fix that hair and get hoops. You needs to be presentable."

"No hoops! I'll be scrunched up at a desk with him."

She gasped. "With all these young men around. What would yo' mama say?"

With great reluctance and muttering, she helped me put on the pale-yellow day dress. Mother said yellow cheers a person's heart, unless you're a blonde, then it makes you look jaundiced, and that ought to rightly give you heart failure.

I sighed as she insisted on fussing with my hair. "I heard tell once of a home where the servants didn't sass their mistresses. Can you believe it?"

Her eyes went wide in that ebony, moon-shaped face. "Oh, Missy. I think that's one of those fairy tales folks tell young'uns, don't you?" She slid in a few more hairpins and changed out my hair ribbon. "There, you not presentable, but at least, well, you go on. We'll do better later."

Mr. Updike, though relieved to see me, wasn't overly gladdened by the sunny dress. Stacks of files, ledgers, and papers normally covered Papa's generous desk. His personal items, including James's wooden horse that had never left the corner of the desk in sixteen years, were all dumped unceremoniously on the floor. Irked at the irreverence, I gently placed the horse on a shelf before it got broken.

"Are you ready?" he asked.

"Yes, sir."

Lemon balm scent flooded in ahead of Zona when she delivered a pot of stress tea and ginger cookies. She ignored my scowl. "Really?"

"Rachel said you need it."

Tea and ginger cookies were the universal cure for stress in the McKenzie household.

Updike had taken off his fine jacket and rolled his shirt sleeves to stay pristine, but his smudged and spotted wrists reminded me of a Dominicker hen.

"I've identified several areas that can be improved," he said without pleasantry or thanks. "Your store needs to be run like a business, for instance. You buy goods wholesale and sell to your people, slave and free, for the same price. Then you buy from them with no profit allowance." His pointer-like finger traced a list in the ledger. "Pottery, fancy work, lace, rocking chair, baskets, herbs, chickens, vegetables, berries, honey, carved horse. A carved horse for heaven's sake?" He threw his hands in the air.

"The store's a convenience to our people, not a business."

"That's obvious."

"We take what our people produce and want to sell to market. It gives them extra incentive and money. Other plantations do this. Surely you're aware of the practice." Mother would chastise me for my wrinkled brow as I scowled at him in frustration.

"Because one sheep foolishly goes over the cliff doesn't mean they all should, and other plantations are not in your position. Surely you realize $78,000 is a substantial fortune." He tapped the page before him. "I read the divorce agreement but couldn't believe it."

"Then you know where the money went. Since Mother lived in Baltimore most of the time anyway, he decided to set her free. I think he was afraid she'd force the sale of everything he'd spent his life building, and I'd be left with no property should something happen to him. It was a cash settlement, furniture of her choice, a carriage and horses, jewelry, plus the home of her choice."

"She also took several slaves?" he said, tapping a paper.

"Yes. He manumitted whomever she wanted if they chose to go."

"Why wasn't their worth listed in the settlement?"

"He didn't sell them."

Updike leaned back in the leather chair that squeaked a protest he must have been feeling. He rubbed the bridge of his nose, then put his hands behind his head. "Even if he were going to free them, he should have allowed their value in the settlement. Does your mother really need thirteen servants?" He leaned forward to look at his notes. "Fifteen."

"No, but we don't separate families if we can help it. If she wanted to take a maid, the family went, too."

He flopped the papers over in disdain. "I see why your father was in such dreadful financial straits."

There it was, the roiling stomach. "He'd have worked his way out with time. Union Bank only called the note because he died."

"If they'd known what he was doing, they'd have called him in sooner. Regardless, Mr. Owens asked me to help. I suggest you sell the eastern acreage Mr. Schoenberger told me about. You have too many slaves and doubtless too many at Rosemount also. The slave market's good."

"Actually, we have very few slaves at Rosemount. Papa tended to collect Irish immigrants who needed jobs and a home."

He waved his hand dismissively again. "Regardless, between the land, horses, and slave sales, you'll have enough operating capital to stay on firm footing. It'll be a smaller, leaner operation, but you might be able to keep enough horses to rebuild a herd."

The cookie in my hand snapped. "I see."

"Sell most of the older slaves and several of the children. Their worth is limited, and they drain resources. A number of prime slaves can go. You don't need that many. Fire your freemen." He slid a prepared list to me.

I finished eating my cookie and washed it down with Zona's extra strong stress tea. Linden, lemon balm, *and* chamomile. Mr. Updike or I might be asleep soon, but right now, my heart pounded my ribcage like a blacksmith beating on a newly fired horseshoe. I glanced at it and folded the paper meticulously into a butterfly while I considered an answer. My nail creased the wings until it looked about to take flight and set it on the desk. "I'm afraid that isn't acceptable."

Updike looked up from the butterfly. "I beg your pardon?"

"My father's will provided for them all to be set free no later than five years after his death. Sooner if the estate was debt free. So, you see, I can't, nor will I, sell them."

"There's no choice. You might lose everything if you don't see reason here."

My fingers traced over the butterfly while my mind went over the promise I made to Papa. I hadn't known what was in the will, but I had vowed to honor it. "We'll do the best we can. I have a contingency plan in any case."

"And what would that be?" he said with great exasperation. "Sell your china?"

"There's a buyer for Rosemount. If I don't make enough money on the land and horses, it'll sell." Fox's plea came back to me as soon as the words were out of my mouth, and I was leaning towards not selling Rosemount, but it was my ace in the hole. Plus, Fox himself had impressed upon me how dangerous the Shenandoah Valley would be. A new school would be safer here. Mostly, I wanted Updike derailed from his gloomy threats.

"I see." He steepled his fingers under his chin. "What do you want me to do?"

"Put together a business plan that doesn't include selling the slaves. Save The Pines."

"I'll do what I can, but this isn't sound business practice."

Saying no more about the slaves, he pulled out the center desk drawer for another sheet of paper. "Out of curiosity, why is the kneehole so wide? Was your father a large man?"

"No, he was quite trim, but perhaps a bit eccentric."

"Eccentric. Yes, that might be one word." He scribbled furiously across the paper.

I rose from my chair and walked over to the wooden horse, caressing the horsehair mane. It had been James's favorite toy. Under that desk we had read and sometimes hidden with Papa, adventured on safaris, explored South America, rode out west to live with the Indians, and sailed the seas aboard the gallant Shillelagh against the damnable English, wreaking "murder and mayhem, hell and havoc," as Papa would cry.

James and I both got our mouths washed out with soap for standing boldly, swords extended, and shouting, "Murder and mayhem, hell and havoc, Woman!" at Mother when she came to claim us for supper once. Our swords confiscated and snapped like twigs, which they were, we were marched to the kitchen for soap and off to the brig without supper. Papa pled mercy, as it was he who taught us the objectionable language, though truly, what else would a self-respecting privateer say? We shouldn't have to go to our rooms without supper when he should bear the punishment. Mother assured him he would. She was going to Baltimore and taking us with her to be around civilized people. The sentence was later reduced to her going to Baltimore with a healthy shopping allowance.

Disembarking from the good ship Shillelagh and back to my present adventure, I glanced at Updike, who was still feverishly transcribing ledger pages. "I need to go check on a mare and see how the preparations are coming. Frank can show you the property and livestock."

He dismissed me with a wave of his pen and a piggish grunt.

With Updike dealt with, I sought out Frank to check on Maddie and last-minute details.

We were just leaving the barn when Frank pointed toward a rider. "Is that Mr. Updike?"

I narrowed my eyes in consternation. "It is. How odd." How could he hope to put a business plan in place for The Pines when all he had done was make notes from the ledgers? Why would he leave before he looked at the property and other livestock and discussed Mr. Schoenberger's plans for the farm?

Papa had mounted a large dragon weathervane on top of the huge mare barn when it was first finished. He christened it with whiskey and told it, "Do ye keep charge over all the horses within, Mr. Dragon, and keep them safe from harm, then."

I looked up when the dragon squealed a protest and swung about in a gust of wind, so it looked like it was flying after Updike.

"Mr. Dragon is screeching," I said. "He needs oiling."

"I think Mr. Dragon is warning us, but I'll see to greasing him," Frank replied.

Chapter Sixteen

I needed time alone and retreated to Papa's office to think, with the warning to the girls I was not to be disturbed unless the heavenly host itself was descending.

My father, in one of his mad escapades and much to my mother's dismay, built an elegant, brick, two-story plantation store. Two stories! A professionally lettered sign announced, so people would know the correct store to enter, *McKenzie General Store and Emporium, K.A. McKenzie, proprietor.* The upper story was Papa's office proper. He tried using the library, but the house was usually in an uproar when Mother was in residence, so he retreated to his emporium office for peace and quiet to work or simply escape. The extra plantation office and two-story building was impressive-looking enough, even in the construction phases, to send Mother sulking to Baltimore for weeks.

Papa even ordered black garters for his sleeves. He could see the back of the house from his office and would rush to play storekeeper whenever Mother came to pry him or the wee McKenzies from his sanctuary. "Mrs. McKenzie," he'd boom, "what can I help you with today? How about a nice penny candy?" He'd whip a peppermint stick out of the candy jar and lean across the counter, waggling it at her.

"For pity's sake, Keiran. Do stop playing the fool. We have a party to attend."

I walked in to the familiar tinkle of the brass bell over the door. James and I insisted on a bell, and Papa let us pick it out. We drove the hardware store owner to distraction testing them all and most more than once. The store smelled of pine. Someone had recently scrubbed the floors with Papa's favorite cleaner. I plundered some peppermint sticks for myself as they were always my favorites.

Papa had deliberately built the stairs to the second story narrow so Mother couldn't navigate them easily in her generous skirts. Since I refused to bow to fashion and wear voluminous skirts without cause, I could scamper up the stairs like a squirrel, and did.

In the center of the office was the library table with his papers, drawings, books, pens, instruments, boxes, and contraptions. All the things that captured his attention lay scattered about in some semblance of order only he understood—chaotic to others, but instantly clear to him. Behind it was the desk of many mechanical wonders, the secret keeper and storyteller. What secrets did it hold today? I traced along the doorjamb until my fingers detected the slightest indentation and pressed in gently. There was a click as a small wooden drawer popped out. I removed the key, then pushed it all back into place.

The secret keeper was more than a desk; it was a marvelous piece of art with exquisite inlaid wood and mother-of-pearl marquetry that told tales. Each flower, bird, animal, mountain, tree, rock, and person told a story according to Papa, and there were thousands of images inlaid into the desk. I asked him how he'd ever tell them all, and he said some were for my children.

"You don't have to bribe me with stories to see my children."

"Ye never know. Ye might forget me."

Never in this life or the next could I forget such a man. I turned the key in the main lock and pulled down the writing table. Such an innocent-looking instrument. Deceiver. I removed two small golden columns, which allowed me to remove a false front and slid out a bank of drawers to access another hidden drawer. Inside that was another smaller key. It slid into what looked like an ornate cherub's flower above the top of the desk. The clock rotated, revealing a fairy tale scene. There were supposed to be two dancers, but Papa asked the maker to install a music box and carousel. I wound it and watched the figures go about with the knights and dragons and fair ladies and unicorns. It was cleverly designed so it looked like the knights and dragons were fighting.

I watched the battle for a bit and pilfered through more secret drawers. Clicks and whirs continued as the secret keeper opened to me, disclosing all the little hidden nooks and boxes, drawers and trays. I lifted out one set of drawers to reveal a smaller set behind it and behind that set a space to hide documents or money. There was more money to join the sizable stack sitting on the table. There were seventy-six hidden compartments; we counted them one day. Money. Jewelry. Photographs of James and me, and even Mother, in happier days. Letters from Grandmamma. He kept them all and tied them in green ribbons. A pocket watch. His father's. He talked little of him. I opened it. There was a faded picture of Grandmamma when she was very young and a young man, I assumed to be Grandpapa, who had died young in Ireland. Drawings and letters I sent to Papa when Mother hauled me north to civilization. He saved all of them. They were bound in blue. Receipts. An old picture of a beautiful young woman I'd never seen before. Nellie was penciled on the back. More whirring and drawers shifted to the side, revealing a keyhole; I inserted the small key. A strong box popped up. I unlocked it. More money and jewelry, and a letter to me.

The letter, unlike many of the things hidden away in the secret keeper, was new.

My Darling Lorena,

If you're reading this, something has happened else you wouldn't be going through the secret keeper. I also assume I've left you bad off as the letter hasn't been replaced. I beg your forgiveness.

I knew your mother would force the sale of both properties on my death to settle her share and hoped to head her off with the divorce. Though money was important, more important was the idea she would browbeat you to move north with her if you had nothing left here and be damned in hell for all eternity if I would let her ruin you with those northern bastards and lose all we worked for. I gambled. I hope by the time you read this I've at least paid off a substantial portion of the debt.

If not, do what you can to keep Rosemount. It will be vital to the coming war. I made an agreement to help and pledged it as a way station. If you haven't discovered it yet, there are manumission papers for Gideon and Tildie in the breast pocket of my brown tweed suit with the plaid pants. The one your mother hated. There are instructions for the lawyer regarding them. Pay them and send them north to live with Rita.

Regardless of what happens, know that I could never have been prouder of you or loved you more than I do. Remember, a man may lose all, but his honor must be given. Stay true to yourself.

My eternal love,
Papa,

P.S. If you let your mother talk you into marrying some damned Yankee I'll come back and haunt you. God above, let me rest in peace.

The peppermint stick dropped from my hand and shattered. "Oh, Papa. What have you done? You've taken away my safety net, and I fear I am doomed."

I rocked back in the chair and reread the letter, then scooped the peppermint shards into the trash before I started crying into them and glued them to the desk. My nostrils were already burning. Tears were on the way, and I let them flow. I was in danger of losing The Pines; Baron was nowhere to be found, and I missed him with every fiber of my being. Finally, with the waterworks done, my head throbbing, eyes swollen, and nose running, I tried to muster my emotion and wits. I had a sale to prepare for, and it was possible Papa may have left me a clue about how to salvage this disaster if I kept searching.

I popped another peppermint stick in my mouth and returned to plundering the secret keeper. The money, nearly seven thousand dollars, and jewelry from the strongbox dropped in with the rest.

A brass rosette pushed in and set more wonders to work. What looked like the bottom of a drawer extended to expose an easel. On the easel was a charcoal drawing of me Papa was working on. It was incomplete, but I was astonished that he had captured me so well. I had been sitting in front of the window redoing my hair that had caught when I was helping him with a project. The secret keeper would go, as would his stories, but how I wished he was here to finish them. My hand caressed one of the carved, gilded legs, and I tied a piece of yellow yarn around it.

A curved section on either side of the upper part of the desk rolled effortlessly around with a gentle touch to reveal Saint Christopher and the blessed Virgin. I pulled out the small prayer stool under the desk, knelt, and said a prayer for the days ahead. When I was done, I closed each section and added the keys to my chatelaine.

Papa's chair invited me to sit awhile before returning to the bedlam house. I accepted and spun about like a child. It was less fun with cumbersome skirts. The photograph of Papa and Mr. O'Neil stared at me when I stopped spinning. Papa learned about racehorses from his master. He learned about raising horses, sawing lumber, and being a man from Mr. O'Neil, who had gathered him from the pile of trash and gave him a home for the next twelve years.

If only the men I'd dealt with recently had learned to be such honorable souls as Mr. O'Neil and the wounded waif he plucked from the rags. Papa was no saint, but he'd never steal a copper from anyone, let alone their life's work. While Papa taught me about horses and farm management, Mr. Mondovi and his crew of cullions taught me about life. It could be hard. It would be harder for a woman. Sometimes the most dangerous thieves weren't the Rascals of the world but men in suits with fine manners and gold cufflinks. Of the many things I'd lost in the past week, I missed my innocence the most.

Chapter Seventeen

I decided to celebrate Easter Sunday at the farm with my people, despite a vague sense of dread that it might be our last together. The cooks prepared a communal feast for the dining hall where all the workers ate breakfast and sometimes supper. Dinner was sent out to the fields when we were working, but it was still prepared in the dining kitchen. Especially with the soldiers, we had a full house to cook for. I would dine in the house with the officers and Frank's family. The soldiers who had families had also been invited, but they would only stay for dinner, as quarters were cramped.

The ladies had boiled dozens and dozens of eggs until I wondered if there was an egg left in the county and then rigged up pots of dye: red cabbage leaves with vinegar for a blue or purple depending on how much vinegar, turmeric for yellow, onion skins for gold, spinach for green, and beets for that lovely pink. Beth and Imogene had the girls at Rosemount painting tiny watercolors of flowers, crosses, and baby animals on little cards and had mailed them for the children of The Pines. I had been in various cottages and seen the paintings over the years kept on shelves as prized decorations. Annie made sure we had some extra penny candies for the little ones. In the afternoon, Reverend Wilkins would baptize any who desired, and we would pray and sing some more hymns before breaking our celebration of life and renewal.

Zona was setting the Meissen china in the main dining room with appropriate crystal and silver. The children's room was set with coordinating Blue Willow so mothers wouldn't get upset if something broke. Though most of the cooking was done in the two cookhouses, the house was already filling with delicious smells from the food they were bringing in. Della was arranging a heaping platter of fried chicken. No special meal was complete without her chicken. Papa had always sliced the hams, the lamb, and roast, but she would prevail on Decker this year. The pickles of various types were already on the table. Outside I heard laughing children who were still hunting eggs, but enough had been turned in to provide platters of deviled eggs. Platters of biscuits and bowls of fresh butter dotted the table. Dishes of field peas, collard greens, corn pudding, and scalloped potatoes waited on the buffet. On a separate buffet sat a dizzying array of desserts and stewed fruits. The girls had outdone themselves. Vases of dogwood branches sat on every table, reminding all of the reason for celebration.

We'd spent frantic days preparing for the sale. Horses gleamed. The farm was immaculate. Arrangements had been made for buyers in hotels and with neighbors since most hotels were already full with conventioneers. Even Papa's friends in town, aware of the dire situation, opened their houses for me. I could not have asked for more divine intervention and hoped it would continue.

Seven people received Jesus after dinner, and we ended our gathering with *Christ the Lord is Risen Today.* The reverend gave a blessing for all, and at the end, he added a special prayer for me and The Pines for a successful sale. I added my own fervent prayer, but a nagging voice reminded me of the last time I begged and pleaded for favor and in the end said, "Thy will be done."

Wednesday was here before we knew it. This would normally be the day of the ball, but there would be no ball this year, nor ever again maybe. Everyone had worked deep into the night for final preparations, but all were up again at dawn the first morning of the sale. Unlike the usual excitement that accompanied our sales, a pall hung over The Pines Thursday morning, heavy and oppressive as the gray flannel skies above. Not knowing how many people would show, they'd butchered a beef to cook outdoors in great kettles over banked fires the day before. Burgoo was an ideal offering for sales. The receipt was inexact, though The Pines had developed a flavor we were famed for: meat cooked slow with spices, vinegar, molasses, and whatever vegetables were available. The girls were dumping in mounds of colorful vegetables now. I stuck a long fork into the meat and pulled off a chunk.

"Moses, that's good," I said. "I'll have some of this and eggs for breakfast."

Zona, ever my shadow, grabbed a crockery bowl from a near-by table. "The girls already got the cornbread goin'."

"Perfect."

A prayer went up for a good sale and thanks for all the blessings the Lord had bestowed on me. Whichever way the day went, the Lord was always good. Today would be no different.

☙

With three long days of sales ended, I hid in Maddie's stall, fingering the scarf in my lap. The black silk was long and narrow, barely wider than my hand and heavily embroidered with long, black beaded fringe. I let the beads slip through my fingers again as if the repetitive motion of picking up and dropping the fringe would soothe me. The barn, even at night, was usually full of noises, soft snuffling and shuffling. Nickers and thumps. Now, there was only the clinking of the beads.

Maddie regarded me with large, intelligent eyes. I'd watched many such eyes regard me throughout the previous days. Bright, inquisitive, excited, adoring. The horses turned to look at me at least briefly in recognition when the grooms led them by. Many nickered as they passed. I was used to horse sales, but this was different. Most of the soldiers staked out favorites while they worked on them. I knew they'd care for them as best they could, but they were going to war. Knowing the value of a good horse in battle, the bidding had been brisk at times.

"Sold!"

There was a whoop followed by a hearty round of congratulations when a young freckled soldier led back a bay, the finest thing he ever owned or might own. He showed the papers to his friends to prove the superiority and stumbled over the grandsire's name, Faugh-a-Ballagh. I pronounced it for him. "It's an Irish battle cry meaning clear the way. That's why we named your horse's sire Clear The Way."

"Clear the way! And that's what we're going to do, isn't it?"

I pulled a dried apple slice out of my pocket, having crammed both pockets full that morning, and gave it to him. "He likes apples. Whistle like this." I whistled like we did to call horses in. "If he's ever away from you and can hear that, he'll come to you."

"Thank you." He grinned wider and fed the gelding his treat, birthing their bond. "He's so handsome."

"It's as close as you'll ever be to handsome," ribbed his friend, who turned his attention back to another horse. He'd already bought three, but like others, intended to buy as many as he could afford. I didn't dwell on the reason they needed several horses, but the dark-haired friend was also sending mares and yearlings home to his father. Praise the Lord, not all were going to war.

Even Major Fox appeared to buy more horses for his ghosts, as he called his men.

Each time the hammer fell, it drove another nail into my coffin until I could barely breathe, and I escaped to the barn.

I let the beads slip again.

"That's a lovely scarf," Carl said from the doorway.

"Yes, I'm trying to decide whether to wear it or hang myself with it."

"I'm sure it's not that bad." He opened the stall door. Maddie shifted around to put her body between the stranger and her sleeping baby. "The girls were worried about you and sent a bowl of burgoo." There was a pewter plate with chunks of cornbread and a covered bowl in his extended hand.

"I'm not hungry."

"You haven't eaten since this morning. It's been a long three days. You should eat and get some rest." He knelt in front of me and pushed the plate closer.

"It has been, hasn't it?" The burgoo was still warm, and I finished every spicy drop of the hearty stew. Maddie shuffled through the straw to lip cornbread from my palm with her velvet muzzle. She flattened her ears at Carl to let him know she was watching him even if she left her post guarding her foal.

Carl extended a tentative hand to her. "What's next?"

"I don't know. Frank said Mr. Updike didn't really discuss our plans for the farm. I let everything go I could, hoping to clear the debt, but even with the equipment sales, I barely cleared $45,000. We'll ship what's left back to Virginia, but the horse operation is done."

Since there were no hooks or posts nearby, hanging wouldn't be convenient tonight, so I wrapped the scarf around my throat instead. Hanging would have to wait.

Chapter Eighteen

Though I was completely drained and desired nothing more than to sleep for a week after the sale, the next day I returned to Charleston to attend evening mass. I needed to recharge my batteries for the upcoming fray and restore my spirit. I'd meet Beddow and Carl on Monday morning for breakfast and finish my banking business. The sale had gone better than I hoped, and with just a bit of luck, Owens would loan me the money I needed to pay Mondovi and keep the Pines. Then, with a little time, I could sell enough land to pay off the loan from Owens. That was the plan, but I still worried about why Owens had been researching the legals on The Pines and why Updike left early. Even with the frenzy of the sale, that cloud had never been far from my mind.

Annie had returned to town to take care of business and handle arrangements for buyers. She pointed to a stack of messages and mail when I walked into the room but pulled out a letter from Baron and handed it to me.

"Thank you, Annie. You've done very well."

She huffed in disdain. "Course I did. I'll be next door if you need me."

I sat and opened the cover carefully.

March 26, 1861
Alexandria, Virginia

My Darling Lorena the Dearest Baroness,

I smile as I write this because I recall how your mother scowled when I called you Baroness. I confess, I'm horrible.

I begged for leave again to come to South Carolina. Colonel has once again declined as he deems it necessary for all to be made ready for war. Even so, I would work thrice as hard later if I could be with you now in your time of need. I should have waited to accept a commission after I resigned from the army. Please finish soon and return.

Two horses were stolen last night. Sad Sally was on the same line, but the thief didn't take her. The popular theory was she was too ugly to steal. Since there was a patch of black broadcloth on the ground near her, I imagine the surly thing took a chunk out of him for waking her. She requires her beauty sleep. Hah!

It was determined the sentry had fallen asleep, allowing the horses to be stolen, and he was severely punished. Suffice to say, it was a lesson to all the import of staying awake on sentry duty. One sleeping sentry could mean death for all.

I'm enclosing a small medal and a pressed flower. A young girl gave this to me and I pressed the flower in my Bible. I was coming in from patrol and saw the poor little thing crying. A dog had chased her kitten up a tree and it wasn't coming down. I sidled Sally up to it so I could stand on her back and jumped up to a limb. I eventually reached the kitten and stuffed it inside my blouse. The trip down was more hazardous than the climb up, but God preserved me even though no one thought to watch Sally, who decided to go grazing and wandered off. We'll have to refresh her memory on ground tying.

I dropped to the ground and rolled, scaring the kitten. She clawed her way out of my blouse and up my face, but all is well save a few scratches, which I'm told improve my looks. The child has her little friend back. Mother and child brought the bouquet of flowers and a cake later. She also gave the colonel a letter insisting I be promoted for bravery.

The men carried me high over this and made me this medal out of a bone button and a bit of ribbon. Someone etched a cat on the button as you see. You may rest assured I didn't share my luscious cake with these clowns.

Sit for a photographer while you're in Charleston. Enclosed find money for it. I promised Mother I would get her another as I brought the one I kept by my bedside at home even though she asked that I leave it so my room might be preserved as it was until I return home. I didn't tell her that had a vaguely ominous sound to it as if she were making a shrine. I think she wanted the ambrotype for herself as you know how she adores you.

Who would not? I have since the first moment I laid eyes on you. My heart was conquered fully. I ache with the inadequacy of words to express how I feel. The longing to touch your cheek, toy with the rebel curls that escape the net and braid. I would free it all and watch it tumble loose. How many times I have dreamt of doing just that and taking you in my arms, but enough. I've been thoroughly indecent in thought and word.

Press your mother about permission to marry. Offer her a bribe. We'll name our firstborn after her. I can live with a child named Lucifer.

I choked on my water, causing Annie to thump on my back. "You all right?"

"Yes," I gasped. "I swallowed wrong." That man was going to be the death of me.

My thoughts wing south on a breeze. Never doubt how much I love you.

In fondest regards and everlasting adoration,
Captain Baron Patrick Callahan, CSA

As always, I inhaled every morsel of scent from the letter: smoke, leather, tobacco, and something sharper. He must have washed just before he settled in to write. Reluctantly, I put it away with a sigh and a hasty prayer for his safety.

Beddow chose to eat breakfast outside the next morning. "There's fewer ears here," he said from behind his menu. "Did you bring me a gift?" He tapped the pastry box.

"They're for Mondovi and his mad minion."

"Is it a bomb?"

"Where would I get a bomb?"

"I'm sure Carl could find you a bomb maker or build you one himself if he were so inclined. I'd prefer he didn't."

Carl stopped buttering his toast and shot him an I-have-no-idea-what-you're-talking-about look. Beddow hmphed and resumed sorting papers, but Carl angled his one and a half brows steeply in contemplation as he pondered the box and undoubtedly constructed a pastry box-size bomb in his mind.

The business at hand stole my appetite, but I ordered food anyway as I didn't want my stomach grumbling in the midst of it.

I pushed the box toward Beddow, who was sipping coffee that looked more like coffee and less like stained cream. "It's lemon cake with raspberry sauce, like the cake I was poisoned with. I included the receipt with strychnine optional at the end."

Beddow choked on his coffee. "If something happens to one of them, they'll come looking for you first."

"Don't open it. If I smell that raspberry sauce, I'll get sick."

"Let's hope no one dies of poisoning before you leave town, though I wouldn't mourn Mahler," Beddow said, still shuffling papers.

The waitress set our plates with a trembling hand and eyes gone wide as the blue-rimmed plates, then rushed away with her little cart squeaking a protest across the uneven brick flooring.

Carl offered me a flask, whiskey by the smell, which I declined. He doctored his coffee and returned to reading the paper. Presently, he lowered it to look at Beddow. "Is there enough money in the retainer for me to kill someone? If they died some other way, that would remove suspicion from Miss McKenzie."

Beddow shook his head.

"I might consider a pro bono."

"Please don't," Beddow said, then fired off a series of questions about the sale and my finances, flipping back and forth through pages and ledgers as he did so.

"Did you sleep at all last night?" I asked. The faint purple shadows under heavily fringed eyes told me he hadn't, but he retained that same edgy energy, like a young racehorse at the starting line he always had. When I first met him, his eyes reminded me of amber tiger eye gems. Now, they had a feral gleam that reminded me only of the tiger.

"Not much. I was looking for every advantage we might use with Mr. Owens. It bothers me that Updike only took inventory and showed no notice in the operation. The question is, how much stock does Owens put in Updike's recommendations?"

That had bothered me also. "He seemed to lose interest after I refused to sell the slaves."

With breakfast finished, Beddow pulled out his pocket watch. "Let's see what the circus has brought to town, shall we?"

⁊

Grand National wasn't nearly as pretentious as Union Bank, and that suited me. Unlike Mondovi, who left me to twist, Mr. Owens was waiting when we arrived and ushered us into his office personally.

Carl remained in the lobby but close enough to keep watch. Mr. Updike waited inside the office, closed as a clam.

I sat opposite Mr. Owens, but Mr. Beddow would take the lead as much as possible. He took his place next to me and laid out our paperwork.

"You had a nice sale," Mr. Owens opened.

"I did," I replied, thankful he felt so.

"$45,000 is more than I expected, but that still leaves us nearly $35,000 short on the note."

"Yes, sir." I didn't tell him about the cash, as the farm would need operating funds.

"We understand that's a substantial amount of money, but the value of The Pines far outweighs that," Beddow said, launching into our case. "Mr. Woodman decided not to buy the land, but given time we can find a buyer. If the bank extends a loan on the property—"

Mr. Owens held up his hand. "Mr. Beddow, save your breath. I received the report from Mr. Updike. He recommends declining credit."

I had leaned forward at Beddow, pleading my case, looking between the two men, trying to read a sign. "Pardon me?" I said quietly and fell back into my chair heavily. "Why?"

Updike sat with his nose in the air as if he'd stepped in fresh pig manure.

"I handed you my recommendations to sell off slaves you don't need and get to the meat of the operation. You sat there like an addled child and folded it into a bird. How was I to take you seriously?"

He couldn't have struck me harder had he slapped me across the face with one of the kid gloves he was drawing on. Standing abruptly, he pulled out a gleaming gold pocket watch. "I promised I'd check on my mother, who is ill. If you don't mind? I'll return shortly."

"It was a butterfly, not a bird," I said, completely stunned.

"Is this true?" Mr. Owens asked.

"See?" Updike shook his head and stalked out in righteous indignation.

"The butterfly?"

"Hang the butterfly!" Owens snapped. "The rest of it."

"I explained we don't separate families if possible, and my father left instructions about the slaves."

Mr. Owens waved his hands expansively. "Miss McKenzie, I understand female compassion, and that's the problem. The farm is a business."

"This isn't female compassion," Beddow protested. "This was her father's directive in his will."

"Either way, I won't be extending a loan. Miss McKenzie's not qualified to bring the farm out of debt due to age and inexperience, especially with the horses gone."

I shook my head in shocked amazement. "So, I sell the horses to reduce the debt as I was advised, and because I no longer have horses, I'm not eligible for a loan. What an elegant trap."

Leaning over his desk, Owens fairly exploded. "I didn't lay a trap for you. The horses are only part of the problem."

"Right, I forgot. I'm a young woman with no experience. Others think that isn't such a hurdle." Looking to Beddow, "Didn't you say another bank is interested? We should stop wasting Mr. Owens's time."

Beddow put the papers back in the valise. "Yes, we should meet with them soon."

"Wait! I have a proposal for you." Unnerved that things weren't going as planned, he pulled out a handkerchief, dabbed at his brow, and swiped across his eyes as if that might clear the vision of a rebellious young woman. "I'm interested in buying it myself." Stepping back, he opened the desk drawer and whipped out a cheque as a magician might a scarf from thin air. His brows jutted up in confirmation of his great feat before handing it to Mr. Beddow, who gave it a fleeting look and passed it to me.

"You must agree that's a fair price considering the circumstances," Owens said.

I let it drop and watched it flutter back to the desk. "And what circumstances would those be?"

"Why you'll lose all if you don't pay Mondovi. Those are dire circumstances."

"Would you mind if I consult with Miss McKenzie in private?" Beddow asked, pulling a few papers from his valise and standing.

"There's an office next door." Owens pointed to a door on the west wall of his office.

"Thank you." Beddow took my arm. "I left some things in my carriage. We can talk on the way."

The banker grimaced something approximating a smile in return. We went outside to the carriage. "I can imagine him standing there with an ear trumpet or stethoscope pressed to that door, listening to our every word."

"You seem to have experience with this," I whispered and looked about. "Where's Carl?"

"Stepped out back, perhaps." He made a show of looking for something in the carriage. "My old law firm was the master of such tricks. That's how I heard the Woodman's conversation. I'm being overly suspicious perhaps."

"Do you have another banker?" I whispered.

"Two more, but they aren't terribly enthusiastic. You need to decide if you want to sell Rosemount. Are you prepared to call his bluff?"

I was drowning in debt, but Papa must have felt strongly to mortgage both properties so heavily. Still, the conversation with Fox invaded my dreams and every waking thought. If I sold Rosemount, there was no turning back. I saw no kind fate in store either way. Plus, the letter in the secret keeper had further closed that path. "I can't sell Rosemount," I said.

Beddow rubbed his jaw. "That puts us at a disadvantage. What happens if we push for more money and he balks? Will you take his offer?"

"No, as much as I despise Mondovi, put it on the block. Let the wolves fight over it."

"All right. Let me shuffle through more papers and hang Owens out for a while. Keep your poker face on. Act like we're in a hurry."

Beddow had wasted a good twenty minutes before we started back. Carl had returned and fell into step with us at the door. "I have news," he said quietly.

"Good, I hope," Beddow responded. "We could use it."

"I followed Updike when he left." We stopped and turned, waiting for him to finish. "He hustled out of here and headed straight to Union Bank. I paid a shoeshine boy to keep watch on him after he left The Pines in such a hurry. He recognized him, and said Updike's been there four times this past week. He was there the second time just after he came back from The Pines, according to my figuring."

I wondered where Carl had disappeared to, but I had been so busy with sales preparations that I hadn't paid it much mind. "Is Owens working with Mondovi?"

Beddow glanced toward the banker's office. "No, he's like all money men. He's so tight he'd try to squeeze the dress off a Liberty half dime, but he hates Mondovi."

When we returned, Mr. Owens asked, "Have you considered my offer?"

"I'm declining."

"I know you're in mourning," he replied, making a solemn gesture toward my weeds, as if using it to excuse my irrationalities.

"I am," I agreed. "I mourn for my father and the lack of integrity of the men I'm forced to deal with in his absence."

Owens clanked his cup of tea down so violently the tea sloshed over papers on the desk. "Be damned," he muttered and sopped the mess. "Now see here, Miss McKenzie," he said as soon as he rescued the papers. "I've been more than respectful toward you. There's no need to be petulant."

Mr. Updike stopped adjusting his coat tail and sat stunned, batting his eyes like a frog in a hailstorm. "You made an offer after my recommendations?"

Mr. Owens recovered from my rudeness enough to remember Updike's return. "How's your mother?"

"Mother?" Updike looked bewildered, then regained his composure. "Oh, fine. You made an offer?"

"Does your mother reside at Union Bank?" Carl asked innocently.

"How ridiculous. Why would you even ask that?"

The relaxed, slouching posture of a man in charge of his world changed to someone preparing for flight as he realized the trap was sprung. Updike's polished boot slid off his knee and hit the floor.

"Because I followed you when you left," Carl said. "You went straight there for a meeting with Mondovi. You've had four meetings with him this past week, including one immediately after you returned from The Pines. A person has to wonder what you and Mondovi talked about so many times."

"That isn't true!" Updike cried out. "I—"

"Is this right?" Mr. Owens barked, his jaw clenching.

"Yes," Carl said, brushing lint from his pant leg as casually as he'd brushed aside Updike's lie. "I had someone watching him, but I followed myself today."

Mr. Owens yanked on a scarlet cord behind him that was nearly the same shade as his flushing face. His secretary appeared moments later. "Get security," he boomed. "Take Updike to the basement. Chain him if you have to. Chain him even if you don't have to." The man's amiable manner turned deadly within moments. I wondered if Updike would make it out of the basement alive. From his trembling, Updike did also. "You're going to tell me everything you've been doing with Mondovi, or by God I'll wring it out of you. And don't think we haven't noticed the accounts gone screwy."

"Mr. Owens, you don't know what Mondovi will do to me," Updike wailed.

"You don't know what I'll do to you. Flashing that damned watch every chance you got. I should have been suspicious."

Two burly security guards rivaling Carl in bulk escorted Updike from the room. I half expected a trail of piss to follow him.

"This wasn't my doing, Miss McKenzie. I extend my apologies. I didn't know he was working with Mondovi." He walked to the window and sighed. "Are you sure you won't accept my offer?"

"We have two counter offers for you," Beddow said. "Either offer her this price, which you know is fair. That's a good property, and you'll make money on it, or this price, and she keeps the brickyard and the riverfront acreage I've drawn off."

Owens took the map Beddow slid across the desk to him and studied it and the offer. "Will you lease it back to me? It would save you having to look after two properties."

"I can do that at an acceptable price and a percentage of the brickyard sales," I replied. It wouldn't give me as much cash as I hoped for, but it would save it from the auction block.

"You'll leave the equipment? I'll buy it and the livestock separate. There's a list here, I believe."

"I'll sell it at market price. There are personal horses and old mares who produced great horses but are retired. Pensioners. I'll take them home."

He waved a hand. "I'll keep them. It'll give me something to do when I'm out there. Besides, it's warmer here and easier on old bones. They'll have a home as long as I do."

"You realize they're too old to breed?"

"I don't plan to raise horses. I just keep a few to ride."

"Promise me if things go bad, you'll put them down rather than let them suffer or go."

"They won't leave," he assured me. Did he share my concern that if the war dragged out, every man and horse in the land would be pressed into service?

"Also, I'll buy the furniture and so forth." He said brightly, changing the timbre of emotion like a snap of the fingers. "I like The Pines as it is and don't want Cora redecorating. The Pines is mine," he declared. "Heaven save me from more rose and magenta, frills and fluff. And especially dear God, preserve me from so many pillows a man can't even sit his fat—" he blushed, "body."

Somewhat surprised at his protective attitude towards The Pines, I asked, "Will she be allowed on the property?"

"I'll issue visitation passports. She won't be permitted to camp out. You know how women are. 'Let me make this little change here, Homer.' No, visitation only, then out she goes. I may not even allow her to bring a satchel."

When I was a little girl, I once thought I saw a woman in my bedroom asking for help. She was weeping and holding a bundle in her arms. I knew it was a baby. I also knew she was a ghost, and though my heart broke for her, I threw the covers over my head and shook with fright until I thought it was safe. I had that same desire now to hide somewhere until it was safe, but I knew there was no such place, and I must drop the sword on my home. With trembling heart, I signed the contract Beddow had ready and blotted my signature.

"What about the slaves?" Owens asked. "I'll purchase them. They can remain in their homes," he added this as if it were a selling point. "I'm easy on my people."

My hand went to the crucifix, clinking the beads together. I didn't feel like the left arm of God. I had just put them out of the only homes some had ever known. Plus, as noble as he might think himself to be, absolute power was dangerous. It was dangerous to the employee, the wife, or the slave. "They go free. About half our people are freemen anyway."

He shook his head and paused with his pen poised above my signature. "You're an abolitionist? What will they do?"

I never thought of myself in those terms. "No. Colonel Lee of Arlington used to write editorials about slavery. He said once, 'There are few in this enlightened age, who will not acknowledge that slavery as an institution is a moral and political evil. It's neither good for slave nor master.'

"He's right in this. Nor is it good for America, I believe, but the practice will die without me. As to what they will do…" I shrugged. "Whatever they want. That's what comes with liberty."

Chapter Nineteen

A truly dismal countenance replaced Mrs. Whimple's usually cheerful smile. Reddened eyes and nose gave proof of recent waterworks that threatened to erupt again as soon as she saw me. My heart plummeted that she might be suffering on my account. Had Mondovi discovered her duplicity?

"Hello, Miss McKenzie." She sniffled and drew a drenched handkerchief from the inside pocket of her jacket. "Mr. Beddow." The damp white flag waved weakly in Carl's direction before she blew her nose. "I'll tell Mr. Mondovi you're here." I handed her my dry handkerchief. A plump, tawny pug scrabbled from beneath her desk to follow her. "No, Gellie. Stay here." She put her hand out, motioning the dog down. The dog whined but dropped to her belly and rolled liquid brown eyes at her. "No, you can't go. Stay here."

"How adorable." I set the cake boxes on the desk and held the leather leash. "Gellie, stay with me. Mama will be back in a minute." The dog gazed past me and snarled deep in her throat so gutturally I rocked back on my heels, then followed her stare to the upper level where Mondovi leaned heavily on his balustrade. He glared at me with such malevolence I was shocked to my very marrow. "Moses!" My hand went immediately to the crucifix.

Beddow looked up. "Don't let him scare you."

"It's hard not to be. That's a face of pure evil."

"Not as evil as me," Carl said from behind me, his voice gravel and grit and barely above a growl. "And I'm on your payroll."

"That's a comfort."

"It should be."

I hadn't seen cleaning women in the bank before, but there one was polishing the brass leaves in the railing near Mondovi. She methodically worked the rag through the intricacies, buffing the brass to a high shine. Mrs. Whimple bowed her head and rushed back down the stairs. He could have let her know he was aware of our presence instead of making her climb three flights of stairs, but heaven forfend he make life easy. He turned his wrath to the cleaning woman and lifted his arm as if to strike her.

"If he touches her, I'll knock him out," Carl rasped. The woman shielded herself with an upraised hand, but Mondovi lowered his. "He just saved himself a broken nose."

"What has him in such a mood today?" I continued to stroke Gellie, who growled the whole time.

Mrs. Whimple arrived breathless, face flushed, but before I could inquire about her, she blurted out, "He says you should come. Please hurry."

Without a word, I gathered the cake boxes and my temper, then shot a quick glance at Beddow. I had no intention of hurrying and leisurely made my way. The cleaning lady worked her way across to the last section of wrought iron before the stairs, meticulously polishing the brass leaves woven amongst the black vines. Carl stopped behind her stooped form, which was all in black aside from the small white apron and caplet. Her bombazine skirts pooled about her, giving the impression she was sinking in despair. "Are you all right?" he asked.

A mourning brooch with a lock of brown hair was pinned to her breast, revealing her cause for anguish. She swiped hurriedly at her eye with the back of her hand. "Forgive me. I was gathering wool and didn't hear you approach."

"No need to apologize," I said. "I hope things get better."

"They will." She cast a quick glance towards Mondovi's office, ducked her head, and returned to work. Mondovi waited until Beddow's second knock to yell, "Come in."

"Even now he has to remind me who has the power?" I whispered.

"Not for long," Carl replied.

Surprisingly, Mondovi smiled when we entered. "Miss McKenzie. Mr. Beddow. I trust everything's ready?"

"Of course," Beddow replied. "We'll need the final number for the cheque."

"It's all here." He handed the paper to Beddow. My face must have betrayed my puzzlement at his change in attitude. "Is something wrong?"

"You seemed upset earlier." There was no need to poke a snake when a person can let him lie. That would come later.

"A regretful matter. Someone pasted the brass last night and neglected to buff it, leaving an ungodly mess this morning. I had to call a woman in. It's deplorable business to see cleaning people. Plus, I'm losing valuable staff. It's not been a good week."

"That would be upsetting," I agreed.

"Yes, terrible." He rocked back in his chair and looked out his window while Beddow read over the papers. Satisfied all was in order, he gave them to me to sign, and I withdrew a cheque to finish filling out.

I took a deep breath. So, this was it. My life as I had known it was over. Thanks to the man sitting across the desk from me and Mahler, it had almost been over entirely. Any misgivings about leaving the pastries vanished when I reminded myself of this. With business concluded, I rose to leave. "I brought you some lemon cake with raspberry sauce and included the receipt for your wife. There's one for Mr. Mahler also. He'll understand."

His face brightened. "How kind." He either didn't know about the attempted poisoning and method or excelled at masking his emotions. "I'll have it with my tea."

"Excellent choice."

Only the business of delivering the release of lien to Mr. Owens and going to the clerk's office to record all the documents remained. Then the final resolution at The Pines. This I dreaded like death, but it had to be done.

The cleaning woman was near the landing, humming *Lowlands Away*, a particularly sad shanty. I dared not risk getting her in trouble for talking to customers, especially this customer, and merely patted her shoulder. Mondovi's cordial act was a bit too contrived.

"A moment," I said as we neared Mrs. Whimple's desk. I knelt to pet Gellie, who squirmed out from under the desk to greet me.

"She's such a sweetheart," I said, stroking the panting dog.

"I don't normally bring her to work, but we gave notice, and Mr. Mondovi didn't take it well. First, he was all honey and sweetness. Then, he tried to bribe Mr. Whimple with a generous raise and a promotion. Such a raise. The fool almost capitulated. I threatened to cut off all comfort to him, and still he wavered." She hurried on in that breathless way she had when she was upset, hands aflutter.

"Mr. Whimple finally told him we were moving to Pensacola. It will be safe from the coming unpleasantries," she said by way of explanation, "plus, we'll be closer to our daughter. Mr. Whimple said we'd give him a month to find replacements." She waved her hands in the air in imitation of an enraged Mondovi. "'A month! A month! Clear out tomorrow. It won't take me a day.'

"I've cried all morning, but after the way he's treated that poor Mrs. Michener, I'm glad to go."

I looked toward the landing. "The cleaning lady?"

"Yes, the brass wasn't that bad. She's new here. Mistakes happen. Came to work after her husband died, poor thing. Petty purse snatcher got thrown in jail and hanged himself. Why would a man go and do that with a pretty little wife and baby at home? It's not like he'd be locked up forever. I guess she needed work, so she took the place of another girl."

Beddow looked at me with a furrowed brow. How many purse snatchers named Michener had hanged themselves in jail lately?

"Yes, I'll be glad to go," Mrs. Whimple said. "That's why I brought Gellie. He avoids me when she's around. No more watching him browbeat people. No more running stairs while he reserves the elevator for himself and his fat friends. No more screaming—"

"You ungrateful bitch!" Mondovi's face was deep pink, the color of the raspberry sauce. He leaned on the railing and flung the cake box through the air. The plate with the lemon cake burst out of the box and sailed away. A metallic screeching drew my eye away from the airborne dessert and back to Mondovi. The top of the railing gave way to his left and leaned precariously forward. Mondovi's arms flailed as if he were backstroking. He swayed there, suspended in air and time, until I thought he might somehow be saved, but he couldn't catch his balance, and over he came headfirst. The tails of his frock coat fluttered after him as he hurtled toward the floor. Horrified shouts from onlookers joined his terrified yowl, followed by the sound of a ripe watermelon hitting a sidewalk.

"He's dead!"

Carl spun me around to face the stair landing. "Don't look."

Mrs. Whimple turned and buried her face in her hands. Everyone ran toward Mr. Mondovi. Everyone except Mrs. Michener. I pushed away from Carl's chest and watched her carefully polish a brass leaf as if a spot of dust or something more nefarious spattered on it. Satisfied it was perfectly shiny, she folded the cloth and set it in the basket of cleaning supplies, rose, and stretched her back. She untied the white apron, folded it neatly, and laid it in the basket also and topped it off with the caplet. When all was done, she unpinned the mourning brooch and opened it to look at the picture inside. Kissing it softly, she gazed at it for a moment, pinned it back on her dress, pulled a small black reticule from the basket, and walked calmly from the bank, never once looking at the banker who had just plunged to his death. Fascinated by the entire scene, I barely breathed as if afraid I might disturb her.

Carl handed me off to Beddow and went to inspect the failed railing. I was still trying to determine what I'd just witnessed with Mrs. Michener when he returned. People milled about in a confused herd, but I caught a glimpse of the inert form covered in several coats. A small pool of blood seeped from beneath one. For all the waving his arms about, he didn't fly, and unlike Bellerophon, the god of commerce hadn't survived his fall. I had an idea a petite gadfly in bombazine had sent him crashing to earth.

Carl slipped through the crowd, including newly arrived police officers. I hesitated to call it an accident, but neither was it a tragedy in my mind. "Someone loosened the bolts," he whispered.

Beddow moved us away from Mrs. Whimple's desk to a secluded corner. I told them about Mrs. Michener's odd behavior. Carl had noticed the same. I should have known he was watching everything.

"I'm sure she's related to Rascal," Beddow said. "I'd be tempted to represent her if anyone ever connects her, but I hope for her sake she leaves town."

I agreed. I couldn't find sympathy for Mondovi, but I was unsure how I felt about outright murder. "It's poor timing, but I need to leave some things with Mrs. Whimple."

She sat at her desk with the plump pug pulled up in her lap for comfort. Her face was bisque white with shock. Gellie looked perfectly content to receive the extra attention. I withdrew some wrapped pieces from my purse and placed them on her desk and extracted the amethyst hatpin from an inner pocket. "Mrs. Whimple, can we call someone for you?"

She looked up, dazed. "No, I expect Mister will be along shortly."

"I brought back that glassware, since I'm returning to Virginia."

"The what?"

"The amethyst?"

"Oh, yes." She waved her hand. "Keep it. You're going back to Virginia. I wanted to speak to you before you sold The Pines. Mrs. Owens told me they were buying. Whatever possessed you? If war comes, it'll be in Virginia faster than you can say scat. You and the girls would be much safer here. That's why we're going to Florida. Lincoln will have no interest there.

"I'm afraid you're going to need amethyst much more than me. Keep it. Buy more. Buy all you can."

"Cassandra! What in thunder's going on here?" boomed from behind us.

"Cassandra? I thought your name was Lou?" I blurted out.

"Cassandra Louise," she answered. "Mondovi disliked the connotations of Cassandra."

It didn't take a seer to realize she was correct about how dangerous Virginia might become, and I questioned my decision as I replaced the amethyst ware in my purse.

"Good luck, Mr. and Mrs. Whimple. And thank you."

Mrs. Whimple gave us a weak wave and collapsed into Mr. Whimple's arms, relaying the disaster through her tears. Gellie waddled off to sit on one of the coats draped over Mr. Mondovi's body. Not satisfied with it, she tugged it from his legs, not unlike the pug tugging at the Mondovi Zeus's hem, padded around in circles forming a comfortable little nest, and plopped down with a satisfied sigh.

Chapter Twenty

Annie insisted she still had to finish buying supplies we were taking back to Rosemount as well as settling my few remaining accounts, but I knew the main reason she wished to remain in town was that she was as busy as a mouse in a cheese factory planning a surprise birthday picnic on the battery before we departed. I was in no mood for a party, but she was determined, and when Annie was on a mission, even Old Nick fled in fear.

Carl met me in the lobby and escorted me to The Pines early the next morning. The appraiser had ridden out as soon as the papers were signed the day before to update inventory lists. Mr. Owens would come out as soon as he could get away from the bank. I was still in shock over Mr. Mondovi, but I found I could not grieve.

We rode by and large in silence, commenting occasionally on the scenery or the events of the past few days, but mostly I mucked through memories and recriminations. I was still in such shock I couldn't comprehend it. I had never failed at anything I put my mind to. The Pines, my heart, and soul were gone, and only emptiness remained.

The staff waited quietly for me on the gallery where, to my shock, black crepe fluttered from the windows. I pulled up my horse and stared, stricken at their countenances that ranged from seething anger to free-flowing tears. Carl must have sensed I was about to topple and hurried over to help me dismount. "Has someone died?" I asked, holding to Carl's arm.

"Don't expect us to be happy 'bout some fat banker gobblin' up The Pines," Zona said, planting her hands on her hips defiantly. "We in mourning."

Though Mr. Owens hadn't given me a deadline, I wanted this over quickly and had sent word ahead of the sale so they could start packing personal items.

"Come inside, girl," Rachel said. "I made ginger cookies this morning."

Bless her heart. How many ginger cookies would it take to get through this? I changed into a day dress and repaired to the library, as that would be the most difficult to sort. All those treasures. "Zona, please show Mr. Carl around the house. I want him to have something to remember us by."

She looked at me like she'd just swallowed a bug but stilled her protest. She couldn't protect me from the chore ahead nor ease the pain. It was simply plowing through hell the best I could.

"I tied yellow yarn about things I'm taking with me, but whatever else you'd like, please feel free." I thought I was only tying the yarn in case of disaster, but now I thanked whatever spirit had guided me to be prepared. I simply didn't have the heart to go through the house now and choose. I might have built a large fire and burnt it all.

"Thank you. That's very kind." Carl replied and then opened his mouth as if to say something more.

"It's all right," I said. "I need to be alone."

He sighed in resignation. It was the first time I'd heard such a sound from him, but there was nothing he could do.

Rachel had followed me into Papa's office, quiet as a ghost, and stood in the doorway, wringing her hands and crying. "You sure you don't want help, Miss Mac?"

"I'm just going to mark a few things to take home to Rosemount." It hit me all over again: The Pines *was* my home. I scoured the tears from my eyes with the apron corner.

"Let me open these windows and get a breeze in here." She lingered afterwards, hesitant and helpless, but turned at last and shut the door.

I meandered, overwhelmed by the upcoming task, and this was only the first room. Bailing into the task at hand at last, I pushed the ladder to one end of the wall of books and went through them, inserting a length of yellow yarn in Papa's favored volumes. Yellow tails fluttered like tiny banners when I finished. Apparently only a handful of books weren't Papa's favorites.

Papa used to read to us from the chair nestled in the bay window. I pictured Baron reading to our children in it. I'd take the two reading chairs and the rugs we had lain on at Papa's feet.

Papa's desk would go. There were desks at Rosemount, but this was the adventure desk. James and I hid out in the kneehole. Sometimes Papa sat there and misdirected whoever was looking for us. I was sure Zona knew exactly when he was hiding us. "Yassir, Marse Mac. I'm sure you hasn't seen hide nor hair o' those chilluns, but when you do, tell 'em to come eat."

Other times he'd hide under the desk with us. The desk was our fort, our castle, our dungeon, and our tiny reading room. Papa had drawn an elaborate, fully colored map and glued it to the bottom of the drawer. There were mountains and kingdoms, jungles, and oceans, and ships, the privateer Shillelagh with three gallant crew members and a plank for sending dastardly foes into the briny deep.

I leaned back in the chair to trace the plank in my mind and let fly the bankers from Union Bank into the ocean, one by one, and waited for a kraken to come by. Finishing the feast with Updike, I sent the sated monster on his way. My murderous mission completed, I laid my hands over my ribs and closed my eyes. All problems should be solved so easily.

"Are you all right?" Carl asked quietly, startling me upright out of my slouch like a suddenly surprised horse.

"Moses, I didn't know you were here. Yes, fine. Just thinking."

"No, you're flogging yourself again. Stop it. You did all you could. Now is the time to fight the next battle."

"You're right. I can do no more except maybe learn and move on like a good little general. Did you find something you'd like?"

"I was on the porch rocking and feeding cookies to a pony a bit ago. I think I'd like one of those rocking chairs for my mother if you don't mind."

"You need a book to go with your rocking chair. Ignore the yarn."

"Would you like me to remove it?"

"Leave it. I got carried away. Most will stay. Someone can use it for bookmarks. I hate it when people dog-ear books, though oddly, I love penciled notes in margins. One mangles and the other expresses love, I suppose. Usually. Papa hated Jane Austen. The things he wrote on those pages. I hope they don't meet in the afterlife. Don't pick an Austen for your mother. She'd be horrified."

I read Austen because, unlike Papa, I did like her in measured doses, but oh, those things he wrote about her. He said once he would cheerfully dig her up and pound her bones to dust just to make sure she never rose again to write another word. I had never entertained the idea that Austen might be a vampyre, but Papa wasn't willing to chance it.

"Take your time," I said. "I'm going to go over ledgers and settle accounts with my people." I said this with a sharp pang of grief, as they were no longer McKenzie people, and I feared what the future might hold for them.

"What will they do?" he asked.

"They're literate and can cipher. Owens will hire some because they know how the brickyard and farm works. He'll be out later to talk to them."

He set two books aside. "Do you mind if I take more than one?"

"Take as many as you like. I'm leaving none for Owens unless he buys them." I felt a twinge of guilt at this, but there was no charity in my heart for bankers. Maybe someday…if I lived long enough. I'd have to take after Mother's side of the family if I did, and they tended to be dotty in old age. I set the pencil aside, stomach and mind turned sour at the thought of bankers. "I'm going to sort some other rooms."

The knob to James's room turned slowly in my hand. The room had remained untouched aside from dusting. Papa used to sit here late at night when he thought no one saw him. I knew the times when grief claimed him and waited for him to slip away to either the cemetery or the room crowded with James's memories.

In the cemetery, he had stood over the small plot, shoulders heaving, and at last collapsed onto the grave as if he could hold his son one more time. Inside, he'd pace, and then the bed creaked when he sank heavily onto it and clutched a toy to his bosom. I peeked through the keyhole once. Once was enough. I slid down the door and kept watch like Argos in his time of sorrow.

I heard the quiet sobs and murmured prayers, or curses, filtered through the door. He blamed himself for not saving his son, but what could a mere man do against that disease? He blamed Mother for insisting on tending the slaves, as was her Christian duty, even after he'd forbidden her to do so. She brought the fever back and gave it to us. I barely survived. James didn't.

I'd scurry away if I heard him rising so he wouldn't know I'd been there. Sometimes he stayed all night. At those times, a maid would find me asleep and carry me back to my room.

The beginning of the end started in this room. The marriage survived, but it was mortally wounded. It just took years to die.

Shaking the memories from my mind, I sat on the bed to the sound of the familiar squeak and looked around the room expecting James to poke his head out of the armoire, as he'd done so many times when we played hide and seek. My eyes closed, and I heard him giggling as he peeked around the door at me. "Are you sure you counted to one hundred, Rena?" Most times I made a great show of running everywhere calling his name and slamming doors in my search, but James had his favorite hiding places, and I knew them all. Sometimes, I'd hear him quietly sniggering as I looked behind curtains or under cushions looking for him and declaring in exasperation, "Where is that boy? I may never find him!"

I'd take his furniture home with Grandmamma's quilt. The wooden rocking horse for children I hoped one day to have.

Over I went to the toy box and poured out memories. Every toy brought back an adventure. There was the one of James nearly drowning as he sailed his boat in the pond and slipped in after it. Old man Robey carved the wooden duck on the string that waddled because the wheels were different sizes. When he told us Bible stories, his deep, booming voice of the Lord spake this or that as he carved. The cast iron banks James loved went in the box. I wound his clockwork train and watched it go around in a circle. James laughed in delight once more. The train went in the crate, and a bank came out, jingling coins inside as it did. Finally, I had the crate full of toys and a stack of books to take home.

Zona stood quietly until the end, then wrapped her arms around me and pulled me down to sit on the bed. "They's nothin' sayin' you can't take all this home."

"I can't keep it all. Do you remember Joe Rough Face?"

"Indian Joe?"

"Yes. Remember when Nachie asked us to help her make food and gift baskets for the poor and do a giveaway in his honor after he died? That's what we're doing. Hard times are coming. They'll need something to hold onto." I looked around the room, batting back the tears. "I want people to remember Papa."

Her almost white (when had that happened?) brows slanted toward the two small lines above the bridge of her nose. "Honey chile, what makes you think anyone could forget yo' daddy? People gonna be tellin' stories about Marse Mac to their grandbabies. Most will be true, cause no need to make up nothin' bout that man."

"That's the problem. I don't want them remembering the crazy Irishman. I want them to remember him kindly."

She pulled me beside her on the bed and wrapped her arms around me like she did when I was a child, then rocked so softly the bed didn't even protest. I buried my head in her shoulder and closed my eyes, wishing I was small again. "'Member when he brought Della and Annie home?"

I nodded. "I was hanging upside down from a tree in the lane when he drove up, and I saw Annie on the wagon seat between Papa and Della. Down I dropped and ran screaming to the house, 'Papa brung me a sister! Papa brung me a sister!' Mother came out wiping her hands on a towel. 'Brought you a sister. Stop speaking like a heathen, Lorena.'"

Zona laughed, shaking her great stomach in waves. "Yes, that poor little girl came in, those eyes wide as saucers, and I ask her, 'What wrong with you, chile?' She looked up at me and whispered, 'Little White girls was fallin' out of trees like rain when we came up the road.'"

"Poor Annie," I said. "What an impression I must have made on her."

With a pat of her hand to comfort me, she continued. "She was already afeared after that auction, poor thing. Her mama told me all bout it later. Mr. Kaine left it in his will for Della and Annie to go free with some money to see to them, but Miz Kaine put them on the block 'fore he was even in the grave. Della told Annie to be brave and not cry when they was gonna sell them apart, but that little girl was wailin' and clingin' to her mama's leg. That's when yo' Papa came by.

"Massa Chauvin wanted Della for his fancy house and was biddin' high, but yo' daddy just kept on until he got her. Then Chauvin said, 'Kieran, what's Bert gonna do when you bring that pretty mulatto home?'"

There was that rolling belly laugh again. "'What are you talkin' about? I thought I bought that little girl.' Then he asks Della if she can cook good fried chicken. She says she cooks the best in the south. 'Good, because Tilda can't cook fried chicken to save her soul. Get that girl and let's go home.' Auctioneer tried to make him pay more for Annie, but yo' daddy threatened him and Miz Kaine too over what she did.

"No, girl. Yo' daddy was colorful, but never fear; people knew how kind he was, and don't discount the value of crazy. Crazy get you through places a right person don't dare go."

"Because they're sane."

"Because they afraid. Marse Mac come up hard and made his own way. Took chances. You got a lot of him in you and you gonna need that. Just because you got money don't mean life gonna be easy. No promise you always gonna have money neither. You best be like a little squirrel and hide some here and hide some there."

She held my hand. "He was a good man, chile. Don't forget that. People won't."

She was right about that. Kieran McKenzie wouldn't be soon forgotten whether I gave his things away or not. I raised my head and looked into eyes filmed blue with age. "Did you get something for yourself?"

She pulled her arm from around my shoulder and folded her hands. "I got a long cookin' fork—"

"But?"

"I'd like to have one of those teacups with the flowers on the sides. I know that's extrav'gant, but I want somethin' pretty for me."

"Take it and a saucer and think kindly of Marse Mac."

Tears welled. "Thank you, Miss Mac." She swiped a hand across her nose.

Owens was keeping her son Randall for the brickyard, so she would stay and have a home…and a cup. Looking around the room once more, I prepared for the final sortings. "Have the girls take the rest of this to the parlor."

"What about the pictures?"

Mother surrounded James with paintings of angels watching protectively over children scattered over the Ye-Frog-He-Would-A-Wooin'-Go wallpaper. I didn't want to be reminded of the failed promises of those paintings.

"Give them away."

Chapter Twenty-One

Mr. Owens hurried out as soon as the bank closed and spent much of the afternoon and evening going over inventory lists and asking me about this or that as I updated it. A grand sum was offered for the secret keeper, but some things weren't for sale. He already had the kingdom; he didn't need my heart on a platter also. I tried to remain genial. No one had forced me to sell The Pines to him, but I brimmed with bitterness at the loss. Zona had baked another batch of ginger cookies and shoved cups of stress tea in my hand at every turn. I stayed up late making sure everything was counted and listed. At some point, I realized Owens had stopped popping in every few minutes to ask about this or that and went looking for him. He was on the west veranda watching the moon rise, sipping whiskey and smoking a cigar as he rocked. He had shed his jacket and tie and wore colorful carpet slippers instead of his expensive riding boots. He was the lord of the manor.

"Are you all right?" I asked.

"Yes, quite. Listening to someone singing down in the quarters. It's so peaceful here I don't ever want to leave. I will die most contentedly here. My heart is full."

My fingers clutched the folds of my skirt as if I were falling. His heart might be full, but I felt the final stitches in my broken heart ripping free. "Yes, it's very peaceful here," I replied and left quietly as a mouse to sob somewhere in silence.

꩜

I was accustomed to being up early, but it surprised me to see Mr. Owens in the kitchen when I descended looking for coffee. The girls had already started breakfast, and the scent of frying ham and baking biscuits filled the air. Someone had bread going in the main kitchen, and that scent also drifted up the path and in through the open door.

He was in high spirits and complimented one and all over the excellent repast during breakfast. The autumn glow marmalade was especially popular. It always was. I was feeling churlish and claimed I didn't know how it was made when he asked for the receipt. It was an odd hill to die on after I had lost all, but I decided I was due a victory no matter how small. Zona raised a censorious brow at me and screwed her mouth up in disappointment, not for declining to share the recipe as we had several we kept under lock and key, but rather for the audacity of the lie, as I knew it by heart, having watched it made since I was knee-high to nothing. She would have me repenting my sin later for fear of my soul.

Mr. Owens missed the unspoken exchange and barreled on in Christmas morning good humor.

He generously offered all the kitchen staff jobs if they wanted to stay. "I've been thinking about holding hunting parties here and maybe some races since you already have a training track," he said. "No sense scrambling for new people when y'all have everything in hand."

They looked at me as if asking for permission to join the enemy camp. "That's an excellent idea," I replied. "I was going to talk to you about the…McKenzie people anyway. Could we make arrangements for them to stay here while paperwork is being settled?"

"I'm sure we could come to an agreement," he said, reaching for another biscuit and more autumn glow.

If he insists on that receipt, I will poison him.

"I can give you a better deal on some of the furnishings perhaps," I said in an attempt to bribe him.

"That would be nice, but I'll need people to keep the place going anyway. Not as many now without the horses, but I may buy some cattle."

Excusing myself before he thought of something else, I retired to the office with Mr. Beddow, who had arrived for a late breakfast. We looked over the books one last time and started paying everyone. As I did so, he discussed their options with them and showed them the legal papers and information from the Colonization Society for any who wanted to resettle elsewhere. Though I hoped they would relocate, I stopped short of telling them I saw no kind fate for coloreds north or south if the nation went to war. It had to be their decision.

Frank came in to tell me he'd finished gathering horses I would take and arranged to sand the two livestock cars to take no chances of cinders from the engine catching a load of horses on fire as sometimes happened with straw bedding. He even fixed a wagon to haul Siobhan to town so the ancient pony wouldn't have to walk and separated her off in a small stall. Bless him. The girls would spoil her silly, and we'd keep her in the barn in the winter. How many more winters could she last anyway?

Since my inventory list was nearly complete, it wouldn't take long to settle on an agreeable price. I left Mr. Beddow to finish up with those who hadn't appeared yet and went to gather Mr. Owens to look for the appraiser, who was wandering somewhere.

He was in the main kitchen visiting Rachel, who was not baking ginger cookies for a change. "Have you seen the appraiser?"

"He went to look at equipment," she replied. "Zona went up to the bee garden to pick peas. Maybe she saw which way he went."

"Butterfly garden."

"Yas'm, but what hangs out there bzzzz, bzzzz, bzzzzing around all the time tryin' to bite people? Bees." She made another buzzing noise and pinched her arm as if she'd been bitten.

"They don't— Never mind. We'll go up there."

"If you goin' to the bee garden, you should take this sugar water I made for them," she said grimly. With a heavy heart, I accepted the jars and put them in a shoulder bag.

At least I could rest easy knowing Rachel would make sure the wee folk and the bees were taken care of after I was gone.

As I stepped away from the warmth and bustle of the kitchen, a wave of melancholy washed over me. Each footfall on the familiar path toward the bees seemed heavier, as though the land itself clung to me, not yet ready to let go. We walked along a well-tended path embanked by a red brick half wall on one side with Mr. Owens making genial conversation about the beauty of the place. He was right. On that point, Mother and Papa had agreed. People should be surrounded by the beauty of nature.

Behind the wall, gardens and flowers in a wild, enchanting sprawl flowed gently up the hill. Bright clusters of bee balm, goldenrod, catmint, salvia, and lavender swayed softly in a delicate dance, their enticing fragrances mingling around us. Butterflies flitted in brilliant pops of color over the flowers, their wings shimmering as they moved from blossom to blossom, pausing only to kiss the open petals.

Bees hummed in a steady, purposeful rhythm, weaving through the blossoms in their unending search for pollen. They moved with the quiet dedication of caretakers, their legs dusted with golden grains as they returned again and again to the heart of the garden.

Owens untied the rope around the gate and unlatched it, looking quizzically at the double closure. "Trying to keep bees in or out?" he asked as he retied the gate.

"A luricawne out," I replied. With such a mild winter, pea vines massed with flowers and pods along the back fence. Zona bent over, picking peas and dropping them in a bulrush basket. "Have you seen Mr. Church?" I asked.

Zona straightened, put her hands on her back, and stretched, then pointed toward the hay barns and machine shed. "Down there, Miss."

"I'm not going to the sheds." He'd be done soon. A dappled yellow mare with silver mane appeared and lipped at the gate rope. Zona gave her the evil eye and returned to picking peas. Owens, on the other hand, stared in fascination. The horse continued worrying at the rope, biting and lipping at it until she got the first part of the knot loose and pulled the tail through. Then she started on the second section. Instead of letting the untied rope fall to the ground, she gripped it in her teeth and waved it like a banner. Flipping it to the side, she opened the gate latch and sauntered in, glancing at me in an accusatory way, knowing it was my fault she'd been inconvenienced. Why did I even bother?

"Meet Luricawne Gold," I said to my astonished companion. The mare moseyed over to the cream bowl beside the bench near the pond and drained it. She similarly emptied the bowl of beer and ate the bread that had been left for the fae folk.

"Papa believed a master should leave out offerings of cream, beer, and bread for the fae folk," I said, turning to Mr. Owens, who was leaning over, watching with rapt attention. "I expect you will want to continue."

A brow rose in surprise, but he nodded his head. "Of course. All traditions will remain."

Zona shook her finger at Luri. "We put that out for Marse Mac's little people. Do you look like a little people? I don't think so. No wonder we havin' bad luck 'round here."

Luri flicked a disinterested ear at her and made her way to the pond. She washed down the dry bread with a deep drink and waded out until she was knee-deep, then kissed her rippling reflection. There she stayed for a moment, contemplating her image, and slowly plunged her head below the water until only the tips of her golden ears remained showing. After a time, bubbles floated to the surface.

Owens stared at her, dumbfounded. "Odd, she didn't look depressed. Should we save her?"

"No, Papa swore she was visiting with the merrows. They'd have to be small mermaids. I can't decide if she's watching the goldfish or if she likes cooling her head. The girls think she's talking to cymbees, water spirits."

"Goldfish?"

"Mmhmm. Papa was visiting with an old sea captain friend of his in New York on one of his horse-selling trips and saw the goldfish in the captain's aquarium. He brought them back from China, and I think they're quite rare. Papa traded a horse for some fish for Jamie and me to keep the merrows company."

Presently, Luri lifted her dripping head, inhaled deeply, and exhaled what amounted to a contented sigh.

"Is she for sale?"

I considered it.

Don't sell thet mare. She's lucky.

Have you noticed how our luck's been going lately? Do I really have to argue with you now?

Don't sell Luri.

"No, and you don't want her. She has an infuriating habit of untying herself and then sets about freeing every other horse she can find. We've sold her a few times, but she's like a homing pigeon and always comes back. Regardless of her eating the little people's food, Papa figured that meant she was McKenzie luck. He was big on signs."

"You certainly can't sell your lucky horse."

"I didn't say she was *good* luck. I said she was McKenzie luck."

I stepped toward her and whistled. "Come on, Luri. You've had your snack and looked at the fish. Let's go." The mare waded out of the pond and strolled through the gate.

"While we are near the bee garden, you should go with me so I may introduce you."

"To the bees?" he asked somewhat incredulously.

"To the bees. You will be their master. As such, you'll be expected to share all the news of your family and people with them. Papa believed they were God's messengers." I shrugged. "Papa held with many mystical beliefs."

I led him to the apiary. "We replaced most of the old hives with Langstroth box hives, which have frames that are easier to extract honey from and upset the bees less. Henry and his family usually do the beekeeping, but I often participated also, as I felt it was my duty to care for the wee ones. Our…your honey will sell well."

I motioned for Mr. Owens to follow me to the rear of the first hive and took the jar of sugar water out of the bag slung around my shoulder. With a deep breath, I poured some sugar water in the bowl on the hive as an offering and then knocked softly on the top. I should have thought about what I was going to tell them.

> "My dear little friends,
> Your master has died, but your mistress stayed.
> And now a new master on your hearth is laid.
> Our journey here ends.
> But be of good cheer.
> Though I must go, please stay here."

Then, sucking in a calming breath, I repeated this over each hive, wiping errant tears as I did with the corner of my apron.

"Do you always announce with a poem?" Mr. Owens asked.

"I do, but it's not necessary. Papa thought they liked music and poetry. He would come out and sing to them, talk to them, and read poetry to them."

"I'll look after them."

I pointed toward the fields where people were ploughing. "It's April 10 and a new moon. We farm according to the moon. Above-ground crops planted in the new moon. Root crops in the full moon." I hadn't thought about it before, but there was so much more to raising horses and crops. I would miss it so much. Rosemount was a farm also, but not like The Pines. Land is unique, as people are. "Mr. Edmund Ruffin is in town trying to play soldier, though God knows he's far too old to be of much use. You might call on him. He's brilliant in regards to soil management. I left his books regarding adding marl and such to soils and crop rotation. Papa was a firm believer in his methods, and

Mr. Ruffin has been out here to analyze it before. You take care of the land, and she will take care of you."

Mr. Owens nodded and looked to the rolling hills of pastures and pine, then heaved a great sigh of satisfaction as if he were a long-gone traveler returned at last. "Miss Lorena, I will ever love this land as dearly as any could."

I took some comfort that my home would be his and not merely an investment.

With everything settled and the giveaway done, we loaded up, mounted, and prepared to leave. Mr. Dragon twisted in the wind atop the stable as if watching us leave. There were many tears and last-minute hugs. The live oaks stood at stately attention on either side of the road, draped in Spanish moss and melancholy—like an old maid's unused wedding veil, hung out to weather the years in silent mourning.

James and I once decided the moss was thoughts and memories that got caught in the trees and cradled bits of it, willing special memories into them so we'd never ever forget. Not even when we were old. I'd gathered moss last night and willed all my memories into it, then put it in a wooden box.

The overarching branches saluted our farewell. Papa celebrated the first year the branches reached delicately over the road, like shy lovers. Mama found him sprawled out in the fork of one of the trees that grand summer, drinking whiskey and variously singing and reciting poetry to the trees. "This will be as majestic as any cathedral in any city, me darlin'," he exulted.

She gave up trying to call him down before he fell and broke his neck. There was no arguing with Papa when he had a vision.

Not surprisingly, Papa appeared for the exodus. He was still riding Dorscha, who looked as irritable as ever for a dead horse.

He was particularly jovial, considering I managed to lose most of our over two hundred horses and the horse farm he loved so dearly. Do the dead get sad?

I'm sorry.

He frowned at me from under his favorite brown hat. It occurred to me he was wearing what he might have if he were going hunting or riding, right to his favorite boots I had packed to take home.

Sorry for what?

Not saving The Pines. Losing the herd. If James had lived, he would have saved it.

Fie! Nothin' ye could do about thet. James would not be after fixin' et any better. Nor would I. Maybe if I'd threatened to shoot them again.

Maybe I should have threatened to shoot them.

An' ye should have, then. Pull yerself out o' the funk o'er the mess. It was me thet got us in the crack. Who would be fer guessin' thet damnable bastard would try an' kill ye an' cheatin' ye out the farm so?

He was going to start swearing in Gaelic soon. *How are you wearing those boots and that hat? They're packed.*

He looked surprised. *I'm dead. May wear what I damned well please now. Surely ye didn't think I'd be fer sproutin' wings or wearin' thet black suit yer mother stuffed me in, did ye?*

I did hope you'd go to heaven.

Eh? By and by. Maybe. I have unfinished business t'be tendin'. I'll be fer makin' Homer's life miserable if he goes changin' The Pines fer one thing. An' there's still a bit of business with ye.

He fell silent. I could tell by the look on his face he'd say no more, and so I shifted my gaze to the people gathering in the neighbors' fields to watch us pass. A called-out farewell over the steady creak of wagon and jangling harness. I waved in return. I was glad I'd chosen the heavier black veil for my top hat.

With the furniture, freight, horses, and people who were traveling back to Virginia loaded on the train, I returned to the hotel to pray and prepare for evening church.

Many of my people had chosen to stay at The Pines as free hires until the legalities were finished, and some might stay on after. It could take weeks to get everyone before the court, so I sold the remaining slaves to Mr. Beddow for a dollar each for their protection. It was the best I could do.

I'd return someday. Mrs. Owens was persona non grata, but I was welcome any time and would forever be the lady of The Pines. I might visit simply to see if Mr. Owens received any devilment from Papa, but my life here was over.

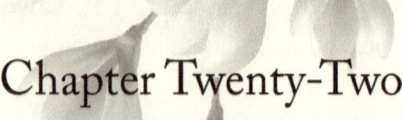

Chapter Twenty-Two

Three weeks in Charleston felt like a lifetime. Perhaps it had been. Like a desperate gambler, I had shoved everything across the table and lost. The one bright spot of the day was a gift and Baron's letter.

April 8, 1861
Alexandria, Virginia

Beloved Baroness,

I am in receipt of your telegram and to say I am shocked cannot describe how I feel. This is hurried as I wanted to get it in the military mail quickly to catch you before you left. I never in life imagined you might lose The Pines. I wish you had contacted my father, but I won't plow that ground again. We broke that field when I was in Charleston.

I am heartsick for you. If only I could be there with you. I would pour my love into your wounded soul to fill the cracks until it is whole again. I would hold you close and let you cry or just lay your head on my chest and be. Stroke your hair. I might be tempted to tell you it will be all right, but how can it be, you may think? You have lost. Not all. This was but one battle. Life is ahead. You will survive.

You're stronger than you believe. I am here for you even if I am not there to hold you and comfort you.

I hoped I might be with you on your birthday. Now even more so. Alas, it was not to be. I woke early before dawn and walked along the river where willows grew and thought of our last stolen kiss. I stopped under one of the green umbrellas and closed my eyes. You were once again in my arms, warm and willing. Your kisses sweet and tender.

Such love in those adoring grey eyes. Was a man ever so blest? I think not. I cannot imagine it; otherwise, no man would ever desire to leave home, and yet, it is for this very love that we must at times. I would move heaven and earth to protect you and stand before the greatest army this world has ever known.

For the hundredth time, I wished some travelling lay preacher had come by so I might have married you, but they are like rain and never around when you need them. Is it not odd I can never find a minister around to marry us, and yet I'm surrounded by them here?

I stepped out to watch the sunrise last week. You were always taken by beautiful sunrises and sunsets and so in my foolishness I imagined I might be sharing this one with you.

Since I couldn't send you a sunrise for your birthday nor flowers, they might be a bit faded by the time they arrived. I determined to find something else and returned to town with a mission.

Billings insisted on helping me since he's an expert on women, having had several sweethearts and seven sisters. I explained being an expert in failed love affairs wasn't the help I needed, but he persisted. You'll be happy to know I resisted the unholy bottles of perfume he picked out and now I know why he has several ex-sweethearts. He picked out a jaunty little white bonnet with violets and rosebuds. I considered it, but it was so fragile I couldn't imagine it shipping well nor you enjoying it. Not that you are indelicate, but you tend to the more practical side, such as the salmon bonnet I bought that you liked because it would wear forever. It also looked quite handsome on you, but you know that.

And so, forgive this meager gift until I can take you shopping for another bonnet or perhaps a new horse, which would be even better.

The lady in the shop with the hats also sold fine work, so I asked if she could embroider a handkerchief. She allowed she could. On the wall was a chart with the meanings of flowers. She helped me pick out the tussie mussie you find enclosed as well as the flowers on the handkerchief.

Forget-me-nots mean remember me forever, and I pray you will because I'll be whispering your name with my dying breath.

Gardenia is for joy, and I do wish you joy, but there is only one as you are not to have too much until I return. We know your mother's nefarious plans to make you fall in love with some black-hearted Yankee.

Ivy is for fidelity and know for all my joking that I am true forever and know you are also.

Magnolias are for dignity, which you abound.

And lastly, red roses for passionate love. I told her to put lots of those. She objected as I kept adding flowers, saying there would be nothing left for your nose. I replied you have a small one.

Speak to Col. Lee and get a letter of recommendation for your mother. We must wed so I may take care of you, but mostly because I love and adore you.

My darling, I seal this with a kiss and a prayer. My love goes with it as always and forever.

With all my everlasting love,
Capt. Baron Patrick Callahan, CSA

My heart broke a little more with longing. If he were here, I would bury my face in his chest and weep until not a bitter tear remained. I would drag him off to the nearest street preacher and wed regardless of Mother's approval.

I smelled the letter, as I always did, eager for a trace of the man I missed desperately. Cigar, ink, leather, and man. My man. Annie rolled her eyes at me burying my nose in the letter but refrained from comment. I tied it up with the rest of his letters, knotting the red ribbon carefully, and stowed the bundle betwixt some clothes in my carpet bag.

I luxuriated in a hot bath, the last one I'd get for days, then set off to pay bills and draw down my bank account, leaving enough to finish legal matters. Annie was flying around like a sheet in a windstorm, coordinating with the kitchen for my "secret" birthday picnic. Luckily, Mr. Humphreys wasn't on duty, as he would be disinclined to help.

"Good Hannah, Annie," I said in sincere disbelief at the quantity of food the staff loaded in the carriage. She ignored me as usual.

At the battery, Mr. Beddow and his wife, Ginny, walked with Carl, who carried their four-year-old son on his shoulders. The boy's legs dangled like a squirmy stole. Those shoulders were clad not in the latest gentleman's fashion but in gray naval uniform.

The armies were still practicing, and I wondered if we were safe but was assured we were. The combatants had, after all, spent weeks firing at each other, testing shot, charge, and trajectory to train their green gunnery crews. Occasionally, one would hit something unintended, prompting a hurried rowing across the harbor under a flag of truce with gentlemanly concern. "Have you declared war? Oh, no, I assure you on my honor I am not. Please accept my profound apologies to all for the accident, and I pray no one was harmed when we set your building on fire. With kindest regards, etc., etc." If it weren't such a deadly game, it would've been comical.

"Carl, what an interesting outfit. No more dapper apparel?"

Beddow's little boy turned loose of Carl's hand and waved at me. "Mr. Carl's a captain." He pointed to the too-large captain's hat on his own head.

"I see. You look good in uniform," I said, unable to keep the surprise from my voice. "When did this happen?"

"This morning. Here, Buster. Let's set you down so I can help Annie and your papa unload the carriage. I was going to sign on with Captain Decie, who has that little racing yacht, the America, that he renamed Camilla. I preferred America, but it's his ship. I love it and would give my right arm to sail her, but he's as much an Irish lord as I am and as much a captain as a lord, I'll wager. The man's nothing more than a swindler.

"Aside from taking care of my mother, my love of fine clothes, and maybe a good horse, I don't have a lot of needs. I found two other investors, and we bought the yacht from him. I renamed her and contracted with the Confederate navy to run the blockade."

While I was happy for him, blockade running was extraordinarily dangerous. There were already rumors that Lincoln intended to treat blockade runners or anyone with a letter of marque from the Confederacy, if Davis issued them, as pirates and hang them. "What's her name?"

"Mother refused to have it named after her, as her name is Antigone, and it would be bad luck. I've named her CSS Faugh-a-Ballagh."

"Clear The Way is perfect for a blockade runner."

"Is there cake?" Buster asked as he prowled through the feast.

"What would a birthday celebration be without cake?" Annie said. "I brought chocolate cake for normal people and peach preserve cake for Miss Lorena because she likes those nasty things. Heaven knows why. All that fuzz bristling against your teeth like a caterpillar? Ugh."

I cocked an eyebrow. "So that's why the hotel got my peach preserve cake receipt."

"Yes, ma'am. Kill two birds with one stone and all."

Anderson's and Pierre's artillery crews were going at it hammer and tong again. A particularly loud crash followed by silence caught our attention. Beddow stood, foot propped on a battery wall, searching the harbor with a brass looking glass. Carl joined him with his own glass. Men, they came prepared for everything.

"What do you see?" Ginny asked, looking anxiously between the men and the fort.

"Nothing serious. Anderson took out the corner of a building. I can't tell which one," Beddow replied. "He's sent a boat under a white flag with bountiful apologies I'm sure. So far the deepest wound has been to the general's feelings when Anderson returned the case of fine whiskey and cigars Beauregard sent his old friend."

Ginny fidgeted with the baby in her lap. "Maybe we should leave. They could be declaring war. Those ships in the harbor might be Lincoln's."

"No," Carl said slowly, sweeping the harbor with his glass and settling his gaze back on the ship. "Can't tell who it is, but Anderson won't declare war. He's hoping to last until the 15th when he can surrender with cause as they'll be starved out. Beauregard won't unless the warships arrive to support the ones already here. As to the ships, one is run up on a sandbar, and the other is trying to kedge her free. It's hardly a fleet."

"Let us pray the ships are delayed further then," I said.

The party lifted my spirits, so I lost track of time until Mr. Beddow pulled out his pocket watch and quickly snapped it shut. "You're about to miss your train! Get in my coach. I'll have you there in a twinkle."

With hurried hugs and goodbyes and no time for tears, we rushed to the coach and were unceremoniously shoved in. Thankfully, our luggage was already at the train and our tickets secure in my bag. Beddow's carriage raced to the depot, picking up a policeman the last four blocks. He shouted at us to stop, but Beddow only urged his flying blacks faster. "Go, go, go," he yelled to us when we slid to a precarious halt at the depot. "I'll handle the ticket. I know a good lawyer."

The firing on Ft. Sumter started the day after I left. What a memorable birthday gift!

At one whistle stop, newsboys raced about on the platform with special editions. Annie rushed out to snag a copy and resorted to sniveling and whining about how her mistress would beat her *turble* bad if she turned loose of the paper when a woman demanded she give it up.

My protestations about the way she made me out to be a monster did as much good as trying to teach a duck French. She lifted her head at the end of my diatribe and blinked as if just waking up. "Are any cookies left?"

Yes, exactly like talking to a duck.

I read through the journalistic dross, picking my way through flourishes, flounces, and adjectives enough to choke a healthy mule to get the meat of the story. After demanding surrender the day before and Anderson politely declining, Pierre began firing from batteries surrounding Sumter at 4:30, an hour before dawn. Ft. Sumter did not return fire for two hours, and some held out hope they might surrender soon. I knew the truth. They were woefully low on ammunition and would wait until they had good light to make the best use of what they had.

With each stop, Annie rushed out like her hair was on fire to grab a newspaper or broadside to get the latest news. Sumter fell 34 hours after firing commenced. At one stop a reporter intoxicated with the romance and lust for war sang the praises of local ladies who banded together and stayed up all night to sew a jaunty banner for the Palmetto Riflemen.

> "Woman, woman, woman
> Let thy light shine.
> The spirit of Joan of Arc, Nightingale, Dix, and
> dear Grace Darling be thine...."

My stars, what dross.

I couldn't go on with the impassioned pleas for one and all to answer the call and honor the flowers of womanhood and scanned further for actual news of Sumter and Lincoln's response.

Ohio reported 50,000 Union troops were gathering, and Ohio was pleased to offer their finest.

50,000 troops!

Regardless of what Pierre and Fox had said about a long and bloody war, I had convinced myself it would be over in ninety days or less and be little more than a minor dustup. Now, I genuinely feared for all I loved.

Soldiers filled the train. Those that couldn't be stuffed in the train or on flatcars rode on top of the cars. The pride of the South answered, raced to their fates. To arms! To arms! If you love your homes, your mothers, your very lives, to arms! Every town and village turned out to cheer them. Ladies waved white handkerchiefs and tossed flowers and packets of food at the soldiers, who cheered back at their adoring throngs. Men fired guns in the air. Children ran alongside the train, waving arms and flags and little wooden swords.

Major Anderson surrendered on Saturday at 2:00 p.m., and Pierre allowed them to fire a 50-gun salute to their flag, but on the 47th shot, a Union soldier was accidentally killed during the discharge. The fort had been burned to ashes from shot. It amazed me more didn't die in flames or from exploding munitions.

Charleston cheered their great victory. They should have donned sackcloth and gone into mourning. But for another three days, Anderson would have been starved out and surrendered. Lincoln's fleet was pressing, but did it matter? The whole country was spoiling for war. If not this powder keg, another.

Had I been there to witness history, one day I might say, "I was there. This is what really happened," but it would have been like watching a train speeding toward a washed-out trestle bridge. Wouldn't history and havoc be in my backyard soon enough?

For now, I tried to smile and act happy for the exuberant young men packing the train.

"My sweetheart said she could never love a man who didn't have the courage to stand for his country. How could I not enlist?"

"My poor old mother begged me not to go, but every boy in my class enlisted. How could I watch my friends march away?"

So the stories went from South Carolina to Virginia. Their faces would remain with me until the end, but I was ready for flowers and embroidery and explaining to my girls why it was necessary to study literature and math and even the detested Latin.

Annie glanced away from the window she'd been staring out. "Miss Mac?"

"Yes, Annie?"

"Am I going to get my dress shop?"

"Yes," I assured her, and yet I didn't know how. There would be no extra money for dress shops that I could tell. With war on the horizon, every dollar that could be saved must be.

She looked out the window at the approaching train station. "I'm not so sure. Not that I mind you and Rosemount, but I want a little dress shop with every morsel of my soul."

"We'll get it. I told you we would, and we will."

She turned on her glory-be-smile, the one that said, All is right in my little garden. "So you did, and you told me when we was girls you'd never lie to me."

"I did!" I said brightly.

Chapter Twenty-Three

"Miss Mac?"

Annie's voice roused me from gazing out the window at the rolling countryside and wondering how I was going to get my mother to give permission to wed. "Yes, what is it?"

"I got a letter from Mrs. Howell while we was in Charleston."

My head cocked in curiosity. "Is something wrong with her or the girls? Why didn't she contact me?" The Howells were neighbors, and I thought we were close.

She waved her hand. "No, nothin' wrong. Bella gettin' married, and she wanted me to make the weddin' dress and maybe help make the bridesmaid dresses. We both know it gonna be a while before I get that dress shop, but this would be good advertisin'. If you'd let me." She looked at me hopefully, hands folded tightly in her lap.

It broke my heart that she realized the dress shop might not be a reality for a while. "I've been thinking about that. I'm sure Gertie would help you if you wanted to go to Baltimore or Washington City. Fashion is booming there, and you would have access to all the Washington ladies."

She shook her head vehemently. "Not after what those men did to me in that alley. I ain't ever goin' back there."

"I understand." I didn't blame her for being afraid of Baltimore and vowing never to set foot north of Virginia again. Two men had grabbed her and dragged her into an alley with evil on their minds. It was only by the Grace of God and a stranger hearing her screams that she escaped. That's when I bought her that Deringer. "Of course, you can make those dresses, but," I shook my finger at her, "you better be available when I get permission to marry. If Mother ever gives in, I know she wants to order something from Paris, but I only want an Annie gown."

She scowled. "Somethin' terrible would happen to your Paris gown. You ain't wearin' nothin' but my dress down the aisle."

If I ever intended to walk down the aisle with Baron, I was going to have to sweeten the pot. Baron had poured on the charm and won Papa over heart and soul. Papa knew how much Baron and I loved each other, but he loved him in his own way. Unfortunately, that way hadn't endeared him to Mother. Papa had only to yell, "Fight!" and Baron would respond, "Where?" and bail in with him, fists blazing. That was not the kind of son-in-law Mother dreamed of. No, it would take more to persuade her now that Papa was gone.

"Annie, I'm going to let you go home. I'm going on to Arlington to get a letter of recommendation from Colonel Lee to take to Mother."

"What about you baggage?"

"We have a healthy layover at Manassas. I'll bribe someone to unload part of it."

"Girls gonna be disappointed, but I think Marse Robert convince her if anyone can."

Annie and I parted ways at Manassas, and I traveled on to Alexandria. I had telegraphed ahead asking permission to stop and visit. The unsavory business of pending war was no excuse for bad manners. At Alexandria, a telegraph waited for me inviting me to come. I'd planned on renting a carriage, but the Lees had one waiting for me. Colonel Lee was ever a connoisseur of good horses, evidenced by the matching blood bays pulling the gleaming Landau carriage. I was sure the carriage was Mary's personal carriage and was doubly honored by the generosity.

Once my decision was made, I had mulled for mile upon mile how to approach Colonel Lee with the request. Baron was sure he would give it, but honor was everything to Lee, and vouching for someone would also reflect on him. When the carriage turned off the road and onto the graveled path to the mansion, I realized I must finalize my thoughts. I would not prevail on friendship and only present the case for Baron on his own merits. Pray God, he hadn't done anything in Texas I would regret not knowing about. I'd heard about a few of his past indiscretions from his mother.

The driver helped me down, and I stood for a moment, just taking in the majesty of the mansion. There was something about the symmetry that soothed my soul. The columns were wood, but plastered and painted to look like marble and fooled even a practiced eye. I touched one as I passed to say hello. Papa had kept the Georgian architecture here in mind when he re-modeled Rosemount. Maybe that's why it was comforting. It felt like coming home.

Selina opened the door and smiled broadly. "Miss Mary sick today, but Marse Robert in the parlor waitin' for you, Miss."

"I'm so sorry to hear that. Rheumatism?"

"That and those headaches again."

"Poor Mary." She had ever been plagued with poor health, and stress did nothing to help it, I was sure.

Selina led me to the parlor where Colonel Lee paced the floor in civilian clothes. He must have been out riding as he still had boots and spurs on. Baron had been with him in Texas when they got orders to return to Washington. His room had been directly under Lee's in the Menger Hotel in San Antonio, and Lee had paced all night long, Baron said. The next morning, he told everyone with him to pack their uniforms and wear civilian clothes to board the train as the militias had been rounding up Federals and arresting them. His jaw clenched as he gave the order as he felt it an act of cowardice, but they were trapped and ordered to return. There was no choice.

The colonel had redecorated the parlor himself in rich red drapes and velvet-covered furnishings. Above the marble fireplace was a large painting of Mary in her youth. It was easy to see where their beautiful children got their looks, as both parents were breathtakingly handsome. Even with age nipping at his heels, Colonel Lee was an imposing man, and the elegant parlor suited him.

"Miss Lorena, I'm so happy to see you, but I cannot tell you once again how sorry I was to hear of Kieran's passing. He was a genuinely good man." He motioned me over to one of the settees. "Selina will bring some tea shortly. Your telegram said something about Captain Callahan?"

"Yes, I notice you were riding. I hope I didn't interrupt your plans."

"No, I took Roany out to do some thinking. Mary's convinced I'm going to pace a hole in her rug, and she may be right." He laughed when he said it, but it was tight and without much mirth. "Callahan wrote me a letter asking me for advice on whether he should resign. I told him I could not counsel him in that regard. I think secession is an abomination, and to take up arms against the Union—" he shook his head. "I cannot condone that. Did he resign then?"

I accepted the tea from Selina and thanked her. "Yes. A major cornered him and demanded he sign an oath of allegiance to take up arms in defense of any and all enemies of the Union. Baron said he would not take arms against his home. Words were said."

He sighed. "It is the question I have been wrangling with. Were it up to me, I would never set foot off Arlington again. I'd never raise a sword or fire a shot except in defense of my home. Trust me, I'd be perfectly happy to spend the rest of my days with Mary and my family. Hopefully, my grandbabies one day. I suppose Captain Callahan did not react well to such a demand at all." Lee smiled knowingly.

Did I dare tell him what happened? I sipped the tea and pondered how much to reveal, but from his smile, he already knew.

"The major called him a coward. Baron signed his resignation. His men resigned. Then Baron asked if that was sufficient, and the dance was on. No one calls him a coward."

Lee laughed. "No, he's not a coward. So, how can I help you?"

With even more nervousness, I explained what I needed. He excused himself and went to his office. Presently, he returned with a letter and a cover and handed it to me. "I'm happy to recommend the captain. I'd be happy for one of my girls to meet someone like him. He does have a bit of a temper, but it's the kind of temper that's directed, and that fellow deserved a dance."

I read the letter over that gave Baron a glowing recommendation. Mother couldn't deny me now, surely. Wiping a tear from my eye, I thanked him profusely.

"Think nothing of it."

We visited a while longer and I had supper with the family. The cook baked Robert's citrus cake, as they called it, and I begged the receipt. Colonel Lee wished me luck again in my mission before I returned to await the train. I wasn't quite ready to hoist the flag and claim victory, but I could hear the trumpets sounding and I was already trying to decide how I would tell Baron. Perhaps I would pay him a visit.

Chapter Twenty-Four

With the letter from Colonel Lee safely stowed in my purse, I hurried on to Baltimore, where Otis ran out of Mother's front door as if he were on fire to take my bags almost before the horses had stopped. He was decked out in the most lurid livery jacket I had ever seen—garish gold and whorehouse scarlet. White stockings tucked into black satin knee breeches covered muscular calves.

I stood for a moment, eyes wide, unsure what to say as I fumbled to pay the driver. "You're looking colorful. What carnival did you rob?"

He rolled his eyes and smoothed the gold brocade vest. "Yes, Miss Lorena. A reg'lar bird of paradise. Missus decided we need to be more uptown."

"I'll talk to Mother."

"Thank you." He deposited my bags inside and returned to hold the door open for me. Mother's home was a handsome three-story, red brick house with crisp white trim and shutters. A black wrought iron fence curlicued its way around the small front yard where mixed flowers sprang up in patches across the manicured lawn in imitation of a spring meadow that made me wish I were back at Rosemount already. I hesitated, not wanting to enter, then gathered some pluck. Otis raised an eyebrow but understood.

Inside, the house was in a dither.

"Come here, darling girl," Mother called from the parlor.

Aunt Gertie intercepted me in the foyer and folded me into her arms.

"Aunt Gertie! I didn't expect to see you."

"How could I not? I was overjoyed when Bert said you were coming and dashed here. I hated that we missed your birthday, but I understood you had business." Whereas Mother had the nervous excitement of a Thoroughbred horse, Gertie had their looks and the elegant carriage.

She released me from the lavender-water hug and held me out for inspection. "You look wonderful. We so feared for you."

Mother stood anxiously by and finally, unable to stand it any longer, pried us apart to pull me into her arms. "I was so terrified they were going to blow you to bits. You have no idea how I fretted. I'm sure I lost ten years of my life worrying."

"You shouldn't have. There was continual practice, but little damage. No one was hurt aside from the Federals during a salute to their flag, and I was gone by then. Let's not discuss it further. I'm away, and all is well."

"Yes, yes." She led us into the withdrawing room where Sallie was serving tea.

I nestled into the settee next to Mother and glanced at Gertie, who narrowed her eyes slightly, suspecting something was afoot as I had encamped so near Mother. Once Sallie finished pouring and Mother sorted pastries, I pulled the letter from my purse and waited for Mother to wind down. Baron had worried Colonel Lee might decline to give a letter of recommendation even though he had served faithfully in Texas with Lee, as Baron had resigned his commission and gone out with Georgia. The dark circles under Lee's eyes witnessed his distress over current affairs, but he had gladly written the letter and wished us well.

"Mother, I stopped to see the Lees on the way here."

"Oh? How are they? I hear he's to be given command of the entire army. I'm thrilled for him. It couldn't go to a better man. Scott's a hero, of course, but he's so obese he can't even ride. He's cooked."

"Such is the rumor. Were it up to him, he'd never draw a sword again and spend his time growing corn."

"Surely not. Wouldn't that be a terrible waste of talent? He was lauded as the champion of the Mexican War." She bit into a petit four, puzzled that a man might not want to go to war.

"Yes, but now he only wishes to take care of Mary and his girls and live out the rest of his days in peace."

"How is Mary? Are her headaches better?"

"She was ill when I was there. Stress, I'm sure, but I think her arthritis is getting worse, too. Colonel Lee is taking her to the Warm Springs Bathhouses next week, I believe." I steeled myself for the coming battle and continued before we got sidetracked in gossip. "Mother, Colonel Lee wrote a letter of recommendation for Baron. He feels he would be an excellent match for me and vouches for him in the strongest terms." I handed her the letter.

She set her tea aside and took the letter as if I were handing her a serpent. The grimace eased, and she passed it to Gertie. The letter was read and shuffled back to me.

"I always liked Baron," said Gertie. "What warm-blooded woman wouldn't?"

"Dear heavens, Gert, for once stop thinking about passions," Mother snapped. "This is my daughter's life we're talking about, not some…dalliance."

"Stop being so sanctimonious. Those broad shoulders, long legs, slim waist, and firm hindquarters? All that riding, I imagine. There's not a woman from thirteen to one hundred who doesn't notice that and don't think I miss you gawking at some fine specimen when he walks by."

Moses, Mary, and Joseph! I sat stunned as a duck someone had just hit over the head with a wooden spoon that my aunt and mother were debating men so. Particularly mine. "I like his eyes," I said to derail them.

"He *does* have beautiful eyes," Gertie said. "I'm sorry if I embarrassed you. Baron's quite the handsomest man ever; he comes from a good family; they're comfortable; he has a good career ahead of him in the military or civilian, and this glowing recommendation from Colonel Lee. We all know your father would have given his blessing, and I've no idea why your mother has set her heels against him."

Mother shot daggers at her. "It's not that! Lorena can do better. If she were to marry someone from the north—"

"Which I won't, and you know it." Why was she even broaching the subject? If she persisted in this, there was no need to unpack. I simply wasn't going to engage in this battle.

"But if you did," she continued, oblivious to my objections, "you'd be safe. I have no doubt you'd marry handsomely, wealthy most likely."

I pushed the letter forward. "Did you read anything he said? I'm not leaving Rosemount. I'm not moving north. I'm not marrying one of your Yankees. Does love mean nothing?"

She looked to Gertie for support, but there was none coming from that quarter. Sighing, she stopped waving her hands in the air and dropped them to her lap. "Of course, love means something to me, but how many poor girls marry for love? Don't be foolish. You can love a rich man as easy as a poor one."

"Baron isn't poor."

"He isn't rich. His granny gives everyone a case of apples she canned for Christmas. Not something you could use like crystal or silver or china. Apples. Apple butter. Applesauce. Apple brandy. At least you won't starve, I suppose."

"How cruel you are," I said. "She's given me other gifts. She gives the apples because it's from the heart, not because they're poor."

"Not yet. How much will his family have if this war proceeds? Nothing. Nor will you if you remain in Virginia and she secedes. You'll be lucky to escape with your life, let alone a silver spoon to your name."

"Enough," Gertie snapped. "Since when did you become Cassandra to know what the future holds? Moses, what a cheery future you predict. We'll support Lorena no matter what happens. She won't be impoverished."

Mother raised her chin defiantly. "I may not. I'll not encourage foolishness."

The letter went back into my purse. "Meaning what?" If the purpose of the trip was wasted, I would spend no more time contending with her browbeating and rose to leave.

Gertie stood also. "It's time for you to stop being so selfish. Momma did you no favors spoiling you. You think if you stomp your foot and throw a fit, everyone is supposed to give in to you. Not this time. I promise if you pursue this selfish route, I'll never speak to you again, and I'll tell Momma and Poppie about your vile threats to Lorena."

Aghast at Gertie's threat, Mother shot back, "Poppie should be the last to say a word after what he did to me."

I called out to the servants shuffling luggage in the hallway. "Don't bother putting those away." Mother might have been slapped for the shocked look she gave me.

"You can't be serious."

"You can't think I wouldn't be?"

"Ignore that. Put those away. Miss Lorena's staying." To Gertie she said simply, "Poppie did it to me."

"You knew I loved Kieran with all my heart," Gertie shot back. "He was fond of me, and you couldn't stand it." Bitterness framed her face and dripped from each word. "You set about to steal his affections just to prove you could, and then when you had him, you were going to turn him down. You were being a heartless piece of fluff. Poppie was right to threaten to cut you off if you didn't carry through, though how many times I wish you hadn't. I'd have been there to pick up the pieces of Kieran's broken heart."

If I hadn't been holding to the trunk in the hall, I might have buckled. Gertie and Papa? I never knew any of this. It was a secret buried deeper than pirate treasure.

Mother and Gertie had argued in the past, but never like this. The two circled each other, nose-to-nose like two snarling dogs, hurling invectives and digging up family skeletons bone by bone.

"He'll side entirely with Lorena, and if I gauge him right, he'll cut you out of his will," Gertie declared. "That's what I'll advise."

Mother gasped, clutched her breast, and collapsed to the settee. "You wouldn't!"

"I would!"

With a quick motion to Otis, who was nearby, I caught his attention and said quietly, "Tell Castor to get the carriage. I'm leaving."

"There ain't another train for hours, ma'am," he protested, eyes wide. Servants, every single one, had gathered in the hall to listen. They looked at me guiltily, but I said nothing, not caring if the laundry was hung out for all to see.

"Then I'll go to a hotel. I'm not staying here."

Mother, with the ears of a fox at times, heard me and hurtled into the hall. "Lorena, come into the parlor. And you people have work to do," she barked at the servants who scattered like mice from an upended shock of wheat.

Reluctantly, I followed her, though my mind was made to leave. I parked in the armchair with the peaceful little shepherdess tapestry. Perhaps the harmony would rub off on me through osmosis.

Sallie bustled into the room with a fresh pot of stress tea and ginger cookies. Were these girls always prepared in case of emergency, but wasn't life with Mother an emergency?

"Miss Lorena, these cookies are fresh this morning. Extra ginger."

Did the tea have extra chamomile and perhaps a dose of laudanum? "Thank you, Sallie. The tea smells quite lemony. Extra lemon balm?"

"Yes, ma'am."

"Mother, I am not marrying someone from up north. I love Baron. If you won't give permission, I will marry without it."

Mother tipped the remnants of her cold tea into a bowl and waited for Sallie to pour, then leveled a challenging gaze at me that might as well have been a nine-pound shot. "Oh, I don't think that would be wise, Miss Lorena McKenzie. You might think you are independent, but not quite. If you do, I will withdraw your trust fund that you put up as a guarantee to secure the loan on Rosemount. The bankers will call the note without that, and then where will you be? Your father died before he could transfer the control of it to Mr. Charles, which means I am the executor."

Though I didn't have access to it until I was twenty-five or married, the bankers had accepted it as additional collateral on Rosemount. I blanched, fighting to keep from fainting dead away. Would I get through the day without hitting the floor? "How did you know about that?"

"Did you think the bankers wouldn't get authorization to use the trust? As much as I despise bankers, I did see to this. I'm not always your enemy, but in this I will be. Tread carefully."

I knew she was manipulative, but to threaten me with Rosemount? Would the bankers call the note? After my experiences in Charleston, I had no doubt they might.

"Bertha," Gertie pleaded, "stop being such a tyrant. Lorena will be fine. You've always trusted Colonel Lee before. Trust him now. Kieran would have given his permission. Baron loves Lorena dearly; that's worth more than gold, surely."

Mother looked between us defiantly, and then her shoulders slumped as if she'd suddenly deflated. "If your heart is set, there's no choice, but trust me, I will extract some assurances from that young man."

I had no doubt she would.

"I hold the Lees in the greatest estimation and won't doubt the colonel. Plus, Poppie *is* so looking forward to walking you down the aisle." She tapped her fingers on her lap. Plans were already forming in her ever-flittering mind. "Might they allow a wedding at Arlington? I love it there."

"Thank you, Mother." I let out a breath of pure relief and wanted to shout for joy. Tears flooded my eyes, and a smile so wide it hurt my face sprang forward. I hugged her tightly, though she stiffened at first, not quite ready to surrender. At last, she wrapped her arms around me. "Of course, darling, but I will expect guarantees from both of you."

I nodded, unable to speak and still amazed at the blindingly swift change of course. My mind screamed at me to flee before she changed hers.

"Maybe we can hold the wedding in Mary's rose gardens. How glorious that would be." She was full bore on grandiose plans now.

Despite wanting to stay on her good side, I wouldn't begin to impose on them as troubled as Colonel Lee was, even if I wished to marry anywhere other than Rosemount. "No, Mother. I'm going to marry at home."

"I'm sure they wouldn't mind. They adore you and apparently Baron."

"No," I said firmly.

"You are so stubborn," she pouted. "I swan, if I hadn't been there, I'd vow Kieran birthed you all by himself without a trace of me. You're purely your father's daughter through and through."

"And praise the Lord for that," Gertie said. "We have two things to celebrate at the ball tonight. Your birthday and future betrothal."

"Tonight?" I squeaked. "Please, not a ball."

"Yes," Mother said. "You said you couldn't stay long, so I planned a full itinerary."

"I thought we might just visit," I said.

"We can visit at the ball."

Gertie rolled her eyes. "Yes, we'll catch up on all the news at the ball because heaven knows, not a single man will notice Lorena nor ask her to dance. We wallflowers will converse the night away, whilst the beautiful people dance their slippers off.

"It's General Scott's Military Ball at the Mechanical Arts Hall. We've been invited. You have too, of course. It's to raise funds for the war efforts. We should take a collection for your mother, too. Apparently, she has fallen on hard times and must dress poor Otis in circus castoffs. For pity's sake, Bert, allow the man some dignity."

"I resent that, Gert. Now I know where Lorena gets her sass."

Raise funds for the war against Virginia, which might still vote to secede? Surely, they were joking. "I've nothing to wear to such an important event." I did, but I was searching for excuses to avoid a ball so quickly.

"We made provisions," Gertie said. "I've had dressmakers working around the clock. This is the one I want you to wear tonight." Sallie and Rita had already fetched three dress boxes from upstairs as if they had read her mind.

Mother looked horrified. "Gertie, I had someone here making her a dress. Prudence, fetch that gown, please."

"Nonsense. You knew I was doing this for her birthday."

Sallie stood behind me, patting my shoulder while I slumped against the pastoral tapestry, and together we watched the battle of the gowns commence. "It'll be all right, child," Sallie said. "You'll look beautiful in whatever you wear."

Prudence hurried into the room holding one arm high with the rest of a gown draped across the other arm. Mother took it from her and pulled the cover loose, unveiling a pale pink taffeta affair covered with hundreds of flowers.

Sallie stopped massaging my shoulder. "Oh, dear."

"My stars," I gasped. "It looks like Mother Nature vomited all over that dress."

Aunt Gertie, standing there surrounded by dress boxes and servants who were equally surprised by the arrival of spring in the form of a ball gown, raised her hand to her mouth to cover her giggle. "Bert, what were you thinking? Lorena's just coming out of mourning. Surely a flowerbed isn't appropriate?"

Mother didn't take kindly to fashion critics, even from her sister. "Mrs. Lincoln loves flowered gowns. They've become the height of fashion."

Regardless of what Mrs. Lincoln favored, I had no intention of being seen in a mound of flowers. "I appreciate it, but Aunt Gertie's right. I have a maroon gown that's more appropriate for half mourning."

"Nonsense," Gertie said. "I told you I came prepared. I knew there would be balls while you were here, and I intended to show off my beautiful niece." She sorted through the dress boxes, looking at the labeling, and pulled out the one in the middle. Untying the twine meticulously, she unraveled the knot and wound the twine carefully around her fingers.

"You drive me insane with your dawdling," Mother cried out.

"And that's your problem, Bertha. Always in a rush." She ignored Mother's glowering and pulled a deep, peacock-blue silk gown from the box and shook the pieces out. The bodice was fitted, dropped off the shoulder with cap sleeves and bugle bead trim. The skirt looked like it had large, transparent peacock feathers laid with the eye pointing down, making scallops around the skirt. The effect was achieved with silk embroidery carefully applied, heavy enough to create the image but not so full as to be solid. There was another row of gold, smaller scallops of solid gold heavy embroidery at the bottom. The effect was mesmerizing. I walked away from it, and the feathers appeared to grow more solid as I moved around her. She nodded, knowing what I was seeing. "Do you love it?"

"I do!" I looked to Mother, wanting her to approve of it. Her head cocked to the side. I knew she was watching the feathers do their magic.

"Good. I have an emerald and topaz necklace and earrings that will set it off to perfection, and your mother has a hairpiece with peacock feathers that would look lovely in your hair. Don't you think, Bertha?"

"Yes, that's it. It'll be perfect."

The Dobbs sisters rushed off to town to shop. I insisted I needed a nap, having been lulled and soothed with copious amounts of ginger cookies, peppermint candy, stress tea liberally dosed with lemon balm and brandy, and a sumptuous soup. "I don't want Miss Lorena disturbed unless Jesus comes calling and then only with proper identification," Sallie declared to one and all. "You best be checking his hands and feet for scars."

Confident I wouldn't be bothered, I quickly drifted away until awakened by a banging on the door by my frantic mother. "Lorena, you should be getting ready."

Sallie had drawn the heavy drapes, leaving the room cave dark. I snatched the clock up in a confusion and shoved it in my face. "Mother, it's barely five."

"I know, hurry up. Your bath's ready." The commands faded down the hall along with her rapidly retreating footsteps.

Two hours was about the right amount of time to get three women ready for a ball, as it turned out. Mother and Gertie decided I should wear my hair waterfalled with shimmering strands of gutta-percha beads artfully arranged among the strands. I protested the peacock comb was enough, and I'd clank as I walked, but I may as well have tried to shout down the north wind when those two had the bit in their perfect teeth.

Gertie's husband George had agreed to meet us there and waited near the door, talking to two young men; one an army officer and another a finely dressed young dandy who was a full head taller than Uncle George, who stood 6'2" in his stocking feet. He was so thin the sun would have to shine twice to cast a shadow.

Mother peered around Gertie. "Who is that death's head on a mop with George?"

Gertie pulled opera glasses from her purse and inspected them covertly. "That's one of his aides, though I don't recall his name. I don't know the young officer."

The valet opened the door, but my attention was still on George and his friends. "I hope Uncle George isn't matchmaking."

"We'll tell him the news later, and that will take care of any good intentions," Gertie reassured me as she climbed out of the carriage.

"Ladies," Uncle George boomed. "May I present Major Richard Tamblin and Mr. Corin Charbonneau?" He kissed Gertie's cheek and held her out to admire her. "Lorena, you get prettier every day."

"Good Hannah, George," Mother exclaimed. "How much have you had to drink?"

I wondered about the same thing myself.

"We may have imbibed a bit," he confessed. "To take the chill off."

Gertie shook her head at his silliness, but I could see from her smile she enjoyed the compliment. "My husband. Thankfully, President Lincoln believes in employing the blind."

He laughed and squeezed her. "How are you, my dear? I've missed you." Pointing me out, he looked to his friends, "This is my lovely niece Lorena McKenzie and her equally lovely sister Miss Bertha Dobbs."

Mother shook her head, but pleasure flushed her face.

Major Tamblin offered me his arm, and my wee mother looked up to Mr. Charbonneau, smiled graciously as if being presented to the Prince of Wales, and readjusted her reticule and fan to hike her arm up to his.

"I understand you know Colonel Lee," Major Tamblin said as we entered and waited to be announced.

"Yes, we're fast friends with the Lees and sell them horses."

His eyes lit. "Oh? I enjoy good horses. Perhaps I could come look at some one day? I was an aide to Colonel Lee for a while and—"

Whatever else he intended to say was interrupted by the introduction by the dance master. We proceeded to chairs, and the gentlemen secured dance cards for us. They asked for dances from the three of us. Tamblin hesitated. "Perhaps if you aren't too engaged, you might do me the honor of a second dance later?"

"I'd be delighted," I replied, as a discussion about horses was certainly preferable to anything else that might be chattered about. George, who was known by everyone in Washington and Baltimore, got pressed into introducing me to a flurry of young men who gallantly offered to dance with Mother and Gertie also. Major Tamblin maneuvered his way back toward me while the latest introduction, a young captain from Maine, was asking if I'd like to visit the refreshment room.

Dismay claimed Tamblin. "I was about to ask you if you'd like something to eat," he said. "You shall pay for this, Richards," he added with a good-natured laugh.

"I'm sure I will, Major, but all's fair in love and war, as they say." He graciously held out his hand to me but winked at Tamblin, who shook his fist at him.

"He seems nice," I said. "Thank you for offering to get something to drink. I was parched." I didn't add hungry.

"He is. I went to school with him. General Scott isn't attending but puts on a fine spread. We should be in luck."

My first thought went to Virginia and war, but I veered away from that. "I hope nothing serious. I heard his health was in decline."

"Nothing like that, just more politics he couldn't beg out of." He leaned toward me and whispered, "If you'll forgive my poor manners, ma'am, I've been on duty all day and haven't eaten since dawn. I might not be gentlemanly."

I tilted my head back to laugh, setting the beads in my hair clattering like myriad little rattles. "Ah, a man after my soul. If you won't tell anyone how unladylike I am as I'm famished. We'll find a dark corner to feast and calm the wagging tongues."

We wended our way through the couples to the food tables. "A dark corner might stir more wagging tongues, but I'll defend your honor from scurrilous rumors to the death, ma'am. Even should Charbonneau be the offender. Forgive me, I couldn't help but notice you walk in with him and Tamblin."

I found myself liking the affable fellow. "Mr. Charbonneau?" I said as I selected sandwiches and cracker bonbons with cheese. "The calf tongue looks delicious, but perhaps later."

"Charbonneau's one of the finest duelists in Washington. The rail is a crack shot and death on call with a saber," he said, adding a generous proportion of sliced fowl and tongue to his plate with jelly. "I'll get an extra piece of tongue or two for you and save your honor."

"Oh, they have blancmange and trifle, too."

"I'm going for the Washington pie."

"Washington pie! I love that with a good lemon sauce." We closed in on the dessert table, and he was right; there was a huge pan of the pie with both raspberry and lemon sauce in chafing dishes near it. I backed away as soon as I nosed the raspberry sauce, which sent my stomach churning. "Yes, perhaps later after the blancmange."

We sat in nearby chairs to eat and chat but avoided dark corners. "Mr. Charbonneau surprises me. By appearances, you wouldn't think him coordinated at all. He looks like last year's scarecrow just stepped down off his post with nary a blade of stuffing left."

Richards deftly forked two slices of the tongue to my plate while no one was looking. "Looks can be deceiving, it appears. And speaking of appearances, I know this is impolite, but that gown is spectacular, and you—" he trailed off embarrassed, "you truly do outshine anyone else here."

"Are you wrangling to get the tongue back, sir?"

He looked appalled. "No, ma'am. I was sincere."

I laughed at his horrified expression. "You're too kind. I owe my grand look to my aunt and mother, bless their hearts. Speaking of the two darlings—" Mother stood waving at me from the doorway with lips pursed and face painted a deep shade of annoyance.

Richards followed my gaze. "That's your mother?"

"The one who looks like she was baptized in vinegar? Yes."

"Ah, here you are," Mother said. "I should have known you'd be near food. The grand march starts soon. We were going to get something to drink."

"The lemonade is good," I suggested.

"How much did you eat?" Mother asked, eying my plate.

"She hardly touched a thing. I had to force food on her," declared Richards, coming quickly to my defense.

"She must be deathly ill," Mother said with uplifted brow.

"Thank you, Mother. I'll have that dessert. Maybe two."

No sooner had I devoured the last creamy bite of blancmange than Tamblin collected me for the march. "You've engaged Miss McKenzie long enough, Richards. Begone, pest."

By the second dance, I was in high spirits and looked forward to my quadrille with Uncle George, who was an elegant dancer. Before he could claim me, however, a messenger rushed in for him. His joviality disappeared along with the message, which he read hastily and stuffed into an inner pocket. He kissed Gertie on the cheek, his face full of genuine regret. "I'm sorry, my darlings. I must return to Washington. I'll be at the Willard if you need me. There's no need to disturb you with my late nights that appear in the making."

My heart sank. Had they attacked Virginia? Would I be able to return home? A hundred questions raced through my mind, and not a one pleasant.

"George, what's happened?" Gertie asked, her normally calm voice trembling with dread.

"You know I can't divulge that, but fear not. I'm going to see if I can unruffle some feathers. Lorena, Mr. Charbonneau has offered to take my place in the quadrille."

"Of course." I didn't feel like dancing, but it was impolite to decline, and I accepted the proffered arm.

"I detect something more than Virginia in your accent," Charbonneau said. My fingers tightened on his arm before I realized it, eliciting a comforting pat with his free hand. "I meant no offense. It's charming. Your voice."

"Forgive me. With…present circumstances. Yes, South Carolina. We have…had a horse farm out of Charleston. I was born there."

"Oh, fortunate child," he cried. "I adore Charleston. "It's one of the most beautiful cities in the world, but don't allow my French mother to hear me say that, or she'll ship me back to Paris until my attitude is properly changed. I'd be eight feet tall if so much of me hadn't turned under, but I'll try my best to avoid treading your toes," he promised most solemnly.

I was laughing like a schoolgirl with his lighthearted banter by the time we joined the quadrille. Afterwards, Mr. Charbonneau escorted me back to my seat via a circuitous route, thus prolonging our conversation.

"You're such a graceful dancer," I said.

He looked at me with a twinkling eye and rascal grin. "For such an ungainly-looking creature."

"Not at all. I seldom dance with anyone as pleasurable, and I love to dance."

"Mother was from France and insisted all seven children take piano and dance from the time we could walk. My dance instructor convinced me dance would also make me a better swordsman, so I threw myself into it. Whether it has or not, I don't know, but I hold my own on both courts. I've yet to find a good use for playing the piano aside from sheer entertainment. Perhaps that's enough. Ladies love to sing if there's an accompanist."

"Having listened to many ladies sing, I'm not sure that's a blessing," I said.

He threw his head back like a crowing rooster and laughed so loudly several couples turned with amused smiles. "An honest woman. What a delight."

I felt the color rise. "I didn't mean that uncharitably. I've been to many events where a lady feels obliged to sing because there's an audience. Just because one can, doesn't mean one should."

"Since your uncle's been called back to Washington, I'm sure I'll be busy, as I'm on his staff, but may I call on you if the opportunity permits?"

"I regret I won't be here long." With permission to wed, I intended to fly back to Rosemount as quickly as possible.

We returned to where Major Tamblin stood waiting for our next dance. A woman behind me gasped as I held out my hand to him, and I turned to see a vision, not unlike a baby girl in multitudinous yards of christening gown with tiny pink ribbons and rosebuds scattered liberally. The overall impression was of a living, if unhappy, baby doll. She raised her skirt enough so everyone could see her stamp her little satin slipper.

"Mr. Charbonneau! I've been waiting for your company while you…meandered with this woman."

"I—I'm sorry, Miss Thackery. Was I supposed to attend you? Didn't we have the German waltz?"

"Does that mean you only attend me for one dance? You've plenty of time for this Southern strumpet with her false hair and paste jewels who's deliberately trying to steal my beau." Her voice and attitude rose steadily, causing people to drift nearer.

Gertie drew to full attention. "Now see here, young lady. Those are *my* jewels, and I'll have you know I don't wear paste. As for Lorena's hair, every bit of that mass is hers. I should know. I spent nearly an hour helping put it up. I don't know what the situation is, but you need to apologize."

Charbonneau looked like a fawn caught in a pack of wolves, stepping one way and another, gesturing helplessly, and gasping for words and air. "Miss Thackery, I've called on you a few times, but that's all."

"See! She has stolen my Mr. Charbonneau. Why was this, this Confederate even allowed in a military ball?"

A bevy of friends encircled her for support. Gertie and Tamblin closed ranks behind me. "Corin," Tamblin said, "you need to get your young lady under control. Deal with your romantic issues elsewhere. This isn't proper."

Law, now the men were involved, but before I could say anything, she sent another salvo. "You side with this Southern Jezebel, major?"

"Dear heavens, please, everyone. Calm." Gertie looked from one to another, seeking to make peace. "Do I need to call a steward?"

"If you are insinuating I played anyone false, Major Tamblin, I'll require satisfaction on the field of honor," Charbonneau replied, his eyes gone cold.

Miss Thackery rushed to his side and clamped onto his arm, thrusting her chin in the air. "Tell him, Mr. Charbonneau. You won't stand for me to be insulted either."

"I suggest you tuck your tongue behind your teeth, darling," I spat. "Your crazy is showing. The last time someone threw a shade on me like that, he was insulting my horse. I liked the gentleman but was obliged to shoot him. You, on the other hand, are insulting me, and I don't like you in the least."

She sniffed. "I rather doubt you're carrying a gun, so don't think to scare me with your empty threats."

"I always carry a gun. I can draw it, but in the south, manners require a person not pull a gun unless they intend to use it."

"My niece is an expert revoluteress," Gertie said to the agitator calmly, as if declaring fish swim, and laid a hand on my arm. "Lorena, please don't shoot this woman. You know how hard it is to get gunpowder out of kid gloves."

Miss Thackery's eyes went wide, as did her pretty mouth, at that and looked to Charbonneau for support, but he and Tamblin were eyeing each other like two Shanghai roosters about to fly with spurs out.

"As to you two cockerels," I declared martially. "If I learn you fought a duel over this mooncalf, I'll come back and shoot you myself. What foolishness to allow yourselves to be drawn into her game to boost her childish ego."

"Are you going to allow this, Mr. Charbonneau? After what Colonel Lee has done, she insults me like this! She's nothing but a...a...Secesh."

"And you are nothing but a fool," I snapped.

Gertie took my purse, no doubt afraid I *would* shoot her. Mother noticed the growing crowd and drifted over to stand beside me. "Who are you threatening to shoot this time? What has Colonel Lee done?"

"Why he stole government secrets by pretending he'd take command and hightailed it to Jeff Davis." Her equally vapid friends nodded their heads, although I was sure none had the slightest clue what she was talking about.

Mother looked at me, astounded. "Is this true?"

"What balderdash. Colonel Lee is at Arlington. He said he desired never to draw a sword again the rest of his days if it were up to him."

Tamblin cleared his throat. "I don't know where Miss Thackery gets her information, but Lee was offered command and declined it. He hasn't resigned his commission, but it's expected since Virginia seceded. It hasn't been ratified, but I expect it will be. Beauregard is still in command."

I clutched Gertie's arm to keep from going down. "Virginia seceded?" I whispered.

"We received word today," Tamblin said somberly as if delivering a death notice.

Mother turned a jaundiced eye on me. "This changes everything regarding our previous conversation, of course."

"Of course it does, Mother." I retrieved my purse from Gertie. "I need to leave before I *do* shoot someone."

"Lorena," Gertie said, "I agree that flibbertigibbet deserves—"

"Her also." I stalked from the room with Major Tamblin in tow.

Chapter Twenty-Five

Major Tamblin escorted me home and waited while servants frantically packed my trunks.

"Miss Lorena, please don't be leaving like this in the middle of the night with this strange man," Sallie pleaded.

"I'm not leaving with anyone. I'm simply leaving. He offered me escort. Less caterwauling and more packing, please, before Mother stops her dramatics long enough to realize I'm gone."

I didn't need an escort, but I hadn't declined, as it was better to separate him from Charbonneau and the idiot woman determined to instigate a duel. He gallantly stayed with me until I was settled in the hotel and promised on his honor not to divulge my whereabouts.

The carriage rattled into Rosemount just past twilight, and I was greeted by the familiar sounds of home: girls screaming as they ran to meet me, dogs barking, and Della's firm voice carrying over the evening bustle. Waiting on the hall table was a letter from Baron, its seal catching the dim light like a beacon.

April 14, 1861
Alexandria, Virginia

My Dearest Baroness,

I had hoped once again to get leave to come visit you, but we are ever in the saddle on scout or training new recruits. I pray you've had a chance to get that letter from Col Lee and talk to your mother as you said you might in a previous letter. It was an excellent idea. I know he holds me in high regard from my days as his aide in Texas, and your mother regards him well also. I have prayed mightily for God's favor in this.

We liberated some nice Federal horses three days ago. Victori spolia. I'm sure their pickets will get a warm discussion about staying awake after this.

Skeeter and I came in from a scout last night and stopped on a hill overlooking a farm at nightfall. It was the most beautiful sunset. Roses, lavenders, golds washed gently across the dusking sky. A woman stood from her gardening and gently stretched her back, illumed in the golden glow while half a dozen happy children swarmed about her. They chased and ran, and I could almost hear her clucking at them like a little hen.

How I wished that was you, and those children a crew of little Callahans. Presently Papa rode down the road and they all raced to meet him. Mama stood there, hands on her hips, but I knew she was smiling, heart filled, to have her man home.

I prayed peace and joy to them, refusing to dwell on what might come in the months ahead.

I felt like a voyeur intruding on their happiness and said, Come, Skeeter, let's go home.

For once, he had nothing to say. Perhaps he was thinking of home and sweetheart also, though I have never heard him mention one. A few nights ago, around a campfire, Brother London made the mistake of asking if a man could kiss any woman he wanted to, who would she be? Several replied the little black-haired girl in Loudon who had brought sandwiches out to us as we rode through. I confess, she was one of the most beautiful girls I had ever seen aside from you, of course. Many are totally smitten with her. Others stayed true to sweethearts or wives. Wise men.

Skeeter said, "Any woman?"

London nodded.

"Then I'd kiss your wife. I think she's got the prettiest mouth I ever seen on a woman."

It was only by the Grace of God, several men holding London back and Skeeter's nimbleness we were spared a bloodletting. I've been taking him with me on scout every chance I get until I'm sure London has calmed down.

And now I am thinking of kissing. I can't seem to find a subject that doesn't lead back to you. If I were there, we would be sharing a sunset and kisses. I would smother you with kisses and hold you close, breathing in the scent of your hair, caressing your skin. You might protest, but don't think I miss the way you raise your chin and surrender your mouth and throat to me. I feel the trembling and know your desire when I hold you.

Ah, my dear. I must close before I am tempted to ride to you now, permission or no.

With all my eternal love,
Captain Baron Patrick Callahan, CSA

I folded it and wept afresh. How could I answer? Before I gave up, many a tear-stained letter describing the fiasco lay balled up in the basket, as I had smudged them to illegibility or fumed so outrageously that I was sure he'd come dashing to me regardless of orders. I tried to focus my mind on bookkeeping that needed attention, but it refused to stay. Just thinking of Mother churned my emotions, and I teared again in bitter disappointment. "Stop dwelling on it. There's nothing you can do."

Manumissions. I could do something about that and repaired to Papa's room to search for the papers. For days after Papa's death, I sat with one of his jackets over my shoulders, as if he were hugging me. The brown tweed I'd avoided, as it was the one he was wearing the day he returned from town after speaking to his attorney. I noticed he looked ill, but it wasn't until the next morning he was fevered and down. I didn't fear the illness, but rather the sad reminder of a life so vibrant now gone. There, as Papa said in his letter, were the manumission papers. With documents in hand, I set about looking for Gideon.

"Don't know," Della said. "He ambled through earlier."

For one old, arthritic man, he got around more than I did at times. I was still searching for him when I came upon the girls in the parlor.

With letters from young soldiers they had met at a ball while I was in Charleston coming in, there was a flurry of embroidering in the late afternoons. One would read, *Ivanhoe* was the current volume, while others monogrammed fine linen handkerchiefs to return in the letters. My very talented assistant manager and language teacher, Beth, could have been Rowena, so passionate was today's reading. I paused in the foyer, reluctant to interrupt the passage, one of my favorites. My eyes closed, and I mouthed the words along with her.

> *"It will not need," said the Lady Rowena, breaking silence; "My voice shall be heard, if no other in this hall is raised in behalf of the absent Ivanhoe. I affirm he will meet fairly every honourable challenge. Could my weak warrant add security to the inestimable pledge of this holy pilgrim, I would pledge name and fame that Ivanhoe gives this proud knight the meeting he desires."*

"Miss McKenzie! Are you praying?" Eagle-eyed Persy noticed my shadow outside the doorway and came to investigate.

"No, Persy. I was reading along with Beth."

"But you don't have a book."

Lucille joined her and was peering at me also. For two such angelic little faces, their glittering, curious eyes reminded me of birds eyeing a worm. "I was reading in my mind."

"You memorized that?" Persy was positively horrified. Lucille looked equally aghast.

I interrupted before the room of romance-struck girls descended on them for blasphemy. "I'm looking for Gideon. Has anyone seen him?"

Persy shook her finger at an imaginary Gideon. "Tilda said, 'You quit lounging around like you got tall cotton in 'lanta and get some work done, old man, afore I whup your skinny ass up one side and down the other.'"

I sighed. "I'll talk to her about the language. Please don't repeat it again."

"You wanted to know where he was!"

"I still don't know where he is, though, do I? All I know is you've acquired more language you shouldn't be using."

"She sent him to the great room to clean the chandelier."

"We'll show you," the two shouted as if I needed help finding the great room in my own home.

"Embroidery's boring," Lucille said.

"So's that dumb story," countered Persy. "Boring as dried dog sh—."

They dashed away before I could deliver another sermon about language. There in the great room was Gideon perched precariously on top of a ladder, wiping crystals with vinegar water. The girls skidded around the ladder, knocking it solidly. The bumped ladder wobbled with the old man clinging for life, twenty feet in the air, eyes wide as saucers, and I not sure at all I could keep it from tumbling.

"Gideon! What are you doing? Come down before you break your fool neck. What happens if this ladder falls?"

With the ladder secure, his usual grin returned. "I reckon I'll turn into a big black bird and fly away, Miz Mac."

"Come down immediately."

"Yas'm. Tilda's in a fuss about getting this house put in order and wanted the chandeliers cleaned. Spring cleaning and all. Pulley stuck on this one."

"Let someone younger do that. I need to talk to you."

He followed me to the library, curiosity brewing. I closed the doors behind us and motioned to the two chairs near the windows. Once seated, I handed him the papers. "Do you know what those are?"

His brow furrowed. He sounded out some of the words, puzzling his way through. "Marse Mac setting me and Tilda free. Wants us to go north to be with you mama and Rita."

"Yes, I'll take you to my aunt in Washington. She can take you on to Baltimore."

"Are we ordered to go?"

It took a moment to process the question, and even then, I was unsure. "No, but Papa set you free. You'll have money to go live with your daughter. I don't think you understand."

"I understand, but there's a reason me and Tilda hid from yo' mama. That woman always crying or dying. Ain't a moment's rest when she around, and Rita flits around with her tail on fire jes like yo' mama. Lord have mercy, but that girl can't be still a second. If she ain't still ain't nobody sposed to be still. Give me peace in my last years."

He looked out the window toward the cottages. "'Sides. Three of our young'uns buried here."

"You said you'd turn into a big, black bird and fly away. Be free. Papa's giving you that."

The green velvet side chair creaked when he leaned back. "They different kinds of freedom. For me and Tilda it's being able to do what we want. Tilda likes being the queen bee. She buzzes around, telling people what to do, feeling important. Who she gonna boss in Baltimore 'cept me? No one."

He pointed at the books behind me. "Me? I want freedom to learn."

I stared at him astounded. He was seventy years old if he was a day, and he wanted to go to school?

"What do you want to learn?"

"Marse Mac used to take me to church with y'all. I like mass. Didn't understand, but it was pretty. I want to be a preacher. I want to learn mass words like the Pope."

"You want to learn Latin?" I was sure I looked as astounded as Lucille had earlier.

"Yas'm. That's what I want. I want to learn how to preach proper. I already do at the chapel, but I want to be able to speak blessings and whatnot in Latin."

A pastor came out on Friday evenings for services at Rosemount, and the elders held prayer meetings, but I had no idea he wanted to go full bore minister. I was too shocked to respond. How was I going to teach him Latin so he could preach like the Pope? "You want to become a Catholic?"

He laughed and slapped his knee. "Sakes no. I'll die a Baptist, but I love the sound of Latin. I want to bless people proper like Jesus did."

"Jesus was Jewish. I'm not sure he spoke Latin."

"I don't think I can learn Jewish, but you can teach me Latin. You know nobody up north gonna do that."

"That's sort of against the law, and Jesus spoke Aramaic."

He swung one spindly leg over the other and rocked his foot. The least of his worries was how I was going to teach him Latin. "Don't wanna learn Aramaic neither. And never stopped you and yo' mama before when you taught us to read and write."

"That was so you could read the Bible and such," I protested.

"Why you think Marse Mac set us free?"

"So you'd be happy. Besides, it's the right thing to do."

"Latin would make me happy."

It would be so much simpler if he'd accept Papa's offer of a new life up north. "All right, but we have to be careful. If the parents find out, they'll withdraw their girls." Not to mention I could be arrested and put on trial.

He stood and tilted forward in a slight bow. "I have faith." He lifted his hands as if he were preaching a sermon right there. "I will raise up for them a prophet like you from among their brothers. And I will put my words in his mouth, and he shall speak Latin to them all that I command him."

Assaulting me with scripture. Rita wasn't the only one who'd been corrupted by Mother. "I don't think the Bible mentions speaking Latin."

"It should," he said righteously and adjusted his coattails.

With that settled as much as it could be anyway, I returned to the ledgers. Two more pages were reconciled when Abigail swept into my office like Atropos on her way to a battle, shears in one hand and one small, terrified child in the other. She appeared about to snip Lucille's life strand in twain. "Miss Boggs, how may I help?"

"Persephone snuck out of Latin class while I was cutting out words, and Lucille won't tell me where she went."

I cleaned the pen nib and laid it aside. "Lucille, what a re-markable child you are. When did you become a seer and take up mind reading? Look deep with your powers and tell us where Persy has gone." I wiggled my fingers at her.

Her owl-wide eyes relaxed into soft crinkles at the corners, and she giggled. "I can't seer where she is, Miss McKenzie."

Abigail, who always spoke with her hands, waved the shears about like a drunken swordsman. "Miss McKenzie, we certainly don't need to be teaching children to mock their elders and speak of dark arts."

"I'm sorry. Would you put the shears down before we have an accident?" I smiled supportively at Lucille, who appeared on the verge of tears. "I forbid you to dabble in the dark arts and do any seering. Now, do you know where Persy might be?"

She looked at Abigail and then at me. "She was hungry."

I leaned back in my chair. "There. I'm sure she went to Della for a treat and will be back before you return to class."

Lucille's black curls shook vigorously. "No," she said, "Latin bored the horse piss out of her. If it—"

"That will be all, Lucille. Miss Boggs, I'll find Persy and bring her to you."

Abigail pursed her mouth and grabbed Lucille's hand. They disappeared as suddenly as they'd appeared, and I set off in search of my missing student. Persy was ever hungry. It's a wonder the girl didn't weigh 300 pounds, but she was like a mink, darting here and there. As her body was, so was her mind. It took a talented teacher to keep her engaged, and while Abigail was classically trained, she was…boring as horse piss.

Miss McKenzie's School for Young Ladies and Fine Arts indeed. We'd discuss acceptable euphemisms for boring. Horse piss wouldn't be on the list, however appropriate.

I made my way into the kitchen where Della and Josie whirred about like bees in a recently knocked hive. It was nearing dinner, and we were shorthanded. "Have you seen Persy?"

Della wiped her brow with an apron. "She ran through here and said, 'Tell 'em I went that way.'" She pointed to the stables.

"And which way did she go?"

She pointed wordlessly to the cookhouse.

"Was anyone with her?"

"Barney was goin' after ham for sandwiches. I told him not to be dawdlin' neither."

They couldn't see me through the rose bushes, but I saw them. Persy skipped along beside him. His wide, round eyes kept cutting to the side, watching the little bandit. By the time they got to the end of the walk, Barney's stride lengthened to a run to escape his giggling companion.

I stepped out from behind the bushes. They stopped dead still, stricken.

"Hello, Miss McKenzie. That's a lovely dress. Is it new?" Persy wallowed the ham around in her mouth before swallowing with a great gulp I feared might choke her. The bushes rustled where she tossed the rest of the purloined ham.

"No, Persy. It's the same one I was wearing yesterday."

"Can I put this down, Miz Mac?"

"Of course, don't stand there all day."

I opened the door for Barney, who set the platter down, rolling his eyes up at Della, waiting for chastisement. "Barney, you may go. I'll handle this," I said.

"Yas'm."

"Della, some ham is missing, but Barney is blameless."

"Hmph."

"Persy, for skipping Latin class, you can study an extra hour."

"A whole hour!"

"A day for five days." Not trusting her, I escorted her to class. The last time she was in trouble, Barney hid her out at his favorite fishing hole. "When you get there, you are to apologize to Miss Boggs for skipping Latin class and for that boring-as-horse-piss remark. After that we'll discuss proper language for young ladies."

Her face was bright red. "Yes, ma'am."

I knocked on Abigail's door and got the "*Intrare*" granting us permission to come in.

Persy stood, her hand still clasped in mine, scowling at Abigail. "I'm sorry I skipped your class," she muttered.

"And?" I prompted, giving her a small nudge.

She looked to Abigail, who wore an even greater scowl. "I'm sorry your class is boring as horse piss."

Giggles broke out.

"I'm not putting up with this any longer," Abigail snapped. "I demand you punish her!"

Persy dropped my hand and sidled behind me like a crab.

"What would you like me to do, Miss Boggs? Hang her from her thumbs?"

"That would be a start."

Persy gasped.

"Persy, I mean apologize for saying her class was boring as...you know."

"I'm sorry I said your class is boring as horse piss," she mumbled.

I sighed. "Please stop saying that."

"You told me to!"

"Never mind. Go sit down. Persy gets an extra hour of Latin for five days, Miss Boggs."

Triumph lit Abigail's face.

"I think I'd rather be hung by my thumbs," Persy mumbled on her way to her desk.

Persy, bless her, presented me with a solution. "Miss Boggs, Gideon will sit in your classes so he can help keep an eye on our young misses."

He'd have to be careful, but he could grasp the basics in class and study a primer in the library when we were alone.

Wasn't it amazing how some things worked themselves out like they were meant to be, and others were like throwing yourself at a brick wall? I couldn't decide if marriage to Baron was a test of our love or a sign we were fated never to marry.

"Another letter from your mother, Miss Mac," Liza said when I returned to my office.

"I'm sure she's still dying."

"The hand getting weaker." She set it on the other unopened letters.

The wax seal was heavier on one side and barely impressed on the other, as if it took the last bit of her strength. The letters were nothing more than spider tracks. I shook my head and opened it. She should have been an actress. "Yes, she's dying. She has days to live."

"My sympathies. Should we get some crepe?"

Chapter Twenty-Six

Baron threw back his blanket, shivering in the cool morning air, and wished himself back in his cocoon and dreaming of Lorena. Harper's Ferry was close enough to Winchester that he was sure he could smell her favorite perfume, but furloughs were not to be had for love nor money.

"Colonel wants you scouting." The gray and gloomy sky showing behind the orderly poking his head in was not fit to be called dawn.

"Yes, I heard you. Any particulars?" he asked, pulling his pants on and turning his boots upside down to knock out any critters that had taken residence during the night.

"Someone saw a bunch of Yankees. Might be that patrol they were talking about."

The flap dropped with no further explanation. If there were interlopers in the area, they'd flush them. He finished dressing, glancing at the letter on the small camp table, and put it back in the kit. Maybe he'd have something interesting to tell Lorena besides nonsense sighings of the heart and idiot pickets.

For his part, Baron was happy to be away from camp as much as possible, even on such a miserable morning when he might have enjoyed a few more hours of sleep. Within minutes, he tracked down men he knew he could depend on, plus some who needed miles and training.

"No, you can't go." He patted the black spaniel who had shown up in camp and adopted them. The pup whined but went back to the blanket someone put out for him under a tree.

"How many you taking?" Billings asked, biting off a chunk of tobacco. He had an extra sense when things were happening and assumed he'd be included, so he was already saddled up. Shadows of the other men moved like apparitions through the mist toward the picket line.

"Ten, maybe twelve," Baron replied, thinking of who else he might take. "Skeeter for sure to scout ahead." Sad Sally flattened her ears when he tightened the cinch. "Don't be such a grouch." He led her out a few steps, waited for her to exhale, and tightened the cinch again. "Shouldn't need more than that." He felt his breast pocket. "Blast. I forgot my Bible. Pick out a few more."

"Not going to a prayer meeting."

"Be right back. Tell the boys to hold."

"Bring food and extra ammunition?" Baron asked when he returned. "It shouldn't take long, but things happen."

"I told them to," London said.

"All right. Let's go squirrel hunting."

He had a disquieting feeling they looked like spirits easing through a spectral plain. The sun would burn away fog and foreboding soon enough.

"We not taking a banner?" a new recruit from Georgia named Rosen asked.

Billings snorted and spat a stream of tobacco over his horse's shoulder. "No, son. We're scouting. We don't want a flag gaily announcing us."

For all her other faults, and they were numerous, Sad Sally was like a rocking chair, and Baron soon nodded off since he'd already pulled a long scout the night before. An hour or so in, he sent everyone into the cover of trees beside the road while Skeeter reconnoitered ahead. Great mounds of white clouds tumbled across a forget-me-not blue sky, marring what otherwise promised to be a perfect day.

Cows grazed peacefully in a lush pasture dotted with new babies.

"I'd make a coat out of that big roan cow," Billings said, surveying the herd.

London's saddle squeaked when he leaned forward. "You take the coat. I'd settle for a juicy beefsteak."

"Maybe the owner will sell us a yearling when we're done," Baron replied. "I could use something besides boiled ham for a change."

"If the colonel doesn't have us training. Playing soldier is wearing thin." London walked over to a tree to relieve himself. "How long are we supposed to wait in Harper's Ferry?"

"I imagine we'll be playing different games soon enough." Baron had joined the Virginia Military Institute at fifteen before transferring to West Point. He'd taken classes from Jackson at the Institute and was familiar with the man and his unorthodox, no-nonsense ways. The military and its regulations were a way of life Baron felt born to. Others, like London, chafed at the regulated lifestyle like a colt fretting at the bit. They'd settle in. They all did. Still, he was so close to Rosemount he could smell it and would be restless enough if he didn't get a pass to see Lorena soon. Could he blame others for their impatience?

He swept the horizon with his field glasses. There was no trace of dust in the air betraying a group of riders or of Skeeter. There was, however, a solitary figure topping the hill. He studied it with interest and turned Sally into the trees. "Someone coming; back up."

They sat in their scrim of light brush and overhanging limbs, watching the figure plodding steadily toward them. An old Negro man ambled along as if he hadn't a care in the world or was too tired to think about them if he did. The men fell silent enough to hear bones moldering in a cemetery. Aged as he was, judging from his nearly white hair, his eyes didn't suffer, and he turned off the road to approach them. His spindly legs made him look like a daddy longlegs spider in a ragged frock coat.

On he came.

"Kill him," Billings whispered. "He'll tell those Yankees if they're near."

There was mumbled agreement. "No, let's see what he wants. I'm not killing an old man for no reason."

"Saving our necks seems like a good enough reason, Cap'n." Billings was firm in his distrust. They'd been betrayed before for gold or patriotic fervor.

"I'll handle it. The rest of you stay out of sight." Baron rode into the sunshine to meet him. "Hello, Uncle." He dismounted so the old fellow didn't have to look up.

"Mornin', Marse. You one of Jackson's boys?"

"Just out riding."

"Yassuh. Mule colicked, and we got the boy sloggin' him through the mud tryin' to save it. Baby colicked, and I got the piles. Not that nobody cares 'bout my piles, but we need help with the colic and Missus. Been on the road a bit going to fetch Miz Anderson. Missus took to bed with fever this mornin'." He scratched at his backside as if reminded of his discomfort. "Used to be a crick runnin' through these trees. Thought I'd get a drink, but didn't bring no food and gettin' kind of hungry. Don't s'pose you got any to spare. I got a few coppers."

Baron ran his fingers through Sally's mane. "No need to pay. Not much, I'm afraid, cornbread and dried beef. Some dried apples." Baron divvied food from his saddlebag and handed it to the old man, who stuffed part in his pockets and ate the corn muffin. He had a good store of hardtack, but that would only break the old fellow's teeth. Baron handed over his canteen and watched him drink greedily.

He looked over his shoulder. "Thank you, suh. Might take care going over yonder hill if you boys don't want a bunch of lead in yer britches. Yankees got a dry camp few miles down the road waitin' fer Jackson's boys."

Baron chuckled. "Nothing wrong with your eyes."

The leathery face, lined as nine miles of corduroy road, broke into a grin. "No, suh. Lord blessed me with good eyes. I can still slingshot a squirrel out of a tree most people can't see."

"I appreciate the warning. Try apple cider vinegar on those piles when you get home. Take care."

He touched the brim of his hat and winked a yellowed eye. "You too, suh. Send them bluebirds packin' back north. Tired of 'em scarin' the missus an' chillun." With that he ambled back toward the road, waving a farewell.

"We going around?" Billings asked when Baron returned to the group with the news.

Baron tore an apple ring in two and gave half to Sally. "Far enough to come in behind them, then straight through."

"Cap'n." London nudged his shoulder. "Skeeter's coming."

"All right." He pulled his hat on tighter. Loose hats invariably sailed off, and he was down to one bedraggled ostrich plume.

Skeeter rode in quietly; he always did unless hell was on his heels. He was one of Baron's best scouts and his deadliest sharpshooter. Many remarked the army should give him a swift kick and send him packing to Mama, but he was twenty, according to his brother and father, who'd enlisted with him. He looked like he ought to be padding down a dirt road in bib overalls with a cane pole slung over his shoulder. A smattering of freckles banded his nose, and about every fourth day there was enough pale, blond peach fuzz on his cheeks to tempt the other men to find a cat to lick it off. "Some men waste their manliness on beards, and others save it for the ladies," he'd reply good-naturedly. As if to prove his theory, at every female sighting, women drew to him like bees to clover, leaving the other men scratching their manly beards—alone.

"Find the Yanks?" Baron asked.

"About fifty or so in a dry camp off the road. Two of 'em walked out to piss under the tree I was in. They're waiting for a Jackson patrol to take some prisoners and find out what's planning. Damned squirrel chattered at 'em and they looked up. Thought they was going to see me."

Baron whistled low. "That would have been bad."

He gave Baron a you-don't-say look. "Yessuh. I waited 'til they left and chunked that tree rat with my slingshot. Squirrel stew for supper."

Baron chuckled. "That'll be a thin stew."

"They was thick as fleas, so I got a couple more." He hoisted a trio of squirrels tied together by their tails.

"Let's pour hellfire and brimstone on them," Baron said. "It'll be good training."

"I don't mind sending a few Lincolnites to heaven or hell, wherever they're bound." London adjusted his collar as if he were about to deliver a sermon instead of rain death. Though he was an ordained minister, as were four more men in the brigade, he preferred active duty to spiritual ones. At a little over six feet tall and so broad-shouldered he looked like a lumberjack, he was an imposing figure on the ground. With the full black beard, eyes like coal, and riding his favorite black mare, he was something from the Apocalypse. His mellow voice could cajole a bird out of the sky with its sweetness until the spirit of the Lord or battle came on him, then it reverberated off the hills and heavens alike.

"Probably sent more men to the promised land with that Colt than you ever did with your sermons," Billings said.

"I do a fair sermon, have you to know, but don't mind knocking a few heads to introduce them to the Lord. They'll go to God or do some quick repenting."

Sergeant Blessing, the Millerite, whispered prayers and scriptures every step of the way, convinced they were going to die because he'd seen a sign. His was the kind of religion that looked for signs the end of the world was nigh. For him, today was it. Signs and figures never lied. End times were simply reckoned again if you didn't die when you were supposed to. London was of the opinion that Millerites weren't very good at math.

"We gonna get in trouble for attacking without orders?" Rosen asked.

"My orders are broad. So, only if we fail." Baron checked his pistols again. "Stick with me." Rosen was from his hometown, and Baron took him out as much as he could to prepare for the real dance. Besides, he liked the kid even if he was underfoot like an orphan pup. Rosen was eager, and it was hard to fault a willing heart. He'd even sent home for an ostrich plume for his hat, which was in much better shape than Baron's, but Baron's hat overall was in sad shape thanks to a picket shooting a hole in it.

"They're over that hill in a little clearing off the road," Skeeter whispered and pointed as they approached.

They moved off the road and through the trees in case there was a lookout. Skeeter hadn't seen one, but anyone worth their salt would post some. "Let's go wide and come out of the trees to chase them out in the open," Baron said. "Ride straight through the middle yelling like hellions, turn around quick, and hit them again before they organize. Cut their tent ropes. Cut the horses loose."

Sounds sharpened. Time slowed. London took out his watch and glanced at it as if to mark time or see if it was still moving. The lid snapped shut with ominous finality. Each man carried two pistols and a saber. Horses shook their heads in nervous anticipation, jingling bits. Leather squeaked. A muffled cough. Snapping twigs underfoot. Birds stopped singing. Baron motioned them forward at a trot. They saw the cook fires and smelled bacon. His stomach growled and heart tripped faster.

He spurred forward, and they burst out of the trees like howling demons, their horses thundering down on the confused soldiers lounging around the camp. Billings cut the picket lines to scatter startled horses. London bellowed and sliced toward a tent with a soldier pushing out. The head disappeared inside just as quickly. With the lines severed, the white tarpaulins floated down like shrouds over the squirming bodies inside.

Blessing was beside him, shooting and spewing Bible verses at terrified Yankees, his voice high, full of fervor and zealotry. "Therefore, stay awake, for you do not know on what day your Lord is coming. Today! Today! He's coming for you today!" One who'd been dancing around trying to pull his boot on and grab a gun at the same time gave up and ran screaming down the road.

Taken by the spirit of prophecy and war alike, Blessing wheeled around to put the fear of God or a bullet in another Yank.

Baron fired at a man, watched him spin like a top, and collapse. Gun smoke and sulfur filled the air. If this wasn't hell, it was close enough. Men screamed in pain or anger, some in fear. They surged through the camp blasting and slashing, leaving dead and wounded behind. Baron curbed Sally sharply to make the second pass.

Their captain rallied those he could for defense. "To me," Baron yelled and spurred toward them. He jumped a fire and landed in front of a terrified cook who'd been trying to save his meal. The man gawked in terror, threw his arms over his head, and dove under a wagon. London's booming voice echoed through the camp. "Virginians, the Lord is with us." He raised his sword. "Split hell open." The dark angel calling on the Lord, followed by his unsettling laugh, sent another layer of terror through them.

"Kill that bastard," their captain yelled.

Skeeter was glued to Baron's left with London on his right. A hail of bullets whizzed and zinged by them like angry hornets. A blow to the chest nearly knocked him from the saddle. He clutched at his breast and leaned forward, trying to catch his breath and his balance. "Damn it to hell, that hurts."

A man jumped out in front of him, pistol raised. He was too far away for Baron to strike with his sword, and his pistol was empty.

So this is how it ends.

Skeeter yelled, distracting the man, and tried to shoot, but *click*, his pistol was empty, too. He jerked the squirrels loose from his saddle and threw them. It was enough distraction to give them time to ride the Yank down. He was either too shaken to move or knocked out as he lay still as death when Baron looked around.

London looked over at him. "Drop back, Cap'n. You're hit."

He glanced at the scarlet blooming on his chest. "No, we need to finish them while they're on their heels." He sheathed his saber and reloaded his pistol.

London roared, calling the men together. Baron could barely breathe, let alone yell. Several Yankees lay fallen. Others broke and ran. "Lay down your weapons," London bellowed.

"Surrender," their captain shouted. "Lay down weapons." Scattered shots reported, slowed, and ceased. Baron stopped in front of their captain and pressed a handkerchief over his wound.

The captain looked at him dubiously. "You going to live, or should I give this to someone else?" He held his sword belt up.

"Hmph. Ruined my Bible mainly." Baron holstered his gun and pulled the sword free of its scabbard. It was an older sword, well-balanced, finely wrought, and engraved. "This is a handsome weapon."

"It was my father's," the captain replied, voice husky with emotion.

"When you're exchanged, I'll return it to you."

"Thank you."

"My men are going to eat. Tend your wounded, then load your weapons and boots in a wagon."

He looked puzzled as if he hadn't heard correctly. "Boots?"

"Y'all can ride until someone tries to escape. Then I will shoot them, and you will all walk. I doubt anyone wants to walk barefoot to Washington." He was too weary to deal with nonsense.

The captain barked out orders. Baron turned back toward the cook fire to see what was still unsullied when Billings called out. "Blessing's hit, sir."

"How bad?" How many did he lose today? He looked around and realized he hadn't seen Rosen since the first pass through the camp.

"Head's bleeding bad, but just took part of his scalp and ear."

"Maybe it knocked some sense in him," Skeeter said. "Hey, I need to find my squirrels."

"Wrap—" There was the familiar pop and ping of a nearby shot. Sally jumped in the air when he involuntarily rammed a spur in her. "The hell?" He pulled the mare up. It felt like a hot poker rammed below his knee. The cook cowering under the wagon held a pistol in his shaking hands and stared at him with wide, terrified eyes.

"Get out from under there before I blow your head off," Baron yelled and leaned over to look at his leg. "Did you not hear your captain? Damn it to hell, I am shot. Again."

"I thought you were going to steal my pans," the man warbled, nearly in tears.

"Law. What do I want with your pans? Blasted fool."

"Want me to look at it?" Billings asked.

"Yes, get some bandages and wrap it tight. Idiot ruined my boot." Turning to the others, he waved at the wagons. "Load the wounded and gather those horses. Someone find Rosen. Get me some food if you please. Collect what supplies we can carry and burn the rest." His chest pain receded to a dull throb, or maybe it was because the leg hurt worse.

The scattered horses hadn't gone far and were drifting back as they grazed toward the camp. Skeeter scrounged him up a plate of biscuits, bacon, potatoes, and scrambled eggs. They must have been trading with locals for eggs as there were no chickens about.

"Can we bury our dead?" the Yankee captain asked.

"I'm not soulless," Baron responded, scooping up a spoonful of eggs.

"I'd debate that, sir. You seem to be riding with the angel of death." He cut a baleful glare at London, who was working on a massive plate of food.

Baron huffed. "Brother London's an ordained minister. If you prevail upon him, he might speak a passing fine service for your boys."

"I am and would," London said between bites. "Imagine I sent some to their maker. It's the least I can do. May not be as elegant as I'd like since it looks like Cap'n needs to get back soon before he needs words spoke over him. Case anyone's interested, that little dance took seventeen minutes."

"Felt longer." Baron wiped the last of the eggs on his plate with a biscuit. He'd compliment the cook if the halfwit hadn't tried to kill him.

"'Cause you was busy getting shot."

With the dead buried and graves marked as best they could so the bodies might be claimed by families later, London gave a respectable, albeit short, service. Wounded were made as comfortable as possible. Baron refused to join them. There was a certain fatal finality to joining the wounded wagon. His boys were good at packing, and they didn't torch much. Aside from Baron and Blessing, two other Virginians were wounded. Thirty-two Yankees captured including the eleven wounded, eight left in graves, thirteen missing and presumed still running. Fifty-eight captured horses and mules. It was a productive but bittersweet victory.

"Rosen, how you doing? Not looking good." Baron sat beside the wagon where the boy lay.

Rosen smiled weakly. Sweat beaded his forehead like dew-drops on a pale petal. "You have a knack for the obvious, sir. 'Magine I look like death. Feel like it. If I don't make it, send my belongings to Ma and my good uniform. Don't bury me in it. No sense letting the worms ruin it when they can eat my patched one. Give my boots to someone. Send my spurs home."

"No talk of burying. We'll get you back to the doc quick as we can."

"Keep my feather," he said in a thready whisper. "Yours done got shot off. What was left of it."

Baron took off his hat and stared at the nub where his plume used to be. "Huh, so it did."

Rosen closed his eyes but nodded. "Yes, sir."

Baron motioned London closer. "Gather the boys; let's pray."

Confederate and Yankee alike circled the wounded. London declaimed God's healing power over the men and spared a special prayer for Rosen.

"How you feeling?" London asked quietly.

"Chest feels like someone hit me with a sledgehammer. Leg hurts, but I'm all right."

They loaded Blessing in the wagon next to Rosen. He insisted he could ride, but his eyes had an odd look as if he were watching something hovering before him, and Baron didn't want to pluck him off the ground when he keeled over. "Today's the day," Blessing said.

Baron nudged Sally to keep pace with him. "For what?"

"The day I die."

"You're not going to die. Head wounds bleed bad. Billings said it just grazed your skull."

"You don't understand. The signs. The numbers. Plus, I saw him again."

London stopped trimming a flap of loose skin from his hand. "Who?"

"The angel. It's the third time I seen him. He motioned me to follow and kept me safe, but today's my day. He's here to take me home."

"Blessing, guardian angels preserve you, not take your life," Baron said. "Besides, you made it through the fight. You'll be fine." He looked to London. "Right?"

"Yep. If he wanted to take you home, he'd do it. Angels don't tarry when they have things to do."

Baron wondered how busy angels were and if they had schedules like mortals. He rode beside the wagon, saying prayers but feeling hopeless. A cold stone of despair settled in his soul. Rosen passed out, and he doubted the boy would rouse again. They'd packed bandages over the stomach wound and wrapped it tightly, but he was bleeding badly.

"I'll take care of him." How do I tell his mother her baby's dead?

Blessing alternately slept or bemoaned his headache before spouting more Bible verses and singing hymns. Despite their assurances otherwise, he was convinced he was dying; it was just taking him a while to get there.

Baron kicked Sally into an easy canter to get away from the ramblings so he could flog himself in peace. The leg ached where they put a tourniquet on. It throbbed and went numb after a while, or maybe he no longer cared. "Billings, I don't know how bad my leg is, but don't you let them take it. Understand?"

"Need to let the surgeon figure out what needs to be done, Cap'n."

"Understand?" He returned the most malevolent glare he could muster.

"Yes, sir."

"Good. It's not that bad, but you never know with those saw-bones. Patch me up and let me go."

Baron drifted on the edge of twilight, even moving at a rapid pace. Had they encountered more Federals, they'd have had to make a running battle of it. Mostly running.

"Get the surgeon!" Billings yelled as soon as they hit camp. Baron woke abruptly and fell away into the sea of hands pulling at him, unresisting, formless, uncaring, his head lolling forward.

Dr. Suffolk looked him over, trying to determine which wound was worse. "Leg's swollen. Need to cut the boot off."

"Don't cut my darned boot. Pull it off. Take care of Rosen first."

"Stop giving me orders. If that bone's broke, you'll destroy it. Rosen's already taken care of."

London reluctantly released the boot, and Baron lay back on the table, too weak to protest further. He watched in detached fascination as blood poured from his boot to pool in an ever-widening circle on the surgery floor. An aide skinned him out of his clothes, and they soon had him naked and shivering.

"An inch or two more and we'd be taking your leg off," the surgeon said as he examined the wound.

"Good thing I have long legs," Baron mumbled.

"Yes. It's also a good thing you carry a Bible and are built like a bull ox. Chest looks bad, but it's in muscle; otherwise, it would've been fatal."

He looked to the leg first. Baron refused to let them chloroform him, not trusting them if he was out.

"You sure?" Suffolk asked.

"I'm sure."

"At least take some poppy milk."

"After you're done."

"Nicked the bone, but it'll grow back." He launched into a story about examining skeletons with previously broken bones and how the bone grew stronger, filling in gaps and reinforcing the area.

"Fascinating," Baron grunted through clenched teeth as the doctor continued to probe the wound.

"Some doctors leave bullets in if they think they won't bother, but they can travel, you know. Cause abscesses and infections." He held a soggy scrap of leather and dropped it in a metal bowl. "That certainly doesn't belong in there. Something else to cause problems."

Baron focused on the clouds meandering past the window, imagining shapes and trying to ignore the Yankee who was threatening to kill a doctor if he took his arm off, the moans of the nearby wounded who were still waiting treatment, and the interminable digging around in his leg. It must be warmer now; he was sweating.

"There," Suffolk said triumphantly, holding the bullet with his forceps, "got it and all the odds and ends." The bullet clinked into the bowl with the other refuse. The rest was a matter of cleaning and wrapping. "Tell anyone who tries to put a poultice on it to keep those things away unless it's onion or garlic."

It didn't take him as long to find the bullet in the chest; however, it still involved more poking about. By the end, Baron was exhausted and accepted the opium without protest. Billings was sitting by his side when he woke with a start in the hospital the next morning. "Gawd, all mighty," he said and rubbed his face.

"Hurting?"

"Some. I need to get up."

"All right. Doc says you can't go out without crutches."

He put on the carpet slippers someone had fetched from his tent. "Let's go check Blessing."

"He's dead, Cap'n. You can see Rosen. Doc says he might make it if he can get enough onion in him to stave off infection." He put his hand to Baron's forehead. "You may be eating onion for a while, too. You're burning up. Wish they hadn't put you in the hospital. Hospital gangrene's contagious no matter how many windows they open."

Baron sat dumbfounded. "Blessing's dead? It was a minor wound."

"Bone splintered off in his brain, Doc said. It didn't look that bad when I bandaged him, but I guess it don't take much. He kept talking about a headache and his angel, then he was gone. War's a funny thing."

～

Despite the doctor's grousing, Baron moved out of the plague house hospital a week later, where a new wave of smallpox raged. Baron had been vaccinated, but only recently.

Billings insisted on hanging around like a stray dog at a butcher shop. The pup Baron had adopted dragged his scrap of blanket under the cot to keep him company also, which didn't sit well with the Shanghai hen who was already in residence there. His tent was getting crowded.

The hen hopped on Baron's shoulder and peered at the letter he was writing as if she were reading it. "I don't need a chicken critiquing what I write, Henri." He set her on the ground and tried to remember what he'd been going to write.

The hen took out her discontent on the dog, flogging him mercilessly. "Consarn it, Pup. If you'd but sally forth and stand your ground, she'd stop that."

"Come on, Sally Forth," Billings said, smooching to the pup. "I'll protect you."

"Don't call him Sally; he's a boy."

"Why not? You call a hen Henry."

"Henri. Short for Henrietta."

"You think she understands the difference? She'll probably start crowing soon."

"Don't you have somewhere to be?"

He nodded to the letter. "You going to tell Lorena?"

"About what?" He continued trying to write the letter and to ignore Billings, without much success in either camp.

"The skirmish. Men dying of bloody flux and mumps isn't that exciting."

"A bit about Blessing and Rosen." He set his raven quill aside, the pup having chewed up both his pencil and his good rosewood pen, and contemplated how he'd broach the subject. The least said, the best. Rosen was a pure miracle. How the bullet missed anything vital was beyond comprehension, but he thanked God daily for it. Blessing was a different matter. Had the zealot truly seen his angel, and should he mention it?

"What about what happened to you?"

"No. She has enough to worry about. Let her believe I live a charmed life."

Billings snorted. "Like Blessing and his guardian angel?"

"Do you think about that? I've been dreaming about Blessing and his angel. It's like he's trying to warn me about something, but I can't hear him. Someone's in danger, and I can't help them."

"We're at war, Cap'n. Lots of people in danger. Surprise!" Billings threw his arms wide. "You're in danger."

"You're not helping. I asked someone to look after Lorena in Charleston, but if she finds out, I may really be in danger." He set the letter aside and pulled out his housewife. Thankfully, his mother had thoughtfully threaded several needles for him to put in the kit, as he still hadn't acquired that knack. "Let me patch this hole in my blouse and we'll go to town in a bit. I need to buy her something."

"Doc says you're not to leave bed."

"He shouldn't have given me the crutches, ill-fitting as they are."

"That was for you to relieve yourself and go back to get dressings changed, not go shopping."

"Should have been more specific instructions."

"*Don't leave bed*'s pretty specific."

Chapter Twenty-Seven

April 22, 1861
Harper's Ferry, Virginia

Beloved Baroness,

I received your most welcome letter and have worn it thin from reading it over so many times. I've inhaled the fragrance of your rose-scented hand until I fear someone would think me mad if they saw me (though Skeeter smelled the letter also and liked the scent), and perhaps I am. I am so mad with love and longing for you that even the faintest scent sets my heart ablaze. I am still disappointed at the turn of events in Baltimore related in your previous letter, but we will find a way.

We are arrived in Harper's Ferry. I think you would like one of the commanders here. He's an old West Pointer and a reverend. Maj. Rev. Dr. Pendleton. Parson Pendleton as all call him. He's a crack artilleryman and busy poaching all the theologians he can from theology schools and various units. It's truly heaven's host. If I weren't afraid of things that go boom, I might join him. Plus, who else would love my surly Sad Sally? We baptized Pendleton's four cannons last Sunday, Matthew, Mark,

Luke, and John, and dedicated them to Saint Barbara, who is the patron saint of artillerymen. I believe God will look out for him.

Brother London is in our unit and also a minister. He says he feels as safe here as in his wife's arms, though he did say once his wife hit him with a frying pan. That sounds rather warlike for a minister's wife, don't you think? We also have a Millerite in our midst who prays continually and predicts various things as they are prone to do.

This must mean I am safe as a babe in a cradle to be in such company, don't you think?

I am constantly in the saddle on scout until even Sad Sally grows weary of me, and I was the only human she tolerated reasonably well. It's a sad state of affairs, I tell you. The woman I love and would appreciate my company is miles away, and the horse who has it constantly backs her ears at my approach.

Were I there, I would give your ears special attention. Do you know you make a funny little mewling sound when I nibble your earlobes? We'll discuss it more when next I see you. There are many places that would get special attention. That hollow in your throat. Your pulsing temple. That place under your jaw. Your lips, of course. I would tarry there teasing promises of love from you.

Fie, and now someone is singing that damnable song Lorena again. Pardon me while I go beat the scullion.

We're going to have some training on pickets shortly. One of them took me for a Federal a while back as I came in. Granted it was foggy and we are all still in blue, but dear God. He wouldn't let me dismount nor listen to me. Then, as he was bringing this prisoner in, he stumbled and jabbed his bayonet in Sally. His gun fired because the idiot had his finger on the trigger. Sally charged off, and who wouldn't after having a knife stuck in them? It wasn't deep, but enough to startle her. The moron reloaded his gun and tried to shoot me. I yelled at him, "I am your captain!

I am your captain!" And the countersign. The next picket ran up to calm things.

The camp was clearing by then, and I was sure I was about to be shot. Thankfully, the first chowderhead forgot how to load his gun, and it misfired when he tried to shoot his escaping prisoner the second time.

The pickets apologized and promised to do better next time. I'm not sure if that means to shoot straighter or what. I had been half asleep when I rode in and was thinking about falling into my cot perhaps to dream of the one I love the dearest, but that woke me up for cert. My face was black from the powder, and my hat has a hole in it now. It singed my durned beard. I'm not happy.

You should be here to comfort me. That would make me happy. There's a peaceful little place down by the river where I go when I have time. I would walk with you and hold your lily hand. Kiss it gently and press you to my bosom. Would that I could hold you wrapped safely in my arms now and forevermore. One day.

Remember when I said I was as safe as a babe in a mother's arms here? Unless the mother is the Amazon Penthesilea, perhaps not.

Tarnation. And now I am being called to scout again. Not sure when I will get this in the mail.

As always, I pray all is well with you and the girls.

All my everlasting love and fondness,
Captain Baron Patrick Callahan, CSA

I folded the letter regretfully and returned to my duties. Beth had kept the books in immaculate order while I was gone, but I was updating them when Gideon knocked on the library door. "Miss Mac, some of the men want to visits with you."

"Of course, let them in." What was wrong now?

Five of my McKenzie men filed in, cleaned up as if going to court or confession. This was serious. "Gideon, would you bring some coffee and whiskey, please?"

"Miss Mac," began John O'Hara, who was apparently the spokesperson for the group. "We been thinkin' about what Marse Mac would be fer doin' were himself here."

"In regard to what, John?"

"The war an all. It bein' upon us." He looked around at the others. "We believe were himself here, he'd be formin' a militia an' join the group gathrin' in Winchester Saturday. We'll be marchin' out Friday with yer permission, ma'am."

I was taken totally by surprise. My thoughts tumbled with all manner of questions and objections. "I see. Have you discussed this with your families? Are they in agreement?"

"Aye, o'course. Well, 'cept Molly Brennan."

"And what did she have to say?"

John put his hand on his hip and shook his finger at an invisible Connall Brennan. "'Ye'll no be marchin' off t'war with me so new fallin' with child Connall Brennan,' says she. 'Be slammed and damned if I won't, woman,' says he. 'Ye're daft if ye think I'll be fer lettin' me boys march off without me and meself cowerin' at home like a wee pisser, then.'" John swung his arm. "'Then,' says she, 'maybe I'll club some sense in yer head fer yer, sure.' An' tried hit him with a fryin' pan, but he dodged an' she only hit his shoulder. So, she picked up his gun an' tried shoot him, but she can't shoot a hole in a ladder, an' he's fast as a cat bein' courted by a fox."

Dear heavens. War had arrived at Rosemount sooner than expected. "Connall outran the bullets, I hope."

"Oh, aye. Then he picked herself some flowers an' butchered the pig. So, they're all sweet again."

"Butchered a pig?"

"He outran the bullets, but thet spotted pig didn't."

"He's staying?"

"Oh, no, ma'am. He's rarin' t'go and she tae be shed of him, though she'll weep enough salt tears when he leaves, I'll wager."

The majority of the men on Rosemount were McKenzie men. Irishmen Papa had either brought over from the old country or stray ones he'd gathered up here and there and taken as his own until he'd formed his own little clan. He always felt Rosemount was perfectly safe, as they were as close to a private army as a person could get. I felt so also, and now that layer of protection was being stripped away.

The corn and wheat crops were mostly in, and calving well underway, but summer was non-stop work on a large farm. I had no idea how we'd get the crops in, the hay put up, and the apples picked and ready to ship. If war proceeded, I didn't even know where my crops that normally went north would go. I might be making lots of cider come fall or letting apples rot with no help.

Still, they were free men, and I couldn't hold them nor lay a blanket of guilt on them no matter how much I wanted to. Above all, was a dread fear for their safety.

Della came in with a tray of coffee and whiskey. She looked around, brows knit in worry at the meeting and mid-morning drinking.

"Would y'all prefer coffee or whiskey?" I asked. "And please pull up chairs. Let's not stand on ceremony."

"I wouldn't be sorry t'get a spot of whiskey," John said, "though I'd take coffee as well, iffen ye don't mind."

Della poured coffee for all and set the decanter and glasses out. She looked at me as if asking if I wanted some also. I nodded and made a motion with my fingers. A large glass. The men helped themselves after she turned to leave.

"What kind of unit are you forming? I know some of you have horses, but not all."

"We had thought cavalry iffen the army will furnish the rest with mounts, then. If not, I suppose we'll be fer the infantry."

I sipped the whiskey slowly, wondering if I should try to talk them out of this madness.

No, ye should not, then. Tis what I would do fer sure an' don't ye know it.

Where have you been? I thought you stayed at The Pines.

Keepin' an eye on Owens who seems tae be mindin' his manners an leavin' The Pines as it should be.

So, I should let them go with my blessings?

Aye, be a good girl, then, an' send them away with all they need. I stored new guns in the root cellar o' the huntin' cabin. Let them have those an' leave theirs with the women.

You know the McKenzie Men were what kept Rosemount safe.

Aye, but these are hard times. No but two things they fear: God and their womenfolk fer good reason. The women will stand fer ye.

If the rest of them shoot like Molly Brennan, I'm not sure what good they'll be.

Buy as much ammunition as ye can and make them practice. They will.

I'll have some supply wagons outfitted for them.

Fie, they ain't goin' t'Oregon. The army will supply.

"Miss Mac?" O'Neil said.

"Yes, sir?"

"The girl's been doing some fancy work fer a flag. We was thinkin' o' callin' ourselves the McKenzie Marauders iffen ye didn't mind."

I like thet.

Yes, I'm sure you do.

"It's a bit to ask, but would ye have a bit of green material for a flag tae sew the pieces on?" He pulled a piece of paper from his pocket and put it on the desk in front of me. In the center of the flag was a golden harp. On either side in semicircles were the McKenzie red roses. Above in gold lettering was McKenzie's Marauders and below Faugh-a-Ballagh.

"That's a handsome design," I said. "But this needs to be on green satin with gold bullion fringe around it. I have a gown your ladies can have. There's enough to make two sides if they can embroider them. I'm sure Annie has some gold fringe ratholed around here."

The men looked at each other dumbfounded. "We couldn't do thet, Miss Mac," John said.

"I'll not have you going off under anything but the best of colors. We'll have a party before you leave. I'll give you some tartan to make cockades for your hats."

The men looked at each other again, surprised perhaps I wasn't protesting their plan. Were it up to me, I'd lock them all up for their own good, but hadn't I warred with my own conscience about duty when I let Baron ride off?

"Papa has new guns stored in the root cellar of the hunting cabin. Take a wagon and fetch them. Leave your rifles for your women and as many pistols as you can. I'll furnish horses for your men. If you want to trade me one of your horses for mine, I'll do as much as I can. You must be mounted. Saddles, I'm not sure about. You may have to buy more if we don't have enough."

Many of the men had already bought horses from Papa and were well mounted, but others had little more than plow horses. They were fine for farm work, but not what they were doing. By the time we were done, I would be nearly out of horses.

"Yer giving away yer treasure, Miss Mac," O'Neil said.

"My people are my treasure. If those horses help you come home, they will serve their purpose."

John shifted uneasily in his chair, like an errant schoolboy. I drank more whiskey and would likely need much more before the week was out, if not the day. "John?"

"There do be one more thing."

"Yes, sir?"

"The ladies would like tae form a lace guild if ye can help them sell it up north or in Richmond, mayhaps."

"I doubt I'll be going north any time soon, but I can contact some dressmakers and milliners in Richmond. They'd be giddy to get good Irish lace."

"Thank ye, ma'am. The women have assured us they will work as hard as any man, so ye'll not even miss us, but if they could get some extra money with the lace, that would help."

"I've no doubt they will." They would work themselves to the bone to take up the slack, and I regretted that, but I wouldn't be able to hire more men and pay them, too.

We got down to business figuring out exactly how many men were going and what supplies were needed. House servants knitted socks for field hands and families when they didn't have anything else to do, so there were two trunks of socks stored up we would send with them. I never realized before what all a soldier needed, but the men had been thinking about this, talking to soldiers, and reading newspapers about calls for supplies.

The week whizzed by, and whether we were ready or not, Friday was here. There were horse races on the practice track and a cross-country race with jumps. Ten dollars gold to the winner of each, plus all they raked in on bets, and there was plenty of that. There was even a women's race. They insisted I join in, which I did reluctantly, but I held Charlie back and allowed one of the other women to win.

Connall Brennan won the greased pig contest but lost a tooth in the process. I doubted he even realized the pig had knocked it out. "How on earth does he run that fast when he's so drunk?" I asked Molly, who was thrilled to have another pig.

"It's from bein' chased by the constable at home, Miss. He does like tae fight a bit when he has drink in him."

No one got the prize from atop the greased pole, but it wasn't from lack of trying.

The three-legged race was a huge success, men teaming up with wives and sweethearts and young single men rushing to grab the girls from the school. More than one couple fell to the ground laughing and didn't bother to get up but rather stayed there, holding each other and kissing. I kept a close eye on the girls later.

After all the games and the feast, which was as bountiful as Christmas, we set out the lights on the back patio and the men began to play.

We danced and drank and whispered words of encouragement and farewell. Some slipped away to spend a few quiet hours with wives and sweethearts while they could. I studied each face, afraid for the future, but forced an even countenance. I would be all smiles and sunshine tonight, though my heart would surely break tomorrow.

The next morning, I wore my green riding habit and top hat with a McKenzie cockade. Looped across my shoulder and over my hip, I draped a McKenzie tartan that was my Scottish grandfather's. The men insisted I ride at the head of the troops with O'Hara, whom they had elected as captain. The girls would not be left behind and rode along. Wives and children piled into wagons behind their men.

"Are ye all right then, Miss Mac?" John asked.

"Not really, John. I'm worried about you. I'll not tell you lies today." I sniffled and put a handkerchief to my nose.

He reached over and patted my hand. "Now, girl, don't be sheddin' those salt tears. Ye know these boys are as firm as the hob o' hell an' by the Grace o' God, we'll all be home afore Christmas, I'll wager."

He was more confident than I. "Yes, I'm sure you will. The flag turned out beautiful."

He looked back at the boy behind him carrying it. "It did, didn't it? Thet gold fringe makes the difference."

Not surprisingly, Papa appeared on my other side, happy as a lark.

You're going with them?

An' why wouldn't I then? They're me boys.

Do you wish you were alive so you could ride with them?

Begob, don't ye know it? We'd raise holy hell in those Yankees.

Someone behind started singing *Leave Her Johnny Leave Her.* Dear God, I was starting to hate that song.

Chapter Twenty-Eight

The next morning, Della tried to soothe my soul with food over my missing McKenzie men and piled enough biscuits and ham in front of me to feed an army. I decided to work it off in the garden. Mid-morning, a shadow crept over me as I viciously thinned rows of carrots. "Miss Mac?" Jacob screwed his mouth around as if he were chewing on words he was trying to spit out along with the wad of tobacco stuffed in his cheek. Jacob had been Papa's overseer here for many years and kept things running like a well-oiled machine. There was little that flustered him, but today he looked like a very tall, gangly teen called into the schoolmaster's office for dipping someone's pigtail in ink and fidgeted with his hat, shuffled back and forth, and kept looking away, unable to hold my gaze.

"Yes, Jacob?"

"Two of the boys was fishing this morning and saw some Federals drive that big roan cow off."

"What?"

He flinched as if I'd struck him. "Yes, ma'am. Put down the fence rails, helped themselves to her, and drove her out. Put the rails back up like no one would notice she was gone."

I leaned back on my heels, looking off to the cow pasture. "Patterson's men?"

He spat a stream of tobacco juice off to the side. "Only Federals I know of."

"All right. Let's pick some vegetables and go visit."

"Pardon?" He scratched at the blonde stubble on his cheek and frowned. "They stole a cow, ma'am."

"Yes, sir. I believe they need some vegetables to go with her. Get some help to pick vegetables."

"Yes, ma'am."

Within an hour I had a cart loaded with vegetables, berries, apples, and eggs. Luri was saddled. Persy and Lucille, like little bloodhounds when it came to sniffing out trouble, had their ponies saddled also. "You two aren't going," I said. "I don't know what's going to happen, and I don't need you in the middle of a ruckus."

Persy raised her little silver trumpet and tooted it twice. "I could warn you if they were closing in on you."

"Yes, and that's exactly what would start a ruckus."

The people in the valley had developed a unique warning system. Just about everyone had acquired trumpets, and blasts sounded from one farm to the next, alerting them of approaching Federals. When Jacob ordered his, Persy insisted on getting a smaller version.

"Miss Mac, you let Jacob take care of this," Annie squawked, tugging at Luri's bridle as I mounted. The mare backed her ears, prompting Annie to shake her finger at her. "Don't you be giving me the evil eye after I called your cymbees."

Her attention shifted back to me. "That cow ain't worth stirring a stink with the army, and you know it. Let them have her."

"She's my cow, and I'll not stand them stealing from me. I won't abide a thief. Not even from the U.S. army. Now turn loose of Luri before she bites you." She'd returned home from the Howells' to fetch some dressmaking supplies, and it would play havoc with her efforts to finish the dresses in time for the wedding if Luri bit a finger off.

Gideon insisted on going with me, though I had no idea what he was going to do aside from invoke the Lord's wrath should they harm me. Perhaps that was enough. I carried my guns concealed but forbade Jacob to take his.

The camp was laid out in orderly rows of white tents, like a small city. Wagons flanked the camp with accompanying horses tied to their sides. Soldiers mostly lounged around playing cards, reading, writing letters, or sleeping. Some were drilling outside the camp. Several perked up when they noticed us, drawn by the food, I was sure. The smell of cookfires and roasting beef hung heavy in the air. My beef.

Fresh food was my passport in. "I'd like to speak to General Patterson, please," I said, flipping my veils over my hat.

"Cooks can help you, ma'am," the sentry said. "General's busy."

I shamelessly cast my most winsome smile on him. "Can you direct me to them?"

He was most willing to lead the way.

A cook unfolded himself from where he'd been bent over a fire tending a pot of simmering beans. He wiped his hands on his apron and grinned when he spied the cart. "Why hello there, little lady. Come to do some trading?"

"Yes, sir. I figured you might like something fresh. Picked it this morning. Tossed in some eggs and a few jars of preserves. Didn't have a lot to spare of those, but there's fresh berries for cobblers or pies. Couple of barrels of early apples. New potatoes. There's some dried apples to flesh out some pies or cobblers. Feel free to look it over."

He rubbed his hands in anticipation and jumped up in the cart. "Looks darned good."

"Would go good with that beef I smell cooking."

"Sure would. How much you want? Willing to bargain?" The other cooks were going through it also, tasting the apples and berries. Nodding and grinning between themselves and already discussing dishes.

"Sixty."

"What? Sixty? Dollars for a cart of vegetables?"

"And fruit and eggs," I added.

"You're crazy." He jumped down. "I ain't paying that for a few baskets of vegetables." He was fair screaming now, drawing a crowd.

"Oh, I forgot. And the roan cow someone stole this morning that you're cooking. Fifty for her and ten for the other goods."

The general and his staff had decided they weren't so busy now and wandered over. "What's going on here?" Patterson demanded.

"Lorena McKenzie from Rosemount. Two of your men stole my Shorthorn cow. She's the best milker in seven counties, and now she's spitted up over your cookfires. I'll require fifty dollars for her. You're welcome to buy the vegetables if you want. I might negotiate on them, but that was my prize cow, so I'll not negotiate on her."

Gideon opened his Bible and began praying aloud, no doubt in fear for my mortal soul at the audacity of the lie. I had just bought the cow three months ago, and she was dry.

Patterson tore his disapproving gaze from my manservant, who appeared to be holding an impromptu camp meeting, and surveyed his men. "Did someone steal this woman's cow?"

"We didn't take no cow with short horns," objected one man. "Just found a big roan cow wandering wild and brought her in."

I rolled my eyes. "Yes. Found her wandering in my pasture, took down the fence, pushed her out, and put the rails back up. Two boys saw you. And Shorthorns don't have horns."

"Pay her," Patterson said.

"I'll take fifty-five for the vegetables and cow, but I want my barrels and baskets back. Keep the preserve jars with my compliments."

"You're too kind," said a major who was counting out money. He kept his wallet out. "Major Clinton Geary at your service. Interested in selling that yellow mare?"

"No, and you don't want her."

He handed the money to me. "I believe I do." He was young. Mid-thirties. Dark hair and eyes, neatly trimmed beard and hair. Everything about him was neat, precise, and of top quality. Wealth and privilege clothed him as completely as did the crisp new uniform and shining knee-high boots. I wondered if anyone had ever told him no before. He walked around Luri, inspecting her carefully. "I'll give you a hundred dollars for her."

"Be still my heart." I clasped my hand over my breast. "A hundred dollars for my Lexington mare. No."

His brow rose. "Lexington, huh. You know, Miss," he said, pulling out a cigar, still studying the mare, "it might be good to learn a little respect. You have an army camped on your doorstep. We could *requisition* whatever we wanted, and there wouldn't be a thing you could do about it."

"Rosemount is well protected. I don't fear your empty threats." I declared boldly, though I knew they could have their way with us if they so desired.

He struck a match on his boot heel, drew deeply on the cigar, and cast a genial smile on me with a hint of wolfish menace. "I'm sorry. That was no threat. Only concern and a word of warning about the ways of war." He ran his hand over Luri's shoulder, who stamped her hoof in irritation. "Four hundred. You can buy two mares like her for that."

Men had drawn in closer to see who would win the war of wills, looking from one to the other. I could see them almost laying bets on their major. They hadn't met me when I was irked, and I was in fine mettle today. Gideon had and prayed louder, tossing in a few Latin words.

"*Vita sine libris mors est,*" he proclaimed with arms upraised.

The major and several others turned to stare at him. Gideon nodded and went back to the Bible. Had he finally lost his mind?

"Then you go buy those two fine mares yourself," I said to the astounded major, who was still gaping at Gideon. "She's not for sale. Jackson's men are near. I hear they've got nigh 40,000 men camped out in the hills. Between you Federals and Jackson's men, I intend to keep a fast horse around in case I need to get away." The number of Jackson men was wildly inflated, but maybe it would keep Patterson close to camp and out of my hair. I motioned to Jacob, who was finished unloading the cart. "Come along. We're done here."

The major said nothing in reply, probably glad to be shed of unhinged people.

"Can't believe the major folded," said one of his men.

"The game's not over," he muttered. "I never lose."

I raised a brow at him as if to ask if he really wanted to play. His teeth clamped tighter on the cigar, and he stomped away.

We were down the road a piece before I questioned Gideon. "What were you doing back there?"

"Why praying for you, Miss Mac. What did you think I was doing?"

"Why the Latin?"

"Your papa always said it. Had those words over the library. Said a man should live by them. Like the golden rule, I reckon. Do unto others. Figured it might soften their hearts to you."

"'*Vita sine libris mors est*' means 'Life without books is death.' From the looks on several faces, they probably thought you were insane."

Jacob, always a man of select words, spit tobacco juice into the dirt beside the cart and replied, "They wouldn't be far off. No offense, Miss Mac, but at times it's a damned asylum around here."

Things returned to normal for the rest of the day. I enjoyed my small victories where I could and decided to buy another Shorthorn cow. Maybe two thanks to General Patterson.

The next morning, Jacob ambled into the kitchen, chewing on his mouth as he always did when he was upset, working it from side to side and back again as if he were toiling to come up with the right words that were simply stuck and refused to choke out of his throat.

"What is it, Jacob?"

Della set him a cup of hot coffee laced generously with whiskey. He picked up the cup and gulped half of it, shook his head, and leaned his lanky frame on the ladderback chair across from me as if he were a schoolboy prepared to take his whipping. "Luri's gone."

"Nonsense. She just let herself out and went wandering. She's probably eating the little people offerings." I buttered another biscuit and offered it to him. He shook his head.

"No, ma'am. We looked everywhere. She ain't touched the little people food. Nobody's seen her. She's gone."

"That's not like her." I finished my biscuit before following Jacob out to the stable. Her stall was empty, and from the amount of water in the bucket, she had disappeared sometime after midnight.

We combed the gardens and were going through the near pastures when Persy and Lucille came racing out to us like their tails were on fire. "Miss Lorena," Persy yelled. "Luri's coming."

Sure enough, Luri was easing down the road at a leisurely trot, that deep gold head with its broad white blaze in the air, nickering at the other horses in the pasture flanking the road as if she had not a care in her happy world. Her mane and tail flowed like spun silver in the light breeze. Luri's swishing tail gave her the air of a dancer moving to music only she could hear, and wasn't she a sight?

She stopped in front of me and put her head down, ready for a pat. "Where have you been, girl?" I let her bury her head in my chest and rubbed her neck. It was then I realized she was wearing a strange halter and lifted her head up to examine the piece. "Luri's stall door was closed when I went in the barn. Who closed it?"

"No, one, Miss Mac," Jacob answered. "That's the way we found it."

"Luri's not in the habit of closing the door after she lets herself out, and this isn't her halter and lead. I believe we had a horse thief with the initials—" I looked at the brass plate on the halter—"C.L.G. who helped himself to Miss Luri. Take her to the barn and care for her. I'll look into this later, but for now I'm going to finish my breakfast. I have an idea who that belongs to."

The game's not over indeed.

Della took one look at me and raised the whiskey bottle after she poured my coffee. I shook my head. "Maybe later. Let's try breakfast again, though."

She could almost read my mind and already had breakfast started. Ham and eggs appeared magically, as did another summons. I sliced at the ham brutally and wolfed down two bites. "Miss Mac?" Jacob said. "Riders coming."

"Yes, I'm sure they are."

And there it was, Persy's warning trumpet.

Picking up the pistol Della had fetched from the library, I stuffed it in my pocket and grabbed my coffee, wishing now I had the whiskey in it. "General Patterson. Major," I said to the troops wheeling around in front of my veranda. "Come to buy another cow?"

"We've come for our horses you stole, Miss McKenzie."

"That's rich. Jacob, fetch that halter."

"If you think for one moment we're going to put up with your thievery just because you're a woman, you're sadly mistaken." Patterson continued with his diatribe until Jacob returned with the halter, which I held up and read off the initials.

"Does anyone here have those initials? My mare returned this morning with this halter on." By now the lace guild had answered Persy's call to arms and was coming in from the fields and chores to surround me. With the impeccable timing of a saint, Luri had decided she'd been locked up long enough and it was time to make her rounds.

"If you will follow me, gentlemen." I had noticed the furtive glances towards Major Moneybags when I read the initials but decided to let it lie for now. When we got to the garden, Luri unfastened the gate as she always did, tossed the rope up and down in victory, and pitched it away in disdain before nosing the gate open. "If you don't mind, tie your horses up at the fence."

Mesmerized by the mare's actions, they did as I asked without question and continued watching her as she made her way from offering to offering and then to the pond, where she waded out and buried her head.

"As soon as she finishes drowning herself or visiting with the water spirits, she'll show you what happened to your horses."

The men stepped away from the gate to make way for her when she ambled out and then peered in astonishment at her as she went down the row untying their horses. I held up my hand when they made to stop her. "No, you need to see what she does. I'm sure CLG had her tied up on a picket line. When she got tired of it, she decided to leave, untied herself and the rest of the horses near her until she got bored and headed home." I wheeled toward the major. "I said you didn't want her. If you'd checked the surrounding hillsides instead of skedaddling over here to accuse me of stealing your horses, you'd probably already have them back.

"My father believed Luri represented McKenzie luck. He died in October. The year is young, and so far, I've had bankers try to cheat me out of my horse farm in Charleston, and, indeed, I lost it. I've been robbed, shot, and poisoned. My dipped and dyed Yankee mother holds the mortgage on this plantation and refuses to give permission for me to wed the man I love. Instead, she's turning over every rock she can to find a Yankee to marry me." I glared at the lot of them. "I will shoot the first one who offers even in jest. I have two armies camped in my backyard and one threatening to *requisition* whatever they want and stealing my cows and horses.

"Now, Major, if you want some of this McKenzie luck, come get it. I could do with a bit less." Luri had made her way back to me, draped her wet head over my shoulder, and gazed at the men. I reached up and patted her.

Now, Lorena, dahrlin. I don't think it's fair t'blame poor Luri fer all this.

Really, Papa? Do I have to deal with you right now? Why aren't you with the men?

Am dead. May be where I please. Bobby Patterson. Betrayed his own people in the Bible Riots in Philadelphia an' put down the Irish Catholics. Destroyed Saint Michael's an' Saint Augustine's churches.

"What?

Aye. Don't believe fer a minute he won't stomp over ye an'
Rosemount.

I clutched my crucifix reflexively.

"As amusing as that trick may be," Patterson said, stepping closer to me. "I'm not believing for a minute that mare turned all those horses loose with no help and no one saw her."

"Believe it or not, that's what happened. I'm not a horse thief. And you need to step back." I narrowed my eyes at him. "I know who you are, Faithless Patterson. Destroyer of Saint Michael's and Saint Augustine's. Rise up against your own Irish Catholic brethren?"

The McKenzie Ladies gasped. Luri stretched, backed her ears, and moved to my side. She always read my moods, and she was getting as irked as I was.

Patterson blanched and ran his fingers through his silver-shot hair. "I was following orders, and I'm not in the habit of taking orders from—"

Just then Luri reached out as quick as thought and grabbed him by the shoulder. Had he not ducked almost as quickly, she'd have had him like a bulldog. As it was, her teeth snapped shut on his uniform, taking the epaulet, part of the uniform, and most likely a little hide.

"Damn it all," he cried out in shock and pain.

Luri snapped the epaulet up and down, golden bullion fringe waving triumphantly.

"Luri," I said, "stop it. Put that down." She ignored me, of course.

Patterson's men surrounded him to see if he was all right. He pushed them away in agitation. "I'm fine. Regardless, young lady, you'll be coming with us until those horses are found."

"Herself will no be doin thet, sir," a woman from the crowd said.

"Oh, and who are you to tell me what I'm going to do?" Patterson groused.

Martha stepped forward. "Martha O'Brien of the Lace Guild. The McKenzie Ladies."

Patterson's men laughed.

The major strode out to meet her and bowed in exaggerated gallantry. "Mistress O'Brien. And why won't we be taking Miss McKenzie?"

She curtsied and smiled sweetly before drawing a pistol from the folds of her skirt, prompting the other ladies to do the same. "Because, should ye touch her, we will blow ye all tae hell. Iffen it please ye."

Mouths dropped and guns whipped out of holsters on Patterson's side. "Jesus Christ," Patterson said. "Stand down. We'll go look for our horses, and we better find them all."

They mounted up, seemingly uninterested in me further.

"Wait, Major. Are you sure you don't want Luri?"

He tipped his hat to me. "Ma'am, I took her as a prank to bring you down a peg or two and maybe convince you to sell her. I never lose. Both you and that mare are quite handsome, but that foul-tempered wench is completely suited to you. I'd hate to break up such an admirably matched pair."

Chapter Twenty-Nine

Heavy gray clouds like smoked cotton hung low and sullen over the valley. Mists rolled up from the river, adding to the melancholy. The weather kept the girls inside, stifling the endless energy that fed Persy and Lucille's mischief. It was no surprise their parents hadn't taken them to Europe. They were enough to keep the saints hopping. Would they be my only students left if war proceeded? There were no withdrawals by nervous parents yet, but it was a daily concern. Would any place be safe now after Lincoln's call for 500,000 troops? I couldn't even fathom that many soldiers. The papers said the entire army only had 16,000, now spread like thin jam across the country.

Weary of worrying, I stepped onto the veranda with Beth's comedy novella, hoping to occupy my thoughts. Rawlins, the redbone pup, and Purdy, my old setter, followed me. Rawlins gnawed at my toes with each step, and Purdy gently thumped my skirt with her tail. She waited for me to settle and laid her spotted head in my lap, content to let my hand rest on her ears while I read. My mind drifted away, pondering myriad things, most of which I could do nothing about. At yet another sigh, Purdy rolled clouded eyes up at me. I patted her and started the same page for the fifth time.

Rawlins abandoned my toes for a bone he'd cadged somewhere and lay down crunching on it next to Purdy. After watching me stare fruitlessly at unfathomed words for nearly an hour, the two were delighted to find something more interesting and ran off barking at an approaching man. He was a gray rider on a gray horse on a gray day. I might have mistaken him for a Rosemount ghost if not for their enthusiastic welcome and the fact that I recognized the horse's three white stockings and bald face.

Like a harbinger of doom, on he came with no glad tidings, I was sure. I walked to meet him with nerves and fears unbound.

"Miss McKenzie," Major Fox greeted, dismounting and removing his hat. The mare had been ridden hard recently, judging from her sweat-caked coat. "Might I visit with you?" Being a gentleman, he waited for my invitation with one dusty boot propped on the lower step.

"Let's go inside." I waved to the boy dashing toward us from the stable. "Levi can care for Sadie."

"Yes, ma'am," Fox said. "Thank you."

Purdy clicked up the red brick stairs beside Fox, who opened the door for me. I checked so suddenly it was only his quick reflexes that kept him from walking over me. At the bottom of the grand stairway were piles of pillows beneath each banister. Girls clustered in the middle of the hall stared upward where Persy and Lucille perched at the top.

"Go!" shouted Cecile.

The two pushed away and slid down the banisters, laughing uproariously with the crowd cheering their favorites. I hurried over as Persy soared off the banister, through the air, and plopped on the pillows barely ahead of Lucille. She sprawled out like a starfish, skirts and petticoats everywhere but where they should be on a young lady and laughing too hard to care that everyone could see her ruffled drawers. She was happy. Lucille was happy. The girls who bet on Persy were happy.

I was not.

The crowd hadn't noticed Major Fox and me until he burst out with a booming laugh that could rattle windows. "Who won?" he asked.

"Where's Imogene?" I demanded.

Lucille was still giggling but stood and straightened her skirts. Wide-eyed, the girls parted, leaving Imogene alone in the middle with a fistful of money. Lucille pointed at her as if I might miss her. "Imogene's taking the bets. She's teaching us math."

"Pity I wasn't here sooner," Fox said. "I love a good race. Will you be going again?"

"I should teach you all subtraction. No, they won't. Please don't encourage them." I glared at him, but having made many a trip down those banisters myself in my younger days, I wasn't inclined to say much lest Tilda or Gideon tell on me. And they would.

"Put those pillows away. It's cleared off enough y'all can go outside and paint." They flew like uncrated doves.

I took him to the library, guessing he'd wish to speak in private. The library's heavy wood gave me a feeling of permanence and held my heart. Annie's sister Liza, on the other hand, had convinced herself it was more like a coffin than a sanctuary with all the polished mahogany and said it was bad luck to be near the place. "Why look at poor Marse Mac. He was in there all the time, and where is he now? Dead, that's where."

Dead or not, I wished he could help me solve whatever Gordian knot Fox was about to lay before me. This time I had to do it alone, and Papa, the problem solver, was the problem creator.

Gideon appeared out of nowhere and took Fox's cloak and hat. "I'll send someone with drinks. Della uncorked lemon syrup this morning. Perhaps lemon soda water?"

"Perfect. Tell her we have a guest for dinner."

We made small talk about Charleston and General Beaure-gard until Tilda brought the drinks. Fox must have impressed her since she not only delivered them herself but had donned the peruke wig she reserved only for special occasions. She was going bald and normally hid the deficit with colorful bandanas, but at times she brought out the worn and ancient wig she'd unearthed in the attic when Papa was remodeling. No amount of cajoling could convince her to part with her treasure, so, over time, the girls helped her restore it as best they could. With its wide white rows of curls liberally sprinkled with little multicolored bows, it now looked somewhat less like a shocked sheep, but it was still a fright.

Fox stared at Tilda for the briefest moment. "Thank you. Do you mind me saying how fetching you look today, Miss?"

Tilda raised a self-satisfied eyebrow at me, patted the wig, knocking it slightly askew, and departed on clouds.

Law. Now I'd never be able to pry that mop out of her hands.

"This is a beautiful library," he said as if nothing unusual at all had just happened.

I decided to follow his lead and looked around as if seeing it for the first time. "Thank you. Papa rescued the woodwork and mantle from a castle that was being dismantled in Ireland. The craftsmen came with it, and what they couldn't save, they built new, but with the same look and feel. You can't tell which carvings are new and which are the ancient. Even as a child I recognized a place of power and would slip out of bed to sleep in the unfinished room. They finally locked it for fear I'd kill myself among the scattered timbers." The heat rose in my cheeks. "Forgive my romantic meandering."

"Not at all. I'd describe it as magical."

First Tilda and now me. I couldn't stifle the laugh, though I was buttressing my will against his charm. "You must be Irish. Papa called it magical also, but I'm sure you didn't come here to discuss my library."

"Indeed I am." He followed me to the conservatory where I could see if anyone was near who might overhear us. "Virginia will ratify," Fox said simply, standing next to me and looking out over the gardens. "We need to step up our operation. I require your service if you're still willing."

There it was. Scanning my face once, he took quick stock of my reaction and looked away, leaving me with my tumbling thoughts.

I sank into a chair next to a pedestaled fern and traced my fingers over the wispy fronds. Fox stood with his back to me as if immersed in something of great interest outside the leaded windows.

"I can't. I will *never* return to Baltimore." Bitterness tinged my words, and I made no attempt to hide it.

He nodded as if he understood completely. "Will you tell me what happened?"

"No."

Long moments passed. In the distance someone chopped a tree. With each thwack I felt my resistance breaking. After several minutes in silence, he let me come to him on my terms, as any good horse trainer does. I resented him even more for this because I knew what he was doing but bowed my head and recounted the debacle with Mother at the ball. The elation at her permission. That duel-inducing idiot and Mother's conviction that Colonel Lee betrayed her, the country, heaven above, and even I was complicit in the deceit.

I only thought I'd cried myself dry over the matter. He pulled me gently to him and clasped me close as a parent might a broken child, letting me sob into his shoulder. He didn't soothe me and tell me it would be all right. We both knew it wouldn't. He simply held me.

I caught a ragged breath. "I'm sorry."

"For what?"

"For blubbering all over your uniform. It's soaked." I wiped at my nose and eyes and stepped away.

He looked at the spot on his chest. "Better a woman's tears than my own heart's blood," he said and handed me a handkerchief. He allowed me a moment to compose myself and looked away graciously while I blew my nose. "Might we sit at the table?"

"Of course." I was anxious to turn to something else instead of my womanly weakness.

At the table, he laid out two carefully folded maps he'd pulled from his pocket and pointed to a small red circle on the first one. "This is Rosemount. Your neighbors in western Virginia are heavy Union sympathizers. The Shenandoah Valley will be like a turnpike for the armies. It'll be deeply contested. Plus, the Union will try to destroy the crops here to keep from provisioning the Confederate army. An army marches on its belly. It has ever been true."

He pointed out railroads, rivers, and roads as he did this, showing how the armies would move. Then he reiterated statistics I'd heard in vague terms in Charleston. These were specific and foreboding. The South was outmanned, outgunned, and outfinanced. The North had more infrastructure and infinitely more manufacturing. It had one of the world's most successful navies. The South had none. I drifted deeper into depression with each word.

"Our only hope is to force a treaty early before they wear us down. I've been a student of war nearly all my life. We don't have castles, but they'll lay siege to us in the same manner, cutting us off from outside supplies and laying waste to crops and materials. They can starve us out and kill us off by sheer numbers, and they will if the war wears on. That's why I need people like you and your Rosemount. I'm not trying to frighten you, but please don't believe you can escape unscathed if you sit it out."

He folded the map and handed it to me. "I don't blame you for not wanting to go, but I'm asking you to rise above it for the sake of the great many lives that may be saved."

"I'm not given to cowardice," I said.

"I know, or I wouldn't approach you."

He stayed at the table, but I needed room and meandered back to the window. My fingers traced out the flowered silver pencil case on my chatelaine. It was a gift from Grandmama for my eighteenth birthday, saying a lady should always carry pencil and paper to keep her house properly organized. How do you organize against war? "How soon will you need me?"

"Soon. Information is already flowing, but I need more intelligencers and couriers."

Sour stomach or no, I drank the lemon soda. "My mother's been sending desperate messages. I could use that as an excuse."

"Excellent." He barreled on before I could retreat and called me to him. "Here's a cipher wheel. You'll need to memorize the key, which changes frequently. For instance, A on the top wheel equals D on the bottom wheel. I'll give you a list until you can memorize them, but if it falls into the wrong hands, it puts all in grave danger."

I fingered the contraption with its two brass wheels, one laid over the other, letters along the edges that could be matched up when you moved the top wheel. It was thin, flat, and about four inches wide. Easily concealed, but not easily explained if discovered. It had but one purpose.

He showed me how to work it and deciphered a simple message with me and then forged ahead. "Stop in Alexandria. The Harbor Brothers Blacksmith Shop will have a new carriage for you. Leave it in Washington at Monroe Farrier and Supply, where they will secrete supplies in the hidden compartments. Someone will meet you in Baltimore and say to you these words exactly." He gave me a passage and my retort. "You'll be the Rain Crow. Don't use your real name in correspondence."

Numbers, letters, statistics, and maps whirled madly in my mind. Pray I would remember it all. It was a tornado of information coming at me so quickly I felt I was caught up helplessly in the whirlwind with nothing to hold on to.

A gentle knock on the door gave me respite from my unruly thoughts. "Miz Mac," Liza said, sticking her head around the open door, "do you want we should bring trays to you here or you to eat with the girls?"

He deftly slipped the cipher wheel inside his jacket. "I'd love to meet the young ladies."

"We'll eat together," I replied.

I could still say no and knew I should. He'd already bought horses for his scouts, but we looked over the horses afterward, and he bought two more to cover his visit. During our discussion in the pasture over this horse or that, he went over the mission again. I would pick up information from his operatives in Baltimore mainly and secret it in various ways. Supplies would be stashed in the special carriage, and I had only to get it from Alexandria into Washington, where it would be stocked, and then back across the river again and to another spot to be stripped. It seemed simple enough, but my stomach was churning at the prospect of what all could go wrong.

In the end, a deal was also struck for me.

Chapter Thirty

Baron had finally wheedled a leave out of Jackson to visit Lorena, pleading an emergency, which seldom worked, but he was still convalescing. Plus, it was possible Jackson was rewarding him for living in the saddle these past weeks on scout. Whatever the reason, he gathered up young Pelham, who was down in the mouth about having to leave West Point weeks before graduation because he refused to sign an oath of allegiance. He was sure a little attention from a few dozen young beauties would raise Pelham's mood. Baron was only interested in one of them.

It had been far too long since his last visit to Rosemount. He and Kieran had walked the fields and discussed rotating crops as per Mr. Ruffins' suggestions and possibly buying the farm next door, which might be available. Kieran hinted it would be a good place for a man to retire after the military. He sighed heavily. They had made so many plans, and now the whole world was upside down.

Taking out the Bowie knife he always carried at his side, he cut an ivory bloom and twirled it meditatively between his fingers. He rubbed a petal gently between his thumb and forefinger. It was flawlessly smooth, as if dipped in wax to protect its beauty, but he knew it could be bruised—like the woman before him. Lifting the bloom, he inhaled deeply, taking in the peculiarly sensuous perfume. Lorena was smiling at him when he opened his eyes over the magnolia.

He studied her as if seeing her anew, struck by her beauty as the first time he met her, and wondered if he was just now truly knowing her. After wrapping the severed stem with his handkerchief, he handed it to her wordlessly, then smoothed stray auburn curls around the rose he'd tucked above her left ear earlier, stroking her hair and cheek. He led her away from the house and out past the lilacs near the stream and willows for privacy.

A plaintive voice drifted up from somewhere near through the gray mists.

> "We loved each other then, Lorena,
> More than we ever dared to tell:
> And what might have been, Lorena,
> Had but our lovings prospered well."

His hand stayed there, cupping her silken cheek. She closed her black lashes against porcelain, murmuring a sigh of contentment. The singer continued, sending Baron deeper into the doldrums until he wanted to shout for peace.

"I despise that damned song with all my being," he growled, dropping his hand, the spell broken. "It puts me so very low, thinking we might never wed."

Lorena's answering fairy bell laugh usually cheered him. Not today.

"Language, Captain." Her laughter faded as quickly as it arrived. "Oddly enough, when Colonel Lee recommended you, before that idiot decried him a traitor, Mother was busy making plans about a wedding at Arlington. She suggested once you come to Baltimore to wed, our problems would be solved."

Baron guffawed. "They'd string me from a tree before my boot hit the ground." He felt her tense and pulled her close. "Calm. Nothing will happen to me. I promised you, with God as my witness, we'll wed. I believe He'll see to it I keep my vows."

As much as he desired to discuss wedding plans, he could put it off no longer. "I know about you and Beauregard."

"Beauregard?" she replied with all the innocence of a babe in arms. She might be good at deception if he allowed it. He had no intention of doing so.

"General Beauregard. Little Creole guy about so tall. Black hair, mustache, and goatee. Olive complexion. High cheekbones. Popular with the ladies. Hard to miss."

She pulled away, indignant and ready to fight. "I know who he is."

"Break it off. I don't want you involved."

It was like watching an untied balloon deflate. Her shoulders slumped. The challenge died from her eyes. "How did you find out?" The question was whispered so softly he might have missed it if the leaves above rustled the tiniest bit.

"Someone warned me about you and Beauregard…and Fox, or whatever name he currently goes by."

She flinched.

"He arranged a meeting with Major Fox," she said.

"You should have declined."

Her chin jutted defiantly. "He didn't talk me into anything."

Baron stalked away. He had to leave before he tried to shake sense into her or the truth out of her. She remained cemetery silent behind him. He batted a low-hanging limb out of his face, pulled a cigar from his tunic pocket, bit off the end, and clamped it between his teeth. There was no need to light it. He simply needed to bite back words he'd regret.

"You're angry," she said.

"How observant," he fairly growled. "I know how persuasive Fox is. Tell him you changed your mind. Find someone else for the Little Creole. You're not to go to Baltimore on missions."

There was a gasp.

"Yes, I know."

She ignored him and charged on. "I can't. He was right. I'm in the perfect position. Besides, you know I must check on Mother."

He stormed back and clasped her hands. "Don't play me! Your mother will likely outlive both of us. Don't you understand? If you're caught, they'll toss you in prison or hang you outright, and don't think for a moment some scallywag here won't take advantage of it to move on Rosemount even if you survive. You'll have nothing."

"What will I have if we don't win! Nothing. Will the North let us escape with anything save our miserable lives?"

"Your life would be enough. Promise me you won't speak to him again."

She slid her hands away. "You would have me promise something I can't fulfill?"

"No, I'd have you promise and do. For the love of God, Lorena, for once don't be so bullheaded. I won't let you put your life in danger."

She glared and drew herself up to her full 5'3". "I fought bankers who hired a robber and nearly killed me. I shot the robber who shot me. The bankers who hired him murdered him before he could talk." Wheeling, she put her hands on her hips and huffed. "Those same bankers poisoned me. It was only because I didn't finish a piece of lemon cake with raspberry sauce that they failed. Surprise!" She threw her arms in the air. "The robber's wife sent the banker flying to his death. I lost The Pines due to their plotting. Pray tell me, how you don't want my life in danger when all I was trying to do was renew a loan on The Pines?" The more she spoke, the higher her voice rose.

Baron watched her hands waving in the air, acting it all out. "I find this hard to believe," he said when she paused for breath.

"That someone would try to kill me?" she asked incredulously.

"No, that you had a piece of lemon cake and didn't finish it."

She halted her agitated pacing and stared at him, mouth open, brows knit in confusion. "Wha—?"

When it hit her, hell's wrath unleashed full force. Her face took on the bright hue of the rose in her hair. She threw the magnolia at him and looked around for something more substantial. He laughed and pulled her to him before she found it. "I was joking." He held her tight, calming her struggles and stroking her hair, murmuring to her. "I'm sorry. I'm sorry. I detest that you went through that without me."

"I hate you so much sometimes."

"I know, and I deserve it. I couldn't be with you, but you weren't alone."

"I don't understand."

"I can't reveal who he is, but I had someone watching over you as best he could. I knew about everything that happened. I tried to desert once to come to you. I was bent on murderous rampage, but Billings clubbed me over the head, and they arrested me for desertion. Fortunately, the major let me off instead of sending me to the gallows since I hadn't actually boarded the train."

Her mouth opened in shock. "Why would you do that?"

"Because I love you. I wanted to protect you. Like I'm trying to do now."

His hand went to the back of her neck, twining his fingers through her hair. He'd love nothing better than to unravel the net and rolls and set it all tumbling. His other arm wrapped around her waist, pulling her closer, and closed his mouth on hers.

She answered every plea willingly with equal fervor. Her knees wavered, and it was all he could do to keep from carrying her away. At last, he pushed her away. "Lorena...."

Men may think they conquer the world, but it was women who mastered the art of conquest, and he was truly lost, heart and soul. "Dear God. Do something about your mother," he whispered. "Until then, please reconsider your actions. I couldn't live if something happened to you." He walked away and leaned against a willow to look out across the water.

It was silent save the cooing of a dove somewhere in a nearby tree. Thankfully, that damnable songster had quit his sorrowful warbling.

Let her come to her senses.

"If I could," she began softly.

Why would she exercise caution now? He lit the cigar, steeling himself for her reply.

"I'd put on britches and join the nearest band of soldiers marching by, but I can't. This is what I can do, and if one small bit of information brings you home sooner, then by all that is holy, that is what I'll do. Do not deny me in this."

"I won't argue more with you and leave with ill words between us." He drew her close to mend the rift and gently kissed the top of her head and then her forehead.

Kieran told him once he planted multitudes of lilacs because the Irish believed lilac scent carried humans into the supernal world of fae folk. He inhaled deeply and wished them away to another world.

"Miss McKenzie! Miss McKenzie! Breakfast soon. There you are." That banshee-bay wasn't the fae he hoped for. The new teacher's voice had a knife-scratching-across-glass quality that set Baron's teeth on edge, compounded by her unfortunate timing.

"Damn that woman," Lorena whispered and slid away from him.

"Language, Miss McKenzie."

Miss Abigail Boggs flitted around a massive lilac bush, waving madly. Her eyes were alight, as always, whenever Baron saw her. Lorena assured him it was the same look every young woman cast on her handsome beau whenever they thought she wasn't looking. He couldn't explain the difference to her. With Boggs, he felt like he was being consumed, slowly, one bite at a time. It wasn't the normal Southern woman flirtations he was accustomed to. He even entertained introducing her to one of his eligible young officers, but there were none he disliked enough.

He stepped closer to Lorena. "Miss Boggs."

"Captain Callahan, I didn't know you were out here! What a pleasant surprise."

That was a lie. The young ladies at the school all went atwitter any time a soldier arrived. Plus, young Pelham was at the house with the horses. The young ladies were probably watching from upper story windows, which is why he had deftly maneuvered Lorena to a spot hidden from curious eyes unless they hid behind the lilac bushes. How long had the creature been there?

"I understand breakfast is ready," he responded. "Miss McKenzie, shall we?" He turned away from Boggs and held out his arm to Lorena, hoping the unwelcome messenger would take the hint. She didn't. Her fingers clawed around his arm, like a bird seeking perch. He masked the profound revulsion and accepted her clutch. "Miss Boggs."

They strolled toward the great house, making meaningless conversation while he passed glances that conveyed more than he dared express in words even had they been alone. There at the steps, Pelham and a new rider argued passionately. The rider's lathered horse champed at the bit, slobbered nervously, and tugged the reins free to steal a bite of grass.

Damnation.

Lorena's hand tightened on his arm. Couriers seldom bore good news and never any exhortations to tarry and spend a few more days of leisure. Her step lagged.

Miss Boggs prattled on with excitement about another dashing visitor. Her hand quivered with anticipation; he could feel even through the layers of his uniform. He withdrew his arm.

"If you'll excuse me, ladies."

Lorena grasped him closer. "Jackson can spare you long enough for breakfast, surely."

He glanced at the hard-ridden horse. "I expect I'm being recalled," he said regretfully.

"Come, Abigail. If the captain must away, the least we can do is send food."

They hurried toward the house *en force*, Lorena lifting her skirts out of the heavily dewed grass. She looked to the upper windows and addressed the house. "Girls! I need you in the cookhouse!"

A half-dozen neatly coifed young heads popped out from behind lace curtains like pheasants being stirred by a bird dog and just as quickly disappeared. Lorena spoke to the rider. "I assume you're here to call the captain?"

He removed his hat and stammered. "Ma'am, I, uh, a message—"

"Do you mean to call him away?" she demanded.

Billings stared helplessly.

Baron shrugged. "Admit your crime, sergeant. She won't be denied."

His hat twisted in his hands. "I'm sorry, ma'am. Captain Callahan has been summoned. We're to leave as soon as I find him. Colonel Stuart has requested he be transferred to his brigade, and he wants him back as soon as possible."

"Stuart? I got the transfer?"

"Yes, sir. But he wants you yesterday. You know Jeb."

"Colonel Stuart can wait a few minutes. Come inside and get something to eat." She motioned to Miss Boggs, "Gather every girl who isn't in the kitchen and fetch the bandages they've been rolling."

She marched up the column-flanked stairs with the men trailing behind like pull toys and, Baron was sure, a surprised young sergeant wondering how he was going to explain the food given his missive.

"We'll make all haste once we leave and recover lost time," Baron said. "You'll find Miss McKenzie is very efficient."

"I'm sure she is."

Lorena swooshed through the door, a ball of energy and irritation. Servants and young ladies scrambled at the barked orders. Baron wished for a few Lorenas in his command.

"Gentlemen, let's sit in the small kitchen. Della can rustle you breakfast while they gather the other food in the cookhouse. Breakfast will be almost ready by the time you've washed."

"Yes, ma'am," echoed from all three of them.

Eggs, ham, and grits with bowls of spiced peaches, jars of preserves, and a heaping platter of toast soon appeared. The women scurried around like ants in a flooded anthill.

"These preserves are delicious," Pelham said.

"Hmmm?" Lorena looked up from a bag she was stuffing. "Oh, yes. Golden glow. Pumpkin and citrus marmalade."

"They taste familiar," Baron said and slathered more on toast.

"Miss McKenzie was eating toast and glow when you rode up," Persy, who had camped out at the corner of Baron's chair as he ate, offered helpfully.

Lorena's blush rose. "Don't you girls have something to do?"

"No, ma'am."

Baron grudgingly set his plate aside before he had to loosen his belt. "We should be going, but that was delicious. Thank you."

"Now," she said, looking at him sternly. "Why were you limping?"

He flinched, dismayed that she had caught it as he had tried to camouflage it.

"A cook shot him," Billings volunteered.

"What?" Lorena replied aghast. "What on earth did you say about his cooking?"

"Nothing, and thank you, Billings. He thought I was trying to steal his pans."

"I have pans if you need them. You don't need to steal pans."

"I wasn't trying to steal his pans," he said in exasperation. "It was a misunderstanding."

"We blew through a Yankee camp like a dose of salts," Billings said, buttering another piece of toast.

"A little more eating from you and a lot less talking, if you please, sir," Baron snapped. "It was a small skirmish and a tiny flesh wound. Barely noticeable."

She hmphed but pressed no further.

Pelham and Billings were still eagerly sopping up the pumpkin marmalade with more toast. He might have to prise them away with a bar, but he didn't begrudge them, as camp food could be terrible at times.

Lorena looked at the sacks piled on the table that were disappearing out the back door. "Come, girls. Help the gentlemen get the bandages. Here." Three bags of cookies shoved across the table toward the three men. "You can eat these on the way. They won't take extra room."

"At your command, my lady. If you'd grant me a moment alone before I leave?"

They wandered to the willow, holding hands, saying little. There was nothing more to be said. Their tightly clasped hands and regretful sighs said it all.

His first kiss was tender on her forehead. He worked his way slowly to her right ear, kissing and pulling the edge of it into his mouth with his lip. She made that little mewling noise she always did when he reached her lobe.

"Moses," she whispered, shuddering in his arms. Fingers tightened against his back, burning a trail of fire up his spine and setting him ablaze. Damn the world. Let them find a bit of happiness in the midst of chaos. She denied nothing. Not a kiss nor embrace. "Ah, Lorena," he said, backing away reluctantly. "I could wear your face off, but for your honor and mine, we should return." He smiled apologetically. "It appears I already tried to. You've got a bit of a rash from my beard, I fear."

She touched her face and looked up, storm-gray eyes still smoldering, half-closed. Damnable honor anyway. He could take her here and now and not have a single regret. Nor, he believed, would she. "We should go."

They walked back toward the house, escaping the cover of the lilac bush. Pausing, he cut a bouquet of flowers for her.

She lifted them to smell regardless of being surrounded by the lilac scent. "Thank you."

"Yes, I'm a generous soul to give you your own flowers. I like to imagine you're walking down the aisle with me. I'd prefer something besides lilacs."

"What would you like?"

"Red and white roses, forget-me-nots, chamomile, ivy," he said without hesitation.

"Chamomile?"

"Chamomile is for patience, which you may need. I've put a lot of thought into this."

"Apparently."

He spied handsome young Pelham sitting on the wide steps surrounded by Rosemount beauties, and Billings leaned against a column, hand on his hip, smoking a cigar, but Baron's horse was nowhere in sight. Baron arched an eyebrow at her. "Madam, if this is some scheme to detain us, Colonel Stuart won't look kindly on you."

"I'd steal your horse if it would do any good, but the boys are only loading the food. She'll be here shortly."

"Loading? I remind you we must travel quickly. Stuart isn't one to wait for man nor beast. And this from someone who moments ago chastised me for trying to withhold you from what you perceive to be your duty."

"I wouldn't detain you nor respect you if you shirked your duty, yet heaven knows I dread you going."

"All right. And thank your young ladies for the attention to Pelham. He's heartbroken about having to leave West Point mere weeks before graduation. This was good for him."

"How dreadful."

"Yes, a politician demanded oaths of allegiance. Pelham and several others refused."

Jacob and a stable boy led two horses around the corner. Sad Sally wore a fully loaded pack saddle; Charlemagne wore Baron's tack. He looked at Lorena. "What's the meaning of this?"

"You need a fast horse. There's few faster than Charlie."

"I'm not taking your horse. It's too dangerous."

"Think what you're saying. I'd rather give you an extra chance at safety."

Sad Sally looked at him with those worried, sunken eyes. Baron laughed in spite of himself. "Don't worry, gal. You won't be a packhorse for long." He turned to Pelham. "Sir, if you'll tear yourself away. We should be going."

A young lady in white poplin looked up from her braiding, frantic. "A moment, please. I'm almost done. I'm tying it off now."

"Hurry, Becca!" another girl in green squealed.

"I am. Shush. There. All done." She handed Pelham's watch back to him with a new watch fob of braided hair tied off with a burgundy ribbon.

"Thank you, ladies. I'll remember all of you." He admired it, then handed it to Baron to examine. It was a handsome piece of hair jewelry consisting of at least six different colors of hair. Eight, judging from the unbound hair.

Baron kissed Lorena quickly amidst the giggling girls and mounted Charlemagne. Pelham quickly kissed each extended hand and bounded to his gelding. Once mounted, he swept his hat off in a grand gesture to the girls and bowed.

Baron grimaced. "You've been hanging around Stuart. His grandiose is rubbing off."

"Nonsense. We ride to war. I might lie dead tomorrow."

Chapter Thirty-One

The confrontation I had dreaded with Baron had come and gone like a bad summer squall, but there had been no letters from him since, and I was heartbroken. I put it down to him being busy with Stuart. I'd get one soon, surely. I busied myself with teaching, the girls, and my gardens. Tending to the plantation. Today I was weeding the herb garden half-heartedly, my mind going to the news of impending war and the man who would be in the thick of it.

Tatters of clouds tumbled lazily across the sky like tufts of cotton across a mill floor. But I smelled no rain. Maybe it was a good day for a ride to ease my mind and take foul-tempered Luri out. I had mostly stopped setting up targets with drawings of bankers for shooting practice. Mostly. Luri wasn't the only one with a foul temper, it seemed.

She still ambled up to me when she was out roaming her little territory but backed her ears at me to let me know she wasn't happy and then would continue past without stopping. She'd then swish her tail at me like a debutante flicking away some peasant's unwanted attention. She still missed The Pines. At first, she refused to go into the pond. Annie said it was because there were no cymbees and she'd have to call them. I didn't ask. Some things were better left unknown. At least Luri was somewhat happier now.

"Miss Mac?"

I looked up from weeding. Jacob was twisting his hat in twain once again.

"Yes, Jacob? Who died?"

"No one, ma'am."

He continued wringing that poor hat until I wanted to snatch it out of his hands. I rocked back on my heels and set my trowel aside. "Then what has you so flustered?"

"Luri, ma'am."

"Hmmm." Thinking about it, I hadn't seen her this morning. The bowl of beer for the wee people nearby was still full. "Is she sick?"

"No, ma'am. We thought she was wandering about, but she's nowhere to be found. We've turned the place over. Even rode the pastures."

Rosemount was a sizeable property, but Luri wasn't one to roam. She had a very small area she traveled and then ambled back to her stall and trap to graze. If ever there was a habitual creature, she was one.

"Saddle Farrell."

"Miss Mac. Please don't go over there accusing them Yanks of stealing that horse again."

"And who else would have taken her? You heard that major. He never loses. He's not stealing my horse and getting away with it."

"Yas'm."

Jacob trudged away as if I were sending him to the gallows. If the McKenzie men were still here, I would have taken a posse of them with me, but they weren't. I would go alone. By the time I changed into my habit, word that Luri was missing had already spread through Rosemount, and people were gathering, including the fully armed Lace Guild. Imogene was also in a habit and waited with her horse, Taffy, popping her crop against her leg.

"What are y'all doing?" I asked. Martha O'Brien stepped forward. "Some of us are going with you. Flynn is on his way in from the fields."

Flynn was Jacob's new assistant overseer since the younger men had left. He was too old for the rigors of war but knew farming and men. "And what is Flynn going to do? He'll be so stove up by the time I get there, I'll have to set him off beside the road like a cairn. You ladies aren't going to challenge the army. Imogene, the last thing I need is you there. They would be on my doorstep tonight, purloining you even if you made it out of camp."

She huffed. "They aren't barbarians."

"Worse, they're Yankees."

Jacob legged me up onto Farrell and started to mount Smokey. "Nor are you going, Jacob."

"But Miss Mac. I promised your daddy I'd take care of you."

Why was I having to argue with everyone on this blasted plantation this morning? "No, if things get warm, they may threaten me, but they won't shoot me. They would shoot a man. If I had several men, it might be different. One, no. Stay."

I was about halfway to Patterson's camp when I heard someone coming hard behind me and turned to see skirts and hooves flying as Imogene bore down on me. She pulled her prancing horse up beside me. "I think you need a distraction as you look for Luri, and I'm a good distraction."

"It would do no good to tell you to go home, would it?"

"None," she replied.

I might as well tell the zephyr to stop whispering o'er the valley as argue with her, and I didn't have time. Her horse blew, and nostrils flared, catching his wind. "Let's see what the rascals are up to," I said. She would ease over toward the picket line to see if she could spot Luri while I engaged Geary. If nothing else, she might be able to worm some information out of someone about where the mare was.

The pickets were once again reluctant to let us into camp. "Listen, you little pismires," I snarled. "I will speak to General Patterson and Major Clinton Geary. I'm not leaving until I do."

Imogene raised her veils and leaned forward, putting her hand on one picket's shoulder, then cast her let-there-be-sunlight-and-roses smile on him. "She won't. She's stubborn that way. I can do nothing with her when she's in a mood."

Another soldier ambled over and asked what the problem was. He escorted us to Major Geary's tent. The sides were up, and Geary was inside the immaculate interior writing a letter or report. He cleaned the pen nib and set it aside, then stood, straightened his jacket, put on his kepi, and walked out with a wide grin. "Miss McKenzie. More vegetables to sell?"

"No," I spat, pushing my veils back. "I'll have my mare now."

"Your mare?" He looked around and reached out to scratch Farrell's nose. "I'm not sure what you're talking about. That's a good-looking stallion. Interested in selling him?"

"No, and should he turn up missing also, I'll know where to come looking. Luri is gone. I know you have her, and I want her back."

Soldiers gathered, sensing a storm. One sat on a crate nearby whittling and smoking a pipe, taking it all in, looking from one of us to the other.

"It's not my fault if you can't keep up with your horses, Miss McKenzie. Are you going to accuse me every time one goes missing?" He lit a cigar and waited with a smirk for my reply.

Imogene had drifted away a little toward some picket lines with horses, visiting with a knot of soldiers. There was genial conversation and laughter from that quarter. None from mine.

"I'm sure I could turn this camp upside down and not find her," I said.

"I'm sure you're right," he said, the smirk growing into an infuriating grin.

He had her hidden where I would never find her. I launched into a string of Gaelic curses ending with. *"Téigh trasna ort féin!"*

The older soldier with the pipe turned crimson, his ears flaming. "Jaysus, Mahry, an' Joseph, girl. An' what ud yer fadder be sayin' about sech language?"

"Where do you think I learned it?"

"Translate it for me," Geary said.

"No, sar. Ay'll no be doin' dat."

"The last bit means to go across yourself," another soldier said.

"Do what?" Geary said, puzzled.

"It means go f—"

"It means," the one with the pipe said, "tae have intimate relations wit yearself, sar."

Geary howled, slapping his kepi across his leg. His brown eyes glittered with dark delight, hair ruffled where his cap had pulled free. "Ah, Miss McKenzie, since we're on such familiar terms, I shall come calling this evening. I'd much rather be intimate with you. I'm rather boring company alone."

"Go hifreann leat!"

He moved to stroke Farrell's neck to further irritate me, I was sure. "Let me guess. Supper at six?"

"Close, sar," the piped one said. "Tae hell wit ye."

Geary was still laughing.

I leaned forward toward him. "You've forgotten what I told you about McKenzie luck. She may carry you for a while, but before the year is out, your men will carry you."

A frisson of fear passed over him.

The one smoking his pipe crossed himself and whispered, "Jaysus."

Geary bit down on his cigar and recovered his composure. "I don't fear your McKenzie luck, Miss. I make my own, and I never run out."

"You should fear it. You'll hear a guinea fowl crying soon enough."

"Jaysus," the pipe smoker said and got up to move away from Geary lest some of that bad luck rub off on him.

"Come, Imogene. I'm done." Luri was gone, and there was nothing I could do about it. I wheeled Farrell around hoping to knock Geary in the head, but he was too quick. Then, I charged through the camp daring anyone to get in my way. Two soldiers strolling and talking and paying no attention barely missed being run down. One bent over a fire looked up in surprise, stumbled, and fell into it. A yellow cur dog barked furiously, then thought better of his bravery, yelped, and darted out of our path. We left the camp in a hot gallop with skirts and veils flying and men whooping after us as if we were in a horse race.

I didn't slow down until well out of camp and out of sight. "I'm furious with the popinjay." I huffed. "He all but admitted he had her."

Our horses blew and danced sideways as if they wanted to keep going. I could have run all the way to Rosemount and still not voided my fury, but there was no sense wasting horses.

"Yes, the soldiers I talked to didn't come right out and say so, but they hinted at it. I believe she's safely hidden at a farm, but who knows where? There are plenty of Union sympathizers about. Plus, he has money, and he's a charmer when he wants to be, from what they say. He had planned on romancing you out of her, but they may be moving out soon, and he was running out of time."

I cocked my head to the side. "Really?"

She shrugged. "Just rumors. No one knows."

"Romance me out of Luri. Phfft."

"Well, soften you up enough to sell her." She smoothed her imaginary mustache. "Why, Miss McKenzie, I fear we got off on the wrong foot. I wanted to make amends and had these candies sent from Maine." She opened the imaginary box dramatically.

"Oh, how kind!" I took one of her chocolates. "Let me sell you my favorite horse and open my arms to you. Kiss me!"

"Oh, no, Miss McKenzie. I just want the horse. Well, maybe one kiss."

We giggled at the absurdity. I was still angry and would be for some time, but Imogene knew how to calm me.

What happened me sweet daughter?

The war, Papa. It's driving me insane. Turning me into a hellcat.

Moses, Mahry, an' Joseph, the words ye did say thet man. What kind o' father they think o' me? I said those things fer sure, but not fer ye be sayin' 'em.

I'm sure they think you're a very colorful father with a broad vocabulary.

He harrumphed in that very Irish way of his.

Sure, an' yer heart-scalded about Luri, but she always comes home. Like a bad penny she is.

Not this time, Papa. That bounder isn't going to let her go. It's not just the horse. It's the idea they can waltz in and take what they want. I feel violated and vulnerable. If I can't protect Luri, how will I protect my girls?

While McKenzie luck may not have been the greatest, it was McKenzie luck, and I had a very real dread of what might come to pass without it.

Chapter Thirty-Two

When we returned to Rosemount, I found a letter waiting for me. Praise the Lord.

May 22, 1861
Harper's Ferry, Virginia

Beloved Baroness,

I pray you are well. I am living in the saddle lately. Col. Stuart purloined a jar of golden glow for himself when we arrived. He maintains a portion should go to him as he is the commander and rank has its privileges. It will encourage others to seek promotion. I'm not sure I believe this, but I will try to become Col. Callahan with all haste to test the theory.

How would you like to be Mrs. Col. Callahan? I would settle for Mrs. Capt. Callahan. You should press the attack on your mother. Send some iced drinks. It must be hot in hell. How is the dear? Still crazy as a peach-orchard boar? I promise I will try to get along with her after we are wed, but so long as she stands between me and what I desire most in life, she is my declared enemy. This is war.

Jeb has thrown a shameless eye on Charlie, but I told him the horse is not for sale for love nor money. He convinced me to let him ride him on reconnoiter earlier. I said so long as he didn't get us into a scrap and get the horse hurt, which would also get me hurt when you found out. He assured me he would care for him like his prize mare.

Off we go, gay as larks, looking for Yanks. Presently, several miles from camp, he spied a friend from West Point.

"Ho, Perk. I'm glad to see you joined Virginia."

His old friend Perkins was wearing Union blue, as we all are.

"Where's your unit?" Jeb called.

"Why, right here, Beauty." Over the hill comes a whole swarm of Union infantry flying old glory.

Jeb leaned forward. "The devil you say."

We spurred away in a hot gallop with bullets flying like angry hornets.

You'll be happy to know Charlie can outrun the warmest Yankee greeting.

As we were returning, Jeb said, "That was quite a hearty how doo back there."

"Yes, sir, it was."

"I confidently believe those rascals were shooting at us on purpose."

"I believe you're right, sir."

He has a knack for understatement at times.

I rode Charlie down to the river bareback afterwards and gave him a bath and myself as well. We earned it. Then I put my britches on and lay on the bank to let Charlie graze while I watched clouds and daydreamed about you.

My thoughts always drift to you. I imagined you were with me, sitting beside me reading poetry. Then you leaned over and stroked my chest as if to smooth the hair into some semblance of order. I closed my eyes, afraid you would stop. Your hand lifted, but I pulled you down to me and wore your face off with passionate kisses. I caressed your

*beautiful throat, kissing it tenderly, lingering more than
I should have.*

*Only the tiniest shred of decency convinced me to
preserve your honor and mine. My heart is breaking with
longing. Please do something with your mother before I
am forced to kidnap you and carry you away to the nearest
minister. Or Brother London, who is calling for mail now
so he can take it to town.*

*With all my everlasting love,
Captain Baron Patrick Callahan, CSA*

I set it aside with a sigh, having no idea how I might work
on my obstinate mother nor when I might see her again. The
problem was best mulled in the garden, so I cut flowers for fresh
arrangements.

My basket was only half full when Della came puffing out to
me like a steam engine. "Miss Mac, some man at the door says
he wants to talk to you about buying a mule." Her face wrinkled
up like a walnut in disapproval that I would stoop to speaking to
a stranger about a mule.

"How dare he! I'll take these shears to protect myself in case
he has nefarious plans. Where did you leave the scoundrel?"

"I set him on the veranda with some tea." She said this with
disdain as if I doubted she'd extend every courtesy on my behalf,
vagrant or not. "No reason Jacob can't do that."

With basket in hand, I wound through the garden, thinking about arranging the flowers, what we were having for dinner,
and the current market for a prime mule. Wasn't life good?

Foolish me. Fox had wasted no time summoning me to
Baltimore with a nondescript mule buyer. We made a show of
looking at mules. After a great deal of haggling, which included
strategically placed information dropped in the conversation in
case anyone overheard us, he bought a young jenny. I would take
the train to Alexandria, where the contraband carriage would

be waiting for me at Harbor Brothers. "Hire a driver at Harbor Brothers to drive to Washington."

"I'll take my own man if you don't mind. I can depend on him, and he's quiet." Jacob would defend me, but I wasn't sure about a stranger.

My contact in Alexandria worked for a dentist named Dr. Styles. Since I didn't know when I'd arrive, he'd fit me in for an "appointment." With any luck, there would be no soldiers in the office who might notice me. He'd give me information for my handler, who would meet me in Baltimore. It was all very mysterious. If all went well, I'd pick up the contraband carriage a few days later to spirit it away along with information that had been passed to me to the people waiting for it.

"Keep your eyes out for someone following you," he added lastly. "Get rid of the information if you feel you're in danger."

"How?" I didn't ask how I would know I was in danger.

"Eating it is the surest way. I always carry a flask of water or whiskey to wash it down if needed. Paper can be tough to swallow."

I stared at him aghast. "This is a jest?"

"No, ma'am. It doesn't happen often, but it can. Be prepared."

❧

Two days later, with nerves fluttering like moths in a wool factory, I was on my way to Alexandria. Thankfully, most of the trip was by train. I took Jacob to drive, and Imogene, who wanted to visit her aunt and uncle.

The Union soldier with wide, unsure eyes, trying to be a man, trying harder to grow a mustache, and barely keeping the squeak out of his voice, halted us at the edge of the train platform where we disembarked. "State your business," he said. He shifted the musket on his shoulder as if to enforce his importance.

"State my business? Since when have I had to explain why I travel?" I waved my hand. "Never mind. Since we've been invaded by the blue horde. I'm here to see my dentist. Imogene's visiting family, and then we're going to Baltimore." Soldiers checked passes of people surging around us in waves and glared at us for delaying their inspections.

"You need passports by declaration of Colonel Wilcox."

"I've been coming here all my life. Now we need passes?" I asked incredulously.

"I'm sorry, ma'am. You need to see the provost, Captain Whittelsey, to get them."

Another soldier, older, with brown, brushy whiskers sprouting down his jaws, stomped toward us. Whereas the first one reminded me of a young sapling unsure of which way to bend in the wind, this one was a gruff old bear. "Private! What's the matter here?"

"These ladies don't have passes. This one," he pointed to me, "needs—"

"I don't need their life histories, interesting as they may be; take them to the provost and get passes or get them out of town. Either way, get them off my damned platform."

"Is it far?" I asked.

"No, ma'am," replied our new guide.

"We'll walk. We've been cooped up for a while."

"I'll wait for the luggage to get unloaded and then be along to get a pass," said Jacob. We'd continue to Baltimore when the carriage was ready, but he wanted to return to Alexandria and stay with his father so they could visit. Though I wasn't crazy about him staying in occupied territory, he viewed Mother as a plague and could tolerate her only in small doses.

Our reluctant guide told him where the provost's office was and hustled us off the platform when he saw his sergeant barreling toward us once more.

Alexandria swarmed with Union troops who either hurried by on important missions or lounged about as if there were nothing to do and nowhere to go. The poor boy tried to herd us along, but we strolled with parasols aloft as I listened for any scrap of useful information.

Civilians crowded the provost's office, complaining about everything from the price of tea to a purloined house. The army possessed their businesses, their homes, and their lives. Our guide looked about for chairs, but none were to be had. "I'm sorry, ladies. I'll see if I can get someone to help you." He whispered to a harried aide who looked at us and nodded. Imogene turned to face the hapless man. Her very large, very blue eyes widened. Then she beamed her let-there-be-light smile on him, the one that made people think all their cares would melt away in her mere presence. He returned a sunstruck smile that showed he was already a believer. They always were. "Yes, ma'am. How can I help?"

After we briefly explained our problem, he promised to assist us as soon as possible.

Our soldier tipped his cap and scooted back to the safety of war, where he might only be shot instead of bludgeoned by irate townspeople. The aide returned with a frowning woman clutching papers in hand and ushered in a young couple with an apologetic shrug to me. I didn't mind waiting as even the complaints bore information. Where supplies were being stored. Where the prisoners were—ironically, the slave pens. Where troops stayed and how many.

Captain Whittelsey agreed to see us at last. He was younger than I expected for such responsibility, in his thirties, no more. Dark, wavy hair and whiskers ran down his jaws to meet his mustache that twitched up following a brief and weary smile.

He stood when we entered the room and waited until we sat to resettle in a tobacco-colored, high-back leather chair behind a walnut partner desk with carved acanthus leaf columns on each corner. Green leather inlaid the desktop, where you could see it, but mostly, it was covered in papers and maps. The office matched the sumptuous furniture. How loudly did the previous owner object when the federals evicted him? Whittelsey was a firm, rod-straight man who would broach no foolery or simpering. The sole softness lay in his eyes, which were puffed with purple shadows beneath, betraying fatigue, and, though I felt some twinge of conscience, pressed my case.

"Captain, my name is Lorena McKenzie, and this is one of my teachers, Imogene Boudreaux. We're from Winchester. Imogene has family here and would like to visit them. I need to see Dr. Styles about a tooth before I go to Baltimore. We'll need a pass to cross into Washington. Plus, my man Jacob is here."

He leaned wearily back in his chair. "What's your business in Baltimore?"

Pressing forward with feminine urgency, I barreled on. "You must be exhausted between your army and all these civilians!" I said, waving my hand toward the commotion beyond the door. "Mother is in poor health. I travel frequently to tend to her. My father passed in October and left me the farm with my boarding school. I divide my time between tending Mother and my business. Truly, I wouldn't trouble you if I had any other choice."

"There's no other family to help?"

"My brother is dead. Once I get Mother situated, I need to see about my school supplies. I hope that won't be a problem."

Imogene bowed her head in solidarity with pitiful me.

"What supplies?" He asked this as if he wished me, my supplies, and the entire civilian population gone, as he had no interest whatsoever but was required by cruel fate to deal with us.

"Paper, watercolors, ink. The normal school things."

"And why is Miss Boudreaux going to Baltimore?"

"She'll take care of school business while I meet with Mother's doctor and care for her."

He pinched the bridge of his nose and closed his eyes.

"Are you unwell?" Imogene asked.

"Just a headache."

"For one thing, you aren't getting enough rest. But try—let me show you." She walked around to his side of the desk and took his hand. "I'm sorry for being forward, but it's easier to demonstrate than explain." Pinching the webbing between his thumb and forefinger, she massaged it in small circles. He at first tried to pull his hand away but was too astonished to object. "Do this for a couple of minutes to each hand. Then—do you mind if I touch your neck?"

What is she doing? I had never seen her be so bold before.

She moved behind him and tilted his head forward a bit. "Feel down a bit from your skull. About two fingers into this hollow on either side. Rub here for a while to relieve stress."

With the captain thoroughly massaged, she returned to her chair. "A doctor in Paris showed me this. The headache should ease soon. When a headache's coming on, try it."

He frowned slightly, touching his neck where she'd massaged it. "Thank you."

Within moments, we had individual passes with broad terms, and he even gave me Jacob's pass.

"Thank you, sir," I said and wished him well.

"Be safe, ladies."

"Well done," I whispered on our way out.

We hurried away before the spell lifted and he changed his mind. A group of loitering soldiers ahead of us watched a young lady passing by. They said nothing; nevertheless, their presence and looks were enough to inflame her. "Beasts," she snapped and spat on one.

The soldier she hit was leaning against the building with one leg crossed over the other. He whipped his hat off with one hand and grabbed her arm with the other so fast she had no chance to escape or cry out. I was sure he was about to strike her, but, to my surprise, he pulled her to his chest and kissed her. He let her loose, pulled her back, and kissed her fully a dozen times. His friends cheered him on until he finally released the mortified girl, who ran screaming with skirts hiked.

I looked at Imogene, who was as astonished as I was. The soldiers were ten feet in front of us. We could cross the street and avoid them, but I was averse to running from trouble. We squared our shoulders and stepped out.

"How about you?" the kissing sergeant asked when we neared. "Would you like to trade a little spit for a kiss?" He was tall and blond, with twinkling blue eyes and high black boots with spurs. I longed for a cavalryman's kiss, but not this one.

"Certainly not! I refuse to have anything to do with a man who has to kiss a woman a dozen times before he gets it right." With the sergeant's game turned on him and his friends carrying him high, we continued. Imogene decided to shop for her aunt, and I hurried to Dr. Styles, who I'd been assured would see me without an appointment. Like the provost's office, this one was equally crowded. The difference was that four Union soldiers and one middle-aged woman primping her hair were busy chatting away. I hesitated, the door open behind me, the bell still ringing, and quelled the urge to flee.

"Come in, Miss McKenzie. Right on time. It won't be long." I stared at the aproned youngster who entered the waiting room from a back hallway. Darcy Hawkins had transformed from a stable boy to a frail, bespectacled dental assistant. He motioned to an empty chair near a Union captain.

"Thank you." I slipped in, trying to recover my composure and hoping to pass it off as nervousness, which I was, but not for the usual reasons. I settled in with my hands primly folded in my lap and my parasol propped up against the white beadboard wall. He ushered me back when the next patient left and settled me into a red leather chair.

"It's good to see you," he said, blocking the door with a chair and tugging out a recalcitrant bottom drawer. Fishing around for a moment, he retrieved an envelope. Replacing the drawer, he returned to me and leaned close as if examining my mouth. "Pass this on to your contact in Baltimore," he whispered. "Keep it someplace on your person in case your belongings are searched." He slipped the envelope into my hand, which I slid under my purse. "So far, they aren't searching women closely, so you should be fine. Your contact in Baltimore will tell you where to get your boots repaired. Ask him to repair them with red glue. They'll put messages in the heels to leave with Bradshaw Shoe Store here." He replaced the dental tool on the tray and set the chair upright. "Good luck."

"Can you watch the door while I put this in my corset?" I furtively unbuttoned my dress and slid the envelope inside, my heart hammering so hard I wondered if he could hear it.

So, this was it. I was a spy. He retied the bow at my throat when my trembling fingers failed and whispered, "You'll be fine."

We continued to the front, where I paid my bill and accepted two bottles of pain medicine. I already knew I was to collect medicine whenever I could.

Waiting outside the door was a Union captain with four soldiers behind him, including the kissing sergeant. Moses, Mary, and Joseph! Soldiers everywhere. I closed the door and stepped in front of the window, hoping Darcy would at least see I was being hauled off.

He glanced at me through the window before escorting another patient back.

Imogene slowed to a stop down the street. She turned to the shop front as if admiring a display, stealing fleeting looks at me.

The captain removed his hat. "I'm Captain Goodtree."

"Captain." I let him take the lead in this dance, volunteering no conversation. Sweat trickled between my breasts.

"I understand you had a confrontation with my men earlier." He motioned toward the smiling sergeant standing beside him.

"I assure you, sir. I did nothing to your men." *Dear heavens. Was I going to get arrested for my sass on my first mission?*

"That isn't what I hear. According to one and all, you cut Smith down to size neatly. I'd like to apologize, as would he. Might we take you and your friend to supper tonight?"

The sergeant removed his hat also. "Indeed, ma'am. I am sorry, all the same; I don't apologize for kissing the young lady who spat on me."

I nearly collapsed in relief. "Oh, I haven't found a room yet, so I don't know our plans."

"The Mansion is lovely. Would six be agreeable?"

I waved at Imogene, who was still playing at window shopping. "Imogene," I called, "come here; you need no more clothes to cram in your trunks."

She looked suitably surprised and hurried toward us. Arriving breathless with her lips and cheeks flushed, she cast her spell on the lot of them. Her eyes went saucer wide. "Lorena! What have you done?"

The captain held out his arm to catch her if she swooned. "Nothing at all, ma'am. My man apologized for the earlier unpleasantness." She draped a gloved hand lightly over his arm and put the other hand to her chest in relief.

The door behind us opened with a tinkling bell, and Darcy swept his way out to the street. He paid no mind other than to sweep around the men.

"Imogene, the captain has invited us to supper," I said brightly. With my all-clear signal delivered, Darcy finished sweeping and retreated.

"Let's get you to the hotel. My name is Captain Aidan Goodtree. This is the infamous Sergeant Colin Smith, and here are Bram Kinney, Len Azza, and Thomas Humboldt."

Imogene's magnetism drew men to her like lacewings to lamps. If I were the jealous sort, I'd seethe at the interest focused on her, but she was here for precisely this reason. Like a magician, I needed a distraction to pull my rabbit out of the hat. My companions were pleasant enough, asking about my business in Alexandria and my school. Imogene's azure skirts before us swished hypnotically with each step, making me believe the men with me didn't mind not being at her side.

"Out of curiosity," I said, "how did you know where I was?"

The men shuffled about awkwardly until Goodtree confessed. "They were all whooping it up when I came out, so I asked what happened. When they explained, I gave a boy a dime to find you. I knew you wouldn't be far."

I gave him an appropriately shocked look. "Why, Captain. I might have been buying contraband tea."

Smith and Kinney shot uncomfortable glances toward the captain when I mentioned contraband. Apparently, this was a grave issue. My overtaxed instinct for survival screamed at me to abandon this fool's errand and flee back to Rosemount. I waited with hitched breath and a nervous smile for his response.

Goodtree's voice took on an official note, but a teasing twinkle remained in his eye. "In that case, I'd have to detain you. Regretfully, of course. Please don't do that."

"Your house, I suppose."

"Of course. The jail is full of scoundrels, and the captured rebels are in the slave pens. That's no place for a lady."

Humboldt, a good foot taller than me, looked down and shook his finger. "The captain is serious about contraband."

Imogene deftly turned the discussion to the men, who all shared details about their lives. They were disappointed to reach the hotel, vowing we were fascinating conversationalists. Soldiers leaning on the balcony railing above us called down to the captain, who responded with a friendly wave. Stars and stripes bunting draped across the balcony, proclaiming the hotel's loyalty. No wonder at the hotel owner's patriotic display, regardless of his personal allegiance. Lincoln's troops had invaded Alexandria on May 24, the day Virginia ratified secession. Mr. Jackson's Marshall House Inn had flown an oversized Confederate flag, taunting Washington in the days leading up to secession. Colonel Elmer Ellsworth, a personal friend of Lincoln's, had vowed the flag would come down and charged into the hotel to seize it. Jackson said it would come down over his dead body and shot Ellsworth as he bounded down the stairs with it, whereupon Ellsworth's Fire Zouaves had killed the hotelier in retaliation. It had been in all the papers. Lincoln had been inconsolable, and the Union army had exacted revenge on the Alexandria citizens. I doubted anyone else desired to die for a flag.

Federals had swarmed through like hungry locusts. Businesses such as hotels were commandeered quickly, but homes left vacant from the hasty evacuation, making the city nearly a ghost town, were also snatched up. Soldiers greatly outnumbered civilians, and locals who remained did so at the pleasure of their new masters.

I had planned to slip quietly into town and visit Dr. Boudreaux before moving on, but our plans shifted like oil on water, and now we were committed to supper with a group of Union soldiers.

With rooms arranged, someone dispatched for our trunks and delivered a message to Jacob. Imogene set off to see her aunt and uncle. He, like many doctors, maintained his practice from his home. When Imogene returned from her aunt and uncle's, she was laden with art supplies and information. Her uncle was seething with the occupation, and her aunt refused to leave the house. There was a killing a day. Homes of God-fearing folk that hadn't been claimed by Federals were being turned into brothels. Saloons sprang up wherever they could cart liquor and chairs. Fights erupted in the streets between soldiers and soldiers and soldiers and civilians. Bored soldiers spent their time drinking and gambling, which led to more strife. The doctor refused to treat them until recently, when told he had no choice. The stress put his wife in bed much of the time, and she refused to eat.

"I don't know that I blame her," Imogene said after recounting Alexandria's chaos. "Uncle confided she has a severe heart condition, and he's worried to death about her. I made her promise she'd eat. I'd stay with her to help with the house, and I had a plan I needed help with."

"And what plan is that?" I watched with interest as she set out pencils, rubbers, watercolors, and papers precisely, along with a bottle of clear liquid and a pen.

"A plan to use this bedlam against them." She sketched out a landscape with quick strokes, tapping the pencil against her chin before drawing another line. Studying the paper and measuring distances with her fingers, she laid in more lines and shades. Hills and trees appeared with dashed lines and triangles.

"What are you doing?"

"Replicating a battle map. I hope." She took a green crayon and filled a corner of the drawing.

"A battle map?"

"Yes. While massaging the captain's hand, I studied the map on his desk. If I get this right, it might be of use."

I rushed to the door to make sure it was locked. Back at her side, I whispered, "Imogene, you can't do this."

"Why not?"

"What if you get caught?"

"What if *you* get caught?"

"What do you mean?"

She put down the rubber she'd taken out a misplaced line with. "Don't play the innocent. Though that was a fine pair of horses you sold Major Fox, I know who he is and what he is. My cousin's been with him for a year. I suspect he's recruited you also, and that's why you suddenly decided to answer your mother's pleas after vowing you'd never set foot in Baltimore again."

The air rushed out of me. What chance did I have among the enemy if I'd been discovered this easily? "Who else suspects?"

"No one. Everyone at Rosemount knows how insistent your mother is, and you raise horses to sell. It was by sheerest coincidence I was at my aunt's farm when Fox and my cousin rode in."

I sat in the chair near the window, pondering how to proceed. Fox hadn't authorized me to add new operatives. "We should get ready for supper," I said, setting the problem aside.

We descended before six, but our gentlemen were already waiting. Imogene chose a peach satin off-the-shoulder gown. Silk rosebuds and pearls sprinkled through her honey blonde hair. The men stood, enraptured—I knew they would be. She lowered her lashes and smiled in that charming, off-kilter way that gave the impression her mouth was still trying to make up its mind if it was amused.

They were all in dress uniforms, trimmed in heavy gold braid with rows of gleaming brass buttons marching up their chests. Gold sashes bound each waist and were cinched with polished black leather belts. The brass buckles with U.S. letters proudly branded them property of the American army. Shiny, tall black boots and spurs further identified them all as cavalry. Six repentant soldiers surged forward to introduce themselves.

The men fell into order promptly. Even a blind person knows a man's looks are improved by uniforms, and all that brass and embroidery positively gleamed in the light of the hotel's gaslight chandeliers, making these particular specimens glitter like knights. They might have been shopkeepers, schoolteachers, students, or farmers weeks ago, but they looked every inch the soldier tonight.

A newcomer to the group named Dublin took my arm. "You ladies look lovely."

"Thank you. You gentlemen polish up nicely yourselves. Had we known you were here, we might have visited sooner."

The hotel prepared a large round table draped in white linen for us. Flickering candles in low silver holders cast a pleasant golden glow on the cordial faces of our escorts. Dublin took his place beside me. Captain Goodtree sat on my other side with Humboldt beside him. Smith, Azza, and Kinney accompanied Imogene. It was a precise maneuver.

Impressed, I asked Dublin. "Are you gentlemen always so organized?"

"Pardon?"

"I'm curious how you arrived at the seating arrangement."

Dublin looked at Captain Goodtree, hesitated, and cleared his throat. "That blackheart Smith got his choice since it was his scoundrel act what got us the invitation. The rest of us played for position except the captain, who pulled rank."

I turned to Goodtree, surprise plain on my face, I was sure. "Why would you pull rank to sit with me?"

"Traitor!" He cast a withering glance toward his lieutenant. "Dublin, we need to discuss how to resist enemy interrogation soon. It's good she didn't ask you for battle plans."

A waiter in a white coat reached between us to serve wine. I lifted the glass and said conspiratorially. "Oh, that comes later."

Goodtree laughed. "For God's sake, someone lock Dublin up. To answer. I'm intrigued by a woman with spirit. I'd have paid good money to see Smith's face when you cut him down."

"I assure you," Smith protested. "I took it in good grace like a man."

"Like a man clubbed between the eyes," said Azza.

The arrival of our waitress interrupted discussions of Smith's manliness. Not that I didn't find it amusing, but my last meal was a bit of fruit. I was famished. "I should order something delicate," I said, not yet decided.

"Nonsense," Goodtree replied. "Smith's paying. Order the biggest steak in the house with all the trimmings."

Imogene giggled. "Don't encourage her. You haven't seen her eat."

I faked a frown. "The captain isn't the only one with a traitor in his midst." I turned to our waitress. "Mary Stuart soup, saddle of venison with the juniper sauce, browned potatoes, and asparagus if it's good. Dinner rolls, please."

"See! I told you," Imogene crowed.

Chowders and the Mary Stuart soup appeared shortly, sending me into ecstasy. I tilted toward Dublin to take in the scent of his clam chowder. My eyes closed, and nostrils flared. When I opened them, everyone at the table was staring at me. "Miss McKenzie?" Dublin said, holding his hand out as if he thought I was about to topple. Are you all right?"

"Moses." I straightened. "I'm so sorry. Your chowder smelled so good—"

"I told you," Imogene said. "She loves food. If anyone wants to lure her away, bait her with food. She'll follow blindly into the trap like a little mouse."

"It's not that bad," I mumbled amidst the laughter. The barley and swirled egg blended perfectly in the creamed soup before me. In between chicken-flavored bites, I inquired where they were all from. Each was from the north except Azza, who was from Florida.

Two of the men were West Point graduates, including Goodtree. Imogene glanced around the dining room, which was brimming with blue, and sighed. "So many soldiers. It breaks my heart to think of what our country has come to."

"Have you heard of General Beauregard?" Goodtree asked. His question arrived with the entrées. I was surprised by both the question and the speedy service.

"I have," I said noncommittally, slicing into the venison. *Was the question a trap?*

"He's from Louisiana. He graduated second in his class from West Point with one of the better records, eight demerits if I recall. That's difficult to do. You can easily get that many for missing church. Beauregard desperately wanted to be superintendent of West Point and petitioned for the position. He was surprisingly named to it in December and assumed command on January 23. Louisiana seceded on the 26th. Beauregard was asked to relinquish command, which he did two days later. It was the shortest command in West Point history. That's the way this conflict will go. President Lincoln called troops for ninety days, and that's all it'll take."

"I pray you're right," I said, hoping he was right, fearing he was not.

"Miss Boudreaux said she might be staying. Are you staying also?" Goodtree asked.

"No, I need to see my mother in Baltimore."

"I see," he said. "I'm from Baltimore. Have you been to the Holliday Theatre?"

"Frequently. I love it but have a boarding school, so I can't travel as much as I'd like. Edwin Booth played Romeo the last time I attended. He was marvelous."

Dublin laughed. "A fellow fan. He's likely America's greatest actor."

"Dublin," the captain growled and shook a finger at him, "are you purloining my game? You're from Michigan. What do you know about theater?"

"I'm from Michigan, not darkest Africa," Dublin protested.

"Miss Boudreaux, would you mind if I posted someone at your aunt's home for security?" Goodtree asked. "I'm sure there'd be no lack of volunteers."

Imogene smiled, but I recognized the faint tremor of fear. She'd already expressed how they felt about being invaded by federals. Still, it was a raucous and unsafe city, and I felt safer with her under guard. Perhaps it would keep her from roaming too much. "Of course," she said. "If it's not an inconvenience."

They rushed to assure her it wasn't. There would be another card game soon to set the duty roster, and I pondered how an officer might explain wanting to stand guard.

"Will you be having dessert?" our waitress asked later, wheeling in a pastry cart.

"Yes," Smith said. "She'll have Parker House Cream Pie."

I nearly swooned at the dessert set in front of me. "Is this your favorite, Sergeant Smith?"

"Yes, my parents used to take us to Parker House in Boston on Sundays after church."

After dessert and coffee, we settled into amiable conversation and more wine. The waiter tried to refill my wine glass, but I declined. "Are you sure you won't enjoy one more glass?" Dublin asked.

"I can't. You'd be carrying me up the stairs shortly."

"I don't think he'd mind," said Goodtree. "I'd pull rank on him regardless."

"He would," Dublin said sadly. "He's soulless."

"Imogene, we should retire. I'd like to leave early if the carriage is ready."

"Yes, and I need to move my trunks to Uncle's."

"We'll move your things," Goodtree offered. "There's no sense paying a porter."

Imogene raised a brow at me. It would be suspicious if one of them asked to escort me to the carriage and it was still being refurbished. "Perhaps 8:00?" I replied.

"Perfect," said Goodtree. "It'll give me a chance to get everyone in order."

"Of course," grumbled Dublin. "No chance you could stay in camp."

"None." Goodtree twirled the end of his black mustache dramatically. Even Dublin had to laugh at that.

"You'd pull rank on me anyway."

Goodtree smoothed his mustache back. "You know me so well."

"It's because you're soulless."

"We've already established that," replied Goodtree.

"We should return to our room," I said, laughing at their good-hearted ribbing. It was hard to dislike them. "Captain Goodtree, I'll pray for you to get a soul."

Despite my desire to hate these men, I couldn't bring myself to do so. If anything, I hated politicians who race to war and never pay the price. And yet, here I was on a mission to confound the same men I had dined with. Maybe I hated myself a bit, also.

Chapter Thirty-Three

True to their word, they were waiting for us the next morning and had gathered a few more to the fold. I wondered if anything got done with all the lollygagging, but with the number of troops encamped in a largely deserted city, there might be little to occupy their time.

I was surprised to see Azza and Dublin step forward to take our arms. "Not pulling rank this morning, Captain Goodtree?"

He shrugged nonchalantly. "I felt magnanimous and declined to cut the cards."

"I'm impressed."

He bowed. "I knew you would be."

Dublin groaned. "Law. I can't win even when I win."

"If you don't mind, we'd like to accompany you to your aunt and uncle's, Miss Boudreaux. I'll introduce them to the men and explain that we'll be standing guard to offer protection. I wouldn't want to show up unannounced and alarm them."

"I think that's wise," Imogene said. "They only live a few blocks from here if you don't mind walking." She pointed to her trunks, which were promptly loaded onto a waiting wagon.

The gentlemen visited cordially and talked about their homes and families, duties, and plans once they returned home as we walked. We talked about the school, our star pupils, and our not-so-star pupils, Lucille and Persy.

"I'm sure the little girls aren't that bad," Smith said in his proper upper-crust Boston accent. "I've never met a Southern girl who wasn't truly a delicate flower. I confess I'm smitten."

"Yes, delicate flowers." I asked Smith if he'd played marbles as a boy.

"I surely did," he replied proudly. "I had two jars of marbles I'd won."

"The last time we went to town with the girls, Persy and Lucille disappeared. We finally found them behind a billiard hall shooting marbles. The girls nearly skunked the boys, but Persy made a particularly nice haul. I was closing in on her when one of the boys lost his marble. He jumped up and accused her of cheating, then threatened to whup her if she didn't give his marbles back. She dropped the marble in her bag, which was filled near to bursting, and hit him in the eye with it.

"I was sure he was about to trounce her, him being a full head taller than her and the two girls surrounded by half a dozen boys. He doubled his fists, but she popped him in the nose and bloodied it before he could blink. The other boys were so dumbfounded they didn't know what to do.

"'Lucille screamed, 'Hit him again! Hit him again!' while we tried to pull the two away," Imogene added with a laugh.

I nodded. "The boy's wail brought Mama and Daddy running. She insisted I punish my ruffian immediately."

The men erupted in laughter. "Did you punish your delicate flower?" Smith asked.

"Daddy said, 'Actually, Flora, I believe I'm going to tan him for fighting with a little girl and especially for getting whipped by her.' Daddy made the boy apologize to Persy, who decided to give him back his prize marble but refused to part with the rest, they being the spoils of victory."

The soldiers raised a cheer. "Hear, hear. To Persy!"

"Indeed," I said. "To our delicate flowers."

"We should pay a visit to the school," Smith said.

I trembled, stomach quailing at the thought of a troop of Union soldiers descending on Rosemount.

Smith looked horror-stricken. "I meant after hostilities are ended, of course."

Though I preferred to leave early, I also wanted to see Imogene safely settled and make sure the Boudreauxs wouldn't be offended by soldiers standing guard. I felt like I was racing on thin ice and feared that if I stopped, the whole of it would come crashing under me.

Imogene drew them out, remarking on this and that and spreading her attention like warm taffy.

Dublin pressed my arm, guiding me away from two boys racing past. "Have you always wanted to be a teacher?"

"In the South, a young lady learns important things like watercolor and poetry, needlework, and how to run a household. We're expected to grow up and marry well. Those who become teachers are either dedicated or unfortunate. I simply enjoy teaching."

"I see. Do you have any other bad habits?"

Imogene laughed, "Shall I list them?"

"I'm capable, thank you. I'm hot-tempered and bullheaded; my mother thinks I'm a perfect heathen, though no one is perfect, and I eat too much. I love good food. Mother contends no decent man will bespeak me if I don't mend my ways, but that doesn't stop her matchmaking."

The affable chatter continued until we arrived at the olive-green Victorian with brick red and cream trim and a neatly lettered sign announcing Dr. Boudreaux's practice.

A. Boudreaux M.D.
Physician and Surgeon
Elixirs
Splints
Remedies
Trusses
Animals doctored when time permits.

Crimson roses, with velveted petals, mounded over the generous lot's white picket fences. Their heady scent so intoxicated me, I might have lingered there awash in it, had I been alone.

We flowed through the gate and up the walk, a sea of blue surrounding Imogene in her virginal white organza. She knocked on the door while the men filed onto the porch. The young girl who answered the door took in the soldiers, and her wide, welcoming grin faded to horror. "Missus B! Missus B! The army's here, and they done got Miss Imogene!"

The alarm rang throughout the house and was quickly taken by others. "Law, let me find my aunt." Imogene raced after the frightened girl. "Nettie, stop!"

I glanced apologetically at Dublin and the others, who stirred uncomfortably, scuffling boots on the wooden porch. Azza whispered he hoped they didn't get shot as someone had last week. Presently, the lady of the house appeared, judging from her finely wrought and pearled chatelaine. She smiled and motioned us into her home, but I noticed the tension straining her delicate features like the wind tugging at a tender line about to snap. Imogene stood to her side, and the house servants flocked closely behind their mistress, eyes wide.

"Come in, gentlemen," Mrs. Boudreaux said. "The doctor's with a patient, so if you don't mind my company?"

I was positive they were pleased simply to be met with a smiling, if slightly unsettled hostess, instead of buckshot. She led us into a large parlor where servants bustled about bringing in dining room chairs, and just as quickly, Mrs. Bastrom, the cook, appeared ushering in trays of drinks like a herd of men appeared in their parlor every morning. Opposite the parlor was a music room with various instruments, including a grand piano, harp, harpsichord, and stringed instruments in cases and on stands. The home spoke to the successful practice of Dr. Boudreaux and his wife's good taste in decor and music, she being a classically trained pianist, according to Imogene. In the corner, a bronze Mercury with caduceus in hand glared sternly from his pedestal.

The nod to medicine was balanced by a bronze of the three muses in the opposite corner.

"Imogene tells me you are her friends," Mrs. Boudreaux said tentatively.

"Yes, ma'am," Goodtree replied, hat balanced on his knee. "I've offered to post a guard for your family's safety until things are more settled if that wouldn't offend you. I realize—"

A woman's scream rent the air, causing several men to jump and dash toward the sound. Azza dropped his glass and clambered after it as it rolled across the thick Turkish carpet.

"Good God. What was that?" Dublin exclaimed.

Mrs. Boudreaux motioned the men down. "Please. Mrs. Loonstra is in labor. It's been a long and difficult one."

Azza dropped to his knees, mopping at the spill with his handkerchief and stumbling over himself with embarrassed apologies.

"It's fine," Mrs. Boudreaux said. "Nettie will get it. With five children, we've had worse spilled. As to the guards, I'll talk to my husband, but given current…conditions, it couldn't hurt."

Imogene turned the full force of her charm on Azza, whose cheeks were flaming from his companion's jibes. "You have the most intriguing eyes. Beguiling, even. I'd love to sketch you if you're willing."

He agreed and immediately rose in stature with his friends. Imogene also offered to sketch the others. They'd be delighted to show her the camps and interesting sights.

I frowned at her, trying to warn her off, but she avoided my gaze like a dog with a hen in its mouth.

For her previous reservations, Mrs. Boudreaux warmed to the men who visited about their homes and families in between screams from the back. Being of good Georgia stock and raised to never slouch, her back remained stick straight, but the stiffness gradually melted from her shoulders. I felt more at ease leaving Imogene in Alexandria; however, if anyone found out she was making sketches and recording troop information, no amount of goodwill might save her.

"I should be going," I said. "I still have a journey ahead of me."

"We should also," Goodtree remarked. "I've some leeway, but duties nonetheless." The men collectively let out a sigh of relief. As gamely as they tried to ignore the painful cries, which were becoming fewer, they were obviously distressed. Humboldt vowed never to have children. Mrs. Boudreaux assured him once the babe was laid in Mrs. Loonstra's arms, she would forget the pain. He was dubious about that bit of magic.

"Lorena, before you go, I want to send something to your mother," Imogene said.

We swept out of the room to the end of the hall that led to the kitchen. There, she lit a lamp, and we hurried to the basement. Lining the walls were shelves of canned vegetables and fruits, various types of meats, sauces, and jellies. Against a far wall was an assortment of traveling trunks and cast-off furniture. "Hold this." She handed me the lamp and knelt to open a dome-top steamer. Setting the trays aside, she sorted through the layers of clothing and pulled out a blue cloth. "Take this with you," she whispered. "They can't get caught with it."

"What is it?"

"The Bonnie Blue."

Immediately, I understood. Many families had been flying the Confederate flag when Alexandria was invaded. After Mr. Jackson was shot, the flags came down. Despite an oath of allegiance, flags would prove they were Confederate sympathizers and lose all. I also understood why they didn't destroy it.

It took finagling, but at last, it was tied around my waist and smoothed under my skirts. Pray God it didn't come loose until I could safely stow it somewhere. I took care to lift my skirts and the underlying flag high as I mounted the stairs. I now understood why Imogene urged me to wear the indigo dress today.

We had just reached the kitchen when someone banged on the door, demanding entrance. "Who on earth can that be?" Imogene asked. We scurried after the rest of the household to find an irate Union major with a paper in his hand and four soldiers brandishing rifles. They were garbed in garish blue and white striped pantaloons, deep blue waistcoats with ornate gold bullion braid, and red sashes. Red silk cords and ostrich feathers adorned the black Hardee hats, completing the uniforms.

"I'll see the doctor now, madam," the major demanded, pushing his way into the hallway. Soldiers from both groups, house staff, Mrs. Boudreaux, Imogene, and I formed a considerable mass spilling into the hallway, music room, and parlor.

"The doctor's birthing a patient, and you'll remove those guns from my house immediately!" Mrs. Boudreaux spat, her face flushed with rage.

"Here now," Goodtree said, "there's no need to threaten these ladies. Stand down." The Goodtree group and the new group faced off as if about to come to fisticuffs.

The major, a man of about forty with the look and air of a pettifogger, puffed up like a toad. "You'd best recognize my rank, Captain, if you want to stay in this army."

"Seeing as I'm career army from West Point, I can smell a conscription officer a mile away. I'm not concerned. What do you want with the Boudreauxs?"

I'd heard the term before in Charleston. What a way to run an army. Regardless, this particular one outranked Goodtree and posed a genuine threat. Thank God the flag was safely hidden.

"Dr. Boudreaux hasn't signed an oath of allegiance." He waved a paper in his hand. "I've been ordered to evict anyone without one." To Mrs. Boudreaux, who paled ghost white and clutched at Imogene for support, he commanded, "You have fifteen minutes to gather what personals you may require."

She looked desperately to Goodtree. "Mrs. Loonstra absolutely can't move. Please explain."

"Major," Goodtree said, "we'll get the paper."

"No excuses. Take me to Boudreaux."

Mrs. Boudreaux sighed and leaned heavily on Imogene's arm. Her complexion waned severely, and her breath labored. "He *cannot* leave," she rasped.

We and the entire mad troop crowded the hall toward the surgery. Dr. Boudreaux's urgent voice rose behind the closed door as we neared. Mrs. Boudreaux knocked on the door, but the major shoved her aside and pushed his way through.

"Get out of here this instant," shouted Dr. Boudreaux.

A young woman, dark hair plastered with sweat, lay in a bed with a distraught man in a chair by her side, a farmer by the looks of him. He looked helplessly between the soldiers pouring into the room, the doctor, and his wife. She clenched his hand. "What's happening?" he asked. "Doctor? My wife."

Mrs. Boudreaux rushed to her husband's side. "Charles, these men are evicting us because we haven't signed the oath."

"Clearly," he snarled, "that isn't happening. Everyone get out of here now!"

Mrs. Loonstra groaned from the depths of her soul and pulled her husband to her. Humboldt looked as if he were going to be sick and fled.

The major motioned his men to level their rifles. "You've had enough time. She can spawn on the street for all I care."

Goodtree stepped in front of one of the men and slammed the rifle down, "For God's sake. Use some common sense."

"Fulkirk's Follies," Dublin whispered to me. "Major Fulkirk and his men are citizen volunteers. Total fop."

Dr. Boudreaux looked up from his patient. "Mary, go find that damnable paper."

She and Imogene rushed into the office. Goodtree whispered something to Smith, who raced out the door. Mrs. Loonstra cried out again as another pain racked her. Two of the major's men lost heart in the operation and slid out the door, taking some of Goodtree's men with them.

Mrs. Loonstra looked near death with exhaustion. Dr. Boudreaux pushed on her stomach, and I knew why the labor had been so difficult. The baby was breech. I glanced away from Mrs. Loonstra and toward the office next to the surgery room, where Mrs. Boudreaux and Imogene frantically searched through papers and drawers in the office next to the treatment room.

There was a strangled cry and thump.

Imogene ran back into the surgery. "Uncle, Aunt Mary fell."

The major motioned to the two remaining soldiers, who pointed their guns at her. "Stop! I'm not falling for this fainting Southern belle routine. Enough stalling. Turn these people out."

"My wife has a heart condition," Dr. Boudreaux said. "Get out of my way." He unlocked the medicine cabinet, snatched a small brown bottle, and hurried into the office. Kneeling beside his wife, he poured medicine into her mouth and massaged her throat to force it down. "You men, make yourselves useful and come in here." He held her wrist, feeling her pulse, and finally nodded for the men. "Follow Imogene with my wife to our room while I look for that damned paper."

Dublin scooped her up and followed Imogene toward the stairs. Fulkirk darted in front of him. "Haul her outside. I told you they've been evicted."

Dublin looked to Goodtree. "Sir?"

"Take her," Goodtree said, stepping between the major's gun and Dublin.

Dr. Boudreaux slammed books and drawers in the office for several minutes. "I can't find the damned thing now." Mrs. Loonstra was having another contraction, and he hurried back to her, lifted the sheet, cursed, and ordered everyone out of the room.

"Enough stalling," Fulkirk said and marched over toward the door. "I have my orders. Everyone outside."

Sliding around behind the major's back, I pulled the Deringer from my pocket and put it to his head. I should have done it sooner, but I had no idea the man would go this far. He jerked his head to the side and into the Deringer. "Now," I said venomously, "this is a gun pointed at your head. It isn't a large gun, but it's big enough to evict what little brain matter you have if you don't shut up. Dr. Boudreaux is going to deliver this baby, and you'll stop harassing him."

He started to turn his head, sputtering profanities.

I drove the barrel into his skull. "Don't move. As you say, we Southern belles are excitable. I'd hate to shoot you accidentally."

The major's two remaining men across the room raised their rifles at me and demanded I drop it. Imogene slipped inside the door, clutching her hands behind her as she sidled behind the major's men. "Lorena, what are you doing?" she quavered uncharacteristically.

"I'm holding this man hostage, so your uncle can finish his work."

Her voice took on a different, deadly note as she pulled a sawed-off shotgun from behind her back and leveled it at one of the major's men. "Good. Drop your guns and move into the hallway, or I swear I'll blow you in two right here."

"You'll go to prison or be shot for this," the major growled.

"That's not—Oh, sweet Mary." I saw what the doctor was cursing. Blood dripped to the floor. She was hemorrhaging. Her distraught husband, who'd spent his time trying to calm his wife during the chaos, buried his head against her chest, sobbing and choking out bits of prayers.

"Doctor," Mrs. Loonstra whispered and clutched him with a bloody hand, "save my baby."

Taking her hand, he squeezed it. "April, they stopped my orders. There's no chloroform."

"I don't care."

"What are you doing?" shouted Mr. Loonstra when the doctor pulled out a drawer of surgical instruments.

"I have to do a Caesarean section. I may be able to save your baby."

He arranged the instruments and took up a scalpel. Motioning to Goodtree's men, he swallowed and angrily wiped a sleeve across his eyes. "Make yourselves useful and come hold her like I show you if you can stomach it."

He took a piece of leather from a drawer and told her to bite on it. She pulled her husband closer to kiss him and whispered something to him. Her clenched knuckles whitened, contrasting even more sharply against her husband's large, tanned hand that held hers. She clamped the leather between her teeth and stared at the ceiling as if trying to bore a hole in it.

Layers of skin and muscle opened under Dr. Boudreaux's skillful touch. Mr. Loonstra looked away, unable to watch. His shoulders heaved. A surprised baby boy slipped into the world and his mother's arms. Her blue eyes locked on his, and a beatific smile lifted her lips, erasing the pain and exhaustion. The baby was still staring into his mother's face when the light left her eyes. It was a quiet, gentle passing like an angel's whisper. She simply took a deep breath and exhaled her soul.

A colonel burst into the house, accompanied by his own guards, and seized the situation after being apprised of what was happening by Smith. He apologized to me and the doctor, Mr. Loonstra. Mrs. Loonstra was dead, but her son survived. The colonel stormed about, livid at the major and feeling his interference contributed to the death of the mother. He ordered the buffoon and the two guards who helped terrorize the doctor's family back to Washington.

"Without orders, Colonel Wilcox?" the major cried, voice quivering. "We'll be shot for deserters."

"I goddamn well hope so. This army could do with a few less fools."

Dr. Boudreaux laid the babe in Mr. Loonstra's arms and stitched Mrs. Loonstra. Then he went to his office and, without the stress of guns and a beleaguered patient, found the oath of allegiance. Imogene apologized for not being able to find it, but he said it was his fault. He forgot they had been praying about it and left it in the Bible.

The colonel asked him out of curiosity where in the Bible it was. "Matthew 26:15," Dr. Boudreaux replied, signing the oath in bold, angry script. He dropped the bloodstained paper and sank in a chair next to Mrs. Loonstra's body, exhausted in spirit and body.

"Judas betraying Jesus for silver," the colonel said with a heavy sigh.

"Yes, now please leave."

The colonel forgave Imogene and me.

I bid a tearful farewell to Imogene. Goodtree's men were heartsick at the events of the day. They walked me back to the hotel with little conversation aside from curses toward the major, apologies, and assurances that not all Federals were that sorry.

Thankfully, Jacob waited for me at the hotel when I returned, as I was well ready to be shed of Alexandria.

Chapter Thirty-Four

With the contraband carriage delivered in Washington, I took the train to Baltimore. At Mother's house, Otis lowered his head like a mad bull and rushed through the door, giving the impression that he feared I might escape. The trio of ostrich plumes rising from the cockade in his silk top hat were tall enough to necessitate the lowered head, but the charge through the door negated the outfit's elegance. Gone was the carnival costume, and he now wore solid black aside from the blinding white shirt with the patricide collar. I stood for a moment, dumbfounded. "We go from one extreme to the other. Are you working at a funeral home in your spare time?"

He rolled his eyes and smoothed the black brocade vest. "Now, Miss Lorena. This is for your benefit. My reg'lar outfit's a black waistcoat with ten pounds of gold embroidery. And the hat. She loves the hat." I noted that in Baltimore, I remained "Miss Lorena." I had taken Papa's mantle on the farms and become "Miss Mac."

"What would you prefer?"

"Duck britches and a fishing pole, but something between Mortician Michael and Duke Dunder might be nice."

"I'll talk to Mother."

"Thank you."

"Lorena, is that you?" The call was so frail that I barely heard it above the luggage shuffling. The call came again, louder this time.

"Yes, Mother. It's me. Where are you?"

I rushed (she was dying, after all) to the parlor, where she was laid out dramatically on a black, red, and gold, mostly gold, ornately carved Chinese daybed that dominated the room. Red lacquer accents highlighted the recesses of the carving. It was breathtakingly gaudy. Mother wasn't physically ill. She'd gone insane.

She raised her hand, expending her last bit of dying energy, then coughed weakly. "I'm so glad you made it in time."

I knelt beside her. "I came as quickly as I could. Have you spoken to your doctor?" Fortunately for her, I needed to establish my contact, or she would have been forced to postpone her death.

She shifted in her pile of satin pillows, lashes fluttering. "Yes," she rasped. "I think he was crying. He's in the kitchen."

I pushed back the bed jacket's satin sleeve, kissed her perfumed hand, and rose. "I'll talk to him. Be strong."

She sank back onto her pillow pile with a dying Ophelia sigh. I wanted to cry out, "Brava! Brava!"

Dr. Frain sat at the kitchen table waving a half-eaten cookie in the air like a weapon, nearly upsetting the cup of coffee in front of him. Then he said dramatically, "'You, sir, are no gentleman. I demand satisfaction!'"

I stood still as a lawn jockey in the doorway, wondering who was being challenged.

"Lorena!" He waved me into the room. "I was just telling the girls about Mr. Blackstone getting shot."

Rita pulled out a chair for me before I dropped from shock. "Mr. Blackstone's dead?"

He sipped his coffee. "No, no. He's married. Marie Beckingham's brother accused him of insulting his sister and demanded satisfaction. Blackstone accepted, whereupon Beckingham shot him in the shoulder. Miss Beckingham called her brother a beast and raced to Blackstone's side, pledging her undying love and hand in marriage if he'd but live."

"Good grief. What on earth did Blackstone do to insult her? I've known Anton for years and never heard him utter an unkind word."

"No idea. Blackstone and Beckingham are closer than brothers. Blackstone was desperate to marry the girl, but she was playing silly games. They hatched the plan to force her hand."

"It's a wonder he didn't die."

"Beckingham's a dead shot. Small chance of serious damage, but there was a lot of blood and tender nursing afterwards." He drained his coffee. "You're here about your mother."

"Yes, I got a message that she was dying. Several messages."

He grabbed a handful of cookies. "Let's step outside."

I followed him, curious and concerned now.

He closed the door behind us. "Your mother's fine. I can't tell her that. If I did, she'd find some charlatan who'd be happy to take her money and give her God knows what kind of poison. So, she has these spells when she needs attention. I give her tonics with fancy labels and send her to a spa for a few weeks to miraculously recuperate."

"I'm familiar. She's done it all her life."

"Let's walk."

While Mother loved city life, it made me claustrophobic. Thankfully, she spent a great deal of money to make the backyard look like a floral kaleidoscope. It didn't compare to my green rolling hills, but I could at least tolerate it here. As confined as it was, there were still hidden niches where people might share a secret or escape, and I knew them all.

Apparently, the doctor did, too, and led me to the fountain in the corner. We sat on the wrought iron settee and watched the fish jump at bits of cookie he threw. He handed me a cookie so I could feed them.

We sat silently, aside from the small splashes of fish jumping for crumbs like trained dogs. Lilacs, paperwhites, and various other sweet-smelling flowers masked the city's stench. By summer, this would be butterfly heaven.

"I heard a rain crow earlier," he said.

I dropped the crumb I'd broken off and stared at him, shock rendering me mute. Fox told me my contact would find me in Baltimore, but I never dreamed it might be Mother's doctor. Frain coaxed me with a smile like you would a frightened child in a school play. I shook my head. "Um, uh, just one? They usually sing to their mates."

"Just one, alas. A rain crow's song usually portends a storm."

I was so surprised that I had to search for the responses. "Fie, uh, a storm from the north, maybe."

He chuckled. "Yes, you'll need to work on that so you don't sound like you're reciting catechism to Sister Mary Magdalen of the Holy Order of the Ruler. I'm the Cardinal. Your contact."

I felt like a child who had bluffed her way to a correct answer. "Y-Yes," I stammered. "I didn't expect that. In which case, there's a message from Alexandria." I withdrew the envelope secreted in my bag lining and handed it to him.

He skimmed it and pocketed it.

I threw the bit of cookie to the fish. "I'd think, your accent, it's hard to hide where you're from."

He twitched a shrug. "I was going to return to Alabama, but Major Fox convinced me I'd be of more use here as I hold the confidence of a great many powerful people. Baltimore, and many in Maryland, have great sympathy for their Southern neighbors, but they can't secede. Lincoln would crush the state. He's already crushed the city with his martial law and arrested half our politicians. He can't allow an enemy that close to his front door."

"Yes, I read about the riots and the aftermath. I barely missed them on my last visit."

The rail line through Baltimore was incomplete, so Lincoln had to march troops through part of Baltimore on the way to Washington. Anti-war and Southern-leaning mobs had harassed the troops along the way, hurling insults, bricks, and paving stones, and waving pistols until their commander told his soldiers to drop any citizen they saw aiming at them. When the brawl between the police, the soldiers, and the mob was over, twelve civilians lay dead, and thirty-six soldiers came away wounded. The soldiers were in a running fight, abandoning equipment, weapons, musical instruments, and any semblance of order.

Governor Hicks and Mayor Brown implored Lincoln not to send any more troops through Maryland or Baltimore, but Lincoln sniped back; Union soldiers were neither birds to fly over Maryland nor moles to burrow under it. He continued to send his troops through regardless of what Baltimore and Maryland wanted, eventually arresting Hicks, Brown, the police force, the city council, and a congressman from Baltimore. It had all been widely and vividly reported in the newspapers.

"*Oderint dum metuant,*" I said.

His hooting laugh spooked a nearby bird into flight. "Hmm, yes, some think him somewhat akin to Caligula, I suppose. But to business, why did I choose this place to speak to you?"

I studied the yard and the back of the house. "Because it's private."

He nodded.

"We can see if anyone comes out the backdoor or in the gate."

"Correct.

"The bushes protect us from sight, except maybe the upper window."

"Which is?"

I looked. "Shuttered. It would be difficult to see anything from there."

"Excellent. Is that all?"

"I—" I scanned the area again. "I think so."

"The fountain. It gives enough noise to mask our voices if we aren't speaking loudly. Even if someone were directly on the other side of the fence, which they aren't, they couldn't hear us. Try to find a way to mask your voice if you can."

"How do you know no one is on the other side of a stone fence?"

"I paid Alton to shimmy up the tree and whistle if he sees anyone. If your mother finds out, she'll think I'm giving you critical information I want kept private."

I leaned back against the settee's iron roses. "It's too much. I don't know if I can do this. If I make a mistake, I could put people in danger." I told him what happened in Alexandria.

"Rise above it. Men like Fulkirk are fools, but it's best not to make enemies even of fools. You'll learn. We're all learning. This is new territory for most of us. Don't let doubt pave your path."

He was right, but it would take time, and I wasn't made of the heroic material in stories and songs.

"I'll return in a few days with information and supplies," he said. "Your mother will mend because you're here. You know she's determined to make you stay."

"Always."

He rose. "I'll prescribe an iron tonic and convince her she needs to get out. Make the social circuit with her. Now, let's get back to resurrecting your poor, dying mother, who may outlive us all."

"So says my beau."

He turned to me. "Miss McKenzie, I hesitate to ask you this, but you'll note I am a man."

My step faltered. "I had noticed."

"I'm not about to proposition anything untoward. I'm happily married."

I gave a small wave as if it never crossed my mind.

"Washington's in a great patriotic furor," he continued. "There'll be many parties, dinners, and the like. It might be best if you appeared unattached. Foolish men will open the gates to the city for a beautiful woman they wish to impress. This will especially be true now with the war lust upon everyone and passions riding high."

We resumed our walk. "I see. I'm sure Mother would be thrilled to ply me with the most eligible bachelors in the land."

"I thought she might." The doctor whistled and motioned to a tree in the corner of the garden, whereupon said tree coughed up one small Black child who dropped to the ground.

The boy ran up and flashed a ten-dollar smile. "Didn't see no one peep a nose around, sir."

"Excellent. Don't spend this all on candy." Frain flipped a bright nickel to the boy, who shoved it in his pocket.

"Thank you. I'm saving for a new fishing pole. Broke my other one sword fighting with my brother. Pap won't buy me a new one."

I laughed. "Perhaps leave the sword fighting to soldiers."

"That's why we was practicing. We want to be soldiers!" He ran to the house, slamming the door behind him.

I couldn't help the escaping sigh. "It's bad enough that children think this is going to be great entertainment, but so many adults share the same fantasy. If this matter is pressed, those giddy laughs will turn to keening cries soon enough."

"Pray it's ended quickly, and people can move on with their lives unmolested," he replied.

Mother was still laid out on the daybed, rattling off instructions to the cook, but her voice suddenly trembled when she noticed us.

He dragged a chair next to the bed and opened his medical bag. Out came some tubing with a small, brass, bell-shaped piece on one end and a cylindrical ivory fitting on the other. I stepped forward, fascinated with the device.

"Come along, Miss Dobbs."

Mother unswaddled herself when she saw the instrument and leaned against a wooden door, confounding me even more.

"Hold," he instructed her. She plopped the bell to her chest, and he stuck the other end of the tubing in his ear. He hmmmed and frowned appropriately and finally removed the earpiece. "Get dressed and go out for a walk today. I'll send a note to the pharmacy to mix you some tonic."

Mother humphed and sank to the edge of the bed.

Unable to control my curiosity any longer, I spoke up. "Excuse me. What is that instrument?"

"It's a Golding Bird stethoscope. You've never seen one?"

"A stethoscope. Fascinating. Our doctor uses a wooden tube that looks like an ear trumpet."

"Some still prefer those. I like this for traveling."

"And why did she lean against the door?"

"Sound travels through wood. It amplifies the effect if a patient leans on it." He clasped the bag shut and locked it. "Are there any other medical lessons today?"

"No, but I think I'd like one of those for Rosemount."

"I can bring one with me when I return in a few days."

Mother waved her handkerchief at us. "What about me?"

The doctor and I both stared at her. "You want a stethoscope?" he said before I could blurt it out.

"For pity's sake, no! What about my care?"

"Oh," Dr. Frain replied. "I discussed your condition with your daughter."

"My condition?"

"I want you to get lots of fresh vegetables and fruit. We need to build your strength, so walk each day. Dance even. Socialize. Invite friends for supper. Do some charity work. Stay active. Take the tonic as directed. You should go to a spa for ten days or so."

Mother looked at me. "Will you remember all that, Lorena?"

"I'm sure I will. Bid adieu to the doctor so he can get your tonic prescribed. Get dressed, and let's get this bed out of the parlor. I wouldn't be caught dead in that hideous thing, nor should you."

Chapter Thirty-Five

With Dr. Frain on his way and me recovered from my shock of discovering he was my contact, I set about getting Mother out of her deathbed. She sprawled out, one hand laid across her brow and the other dramatically at her breast.

"Moses, Mary, and Joseph. Get out of that monstrosity. Someone fetch Castor to help Otis get this out of the parlor. And speaking of Otis, what's wrong with you? I near had heart failure when I saw him. I thought the funeral home was here to haul you away."

"You wanted professional attire."

"Professional, not funereal. Beth and Imogene subscribe to newspapers from France and England. They have pictures of royal servants—royal, mind you, and they aren't in these get-ups."

She bolted up. "Berating my servants and demanding I get out of my sickbed, too. It's not like I can recover instantly."

"You heard Dr. Frain. You need to be moving. The next time I see you laid out in that thing, you had best be well and truly dead because I'm going to have it carried into the yard like a Chinese bier and set it alight."

She waved a hand dismissively, shooing servants and idea alike away. "Don't be foolish. I'm positive lighting a funeral pyre in the yard is against the law."

"Then we'll take you to the bay at sunset and cast you adrift on your bed like Charon ferrying you across the Styx. It will be *très* dramatic."

"The bed would sink, and I'd bob around the bay like an untethered buoy in my shroud with ravens pecking at my bones."

"Even better. You'd be legendary. Your tattered corpse would bob against a ship, tap, tap, tapping like a portent of doom.

"The lookout nodded, nearly napping; suddenly there came a tapping.
Bad News Bertha gently rapping,
Floating 'bout from ship to shore.
Death, disaster, and nothing more."

"Bad News Bertha," she huffed. "I told your father not to let you read that horrible Poe. He's positively corrupted your mind." She dragged herself out of the bed and threw the brocade robe about her like a great cloak.

"It's the best I could do off the top of my head. Either way, I don't want to see that thing in the parlor again, nor you claiming it for a deathbed."

"I'm not speaking to you." She plopped into an overstuffed chair near the bay window to oversee the dismantling but pointedly ignored me much as an aloof cat might.

Presently, Castor appeared, and even with the generous ceilings and doorways, at nearly seven feet tall and stout as an oak, he seemed too large for whatever room he was in. "Miss Lorena," he said, grinning broadly. "Good to see you."

"It's good to see you also. We miss you at Rosemount. The mares and babies miss you."

He sighed wistfully. "I miss all those fuzzy babies. Maybe I can come for a visit."

"I believe you needed to get my monstrosity out of here?" Mother scolded. I felt sure she'd talk him out of coming to Rosemount lest he be tempted to stay. "Move that to Lorena's room. It's the biggest."

"If you put that in my room, I'll chop it into kindling and burn it."

Castor and Otis ignored the storm and examined the bed to see how it might be dismantled.

"I spent a great deal of money on that bed, young lady," Mother said. "The antique dealer assured me it's from a Chinese royal family."

"Oh, no doubt you spent a young fortune on it. As for the Chinese royal family, it's most likely from one of their opium dens."

A hidden drawer in the corner post popped out, and Otis jumped backward. "I was trying to get the side rails loose, but I didn't do that."

"I told you so," I crowed exultantly. "The bed's no doubt filled with drugs."

"Dare I hope?" Mother huffed. "I could use some right about now." She looked like a figurehead leaning forward. "Is anything in the drawer?"

I moved closer and looked. It was a cleverly disguised wooden drawer carved into the solid post. The interior was dark, but I saw a small glint in the bottom and probed with my fingers. The object was smooth and cool, with carved trenches. I traced the rounded edges and the metal pin protruding from beneath. The drawer was small, barely room enough for my fingertips, and it couldn't be pulled free without breaking the mechanism. After some fishing, I triumphantly pulled out a beautifully carved jade butterfly with two blue eyes and a blue body. It was a lady's brooch.

Curiosity claimed her, and Mother eased over to see what everyone was oohing about. I laid it in her hand. "It appears you have a lovely butterfly to keep you company."

Walking to the window for a better view, she held it up to the sunlight and admired it. "It's a gorgeous little thing, isn't it? The Chinese believe butterflies are a symbol of enduring love."

"How did you know that?" I asked, impressed.

"Your father told me years ago. He bought me a beautiful cloisonné butterfly hat pin my heart was set on. He could scarce afford it but moved heaven and earth to buy it. I broke it later. I suppose that was an omen of things to come." She laid the brooch in my hand and closed my fingers around it. "Keep it. Let's get that bed moved. Aunt Gertie will be here soon, and I don't want the house in an uproar."

Mother disappeared with her retinue to prepare for Aunt Gertie while Castor and Otis continued dismantling the bed. My curiosity was piqued. As ghastly as it was, I wanted time alone with the daybed to see what other secrets it held. They reassembled it in the room next to mine, so all sides were accessible. I intended to examine it closely later with a magnifying glass for seams or compartments. If they found it odd, they said nothing and simply shuffled things around as I directed, being accustomed to intemperate and illogical women. "We'll rearrange this shortly," I said.

"I assumed so," Castor replied with a knowing look. "Might probe about the bottom panels."

With Mother safely occupied, I unpacked and untied the flag in my room. Lovingly, I spread it on my bed and caressed the embroidered gold star and heavy gold bullion fringe. *Ah, Virginia, what will become of you now that you've taken the Bonnie Blue?*

Nothing if I had anything to do with it.

A gentle knocking on the door set me quickly folding the flag and tucking it under my mattress. "Miss Lorena," Prudence called, "your mama wants me to sweep the floor and dust."

God help a speck of dust that drifted in, but my mother was determined neither dust nor city air would drive me home prematurely.

"Come in, but there's no need to sweep. I'll talk to Mother."

"I don't mind."

"It's fine. You can gather fresh flowers instead of sweeping clean floors."

She grinned that gap-toothed grin, which reminded me of a white picket fence with a slat missing.

"That sounds good. You know how I like flowers."

The clinking of glass jars drew my attention from staring out the window to her unpacking the vanity trays I had deliberately overpacked. I hoped to overwhelm whoever might search our things so that they would weary of looking at womanly things and wave us on.

She stared slack-jawed at the collection. "What you gonna do with all this?"

What to say? "I had help packing, and they insisted on loaning me things."

"You want I should unpack it all?"

"No, just the things in the top two drawers. My dresses are wrinkled to a fare-thee-well, though."

The doorbell interrupted Prudence's exclamations about the various creams and pots.

I recognized the voice and plunged down the stairs like a child on Christmas morning. There was the familiar lavender water scent, albeit tainted. I pulled away from the warm embrace. "Aunt Gert! What's that smell? Have you taken up smoking?"

Her hand went to her hair. "My poor hat and hair are thoroughly smoked, I fear. I'm surprised my face isn't black and my clothes in tatters from the cinders. I hung out the train window nearly all the way here from Washington, waving at soldiers."

As if summoned by the mere mention, a faint tattoo of drums and trill of pipes floated down the street.

Mother perked up like a Pekingese spying an empty lap. By the sound of it, a sizeable army was marching toward us. "Someone get the flags," Mother cried, hurriedly smoothing her dress as if she were about to receive a gentleman caller.

Crowds gathered on the sidewalks to watch the troops. Mother snatched up the little American flags from Rita and passed them out to everyone. I looked in dismay at the one jammed in my hand. "Come!" Mother said, "Everyone outside before our sidewalk fills."

No one noticed me hanging back. I couldn't believe Mother was cheering them on after what had happened mere weeks ago on the streets of Baltimore when Lincoln's thug general had declared martial law and taken over the city. I knew I would associate with Union soldiers as part of my new job, but I had no intention of hooraying them. Not today. Mrs. Loonstra was still too fresh in my mind. I sprinted up the stairs to my room.

The closer the drums and pipes got, the more my blood boiled. These jaunty boys in blue would soon be joining the invasion of my homeland. Damn them all, anyway.

Troops passed below the house, banners waving, crowds hurrahing or booing depending on where loyalties lay. I pulled the Confederate flag from under the mattress and threw the sash open, further disarraying my hair, which had come undone under the mattress when I scrambled for the flag.

"Dash it all anyway!" With my net destroyed, my hair loosed, I let the rest down as I refused to take time to rearrange it. Though no match for the drums and marching feet, I rebelled as fully as I might in my own way. Leaning out my bedroom window, I waved the flag and sang Dixie as loudly as I could. The wind picked up, whipping the flag as if trying to keep time with the jaunty song.

At first, no one noticed. Then a few people pointed, shocked, unsure what to do. There were a few boos, but they were scattered in the face of their troops. There were also cheers cast my way. My door! I dashed across the room to lock it and wedge a chair under the handle. For good measure, I shoved a heavy chest of drawers across as Mother would surely order Castor to drag me away from the window as soon as she discovered my treason.

Back to the window I ran and continued with *Baron's Marauders*, a song the girls had written to surprise Baron. I sat precariously in the window with my unbound hair and flag flying. When I launched into *Maryland, My Maryland*, there was a stir in the crowd, and several joined me, picking up the call to rebellion.

A young aide sitting below my window next to his captain pointed to me, scowling in distaste. "Should I arrest her, sir?"

Go ahead, you little pismire. I waved the flag harder.

The captain, all Yankee blue and polished brass buttons, looked up, cigar clenched between his teeth. No shopkeeper he. This man was rugged and deep. His beard was neatly trimmed and the color of good chocolate, not the cheap stuff, but dark and rich. His hat brim tilted low over his brow, but I could see his eyes narrow, studying me as if he were making an important decision. I tilted my chin up and continued singing. I'd sing my way to the stockades and damn them every one to hell.

"No," he said at last. "A woman that beautiful may do as she wishes." He drew on his cigar, studying me further. "Sing about the Baron again," he called up.

I blinked in surprise and stopped in mid-chorus. Blowing a kiss to him, I resumed waving the flag and sang *Baron's Marauders*. The aide glared at me, prompting me to sing louder, though it threatened to steal my voice. Mother had discovered my actions and sent Castor to demand I stop my recreant works. He shouted and banged on my door, but I only sang louder and launched back into *Maryland, My Maryland* since the aide particularly hated that song. The crowd joined in with more enthusiasm and cheers this time.

"Miss Lorena, please stop. Don't make me break this door down."

"They'll be gone soon," I replied.

He continued banging but without much heart.

I finished my repertoire with *Dixie*, though my voice was nearly gone. As the troops' parade neared its end, the captain looked up once more, beamed a brilliant and amused smile, and touched his hat. Boldly whistling Dixie, he turned his horse away—one small victory for the South.

Satisfied I'd stirred enough trouble, I unstacked the furniture from in front of the door and let Castor in.

He leaned against the doorjamb and sighed. "Miss Lorena. What possessed you? Missus running around in circles like a chicken with her head cut off, hollering 'bout her reputation."

Prudence and Sallie peered around him as if I were indeed mad.

"I'll go soothe her as soon as I put my room back in order."

"We do that," chirped Sallie. "Go calm you mama afore we have to 'range a funeral round here."

"Prudence, you come with me. Castor, you help Sallie with the furniture."

Downstairs, Mother screamed frantically. Aunt Gertie sat in the burgundy velvet chair near the bay window, tea in hand, gazing out.

Mother whirled to face me, the bouquet of small American flags in her hand ruffling as she did. "Lorena Dobbs Fiona McKenzie!" All four names. Impressive shades of fury. "What were you thinking? We'll be lucky if we aren't all arrested by day's end. I'll be blacklisted from the garden club, and they just elected me vice president. Must you always pepper my pudding?" She paced dramatically in front of the windows, waving her arms about. I was sure neighbors gathered outside, watching and listening as best they could. Knowing people as I did, at least one small child listened under the window.

"I'm sure no one will arrest you. You had nothing to do with my treachery."

Gertie leafed through an issue of Godey's and glanced occasionally at something outside the window, confirming my suspicions of a spy. "I'm sure no one will be under arrest, Bertha. The young captain enjoyed the singing. He even asked her to sing that one song again."

Ignoring the reassurances, Mother barreled on. "Please stop making excuses for her. I'll never be able to show my face in the garden club."

Sallie appeared with a heaping plate of ginger cookies and a fresh pot of tea. At this rate, she'd be baking again before the day was out.

"The garden club won't remove you," I said. "Mrs. Blakely's husband embezzled thousands from the bank and fled to Canada. Mrs. Thompson's husband got his secretary with child and moved her to another town, where he still visits frequently. Mrs. Sorrelson must be poured into her carriage nearly every afternoon after spending too much time in the tearoom drinking Mosley tea. Trevor Jackson left his wife and ran away with their groom."

Mother's face flushed fair crimson. "Where did you hear all this nonsense?"

I couldn't tell her the servants had filled me in on all the latest gossip the last time I was in town. Servants knew every intimate secret of every house, great and small.

"Bertha, every drop is true and more," Gertie said. "Why people think they can keep these secrets is beyond me. I know all about the Baltimore Garden Society gossip and don't even belong to a garden club. I doubt Lorena can hold a candle to the rest of the misfits. You've probably grown in stature. People will sympathize with you about your wayward daughter.

"Besides, Rose Greenhow is the biggest Southern sympathizer this side of Virginia, and she entertains politicians, diplomats, military notables, and royalty regularly. If they haven't arrested her, they're not going to arrest anyone. Half of Congress is in love with her."

"What drivel. You sound like an admirer. You should be more careful with your support."

"If she weren't a woman, she'd be one of Washington's most successful diplomats or politicians. She has a brilliant mind."

Mother, not being so impressed with brilliant political minds, sniffed. "If you think I intend to let this go one step farther, you're mistaken. Lorena will appear at that ball and be properly supportive of the war efforts."

Dear heavens. Was there ever anything on her mind but balls? "I'm sorry. I don't know what possessed me." With a furtive flick of the wrist, I motioned Sallie closer and whispered to her to bring me the slop bucket from the kitchen. With Mother's rant out of her system and my obeisance, I determined to finish the neighbor's interest. Bucket in hand, I marched out the door before Mother could question me, tossing the contents in the bush Gertie had been watching. A thoroughly soaked boy covered with bits of kitchen refuse tore from behind a bush, yowling like a scalded hound. A woman across the street scuttled into her house. The boy darted between carriages and horses, yelling, "Mama! Mama!" but Mama was hiding behind her door, peering out through a small crack. The child ran up the stairs and was quickly ushered in. His mother looked around to see if anyone was watching and cast a wicked glare my way before slamming the door. The small gathering on the sidewalk broke up laughing.

"Lorena, what did you do?" Mother asked. "Why is that boy yelling?"

"The rotting vegetables are good for your plants," I replied.

"Missus, won't you have another cookie?" Sallie offered.

Chapter Thirty-Six

That night, I sat at the edge of the ballroom enjoying the music, which banished thoughts of war as far away as the abundance of blue and polished brass would allow. Mother motioned to me with a flick of her black, feathered fan, delicate at first, then more insistent, like a one-winged crow trying to take flight. Giving up, she sent a steward to collect me. I meandered over, acknowledging one and then another as I did.

"Lorena, have you met Colonel Orwyn and his sister Miss Emalee Orwyn?"

"No, I haven't." To Miss Emalee's annoyance, I extended my hand, which the colonel graciously kissed. "Miss Orwyn. Are you enjoying the party? What a lovely gown. The color is quite dramatic."

Her features softened like summer butter. "Thank you! I'm fond of yellow. Bert thinks it looks horrible on me." She shot her brother a triumphant glance. In truth, she should have listened to him. The hue heightened her sallow complexion and did nothing to set off her pale blonde hair.

"If you don't mind me remarking," Colonel Orwyn said to me. "Your gown is exquisite."

My own gown, a deep sapphire-blue satin overlaid with matching tulle, had embroidered gold bees and star flowers with seed pearl centers drifting across the skirt as if carried on a faint breeze. Annie carefully designed the off-shoulder sleeves and beading to cover my scarred arm from the shooting that she found mortifying for a young lady. The dress was typical of Annie's magic.

"You're too kind." I bowed my head.

"Your mother says you'll be returning South soon?" Orwyn said. "I hope you'll have a chance to enjoy some social life during your visit."

"We're to attend a recital on Monday. I planned on taking Mother to see The Lady of Lyons, but it's sold out, and I can't wait for an opening."

He stroked his salt-and-pepper-bearded chin as if thinking.

"I happen to have two tickets. Emalee has no interest, and I've been called to meetings."

My eyes widened, and I poured on the Southern. "How sweet would you be if you let me buy those tickets?" I topped it off with my most gracious Southern smile. There is a difference between a Southern smile and a Northern smile. I learned at a young age mine was one that melts hearts and captures souls.

"Nonsense. I'll have a runner deliver them tomorrow. I hope you and Miss Dobbs enjoy the play. I only wish I could be there to partake with you."

"Oh, Colonel, that's uncommon kind. We must take in a play together the next time I'm in town." I gave him my calling card with Mother's address, which he tucked away in an inner pocket like a treasure map.

"Bertram, this is our dance." Emalee snipped and steered him away before he could say more. "I can't believe it. You folded like a cheap suit."

"Sister dearest, be thankful I'm not ten years younger, or I'd be whistling Dixie and waving the Bonnie Blue all the way to Richmond."

I did my best to ignore Mother, who glared a hole through me. "Good grief, Lorena. Could you have been any more flirtatious? That man will be camped on my doorstep."

"Good. You could use the company."

She beat a hasty retreat, refusing to engage me further. Life is all about the little pleasures.

"I almost didn't recognize you without the Bonnie Blue waving madly from your fist."

The voice jolting me out of my meanderings was pleasantly mellow and faintly familiar. I looked around to find the chocolate-bearded captain who decided I wasn't worthy of arrest. "Good evening, Captain—"

"Lucian Simmons at your service." He held a punch cup out toward me.

I folded my fan and accepted the drink. "I'm pleased to meet you. Lorena McKenzie, and you already did me a great service. Your aide was hell fire bent on having me arrested."

He gave a small shrug. "Yes, he's stirred up with righteous patriotism. Put some miles on him in the mud and the blood, and his fervor will settle to an acceptable simmer. Even so, there are enough zealots around who will put your pretty head on a pike for less, so perhaps exercise a bit less exuberance in the future." He gently nudged me away from the crowd as we talked.

"It was foolish of me. In truth, I haven't much of a mind for politics. I'm corn pone simple, as most Southern women are."

We drifted away from the fold and toward the French doors. "I somehow doubt that, but for the sake of conversation, what are you gifted at? Besides charming my colonel?" He grinned.

"Is he yours?"

"Yes. He's top-notch in all things, including his excellent taste in ladies."

"My mother was the one who garnered that introduction, but to my expertise—" I pointed my fan at a young lady swimming in pink ruffles. "It took fourteen yards of silk taffeta to make that dress. I know precisely how many beeswax candles light a room this size and how long they'll burn. I can look at a rice field and tell you how much gravy it'll take to cover it."

His booming laugh caused people nearby to turn smiling. "I see you've been to Louisiana also. I love the place."

"New Orleans is one of my favorite cities in the entire world."

He stopped to watch the dancers. "I love the way New Orleans melts off your tongue. I'd like to visit again…when things are settled. I was sublimely content there." He huffed a bit. "But we'll be moving in a different direction, I fear."

I raised my fan. "Please, don't tell me where you're going. I won't have some busybody arresting me for a Confederate spy. I deplore the idea of our boys dying on either side." There was truth in that; however, I would do what I could to protect my homeland.

He inclined his head and opened the doors so I could pass through. "Of course, madam. Please, continue telling me what you know."

"I know several ladies will swoon tonight, and some handsome beau will come to their rescue, taking them outside to get fresh air…as we are." It didn't compare to my magnolias, but the pale mock orange refreshed after the stuffy ballroom. I inhaled in contentment. "The more inexperienced ladies will return with grass stains on their skirts, but they'll have indeed caught their air."

He rolled his tongue in his cheek. "And do you swoon, Miss McKenzie?"

I drained the last of my punch. "I might if the right handsome gentleman were around, but I'm not the kind to get grass stains on my skirts. I think some things are worth spending time on, don't you?" I held my cup up. "I have no punch."

"Oh, I wouldn't say that, Miss McKenzie," he said, taking my cup. "Would you honor me with a dance if your card isn't full?"

"It's the least I can do for someone who saved my life." I took the dance card from the velvet pouch at my wrist and handed it to him.

"The German Waltz, perhaps?"

"I'd love that."

"Perhaps we should go back inside so I can save your honor, too." He offered his arm, and we strolled toward the doors. "Will you be staying in Baltimore?"

"For a few more days, but I must return to Virginia soon."

"A shame. I hoped I might call on you before I left."

"Mother's having a small supper—"

"Luke! There you are. And who is this beauty? No wonder you were hiding." The man, an escaped character from an Austen novel, bowed and kissed my hand. He would have given De Wilde a run for his money with his pale blond wavy hair, meticulously trimmed Vandyke, and curious ice-blue eyes. I almost expected him to say, "Hello, I'm Beautiful, and you are?"

"Garry, this is Miss McKenzie. Miss McKenzie, my younger brother, Garrold Simmons." The irritation in his voice was plain.

"Esquire."

"Yes, I always forget that. Esquire."

Instead of releasing my hand, Garrold attempted to steer me away from Lucian and into the ballroom. "I'm sure my brother won't mind if I steal a dance."

"I'm sorry, I've promised him my last two dances."

"Surely he wouldn't mind sharing one dance."

"Alas, my father would turn in his grave if I reneged on my word. I'm sure a man of the law appreciates this."

"I'll hold you to your word, Miss McKenzie," he said and sauntered away.

Lucian had drifted away to lean against a tree and light a cigar. He raised an eyebrow when I came near, seemingly surprised I was still there. "You should have gone with him. He has a promising future, and you're everything he looks for in a woman."

"He's nothing I look for in a man. Frankly, I think his interest in me was that I was with you."

"That's a very great attraction, but I assure you, not all."

"Since I told your brother you have my last two dances, would you pencil another dance in for the second set if you have an opening?"

The end of the cigar glowed as he inhaled. "I believe I could force myself to enjoy your company." He studied me. "Tell me, Miss McKenzie. What *do* you look for in a man?"

"That's an interesting question. I'll ponder it a bit and give you an answer at Mother's supper party tomorrow if you're free."

"I can arrange that."

I passed him my calling card. "Tomorrow at seven."

He took it and bowed. "If you'll excuse me, I owe a dance to a young lady. Let me escort you to your seat."

As soon as Captain Simmons departed, Mother swooped in on me in a cloud of charcoal taffeta like an avenging angel. I continued to study my dance card and pretended not to take note, though she cast a complete shade on me.

"Lorena, I noticed you visiting with Captain Simmons."

"I was sure you would."

"He's educated. West Point '56. He studied engineering. His family's from Boston, the finest lineage available going back to the Goodspeed. One uncle owns five banks and heaven knows how much property."

I cast a withering glance at her. "No doubt. Bankers tend to acquire property."

She flipped out her fan and waved it about as if someone had farted in her vicinity, and she was shooing the stench away. "I know you're upset about The Pines, but Mr. Simmons had nothing to do with that. If he'd held your note, I dare say he'd have given you generous terms."

"Yes, I'm sure. Can we talk about something else?" I was still seething about The Pines and divided my time between sulking at home, crying over the loss, or riding out someplace alone so I could shoot at targets with drawings of bankers and cursing them to heaven and hell. Annie had refused to share her magic with me, saying it was not for me to dabble in. She was right. There are some paths better left untrod, but there were still times I wished I could plague them unmercifully.

Mother laid a delicate, gloved hand on mine. "You've successfully dodged my previous attempts, but we must discuss your future. Your heart is set on Captain Callahan; heaven knows every girl south of Richmond has, but you must listen to reason. This war will ruin his family."

I opened my fan and waved it lazily, brushing away each argument against Baron. I made nondescript hmmms and inclined my head at the proper times. Mother, emboldened by her great oratorical progress, left off the cons of marriage to Baron and returned to the sale of one Captain Simmons.

"His grandfather served with Washington. Two of his uncles are senators. His younger brother's an aide to the secretary of war. Simmons won't be a captain long, I assure you."

She gave me a full dossier on yon Adonis approaching with three punch cups. "Besides, look how handsome he is. There isn't a woman in this hall who wouldn't give every tooth in her head to be on his arm."

Mother was right about that, as evidenced by several ladies, adolescent to ancient, turning to watch him to the great displeasure of their escorts. "Yes, but don't you think that's because he's viewed through the veil of war? Every man, especially one in uniform, is the handsomest thing ever. Each lady a goddess. Don't you know Eros is worn out?" I made a small motion, like shooting an arrow.

"If he'd but take better aim," she muttered.

"Ladies, I hope I'm not interrupting anything. I noticed your mother and went back for more punch. I hope you don't mind."

"Not at all," I said, accepting the cup. "Mother was telling me about you. Your rare looks and pedigree are comparable to the finest breeding stallion coming out of Kentucky, it seems."

"For heaven's sake, Lorena! Are you trying to put me in the grave?" Her skirts eddied about her as she bolted.

Lucian guffawed. "Oh, if only my brother could hear that. How he would laugh. I'm sorry I frightened your mother away."

"No, sirree Bob," I said, watching my mother's retreating form, "I'll not allow you to take credit for my victory."

Chapter Thirty-Seven

I foolishly imagined I might escape the house without Mother's notice the next morning, but she was no less vigilant than in my youth, even for her complaints of going blind and deaf. "Lorena, where are you going so early? It's not a decent hour for a young lady to be out."

"It's after ten."

"I know what time it is."

"I have a business to tend to and want to buy a new bonnet."

She brightened. "I'll go with you. You can't go out alone in any case."

"I'm going to an accountant's office. You'd be bored silly."

Her face soured as if she were eating early persimmons. "How perfectly ghastly. No, I refuse to enter a money counter's den. Take Castor with you. Buy a pretty bonnet. Your salmon one looks like you've been to a dog fight, and it was the bait."

I took it off and examined it. The milliner might have freshened it, but it wasn't ready to retire. "Baron gave me this. I love it."

She eyed the bonnet so evilly I expected it to burst into flames.

With my guardian summoned, we set off to town. Mother wanted me to take the carriage, but I preferred the fresh air and more time away from Mother.

I stopped to window shop here and there, studying the reflection for any figures keeping pace with me.

"Kinda odd that man with the frumpy frock coat and slouch hat stops every time you do," Castor said.

I was surprised he'd noticed, also. The nondescript little man might have melted into a crowd normally, but there was little traffic today. "Isn't it? Pay him no mind. Probably an admirer."

"Uh-huh."

Mr. Abrahamson was elated to see me. Nothing was changed in the modest account Papa left with him, but he advised a switch in investments to a steel company due to the expected war contracts. I felt like Judas for doing so, but I told him to do as he saw fit. Papa trusted a few people in the north, but their relationship had lasted for many years.

My shadow had disappeared when I came out of Abrahamson's, so I continued to Madame Gaspard's Fine Hats and Accessories.

To this day, Madame Gaspard, a willowy woman in her fifties, wore a red ribbon around her throat to commemorate her relatives lost in the French Revolution. Every now and then, she made a spitting motion and sliced her finger across the scarlet ribbon. "*Vive la France! Vive le Roi!*" she exclaimed in dramatic, if imperfect, French.

It was all quite impressive. She adored me mostly because Mother was a generous customer, but I appreciated her skill and attention. Oddly, Doctor Frain had also recommended her, and I suspected she would be a future contact.

"Mother thinks my bonnet's bedraggled. Can you fix it?"

"Eet ees not bedraggled. Eet ees loved. I will nurse eet back to life. But! You need a new bonnet, *ma pet*."

She pulled a dozen hats from displays. I particularly liked a black one with lavender roses and black veils.

"*Non! Non!* Why would you wear zat? Eet makes you look so dreary." Madame fitted a gay little piece on my head with a flurry of ribbons, lace, feathers, and two silk flowers arranged so it looked as if they grew straight out of the top of my head.

"Oh, madame," I gasped, watching the two stems wave at me in the mirror. "You have truly buttered the bacon with this, don't you think?"

She noticed my horrified look and clucked in agreement.

I settled on a navy with ostrich plumes and veils I intended to wear, one for Gertie and a flowered spoon bonnet for Mother. I also purchased two new ostrich plumes for Baron's hat and peacock feathers to replace the missing ones in my top hat. Madam Gaspar would deliver them along with my repaired bonnet.

With my two business details taken care of, I'd wasted enough time to go to the tearoom at the appointed time. In front of the tearoom was a vagrant handing out tracts for donations. He was as squabby as the Shetland pony I kept for the girls. He even had that shaggy pony look about him. His hair and beard were unkempt, as was the rest of him, and unfashionably long. No two buttons on his tattered vest matched. Certainly nothing that might identify him.

I picked out a few tracts and noticed a man nearby in a pulled-down derby hat watching us.

"Please do take this one also, ma'am." The tract featured a lamp on the front and Luke 8:17 written in large gold letters.

"Thank you." I fished some coins out of my purse and paid him. He doffed his ragged slouch hat. "Thank you. Oh, thank you. First Corinthians chapter thirteen, verse thirteen for sure, beloved baroness." He flashed an are-you-surprised grin, ducked his head, and shuffled away, all rags and rumples, to gather up a familiar frock coat lying in a heap by a box. My shadow from earlier!

I was too astounded to breathe. Was Baron here? I looked around quickly, but of course, he wouldn't be. Even the little vagrant had disappeared by the time I finished glancing around. He was sending me a message, though.

"Are you all right?" Castor asked. "You look like you saw a ghost."

"I'm fine," I lied, feeling like I had seen one. "Are you hungry?"

"Think I'm going to the cobbler first," he said, still looking at me in consternation.

I needed to go to the cobbler before I left to have the message inserted in my heels as instructed, but not today.

"I'll get some tea," I said to Castor, still pondering the messenger and the message.

"Don't you stir. I don't want your mama on my tail for losing you."

"Trust me. I'm not moving." Could that have been Darcy? Surely, I would have recognized him. Who would know about beloved baroness?

Mrs. Smythe's Tea and Reading Room was popular for its excellent sandwiches, pastries, and teas but also because she served Mosley tea, which meant ladies could get a bit of gin with their Earl Grey. She did a brisk business. Tempting as it was to sink into the nearest chair, I went to a far table so I'd have no one at my back, and I could watch the door. No one aside from Queen Victoria, who scowled at me from her larger-than-life portrait above the marble fireplace.

My usual waitress came over with a bobbing curtsey and smile that made her look like she had too many teeth. On second glance, one realized they were just overly large in a too-small mouth, made more noticeable because everything about her was simply tiny, as if she were stuck at fourteen by some magical spell, though she was married with children. "Mornin' Miss Lorena," Patty said. "Wot can I get fer yer? Got a nice selection o' sandwiches terday. Apple tansey fresh out the oven. Course, the reg'lar menu."

"Lady Earl Grey citrus. Ham and cheese sandwich with tomato. Champagne wafers afterward. Will you bring me a Bible also?"

"Course, Mum."

Mrs. Smythe kept a credible selection of reading material, including novels disapproved of by many households and Bibles to soothe gin-soaked consciences.

My tea and Bible arrived shortly. "Patty, I'll also take two dozen almond cream cornucopias and a dozen assorted other dainties for a party when I leave."

"Yes, mum."

I started leafing through the King James just as Derby Hat entered. Looking up, as anyone might, I took quick note of him. Clean, pressed, tan Angola trousers covered well-made boots, but I noticed the marring where his spurs normally rode. He should have swapped into shoes to complete his city costume. The question was, whose side was the rider on? My interest returned to the Bible.

> *And now abideth faith, hope, charity, these three; but*
> *the greatest of these is charity.*

Now I was even more flustered. Baron often quoted that to me, saying if I were truly charitable, I'd share more kisses with him and be less niggardly with my affection. How could that slip my mind? I looked around the room again to see if he was nearby. The newcomer was certainly not my missing love. He wasn't ill-made, but Baron was broader in the shoulders with long legs, like a Kentucky Thoroughbred. This man was compact, muscular, and suited to skulking around.

The man had given me a message in the tracts, but I couldn't decipher it. It would have to wait until I got home and dug out the cipher wheel.

When Patty returned to check on me, I took the opportunity to steal another glance at the man. "Patty," I whispered, "Who's that gentleman in the corner reading Harper's Weekly?"

She had good sense enough not to look. "Mr. Benjamin Byles, so says 'e, and 'e's single, but I don't think 'e's proper for a lady such as yerself, miss. 'e's a strange un."

"He's not a businessman?"

"Don't sees 'ow 'e can be. Wanders about doin' nothin'. Comes in 'ere ter read 'is paper an' watch people. Don't dress that fine now, does 'e? Not even a looker ifin you ask me, but not speakin' ill o' payin' customers. Don't want yer gettin' mixed up with the wrong sorts all."

I looked at him again. He was an attractive man, but something about him unsettled me.

"Thank you."

Castor wasn't hungry when he returned, so I finished, gathered up my box of pastries, and paid out. Mrs. Smythe hurried out from the back to hug me.

"Lorena, you get more beautiful every time I see you."

It would be flattering if she didn't tell every young lady the same thing. "Mrs. Smythe. Such kindness, but look at you. You're positively glowing."

She twittered and leaned closer. "It's Monsieur Bandeau's magic. He has The Beauty Emporium, you know. You can get enameled for only $25 a week, and his masters will remove all that unwanted hair on your face and décolleté." She motioned vaguely toward her generous bosom and caressed my cheek. "He could get rid of that peach fuzz and tame those brows. They're beautiful little dove wings, but a few wild feathers look about to take flight."

Mrs. Smythe's perfectly plucked and penciled brows were so thin and highly arched that she looked like a permanently surprised corpse.

I touched my wild brow. "Oh, I think I can bring them to order, but thank you."

"I included extra cornucopias in the box and a sampling of new pastries we're trying out for your mother to enjoy. Maybe she'll think of me for her next soiree?"

"I'll be sure to remind her. She loves your confections."

I waited until we were safely away from the shop and prying eyes and ears before I stopped. "Castor Samuel Adams," I said in a low tone, "if you whisper a word of this business about 'beloved baroness' or that man following me, you'll never play another game of cards or toss dice in the stables as long as you live. *Comprende?*" I certainly didn't need Mother thinking

Baron was trying to sneak north to see me or send messages, nor compromise my mission with servant's gossip.

His eyes shot open, silver dollar wide. "Miss Lorena. I don't know what you talkin' about." He was a goliath with nary an ounce of fat, but he shifted the pastry box between us like it was a shield and I a dragon. The dress shop across the street suddenly stole his interest.

"Don't play me for a fool. You have gambling parties in the stables on Tuesdays and Fridays, regular as clockwork. Trust me, I'll have the police, the pastor, and my mother descending on your den of sin if you breathe a word of what transpired today. When Mother isn't dragging you to church to repent, Pastor Dykes will be at the house. You'll be eating, dreaming, and pissing fire and brimstone."

"I swear—" His shoulders slumped. He made a locking motion to his lips and handed me the imaginary key. "My lips are sealed. And folks think your mama's scary."

"Only because they haven't crossed me."

"How did you know? Never mind, Prudence."

"She keeps me well informed about the goings-on here."

As a peace offering, I opened the box and handed him one of the cornucopias. "Is it good?"

He rolled his eyes. "Mmm mmm mmm. Yes, ma'am. It's delicious. You should try one." His voice lowered. "Derby Hat just came out."

"Mr. Byles. I wondered if he would."

We strolled leisurely, him enjoying his pastry and taunting me with it until he broke off a piece and handed it to me. He dropped his twine-wrapped bundle when he did. "Oops. Gettin' so clumsy these days."

I popped the chunk in my mouth.

"He's followin'," he said. "Let's mosey on home."

"We'll keep an eye on him."

Our pace quickened, but I didn't want him to think we were aware of him, so I pointed here and there occasionally and kept up a string of nonsense feminine chatter. If only I hadn't insisted on walking.

"Castor—"

"Don't worry, Miss Lorena. I ain't gonna let nothin' happen to you."

What if Byles was a Federal man? How could I dispose of the tract if worse came to worse? "I have a paper I need to get rid of if he takes me, but it needs to be kept safe; else I'd eat it."

"You pass it to me when you ready, and I'll tuck it down my drawers. Men always diggin' at their privates like heathens. If anyone stops me, I'll jess be a poor ole skeered Negro." He balled his hands before his face and shook, emphasizing his words with a properly fine warble. "Fine Mr. Byles won't want to go diggin' around in my drawers. If he does, I'll act surprised and ask if he knows Monsieur Bastien Joubert."

"Who?" I turned my head to cover an affected sneeze and gauge Byles' distance.

"He's a fancy man who works for Dr. Cameron. That little guy loves to gamble and flirt. Times I think he does it to throw them off their game. Reckon that'd discourage Mr. Byles. Everyone knows French Tien. Dr. Cameron dresses him up in fancy livery costumes to irk the busybodies, much to Tien's amusement."

We traveled four blocks with Byles keeping pace. Shops gave way to upscale homes. "Do you think we can ask someone for sanctuary if he tries to stop us?"

"I'm sure we could. If I need to leave you somewhere, I'll hurry home and get the carriage."

As if in answer to prayer, a hack stopped beside us. "Ma'am." The driver tipped his hat. "A rain crow was singing earlier. Heard that means rain. Would you like a ride?"

Rain crow. How on earth did someone know I needed help? Fox said he'd have men watching over me, but I never dreamed this closely.

"I believe I would."

I clambered into the carriage while Castor guarded the door as if we might be accosted at any moment, and stole a glance back at a plainly irritated Byles.

Chapter Thirty-Eight

"I t's just supper, Mother," I said to no avail as she fussed about my dress and hair and jewelry, none of which were sufficient for dinner with Captain Simmons.

"Can you not take a little more care with your hair? An extra rat, maybe?"

Sallie reached for the silk net filled with cast-off hair that did look like a dead rat at the moment. "No, my hair is fluffed enough. No more feathers and frills. No more anything, or I will plead a headache, and you can entertain him yourself. I invited him because he did me a kindness, not because I'm interested in him."

Mother huffed but desisted.

Captain Simmons was a charming guest, delighting everyone with his easy wit. He immediately captured Mother by recognizing her newest art acquisition and discussing the artist with her. "Buy more," he urged. "Homer is going to be famous one day soon, and you won't regret having a house full of his art."

Maybe it would keep her out of antique shops with Chinese opium beds. I agreed with the captain. At the end of the evening, Mother regretfully bid him adieu and sank against the wall, holding her hand to her breast. "Oh, Lorena. Why can't you see fit to open your heart to that young man?"

"Mother, I'm not having this discussion with you tonight or ever again."

"If you would but—"

I stalked away to my room with Sallie in tow, stress tea brewing in the kitchen, I was sure. I retrieved the tracts from where I'd hidden them and slipped into the guest room. I'd already deciphered them with the wheel but hadn't had time to stash them and the wheel again with all the supper preparations. With my usual misgivings about tight spaces, I wriggled under the opium bed and fiddled with a panel until it slid sideways. Clawing down my growing fear, I took calming breaths and maneuvered three more jigs in the right sequence to get a larger panel to unlock. It slid open, and I stuffed the envelope in for safekeeping. I despised this niche, but it was the safest. There were seven compartments, possibly more if I'd been more diligent in searching. Most were tiny caches barely large enough for jewels or drugs, but some were larger and seemed made for documents. One was a tray at the foot of the bed, a hidden desk judging from the ink stains. I slid out from under the bed with difficulty, having to ease myself out with little pushing motions of my hands. If someone ever caught me under there, I wouldn't escape.

The next morning, we rose early for breakfast and church while I plotted leaving. Church was a welcome respite for the message, and because Mother ceased operations regarding Captain Simmons. We spent the rest of the day relaxing and puttering in the gardens. I would attend the play with her Monday evening and flee home Tuesday morning. Five days was my limit with Mother.

꙳

Doctor Frain rescued me from more pleadings on behalf of Captain Simmons with his most welcome arrival the next morning. As before, he gave Mother her obligatory exam and then took me to the garden for private instructions. Though Mother was convinced he was giving me urgent information about her health, he was actually training me. He'd shown me how to hide messages and use various phrases to denote different things. It was all fascinating but had to be done surreptitiously so as not to raise suspicions, and Mother demanded most of his attention, so our time was limited. The main trick was to use poetry with keywords and pen it on the lining of my garments; thus, no one would understand it even if it was found.

I found that I liked the man more each time I met him. He was kind to a fault and unfailingly patient with Mother, who could drive a saint to drink. Once, he had brought the Frain train by to visit as his wife was busy with something, and he had volunteered to care for the five wee Frains. We accomplished little, I thought, until Doctor Frain grilled me on what each of the children had been wearing and doing in the yard as we visited. I realized I had become more peripherally observant than I realized due to him coaching me to watch my surroundings. Hoorah, I passed the test.

Mother waited at the back door, watching anxiously as we approached. Dr. Frain had opened the door for me no sooner than Sallie dashed in. "Miss Bertha, there's a man with some soldiers and a carriage out front."

Mother looked at me quizzically. "Did you invite Captain Simmons to take you for a ride? You can't go looking like that. You're a perfect shamble."

"I assure you," I replied. "I have no plans for this morning aside from packing. I hadn't even planned on visiting with Doctor Frain. I thought he was coming later, or I'd be dressed proper."

We all went to the door to answer the insistent knocking, adjusting our hair and dresses as we did. My hair was still in its loose night braid, with tiny renegade curls framing my face in a most unruly fashion, and all three of us still in day dresses.

"Yes?" Mother said as soon as Otis opened the door.

"We're here to see Miss Lorena McKenzie," Mr. Byles replied, removing his hat and bowing slightly. He was flanked by four Union soldiers bearing bayonetted rifles who did not remove their hats, shuffled uncomfortably, and shifted their gazes away when I looked at them. I caught the eye of one on the right, and he gave me an I'm-sorry look that told me all I needed to know.

"For what purpose?" Mother demanded.

"She's under arrest for sedition against the United States," he replied. "My name is Benjamin Byles of the Pinkerton Agency." He was meticulously dressed and recently groomed. Had he visited the barber shop, especially for this visit? I being such a notorious criminal and all.

"Preposterous. My daughter isn't a seditionist."

"What authority do Pinkertons have here?" Gertie asked, not bothering to hide her disdain.

"President Lincoln has given us wide authority to stamp out traitors and treason," he replied.

Sallie, in the meantime, had fetched a brush and was trying to pomade and brush my wild curls into order. Being hauled off to prison and possibly hanged required your hair to be properly coifed, after all.

He looked back to Mother. "I'm not here to argue. I simply require Miss McKenzie to come with me."

"My husband is with the State Department," Gertie said. "I'm sure if you contact him, we can sort this all out. There's no need to arrest my niece."

Byles motioned to four more soldiers who waited on the sidewalk. "Search the house. Miss McKenzie, you will come with me now."

I prayed the tracts and wheel I had stashed in the opium bed would remain hidden as it was damning if found. I'd already relayed the information to Dr. Frain, but it needed to go south to my contact in Alexandria. The flag, though, was in my trunk as I planned to take it home to Winchester. My goose was cooked on that account. My heart suddenly took wings and began fluttering madly about my chest.

Mother grasped at his lapels. "Madam!" Byles growled, seizing her wrist in a powerful, vicelike grip. "Turn loose of me, or I'll arrest you also."

"Don't hurt my mother!" I cried, trying to peel his hand off her.

He pushed Mother away and snatched up my arm. Mother grabbed my other arm as if she might wrest me from him. Sallie started to re-braid my now unbound hair amid the tug-of-war.

"Sallie, for God's sake, let go my hair and get me a cloak."

Someone shoved a cloak into my hands as I was hauled out the door with Sallie in my hair to the last.

I caught Doctor Frain's glance, but he could do nothing.

Gertie pulled Mother away. "Bert, let go. I'll fetch George, and we'll get her back. It's a terrible misunderstanding." With Mother cradled in her arms, she wheeled her attention back to Byles. "Where are you taking her?"

"Fort McHenry," he replied shortly, releasing me to the nearest soldier.

Two soldiers took me, one on each arm, as if afraid I might suddenly take flight. Sallie gave up the fight and berated Byles for the heathen he was, dragging a lady out of the house in such a state. She thrust two tucking combs and some pins in my hand as they hauled me away to the rattle of bayonets and ramrods.

Mother was now in a frenzy, screaming as I hadn't heard in years. I looked over my shoulder just as she collapsed to the ground, and I tried to wrench free to run back to her, but the soldiers held me firmly. There was nothing I could do but go along without creating more disturbance.

I shoved Byles' hand away when he tried to help me into the carriage. "Keep your hands off me."

"Perhaps a few weeks in a cell will make you more agreeable."

"I doubt it." I buried my hands in my skirt to hide the trembling and stared out the carriage window to distract my terrified thoughts of what lay ahead. From time to time, I glanced at my captor and then returned to watching the passing scenery and fought to keep from crying. City air was only agreeable to me briefly before I choked down. How long would I last in prison?

He tried to make small talk, asking about my family and home. I remained still.

"I regret we had to do this, of course. I'm sure as the lady said, it's just a misunderstanding. Perhaps someone has led you to believe you should support the South?"

Did he really think I was going to decry someone to save my neck?

Byles was younger than I first thought. Mid-thirties with dark blonde hair not unlike Baron's, aside from Baron's odd dark streaks and auburn beard. Byles had a full blond mustache and chin goatee with trimmed side whiskers. Odd how both men wore nearly identical facial hair. It somehow irked me. His features were even, classical almost. But the eyes, that was where I held. They were the palest gray I ever saw, the color and depth of winter ice.

His cologne might have enticed me on another day. I breathed in deeply to pick out the notes of cinnamon, cloves, rose geranium, and musk. It was an intoxicating Oriental blend I found particularly appealing. On anyone else, it would have been a favorite.

He tapped out something on his knee as he looked out the window also, having given up speaking to me. Morse code? It was too rhythmic to be random. No, I realized he was playing the piano, but what? Every now and then he would glance at me, and the playing would stop. The fingers clenched and eyes narrowed, assessing me. He'd rub his thigh, then resume the concert and return to watching out the window.

I shuddered each time he studied me.

Fort McHenry was on a peninsula of land in the harbor, an odd, star-shaped fortress with grassy embankments people often picnicked upon. It wouldn't look that intimidating if I weren't bound there.

The sally port into the fort was not massive, but it was foreboding like a red brick maw about to swallow me. Not for the first time, I thought of flinging the carriage door open and fleeing, but with mounted Federals escorting me, it would be a short-lived escape and only raise more suspicion.

At the fort, I accepted the soldier's hand to disembark the carriage, not wanting to stumble and humiliate myself. I drew my cloak hood up around my face so I didn't have to look at anyone, nor could anyone see the fear I was sure betrayed my features. I had to control my emotions and tongue.

Byles stepped in to take charge and held out his arm as if he were escorting me to a garden party.

"If you lay a hand on me, you'll regret it," I growled. So much for controlling both tongue and emotions.

He laughed but lowered his arm. "Is that so? And what will you do, Miss McKenzie? Slap me with prejudice?" He swiped the air prissily.

One of the soldiers behind me sniggered.

"I will bite your hand like a rabid badger and not let go. You'll have to cut my head off to get me loose."

"Charming."

"I'm sure you were expecting simpering and batting eyelashes."

"I was expecting a bit more ladylike behavior."

I pushed back the hood and fluttered my lashes at him, then stared straight ahead. We marched without a further word into a nearby stone building.

The room had a small cast iron stove with a simmering tea kettle on it, cabinets, a table, and several chairs. It smelled of wood, both burned and fresh from the stack near the stove, and leather from various pieces of equipment being repaired in a corner. The stale odor of unwashed bodies warred with bodies washed recently with bay rum soap.

Underlying all was that undefinable scent that was simply man, and it was nearly overwhelming as it always was around men of war and power.

Byles motioned to a chair at a table large enough to seat six people. One of the soldiers took my cloak and hung it on a peg next to their coats and cloaks.

Another soldier, the one who had cast the apologetic look at me to begin with, brought me a cup of tea that I gratefully accepted. He was beanpole tall and thin with a shock of pale hair that curled down over his forehead, and I could imagine a mother fondly pushing it into place. He pushed it back under the cap as I thought this and smiled shyly. "Thank you, Sergeant—"

"Gatlan, ma'am."

"Thank you, Sergeant Gatlan."

"Yes, yes," Byles said irritably, pulling out a small leather-bound notebook to start his interrogation. I gave him my name and age, where I was from, and Mother's address. Why deny that or that I was from Virginia?

"Did you not realize there is a war?" he asked gently as if he were soothing a frightened child.

"Yes, but my mother's illness hadn't been notified. When she alerted me she was sick, I came to tend to her."

"And her doctor's name?"

"Frain."

"Have you had any contact with rebel supporters while you've been here?"

I leveled my gaze at him. "Since you are aware of my actions, I assume you also know of the many others who were engaged in similar actions of waving Rebel flags. How would I know if I had met such miscreants? I refuse to discuss any more of this foolishness with you."

He asked a few more questions, but I remained still as stone and pulled the tucking combs and pins out of my pocket so I could finish braiding my hair and put it up. A last question met with a tight-lipped mouth bristling with pins like a porcupine. He began tapping the music on the table again as he watched me. I tried to smooth my wayward curls into submission, but they were as stubborn as their mistress and refused to be subdued. Gatlan handed me a small looking glass that had been hanging on a post. Little curls were everywhere; the humidity must be soaring. "Moses, I can't do anything with this nest."

I finished with a few pins and the tucking combs and handed the mirror back to him.

"What are you playing?" I asked.

"Pardon?"

"It looks like you're playing piano."

"Does it?" Byles shrugged. "I do this when I'm thinking."

I turned to watch soldiers outside the window. The thinking and recital continued.

"I'm sure we can put all this unpleasantness behind us if you will but sign an oath of allegiance," he said, giving up on interrogation and pulling a paper from the desk against the wall.

I tore my gaze from the soldiers drilling and leveled it on him with viperous intent. "I'm sure you may go to hell."

"Oh, where are my manners?" he said brightly. "Let me give you a tour of Fort McHenry."

As if preparing to take me to the gallows, Sergeant Gatlan picked up my cloak with a glum look and placed it over my shoulders.

"Thank you, sir."

I wasn't really in the mood for a tour of the fort, but if it would get me out of there and back home, I would entertain him for a time. Byles pointed out the historical features and the beautiful view of the bay. "Did you notice?" he said, turning me around gently. I had decided not to be so prickly and allowed him to guide me and take my arm. "The fort also has a spectacular view of the city." His hand rested on a cannon as he said this, and I didn't fail to notice it was aimed at the city. An amused smile met me when I turned. "The commander decided to broach no further insurrections from the townsfolk. What was the conversation when he showed this to Police Commissioner Davis? Let me think. Oh, yes, something about he should be very sorry to fire on the city but not hesitate a moment to hold the fort. Dire times call for dire measures, don't you agree?"

"Yes, because singing Dixie is the direst of offenses." I laid my hand on his arm companionably and smiled sweetly. "I hear Dixie is Lincoln's favorite song. Will you be arresting him also?"

"I doubt he waves the Bonnie Blue as he sings it," Byles replied acerbically, removing my offending hand.

Gatlan had been picking wildflowers as we spoke and shyly handed me a small bouquet. I thanked him quietly, not wanting to draw too much attention to him as Byles was already rolling his eyes at the gesture.

"No fort is complete without its prison, of course," Byles said as we returned from the ramparts and took my arm. "Dank, dismal affairs, but I would be remiss if I didn't show you."

So, this was the purpose of the tour. He was trying to break my resolve. I raised my chin. He must have noted the motion because he smiled, and his grip on my arm tightened just the tiniest amount. The tunnel into the cells smelled of fetid mold and human waste. I refrained from covering my nose, but my nostrils flared in protest. A few prisoners looked up from their tiny cells in mild interest. Mattresses barely big enough for a grown man were stacked on end in the cells, and the men sat on bare floors. The cells weren't much larger than the mattresses and reminded me of nothing more than mausoleums.

"The floors are damp, alas," Byles said. "The prisoners find it necessary to stand their mattresses up in the daytime; else they'd be sleeping in a swamp at night. As you can see, the cells aren't big enough for chairs or tables. Quite depressing, really, but then prison isn't supposed to be pleasant, is it?"

"I don't suppose so." My discomfort with small places had already seized me. "Who did this man murder?" I asked at the end of the tunnel.

The man stood and bowed. "I dared to write an unflattering newspaper article about Mr. Lincoln, madam."

"President Lincoln," Byles growled.

"When he acts like a president and not a tyrant, I shall address him as such," the man challenged.

When Byles tried to lead me closer to the cell adjacent to the man, I balked like a colt in its first halter.

"Now, now." He clasped my arm firmly and nodded to the sergeant. I realized with great horror they meant to put me in it and screamed. The black metal door clanged back against the brick wall when I flung myself against it. I fought them, digging in my heels, flailing, kicking, and clawing at his face, but I was in the cell within short order, and the door slammed shut. I stood panting inside my cage, glaring at Byles, seething. He reached up and felt the side of his face where I had raked deep scratches across one cheek. The blood on his hand seemed to surprise him. He sighed. "Oh, Miss McKenzie, you've marred my boyish good looks, but then I'm told some women enjoy a more rugged countenance." Motioning to Sergeant Gatlan without taking his eyes off me, he said, "Sergeant, would you go get Miss McKenzie her accouterments? She'll be staying with us for a while."

Gatlan hesitated as if he were reluctant to leave me alone with Byles.

"Now," snapped Byles.

"Yes, sir."

He touched his face again. "You're going to pay for this, of course. Not that I care about a scratch. I'm not delicate. It's just a matter of principle. I think if we let you cool your heels a bit, your fine temper may settle. What say you?"

My heart still pounded in my chest. My breath was still ragged. My fury raged. "Go to hell."

"Oh, I'm quite sure of that. I've earned my way."

He stood back, appraising me. He wasn't tall, but on closer inspection, he was quite muscular, a shorter and smaller version of Carl. He could have easily snapped an arm in two had he wished. The cell was so small there was no way to escape his gaze, and so I stood, staring back at him, arms over my heaving chest. If only I had my knife. I imagined planting it in Byles, deeply, with great malice and satisfaction. A smile flitted across my lips.

Byles laughed. "You're imagining murder. Did I die screaming?"

I felt my cheeks flaming. "Very much so."

"Honesty. I appreciate that." He turned to look down the tunnel. "Ah, here comes your young knight, and he's even picked you more flowers. Isn't it a shame all men aren't as considerate? Maybe I'll bring you flowers someday."

I opened my mouth to respond.

He waved his hand. "I know, go to hell. You need to expand your repertoire."

Gatlan stopped in front of the cell with a blanket, a tin cup, a knife, a water flask, and a fistful of flowers to replace the flowers that had been trampled in the fight. Byles unlocked the door and allowed Gatlan to duck his way into my cell, for the opening was so low that I could only enter without bowing. He slunk into the cell like a whipped dog and laid the items in my arms. His wayward curl had escaped his kepi again, and he looked so much like a little boy right now that I wanted to brush it up for him, even if he had helped toss me in here.

"Thank you, Sergeant. You've been most considerate."

"Yes, ma'am."

"Come along, Sergeant. I'm sure madam would like to set up housekeeping."

Their footsteps faded hollowly as I looked about my new home. Like almost everything else here, it was made of brick. I was in a brick box with a rounded top, not unlike some coffins. I counted the bricks in the floor. Five and a half wide, so about forty inches. I leaned one shoulder against a wall and touched the other wall with my fingertips.

Dear God. I won't survive this.

Chapter Thirty-Nine

I wanted to weep for fear and exhaustion and anxiety of what was to come, but surely Gertie was moving heaven and earth to get me out. Mother would call on all her high friends.

"That was quite a fight you put up, Miss," came from the next cell.

"Thank you. Not that it did any good. Lorena McKenzie of the Fighting Clan McKenzie."

He laughed. "So, I see. Brian Kingston at your service. I would say don't let Byles frighten you, but he's a genuinely bad character. That being said, I'm sure Major Morris will return soon. I can't imagine Byles would be plowing roughshod so if he were here."

That was some consolation. "Are there many women confined?" I sipped the water and poured some into the cup for my flowers. Frivolous, perhaps, but they wouldn't drink much, and I needed cheering.

"Parson," Kingston yelled. "Are there any women here?"

"No. They aren't that godless yet."

"They are now. Meet Miss McKenzie."

"Hello, Parson," I called out. Then to Kingston, "Is he really a parson?"

"Yes," he replied. "He refused to bless Lincoln in his services, and someone reported him."

I dropped the thin gray blanket on the floor and sank down on it. My cloak I folded to make a padding to lean against.

"I'm afraid," I admitted.

"Don't be. I'm sure they'll have you out quickly, and Byles can't really do much to you other than try to scare you into a confession. What was your crime?"

"Waving a Bonnie Blue at some passing troops and singing Dixie and a few other Rebel songs."

His laugh echoed down the tunnel. "The prison will fill up quickly in that case. There are dozens, if not a hundred or more, young ladies doing similar things in Monument Square."

"Byles is just a vile man, and there are plenty of those in the world, but I'm afraid of small spaces. I fell down an embankment once when I was a child and was trapped for hours under the dirt. I thought I was going to die. This cell feels very much like a tomb. I'm afraid if I start coming undone, I won't be able to breathe."

"I see. We'll have to keep your mind off things. You may have to bang on the bars with your cup if you have difficulties at night. I am dead to the world once I go to sleep. I once slept through an earthquake. It drives my wife insane."

"Thank you, Mr. Kingston."

"Brian. Let's not stand on formality."

We discussed families and friends, the current political climate, and the weather. And before I knew it, they were bringing dinner.

"Did my wife not send a food packet?" Kingston asked.

"Not today," the servant answered.

"Rubbish. How about some extra food from the Ladies' Aide for Miss McKenzie?"

"Marse Byles say she to get standard fare. Nothin' else, sir."

"All right, Boyd. Thank you." There was a pause. "Stop calling him marse."

"Yassuh."

I thanked Boyd, who was an elderly Negro, definitely from the South at some point, with knobby, gnarled fingers and a ready, if toothless, smile. Dinner consisted of a bowl of watery bean soup lacking flavor and beans to speak of, a cracker called hardtack, and a cup of coffee. Not knowing if I would be fed again or what, I choked down the flavored water and nibbled on the cracker.

"Should I save the hardtack for later?"

"Law, no," Kingston exclaimed. "Rats are bad enough. Don't draw them to your cell with food."

And that was it. Drawing my knees up to my chest, I laid my head down on them and sobbed with my arms over my head as if I could hide from my new reality.

"Miss McKenzie, Lorena. Don't cry. It's not that bad if you don't keep food around. My wife brought me a tin to keep food in, and that solved the problem."

I continued weeping. "All this over waving a miserable flag. When I was a little girl, I saw a baby who lost her toes to rats." I blubbered out between sobs.

"I sometimes sleep with my shoes on and take them off in the daytime to let my feet breathe, but you'll be all right. We'll get you through this. It's not like you're a reporter."

I laughed and sniffled. "Yes, thank you."

"Sing for me."

"What?"

"I love 'Shenandoah.' Do you know it?"

"Yes."

We spent much of the afternoon singing until I forgot to be afraid. Even Parson and some of the other prisoners joined in. Parson had a beautiful baritone voice. Someone down the line sang slightly off-key but with great joy. A soldier outside the window stopped on his rounds to join in one of the songs.

Boyd returned late that afternoon with a small lap desk and an oath of allegiance. "Marse Byles say he want you to sign this an' you can go free, Miss."

"What did I tell you about calling him marse, Boyd?" came from the next cell.

"Yassuh, but you know what they say bout teachin' an old dog new tricks, an' I'm a pretty old dog."

"I'll have Mrs. Kingston bring me some dimes the next time she comes, and every time you call him Mr. Byles or that Devil Byles, I'll give you a dime."

Boyd laughed. "Don't reckon I better call him Debil Byles, but I'll try Mistah."

While they debated Byles, I signed the oath "Mrs. Mary Todd Lincoln" and wrote *in infernum* below it.

Brian and I visited about my school and The Pines until I curled up on my blanket to take a nap. I didn't think I could sleep, but I did until Boyd reappeared with supper, boiled salt pork, hardtack, and coffee. I sliced off a bite of the salt pork and tried to choke it down but could bear no more and ate the cracker and coffee. Boyd admonished me about not eating, saying I had to keep my strength up, and I promised to do better tomorrow. I knew I most likely wouldn't; the meat was near rancid, and I could last on hardtack until I was released. With little else to do, I lay down again and tried to sleep.

"You didn't eat your supper."

I opened my eyes and saw Byles standing outside my cell with a paper in his hand. Judging from his fawn breeches tucked in knee-high black boots, spurs, and a close-fitted jacket, he'd been riding.

"I wasn't hungry."

"Need to keep your strength up."

"So Boyd said." I stood to face him. "Is there something I can help you with, or do you check on the dietary habits of all the prisoners?"

He held up the paper. "Mary Todd Lincoln. My heart is warmed that she's so loyal."

I inclined my head.

"And you sent me a note. A love note?"

"Of course."

He laughed. "I'm sure." One leg crossed over the other as he leaned against the wall, arms folded across his chest. He studied me, half smiling with a toothpick angled from the corner of his mouth as if imagining something amusing. "What are we going to do with you, Miss McKenzie?"

I took a step toward the barred gate. "Let me go. This is a spurious charge, and you know it."

"You're a seditionist. My men found the flag. So, I not only have witnesses but also the flag." He started tapping his fingers rhythmically against one arm again in that odd way of his. "Would you like to ask a favor of me? Can I contact someone for you?"

I wanted to cry out, "Yes, anyone. Uncle George! Get me out of here." Then I looked at that infuriating smirk and said, "No, I require no boons from you. Let me rot." As soon as I said it, I could have bitten my tongue.

He grinned and rolled the toothpick across his lip. "As you wish."

Fool.

I listened to his footsteps fade and then slid down the wall of my cell into a heap.

"Tell me, do you poke bears in Virginia for sport?"

"No, Brian," I said miserably. "I'm an idiot. The man infuriates me."

Brian offered to light his candle that night to assuage my fears, but there was a bit of moonlight streaming through the barred window nearby, and I didn't want him to waste it. The blanket was of the coarsest wool. There were no linens on the mattress. I thought about sleeping in my clothes, but I also didn't know how long I would be here, so I undressed to my chemise, used my petticoats as best I could for linens, and laid out my dress over the blanket for warmth. At last, I dozed off, and though I slept fitfully, I did sleep.

Breakfast was hardtack and coffee. It wasn't good coffee, but it was coffee, and I wished for more. I also wished mightily for a brush and a bath. Later that morning, Sergeant Gatlan came bearing gifts. He'd told his sister about me, who was mortified that a lady was confined. She sent a brush, looking glass, small pitcher, wash basin, washcloth, and soap. Never was a man more welcome in life than this gangly young fellow with his sack of delights.

"Patience apologized for the meagerness of the items, but she was in a hurry to gather them and had to take what she could buy quickly," he said.

"Oh, no," I cried. "This is more precious than gold. Please thank her, and thank you."

He blushed and mumbled something, then excused himself, regretfully locking me back in my cage, but I didn't care. I could brush my hair and wash, and that would be heaven.

Brian chuckled. "You sound like a bird in a bath over there with all that splashing about. If birds hummed happily."

"Oh, you have no idea how joyous this is. I can't wash my hair, but I won't be here that long."

"Another day at most, I would think," he replied.

I had leaned my mattress up against the wall and was sitting on my folded blanket close to the door, brushing my hair, when Byles appeared in person with the lap desk and another oath of allegiance. I stood and backed away from the door, my heart sinking. This could only mean I wasn't being released.

"Miss McKenzie. I'm sorry to interrupt your ablutions, but we have some business. If you'll but sign this, you can be on your way." He glanced down at the wash basin and looking glass. "I didn't realize Gatlan also brought you a looking glass. I can't allow that, of course. You might have an accident with it and cut yourself…or someone else."

He smiled knowingly as I envisioned slicing his throat with it at this very moment.

"I assure you—of course." I wasn't going to plead with him over a mirror.

"Is there anything else you require? Anything I can do for you today? You'll be careful with the wash basin?"

"Very."

I snatched the desk and paper away from him and knelt to sign. *Mrs. Abigail Adams* and below *Ne cede malis.*

He took a toothpick from a silver case inside his vest pocket. I realized now that the pick was a sliver of cinnamon stick when he pulled it out, and the cinnamon scent wafted to me. My stomach growled in response as I recalled Della's wonderful cinnamon rolls. An eyebrow rose, and the smirk returned. "Are you sure there's nothing you require? Nothing I can get you?"

"Nothing."

I stood and handed back the oath and desk.

"Ah, one of my favorites. And another love note. How thoughtful."

I curtsied with a malevolent glare and wished him to hell.

He laughed and locked my cage. "Oh, I'm already headed there, my dear."

"Stay out of my head," I whispered as he whistled away.

"You two have an interesting relationship," Brian said later.

"He's just trying to frighten me. I'm not going to let him." They were brave words, but I wasn't so sure. My voice quavered even as I made the bold declaration. The close quarters and hunger were already wearing on me. He could last longer than I could in a war of wills, but surely George wouldn't let me sit long.

"What note did you send him?"

"Yield not to evil in Latin."

There was a soft snort. "Let's hope he doesn't read Latin or find a translator. Tell me more about your school."

I was sure he couldn't care less about a boarding school, but I scooted close to my gate to see the window and not feel so confined, then spoke of it and the girls. It took my mind off the walls that crept ever closer.

Later, Boyd surprised me with a bowl of real bean soup. It was delicious and filled with beans, bits of onion, carrots, celery, ham, and spiced to perfection. I drank down every drop. Though the bowl was small, my thankful stomach was soon full. Brian thought I was hallucinating as he had been served the same bean water as usual, but thankfully, his wife had sent along a food packet today, so he didn't begrudge my good fortune.

"Missus say she was sick and de maid forgot to send you food," Boyd said. "Won't happen no mo'. She done run dat mutton-headed cullion muncher off."

Kingston snorted. "Ah, my delicate Rosie. I'm sure that little speech impressed one and all."

"Two of de men got up an' left de room laughin'. One man choked on his coffee."

After Boyd left, we pondered my good fortune and whether it might continue. "Maybe someone took pity on you?" he said. "You may be wearing Byles down."

We both laughed at the thought. Not long after eating, I begged off further discussion or even our customary singing to pass the time, saying I was exhausted and only wanted a nap. I pulled down my mattress, chancing it becoming soaked, and lay down, dead to the world.

Boyd woke me up at suppertime, but I declined through a fatigued haze, saying I only wanted sleep. After he left, I managed barely to undress and undo my hair. With my petticoat spread to sleep on, I pulled the blanket over me and fell back into a deep slumber.

"There, there, darling. It'll be all right."

Through the fog, I felt a hand gently stroking my face and hair. My head was in a warm, comforting lap. "Mama?"

A soft chuckle. "Not quite." More stroking. "Shh, shh. Just rest. I have you."

I fought to open my eyes, but they were like lead. A hand patted my bare shoulder. There was a muted golden glow. I tried to remember where I was. My cell, but it was night. My eyes forced open. A candle flickered nearby. Cinnamon and cloves. I knew that scent. Looking up, I saw what I feared. Byles peered down affectionately at me.

"Hello, darling. Are you feeling better?"

I tried to sit up but floundered. He pushed me gently back down. "No, no. It's all right. Ben will take care of you."

"What are you doing here?" I pulled the blanket up over my chest and pushed his hand away. "Leave me alone."

"A guard came to me and said he thought you were distressed. I had to come, of course. I brought you some chamomile tea with a bit of brandy. That's what my nanny used to fix me when I was sick. I still drink it when I can't sleep."

He resumed stroking my hair.

"Moses! Stop petting me."

"Of course. You're upset."

"How long have you been here?" Heaving myself into an upright position, I tried to clear my head.

He touched the cup near him. "Your tea is stone cold, so I would say for quite some time." Picking it up, he offered it to me.

I shook my head.

"Drink your tea, and I'll leave. It's not poison. Look, I'll drink some first." He smiled benevolently and drank, then put the cup to my lips.

Knowing he wouldn't leave until I drank it, I swallowed the tea and looked at him to see if he was satisfied.

"Good girl. Now see. That wasn't so difficult, was it?" He stood and picked up the candle, then quirked a brow at me. "Would you like me to leave this? Are you afraid of the dark?"

I desperately wanted him to leave it. The absolute darkness of the cell terrified me when the moon didn't shine, and the clouds hid all light tonight. I shook my head.

He sighed. "Oh, darling. Would it really have hurt you to say yes this once? As you wish. Into the darkness once more. I'll send the doctor to check on you tomorrow and allow your mother to send a fresh change of clothes. I'm not without heart."

I watched the light fade and pulled my mattress to the edge of my gate to sit in the corner and stare at the window, hoping for a glimmer of moonlight. Then I wrapped my blanket around me and forced myself not to cry. I felt as if I were suffocating, and I would not survive. I sat curled up in the corner until nearly dawn, breathing raggedly and staring at the window. I should have stirred Brian, but he either woke on his own or sensed I was in distress.

"Lorena. Miss McKenzie."

I didn't answer.

"Lorena, listen to me. Focus. You're going to start panicking if you don't listen. Now pay attention."

"Y-yes—what do you want?" I said between shuddering sobs.

"Think. Tell me about Lucy and Persy. Focus. Tell me about the marble game."

"I can't. Leave me alone."

"Yes, you can."

"What does he want with me?"

"Don't think about him. Don't think about the dark. Think about Lucy and Persy. Talk to me."

He pressed me to talk about the girls, describing each of them, what they liked, how they spoke, the help, the farm, and the horses. I objected to him digging for pointless details about what kind of dresses they wore in each adventure, and he'd say, "I'm a reporter; I require details." I'd have to stop and think, remember until I realized my heart had stopped racing and my mind had calmed.

"How did you know to do that?" I said at last.

"I covered the Crimean War," he replied. "I suffered from nostalgia afterward, and a doctor showed me how to focus on mundane things from my past to get control of my terrors."

I sank into slumber and didn't wake again until Boyd announced he had a surprise. "Lookee here, Missie. Mistah Byles say he worried about you health and had the cook make you up some nice, scrambled eggs an' a bit of fried apples with cinnamon. Even sent along a slice of light bread with butter. Mmm, mmm."

I eyed the plate suspiciously but was too hungry to turn it down. "Thank you, Boyd. I'm sure Mr. Byles will be along directly with his oath, and I'll thank him in person."

I might survive. Though I flinched at the apples as the cinnamon scent reminded me of Byles, I wolfed them down. It was a light breakfast, but that's all my stomach could handle. Byles knew what he was doing. It reminded me of people who starved horses they couldn't control. When they did start feeding them again, they had to feed slowly. I resented being trained.

Sergeant Gatlan arrived later with a fresh set of clothes. Praise the Lord. He was grinning like a possum when he delivered them. "I thought these might cheer you up."

"Oh, clean clothes," I crooned. The dress was bright mint green with pink rosebuds and dark green ribbon trim. It wasn't perfect prison wear, but Mother was trying to cheer me up. Inside the package was a full set of innerwear. Even a hair net and matching ribbon. Sallie, bless her. Gatlan turned his head when I opened the package with inner clothes, and I tactfully laid it aside to examine more fully later even though I was sure they had already inspected it for contraband.

"I'll see if we can get you some fresh water to bathe," he said.

"Thank you."

"I wish you could see me," I said to Brian after I had bathed and changed clothes. "I look like I'm about to go out for a walk in the park." I clasped the bars of my gate and looked toward the window. "Oh, how I wish I were. I long to feel grass under my feet. I can't imagine how you feel being in here so long."

"Extend your arm. Let me see you."

I stuck my arm through the gate as far as I could.

"Yes, I can barely see the end of your arm, but you look divine, Miss McKenzie. Divine, I say. I'm going to write a fashion column about you."

We were in such high spirits that we decided to sing some favorite songs, starting with Dixie. That always earned a "Shut that up" from somewhere down the tunnel and only prompted us to sing it again and louder.

The doctor came to see me and brought the lap desk and oath with him.

"Mr. Byles is busy with other things and asked me to bring this. You are to sign it with your name if you please. Now what seems to be the problem? He said you were indisposed?"

I told him about how I had felt groggy and unable to focus during the night. Unable to move or think coherently. He examined me and tapped on his chin a bit. "You're a bit fatigued, but mainly I think you just overmedicated yourself, Miss."

I looked up from signing Martha Washington's name to the oath. "What?"

"You took too much sleeping powders, I think."

"I don't have any sleeping powders."

"Oh? Then perhaps a reaction to food. You seem fine now."

I added *anguis in herba* after Martha's name, for he was truly a snake in the grass, and handed the oath and desk back to the doctor. "Thank you, sir."

I refused the soup for dinner, accepting only the hardtack and hardtack again for supper. How long I could subsist on crackers, I didn't know, but I wasn't giving him another chance to drug me.

Byles didn't come by until after supper. Though he wore it in moderation, his cologne was distinctive, and I smelled it as soon as he stepped into the hall leading to our cells. I had hoped he would stay busy, and I would be spared a visit. My disappointment was palpable.

"Good evening, Miss McKenzie," he called out cheerfully as he unlocked the gate. He didn't bother to pull it shut. Even though the opening was tempting, where would I run?

"Good evening, Mr. Byles. Thank you for breakfast." I wanted to add "and the drugging," but thought better of it.

"I was concerned about you, but you're looking much better today. Quite lovely in fact. You'd look much prettier outside this dreary prison, don't you think? All you need do is sign this oath. Properly, of course."

He waved the oath and laughed. He laughed too often, and it annoyed me. Everything seemed to amuse him as if the world were his plaything. "Very clever. I'm glad Martha Washington is also so loyal to the cause."

I curtsied. "I'm glad you enjoyed it."

"Oh, I enjoy a great many things about you, my dear. That's why I brought you a gift." He held out a spoon.

I accepted it with thanks and motioned to the cell with an apologetic shrug. "I'd offer you a seat, but I seem to be out of—" Had I not been turning back at just that moment, I would have missed the predatory shift in his eyes. I backed up toward the corner where the cup and knife lay, but in a quick stride, he was there before me and snatched up the knife. "No, no. That's why I brought you the spoon. No need for this."

"Why did you let me keep it this long?"

He shrugged. "It gave you a sense of control. If you really wanted to, you could dispatch your monsters. Of course, some monsters could have you on your knees and begging for mercy in a matter of seconds."

A flash of defiance flared.

"Don't tempt me, Miss McKenzie."

I willed myself to think of something else besides the abiding hatred I felt for the man.

With a fluid motion, he slipped my knife into his pocket, pulled out a switchblade instead, and flicked it open. "It wasn't that useful anyway. One with a longer, sharper blade, like this, is."

Was he going to kill me? I shied away from him, but the cell was so small that I was soon up against the wall.

He smiled but stood where he was and only retrieved one of those odd cinnamon toothpicks. The spicy scent filled the air. Then he stepped forward, blade raised.

Dear God. He *was* going to kill me.

I drew breath to scream, but his hand was over my mouth before I could make a sound.

"Oh," he sighed, pressing his body against mine, driving my back against the rough brick. "I love it when a woman screams. I can always tell when they're going to. Their eyes give them away. The fear, you know. Then they fill up their lungs. Their ribs expand. Their breasts rise in the most desirable way. It's exhilarating. I'm particularly good at cutting off that scream if I want. Practice.

"Then," he moved his hand up over my nose until I couldn't breathe. I struggled against him, clawing at his arm. The blood pounded in my ears. My chest felt as if it might explode. I saw stars, and my hand dropped from his. He let his hand slip. "I could stop you from screaming altogether, couldn't I?"

I slumped against the wall, gasping for breath, but nodded. He remained pressed against me, preventing any struggle or escape, and counted down my ribs with the knife. "Did you know if you stab someone between this rib and this rib, it goes into the lung, and they can't scream at all? They make not a sound. Not much of one anyway. But then my lady is dead, and what fun is a dead lady? Sometimes, though, it's just a regrettable necessity. It won't be with you, will it?"

I shook my head.

"No, I didn't think so. It would be such a waste of a beautiful woman." He rubbed his cheek against mine as gently as a lover might and closed his eyes. "Dear God. You have the most pristine skin. Like silk. The things I can imagine doing to it." He laughed giddily and leaned back, looking into my eyes. First, he caressed my cheek with his hand, then with the knife, and smiled. "Such beautiful skin."

I felt a scream rising.

"No, no. Mustn't scream. You think I'm a beast, but I'm not. I can be quite charming. I love Southern women. They're my specialty. They love me. I know what they like," he paused, "for a while. You might even enjoy me. I would certainly enjoy you. I would be exceedingly attentive to you." He said all this in a soft, almost sing-song voice as if whispering the sweetest lover's promises to me.

I turned away in revulsion at the thought of him touching me.

"That shiver. Is it anticipation?" His head lowered to my throat, and he inhaled deeply. "I've investigated you. You raise horses. So, you understand how a stallion smells a mare when she's in season. Did you know a sensitive man can smell a woman too?" He inhaled again and sighed. "The smell of fear is almost as exciting."

Pushing my chin back toward him with the tip of the knife, he gazed deeply into my eyes. "Yes, Miss McKenzie. I would enjoy you very much. You think I'm going to rape you, but this isn't the place for it. I just wanted to pay my respects and bring you the spoon."

He lowered the knife and wrapped his other arm around me, then kissed me. When I started to struggle, he pressed the knife into my ribs. The kiss was long and probing, gentle at first, then more insistent, thrusting, exploring my mouth with this tongue. I wriggled under him again, trying to get away, but he pressed his body into me harder and slid the knife across my rib. He tasted of cinnamon and rum tobacco. His lips were surprisingly soft and warm, biting with the tang of the cinnamon stick he chewed on. His beard and mustache were so like Baron's. I hated him for the deception.

It was a kiss, but that was all he wanted. It could have been worse. I could survive this. Don't think about it.

When he was done, he smiled at me—almost sweetly. "You have a lover somewhere."

I glared at him and tried to push him away.

He pocketed his knife and caressed my throat. "Fortunate man." Before I realized it, his fingers tightened. I raised my hands to pull them away, but my vision narrowed. The smile broadened. Fingers tightening. His eyes were pure ice, soulless. My vision shimmered and went black.

"Here, what's going on in there?" I heard through a haze.

"I came to check on Miss McKenzie and found her in a faint. Go get some fresh water and brandy."

"Yes, sir."

I wanted to scream at him not to leave me alone but was unable to move, let alone cry out.

Byles gathered me up in his lap and stroked my face. "There, there, darling. It's going to be all right. Ben's going to take care of you."

I struggled to sit up but had neither the strength nor coordination. It was as if I were drunk.

He held me closer and crooned at me, stroking my hair. "You wanted to tell me to go to hell a bit ago but didn't. You're learning. I think just a little time with me, and I would have you trained. Breathtaking to think about."

"Leave me alone," I whispered, imagining what kind of training he had in mind. Tears sprang to my eyes, and he wiped them tenderly.

"There, there. Don't cry. It's going to be all right."

Byles gave me the cup of brandy and water and left me with a promise to visit the next day. I spent the night curled up in the corner of my cell, staring at the window. Brian made me talk about the girls and their embroidery. What was Beth reading? Could I recite some *Ivanhoe*? I wanted to scream at him to leave me alone in my tomb, but he wouldn't. He kept me talking until sleep overtook me.

The next morning, after breakfast, I was escorted to the commandant's office. Colonel Orwyn, Captain Simmons, an unfamiliar major, and Byles were all embroiled in an argument when I walked in.

"Miss McKenzie?" the major said.

"Yes."

"I'm Major Morris, commander of Fort McHenry when I'm allowed to be here. I'm sorry I was away when you were brought in."

"Yes, sir."

"Please sit down, all."

He sat behind his desk, and we all took seats around the room. Orwyn and Simmons looked at me and each other, somewhat aghast. I sighed, knowing I must look a fright. With any luck at all, this ordeal might be coming to an end. The flag was folded neatly on the corner of Major Morris's desk.

Byles sat near me, one booted leg over his knee with a small table between us.

"You're accused of sedition." Major Morris continued, consulting a paper "You waved this flag and sang various Rebel songs while troops passed below in the street. Is that correct?"

"Yes."

"You aren't denying it?"

"Not in the least."

"And you refused to sign an oath of allegiance."

"I signed a few."

"So I see," Morris said, flipping through the signed oaths. "But none with your name."

"Nor will I."

"Major," Colonel Orwyn said, "I passed a girl wearing a dress made of a Palmetto flag this morning. While she ought to be arrested for questionable fashion sense, if we start arresting every one of these Monument Square Girls and others who wave Bonnie Blues or sing Dixie, there won't be an open cell in Baltimore."

I arched an eyebrow. A dress made of the first Confederate flag. Brave girl.

"Then we'll start filling other prisons," Byles replied irritably. He was drumming his fingers in that odd rhythmic pattern again on a table next to his chair. He caught me watching his hand. "Mozart's 3rd, Miss McKenzie. I have an unfortunate habit of tapping it when I'm thinking. My grandmother always decried my short fingers for playing piano, but they're long enough for other things, don't you agree?"

I stared at him, remembering those fingers around my throat.

"I'm releasing Miss McKenzie," Morris said, looking between us. "I would think you have more important things to do, Mr. Byles, than harass young ladies."

"Thank you, Major," I said most sincerely.

"I better not find you harassing her again," Orwyn grumbled.

"Careful where you tread, Colonel," Byles said. "Allan Pinkerton has the ear of Lincoln, and colonels can be easily replaced."

"As can two-bit agents," Captain Simmons said indignantly. He looked closer at me and frowned. "How did you get those bruises on your neck?"

I heard a click and saw Byles cleaning his nails with his knife. He glanced up at me.

"Bruises? I must have been thrashing around in my sleep." His game was done, and I was free. Captain Simmons and Colonel Orwyn stood up. Simmons took my arm when I stood, but I kept my gaze on Byles. "*Acta est fabula, plaudite!*"

Byles laid down his knife and started clapping slowly. A smile crept over his face. To anyone else, it was a simple, genial expression, but I recognized the truth. *I am the wolf waiting in the dark, Kitten, and you are mine.* "Really, Miss McKenzie? The last words of Augustus? The play is over? No, I believe the play has just begun."

Had Simmons not been holding me, I would have fainted. The blood drained from my face, and my knees turned boneless. Byles held my gaze, those icy eyes plumbing my soul. I stood thus transfixed until Simmons squeezed my arm and turned me away. Leaning heavily into him, I let him put his arm around me. Behind me, I heard the familiar laugh and shuddered.

Chapter Forty

They loaded me into a carriage and took me home with an escort of soldiers. "Why are you here?" I asked when we were safely away.

"Your mother prevailed on anyone with rank to save you, but we could do nothing until Morris returned," Colonel Orwyn replied. "Your aunt had the diplomatic corps raising hell in the White House, but Lincoln has other things on his mind and refused to get involved with Pinkertons."

"Thank you. I'm in your debt." I didn't dare tell them how dire my situation had been.

Mother and Gertie dashed out the door to swoop me up nearly before we stopped. Colonel Orwyn and Captain Simmons trailed along and accepted a flurry of thanks and a supper invitation but said they should return to duty. I feared them leaving but thanked them again and let them depart.

Mother insisted I be bathed and fed, proclaiming I looked like an escapee from a cemetery. My clothes were promptly tossed in a roaring fire, fearing lice infestation, no doubt. She was probably right. A shampoo of lye soap, brandy, olive oil, and eggs twice and a vinegar rinse just to make sure, plus a thorough raking with a fine-toothed comb, and I was sanitary once more. Even with the lavender talc, I wasn't sure I would ever get the prison stench from my nostrils. I was peppered with questions from all fronts. Gertie and Mother shooed the servants away and then delicately inquired if anyone had touched me. I assured them I had been treated well and made up an excuse for the bruises on my throat.

Doctor Frain arrived shortly after I finished eating, his medical bag in hand and a calm air that belied the storm still brewing. He endured Mother's hovering and frantic questions with patience that belonged to saints and physicians alone. At last, he insisted on seeing me privately.

Once in my room, he motioned for me to sit near the window. Sunlight poured over the instruments unpacked with quiet precision. The small, familiar care routines settled some part of me that still felt raw and jagged.

"How are you?" he asked.

"I'm not sure," I admitted, my hand instinctively brushing the bruises on my neck. "I made as brave a front as possible, but the man terrifies me."

Frain's expression didn't change, though his eyes sharpened. "That's expected," he said, examining my throat. "No woman should have to endure what you did. I'll leave you some arnica salve for those bruises. Tell me what happened."

The words caught in my throat like thorns, but I told him everything. Then, I stared out the window, pondering what weighed heaviest on my mind. "Doctor?" How did I even ask this? "The kiss?"

"Yes?"

"I struggled at first, but he reminded me of the knife by sticking it in my ribs again, and I stopped. The kiss was tender, like a lover's kiss. It wasn't violent. Seductive almost, if I can use the word. I don't understand."

He folded the stethoscope and put it in his bag. "I'm sure from what you said, he's a predator and a practiced one. It's another form of torture to keep the captive off-kilter. He means to make you doubt yourself. Don't let him. Stay a few days and recuperate."

It fit. "I don't want to let him win."

"We'll talk soon, but rest now." He mixed up some sleeping powders. "This is a mild dose. I'll leave some more. You'll nap and not feel groggy when you wake."

Later that night, supper was pleasant if subdued. Colonel Orwyn and Captain Simmons were hailed as conquering heroes and assured they would always be welcome in the Dobbs/McKenzie houses. Gertie protested the McTavish house also.

Gertie left the next day to return to Washington after extracting a promise that I would see her before returning home.

Before the arrest, Mother had planned events for each waking moment, introducing me to every eligible, wealthy, powerful, or influential young bachelor and a few who weren't so young or eligible until I threatened to lock myself in my room if she didn't cease operations. Now she hovered over me, certain I was going to shatter into a thousand pieces at any moment. My only social regret was missing the play Colonel Orwyn had graciously sent tickets for.

Doctor Frain stopped by the next day as promised. "Did you sleep?" he asked as he examined me again.

"The sleep of the dead. Thank you."

"Let's walk in the garden."

I gathered the messages secreted in the daybed and the cipher wheel. Since I was leaving and didn't want to chance Mother being caught with the cipher wheel, I gave it to him to keep for me. He secreted it in the false bottom in his bag. I couldn't leave it at Mother's with Byles and Simmons snooping around. Unless someone noticed the misspelled words and strangely organized scriptures, the tracts might be explained easily enough. The cipher wheel would hang me.

We strolled, coffee in hand, Mother peering anxiously out the window. "I'm going to have to do something with your mother," he said.

"Knock her in the head?"

He chuckled. "I was thinking more of sending her to a spa for a few weeks. I wish sending you to a spa would fix everything, but it's not that simple."

"No," I replied, sitting down on the iron settee. "A spa won't fix me, but I'm starting to regain some of my starch. How dare he!"

"He dares because he can. A twisted man with power is a dangerous combination, but there's only so much he can do. The question is, do you continue now that you've garnered his attention? Another question is, *why* did you attract his attention? The Monument Square girls do that and worse every day."

I sipped my coffee slowly, surprised Sallie hadn't laced it with whiskey or brandy as she had everything else, convinced I needed calming. If she calmed me more, I was going to turn into an alcoholic. "I'm curious about that also, but the situation remains the same regardless of Byles."

"It's changed a bit since you were arrested, actually."

"How so?" I asked, afraid to ask, but I must know.

"Have you heard about the Phillipi Races?"

Another sip of coffee, wishing I had the whiskey now. "No."

"A Union force under General Morris surrounded an ill-equipped and poorly trained Confederate militia in Phillipi to take control of the B and O and the turnpikes in the area to keep Rebs from disrupting their supply lines. At dawn on the day you were arrested, they attacked. The Rebs were ill-prepared to defend and fled, abandoning weapons and supplies. Twenty-six Reb casualties to two Union. The North named it the Phillipi Races and said this was exactly how the war would proceed. The South has not a prayer, they think."

Byles wormed his way into my mind, but now I was mad, and while that didn't always lead to sane decisions, the anger had pulled me out of the swale. And here was a renewed fear for my girls. "Phillipi isn't that far from Winchester. These missions must proceed. How do we throw him off my trail?"

Doctor Frain lifted a brow as if to ask if I were certain.

"I realize what kind of man he is. I fear him but refuse to live *in* fear because of him."

"What would you do normally if you had no fear?"

I thought about this, twisting my coffee cup in my hands. "Proceed as if that whale waste had never crossed my path; be aware he might be lurking around every corner."

"My thoughts exactly. Next time you're here, we'll hide you in plain sight. Go down to Monument Square and associate with the rest of the rabble-rousers. I'm sure the other rings pass information there, but we'll hold off until we see what he does. We'll vary your routine. Give him ghosts to chase if he decides he's still interested."

If Byles arrested me again with contraband or information, I would not be saved. "You know Fort McHenry has cannon trained on the city, specifically the square, don't you?"

"Yes, but I doubt if Morris will do anything with them unless there are serious riots. I'll have people watching out for you as I did when the carriage picked you up the day Byles followed you."

It eased me somewhat, but I now realized how serious my stakes were.

"I have people observing checkpoints. You'll undoubtedly go through one or two on your way out of Washington or Alexandria. Southern ladies are irritated about being searched and not mincing words. If you act afraid or nervous, it will make them suspicious, and they'll inspect your carriage closer. Are you sure you can deal with this so soon after your experience?"

My stomach knotted at the thought of soldiers laying hands on me again, but I soothed it with the thought of thwarting Byles. "I can do it."

"I'll give you some extra medicines you can put in your bags, but they might get confiscated." He then instructed me where and how to drop the contraband carriage and where my second drop point was if the first was unsafe. He described the Johnson Farm and the owners, who were close friends of his. I could trust them as dearly as he did. I would know by the passwords given at a stop if it was safe to proceed or if I should go on. I wasn't sure I would ever unknot my nerves after all this, but I listened intently and wished him well.

Mother insisted I spend another week, but I was done with Baltimore. My only regret was declining a supper invitation from Captain Simmons, who would be in Washington. I needed a quiet rest day and planned to spend it peacefully with Aunt Gertie and Uncle George before leaving.

At The Fortress, the gray-tiled cupola with its black wrought iron–enclosed widow's walk topped the stone manse like a crown. Inside the fence paced a woman, waiting not for her seafaring captain but for my approaching carriage. I opened the carriage window. "Hiram, how long has she been up there?"

Gertie's long-suffering driver, stableman, and gardener *tched* to the horses. "Get up, boys. I reckon since I left, and she told me to leave early to make sure you didn't have to wait in case the train arrived early. Like any train ever gets in on time, let alone early."

Settling back into the seat in exasperation, I gathered my belongings. If she could rush me in on angel's wings, I'm sure she would. At the house, she raced out the door to meet me. "I'm so glad to see you!" Her arms wrapped around me as she kissed me soundly on both cheeks.

I giggled and hugged her back. "Gertie! I missed you so much. It's been two days, I'm sure."

"I can't help it if I'm delighted you made time to spend a few days."

"One day," I said sternly. "I must get back to Rosemount."

"We'll see."

"I'm serious. One day."

Uncle George wanted to buy a townhouse, which would be easier for Gertie to maintain when he was away on missions. Gertie insisted she needed room and gardens. They settled on the rambling limestone mansion on the outskirts of Washington. The city grew up around it, but Gertie fiercely protected her independence and privacy with stone walls so formidable that the house became known as The Fortress.

"Take her things to the India room," she told the assembled servants after Hiram toted my luggage in. Taking me arm-in-arm, she led me through the house and out the back door. "The girls placed refreshments in the garden. Maybe you can nap before supper."

"I'd like that. I'd forgotten how exhausting it was to simply exist in Mother's chaotic sphere combined with the other affair."

We settled into the seclusion of the gazebo. "Yes, I enjoyed our time in Baltimore aside from the other situation, of course," Gertie said, wasting no time. "Captain Simmons is charming. Heroic even. Your mother's quite enamored of him."

"She has her sights on him as a son-in-law."

"You could certainly do worse. I know your heart's set on Baron, but sometimes life leads us down paths we hadn't planned."

"He asked me to supper this evening, but I told him I was spending a quiet evening with you and Uncle George."

"You should have gone. We have all of tomorrow to visit."

"I wanted time with y'all. As for Captain Simmons. He's nice, but I'll not take your path." I had asked God and Captain Simmons' forgiveness for my bold remarks about grass-stained skirts at the ball, and we had since settled into an honest friendship. I simply wasn't going to play the man.

She waved a hand as if it were nothing, but how can your sister breaking your heart be nothing? "I forgave her a long time ago. She's the product of her raising, as we all are. She nearly died when she was two and was terribly sick for a year. After Mother had already buried three children, she was frantic about losing another and spoiled her terribly. She is who she is, as we all are, but that doesn't mean we must allow her to ruin your life.

"She has this idea all laid out of you marrying some wealthy and powerful man. You'll invite her to live in your mansion to help care for your children, and she'll go with you on all your vacations to Europe, Egypt, and other exotic locations. She'll accompany you to the opera and balls like a dowager queen. Life will be grand." She waved her hands through the air as if conducting orchestras, sashaying around, nodding to this imaginary person and that as she related Mother's grand scheme.

"Dear Father in Heaven. You can't be serious. We can't be around each other for more than a week before she's pleading her deathbed."

Her head tilted. "If you were married to Mr. Moneybags, you'd have the *best* doctors who would send her to the *best* spas where people would whisper about her fabulous clothes and say, 'That's Bertha Dobbs; her daughter married Mr. Moneybags!'"

"Why doesn't she marry Mr. Moneybags? I'm sure there are many older ones."

"It's a universal truth that old men grow exponentially more attractive with wealth and power regardless of age or physical appearance. Hence the twenty-year-old wives married to octogenarians who wouldn't get a by your leave otherwise." She shrugged. "Your mother enjoys socializing too much, and who would hold her attention?

"But to you. The Fortress would make a lovely wedding venue. The fountains would be exquisite lighted and draped with flowers."

"The trees draped with the bodies of hanging Confederate groomsmen, including the groom," I added. A bee buzzed around my drink and then circled off to some nearby flowers. "I doubt a wedding will happen now. At least not with Mother's permission. Baron thinks we should elope." I bit off the head of a gingerbread woman viciously and ground her raisin features to a pulp.

"Please don't do that. Poppie is so looking forward to giving you a big wedding and walking you down the aisle. You know how Meemaw dreams of this wedding and puts things away for your trousseau. It would break their hearts to deny them. I think it's the only thing that keeps them hanging on at times. They so want to see you wed with babies. Give me time to work on your mother."

"I doubt it will do any good. I'm positive she danced with glee when I lost The Pines. That just put me one step closer to homeless."

Gertie picked up a cake and considered it. "I'm not so sure. Your mother saved The Pines. Twice, actually. I think it held a special place in her heart once."

"I thought Mother hated The Pines."

"Oh, no. Not at first. Kieran struggled for a while, but he built her the cutest little home. It wasn't what she was accustomed to, but it was genuinely nice. I think Poppie realized there were financial problems, so he sent her money to come home after you were born because they wanted to see you."

She took a bite of the spice cake and smiled as if remembering the homecoming fondly. "We were so excited to see you both. Kieran couldn't come as he had to take care of the farm. Who missed him anyway with such a pretty baby to make over?" She laughed.

"I decided to go home with Bert and help. I had nothing else to do, and she was mad for company. Imagine our surprise when we walked in the door, and it was vacant as if someone had robbed it. Not a stick of furniture!"

I set my drink down in shock. "Someone stole the furniture while Mother was gone?"

"Not quite. 'Bert! Yer home.' Kieran boomed. 'I'll be fer explainin'.'"

I got a sinking feeling in the pit of my stomach. I'd heard the "I'll be for explainin'" many times.

"'Mr. Farrow passed away, an' Mrs. Farrow wanted get rid o' thet herd o' horses fast. I had t'be after raisin' money afore someone else swooped in an' got 'em, doncha see?'

"Your mother wandered around the empty house looking for her furniture. She was in shock. 'But where's my furniture?'"

I knew what Gertie was going to say. "I sold it t'raise money."

"'You what? Everything?'"

"'I did not, then. Kept the beds, an' the table, an' the stove.' Then she wheeled on him. Luckily, I was holding you, or I fear she might have thrown you at him. "'Where's my wedding china?'"

I prayed Papa hadn't sold her china, as I knew how much store she set by such things.

"'Dahrlin,'" Gertie continued in a perfect imitation of my father, "'I would ne'er do thet.' Then your mother spied her piano and sat on the bench. 'My piano,' she cried, hugging it. 'Thank God you didn't sell my piano.' Just then, two men came clomping into the house. "'We're back for the piano, Mr. Mac.'"

"And I'm sure that's when Mother went insane," I said.

Gertie nodded. "'You bastard!' She grabbed the shotgun from above the mantle and tried to kill your father. Luckily, he's fast as a rabbit, and she'd never shot a gun. He ran through the dining room, and she only managed to kill the table, blowing a leg out from under it. Unfortunately, the china was stacked on the table, and when it went down, so did the dishes.

"He returned to the house later and tried to show her the china might be glued back together, but she just sat there on the floor crying and told him to leave her alone."

"It's a wonder she didn't pack up and move back home to Baltimore permanently," I said.

"Her pride prevented that, but she went home for a while. Kieran had a good nose for horses and opportunities, however. He hauled those horses north and made a killing. Two of them turned into top-notch racehorses, and half of the eastern seaboard was trying to get him drunk and gambling to push one little mare across the poker table, but your father was smart enough to know when his luck was turning and when people were playing him. He made a lot of money with that yellow mare on and off the track. That's why all her offspring were named "Gold" something.

"Your mother forgave him and returned, but he paid a heavy toll in furniture and china."

I filled up our drinks again, curious now about this history I hadn't heard before, though I was familiar with my father taking crazy chances. "And the second time?"

Gertie's face clouded as if a storm passed in her memory. "The second time, you will identify with. Kieran had mortgaged

the property to buy more land, but the crops failed that year."
She shook her head. "After Bert paid such a terrible price for it, I
never thought The Pines would belong to anyone but McKenzies."

I tossed the cookie to a curious bird and looked sideways at
her. "What do you mean?"

"Your daddy's gone now, and so is The Pines, so there is no
sense keeping this cursed secret. He had speculated heavily on
some land, always looking to improve himself. No one made
money that year, but the bankers gobbled up land like vultures."

I understood that. She told me how Papa had donned his
best suit, as he always believed clothes made the man, and went
to town to get an extension on the mortgage. The bankers had
not only declined him but laughed at his request. He had pulled
a gun on them and threatened to shoot them, whereupon they
had him arrested.

Papa had sold all the cattle and horses except his personal
horse to raise money and come up short. No one was buying
land. Mother put on her best dress, gathered her jewelry, and
coerced Zona into helping her hook up the lone mule left on
the place to the carriage. Off they went to town with baby Jamie
and me. She was determined to sell her jewelry and charm one
of the bankers who had always been sweet on her into extending
the note. She sold most of the jewelry and got her appointment
with Mr. Dickinson. Private, he insisted, so they could discuss
business. Yes, he might be interested in the rest of her jewelry
and the cash she'd raised.

"Zona said she came out of that bank wobbling like a new
kitten and white as a sheet. Bert ordered her to get home quick.
He took her so hard he tore her up and told her to put some rags
in her drawers so she didn't bleed on his carpet. She kept telling
him she was with child, so he said he guessed he better take her
from behind then and did that, too."

I sat aghast. I was too numb to process what my beautiful,
sheltered mother went through. My breath caught. Uncon-
sciously, I touched my own stomach, feeling her pain.

"Zona sent for the doctor when they got home. He asked her who did that, but she wouldn't tell. She lost the baby three days later and stayed in bed for months. We thought we were going to lose her." She laughed bitterly. "The banker gave him the loan and dropped the charges. So magnanimous, considering."

Too stunned to move, I stared across the yard. "I never knew."

"It was never spoken of. The banker made a disparaging remark about your mother later, and your daddy near beat him to death, but no one brought charges against him because witnesses say he justified."

I nodded. "Did Papa know what the banker did to her?"

"Oh, no. If he had, he'd have killed him, but he knew something was wrong."

I sat benumbed, shaking my head. "I never realized this happened to her or that she was so affected."

She reached for her drink as if to fortify herself. "That's because in her times of insanity, when she took to her bed or spent days crying, your father bundled you up and shipped you North to stay with Meemaw and Poppie. I'd go down and get her settled. Your father didn't want you children to have memories of an impaired mother. It's why she was so frantic about your arrest. She fears the same kind of attack might happen to you. Especially with war on your doorstep."

I thought about Byles and felt he might certainly have done so under different circumstances. "No, I was perfectly safe." There was a twinge of guilt for the lie, but they must never know the truth. Byles must remain hidden and hopefully forgotten.

She peered at me with a slight frown as if searching the truth of my words. "We all deal with these things in our own way," she said. "Your mother's trying to save you from making poor decisions or becoming prey to a monster. She has a horror of you landing destitute as they nearly were many times in the beginning. Your father could handle the gambling and losing and rebuilding. She couldn't. It drove her insane then. It drives her insane today to think of you going through it. She will destroy you in the South to force you to marry well in the North for your own good if that makes any sense."

"It does in a twisted way, but it's not her choice."

"I know, dear." She reached over and patted my hand. "But you should think about what you stand to lose."

"Miz Gertie. Mister is home," announced Suella breathlessly after hurrying down the path.

The various trinkets on Gertie's chatelaine tinkled as she looked for her watch. "Hmmm. He's home early. I hope nothing's wrong.

"I know you wonder about me and your father. I loved him dearly all my life, and it hurt when your mother took him, but I've never regretted my marriage. George is a good man. We've had a good life and four perfect sons. If your mother and father hadn't married, I wouldn't have had you and little Jamie." She hugged me and stood.

"I was at The Pines once and rode out to find your father at your mother's behest. He was in a tree, drinking whiskey," she said as we walked. "'Let me guess,' he said. 'Yer here tell me get out the tree afore I break me fool neck.'" Gertie said, imitating Papa.

"Actually, I'm here to drink whiskey, you selfish man."

"'Knew it!' your father said, dropping from the tree. 'I married the wrong Dobbs girl.'" She grabbed hold of my hand and swung it. "'But then I wouldn't have me dahrlin' Lorena,'" he said and grandly offered me his whiskey, which I drank with him all the way back to the house. Much to your mother's chagrin."

"Thank you. I needed to know he had no regrets."

"He didn't. He adored you and Jamie and knew you were part of your mother's blessing. Plus, they were happy once. You will be, too."

We went to the parlor where Uncle George waited impatiently, pacing in front of the great red rose marble fireplace with the cherub mural above it. He paused beside the five-foot-tall, white-bearded statue of Zeus holding up the right side of the mantle and made to strike a Lucifer against the god's beard.

"George MacTavish! If you do, I'll snatch your beard out."

"Hello, darling. I didn't see you there."

"I'm sure you didn't."

Still tall and slim, even at nearly sixty, with dark hair graying at the temples, he was an imposing figure. He was older than Gertie by thirteen years, but if it ever bothered her, I couldn't tell. He was as vibrant as ever, and they were a lively match. "How are my two favorite girls?" he boomed, hugging us in turn.

"You're home early," she said. "Are there no political disasters to avert?"

"There will never be a shortage of those, I fear. However, I have a surprise." He grinned at me and waved tickets in the air.

I frowned as my hopes for a quiet evening disappeared. "What are those?"

"These, my darlings," he said as if he'd just won the Louisiana lottery, "are tickets to see Macbeth at The National, which is sold out until kingdom come."

"How on earth did you get them?" Gertie gasped.

"Cameron's aide Garry Simmons stopped by my office. A little birdie told him my beautiful niece was visiting. He said he befriended you in Baltimore but was too busy to pay his respects and wished to make it up with supper and the theater tonight." George clapped me on the shoulder. "I can see the attraction. What a handsome and courteous fellow he is! Half the girls in Washington must be panting after him."

"I assure you I didn't," I said, trying not to spit out how I felt about the conniving snake. "I'm friends with his brother, and he inserted himself into our conversation."

Uncle laughed. "Leave it to Lorena to start a war for her affections. No matter. We leave in an hour, which is scarce time to prepare."

"Come, dear," Gertie said, taking me by the arm. "It'll be good for you to get out."

"Yes, because I've been a recluse for a week and more."

I had no appetite at all, simply thinking about Simmons, but I couldn't graciously decline. Heading up the ornate stairway to my room, I paused at each newel to touch the bronze saints that perched atop them. The first, possibly my favorite, was Saint Philomena with her flower crown. "Pray for me, Saint Philomena, and all the children," I whispered. "Watch over my girls." My journey, like the stations of the cross, ended with Saint Michael the archangel, appropriately enough. "Saint Michael, defender of the realm, leader of the heavenly host, watch over us in our time of need. Protect Baron and Rosemount. Protect those I love. Protect me from vipers and their plans for evil." I paused. "Knock some sense into those hardheaded politicians. Amen."

I tried to wear the black moiré silk gown, but Gertie would have none of it, so we compromised on the indigo with the modest neckline and elbow-length sleeves. Uncle frowned when I descended the stairs. "I'm sure we have some sackcloth somewhere, Lorena. Shall we stop at a cemetery to pay your respects?"

"My husband, the diplomat. Shush, George. I was doing good to get her out of the weeds."

He looked at her helplessly. "I hoped she might wear something more—"

"Fetching?" I said, fluttering my fan and lashes.

"He's an influential young man, and I have no doubt he has a bright future in politics."

"Yes, Uncle George. That's exactly what I want, a Yankee politician. Are you and Mother related?" I flung the opera cape across my shoulders.

"You know, George," said Gertie as she put on her cloak, "I've always thought a person should stop digging their grave at about six feet. You're well below that."

He humphed but wisely took her advice.

We met Simmons at the Willard, a highly coveted hotel and restaurant. Compared to the other women, I looked like a mud hen amongst a flock of peacocks, which suited me admirably.

Simmons waited, top hat in hand. "I'm so glad you could join me tonight," he said. "I hope you don't mind me making reservations here. It's one of my favorite places."

"This is marvelous," replied Uncle. "I'm surprised you could get reservations on short notice."

He waved his hand airily as if working miracles were an everyday affair. "I called in a favor or two. Mrs. McTavish, you look divine, as do you, Miss McKenzie."

We didn't compare in splendor to the dandy, who was impeccably dressed in the latest fashion: white kid gloves, a black silk top hat, an ornately wrought cravat, and not a wavy golden hair out of place. The Willard, palatial in style, played host to every person of note who'd graced Washington for the last fifty years. The failed peace convention had occurred there in February, and had rescheduled for June, but that was before Sumter. Pray it would be more successful then.

The dining room was filled with a wide assortment of important people, not a few generals and their accompanying aides and companions. Simmons veered away from our waiter toward a large gathering of soldiers and ladies to our left. They stood at our approach. The most elderly one of them rose with difficulty. He was a massive man decked in gold epaulets and glittering gold braid about his collar and waist, which was substantial. Fuss and Feathers Scott in person. To his right was one Captain Lucian Simmons, similarly clad in his best dress uniform. I wavered, my breath catching as I cursed Garry Simmons once again. Lucian's eyes narrowed briefly before looking away.

"General Scott, may I present Mr. and Mrs. McTavish and their niece Miss McKenzie?" Simmons went around the table, introducing us to the remaining officers and their companions, ending with his brother, who had no one. "I believe, Miss McKenzie, you know my brother?"

"Yes, thank you," I replied icily. "Your brother surprised my uncle with supper and theater invitations."

"Yes," Lucian said in clipped tones. "He's good at surprises."

"And we surprised Lucian with a birthday supper!" said General Scott. "I couldn't let my godson go unremembered. He's

named after me and all. Lucian Winfield Simmons. Fine name
if I do say so."

The soldier to his left chuckled. "General, I hope you keep
military secrets better than this one. Everyone in Washington
knew about this party."

Scott huffed his disdain.

"Surprise or not, happy birthday, sir," said Gertie.

"Happy birthday," I said. "I wish I'd known."

Lucian responded to me with a withering look. Garry
inhaled sweet victory through distended nostrils, raising his
head and gripping my arm possessively. I couldn't draw away
without creating a scene but glared up at him. If he saw me, it
was ignored.

"If you don't mind," Scott said, gripping the table, "I must sit.
My knees."

"Of course," replied Simmons. "I think our waiter grows
impatient. Happy birthday, brother."

Lucian said nothing.

At our table, I settled into a slow seethe, glancing occasionally
at Lucian, who spared me no thought or look. The Willard's
menu looked enticing as always, but I took little pleasure in
perusing it. "The blue point oyster cocktail, I think. Tenderloin
done, mashed potatoes, buttered carrots, and ribbon cake for
dessert." I accepted the waiter's suggestion for wine.

"The tenderloin's nice, but I think the lady would prefer the
lamb," Simmons said. "It's particularly good, and you'll find the
sauce heavenly. He finished changing my order and smiled at me
indulgently.

"If you bring that lamb, the gentleman will be eating it. It's
not what I ordered."

The waiter swiveled from me to Simmons, pencil poised in
the air. "Bring the lady what she wants," Simmons said sourly.

George started to say something and thought better of it
when Gertie shot him a warning glare and probably a rap under
the table.

"Thank you," I responded coolly.

Polite conversation pattered throughout the meal. Questions about Virginia and my home and school, which I'm sure Simmons had little interest in aside from value. What did we raise? Was that prosperous? Not at all, hence my need to have a school. Rosemount was successful, but my finances were none of his business.

"Now might be a good time to sell," Simmons said. "You could buy a nice home in Washington or Baltimore."

"That's a good idea," Uncle said. "I know Gertie would love to see you more."

I sliced savagely through the beefsteak. Fool men. I happened to look up at Lucian, who was looking my way laughing, and then turned back to Scott, who was telling an animated story.

"I've sold all I'm going to sell," I replied resolutely. "I'm not selling Rosemount."

"Let me do the next best thing." Simmons was the soul of concern. "I'll contact the commander in Alexandria and get you an open passport to visit your family any time you need. I understand you must return frequently due to your mother's declining health."

"Mother's what?" I nearly dropped my knife.

"She didn't want to tell me, but I pried it out of her as she looked so frail the day I stopped to inquire after you."

"Yes, she's such a private person. She told you I was coming here?"

"Again, I pried it out of her."

"Like a clam she is. I'm surprised you could wedge a single secret from her."

He smiled and sipped his wine. "I told her I'd check on her again."

"There's no need for that," I said, seized by dread. With a little butter, my mother would lay open every tidbit there was to know about me.

I looked to Gertie for help, but she shrugged imperceptibly, not knowing what to do.

"I'm in Baltimore frequently. It's no trouble," he replied. "Use the pass as you see fit."

There was no denying him, and further debate was useless. Besides, it might be useful for the next mission.

We finished dessert in relative peace and headed to the theater for an impeccable performance. Outside the theater, the rain eased to a fine mist sufficient to curtail prolonged conversation. Simmons asked if he might see me again, but I declined.

"That was an interesting evening," Uncle said in the carriage, twisting his top hat about in his hands as if he were wiping rain droplets off even though we'd been under umbrellas.

"It was," I agreed. "The food was excellent, and Macbeth outstanding."

"Did you have to challenge him about ordering?" He plopped the hat on the seat.

"Did he have to treat me like a witless rube?"

"Dear heavens," Gertie said. "The man is obviously used to being around simpering, clinging vines who enjoy being controlled. Maybe it was good for him to meet a rose with thorns."

"He certainly met the prickly side of our darling niece." He looked out the carriage window as if something mesmerizing in the haloed reflections of passing streetlamps caught his attention.

"I'm sorry, Uncle George. You're a marvelous diplomat but truly abysmal at matchmaking. This was absolutely the worst timing. Greek tragedy bad timing."

"Bert permitted Lorena and Baron to wed based on Colonel Lee's glowing recommendation the last time she was here until some nitwit at the military ball told her Lee betrayed the army. He hadn't even resigned yet," Gertie said. "Bert all but damned both Lee and Baron to hell in a spectacular come apart."

He looked horrified. "She told me you broke it off. I thought this might take your mind off things."

"That's her fondest wish. We aren't engaged, but I don't wish him mentioned to anyone if you don't mind. It could put him in more danger and possibly myself."

"Of course, darling."

We finished the ride home in silence, and I quickly retreated to my room, which was already prepared with a cozy fire to allay the chill.

It was still faintly drizzling in the half-hearted way heaven does when it can't decide whether to stop or wring out the last few drops before giving up. I walked onto the balcony to finish brushing my hair and scanning the night sky. Stars glittered here and there across an ebony mantle where the storm had cleared while raveling clouds scuttered across a full moon. With the moon out, shadows in shades of blue and black flowed across the gardens below as if a depressed painter were at work. Beyond the wrought iron gates was another shadow. I slowly lowered the brush from my hair. A cloaked figure on a horse sat beside the road, gazing up at me. I saw no features; it was too dark, and the hat pulled too low, but from the figure's angle I knew he watched. Then he turned his horse and disappeared into the darkness.

Chapter Forty-One

"Not my doing," Uncle George replied the next morning when Gertie quizzed him about hiring someone to watch the house. We had gone to early mass and then spent a day in quiet conversation, playing euchre and whist and puttering in the garden until George insisted we go for a carriage ride. "Stop, please," I called to Hiram when we neared the area where the rider watched the night before.

"What are you doing?" George demanded, aghast, as I clambered out of the coach nearly before it stopped.

"I want to look at something." I scouted the area, stooping to inspect the ground and eventually returning to the coach with its anxiously peering heads sticking out.

Hiram guided me back in with a disapproving frown. "Please do wait next time, Miss."

"The horse shat twice, so the rider was there for a while. He was riding a gelding or stallion, judging by the way the horse stretched out to piss and was freshly shod, but that could be anyone. I think the man wore about a size eight boot since it looks like he also relieved himself by the boot tracks. He was polite enough to turn away from the house even in the dark."

George *tched* in disapproval. "When did you become a Pinkerton?"

Gertie gasped. "Pinkerton! George McTavish. What a perfectly horrid thing to say."

I waved the insult away. "I was curious."

"It was just someone sitting out the rain under the trees." George fidgeted with his cane. "Lorena, are you sure you won't consider moving north? It would be much safer."

I shook my head as if to clear an annoying bee inside. "My home's in Virginia. That's where I belong."

His sigh was heavy and resigned, like an executioner who asked one last time if I wouldn't repent. "Lieutenant Merryman is still imprisoned at Fort McHenry even after Chief Justice Taney issued the writ of habeas corpus. Taney cited General Cadwalader for contempt, but the reprobate refuses to charge or release the man, and Lincoln backs this sordid illegality. It's a mess. These are trying times when martial law can do what it wants, and the president gives broad authority to enforce it. You should realize this by your recent experience."

His eyes bored into me with serious intent. "I requested the carriage ride in case you wanted to divulge anything to me in private. I trust my servants, but I've been in politics long enough to know that to trust anyone is to place your life in their hands."

"Such as?"

"Gertie told me you vowed never to return, and I don't blame you. I suspect you're transporting contraband, as I know your love of food. You may be forgiven a stash of coffee, tea, spices, or needles, but they will arrest you if you get caught with medicine or information."

The landscape passed, holding my gaze but not my attention. I'd heard of Merryman's arrest but not the legal wrangling. A small huff escaped. "And you think I'd be safer here where the law no longer applies? I have nothing to divulge."

"He *was* accused of burning bridges." He said this as if it excused all.

"Accused." I said no more. What was there to say? I was doing worse.

"For God's sake, be careful," George cautioned me. "You know you have a home here if you need one." Gertie sighed again as she had all morning.

I left with many tears and fond hugs as if I'd never see them again. Gertie held on to me until the last, begging me not to go, convinced I was bound for doom. If only she knew how close I might be to riding a rail...or worse. Monroe Farrier, who had been refitting the contraband carriage with hidden supplies, arranged for a driver to pick me up at The Fortress and drive me across the river to Alexandria to meet Imogene and Jacob.

We passed out of Washington City with only a cursory inspection of passports and carriage and none of the luggage due to heavy traffic at that hour of the morning, I was sure. Safely arrived at the Boudreaux residence, I collected Imogene. Jacob had stayed behind in Alexandria to visit with his father and look after Imogene, but from the gathered soldiers wishing her farewell, it was plain she had been perfectly safe without him. We had tea while our luggage was loaded into the contraband carriage. My stomach quailed at the journey ahead. Mrs. Boudreaux pleaded with her to stay. I almost left her in case things went horribly sideways, but Imogene insisted on leaving and would only be released with a promise that she'd return soon. Mrs. Bastrom insisted on sending us off with a basket of food. Her grandson J.B., who seldom left her side, declared he would tote it for us. With some difficulty, he pushed it into the carriage and then beamed with pride at his accomplishment. It didn't take much to make him happy, as he was either gifted or cursed with being simple.

"J.B., thank you so much," I said. "You're always such a big help. Can I give you a dime for your bank?"

"Yeth, ma'am. I'm thaving for a pony."

"Ponies are good. Let me give you two dimes, then."

We stopped at a checkpoint at the edge of a new camp outside Alexandria, where a Zouave in scarlet pantaloons, heavily corded blue jacket, silk sash, gaiters, and scarlet fez opened the carriage door and looked in. "Ladies, would you be so kind as to step out of the carriage?"

"I have papers." I was prepared and pulled them from my purse.

"Yes, ma'am, but we need to search the carriage for contraband. Orders."

Putting on my best frown, I pouted prettily. "I see."

The Fire Zouaves from New York were pomp and puffery, but I knew their fierce reputation. "Thank you, sir. What a gorgeous uniform."

He set the step and held out his hand to me. "Thank you, ma'am. It shouldn't take long."

I lifted my hem higher than necessary and stepped down. The man next to him regarded my ankle with approval and offered to escort me. I strolled to the stool they considerately moved to the shade of a tree and sat like an obedient lapdog. Imogene peeked out of the carriage, her large blue eyes abnormally wide and golden curls shining in the sunlight. Two young soldiers dashed to assist her, bobbing gold tassels on their fezzes marking their haste. The footrace culminated in a tie, and both held their hands out to her. Imogene, ever the diplomat, let go the carriage door and took a hand in each of hers. She expertly kicked the dress hem out of the way and descended like a Botticelli goddess. I noticed she left her bolero in the carriage. When she leaned forward, her chemise lace showed faintly through her blouse.

She took a few steps forward, graciously thanking her rescuers and smiling widely, deepening the dimples alluringly.

A captain some distance away bellowed. "Here, you men. Give that woman air!"

"My parasol! I'll simply fry to a crisp in this sun." Imogene started to turn, twisted, yelped in pain, and fell into the arms of a stunned young lieutenant. I rushed forward to check on my teacher, who was now half sprawled in the dirt and half clinging to the soldier. He deftly scooped her up and carried her to the chair beside mine. The other Zouave ran off, red legs churning, shouting for the doctor.

"Imogene, what on earth did you do?"

Impressively, tears sprang to her eyes. If acting weren't such a vulgar profession, she'd excel. "I think I've broken my ankle, Miss McKenzie. How will I teach? Get my parasol!"

Her rescuer patted her hand. "There, there, miss. At least you're not a horse. We won't have to shoot you."

"Shoot me! Get my parasol."

Was she going to fend them off with it?

Imogene wailed, drowning out his desperate explanation that he was joking.

The captain strode up, sending small puffs of dust up with each step. "What in tarnation is going on? Search that damned carriage and let these women go."

"Captain! I must protest. Language. My teacher has broken her ankle. Your lieutenant's threatening to shoot her, and you stomp around like we left the gate to Hades open."

"Sir, I was joking," the lieutenant complained plaintively.

"Miss, please stop crying. No one's going to shoot you," the captain said.

Imogene calmed to noisy sniffles.

The captain looked around. "For God's sake, someone get the doctor."

"We found secret compartments in the footrests," a soldier from inside the carriage called.

Imogene broke out into a fresh wail.

"Never mind. Cormack, carry her out back."

"Out back?" Imogene wailed afresh.

"Miss, the doctor's out back," said the lieutenant, who must have regretted his gallantry.

"Captain, I must protest tearing up my carriage."

"Ma'am, please do stay out of my way and save your protests. Sit down, damn it."

I sat with a huff while they unloaded my contraband. The captain turned to me with an accusatory look. I adjusted the lace on my bonnet.

When they were done, six crates lay on the ground. The captain knelt with his knife to pry a lid loose. It came off with a screech of bending nails. I fanned lazily and kicked my foot. He lifted ink bottles out one by one, scrutinizing each. Frowning, he opened one and smelled the contents, dabbed a bit on his thumb, and wiped his thumbprint on the crate lid.

The frown deepened. "Ink?"

"Ink."

"Why'd you hide it?"

"I didn't. My girls get cold. This carriage was specially built with lined footrests to put warmers for their feet in the winter. This was simply a convenient place to put ink."

"You need six boxes of ink?"

"I have nearly three dozen young ladies in my boarding school. My mother believes in education, so she stocks me up."

He huffed. "A woman's education should be confined to reading the Bible and keeping a household. I can't let you take this."

I stopped fanning. "I spoke to the commandant before I left."

He motioned to the rest of the crates. "Open them."

I flounced to him. "Captain, really, I—"

"Yes, I know. You must protest."

While the rest of the crates were opened, two soldiers pulled our trunks from the back of the carriage.

"Moses, Mary, and Joseph. What do you think we're going to carry in our trunks? We could barely get our clothes in. I had to get a healthy maid to dance on the lids to close them."

"Four trunks for two women? I could stuff a small army in there."

"I'll refrain from comment."

"Please do."

The trunks were unloaded and unlocked. Dresses taken and shaken. They opened every drawer, holding up each item for the Captain's inspection. We carried a dizzying array of vanity items. The soldiers doing the unpacking were, by turns, bewildered and embarrassed.

"Is all this necessary?" the captain asked peevishly as the third row of drawers was unpacked.

"Not if you prefer unkempt women who care nothing of their appearance. There's a reason Southern men don't stray."

"Because they fear for their damned lives mostly."

"Language." I continued to fan myself and watched with mild interest as the soldiers grew more agitated the deeper they dug.

"Miss?" Lieutenant Cormac inquired timidly. "We can't get Miss Boudreaux's boot off. Our button hooks are too large, and she refuses to let the doctor cut the boot off."

"It's a Boucher; I'm sure she does. I'll fetch her hook, providing it's still where it was. Heaven knows there's a summer storm blowing through everything from caplet to corset."

"I ain't touched no corsets, ma'am," one of the conscripted soldiers protested.

"The day is young." I pulled a button hook from a top drawer and handed it over. "Is there anything else she requires?"

"She's upset and in pain. Perhaps you can comfort her?"

"Tell her I'll come as soon as we've been searched. Do *not* tell her your comrades are rifling her unmentionables."

"Dear God, no, ma'am. I would never in life tell her that. Trust me."

"Ma'am! I'm not rifling no unmentionables! I ain't even got a gun near 'em."

The captain sighed. "Jameson, ignore her. I know it's difficult, but ignore her and finish the search."

"Sir, the rest of this stuff is ladies' wear."

"It's all ladies' wear."

"I mean private ladies' wear." Jameson's face was flaming.

"For pity's sake!" I pushed them away from the trunks. "Handkerchiefs, fourteen. Drawers." I shook each heavily laced pair out as they had the dresses and laid them on top of the growing pile of clothes. "Chemises." Brandished boldly. A few in the gathering crowd whistled. "Corsets." I waved them like banners, laces flying. More whistles. "Corset covers." More men and even more whistles. "Camisoles." Clapping and whistles. "Nightgowns." We'd packed our prettiest, laciest gowns. They also fluttered in the air. Cheers. "Robes." The robes were the daintiest lace, satin, and silk. Rousing cheers. "Silk stockings." I unrolled them and shook them madly. Wild applause.

"Does she have to do that?" Jameson was as scarlet as his pantaloons.

"I believe that's enough," the captain said. "You, madam, are no lady."

"And you, sir, are no gentleman. I'm not the one who demanded to look at drawers. Where's my teacher?"

Jameson gratefully volunteered to get me away from the clothing display, but some of the other soldiers booed him. We hurried through the camp. I kept my chin up in a proper haughty expression while trying to take in as much as possible. They were strongly provisioned and organized, but this was a fresh camp.

French conversation and laughter bubbled from the direction of the medical tent. Where on earth had Imogene found a Frenchman? Jameson delivered me to a tent with rolled-up sides to catch the breeze.

"Ma'am."

"Thank you, Mr. Jameson, for being such a gentleman in difficult circumstances."

He touched his fez and hurried away, undoubtedly glad to be shed of me.

Imogene sat in a camp chair, her foot propped up in a man's lap, a Zouave fez parked jauntily on her head. The man had a full head of curly black hair and capable hands by the way she smiled as he massaged her foot. The animated conversation and laughter flowed. They were in Paris at their favorite cafe, discussing an odd little artist who painted nearby and insisted his muse was a monkey in a red fez, much like the Zouave fez. He had painted a miniature of Imogene once and asked her to pose nude. No, no. Of course, she hadn't. The little painter threw himself into the Seine when his monkey died. How could he ever paint again without his muse? The gentleman knew the painter but hadn't known what happened to him.

I cleared my throat, and the conversation went from perfect French to Imogene's soft Tennessee drawl. "Miss McKenzie. Dr. Auclair and I were discussing this little cafe in Paris."

The doctor stood and bowed. "Mademoiselle, *enchanté*. Mademoiselle Boudreaux has a badly sprained ankle. I've massaged the oil and will wrap it for her. She mustn't walk on it." He shook his finger in warning. "Get some crutches. I showed her exercises for when the ankle she is better. We must have her dancing. She has promised me a dance. Many of them. Don't wrap the ankle too tightly. Rest with it up, like this." He kicked his heel up chest high. "It drains the humours." He wagged a finger at her. "Remember the exercises. And the letters."

"Letters?"

"I promised to let him know how I'm doing."

"It will have to be in pencil since our ink's being confiscated." She wrinkled her nose.

The doctor looked scandaled. "Who is confiscating your ink?"

"Your captain thinks it's contraband."

"Nonsense. Come. I will see about this." He wrapped her ankle and set the fez straight on her head. "To remember me by."

"But what about you?" Imogene protested. "Won't you get in trouble for being out of uniform?"

"I have another. It looks better on you, *ma chère*."

From the size of her pupils, he'd also gifted her with laudanum. I followed the doctor who marched through the camp carrying his patient back to the carriage where Jacob was repacking the trunks. The captain waited, chewing on his cigar, eyes narrowed, leaning against the carriage with one hand on his hip. He touched the brim of his kepi to Imogene. "Ma'am. I hope you're feeling better."

She giggled.

Law. How much laudanum did the doctor give her?

"Much better, thank you. Paul has lovely hands."

The captain shot the doctor a questioning look. "Does he now?"

"I massaged her foot with oil before I wrapped it!"

The captain took the cigar out of his mouth and spit out a bit of tobacco. "If I ever sprain my ankle, just wrap the damned thing. Don't be rubbing it." He jabbed his cigar toward the carriage. "You can set her down."

The doctor reluctantly unloaded his patient and then drew himself up to all 5' 7", I judged, and addressed the captain. "I understand you are taking their ink?"

"I am."

"You will please to find a new doctor, *au revoir*."

The captain's eyes narrowed. "The hell you say."

"The hell I say. I am not enlisted. I serve at my pleasure. My pleasure is not to serve someone who would steal ink from innocent teachers."

"That woman," he stabbed his cigar toward me as I finished packing, "is about the farthest thing from innocent you may ever see, doctor."

"Captain! I must protest! I've done nothing to you."

"Madam, you've done nothing but rankle me from the moment your size five hit the dirt, and now you have my doctor in mutiny. Take your damned ink and be gone."

"Jacob, load the ink, please."

"Yes'm."

I politely kissed the doctor on the cheek and thanked him in French for saving our ink and treating Imogene.

He beamed. "It was my pleasure to serve, *mademoiselle*."

"Captain, I'm sure you inspected the box on the seat in the carriage?"

He struck a match against the wheel of the carriage and lit his cigar. "I did. It appears to be about a thousand cookies."

"Six hundred. Jacob, when you're done with the ink, would you get out the cookies?"

He handed me the box of cookies, which I presented to the doctor. "My mother loads us with cookies for the girls. Take these as thanks for rescuing my ink and treating Imogene so tenderly. You may distribute them as you see fit." I cut my eyes to the captain.

"I can't take these!" Auclaire protested.

"Of course, you can. You've earned them."

"Then they go to the men. They shall sing your praises."

I smiled sweetly at the captain. "And shall you sing my praises?"

"I'll sing something about you, madam." He drew contemplatively on the cigar. "Tell me, are you married?"

"That's quite personal, Captain. Are you asking?"

He growled.

"It's Miss McKenzie."

"I can't say I'm surprised. Might I make a suggestion? Should you find a man so inclined to propose matrimony. When the preacher asks, 'Do you take this man?' the proper response is, 'Yes.' I know you'll be inclined to say, 'I must protest!' but the answer is, 'Yes.'"

"Captain, I—of course. I shall heed your advice."

I took poor Jameson's hand and stepped into the carriage, carefully lifting my skirts to avoid another accident. "Thank you, kindly. I wish you a good day."

"And you, ma'am."

The door shut with a satisfyingly solid click, and Jacob popped the reins, setting the carriage rocking into motion. I sat, rail straight, chin up until we were out of sight, and then, with the soul and energy sucked from me, I could do nothing but slump like a ragdoll. At last, I opened my eyes. "What were you thinking? You were supposed to pretend to turn your ankle."

"I didn't plan on it! My boot heel caught on something, and down I went, burying my face in that poor man's chest. I've never been so mortified in all my years."

"How do you feel?"

She waved her handkerchief. "I'm fine. He gave me laudanum and a bottle to take home with me." She pulled her skirts up to look at the puffed ankle. "He said it might take two months to heal, but wasn't he nice?"

"Yes, he was." With my first wave of exhaustion passing, I wanted to tell Jacob to lay the whip, but I knew we needed to continue at a normal pace. If anyone were suspicious, they'd wait for us to do that.

"How far is it to the Johnson farm? My eyes are floating."

"Ten miles, more or less." I leaned out the window. "Jacob, we have to necessary. Can you stop soon?"

"Yes'm. There's some bushes up ahead."

Once discussed, the urge grew, and I peered out the window to spot the bushes. I counted the hoofbeats and crossed my legs. More hoofbeats coming hard from behind us.

They've discovered us!

I took Imogene's hands in mine, desperate to get through the drugged haze. "Listen to me! If they challenge me, you know nothing about it. Nothing. Do you understand?"

"But—"

"But nothing. You're no use in prison. Cry, plead innocence, faint. Do whatever you must, but admit nothing!"

She nodded silently, her face ghost white.

"Jacob, who is that?"

"Looks like two of the Zouaves are surrendering, ma'am."

"What? Stop the carriage."

"They're coming hard and waving a white flag. Can you take prisoners?"

"Ridiculous. Of course, I can't."

Now that idiot captain would accuse me of subverting his men. I leaned anxiously out the window, the hoofbeats and laughter getting closer. It was a horse race. The two men skidded to a stop at the carriage, boiling up dust.

"Doctor, by a nose, because your horse has such a long head."

"Do not insult my Jennie so!"

The men laughed, their horses dancing in circles and blowing hard from the run.

"Dr. Auclair! Lieutenant Cormack! What are you doing?"

"*Le demoiselle* left her boot behind," Auclair said. "I knew she'd be distressed."

"My boot! Thank you, doctor. The second time today you've rescued me." She leaned around me, fez still on her head, golden tassel dangling across her face. "I am in your debt."

"*Oui, mademoiselle*, you are, and I won't allow you to besmirch your honor by being a debtor. I shall return and collect it one day." He spurred around to her side, gallantly handed her the boot, and kissed her hand.

"I look forward to that day, sir."

Cormack reined his dancing bay horse closer to me and held up a chemise. I recognized the lavender ribbon and lace. Thankfully, it was mine and not Imogene's. "You're not surrendering?"

"Not today, ma'am. This got left behind. I thought you'd like it back. I was offered a fine price for it, however. They said the rose scent reminds them of home."

"Yes, I'm sure that was the reason. I'm surprised anyone could smell it."

"Uh...it did sort of make the rounds before I offered to return it when the doctor found the boot."

"I see." I folded the chemise and set it on the seat.

"The men greatly appreciated your cookies and sent you a gift. He pulled a fez from inside his blouse and offered it to me. "They thought since Miss Boudreaux had one, you should also."

I was thoroughly and pleasantly surprised. "Please thank them. I'm amazed your captain allowed it."

"The men petitioned for a captain's kepi instead of a fez."

I laughed most unladylike. "I'm sure that was agreeable."

"He said," in a perfect imitation of the captain, "you may all go straight to hell."

Auclair and Imogene were still laughing and whispering when Cormack reminded the doctor they should return. They trotted off, laughing and hurrahing, not a care in the world, forgetting for an afternoon that war was a short march away. What harm would a rose-scented chemise do?

"Jacob, holler the men down."

They hadn't gone far and hurried back to us in an abbreviated race.

"Cut it up for those who have no one," I said and handed the chemise to Cormack.

He grinned and touched his brow. "Thank you, ma'am. Good day."

As if he could intuit our need, Jacob smooched the horses into a brisk trot. The man was a saint on earth. He stopped none too soon and hurried as much as Jacob ever hurries to carry Imogene a discreet distance away from the road.

"You ladies gonna be all right?"

"We'll be fine. Thank you."

"All right. I'm gonna water a tree across the way. Holler when you need me."

Chapter Forty-Two

I rode in the right side of the carriage, anxiously watching for not only my contact but also signs of Federals in the area. Once at the farm, Confederate soldiers posing as "new hires" would quickly strip the carriage doors and other compartments of their hidden cargo in the barn and put it back together. I was curious about how the carriage was constructed but decided not to watch. One careless glance at a hidden compartment during a search might doom all.

When all was done, Jacob would drive us to Fairfax to the train, and our contact there would take the carriage back to Washington to repeat the operation. It was too valuable to reserve for just my missions. It was all remarkably well thought out. All I had to do was get the carriage and information out without getting caught.

Some distance down the road, I spotted a little blonde girl in a white bonnet with a brown and white goat and called for Jacob to pull over. Pardon me," I said. "We've come a good distance. Is there a place to water my horses nearby?"

The girl tugged her goat nearer. "Our farm's to the right. Ma has fresh goat milk if you've a mind."

"That would be delightful. Goat milk is so good for the skin."

She waved the doll at us and dashed through the pasture with the goat bounding behind her.

The invitation for fresh milk meant our contacts were waiting and no one else; my response was the countersign. Even so, I kept a watchful eye on the nearby woods. Our recent encounter with the Zouaves had put me on edge, and I couldn't relax until the carriage was plundered and we were safely on our way. I clung to the carriage door, listening for unusual noises and watching the trees for flights of birds suddenly lifting. Thankfully, Imogene's nap had worn some of the laudanum away, as I didn't know what intelligence she'd gathered nor what she'd done with it. Most of what I had was troop movements and strength.

The farm was as pretty as a painting, but for how long with war boiling so close at hand? Would it be preserved even without Southern sympathies? The house, a brilliant white two-story, boasted a generous veranda that flowed around the sides as if hugging it. Numerous curtained windows with stark black shutters testified to a certain amount of prosperity. On the porch was an assortment of rockers. Two sat side by side at one end.

Mercy Johnson came out, drying her hands on her apron and smiling genially, but I recognized the tension about her. She wore a blue calico dress that matched her vivid eyes. Her face was tan from working in the sun and lined from fretting about six boys and, finally, the one girl Seth so desperately desired, and yet it was still an attractive face. It was the kind of face that aged well. In youth, it turned a man's head and heart. In age, she'd have those same apple cheeks, glittering eyes, and a comely smile that said, "I know a wonderful secret."

"Raynie says you need to water your horses. We've got a trough by the barn. Come in out of the heat, ladies." She patted the girl. "Go to the crick and get that milk."

We followed Mrs. Johnson inside and sat at the table with a plate of sugar cookies. The house inside was as neat as the out-side, with an impressive collection of family portraits hanging in the hall. She pointed out the new portraits of her sons in new uniforms, looking properly grim for the photographer. Raynie dashed inside with the milk and carefully propped her doll in a corner chair. The doll matched her mistress with yellow yarn braids tied off with ribbons and a blue ribbon sash. She poured three glasses and served them with care.

"Thank you, Miss Raynie, I love that silk sash. It matches your eyes perfectly."

Beaming back at me, she sketched an awkward curtsey. "Thank you. Daddy gave it to me for Christmas."

"It's very pretty," said Imogene. "I wish I had one like it."

"You're too kind," Mercy said, smiling at the girl. "Now go outside, sweetheart, while we visit. See if Grandpa needs help in the garden."

"Yes, ma'am." She gathered her doll and scurried away.

"Seth was so proud to finally get a girl. Couldn't wait to buy frilly things like that sash." She took a long drink of milk and twisted the wedding ring on her finger. "Since her brothers enlisted, she's afraid. I reckon we all are. Has nightmares about the boys dying and Seth leaving. Wears that sash every day to remind her of her daddy and packs that doll around like a toddler with a blanket." She looked out the window across the yard. "Sometimes I wish I had a doll to curl up with instead of my fears."

I wanted to comfort her, but there were reasons to fear. "The Union army in Alexandria was mostly civil enough, but more are on the move. You should be aware."

"I figured they were. Riders thundered by last night."

I took off my boots and retrieved the messages in the heels, then tapped them back on with the butt of my gun. The most recent missives were stashed in my corset, so I excused myself to pull them out. Imogene was drinking coffee when I returned.

"Feeling better?" I asked.

She grimaced. "The ankle is throbbing, but I need a clear head, and Mrs. Johnson is steaming my parasol handle."

"What for?"

"I put the handle on with thin horse glue. The maps are in the parasol."

That was a brilliant idea. I might use it in the future.

She returned with the parasol, and Imogene wriggled the handle off the shaft, then shook the wax-paper-wrapped tube loose. Inside were detailed maps of Alexandria and surrounding camps. A list of troops and notes about rumored movements followed the maps.

"Imogene, where'd you get all that?"

She shook her head. "It's frightening what they tell you in innocent conversation. If I'd been seeking information, there wouldn't have been a secret left in that city. I wanted to go to confession due to guilt, and I'm not even Catholic."

We passed the information to our contact who had come in from the barn while I was retrieving messages. He glanced at it briefly with some surprise and put it in a messenger bag at his side. "I hope paper is acceptable," he said and peeled off a stack of bills.

"I didn't do it for money," I replied.

"Take it with our thanks. I expect you had expenses." He bowed and replaced his hat. "Ladies."

The *hires* were gone in a hot gallop. Jacob drove us to the train in Fairfax Station. We had survived our first mission.

Chapter Forty-Three

I assumed Frain would not use me often, as I wasn't within convenient distance of Baltimore, but a week later, I received a message begging me to return to Baltimore. The telegram was short but urgent: "Come quickly. Short stay. ABW" I knew Frain was the Avid Bird Watcher, but he had never urged me to hurry before.

Though I hoped to spend time teaching and relaxing at the farm, I returned, much to Gertie's and Mother's delight. Doctor Frain arrived shortly after I did. He was checking on Mother's sore throat or some other dire malady. As usual, he took me to the pond in the backyard to explain her treatment. Honey, lemon, whiskey, hot toddy. I had fixed enough of those to clear an orchard when Papa got sick, so I didn't need further instructions in that realm.

"You're wondering what was urgent," he said.

"Yes, I told you I needed some time. My aunt and uncle are already suspicious."

He had made such a habit of coming to the pond; the fish were already jumping and vying for his attention, so he broke up a cookie he had pilfered and tossed it to them. "The person requesting you said she would only deal with you."

Fear clawed up my spine with icy fingers until I feared to breathe. This had to be a trap. "How does someone outside the circle know me?"

"She found out Byles had you tossed in prison. Her sister was involved with Byles a few months ago and then suddenly disappeared without a word. She begged the police for help, but they said they could do nothing; she was a grown woman. She appealed to everyone in power she could find, but no one would challenge Pinkerton. Finally, she told her husband she was returning to Mississippi to her family to grieve among loved ones. Colonel Collins refused, saying it would damage his reputation and his chance for advancement. He cut off all her funds to make sure she couldn't leave.

"That straw broke the camel's back, as they say. Now Mrs. Collins wants to ruin him and put a stake in Byles. In covert matters, she will be known as the Goldfinch, but you'll meet her often in social situations."

I felt Byles counting up my ribs with his knife and telling me how he could stab a woman just so, and she would never make a sound…or how exciting it was to watch one scream. I had no doubt he was responsible for the sister's disappearance. "Tell me what I need to do," I said, even though I realized I might just as fully disappear as the sister if Byles caught me again.

Frain continued dropping information. Colonel Collins frequently hosted high-level meetings in their house, so Mrs. C. was privy to important intelligence. She would transcribe the information on a handkerchief as she could. The message could only be revealed with heat. I had to pass the handkerchief on without knowing what I held as heat would expose the message permanently. He told me to go through my routines with Mrs. Smythe at the tea shop, Abrahamson, my accountant, Bouchard's Shoes, and Madame Gaspard's.

Mother sent me to Mrs. Smythe's for pastries, which gave me the perfect excuse to put our plan in motion. I varied the stops but included my contacts, though they had been warned not to pass information to me. At Madame Gaspard's, I was admiring a display of lovely lace-trimmed handkerchiefs when she pulled a box from under the counter. "A friend ordered these for you." Then she urged me to buy some for Gertie and Mother, as they were much in demand. I was to carry one unused and neatly folded at all times. These were the ones I would exchange with the Goldfinch. I left some lace from the lace guild, collected needles, thread, and payment, and returned home leisurely in case someone followed.

So it continued for several days. Eating at the tea shop, going to this shop or that, running silly errands, spending afternoons with the rabble-rousing Monument Girls. I would often take baskets of tasties from the tea shop and exchange notes or receipts with them, gossiping and laughing. We made a game of guessing which casual dandy reading his newspaper or walking his dog, flirting with the women, was a Pinkerton. "Be careful," one girl warned. "Pinkerton has some female agents, also. Absolute traitors to everything holy. A pox on them."

It put me even more on edge, but the race was started and must be run.

Mrs. Collins hosted a tea party in Washington that Mother had been invited to as she was the chairlady of one of the groups raising funds for a military hospital.

Interspersed with all the silly errands, Mother dragged me to one event after another. So many charities and teas! I met Mrs. Collins the socialite immediately. She was inordinately friendly and charming, but I was told that was her nature. It wasn't until the second meeting that she quietly slipped me a handkerchief, and I exchanged an identical one that I carried with her. The only difference between the two was that hers had a tiny ink stain on the tip of one corner.

Byles sent a boy to retrieve the pastries twice, saying there had been a mistake with my order. When questioned about this, Mrs. Smythe revealed Byles had duplicated Mother's orders. It wouldn't be hard to find out about delivery orders if someone were dedicated. She hadn't sent anyone to retrieve the original. One day, I noticed him lurking in the tea shop and asked Patty for the same box of pastries. These I delivered to his table.

"Since you enjoy what we order so much, I thought I'd save you the trouble of sending a boy to retrieve my pastries. Which box would you like, Mr. Byles?"

He glowered briefly at me, flashing steel before regaining his composure. "That's exceedingly kind, Miss McKenzie. Perhaps we can enjoy a relaxing evening at the Willard sometime. I understand you favor the beefsteak there."

My back stiffened, but I kept my face impassive. I'm sure my eyes gave me away as I noticed his twitching smile in response. "I'm afraid I won't have time, nor do I imagine you will, with all the skullduggery taking place at Monument Square."

He grimaced. "Yes, you girls are leading a merry chase, but I would make time. The marmalade cake was delicious, by the way."

I bowed my head. "I'm glad you enjoyed it."

The Monument Square Girls had taken to passing false messages to tie up Pinkerton's men, and I had joined in by passing messages, mostly receipts, in a very covert manner so as to attract the attention of any spies who might be watching. One girl had been arrested after I passed her the receipt for the marmalade cake. Though I hated giving it up, it had to be good and unusual.

With our cat-and-mouse game finished, I took my leave, knowing he might still watch me from time to time, but with the war heating up, he had bigger fish to fry, and I had given him nothing but smoke and whispers to chase.

But as they warn, where there's smoke, there's fire, and so I didn't dare fan the coals too much, or Byles would be sure to investigate. I had no desire to be his guest again nor smell that cologne preceding him down a dark alley. It was not only a fear but also a frequent nightmare.

෴

By the first week of July, I had been accepted to the inner circle, which was rich with important information, and had made more trips as required, but I was happy to be relaxing back at Rosemount now with nothing to do but take care of my girls and business. I had ignored both far too much lately. I was sitting at the kitchen table sipping coffee and sorting through mail when I looked out the window toward the gardens. It was too nice to be inside today. "Della, don't you think it's time for a practice?"

She rolled her eyes. "Yes'm. Like they wanna stay inside 'citing math and Latin on a pretty day when they can be racing like the wind. Want me to pack a picnic?"

"Please."

Even with Baron constantly on the move, his letters had been steady as a rock, and a new one had arrived today. I eagerly tore into it while the girls fixed picnics.

Once Della started clanging the alarm bell, every student and teacher would drop everything she was doing and run to the stable to fetch her horse and race to the woods where the hunting cabin stood. We had been drilling so all might be saved. The household staff knew the main places to hide the valuables. Everyone in the stable would hide the horses and mules, not that we had many left. I was determined to save what I could if we were raided. I set out my watch to time them.

July 6, 1861
Somewhere in hell since I'm without you

Beloved Baroness,

Mrs. Murray has opened a small ladies wear in her husband's general store. She's claimed over half his display window with her finery, but among them were satin dancing slippers that caught my eye. I was bent on buying you a gift, and this seemed perfect, so long as you don't wear them out dancing with Yankees!

In the store we go. I had no idea what size shoe you wore, and I was trying to recall how my hands lay when I had to take your boots off the time your horse fell in the muddy stream. I'm going from one shoe to another, feeling it, eyes closed, trying to remember the size of your foot. I had

Skeeter with me, who you will recall looks about fourteen and acts the same at times. Then I heard a gasp behind me and looked around, thinking Skeeter had upset something. No. Mrs. Murray stood behind me, eyes wide, handkerchief at her mouth in horror. "What are you doing?" she cried.

"What's wrong?" her husband asked.

"This, this degenerate was fondling these shoes."

"I most certainly was not," I replied. "I was just feeling them."

"You was kind of fondling them," Skeeter said unhelpfully. "What's a degenerate?"

She blushed and stuttered, then declared I should be ashamed of corrupting my son before fleeing to the back of the store. Mr. Murray screamed. "Out! Out! Out!"

Skeeter said, "Come along, Pa."

I told him to shut up before I had him whupped.

Just about then Billings wandered in, and Murray noticed his uniform. "Out!"

"What? I just need some tobacco."

"Out!"

Skeeter told him what happened. Billings told us to go find a tavern somewhere so he could finish his shopping. You would think being a captain would earn you some respect, wouldn't you? It doesn't; I'm here to tell you.

So, my dear, you did not get those pretty satin slippers, but I trust you will enjoy this Florida Water another shop sold me and was assured any lady likes. Slippers aren't proper gifts to an unmarried lady, she said. We should fix that.

I had romantic visions of coming to Rosemount and stealing you away to the willow, where I would hum the Cavalier's Waltz because I am your cavalier, and we would dance. You in your satin slippers. Then having danced, I would drop to my knee and ask you formally to marry me, and you would cry, "Yes, yes!"

Brother London would appear as if by magic and wed us on the spot.

With the way my luck has been running, instead of London, Miss Boggs would appear screeching your name and interrupt our sweet interlude as always.

I must adieu as I am ever in the saddle. For now you must content yourself with scented water and a heart filled with love and longing that will forever belong to you,

Yours eternally,
Captain Baron Patrick Callahan, CSA

I smiled and put the letter back in its cover, smelled the Florida Water, and sank back in my chair.

"Picnic's bout ready, Miss," Della announced. "Get that bonnet on."

Four minutes and thirty-three seconds. We needed to improve, but a ride with the girls was exactly what we all needed. We even found a few jumps to take near the hunting cabin for those so inclined. The hay meadows spread like verdant quilts across the valley and hills, as did the wheat and oat crops. We'd have a good corn harvest if the worms didn't get it. I hoped the market held for apples as it looked like the orchards would be laden come fall. Being unable to ship north would be a problem, but I'd deal with it when I came to that bridge. If nothing else, we'd press them. I might be able to make all my payments at least, and that would be a blessing. What more could I ask?

After eating, Lucy and Persy sprawled on the blankets to cloud watch. "I see a horse," Lucy said.

Beth looked up from her book. "You always see horses. I see a flower."

"I see a rider," Persy said.

"A rider? Where?" I couldn't imagine where she got that from, such a mound of clouds.

"Coming up the tree line," she said and pointed.

Sure enough, a man on a dark horse rode steadily toward us. I mounted Farrell. "Wait here."

"Your mama's sick," Lucy said.

"I'm sure it's not that," I replied, though I wasn't sure at all.

The man stopped in front of me and looked at the sky. "Miss McKenzie, I'm sorry to bother you." He began the familiar conversation about rain crows.

Frain had found a couple the Goldfinch trusted and promised me I wouldn't be pressed into service soon. "I said I needed time," I replied peevishly.

He shrugged a sheepish apology. "I know, but this is important. We lost the lovebirds."

My heart caught as if it had forgotten the rhythm. "Lost?"

"She and her husband caught typhoid. We lost them both. The Cardinal requested you."

"There's no one else?"

"No. It's getting hot, and there's no one else she trusts. There's no contraband."

I should have asked why it was getting hot, but if I knew, I might choose to hide. Thoughts of dark hallways and the scent of cinnamon flashed through my mind. I buried them as deeply as Byles had his stolen women and nodded mutely.

The girls were already packing, mounting, and looking my way as if they might ride to rescue me at any moment. I wished they could, but there was nothing to be done.

I was to come alone this time, much to Imogene's displeasure, as she had on the last two missions and was turning into the angel of Alexandria. If they only knew.

Chapter Forty-Four

"Darling, I'm so glad you're back," Mother positively sang with delight. "It's that handsome Captain Simmons, isn't it? You'll be happy to know he's still in Baltimore. I invited him for supper when I got your telegram."

I had business to see to that didn't include her packed social calendar. Mother directed the driver and servants about with my luggage as she continued with the social itinerary. "Yes, thank you. Is that all the luggage?" She looked at me, frowning. "That's not enough clothes for anything."

I paid the driver, who made good his escape before Mother asked him to go search the cab again.

"I'm not staying that long."

She waved a hand. "Pish. We have things to do. There's a clothes drive this afternoon for the war effort. We can—"

I stopped her. "Mother, I'm going to pick up some pastries for you, and I need to get supplies for the school."

Gertie gave me a quick hug but remained in the background, uncharacteristically quiet, with a Vee furrowed between her sable brows. "Bertha, why don't you finish gathering your clothes for the drive while I show Lorena that gown?"

"Yes, that's a good idea."

I hadn't been taken out back often, but I felt as if we were heading to a tree for a switch now. She motioned me to a chair in her room and stood at the window looking out, saying nothing for a long time as if measuring the words in her mind carefully. "What are you doing?"

"Pardon?"

"You've been here several times since April. Don't tell me you're concerned about your mother."

"She keeps sending—"

Gertie held up her hand. "Please don't. We both know you wouldn't come flying north every time she claimed her deathbed. You're up to something, and I'm afraid for you."

"I've been carrying mail." That part was true. Some people were afraid it was being read, and I'd been pressed into service to deliver letters to loved ones on either side of the line. While the letters might get confiscated if they were found, there was nothing incriminating in them. "Plus, I'm stocking up on supplies we may not be able to get if Lincoln's blockade is successful, and bringing the lace, of course." She couldn't object to the lace as she was complicit in that.

"Foolish girl. I don't know why you don't let your overseer take care of Rosemount and move north. Sell it while you can."

"Why don't you sell the Fortress and move south?"

"That's not the same at all. The Fortress isn't going to be destroyed." She clasped a hand over her mouth. "Lorena, I'm sorry. I didn't mean to say that."

I stood, irked that even Gertie would declare Rosemount a corpse. "I need to get pastries for Mother's party."

"I brought you a gown; let me get it."

"Thank you," I replied coolly. "Leave it in my room."

Mother protested my leaving when she was anxious to show me off to the Ladies' Aide Society, but I insisted I had to see my accountant and take care of the other business. She never asked why I couldn't find an accountant in Virginia, thankfully, and I escaped by taking Castor with me.

"Where to today, Miss Mac?" he asked, holding the carriage door open. He was dressed in a black suit, like Otis' funerary garb.

I shook my head. "I'll talk to Mother about these getups. I swan, there's no middle ground with that woman. I believe I'll walk. Leave the carriage for Mother."

"I'll tell Otis we're walking." He tugged at the black brocade waistcoat "I don't mind this so much. I think I cut an imposing figure."

"You'd cut an imposing figure in your altogethers, but, yes, you look quite nice. Just like the grim reaper's apprentice. Let's make the rounds. Mr. Abrahamson to check my accounts, Mrs. Gaspard to pick up a bonnet and an ostrich feather if she has one, Boucher to drop off Mother's slippers, and Mrs. Smythe's for pastries, and we'll get an early bite to eat since Mother's going to Ladies' Aide. I'll find the school supplies I need."

Mr. Abrahamson reported some modest gains. I gave him some more jewelry to hold for me. "Invest where you will."

"You know I do. It's as safe with me as if you were my daughter."

His son walked me to the door and whispered. "There's no message for you today. Come back before you leave."

Castor waited outside during my accountant business but decided to come in with me at the millinery shop. Madame Gaspard buzzed about me like a bee to balm and patted Castor on the chest, sighed wistfully, and primped her hair, though it was perfect. Perfect for Madame Gaspard meant it looked as if she had carefully coifed it, but a later vigorous romantic encounter disheveled her. I felt guilty for my assessment but was positive it was a carefully planned look. From the glances male companions of female shoppers shot her surreptitiously, it worked. Castor rewarded her with a wicked grin.

Dear Father in Heaven. Don't fall into her web.

"Madame, I need a new empress bonnet. Some blackguard shot a hole through my other one, and it simply can't be mended. We've tried everything, and it looks ridiculous."

"*Mon Dieu!* Who would shoot you, *ma pet*? Did you shoot him back?"

"To be sure."

"*Bon.* Why would a man shoot at you? Or maybe a jealous woman?" She shuddered, giddy at the idea of such a scandal.

An array of bonnets from shelves and disembodied wooden heads appeared, few of them empress hats. "It was a robber. Just an empress hat, Madame."

"Pish." She waved the hat in her hand, dismissing the ridiculous idea. "Hats are like lovers. One can never have too many."

"One is sufficient, of either," I replied. Castor held one up in front of him in a mirror, turning it this way and that. "That isn't your color at all, Castor."

He frowned. "I was thinking 'bout Miss Annie. Do you think she'd like it?"

"Purple's her favorite color, so she'd love all those violets. Before you set your cap for her, however, I'd reconsider your colorful side business. She won't have much truck with that. Plus, how are you going to court her from up here?"

My advice was shrugged away like an annoying gnat. "That's to save up enough money to buy her a house. I aim to be a man of property before I approach her. I expect I can convince her to come north with enough coaxing."

He could have pushed me over with the purple plume trailing from the bonnet. "I'm not so sure of that. You know there's a reason I bought her that Deringer."

"If she was my wife, wouldn't no one ever lay an eye on that girl."

Madame Gaspard drew my attention back to a perfect replacement for my empress with adjustments to feathers. I refused the inverted pot festooned with feathers, flowers, lace, and ribbons. "My stars, no. Do I look like a politician's wife? Too much…everything." When had women decided overflowing fake flowers were the epitome of fashion?

"You must take this hat," she said and handed me a Glengarry in McKenzie tartan with a colorful cockade. "These are *your* colors." By the end she talked me into three hats, which she would have delivered. I'd deconstruct the Glengarry later in private to safely retrieve the message.

I left a good supply of lace from the Lace Guild. The ladies would be thrilled with their tidy profit. She promised to send thread and needles to the house later to make more lace.

Castor escaped with one bonnet and an invitation to come again—soon. I felt I should warn him about spiders and webs, no matter how attractively spun, but he was a grown man.

I left Mother's slippers at Boucher's to be repaired and would retrieve them the next day. Not every stop there was for messages.

Off to Mrs. Smythe's to eat and buy pastries, but Castor went across the street to visit with a friend and order something. I scanned the room casually before sitting next to a wall where I could keep anyone away from my back and watch people coming in. There was the usual assortment of customers. Couples, businesspeople, and ladies chatting genially; a man in the corner reading a paper. I looked up from the menu that already had my mouth watering when my waitress arrived. "Hello, Patty."

"Tea terday? With?"

"Lady Earl Grey. Without. What's your special?"

"Beef an' noodles with a cup of tomato bisque."

"That sounds good."

Mrs. Smythe bustled across the room and hugged me. The proprietor positively glowed with pearl powder and heaven knows what else to give her an eerie blue cast. "Mother's having a supper party tonight," I said. "What pastries do you recommend?"

"I can send an assortment of desserts plus some nice savories. There's a special box of peach pastries for you also. You'll simply crow about them."

"Thank you so much. You know I love peaches."

Peaches and crows. So much information passing this time. Usually, it was one or two. A man hurried in and sat next to the fellow reading the newspaper. Whatever he had to say must not have been too interesting, as the man kept reading, only letting go of one side from time to time to sip his coffee. A few others filtered in. Some finished and left. It was a very ordinary crowd. The kind I liked.

With the excellent meal ended, I went to pay and collect the boxes of pastries, including the peach ones with the information. "Oh, it's already paid," Mrs. Smythe twittered. "That gentleman in the corner with the newspaper got it for you. He even paid for your pastries." She raised a conspiratorial eyebrow as if to say, "Well done, my girl."

I marched over to the man who lowered his paper upon my arrival. "Miss McKenzie." He beamed as if he expected my visit. "You're looking lovely."

My breath caught, but nothing like my heart, which threatened to stop beating altogether. "Mr. Byles."

He smiled and tilted his head, then drew one of those cinnamon toothpicks out of his silver case. "I hope you enjoyed your meal. The tomato bisque is quite good today, isn't it?"

"Why would you presume to pay for me?" I fumbled in my reticule for my coin purse. People around us were turning to look, curious at the brewing storm.

"I don't see why you should object at all. You were certainly more than happy to accept the nice meal I gave you and then breakfast the next morning when you, uh, shall we say, stayed with me."

The old woman at the table next to me gasped, eyes wide as platters and mouth just as gaped.

"How dare you!" I sputtered.

His infuriating smirk tilted up higher on one side, shifting the toothpick like a tiny orchestra leader's baton directing my rising fury. "*Acta est fabula, plaudit*, indeed. Which act do you think we're in now?"

I tossed some coins on the table. "*Go hifreann leat!*"

With infuriating calm, he sipped his coffee, his eyes never leaving mine. "We've already discussed this. I'm quite sure I am. You really need to expand your sentiments, though the Irish is a nice touch."

My mouth dropped open.

He waved a hand dismissively. "I speak a bit, but it was a guess. You're so predictable. I understand you're walking today. Would you like me to summon you a hack?"

An ice worm crawled into my stomach, spreading icy tendrils of fear, but I was too furious to respond. All I could do was huff and spin in hasty retreat. His laugh followed me like a plague I couldn't escape. "Mrs. Smythe," I said under my breath, "please have the same number of boxes delivered. The special peach pastries tomorrow, discreetly."

When I got home, Mother and Aunt Gertie were gone, so I took advantage of the solitude to remove messages and scan them: troop movements, changes in leadership, troop strengths in various areas, and anticipated campaigns. I wriggled back under the opium bed again and stowed the documents and cipher wheel that Frain had left with me at our last meeting.

I'd barely finished stashing the documents when Rita announced Doctor Frain's arrival. *Perfect timing, Doctor.* Now I'd have to fetch the documents for him.

To the backyard as usual for privacy. He declined the information because he was between appointments and didn't want to carry it. All would pass tomorrow after I received the information from Mrs. Smythe. We sipped lemonade and ate cookies in the gazebo; by all appearances, we laughed and joked like old friends to anyone who was watching.

"I'm sure you're weary of balls and fundraisers," he said, tossing a bit of cookie to a goldfish who leaped into the air to catch it expertly. "There are three tomorrow. I made sure your mother had invitations to the Blue and Gold. She probably has invitations to others, but be at the Blue and Gold through the second set at least."

"I'm going to stay there, regardless of what she does. I refuse to traipse all over town."

He offered me a cookie and then tossed another bit to the fish. I noticed him glance around, taking stock of our surroundings, and then he lowered his voice. "Go to the powder room on the first floor after the first set, the one near the French doors. The

Goldfinch will be there. It's the last bit of the puzzle we need. Make sure you keep it safe."

I set the cookie down and ran my finger pensively around the rim of my glass before setting it down also. Passing information so publicly always made me nervous. I was more on edge after this afternoon. "You should know Byles approached me at Mrs. Smythe's earlier. He knew I was walking, so he's been watching me."

"I'm not surprised, but we need this information. Go to your aunt's the day after tomorrow, and I'll get you out of Washington with the information. We'll distract Byles away from you to make your escape. Maybe a protest at Monument Square or something. Just a small affair, but enough to draw his attention."

My stomach churned at the thought of meeting her so openly after Byles had all but announced I was being followed. "Can you not find another agent?"

"She only trusts you now with the couple gone, and this is vital. She may destroy it if we don't meet her."

I looked down at my hands and noticed my fingers tapping nervously in my lap. *Stop it! That's too much like Byles and his piano playing.* "Then a-dancing we will go, I suppose. Is there anything else?"

"Nothing of note," he said. "I'll give you information about your mission in Washington. Try to get some rest before your supper tonight. Relax. Pick some flowers. Take your mind off the mission and Byles."

"I'll nap." I looked around at the flowers as tempting as they were. "If I putter in the garden, my mind will just dig up worry weeds."

We parted company, and I napped until Rita poked her head around the door to rouse me from a lovely dream of Baron and Rosemount. "Miss Lorena, yo' mama and Miz G want to see you. You want help dressing?"

"Is anyone here?"

"Just family."

"I'll wear my wrapper."

Rita led me to the parlor where the Dobbs sisters sat together on the settee surrounded by piles of boxes and packages. Was there a shop in town left unraided?

"Lorena," Mother said, folding her hands primly in her lap. She looked to Gertie for support. "I know you love me."

Don't reply.

Rita brought me tea and ginger cookies. I sank into the shepherdess chair warily.

"But let's be honest, there's another reason you visit so frequently." She looked at Gertie for support. "I know you like Captain Simmons, and so do I. He's nice—"

"And handsome," Gertie added.

Mother nodded enthusiastically. "He comes from a good family of considerable wealth. It would be a good match."

"Mother—"

She held her hand up. "Before you make any decisions. We think you should seriously consider Colonel Orwyn. He'll make general soon, we're told, and is of even finer stock. He may be a bit older than you, but I assure you a man may remain—" she looked to Gertie for help.

"George is still, uh, romantically *active* if you take my meaning, and he's twenty years Colonel Orwyn's senior, is what your mother's trying to say."

"Yes, you shouldn't worry in that regard if it's important to you."

Dear Father in Heaven.

"Why are you two bringing this up to me?"

The two conspirators looked at each other. "We think Colonel Orwyn may ask formal permission to court you," Mother said.

"And why would he think this a good idea?"

"Well—"

"Well?"

"Well, you were visiting so often I was sure you were interested in one of these gentlemen. Gertie said you aren't interested in Garrold Simmons; however, you should reconsider him. He's the best of the lot, but I know you love uniforms. If you insist on such, that leaves Orwyn and Simmons. Captain Simmons is heartbreakingly handsome and, uh, vigorous, I'm sure, but there's a lot to be said for age."

"They're closer to the grave?"

"No!" Mother snapped.

"Cease, both of you. I refuse to discuss this."

They looked like children who'd been caught in the candy jar. Mother opened her mouth once, then wisely closed it without saying anything.

"We went shopping," Gertie said, changing course.

"So I see. Stop buying me clothes."

Rita brought Gertie's gown down for my inspection. "Didn't you show that to her earlier?" Mother eyed us both suspiciously.

"We were talking, and I forgot."

"I love it," I said, interrupting further questioning. The gown was uncharacteristically ethereal and understated. Its bodice was dove-gray silk, embroidered with the same tone thread and embellished with seed pearls. Below, the same color silk and three layers of tulle cascaded down with delicate peach and lavender hand-painted roses that encircled the hem and floated up the front of the gown toward the waist. It was a misty, magical thing as if viewed through a fog, a fairy maiden dress.

Gertie raised a knowing brow. "I knew you would the moment I saw this gauzy material. I mailed it to Annie and told her to do her magic. The silk matches your eyes. We bought accessories to go with it."

Though the gown was truly beautiful, I did wonder about Annie's magic since she had been so busy with the wedding party dresses. Gertie must have offered her a fabulous bribe. I further pondered if any commitment on my part was included in the bribe.

Chapter Forty-Five

"Captain Simmons," George said that night, "I understand you may be deploying?"

"Yes, sir. We'll be leaving soon. I was especially grateful for the invitation tonight as I wasn't sure I'd see Miss McKenzie again before we left. And the rest of you, of course."

"You can visit even if Lorena isn't here," Mother chirped. "Your brother stops by frequently."

Simmons's eyes turned murderous, and his fingers clenched about his knife with whitened knuckles as if he were about to murder someone. "Does he now?"

We finished eating congenially, but a subtle chill settled over the mood like a lightly rimed window in October.

The men retired to the library to smoke and talk politics after dinner while we ladies disappeared into the withdrawing room.

At the end of the evening, Mother and Gertie conveniently slipped away so Simmons and I might visit privately. We strolled into the garden with Mother's *elf* lights. They were actually skater's lamps with blue globes and punched tin lamps artfully arranged in the plantings to make it look like there was a ghostly blue glow or dozens of fireflies. Had she suggested Simmons take me for a walk here with its decidedly romantic effect?

"You look exceptionally lovely tonight." There was a bashful, embarrassed half grin. He laid his hand across my hand I'd placed on his arm. "I'm sure you've never heard that."

"Thank you. A lady isn't supposed to say so, but you're quite handsome yourself."

"I admire that you speak your mind rather than play games."

If you knew the dangerous games I play.

"Your mother hopes I'm proposing something of a romantic nature, I think," he said without guile.

"Undoubtedly."

"Trust me when I say I'd like to, but I sense a reserve in you that I've not been able to breach. I believe any declarations on my part at this time would be rebuffed."

The "at this time" was noted.

I saw a glimmer of hope in his eyes that I might deny this. "Captain Simmons, I *am* fond of you—"

"But I'm correct."

"I can make no commitments." *Because I'm madly in love with a Rebel captain, and this shameful subterfuge is killing me.*

"I pray you'll permit me to remain your friend. As a friend, may I write you when I deploy?"

"Of course. I'd be delighted to correspond."

He stopped in front of a gazing ball with one of the punched tin lights behind it. "And, as a friend, please take some important advice. My brother isn't to be trusted. He'll try to woo you because you're a desirable woman, but also because he knows I'm interested. It's a game. He'll do all in his power to take you, and he has a history of leaving broken women in his wake. You might think I speak this out of jealousy, but it's the simple truth. I care enough to not want you hurt. If you can convince your mother to be shed of him, do it."

I doubted not for a minute what he said was true. Unlike Mother, I had an innate sense of people that was usually sound. Garry Simmons was like a beautiful snake. "I won't be lured by him, but Mother's convinced he cares about her."

"He cares about the information and advantage she brings him." There was a difficult pause. "I followed you home the night of my birthday," he said quietly as if I were taking confession. "Garry's been known to show up at a young lady's home on some pretext or another after an engagement or even romantically climb into windows. Some women find it endearing. I'd have shot him had I seen the blackguard scaling your wall."

"So, you were the watcher." I exhaled a relieved sigh.

"Yes, forgive me."

"There's nothing to forgive. Thank you for looking out for me. If your brother tries to climb in my window, I'll shoot him myself. I can be convincingly frantic."

"I have another confession to make that you might not forgive me for." His jaw clenched as he said this. What could he have done?

"It's my fault you were arrested."

"What!" My hand dropped from his arm.

"Not my fault directly, but in a way. Do you remember when I first saw you and you were singing and waving the Bonnie Blue?"

I nodded warily.

"My aide wanted to have you arrested. I refused. The viper is a senator's son. He was angry that I didn't have you arrested, so he cried to his father, who complained to Lincoln. I'm sure the weasel thought he'd get a promotion, and I'd get busted. All that happened was Lincoln siccing Pinkerton on you and me, making sure that little—" he caught himself. "Fool doesn't make that mistake again. Several of my men happened to tell stories about an ambitious snitch who got blown away by his own men at first opportunity. He has permanently chained himself to a desk, afraid if he pokes his head up, someone will shoot him."

"Well, that solves that mystery. With everything else going on, we were all wondering why I caught his attention."

"Yes, and I owe you everlasting apologies for that."

I waved a hand away, though the damage was permanent, I feared. "It wasn't your doing."

He looked to the house where shadows of people were silhouetted in the windows. "I should take you back in before they think I'm inappropriate."

"Knowing Mother, she's probably hoping."

He laughed. "I hate to disappoint your mother. If I may?" He tenderly kissed me without waiting for an answer.

Since I'd all but invited it, I couldn't object. I bid the captain to take care of himself but didn't ask where he was going or when, and he didn't volunteer. Simmons I kept carefully off the playing board in case anything should ever go wrong.

Having made the information rounds in Baltimore, I returned to Washington with Gertie and George the next day. Mother would come up later and join us for the Blue and Gold.

For once, Mother didn't object to Gertie's gown selections. Together, they adorned me to perfection, accenting the gown's glory. Draped in silk that shimmered like mist in moonlight, I felt as if I were slipping through smoke with gossamer blooms rising up to meet me. Suella brought down a velvet jewel box with Gertie's magnificent sapphire and diamond parure.

"I can't wear this," I objected as Gertie pulled the necklace out.

"Of course, you can," she replied, adjusting the center gem just so. "Bert, put that hair comb in while I get the ear bobs."

At last, decked out in the entire set, they stood back to admire their handiwork. "Lovely," Gertie said. "This necklace does wonders for your décolletage, my dear. A woman should flaunt her jewels—and her charms—before time and gravity conspire against her."

Suella giggled. Mother chastised Gertie about vulgar talk, then adjusted the dress to showcase me even more perfectly.

"I'm going to find a scarf for a modesty panel," I said.

"You most certainly are not," Gertie replied. "I want you shining tonight." She peered at me closer. "That bracelet could be fuller, but it will do. Now sit pretty while your mother and I finish dressing. Or stand. Don't wrinkle that dress."

Even Mother and Gertie had donned new gowns and their best jewels. Someone important was coming to the ball. It made me even more nervous. That meant more security.

Rumors that the Prince of Belgium was in town whispered on every lip, but no one had seen him or any foreign dignitaries yet. George affirmed that something was up but didn't have the details. We could only wait and wonder. Willard Hall was tastefully decorated with hothouse flowers in grandiose arrangements. If not for my nerves, I would have wandered about like a bee smelling the various blooms. As it was, I would feign illness and escape as soon as I had the information. There were guards at every door, plus who knew how many Pinkertons in civilian garb. The Goldfinch and I had no chance of slipping away unnoticed should things get warm.

With her usual grace, Gertie introduced me to every young man she knew, and apparently, she knew them all. Mother stayed focused on rank and wealth with her introductions. "Wouldn't it be exciting if you caught a prince's eye?" she sighed wistfully after one man departed.

"I think I'm not feeling well," I said.

"Do you see those guards?" she said. "I will give every one of them orders not to let you escape."

My heart stopped and fell to the floor. "Dear heavens, Mother. Don't even joke about that."

She waved her fan lazily. "I'm not."

If her meddling got me arrested again, this time with information, I'd be dancing on air soon enough and be dipped and dyed if I'd invite her to the dance.

There was still no prince at the end of the first set, but I noticed the Goldfinch making her way to the powder room and excused myself from the two gentlemen who had been conversing with me. Goldfinch and I entered the powder room separately, careful not to draw attention. A troop of giggling girls primped in front of mirrors and pined over this young man or that, but they were waiting for the prince. Wasn't it all so exciting!

The attendant stood quietly near the door, watching attentively in case anyone needed anything. I had no idea how we would exchange the handkerchiefs without notice. We exchanged brief pleasantries and commented about the music. Goldfinch nodded slightly toward the screens hiding the water closet and made her way to one. I fussed with my hair a bit before claiming the remaining one next to it, and we passed the handkerchiefs under the dividing screen.

My heart thudded as I tucked hers away. Without a word, the attendant stepped forward to hand us each towels. We washed our hands with delightfully perfumed soaps, tipped the girl generously, and returned to the fray with practiced indifference.

"Mr. Charbonneau is very much looking forward to your company," Uncle George said when he led me to the dance floor. "Could you not spare him a second dance?"

"I'm not really feeling well. I think I may leave early."

"Oh, please don't. I know you're going home soon, and Gertie so enjoys your company." He leaned closer and winked conspiratorially. "Plus, every woman in the hall is raving about her jewels, which haven't looked so lovely in years."

I had caught many admiring glances from men who also enjoyed fine jewels, it seemed.

There was a stirring among the guards when George led me back to my seat, where Mr. Charbonneau and another man waited. A man came up to George and handed him a message that he read hurriedly. "Damnation."

Before I could ask what was wrong, Mr. Charboneau turned, bowed, and kissed my hand. "Miss McKenzie. I regret deeply that I must forfeit this dance. Your uncle and I are being recalled to the White House. However, my friend has offered to fill in for me."

I was paying little attention as I watched George hurry over to a plague of guards arguing with a military officer.

"Miss McKenzie?"

"Oh, I'm sorry. Yes, of course, Mr. Charbonneau. I hope it's not serious." It might be my chance to escape, but I suddenly realized I was enveloped with a familiar cologne and started to shrink with dread.

"Miss McKenzie," Byles said, turning to face me. "We mustn't disappoint your uncle and his aide." His hand was on my arm, tugging me toward the dance floor before I could object.

"I'll just sit this one out," I said, trying to pull away from him.

"I insist, and believe me, you do not want to make a scene right now."

With guards converging on the area, I was sure something dreadful was about to happen. Suddenly, the sea parted, and I saw the Goldfinch arguing with the guards and officer.

I was too numb to resist and followed his steps blindly while trying to keep my eyes on the scene. Her voice raised. "Do something, Ambrose!" He said something to her, raising his hands helplessly, whereupon she slapped him as fully as she could and spun around to face the guards. "Take me to prison, you worthless bastards. You can't be bothered to look for a missing woman, but you can harass me? A pox on all of you."

The music faltered, and people stood staring. Byles motioned to the band that started playing again. I leveled a baleful glare on him. "So, this is your dance."

"No, this is the Blue and Gold. I just provided some brief entertainment."

"Is that what you call it? Unhand me, you…" I cast about for the proper contemptible word.

"Beast?'

"Let me go."

"We will finish this dance. Afterward, I'll have you searched. I noticed you speaking with Mrs. Collins earlier—exchanging marmalade recipes, were you?"

"Don't be ridiculous." I tried to pull away again, but he held my arm firmly.

At the end of the dance, he waved away a young man who came to collect me for the following dance and led me to the powder room where a woman waited. "Search her like you did Mrs. Collins. Thoroughly."

I recognized the woman from Monument Square. I'd have to get a message to Frain to warn them. The woman introduced herself and set about searching me from toe to head, slippers first. She looked under my hoops, checked for pockets, patted me down, ran her hands over my bodice thoroughly, and even ran a thin ivory busk down my corset in several places to feel for messages. Lastly, she dumped out the contents of my reticule on the small vanity table in front of a mirror. Then she went to the door that had been guarded to this point and called Byles in. "I didn't find anything, and this is all that was in her bag."

Byles checked for secret pockets in the reticule, opened the hair and lip pomade tins, and even examined my comb. He tapped the Deringer. "Expecting trouble?"

"This is Washington. Crooks and scapegraces are its lifeblood, as tonight proves."

He examined the handkerchief. My bones jellied, but I willed myself not to waver. "Mrs. Collins had a handkerchief like this."

"I'm not surprised," I replied. "I'm sure half the women in Baltimore and Washington have them. Madame Gaspard said she can barely keep them in stock."

He turned to his agent. "Is this true, Emma?"

"They're expensive, but everyone wants one, it seems. The linen is very fine."

He rubbed it across his cheek. "Yes, I can see why a lady would favor them. Delicate skin deserves care." He waved toward the door. "Give us a moment."

She hesitated, glancing at me with worry tracing through her eyes. "Yes, sir."

Then he turned on the attendant. "Did you see her talking to anyone earlier?"

My eyes closed, and I said a small prayer. I watched her shrug. "They said hello as any civilized lady would and remarked how nice the music was."

"Nothing else? They didn't exchange anything?"

She frowned. "Smiles?"

"Get out."

She curtsied and left, but I noticed the small smirk as she was leaving.

"I'm quite sure you're involved in something," he said after the door closed. "I just haven't figured out what yet." He pulled one of those damnable cinnamon toothpicks out of the silver case. "Besides the lace running operation, I mean."

I backed up to the vanity table and gripped it with one hand. What else did he know?

There was that smile. "Of course, I know about you smuggling lace to Madame Gaspard and her giving you needles and thread. I care not about those petty crimes. I'm not even sure needles are contraband yet, and I wouldn't care if they were. Women deserve to be beautiful."

His hand slipped under the necklace and lifted it to admire it seemingly. The back of his hand rested against my chest, sending a shiver of revulsion down my spine. I stiffened, leaning back instinctively. "Unhand me," I said, my voice tight with controlled fury.

He let the necklace fall but brushed the hand across my chest slowly. "You look quite lovely tonight, my dear. The necklace is exquisite on you. If we were on better terms, I would cloud you in lace and jewels."

"If you have nothing else?" I turned my back and began scooping my belongings back into my reticule. Then I made the mistake of glancing in the mirror before me, catching my reflection and his rapacious gaze.

"Not tonight. You're free to go."

Mother and Aunt Gertie waited at the end of the hall leading to the powder room. They argued with guards blocking their path to no avail and called out to me as soon as I set foot out the door. George was still missing, but they shoved past the guards who parted to let them through.

"No goodbye, Miss McKenzie?"

"*Téigh trasna ort féin!*" I said.

He answered with that annoying laugh. "Not tonight, my dear."

Did he understand what I said?

"Lorena!" Mother gasped.

Mother did.

Mother and Gertie peppered me with questions all the way home, but I assured them he had only questioned me because I had been seen with Mrs. Collins earlier. Mrs. Collins, I learned, had been accused of adultery. That was when she slapped her husband. The man she was accused of having an affair with was suspected of being a spy. How close were they to the truth? I listened to the excited, outraged chatter but said little. Mother insisted on returning to Baltimore, claiming she was nearly on her deathbed from fright and needed her medicine.

Waiting for me at the Fortress was a letter edged in black resting ominously on a silver tray.

Chapter Forty-Six

I could not bring myself to open the seal and stumbled into the withdrawing room, where I collapsed onto the settee, worn in body and spirit and unable to deal with death at the moment. My first thought went to Baron, though wouldn't someone telegraph me? I pushed the thought away and cradled the letter in my lap like a baby viper, afraid to let go and terrified to hold on.

Gertie sat down beside me and gently peeled it from my hands. "Mrs. Tattenham has died," she said. "This is an invitation to her funeral tomorrow."

"What?" I said, roused from my nightmare. "Mrs. Tattenham?" I took the announcement from her and noticed the red Cardinal inked at the top of the announcement. "Oh, I didn't even know she was ill." I had no idea who Mrs. Tattenham was or why I would attend the funeral the next day, but I'd follow Dr. Frain's lead.

Gertie frowned. "I've never even heard you mention Mrs. Tattenham."

"I went to school with her daughter," I said by way of explanation. I read the enclosed note penned in delicate hand and signed by someone named Sissy. "I'm not sure I spoke much of her. Her daughter asked if I might stay as she's very distraught. I'll be gone a few days, maybe." I feigned a headache and retired before she could quiz me further and took a small bath. My head was still swarming with questions, but I was near to collapsing with relief that the announcement was not about someone I cared for and surprisingly fell asleep quickly.

When I came downstairs the next morning, Dr. Frain was waiting in the kitchen, surrounded by a flock of hovering women.

"Is Mother all right?" I asked, noting the tension about his mouth.

"Yes, she's off to the spa."

"Might I speak to you in private for a moment?" Frain asked and led me to the gazebo. "The funeral is a ruse to get you across the river without question. This information from the Goldfinch must get to General Beauregard immediately."

I fiddled with the folds of my dress, burying my trembling fingers deep in the recesses to hide my fear. "You know Byles interrogated me in the powder room after he arrested her."

"Yes, I had people watching you."

"You're not afraid he will be watching me even closer?"

One of the fish in the pond jumped as if vying for his attention. He laughed. "Sorry, boys. I forgot to bring you a treat. As for Byles, he's been called on the carpet for her public arrest. She's very popular with the military and the society ladies for her charity work. His attention is on saving his own neck right now."

I couldn't have been more surprised had he slapped me with one of the goldfish. "I thought he was beyond control. Will she go free?"

"No, even Pinkerton has a leash. We'll have her out today, and she'll be out of town tomorrow, I would think. We need her gone before the fireworks start. Take a bag with a change of clothes with you."

Luckily, I had left some sober clothes here from earlier when I was still in full mourning for Papa.

"Give me what information you have. Castor will drive your carriage. Stand away from the crowd. Sniffle a bit and nod if anyone says anything. The carriage will break down on the way back from the cemetery. As soon as things are clear, they'll bring you a horse. You must get this message to General Beauregard.

Go to Fairfax. General Bonham's in danger, and General Johnston will be cut off if we don't get this message to them. We could lose the army."

I sat stunned, unable to twitch. I wanted to scream in frustration and fear. Baron was with Johnston.

"You look like you're about to pass out."

"Someone I care about is with Johnston."

He held my arm and patted my hand. "Even more reason to succeed, and you will." Servant and master alike waited anxiously at the back door when we entered.

"Is everything all right?" Gertie asked.

"Yes, I need to get ready for this funeral. Dr. Frain will take me to the livery to rent a carriage. Can you see about rearranging my carriage to Alexandria?"

After breakfast, I hugged everyone and made goodbyes. The horses trotted smartly away from The Fortress, with Gertie standing in the drive looking after us in consternation. Frain secreted the information I had in a hidden compartment in the carriage. He delivered me to a carriage house on the outskirts of town where a woman unbound my hair, wove two small side braids, and pulled them to the back of my head. I read the message lying on the table next to me while she was stitching. She put it in a silk net and sewed it into the braids, pinned it tightly, and rerolled my hair, finishing it off with my tortoiseshell tucking combs. "How do I get that loose without cutting my hair?"

"Ask for help." She slipped dainty embroidery scissors in my hand. I imagined this mild, middle-aged woman with her delicate hands and voice in a life of "Yes, dears," needlework, and watercolor. What had spun her to espionage? "Take these with you," she said. "Knowing men, they'll only have whittling knives."

The funeral was nice, if long, as funerals go. No one questioned my invitation, and we were off to the cemetery. Ladies fanned and leaned heavily on their men until I feared someone might topple into the open grave in a faint as the commentary wore on. Afterwards, with my carriage broken down, people kindly stopped to offer assistance, one after another, further delaying my escape. Luckily, my heavy veils masked my frustration.

"No, sir," Castor replied over and over. "I sent my boy for help. He should be back shortly."

"Are you sure you don't want to ride back with us, Miss?"

"No, but thank you. I'll be fine."

With the last of the carriages out of sight and no one to hear us but the dead, I addressed Castor for the truth that had been niggling at me for some time. "You've been playing me."

"How so, ma'am?"

"Why did you come north with Mother?"

He looked surprised, flipped the coattails of Mother's Grim Reaper suit, and sat on a nearby gravestone. "Your daddy asked me to come up here."

The stirrings of betrayal churned. Papa was more worried about taking care of Mother than me? He knew how much Castor loved the horses and took him away from the farm for what? "I'm surprised he asked, and you agreed."

"I'd walk through hell and back for that man, Miss Lorena. When he bought me, I was beat bad. They'd nurse me back and put me to fightin' again like they fight dogs or roosters. Yo' daddy paid a lot of money for me. A fortune. I figured he wanted me for a stout field hand...or somethin' else." He looked away.

"Breeding stock," I said plainly.

He ducked his head, embarrassed at my bluntness, but there was the awful truth. "Yo' daddy called the doctor to look at me and did what he could. When I was healed, he took me to the foalin' barn. He showed me how to make friends with the mamas and get the babies used to bein' handled. Some days I'd sleep in the stalls with them, my arm around the little ones that was skittish.

"I asked him once how he knew I needed that. He said because one time someone did it for him. He spent the first few years thinkin' when he grew up, he was goin' back to kill the man that near whipped him to death. One day he realized he didn't care. That man an' his family had to live with what they done, and he wasn't gonna let them ruin the rest of his life eat up with hate. He wanted me to have a life without hate, too."

That would have been Papa.

"His mama sent him to America with her sister to make a better life for him, and then the sister hit on hard times and indentured him. He'd been fished up, he said, and so he became a fisher of men. He fished me up, and if he needed me here, that's where I'd be."

"But are you happy?"

"Mostly. I work with a lot of horses, an' I like that. Mr. Lincoln had lots of soldiers answer the call, but they ain't a lot of good farriers to take care of all those horses, an' I'm one of the best. I get as much work as I want. I'm gettin' prosp'rous. Someday I'll have enough money to raise a few horses."

"What!" I dropped the funeral program I was fanning myself with.

He giggled, which was disturbing from a man the size of Castor. "Yo' daddy put me here to protect you. It time for slavery to go, but he knew you'd be alone when you came to visit yo' mama an' needed me. You know he don' trust these damn Yankees or yo' mama."

He could do little to protect me from Mother and her plotting ways, and could anyone protect me from Byles? I didn't think so. Not even Castor, who would go to his grave trying.

Chapter Forty-Seven

The rider brought a spare horse who looked like a distance hunter. I was glad for that as I might have to go cross-country part of the way. "You know where you're going?" the man asked.

"Yes, sir."

"Get to General Bonham at Fairfax Courthouse. If they deny you, go on to Manassas. Beauregard needs this information. If they don't move, Bonham and Johnston could be trapped."

"I'll get there." I had to put recent events behind me. Lives depended on it, including Baron's.

"I'll stay here with Castor and tinker on the carriage so it doesn't look suspicious to the grave diggers over there covering that grave. Godspeed." He gave me a leg up. "Wish we'd brought riding clothes, but you look imposing in the black. That might be an asset. Bob's a good horse." He saluted me with a crop before handing it to me.

Castor offered me his funeral biscuit. "Might get hungry. Be careful, girl. Don't want yo' daddy hauntin' me for not takin' care of you."

The sun drifted lower into the afternoon, and I hadn't eaten since morning. His wrapped biscuit went into my purse with my own. If I'd only thought to bring food to go with my small water flask. "I'll see you soon."

Having ridden this country in years past, I was familiar with it, but I still wanted to reach camp before dark. Bob was a stout chestnut Thoroughbred with a pleasant gait and manner, but such eagerness to be away I had to keep him under tight rein the first few miles. We might need to fly like wild geese later, so I needed to save him as much as possible. Blackberry bushes beside the road beckoned and any other time I'd happily gather them by the bucket. A few rare red apples from the orchard flanking the road to supplement my funeral biscuits would have to suffice. With Bob settled and dinner far past, I paused to pick some apples.

Bob lowered his head, nostrils flared, taking in the apple scent. I'm sure I was sniffing them out as eagerly as he was and sighed in contentment. Some apples had fallen to the ground, but the fermented fruit aroma wasn't unpleasant. I reached through the branches to pluck particularly rosy, red cheeks while Bob nosed out treats on the ground. With my purloined fruit cradled in my lap, I eased out onto the road, partly because I didn't want Bob eating too many green apples and partly because I didn't want to get caught in my thievery.

Pushing guilt aside, I polished one to a high shine and bit into the firm flesh. Heaven. I wiped juice flowing down my chin away with a handkerchief and continued the feast, then thought of the funeral biscuits in my purse. The combination might be almost like apple pie.

A blob of black wax impressed with a skull and crossbones sealed the biscuit wrapper. I flicked the seal loose on one and unwrapped it carefully so as not to lose my precious meal. They spared no expense with the rich cardamom, cinnamon, and molasses cookie stamped with a cross and twice as big as most such grave offerings. I'd light a candle for Mrs. Tattenham when I got home. I could do without the cinnamon, but I was starving, and it was delicious.

My mock apple pie munching stopped when Bob raised his head and pricked his ears. Someone was coming. The orchard was too open for protection, but there was a copse of trees with thick brush I could disappear into across the road. I popped more of the cookie in my mouth and urged the horse forward. He cleared a split rail fence easily, and I threaded him carefully through the brush. We waited, watching the road. There was no disturbance to a still afternoon save me crunching my apple. I leaned forward and fed him the core, then started on my second apple. It was even more succulent than the first. The flesh was almost wine-like in flavor. I hated to admit it, but these might be better apples than our Rosemount's.

Was the horse wrong? No, he kept staring down the road. Presently, fluttering banners topped the hill. I backed further into the brush and absently started my last apple. Federals, but which unit? Did it matter?

Reaching down reflexively, I stroked Bob, "Shhhh, no calling out to them." New Yorkers. Was that Simmons's unit? No, these weren't dragoons. The horses in the lead evened with me. The men were dusty and tired and sweltering in their new woolen uniforms. Instead of marching in orderly rows, the soldiers broke away to pick apples and berries and throw themselves down to check this or that or simply declare they were done marching.

Moses, what a rabble.

I continued to stroke Bob. He raised his head. "Shhhh." No use. He nickered, and the young soldier pushing through the brush looked over, astonished, dropped his cap full of berries, and snatched at his gun. The troop stopped—as did my heart.

"Who's in there?" the leader bellowed. "Show yourself before we blow you away."

The soldier gathered his cap and berries and scuttled away like a crab. I guided Bob out and held up my hands, with the crop and purse dangling from my right wrist and handkerchief and reins in the left as if waving a white flag of surrender. Bob stopped before the fence and scratched his nose on the top rail as if nothing at all was wrong. I suppose for him there wasn't.

The officer, a lieutenant, called out, "What were you doing in the bushes? Spying on us?"

I thought to play a poor damsel and pour on the charm, but this comment sent my plans and temper sideways. "To what end? I saw a bunch of Yankees picking berries and apples? We best be on guard, for I fear they might be going to make pies?"

He scowled at his meandering troops. "Get those men back in line," he yelled. "What were you doing in the bushes?"

"I'm returning from a funeral and went in the bushes to tend to necessaries."

"How did you get there?'

"I jumped the fence."

He motioned to nearby troops. "Take these rails down so she can come through."

"For what reason?"

'We're taking you with us. I don't need you reporting my activities to Confederate armies."

"I've spent half the day at a funeral. It's blistering hot. All I've eaten since this morning is a funeral biscuit and some apples. I'm sure no one cares about your fruit pickers aside from the farmer who owns this orchard. I don't intend to be kidnapped by you nor anyone else today. I'm going home. I'm going to eat. I'm going to take a bath and try to forget this miserable day. And what, pray tell, will you do with a woman when you get wherever you're going anyway?"

"I'm not giving you a choice. You, madam, are coming with us. I don't need reports about us going to Beauregard." If he couldn't control his men, he was at least going to control one recalcitrant Rebel woman.

I pushed the veils back from my face in a last effort to worm my way out of capture with cheap womanly wiles. Softening my tone and demeanor. "Please, I'm already upset enough with the funeral and all."

He huffed. "Likely story."

I pulled the second funeral biscuit out and waved the black seal toward him. "Do you carry these around for good luck?"

"You're coming with us," he said. The major looked sympathetic and might have freed me, but he wouldn't undermine his officer.

Men leaned on their guns, wondering which way the test of wills would go. I might garner more sympathy if I were one of those women who could cry on demand. Since I wasn't, I dabbed at my eye and poked a fingernail in the corner of it. Tears welled up. Even the private holding Bob's bridle sighed and looked to the lieutenant, who puffed up with indignation and manly fortitude.

"Here, no crying!" he barked.

I sniffled. "Yes, sir. If you insist I must go with you, there's no other choice."

"None."

"Berry picking we shall go. By the way," sniff, "the men scoffing down those green apples may regret it before long."

A few men had been herded into line; others were already easing back out to the apple trees like a flock of guineas searching for ticks.

"Get those men back!" he yelled.

The private holding Bob crooned with affection and stroked the horse's nose.

"I'm sorry," I said regretfully.

He scratched his forehead. "For what, ma'am?"

"For this." I jerked back the whip and sliced him so sharply across the hand that he yelped and dropped his grip on the bridle as if it had caught fire.

In the same instant, I kicked and flailed Bob, who leapt forward like a horse at the starting line. The men leaning on their guns were mostly so surprised they dropped them; a few snatched them back up and looked to their astounded officers for directions. I continued whipping Bob and any unfortunate soldier who tried to grab me or the horse. I screamed at Bob. They screamed at me and each other. Bullets pinged past. I leaned low on the horse's neck, his mane stinging my face. With my skirts billowing like a black cloud, we flew for dear life. Men who'd been ambling off the road scrambled to stop me but scattered like leaves before the wind when we raced through them. Over the fence we went, close to the edge of the trees, and cut across a pasture. The mounted officers gathered their wits and took the fence also. My hope was for a better, fresher horse. With luck, the shots were mainly to frighten me, and none were shooting with serious intent, but luck was in short supply lately. I was a small target, but Bob wasn't.

They gave up after a mile or so. There were more important things on their mind than one Secesh woman. If they only knew. Safely away from the Yankees, I slowed to an easy trot and back to a walk to cool Bob. God bless him.

It was dusk when I hit Bonham's camp.

"Ma'am, can I help you?" asked a picket.

"I have a message for General Bonham."

He looked at the picket on the other side of the road and smirked. The only thing missing from his irritating display was a bawdy wink. "Yes, ma'am. I'm sure you do. We've been instructed to decline information from young ladies."

I flipped the veils over my hat that miraculously survived the wild ride and leaned down as if I might grab him by the throat. "I slipped out of Washington by attending some woman's funeral I don't even know. I've ridden here in the broiling heat. I've had two funeral biscuits and some apples to eat, and while they were good, I'm hungry enough to eat that smile off your face with or without catsup. I've been stopped by Yankees that wanted to take me prisoner and escaped them amid a hail of bullets. Now you stand there with a smarmy look, like my purpose is to flirt with one of you fine young specimens. You either get me to Bonham, or I'll ride on to Manassas and G.T. This information must reach him, and if you jackanapes won't help, by all that is holy, I'll do it myself."

He straightened during the tirade and tugged at his collar. "Uh, yes, ma'am. Let me see if he's available." Without setting foot to stirrup, he leapt on a nearby horse and galloped away. I had begun the day determined to use charm to my advantage and had failed utterly so far. I blamed it on starvation. The picket

cut a surprised look my way when my stomach growled loudly but politely said nothing. I clearly wasn't meant for delicate
feeding.

"Ma'am, if you'll follow me?" The returning soldier led me
through the camp, where I received several curious stares. I'm
sure I looked like an angel of death in my funerary garb and
scowling countenance. He stopped in front of a two-story house
with mounds of pink roses cascading in happy profusion over a
neat little white picket fence. Horses lined up along the fence
with hooves cocked in relaxation, swishing flies, heads down and
mostly asleep or nipping at grass. The picket held his arms up to
me to help me dismount.

Like a swift summer squall, my irritation faded, and I was
simply thankful to be on the ground. While I stretched, he
fetched a water bucket for Bob, who drank greedily and then
nosed out his new neighbors.

The house, a pristine white square with green shutters,
boasted a generous gallery with square wooden columns, also
sparkling white. Two soldiers rocked and smoked at the north
end. Others leaned against the columns or sat on the steps and
whittled, a perfect picture of leisure as if war was a distant rumor.
Pink petunias tumbled out of hanging baskets swaying gently in
the dusk breeze. The home was a portrait of peaceful pink and
white with slashes of gray, and then blue uniforms added for
contrast. My guide knocked on the door. The lounging soldiers,
who were no doubt also aware of the order about admitting
young ladies with information, perked up.

He knocked once more, and at last an elderly Black man with
snowy white hair opened it and hobbled backwards. "Yassuh?"

"We need to see General Bonham."

The old man closed the door behind us and slow-shuffled
away, one slippered foot barely rising in front of the other.

"Who is it, Caesar?" A woman as square and pink and white
as her house fluttered toward us like a butterfly. Wispy little curls
peeked out from under a starched white caplet, framing her face

in a pale gray cloud. Pink cheeks of a natural blush some women are blessed with completed her cherubic impression.

"These people needs to see the gen'ral, Miz M."

"I'll take them. Ask Nana to get food for this girl." She peered up in my face with round blue eyes made larger by the round, brass-rimmed spectacles. "You look famished. Are you famished? Yes, I'm sure you are."

"Food would be nice," I replied.

Without another word, she hustled us into a library where five officers leaned across a large library table littered with maps and papers. On either end of the table, two matched kerosene lamps glowed brightly, casting golden pools of light on the table. Their glow extended to six sober faces, sharpening features with exaggerated shadows and brightened highlights.

"General? This is the young lady I told you about," the picket said hesitantly.

A general with full, dark blond hair that looked as if he'd been running his hands through it more than once looked up. "Oh, yes. Thank you." He quirked an eyebrow in surprise and attended to his skewed jacket and hair. "Mrs. Milton, could you bring refreshments?"

"Of course. Caesar is probably still dawdling. I swan, he's never hurried in his life, and now that rheumatism has him—let's say if he dies on Tuesday, Saint Peter will still be waiting on Friday."

The young picket snapped a quick salute and made his escape. I hadn't planned on a group, as the message was for General Bonham, but I couldn't ask him to dismiss his war council, which included James Chesnut, colonel now, and aide to G.T. Foreboding stirred deeply at revealing my identity to so many as if someone trod my grave. Mary Chesnut was the biggest gossip south of Boston, and I had no doubt James spilled everything he knew to her to curry her wifely favor. "I have a message of great importance from Washington," I said, hoping Bonham would speak to me in private. There were some rolled eyes among the assemblage, and, to my dismay, he made no attempt to excuse his men, including aides lounging about the room.

I ignored the rolled eyes and removed my pinned hat. I had to deliver the message or ride to Manassas at the risk of Bonham being trapped. My hair was securely bound, so it took a bit to pull the pins. Fingering through the roll to make sure I had them all, I removed the tucking combs and let it fall. There was inhaled breath behind me. I'm sure they thought it most inappropriate. With some apprehension, I pulled the embroidery scissors from my bag and held them up. "If someone could cut the message from the braids."

*Hmm*ing, Bonham held the hair up and guided me to the table. "James, hold that lamp. I don't want to cut this young lady's hair."

"Please don't."

With my head pushed down gently, he snipped the threads. I instinctively felt my hair, eliciting laughter. "He was cautious, Miss," said one young officer. "Lucky for you he was cutting and not me. I was thinking what a beautiful watch fob the end of one of those auburn braids would make."

"Oh, my maid would hunt you down for such an affront."

He bowed to me in good humor.

Bonham pulled a chair up to the table for me while he read the message. "Is this true?"

"I assure you it is. Patterson's 20,000 will hold in Harper's to cut Johnston off. McDowell has three columns with 50,000 men advancing and means to take Fairfax and you. If you tarry, you'll be trapped. You must get the details of McDowell's army and movements to G.T., General Beauregard, as quickly as you can. They mean to take Manassas." I looked around at the men staring at me. "That information was acquired at great cost. And, as I've already seen, no one wants to trust the words of a woman, so the message had to be committed to paper and verified with that signature for you to take it seriously, but it very much is the truth."

Mrs. Milton and an elderly Black woman knocked and entered with a plate of stew, cornbread, and a tea tray. I looked longingly at it but waited for more questions.

"Please, enjoy your supper," Bonham said, his hand rumpling through his hair again.

Mrs. Milton put the lamp back in proper position, that being the exact opposite of its mate. Even in war, nothing must be out of order in the Milton household. Then, having the good sense not to linger, she quickly disappeared.

Colonel Chesnut snatched a campaign desk open and began a letter. Bonham moved maps to the end of the table where the officers gathered around, pointed, and set chess pieces on the map in a different and deadly game. "Send scouts out to see if they can find McDowell," he said, moving several pieces to the Little River Turnpike coming out of Alexandria.

Piano music and a high-pitched hymn curbed even their sonorous tones. The officer who coveted my hair put his hands over his head as if trying to hold his brains in, "Dear God."

"What is it?" I asked.

"She thinks music soothes us," he replied.

"Let me help." In a nearby parlor, Mrs. Milton enveloped a little mahogany ball and claw piano stool in front of an exquisitely carved Chickering square piano. I couldn't help but think the stool's poor eagle claws were clinging for dear life to the crystal balls and chided myself for being so uncharitable when she had been nothing but kind to me. Several superb portraits smiled at me from the wall behind the piano. On a cushion beside her lay a great golden tabby, enjoying the concert. "Mrs. Milton! Is this your wedding portrait?" I said, pointing to an ornately framed painting.

The hymn stopped mid-note. Giggling like a schoolgirl, she held her hands to her flushed cheeks. "Wasn't he the handsomest thing! Every girl in three counties set her hat for Mr. Rufus Milton. I near died of happiness when he asked Father if he could pay me court."

"I don't doubt he did. Look how beautiful you are." It was no exaggeration. Mrs. Milton had been a wee bit of a thing with angelic features, made lovelier by the way she gazed adoringly at the dapper young man in the chair.

"Not anymore, but I used to turn a few heads. Ruff, his friends called him Ruff, and I were together for fifty-one years. I lost him two years ago and consoled myself with food until," she sighed. "Until I'm eating myself into a stupor. He liked me to sing to him when he was deciding a case. And that's our Billy, but he passed years ago. Ruff bought me this piano for an anniversary gift." She caressed it lovingly. "He said I wore out the one he bought me for a wedding present. I thought music might help the generals."

"Alas, military men aren't as sophisticated as a judge. As gorgeous as that piano is, and your voice, what they need is prayer. Could you find a Bible and read scriptures for protection? Maybe the Psalms. My friend Baron's in danger also, so perhaps pray for him."

Her face lit like a lamp. "Yes! I lead our Sunday school group. We'll start a new prayer circle."

"Perfect."

"What did you do?" Bonham asked when I returned.

"I asked her to pray for you."

"That's a neat solution."

"It doesn't need to be complicated to work, and who doesn't need prayer?" I finished the last bit of stew and sank back in my chair as contented as a cat in a milk house.

"Abel, get Pende," Chesnut called out as soon as he sealed the letter. "I need a message to go to Beauregard tonight." A young aide jumped up and dashed out the door.

"I should return if you have no further need of me."

"Nonsense," Bonham said. "Mrs. Milton has a spare room. I'll have someone stable your horse.

Chapter Forty-Eight

"Miss McKenzie, Miss McKenzie." Mrs. Milton's frantic shaking startled me awake. She bent close, a wobbling candleholder in her hand and papered curls flying about her faint and frightened face like tethered moths. "Hurry. You must get dressed. The Yanks are coming. They're evacuating the army and told us to leave if we can. You don't want to be here when those Philistines beleaguer the place again."

"Philistines?" I said groggily, wiping my hand across my face.

She waved a plump hand. "Philistines. Yankees. General Bonham sent someone for your horse. Nana's packing sandwiches and a bag of gingerbread."

I dressed hurriedly and checked to make sure I left nothing incriminating, then hurried down the stairs like a scalded cat.

"I ain't settin' foot outa this house, Miz M," Caesar declared. "My rheumatism and me stayin' right hare. What dem Yankees gonna do to an ole colored man?"

"You don't know what those devils might do, Caesar. Remember last month when they rode through here shooting the place up? I order you to leave."

He plopped into a chair in the hall and folded his arms across his chest. "No, ma'am. Stayin' right hare. We watch de house till you returns. All dese Quakers hare? Phfft. Dey ain't gonna trouble us."

"By God almighty, if Ruff was here, you'd leave. You think they're going to care about those peace-loving Quakers or even know who they are? No, sirree, Bob. They'll die along with the rest." She threw her hands up in the air. "Ruff!" Forsaking her wayward servant, she ran to the parlor with Nana on her heels. "Leave my painting. Get Ruff. I'm not leaving him. And our wedding portrait. No one will bother the others."

"No room, Miz M," Nana protested. "That cart already spilling over."

I needed to be away, but I couldn't abandon her. "Mrs. Milton, who's going to drive you? Where are you going?"

"A neighbor loaned me her son. I'll stay with my sister in Germantown until they march through. We'll be safe."

The grandfather clock in the hall struck three. The witching hour, according to some. How appropriate. I took Nana's bag of food and hugged them all, including the glowering Caesar. Bob danced and pranced with excitement, eager to join the flight. Stalwarts who were staying stood on porches in various stages of dress, waving at neighbors and kin. Babies squalled, men cussed, dogs barked. Mothers called out for missing children. Somewhere a confused rooster crowed. Everywhere people cried, and stitching it all together was the steady tattoo of drums beating out orders.

A boy, barely in his teens and washed white with fright, helped Mrs. Milton into the cart. "I put an extra pillow on the seat," he said. After she shuffled around like a setting hen, he laid a quilt over her lap and slid Ruff's painting in front of her, where she clutched it like a shield. Nana wrapped the other painting in quilts and rearranged things until she could wedge it safely in the cart. Bob fought his head, anxious to go until my arms felt about to give out, but I wanted to wait until I knew she was away.

Mrs. Milton smiled tremulously up at me.

"Are you all right?"

Her frightened smile faded, and she looked at me steady and deep. "Panic shreds my soul, but I must be. Thomas has abandoned me, Caesar refuses to budge, and Nana stays by his side like a rock." She threw her hands in the air. "Oh, my dear. If you have tears, prepare to shed them now."

Gently, I patted Bob's neck, taken aback by the odd bit of Shakespeare at such a time, and wished I could hold and comfort her. Our parting had come, however, and we must each meet our fates.

"Farewell, Mrs. Milton. Be well." I gave her a wave with the crop and turned the horse away from her faint and frightened face.

Clouds drifted aimlessly across a Stygian sky like plump old dowagers wandering a familiar garden path. A storm might rise later, but for now it was peace in the heavens.

I rode carefully, listening for nightriders or the approaching tramp of feet. Three times riders raced past me, but they either didn't see me skulking on the side of the road or didn't care. Exhausted troops lay scattered like cordwood up and down the road, beside the road, and even into the surrounding pastures. A few roused and tried to challenge me, but they were too tired to put up much resistance or shoot straight when I did. My fortune couldn't hold. I had never been lucky except at cards, and tonight I was running a weak bluff. Someone was sure to call my hand. The nearly full moon had shone brightly all night, lighting my way, but it also illumed me for anyone with eyes. I moved further out into the pastures as dawn gilded tree and pasture alike and stole with it what little cover I'd had. On the road, the army resumed its march, writhing purposefully toward Manassas. Purely by the grace of God, I was back to the carriage house without further incident. Castor waited with another funeral carriage and the man who had delivered Bob. "You make it through all right?" Castor asked.

"Yes, but barely in time. McDowell will be in Fairfax today. Luckily, Bonham was already moving his troops out during the night."

I pulled a piece of gingerbread from the bag and fed Bob. "He deserves a special reward. He saved my life." The horse rubbed his head on me as if agreeing.

"We'll take care of him," the man said. "Don't you worry about that. He's one of my favorite horses with good reason."

I needed a hot bath and sleep before I made my escape tomorrow, but right now I craved a hot cup of coffee. Gertie would find some excuse for me to stay, but my carriage was rented, and I would be in it come the devil or the deep blue sea. I was going home. I didn't even know if Rosemount still stood with Patterson, possibly warring his way through Winchester.

Frain met me in the carriage house and took a brief report. I changed clothes and wished him well, not daring to voice my fears for the coming battle. There would be no more Philippi races with Confederates running away. I'd seen the army making its way toward destiny and knew another one trailed behind to make their stand. The Titans would soon make the world tremble in their fury.

Chapter Forty-Nine

Gertie was uncommonly withdrawn and I spent a quiet day puttering in the garden, napping, and avoiding all discussion of war, but that night, I dreamt of battles and wandering through the haunted waste looking for Baron, turning one terribly ruined body after another. He was nowhere to be found among the living nor the dead. Gertie insisted the nightmare was an aftereffect of going to a funeral. "They are to be avoided at all costs. That's what was wrong with Mr. Poe," she said with authority. "He was around death too much as a child, and it affected his mind and spirit. Thus, you see the effects in his ghastly writing."

I said nothing, as I was a Poe fan, which must mean my mind and spirit were off-kilter also. As Gertie set little stock in the McKenzie stress cure, she bustled about drawing a lavender bath and lighting lavender candles. Even through the lavender fog, the smell of fried apples with cinnamon drifted in. Cinnamon. Would that she leave off that infernal spice, but she was pulling out all stops.

"Let's eat in the kitchen," I said. "I want to look at the garden."

Gertie sent the girls scuttling into the dining room to fetch the candles I was trying to escape and surrounded me again until I felt like I was at a vigil. Martha set a bowl of oatmeal and fried apples along with a large mug of Mexican chocolate with, of course, more cinnamon.

"Is there any coffee?"

"Chocolate's more soothing. Green apples ease a headache, and oatmeal—it's good for you." Gertie explained her unusual breakfast menu like a doctor prescribing the cure for some dread disease.

"I don't have a headache. If I smell much more lavender or drink any more chocolate, I'll be asleep before I hit Alexandria."

She made a light, airy movement with her hands that was totally unlike her, betraying her disquiet. I didn't argue further and let her bustle about soothing me. Most of it, I suspected, was to cover her own frazzled nerves about me going to certain doom.

Gertie gazed at me across the table while I ate my oatmeal, memorizing every strand of hair, every feature, every mannerism. "I'm five foot three," I said between bites.

"What?" She said as though waking from a daze.

"I'm five foot three. You're studying me as if you're trying to fix me in your memory. If things are this dire, you should know my measurements, so you can order a coffin. Rosewood with brass trim is nice. Certainly not a Fisk metallic. Who wants to be preserved forever?"

Everyone in the kitchen froze like wax statues. Even the black cat sitting on the stool next to the door stared with his great yellow eyes, much like a Poe character. It was a perfectly poetic scene. "Good Hannah," Gertie gasped when the shock wore off. "What a horrid thing to say."

"Then stop acting like I'm going to the gallows. I'm not. I'm going home. It's not fatal. I left some clothes."

"But you know how I enjoy shopping for you," Gertie said.

"Yes, I do." With her successfully diverted to thoughts of shopping, she brightened considerably. "I'll bring you more lace from the Guild when I return."

"Lace!" The cry couldn't have been more delighted if I'd promised her a glass carriage. "Oh, I forgot. You have a message."

"From who?"

"I don't know. A military man delivered it this morning. Maybe Captain Simmons or Colonel Orwyn sent an invitation to something."

I opened the cover and read it with dismay. "Colonel Collins requested that I remain in town to testify for his wife."

Gertie frowned. "I'm not sure it's a good idea to get further involved in that sordid affair. Suella, we need more hot chocolate."

"Unfortunately, I'm already involved." I had escaped Byles twice; tarrying to give him a third bite at the apple would be suicide, but what choice did I have?

Dr. Frain stopped by later to give me a report on Mother.

"Has something happened?" I asked.

"Not really, but a doctor at the spa wants to run some tests on her."

"That's ridiculous," Gertie said. "Bert is as healthy as a horse."

She was right. My mother might claim every disease known to *Gunn's Domestic Medicine,* but illness fled from her in terror. "What kind of tests are they doing on her?" I asked.

"I have no idea. That's why I'm sending my nurse to check." He sipped the hot chocolate Suella had offered him. "Lorena, would you join me in the garden to discuss your mother?"

Gertie raised an eyebrow. "Is it that serious?"

"It might be," he replied. "I'm going to discuss it with Lorena."

She screwed up her mouth in disapproval and probably a hint of suspicion, but I followed Frain out the back door.

"You know your mother's fine," he said when we settled in the gazebo.

"I assumed that. This has something to do with Byles?"

He sipped his chocolate. "This really is delicious. I need to get the receipt for my wife." Then looking toward the house to assess our surroundings again, his voice lowered. "Yes. Byles and the Goldfinch. You've been asked to stay and testify for her."

"Yes, but I don't know what I can say."

"The less said, the better. We orchestrated her coming under suspicion, though I hadn't planned on her being picked up so soon. The man she's been meeting with clandestinely is her cousin, who is a police officer from Mississippi. He came out to help look for the missing girl, but Goldfinch purposely met with him in compromising ways to cast suspicions. We knew Pinkerton would bite and pick them both up sooner or later."

I couldn't keep up with Frain and his plans upon plans. I wasn't comfortable staying any longer than I had to, and it was only sheer luck that we had made the exchange before Byles arrested her. "How will they prove he's her cousin?"

"Pinkerton already wired Natchez and confirmed his identity. Goldfinch is packing to leave as we speak. They'll hold her a couple more days at the most. Collins is bringing as many witnesses as possible to clear her, meaning his, reputation, but she's done. She'll make a very public denunciation of her husband, who refused to defend her, and leave town."

"I thought he had taken all her money?"

Frain laughed. "Oh, he did, but all the charities she's been working with did some remarkable fundraising on her behalf. The ladies are a formidable force."

"Good. Then she'll be safe, but her sister is still gone."

"I have no doubt Byles killed her," he said, his voice dripping venom, "but there's no way to prove it. However, her very public arrest will keep him out of our hair for a while. It's a huge embarrassment to Pinkerton, and Byles has been relieved of duty. It won't last. He's too good at what he does, but he's on ice for now."

An immense weight lifted off my shoulders, but fury raged like steamboats feeding the beast by throwing bacon into the fires to generate infernos. Byles would escape justice, and Mrs. Collins would never know for sure.

Byles presented formidable evidence against the Goldfinch, but newspapers had latched on to the story like a bunch of fishmongers and were crying the story on every street corner. Character witnesses were called in by the dozens until they finally got to me two days later. I confirmed what the attendant said but added no more. I might have had Byles not been sitting there cleaning his fingernails with that knife and watching me intently.

At last free, with more tears and hugs, I loaded into the hack the next day. It was a short and pleasant drive, and I felt like a child on Christmas Eve at the thought of Rosemount. The messages in my bolero that were destined for Richmond were more of a housekeeping affair than military and nothing time sensitive. They consisted of rearranging birds, finding lost shoes, and a flower garden written as a poem, which would be nonsense meanderings even if found. To the recipient with the key, however, it would make perfect sense. We passed through the checkpoint with little problem, thanks to Garrold Simmons's pass, or maybe they had other things on their mind than further bogging a road already congested with carriage, horse, and foot traffic.

At the doctor's house, I knocked and waited, slightly amused that Gertie sent a bouquet of flowers to Mrs. Boudreaux, whose flower gardens were in full and glorious bloom. On a more practical note, she also sent tins of coffee, tea, and a loaf of sugar. A curtain raised in the bay window beside the door, and a small face beamed with a gap-toothed grin. J.B. thundered to the door, which was surprising, given he wasn't that large but managed to sound like a herd of elephants and wasn't supposed to answer the door. Some of the more respectable citizens felt his condition might be contagious, and therefore he was normally kept in the back with his grandmother, Mrs. Bastrom.

"Hello, J.B. Where's Nettie?"

His expressive eyebrows shot up to match the corners of his mouth. "With Mithuth B. in Lanta."

"Boy!" Mrs. Bastrom shouted and came barreling down the hall toward us like a boulder rolling downhill and threatening to take out one small, helpful child as soon as she finished wiping her floury hands on her apron. Murder is best done with clean hands, after all. "What have I told you about answering the door?"

"Ain't people, Gammy. Ith Mith Lorena."

I shoved the sugar loaf in her hands before she could do bodily harm to the child; nevertheless, from her *humph*, she agreed with his logic, and he was safe. I wasn't people; I was family. "Mrs. Boudreaux is gone?"

"Doctor sent her to Atlanta to stay with their daughter and son-in-law, where she'll be safe. She took the help with her except Beula, me, and Silver. Who knows how much help he is? And, of course, Boy," she looked at him sternly, "who is not the doorman."

"Yeth, Gammy." He hadn't stopped grinning through all of this. Imminent demise at the hands of his grandmother never crossed his mind.

"My aunt sent flowers. There's also tins of coffee and tea stashed in my carpet bag. I kept the sugar near my person lest it get waylaid. I'm sure you can still get supplies, but Gertie's convinced you're under siege."

"You should take the tea and coffee with you, but sugar was short last week. This is welcome."

The driver and Silver lugged a trunk in as we discussed staples. "Gentlemen. I'm sorry. I'm not staying."

Doctor Boudreaux strolled out from his office with a young mother and a boy in a cast. The mother swiveled between being eternally grateful to the doctor and threatening to break the child's other arm if he climbed that barn again. She swatted his butt and swooshed him out the door. He was no doubt already plotting his next adventure as they hurried away. Freckles and falls go together.

"Lorena, what a pleasant surprise. Are you here for a spell?" He glanced at the trunk Silver was leaning against.

"No. They unloaded that by mistake. I'm catching the afternoon train, but I wanted to visit before I did."

With deliberate motions, he unrolled his white shirt sleeves and buttoned the cuffs, straightening everything just so. "You have a ticket?"

"Not yet. I was going to leave these flowers and go to the depot."

"I doubt you'll get one. Trains have been booked solid for days, and soldiers take up every inch left over. I can send Silver to check for you."

Silver stood and pulled the bedraggled palm leaf planter's hat on. "Si, I, Benito Silvestri, will go for Miss Lorena."

One of the young Boudreaux children, unable to pronounce Mr. Silvestri, had shortened his name to Silver. Years later, he still announced, "I, Benito Silvestri," was about to do something whenever he deemed the deed of import. It put me in mind of Don Quixote off on some gallant quest. If only he had a Sancho.

"Take Boy with you," Mrs. Bastrom said. "He needs to get out."

And like that he had his Sancho.

"Through to Strasburg?" Doctor Boudreaux asked.

"Richmond, then Strasburg."

He frowned and pulled at the goatee as if he were stroking a cat's ear. "Richmond's going to be tougher. Let me see if I can find you a carriage. In the meantime, you'll stay here." He turned to Mrs. Bastrom. "One more for supper, if you please, and something respectable. No boiled cabbage with its unfortunate side effects." He cast an accusatory eye on J.B., who giggled.

Chapter Fifty

July 21, 1861
Manassas, Virginia

Beloved Baroness,

I steal a moment to scribble these lines to you before battle. It's begun, but the cavalry is held in reserve. We're cautioned not to discuss military matters, but it will be over before you receive this. I pray you're home safe. You were gone from Rosemount the last time I begged leave, hoping to see you again before we left.

If all went according to plan, Patterson believes we are still trapped in the valley. Johnston slipped his army out, and our cavalry held the line to cover him. You may have heard of the Falling Waters incident. We engaged Patterson until we had to reluctantly fall back, but it was at a heavy price for him. Scuttlebutt has it he believes Stuart has a far greater force, and that may make P. cautious. It amuses Jeb no end that we so impressed him. We rode straight from Winchester. Johnston hit the rail at Piedmont, but there were still miles to make on foot. Soldiers falling out all along the road as we neared Manassas. Our horses were as tired as we were, so we weren't always successful in avoiding them. There were no serious injuries, but it spooked a few horses and riders when a "log" stirred up cursing at the horse tromping it. Only one bucked off. Hoorah! As tired as everyone was, there was no lack of whooping, hollering, and scrambling out of the way.

Thirty-six hours in the saddle and precious little sleep before the guns woke us at daylight. Jeb still sprang up instantly awake and looked toward the cannon shot. "Hello! What's this?" The firing came from Sudley Creek, where we hadn't expected it. We're camped opposite Stone Bridge, and the fighting was coming toward us.

I rode out with him to scout the battle and will describe it more fully later. It's early afternoon, and the fighting has been raging all morning. Shanks Evans will be the hero of the fight if anyone is honest. He and his men have fought like demons and have paid a heavy price. Stuart paces like a caged tiger, anxious to get in the fray. He sends me to Jackson to remind him we are ready to go, remember us, to which Jackson replies, That's good. That's good. Tell him yes, I will. That's good.

Charlie has taken up Sad Sally's bad habits and sleeps lying down whenever he can. He's sprawled out with his head in my lap like a dog. I asked him if he wouldn't be more comfortable on the picket line, but he said, No, this is fine. Hah. I thought about trying to nap, but I'm sure it's time for Jeb to send me to remind Jackson we are ready, and Charlie is snoring so loudly I'm not sure I could sleep anyway. Oddly, the sound of cannon fire doesn't disturb my sleep unless it changes.

The elite of Washington came out in their fine carriages, and the profiteers came out in their carts and sutler wagons with picnics and even children to watch the show. That's all this is to them. Word is there are somewhere around 500 of the vultures gathered to watch. They settled on blankets on the hillsides as opposing armies gathered to deal death. They know not what a horror war is, but shall soon learn *regardless of the outcome today. The butcher's bill will be paid, and it's a dear price few have ever tallied.*

I've put off saying what I wanted and needed to because my heart is so conflicted with emotion I cannot find the words to express myself.

No doubt we'll be called forth soon, and I look forward to doing my duty. Know that regardless of what happens, no man could ever love you more than I do. I go to sleep at night with your image in my heart and an eternal prayer for your safety and joy. When my last breath leaves my body, it will be to sigh your name. My soul is fastened to yours with bonds that not even death can sever. I haven't deserved a woman such as you, but I thank God daily for the blessing he bestowed on me when he brought you into my life and heart. My love flies to you on a soft summer breeze, warming your cheek and whispering, I love you now and until the end of time. If I do not survive, know that my only regret is being parted from you and the future we might have had together, but we will meet again, I am sure.

Forever and always your beloved,
Captain Baron Patrick Callahan, CSA

Baron slipped the letter into the prepared envelope and sealed it. He added it to the other two letters he'd written and folded the rest of his paper into his writing kit. Charlie opened an eye and looked at him when he moved to put the leather packet in his saddlebag. The letters went in his breast pocket. He'd leave them with someone before they rode out in case—he'd leave them to be posted.

"Nothing disturbs that horse, does it?" said Rosen, who sat quietly this whole time, alternately reading a letter from his girl, fiddling with his new spurs, and peering through the woods as if a Federal might pop up at any moment.

"Not much," Baron agreed. "He doesn't like being left behind, or I'd take Sally. Course, she doesn't like getting left out either. Spoiled children. You should follow his example and rest."

Skeeter sucked clean a squirrel leg and grinned wryly. "Or write love poems to your girl."

Baron felt a schoolgirl's blush coming on. "Love poems. I wish. I prattled on about nonsense only an old man might care about. A poet, I'm not. God help me if some silver-tongued Yankee ever captures her fancy."

Skeeter sucked off another bone. "Uh-huh. We could kidnap her and have Brother London marry you two."

"Don't give me ideas."

"He gave a nice sermon earlier," Rosen said. "Gives a feller hope, don't it?"

"Always need hope," Baron replied.

Rosen's eyes were wide, childlike in a sweat-sheened face. Not all of it was from the heat. He lay down with his ear to the ground as if he were listening and closed his eyes. "This is good soil, virgin, rich. I wouldn't mind owning land here. You can smell good land. Pa says you can taste it. I can't taste the difference like he can, but I can smell it. I'd build a cabin for Lou up in these pines with a narrow road, so it was hid away from people." His eyes popped open. "Did I tell you she agreed to marry me?"

"Yes, I believe you mentioned that," Baron said.

"Only 'bout a hunert times," Skeeter said and squatted in front of them with three roasted squirrels he pulled out of his hunting bag. He'd been waging his own battle.

"How'd you cook these with no fire?" Baron asked.

"Cooked 'em last night afore Jackson made everyone douse the fires and stowed 'em away just in case."

"Any of those tree rats left in these woods?"

"Thinned out the population a bit, I reckon. Beats sitting around thinking and playing what-ifs or watching the louse races. Cam's greyback won again. I'm sure he's turpentining that louse."

Baron rolled his eyes at the idea of doctoring a louse race and started to ask how to turpentine a louse but thought better of it. Some conversations were better left alone.

The conversations were mostly muted and dwelling on mortality throughout the morning, but everyone was still anxious to see the elephant. Men checked guns, checked horses, wrote letters, and sometimes the more practical wrote out their names, units, and addresses so their bodies might be identified if they fell. In between all this, they slept or tried to. There were a few braggadocios with loud claims of what they had done and would do. It was Baron's experience these were most likely to run. There's a difference between bold confidence and empty crowing. Stuart expected to win. He prepared to win. It wasn't in his code to fail. If Jackson told him they needed to take hell, Stuart would answer, "When do you want it delivered?"

Skeeter finished off his squirrel and wiped his hands on his pants. "Ma'd skin me if she saw me do that, but I lost my handkerchief. Durned fool Germain was sprawled out in the dark, and his horse stepped on his hand. Near cut off his little finger, so he lopped it off. I gave him my handkerchief to wrap it up."

Baron's finger twitched in sympathetic response. "He go to the doctor?"

"Nah, he's afraid they'd hold him back."

"Not stopping Jackson," Baron said. "He had his hand in the air and got a finger shot."

"Pointing to heaven again?" Rosen asked.

"That's not why he raises his arm," Baron said. "He used to do that at the school and stands a lot because it feels better. I think he has trouble breathing or something. Don't believe he's healthy. Not healthy enough to get old anyway."

"Looks like we will. We ain't even going to fight," Rosen said. "Day's half done, and they been fighting since dawn. Someone said we're in retreat."

"I don't know," Baron said. "This isn't like anything most anyone has experienced. I think we're going to be in for a grinding before it's done." He tossed the bones away to keep the ants busy elsewhere. Squirrel was all right, but there wasn't much meat on one. It beat the greasy possums Skeeter foraged up a few nights ago. He wiped his hands in the grass. They'd been in several skirmishes, but everyone was spoiling for a real fight. God help them. "If the cavalry isn't scouting, they hold us back to protect a flank or cover the rear. We'll get called. Battle's been going back and forth. It looked bad earlier, but Johnston's troops keep coming in. That'll help."

Baron checked Rosen's gear. "Be sure your guns are clean and loaded and tighten the straps on those shiny spurs your Ma sent." The spurs were engraved silver with Rosen's name etched amongst the scrollwork. Even Stuart, with his gilded spurs, had complimented them.

Skeeter buffed one of the spurs with his sleeve. "You got a speck of dust there." He jammed a wad of tobacco in his jaw. "Not sure how much Johnston will help. Forced march wears a man out even if they did come partway on a train, but no food or water for those poor devils makes it worse."

"Federals are bound to be tired, too. Everyone's green and wore out." Baron had been up to the hill with Stuart to survey the battle with the generals. The Union put them on their heels early on, but they were holding now. It could go either way with a stupid mistake or a bold stroke.

Skeeter and Charlie looked up at the same time. "Rider spurring in hard," Skeeter said. "That's our call." The horse scrambled to his feet and shook from his nose to his tail, sending pine needles and dead grass flying as if he knew it was time to go to work. Men tightened girths and mounted up. Stuart had positioned Beckham's two commandeered artillery pieces in the pines above the field. They weren't mobile, so he situated them where he calculated they'd do the most damage while remaining hidden. It would take a keen eye to sight the cannon even when they fired. The cavalry would make their presence known soon enough, but by then it would be too late to counter their move.

Such was the plan, but the gods of war were notoriously fickle.

The messenger slid to a stop, showering dirt and debris. "Where is Stuart? I need him!"

Stuart bolted toward the rider. "Here, here, I am. What's the news?"

"Beauregard says to take your men where you will. Find the hottest fighting."

There couldn't have been better news if angels from heaven descended with it. Stuart rubbed his gauntleted hands together, a delighted grin splitting the full, auburn beard. His bright blue eyes lit like lightning. "Let's go, boys. This is what we've been waiting for. If we cannot bend the will of Heaven, we shall move Hell."

Chapter Fifty-One

Rain changes the way the air smells and feels, sometimes sagging and oppressively heavy. Clouds change. Birds fly closer to the ground. Butterflies and bees disappear from gardens. Flies turn into biting pests. We had sat on Doctor Boudreaux's porch the night before and remarked on the variety of butterflies fluttering among the flowers. Awakening the next morning to the distant sound of thunder confused me. Thunder rolled, deep, ominous, rhythmic, rumbling. I rolled over in bed and stared out the window. When had God become so precise?

Another peal answered as if clouds were trading—

Instantly alert, I threw back the covers and vaulted out of bed. That wasn't thunder. It was cannon fire. With my wrapper hastily thrown on and feet barely crammed into my slippers, I raced down the stairs and onto the veranda. Doctor Boudreaux and his household were already there gazing to the west. J.B. stood wrapped cocoon-like in Mrs. Bastrom's skirts, his little fists clutching them closely around him.

"Where is it?" I asked, already knowing.

"Manassas," Doctor Boudreaux answered.

We drifted into the yard, listening to the battle twenty-five miles distant and flinching at each volley. Every yard was as full as ours, and the streets thronged with civilians and soldiers alike, all looking west with faces awash with emotion. I should have been accustomed to it after Charleston, but this was different. In

Charleston we only feared when the constant cannon fire might proceed to war. This was real, and somewhere in that fury was Baron.

"We're not doing them any good out here in our dressing gowns starting at each shot," the doctor said. "Let's get breakfast and go to early church."

Mrs. Bastrom sent Beula to help with my toilet, but the girl broke down in tears after unsuccessfully trying to pin the braid into some semblance of fashion. I dismissed her softly and removed the untidy attempt. I could hear Annie nattering on about what a mess I was.

Breakfast was quickly dispatched, and we loaded into the carriage for church. Even beneath his trim beard, Doctor Boudreaux's jaw tightened at each distant report. His large brown eyes, normally warm with good humor, narrowed as though he might bolt at any moment—but to where?

"This is a lovely church," I said, admiring the stately Gothic arches.

"Hmm, yes. The heathens have taken Christ Church, scattering our congregation to the wind, but we've found sanctuary here at St. Paul's. It is still Episcopal, still familiar. Reverend Norton left to minister to the army, and the community mourned his departure. But Stewart has proven a dedicated shepherd, embracing all us wanderers in need of a home."

An elderly couple greeted us at the doors. "Hello, Doctor. Hello, Boy," the lady said.

Doctor Boudreaux rolled his eyes. "Law, Mrs. Bastrom, must everyone insist on calling the poor child that abominable name?"

The couple chuckled and tousled the child's hair, which needed no encouragement to the wild side.

"Who named him Boy?" I asked since the subject was broached.

"They named him James Boyton Bastrom after my son James," Mrs. Bastrom said. "Boyton being his mother Ella's maiden name. We called him Jamie Boy instead of Junior, and it got shortened to Boy. He wasn't a junior anyway. Doctor says it's like calling a pup Pup."

"My children did that once," the doctor groused. "It was horrible, as if they hadn't a creative thought in their heads. I changed it to Puppers."

I grimaced. "I'm not sure that's better."

"No, but it was so bad, they renamed him."

"To?"

"Agamemnon."

"Dear heavens."

"Yes. It's my middle name, which I detest. I learned my lesson, but really, Boy?"

"Yeth, thir?" J.B. looked up.

"Here's our pew." He opened the door to the box pew. "Sit next to me."

St. Paul's was quietly elegant in that reserved Episcopal way, with banks of leaded glass windows bathing the parishioners in golden sunlight. Three stone arches in the front mirrored the wooden arches behind the altar in the chancel. A soothing incense permeated the air. Even with war raging so near, I felt a sense of peace. Reverend Stewart delivered a message of hope and an appeal for service in the coming uncertain days. Pray for our country, but which country? Unlike most services, he didn't pray for the president in the litany, and no one seemed surprised.

༜

"We'll go to the hospital after dinner," Doctor Boudreaux said. It barely registered until he cleared his throat.

"We?"

"You doubtless have friends in the fight, but busy hands are better than sitting here imagining all sorts of horrors."

Instead of imagining horrors, I could see them firsthand. "I'm being volunteered?"

"Or impressed if you prefer. Wear sensible shoes. A plain dress you don't mind getting...soiled. For God's sake, no hoops. Simple jewelry."

My hand went to the crucifix.

"Mrs. Covington will disapprove, but keep it. Ordinary earrings maybe. Try to look plain."

He glazed some bread with a thin sheen of butter and peach preserves. "Bring your Bible. The Christian Commission supplies them, but you'll be more comfortable with your own. Get a book from the library. The men like to be read to. Nothing maudlin."

I changed into my blue calico gardening dress and left off my earrings since I was standing my ground on the crucifix.

"It might be late when we return," Doctor Boudreaux said, handing me one of his wife's woolen cloaks.

At St. Catherine's School for Young Ladies, now serving as a hospital, was a large desk inside the door, and to the side of that, an office with a large window overlooking all. Behind the hall desk sat an older woman methodically logging stacks of supplies into a ledger. In the office was a hawkish woman in her mid-fifties, lean of limb and humor and not at all in the mood to deal with me, judging from her gimlet gaze. A miserable young woman in a pale blue muslin dress sat in the hall like a miscreant sent to the schoolmaster. Doctor Boudreaux gave the girl an encouraging smile and ushered me into the office.

"Doctor Boudreaux, I'm so glad you decided to make an appearance today." She-hawk looked at her watch. He looked at his.

"I wasn't scheduled for duty. Is there a problem?"

"Aside from Doctor Bainbridge being sick, Doctor Craig going to the battle, and the wounded pouring in like Noah's flood soon—no, nothing at all."

"I fail to see why this is my fault. Regardless," he said cheerfully, "I brought help," and gestured vaguely in my direction as he looked over some papers.

"I doubt that. You know my rule about young ladies." She put the emphasis on "ladies" as if it were a profanity. A woman about town might have been more welcome.

"I'm happy to occupy myself elsewhere," I said, sick with worry about Baron and not interested in attitude or insults today.

"We can find *something*. Do you faint at the sight of shit, blood, or whiskey?"

I snorted. "Never in life. I'm from the country."

"We'll see."

A distraught woman dragging a teenaged girl by the hand coursed through the ward door and into the office. The cleaver-faced woman appraised me through brass-rimmed spectacles, chin raised imperiously, "You look like a proper young lady. As such, I suggest you leave immediately. There are men in their shirts who refuse to get dressed when a lady enters, and the attendants are besotting them with whiskey."

"They are convalescing," Doctor Boudreaux said with a sigh. "This is neither a parlor nor a saloon. It's a hospital. The whiskey is medicinal."

Mrs. Covington rolled her eyes, her lips disappearing to a thin, censorious line.

The woman humphed her dismissal and returned to saving me. "I'm sure you don't want to be exposed to such."

I shrugged. "I'm Irish. I was weaned on whiskey and uncouth men."

"Come along, Prissy," she said to the girl, presumably her daughter. "Leave the Paddy to the boors."

"How much whiskey do you give them?" I asked as the woman stormed away under a full head of self-righteous steam.

"A tot," Doctor Boudreaux replied. "It's for medicine that doesn't dissolve readily in water. Some refuse to take even that, saying they swore to their beloveds not to touch liquor. Others complain they need more to kill the medicine taste or pain or whatever creative excuse they come up with. Either way, it's neither enough to corrupt a man nor pleasure him."

"Ladies," Mrs. Covington said as if she were spitting out a mouthful of dog droppings, and looked back to me. "At least you held your ground. Fill out this form and give me your personal possessions." She pointed to the *No Weapons Allowed* sign.

"Two guns."

"Two?"

"Yes."

"What are you afraid of?"

"Nothing."

"You can't have them. We have guards for protection."

I looked to the doctor for appeal, but he raised his hands as if the matter were beyond his control. With great misgiving, I surrendered all.

She put my items in a drawstring bag and locked it in a cabinet. "I'll put the ladies on the ward."

He frowned. "Not yet."

"We're shorthanded on the floors. I'll either put them to work or dismiss them."

"I don't want them in the wards yet."

"You wanted these young ladies. I told you older women. I'll show you why." She grabbed up a paper-filled folder and a pencil and herded us out of her office.

"Miss Adams, come with us," she said to the young woman.

Blood wouldn't come out of that delicate frock easily, but perhaps the white aprons Mrs. Covington slapped into our hands might help. She pointed to a cart stocked with medical supplies. "One of you grab that. Don't smile and carry on with the men."

"Let them clean bandages or pick surgical lint," Doctor Boudreaux pleaded.

He retreated from Mrs. Covington's answering glare with his papers and one nervous steward. "Have a good day."

Even inside the brick walls we heard the rumble of battle, and I couldn't keep from flinching at particularly loud volleys. Mrs. Covington was made of sterner stuff and huffed her disdain at Miss Adams, who looked about to dive under the nearest table or bed at each shot. Regardless of every window flung open to dispel miasma, the stink of vomit, urine, blood, shit, and the cloying sweet smell of gangrene combined with the stinging carbolic acid cleanser used to clean the floors was overwhelming. Once my nose adjusted to the onslaught of scents, I caught familiar sweet undertones of ladies who had been ignominiously evicted. It was faint, but the ghost of their perfumes over the years still lingered. Ten steps into the ward, Miss Adams fainted with the merest butterfly sigh.

Patients watching us with great interest cried out in alarm. One jumped out of bed and ran to her side, cradling her head in his lap with his good arm. His other arm was cast and in a sling, making it difficult for him to lift her. "Hook your arm around her feet, Tom," a nearby orderly with a mop said. "I'll get her arms."

"I've a mind to leave her in a pile," snapped Mrs. Covington.

"I'll get one foot, you get the other," I told Tom, who was trying to wrangle her ankles into the crook of his arm. It would be easier for me to do it, but how could I deny his gallant effort? I wrapped her skirt around her legs, not wishing to give the men a gape at what might be under the trailing skirts, particularly if she was sans drawers. With such done, we lifted the unfortunate girl and carried her to the bed. Tom insisted on staying with her. I expect it did him good to feel useful. Plus, Miss Adams was a pretty little thing with hair like spun sunbeams.

"She'll come round before long," the orderly said. "Alvin Calvin. But dear Lord, what a name to tack on a child. A.J. will do."

"Your middle name isn't Jalvin is it?"

He laughed. "Nearly as bad. Japeth."

"Lorena McKenzie. Pleased to meet you. Do many ladies pass out like this?"

"More than you'd think. The smell, I reckon. It takes getting used to. Plus, the misery can be appalling to ladies who've never been around this." He looked around. "But how many people have?"

"All right. Tell me what to do. I'll try not to faint."

"They've already been fed and dosed. The Ladies' Aide Society swooped through earlier and washed faces. You might ask if they want further washing. Some can't bathe easy. Write letters. I expect you're on bedpan duty since Mrs. C. wasn't pleased with you."

"I gather she doesn't want young women helping."

"She barely tolerates the Ladies' Aide because they tend to be older and married. Plus, they do a lot of fundraising and provide surgical lint and bandages."

He showed me where to empty bedpans and urinals, so I set off on the most disagreeable duty first. Many were embarrassed by using them. Others were beyond caring, with one foot more in the grave than out. I flitted in and out, avoiding eye contact and pretending not to notice the flushed cheeks. Miss Adams was awake by the time I finished and washed. *Perfect timing, young lady.*

"I'm sorry," she stammered. "I didn't eat this morning because I didn't want to be late. The smell hit me wrong on an empty stomach."

"Come along," Tom offered. "I'll take you to the kitchen. You too, Miss McKenzie. You need a break."

I was afraid of being caught shirking, but then, I was pressed labor. What could she do? Dismiss me?

A harried woman with kerchiefs about her hair and shoulders looked up from a pile of carrots she and her girls were scraping most vigorously.

"Mrs. Brodie?" Tom said from the doorway as if entering sacred grounds.

"Aye, Thomas?"

"Miss Adams didn't eat this morning before she came to help, and could we maybe get a cup of tea for Miss McKenzie?"

She waved us into her domain. "Aye, come sit with ye."

Before I could even adjust my skirts, she shoved a carrot and a knife in my hand. "Scrape. I'll be for getting tea and bread."

Miss Adams was rewarded with two fat slices of bread and cheese. Tom must have been a favorite because he was also plied with hot bread and cheese.

"I'm not hungry, but thank you." He pushed the plate away.

"Eat to keep from getting hungry," Mrs. Brodie replied. "You, too, Missy."

I obediently ate a chunk of bread and continued scraping. "Mmm, this is delicious. I'd love the receipt."

Mrs. Brodie, who was nearly as wide as she was tall and assuredly followed her own eating advice, beamed with pleasure. "It's my sourdough honey wheat bread. The secret's a bit of orange zest. Do ye bake?"

"Me? No, but I collect receipts for my cooks."

"Learn ye to bake, and I'll share it."

With bodies refreshed and carrots scraped in payment, we returned to the ward.

I set about offering to bathe men. Miss Adams tried to wash one handsome soldier's face, but he held up a hand. "The Ladies' Aide was in earlier. It's already been washed fourteen times. Maybe help me write a letter?" Letter writing was the most merciful service and one least likely to cause more fainting on her part. So I believed. Sometime later, while helping another soldier with a letter, she screamed, pointed at his missing arm and mangled shoulder, and ran backwards as if the man had turned into the devil incarnate.

I dropped the clean bedpan I was returning and ran to them. The man sighed and picked at his bandages. Coming closer, I saw the problem. Maggots were wriggling out from between the layers of bandages and dropping from his arm. I yelled for A.J. to get a doctor and retrieved the empty bedpan. Mortified, as if this were the utmost social disgrace, the man tried to pull away.

"Stop it. I'm from the country. I've seen worse." I hadn't.

I carefully started unwrapping the arm with fat little maggots making small pinging sounds as they dropped in the bedpan. I looked away once, steeling myself to the putrid smell, and swore never to eat rice again. The shoulder was fiery red.

"What are you doing?" The voice echoing through the ward like a foghorn on a shrouded inlet startled me into him. He groaned when I hit his arm and jerked away.

"I'm so sorry," I cried.

Mrs. Covington, she of the foghorn call, was quickly upon me and jerking at me with frantic fingers. "What did you do, you stupid woman? I told you not to touch these men."

"Maggots were dropping from the wound. I had to help."

"No, you didn't. Who knows what kind of damage you've done? Get out of my way."

Nearly in tears, I backed into Doctor Boudreaux. "Has a suture come loose?" he demanded.

"I don't know," Covington snapped. "That idiot was clawing through the bandages like a hen looking for grain."

"I was not," I said, now fully in waterworks.

"No, she wasn't," the man said irritably. "Miss Adams was writing a letter when they started dropping. It was itching fierce, but I had no idea I was worm food. Miss McKenzie was helping me get those rotten things off."

Doctor Boudreaux finished unwrapping the arm and dropped the writhing mass in the bedpan. He scraped the remaining maggots away and examined the wound. "When were these changed last, Haddock?"

"Yesterday," Mrs. Covington replied.

"Three days ago," said Haddock.

"Impossible. Mrs. Ellison changes these dressings."

"Not meaning to cause trouble, but perhaps if she stayed out of the whiskey, she'd know who she changed and who she didn't," Haddock replied.

I gathered up the bedpan and quietly asked A.J. what to do with the bandages. A few maggots tried to escape, but I flicked them back in the pan with justifiable malice.

"Follow me."

He took me to a patio with wash pots and clothes lines. "We wash all the bandages. There's soap on the table." The fire was out under the largest wash pot, but I lifted the bandages out and shook out the remaining worms from the bedpan into the remaining coals. Customary to save the bandages or not, I dropped the putrid bandages also and restoked the fire to heat the water and destroy evidence. There were plenty of other bandages to wash, and into the pot of warm, if not boiling, water they went. A layer of ash from too much lye coated the fresh bars of ivory-colored soap. Mother would have heart failure if she saw me abusing my fair skin so.

I returned to washing after dinner and finished hours later. My aching back popped when I straightened it before stirring through the gory water one last time to make sure I had all the bandages. More maggots rose to the surface and swirled around in a wriggling mass. I scooped them up with a bucket to put out my fire and tipped the pot.

With laundry finished, I washed my pruney hands and went to find a new job where I could sit for a while. A.J. suggested I read to men who were on a covered patio. "There's novels on the table and a few Bibles." I picked up the books and discarded them, as I was sure the men wouldn't particularly enjoy the Brontë sisters. The Bible it was. I'd fetch *Ivanhoe* or Poe later.

I stayed so busy reading and visiting with the men I didn't notice the far-off rumble of cannon until it stilled ominously. My watch said nearly six o'clock. "The quiet. What does that mean?"

A soldier from Maine cocked his head, birdlike, and listened. His eyes narrowed. "Ayuh, theyah done tryin tah kill each othah at lahst. Least wise fah now. Pissahs gettin up for anothah go, mebbe."

"Pardon?" I said, puzzling through his explanation.

"Yes, they're done trying to kill each other at last. Least wise for now. Pissers—" The Confederate patient who'd declined all contact previously blushed. "Beg pardon, ma'am," he said with the soft Texas drawl I immediately recognized. "The, uh, men, getting up for another go maybe. Travis Bowie Crockett Williams at your translating service."

He noticed me mouthing the names, trying to get them straight.

"My parents were admirers of the Alamo defenders."

I hadn't expected a translation, nor the names, and laughed. "Justifiable cause for admiration. Thank you."

The Mainer spit tobacco into a jar. "Ayuh, I jest said thaht, ya idjit."

The Texan winked at him. "Yes, Fred, but no civilized person can cotton that. I, not being civilized, can." He looked back at me, leaving Fred to complain about damned Texans. "It's still light.

Either the battle ended, or the armies are repositioning after heavy losses, is my guess. They won't fight after dark, especially in a wooded area."

I felt all strength fleeing my limbs, but willed myself steady. "Let's pray there are few losses."

"Small chance of that, but so we shall."

I called on the Lord for help and mercy and read from Psalms with many repeating the words they knew by heart.

"There you are," Doctor Boudreaux called from the doorway. "Supper's coming for the men. Grab one and I'll grab another. The orderlies will get the rest."

As soon as all staff was assembled in the dining room, Mrs. Covington clanged a spoon on a cup for quiet. "Mrs. Ellison was found sleeping in a supply closet in a cloud of whiskey breath. She proclaimed innocence, saying she nipped a bit here and there to steady her nerves, and it was only the portions allowed for the men who declined liquor."

Doctor Boudreaux snorted. "That's enough to keep a healthy Irishman drunk, and I insisted she go. We have enough problems keeping the men out of the liquor. I'll not tolerate staff nipping whiskey or medicine. Understood?"

There was a chorus of, "Yes, sirs." From his tone, all knew he was serious. After today, I could use a draught of whiskey or sherry when I got home, however. It had been disheartening, exhausting work, and try as I might, I could not help thinking each one of those mangled men might be Baron. It was wearing on my soul, and I wished to be anywhere but here, no matter how noble the work.

Supper was served on long tables in the dining room. It was plain but hearty stew loaded with vegetables and tender chunks of beef and served with trays of corn muffins. Mrs. Covington scowled at me in between bites. Miss Adams kept her head down to avoid notice.

When we were finished, Mrs. Covington fired. "You two may go and don't return. I don't have time for troublemakers."

Miss Adams looked at me, stricken.

I wanted to shout, "Praise God," but instead gave the girl an encouraging pat and mixed celebratory butter and sorghum for another muffin.

Doctor Boudreaux didn't bother to look up from dipping more stew. "We've just had a major battle. This hospital and every other structure in this town will likely be flooded with wounded. If they desire to come back, though I don't know why they would, we won't turn away willing hands."

I'd been dismissed, but with two missing doctors, Doctor Boudreaux opted to stay and finish as much as he could. I did also. There was no shortage of things to do. I wrote letters, shaved a few, read the Bible, prayed with all, and gave each of them my most generous smile and a word of encouragement. They needed that as much as anything. I spent extra time with a patient named Constant, who had stolen my heart earlier with his sweet attitude, though it was plain to all he was dying and not going easy.

I could afford to let my guard down and be friendly. I wasn't returning, after all.

The Texan, Travis Williams, stopped me on one of my rounds later and asked if I would help him with a letter on the morrow. I noticed earlier he had refused all offers of help with bathing, so I was surprised at the request for help now.

"I don't think I'll be here," I replied. "Mrs. Covington rejected me."

He waved his hand across the ward. "Your smile has meant more to these men than an army of Mrs. Covington's scowling, trained nurses. Take the bit in your teeth and do what is right, not what is proper."

Chapter Fifty-Two

The call to arms was swiftly answered, and Stuart's men mounted at once, eager to join the fight. Unlike many, Baron knew what lay before them, but he was still glad the waiting was over. Knowing the battle was going badly, and they were helpless to do anything but watch, shreds a man's soul.

It was their misfortune to ride past a field hospital on the way. The sides of the surgeon's tents were rolled up, revealing men lying inside cheek by jowl until not another could fit. Miserables who'd already gone under the butcher's knife and those still awaiting treatment groaned in pain or screamed at learning they would be amputated. Some gazed unfocused with glassy eyes through the fog of pain, shock, and receding medication like mangled dolls. Others stared lifelessly, jaws slack, beyond pain and caring, with flies swarming in and out of their mouths and around their wounds. Many lay quietly enduring what had been laid upon them with stoic determination in the shadow of death. One man leaning against a tree with a bandaged head drew his hand to his face and away, repeating the motion as if his unseeing eyes might magically be cured if only he stared hard enough. The surgeons and aides, naked to the waist and covered with blood and gore and sweat, rushed fresh victims to waist-high tables. Under each table ran rivulets of blood. In his most fevered dreams, Dante couldn't imagine such horror.

A pair of men pounced on a waiting wounded and clapped a cloth over his mouth and nose. The man shook his head back and forth, violently trying to fight them off. A third man jumped in the skirmish to hold the man.

"Good God," Rosen gasped, starting off his horse. "They're suffocating that poor devil."

Baron grabbed his arm. "Hold. They're chloroforming him. It takes a while for it to set in and sometimes causes a violent reaction."

"Breathe," the man said, clapping a funnel-like device on the cloth.

A surgeon wiped his arm across his brow and swiped his bone saw across his bloody apron, then laid it aside and leaned heavily on the table. A steward handed him a cup of water. He gulped it greedily and tossed the cup back. "Next!"

Two men were already packing away the man who'd lost his arm. The arm lay in a pile of spare parts piled as high as the table. A golden band glinted in the pile of gore. "Hold that man," Baron barked to the two soldiers carting the patient away.

Baron grasped the arm by the wrist and pulled the ring off. The fingers curled in reflexively as if trying to hold his hand. "Gawd almighty." Baron gasped and threw it back on the pile in revulsion. Recovering from his shock, he strode to the two soldiers and shoved the ring in the unconscious man's pocket. "Can y'all at least remove their wedding rings?"

The doctor looked up from his new patient in pure exhaustion. "In case you haven't noticed, we're a mite busy here, Captain."

"I can do it, sir," said one of Jackson's young couriers who sat nearby unpacking a box of bandages.

"Thank you. Can you post these for me?" Baron glanced at the letters once more, wishing he'd been able to write something more inspiring.

"Yes, sir. Take care."

"You, too. Keep your head down." He galloped back to where Rosen was retching violently. Rosen wasn't alone. Baron felt the dead fingers curling around his and Skeeter's squirrel rose in a tide of sour bile until he had to spit several times.

"Sorry, sir," Rosen said. "I—Dear God, that was awful."

"*You did thirst for blood, and with blood I fill you,*" Baron replied.

Rosen frowned. "I did what?"

"It's a line from an ancient poem. I'm full of odd thoughts today, it seems. There are worse things than death, but if I die, someone bind my head, so my mouth isn't gaping open. I can't bear the idea of flies crawling around in my mouth like that."

Skeeter cocked his head sideways in regard. "Don't imagine you'd feel it, Cap'n. 'Sides, I did your numbers. Blessing showed me how. You're going to live to be eighty-two."

"Not sure I want to live that long."

He drew numbers in the air and refigured. "Maybe it was. Twenty-three"

Baron scowled at him. "Dolt. I'm already twenty-three."

Unmoved, Skeeter shrugged. "Guess your number's up."

"Moses. Don't be doing my numbers anymore."

Stuart, who'd been calculating every detail of the country and the unfolding battle coming before them, seemingly hadn't paid attention to the banter until he said, "If it is, can I have your horse?" His shoulders bobbed, betraying laughter.

"Sure, Colonel. You take Charlie. Rosen gets Sally."

"Law," he exclaimed, "what did Rosen ever do to you to merit that foul-tempered wench?"

"She bit you because she thought you were trying to steal her oats."

"I was trying to move her," Stuart protested.

London stared at Baron as if he'd lost his last vestige of good sense. "Good heavens, Captain. Don't tell him that. He'll shoot you himself."

Stuart laughed out loud at that and held up his hand. They stopped at the edge of the woods to get their bearings. Confederates were giving way on the left flank and slowly retreating. Common sense dictated that was where they would shore Jackson up.

Baron glanced over at Rosen, who looked like he was going to be sick again. Beside the road a man lay curled up, clutching his torn and bloody gut. His face was hard and plastic-looking, frozen in agony and already turning black. *People say dying's easy. Not for all.*

Wounded and others simply walking away shook their heads as they passed. "No sense going, boys. We've lost. It's over. We've been cut to pieces. Shredded. There's nothing left."

Stuart glared at them. "It's never over. I'll hear no more of that." He turned away from them as if they didn't exist in his universe, then turned his attention back to the battle. Below, blue mists demarked positions of infantry dealing death one volley after another. Cannons spit lurid flames through heavy white cloud banks. "Who are those Red Legs?" Stuart asked when a breeze cleared the smoke to reveal a bright scarlet line, advancing toward them across the battlefield, quick time.

"I'm not sure," Billings said. "I heard Beauregard brought in some Zouaves from New Orleans. Hard to see with all that smoke. Might be them."

"Hold on, boys, no need to run; we're coming," Stuart called out and laughed. "Find out for sure. We can't fire on our own men." Stuart leaned forward intently and scanned the battle with his glasses while Baron kept his eyes trained on the troop.

The wind cleared the haze and snapped open the Stars and Stripes along with the ornate New York banner. "That's the Eleventh New York. Fire Zouaves. Union," Baron said. He was at odds with how he felt at the moment. He'd been loyal to and served that flag most of his life, and now the enemy carried it.

Three hundred men of the first Virginia Calvary filed from the trees in an orderly trot at four abreast as if they were going to a parade instead of a battle. Stuart signaled to Beckham's artillery, who laid down the middle of the Zouaves with deadly precision. Bodies, parts of bodies, dirt, and debris exploded into the air. The hapless men on either side of the strikes flowed away like Moses parting the sea. Seventy yards out, Stuart's cavalry broke into a full gallop and flooded through like the wrath of God. Red vapor rose where cannon shot hit, and once a man stood. The Zouaves knelt and loosed a volley. A sheet of fire exploded across the line, and the Zouaves disappeared in a haze of sulfurous smoke. Wounded horses screamed, shrill and terrifying like a falling woman. Men yelled in pain, cursed in anger, shouted in rage, and fell, wounded and dead. A cannonball whistled in, taking the head off the horse ahead of Baron. It galloped on several yards before collapsing and vaulting his rider into the air. Baron leaned forward to grab him, but the man's chest was riddled with shrapnel from the cannon shot. He had died with his horse.

Through the haze, Zouaves knelt to reload instead of fixing bayonets. It was a fatal mistake. Stuart's cavalry closed the gap with devastating speed.

One man looked up from his gun in surprise. Black, sweat-soaked curls framed his handsome face under the scarlet fez. Shock passed, and he shifted to use the gun as a club. He clutched his bleeding throat instead, as if he could hold in the life's blood spurting out in streams where Baron shot him. The rifle fell across a fallen companion, and then so did he. The first face, the handsome, surprised face, was the only one Baron clearly registered. After that, it became a blur of firing until he emptied both revolvers. Firing on an empty chamber on his last victim, he clubbed him with the gun barrel, and the man crumpled. He shoved the second revolver in his belt and pulled his sword to continue the slaughter. They cut a wide swath through the Union line, but the close-quarters fighting also took its toll. Regrouping after the first bloody pass, they surged back through.

Jackson's line was holding. Bee's men had rallied behind them. They'd fought their way man by man twice in hot, dirty, exhausting, death-dealing charges. Baron looked around to see where the lines were positioned. When he looked back, he couldn't believe what he was seeing. The line they'd charged through was in flight. Three hours of hammering this flank had broken it. When it collapsed, panic spread like a contagion.

"Go to Beauregard and see if our orders are changed," Stuart called out to his adjutant. "We'll stay on their tail."

Expecting to be reinforced at any time, they pursued their quarry halfway to Washington. Small detachments of riders peeled off with captured prisoners until there were no more to carry forward, and the foxhunt ended.

Unwilling to accept anything but full victory, Stuart declared, "I will wait on this hill until I get further orders to press the attack," and sent his adjutant to find Beauregard or Jackson for permission.

The adjutant returned, but there was no message arriving to attack. Gone were the flying hooves and clouds of dust this time; instead, his exhausted horse could barely manage a shambling trot. "Beauregard wishes to pursue, but he was denied," the man said glumly, stepping off his horse and dropping the reins to let it graze. "Jeff Davis and General Johnston declined, saying we had not the forces, and Davis didn't want to alienate the goodwill of our northern brethren."

Baron turned away at this and wiped angrily at the welling tears of frustration. "Alienate the goodwill of our northern brethren? Has he lost his mind? Our northern brethren just tried to slaughter us. The devil take every politician on earth. I despise them all. Davis has just condemned us to hell. I will despise that man until the day I die—which will probably be sooner rather than later, thanks to him."

"And what of Jackson?" Stuart demanded.

"Jackson was having his hand treated. I heard him tell the doctor if he had 10,000 fresh troops, he would harry Washington. There are no fresh troops, of course. Still, I believe he would press on if unleashed. His blue eyes were still flashing lightning at the idea of being denied the opportunity to pursue. He told the doctor, 'We have been committed to the crucible. This is a fatal mistake.' Having overheard this, I didn't bother to ask him for orders. We are done."

"Well, I'm not done," Stuart declared vehemently. "I will wait right here on this hill until Jackson sends me."

Baron tightened the girth on Charlie and mounted up, thoroughly disheartened. "It'll be dark soon. I'm tired and thirsty. Let's get these prisoners in and find Rosen."

All along the road, muskets stood, bayonetted into the ground where soldiers were captured, and the weapons stuck for someone to collect later. The ground was so heavily littered with equipment in places the horses couldn't step without trampling shiny, new, valuable gear tossed aside in terrified flight. Soldiers might arrive in Washington naked and tired, but happy to be home.

"Cap'n," Billings said, "some men under that oak yonder. Wounded. One's a Reb."

"Check it out. Could be Rosen," Baron replied.

It was two men, and a drummer boy with large, frightened eyes, who had managed to save his drum. The drum, smaller than a standard, lay next to the boy as he leaned against a tree. The drum was new and shiny before shrapnel ripped through it, tearing the right wing off the Union eagle. Blood spray across the side made it look like the bird was mortally wounded. The eagle would fly no more, nor would the little drummer march again.

The men dismounted to check the wounded sprawled under the oak. The Rebel sitting next to the boy was gut shot and already dead. Underneath the photo of a woman in his right hand, a letter fluttered in the slight breeze, dead fingers clasping them tightly. It was as if he'd read the letter one last time and bled out his life staring at her. Even now his lifeless eyes locked on her. Had she felt his passing? Before dying, he'd taken off his galluses and tied off each of the boy's legs below the knee. No need to worry about your britches falling when you're soon to exchange them for a heavenly robe. On the other side of the boy was a Yankee with a hole in his thigh.

The boy looked up, fear widening his already large brown eyes in a ghost-white face. He clutched his little plumed hat.

Baron knelt before him. "We're not going to hurt you."

"That Reb who tied my legs said you have doctors who can fix my feet as good as new."

Baron avoided looking at the bloody stumps where the boy's feet used to be. "We have the best. I'm going to take you to him."

The child blinked away tears. "I can't walk. Reb carried me here, but—"

"No need. I'll take you. You can ride with me. I have the prettiest horse in the army."

That drew a smile. Baron never met a boy who didn't like pretty horses. They were still five miles from camp and help, but neither the boy nor the exhausted horses could take a hard ride.

Billings led Charlie up. The horse offered a velvet muzzle for the boy to pet and stood quietly while Billings lifted the child up to Baron's arms. He handed his canteen up, eyes squinting and watery. "Sun's bright."

Baron nodded and unscrewed the top, giving the boy a drink.

The boy finished and pointed to the wounded Yank London was helping mount a captured horse. "John fetched me water from the creek. I didn't want him to leave me alone, but he said he'd return, and he did!" He raised up and looked around. "Don't forget my drum, sir. Mama bought it with her egg money."

"We'll get it," Baron replied.

"My legs hurt where he tied them off. Can you loosen them?"

"Better not, but the doctor will shortly. He'll make you all better. Tell me your name and where you come from." Even with the tourniquets, blood still seeped. Baron's leg was sticky where the boy's legs rested against it. He brushed away the buzzing flies who made the journey.

The Yankee prisoner trotted up beside them. "Hey, boy. Reb wasn't lying. That's the best-looking horse in the army." He squeezed the little fellow's hand.

"I know!" That small burst of excitement was all he could manage, and he sank back wearily against Baron's chest. "My name's Josiah James Johnston, but everyone calls me J.J. I'm ten." He took a ragged breath. "We're from Pennsylvania. You got any children, mister?"

Christ. Who would send a ten-year-old onto a battlefield?

"No, but when Miss Lorena and I get married, I'll have a boy as brave as you and name him Josiah." He could almost feel the boy smiling.

"I'd like that. They told me to stay back, but Danny got hurt, so I ran up to take his place. Didn't want no one thinking I was scared."

He grinned up at Baron and talked about his mama and her brown eyes like his and rhubarb pie. He liked rhubarb pie. His words became slower and slurred. Baron thought he should tell him to save his strength, but he seemed to want to dwell on Mama, and perhaps that's where he needed to be.

About two miles from camp, the words stopped.

Billings dropped back and glanced over. "He asleep?"

"No."

Chapter Fifty-Three

Baron left the boy with a group who had wagons of wounded. The major took his information and promised to keep the drum and hat so Baron could return it to the family. He'd write them a letter and tell them about their brave boy, though he didn't know how welcome it would be from a Reb. There would be other letters to write when he knew how many men he'd lost.

Rosen was still missing.

The battle was over. The rout was done. The looting continued. When the Federals broke, they surged over their congressmen, reporters, families, various quick-buck artists, vendors, and the curious from Washington who camped on the hillsides to watch their vaunted Federals wipe out the Rebels. The civilians added to the chaotic retreat, if such a disorganized scramble could be dignified with the word.

An enterprising woman had brought a pie cart. When the panicked army took flight, she cut her horse loose and left her cart. Men gathered around, sampling her goods. He wanted something more substantial than pie, but that would do for a start. In some bushes he spied an abandoned picnic basket and sidetracked to see if anything was left. Surprisingly, it was filled with fried chicken, bowls of German potato salad, pickles, stuffed eggs, and fresh fruit. He quartered an apple and fed Charlie, who chomped greedily and nosed inside the basket for more. Grabbing the basket before the horse cleaned it out, chicken and all, he headed to the pie cart.

"Anything good left, boys?"

"Quite a bit, captain. There's a rhubarb pie in the corner. I'm partial to blueberry."

I like rhubarb pie, he heard Josiah whisper.

"I'll take the rhubarb."

What a way to spend the Lord's Day.

Not bashful, he grabbed the rhubarb pie and found a quiet place to eat. Like filings to a magnet, his men drew to him, and before long, a dozen had regathered.

"What's the butcher's bill?" he asked reluctantly.

"Nine dead, sixteen wounded, eighteen horses, five missing," said Skeeter. "What I heard anyway."

"Anyone seen Rosen?" He'd been missing since the second charge. "There's pies left in that cart." He pointed to the pie cart with his fork, though several of them had already gathered abandoned picnic baskets.

They finished eating and wanted nothing more than a nap, but the day wasn't done.

"Let's gather some food and see about rounding up more Yankees. Keep an eye out for Rosen."

They raided sutler wagons that were brimming over with tins of food and various necessities. Baron snagged a box of metal identification tags along with the stamping machine and crammed it in a bag on a whim along with tins of sardines and various other provisions.

"Captain," Skeeter called out from the back of an army wagon. "Look what I found."

Baron eased over to the wagon with severed traces, where Skeeter rattled a pair of shackles at him. "Reckon what they needed with all these? Three wagons full so far."

"Huh. Take us prisoner, I imagine."

"That didn't work out so well, did it?"

"Not today. Toss me a pair." The chains clinked together as they flew through the air. He tied them to his saddle. A souvenir for someone. He contemplated picking up a white lace parasol rocking gently under a nearby tree for Lorena, but didn't know where he'd put it. Another soldier snagged it.

They filled their canteens and watered their horses from another enterprising sutler selling ice water and lemonade. Would the Federals appreciate knowing Fuss and Feathers had been here in his finest carriage and fanciest uniform to have oysters and champagne while the army had dry marched, drinking water from mud holes in the road according to prisoners desperate for water? Spectators had sipped their iced drinks and picnicked while exhausted men died below them. Damned ghouls.

A scout had gotten close enough to watch Scott and his entourage enjoying their feast until all hell broke loose. Then it wasn't so much fun. It was even less fun when a lucky shell hit a wagon going across Stone Bridge and blocked the exodus.

Worthless, the lot of them.

Nearby a man screamed in terror. Another yelled at him to hold.

"Fie." Baron galloped toward the sound, expecting to find a late skirmish. Instead, he found a mounted Yankee major who had been left behind, gun drawn, chasing a civilian around another mounted soldier.

"Hold still, you rotten bastard," the major shouted. "You murdered my men, and I intend to murder you!"

The civilian shrieked again and dodged around the sergeant, who was whirling his horse to shield him. "Major, Darling. Ye know ye don't want tae kill the son-of-a-bitch, deservin' he may be."

"Be damned in hell if I don't, Donnelly. Get out of my way."

The man spotted them. "Help me. He's crazy; I'm a senator—"

"If you say you're some lowlife politician," Baron said. "I promise you; I'll shoot you myself."

"Stay out of this," the major growled. "By God, these worthless politicians started this damned war, and one of them will pay today."

Skeeter nodded in agreement as if some profound truth had been revealed. "Can't disagree with him."

"Major. Darling. Think of yer wife and children."

"Damn it to hell, Donnelly. Shut up. Are you drunk again? I'm not even married, and stop calling me Darling." He fired across the horse's neck at the politician.

"That's precious close tae me equipment, Major. I'll be thanking ye tae not do that again. Think of yer future wife and children."

Baron sighed. "The world would be better off without another politician, but there are too many witnesses. No sense in a good officer, Union or not, swinging for him." He spurred up to the major. "Stand down, sir. You are my prisoner."

"Thank you, sir," the civilian stammered, spittle flying from his fleshy lips. "Thank you. If you'll supply me a horse. I can be on my way. I'll see that you're rewarded."

"On your way? I think not. Skeeter will escort you to the holding area about two miles back."

The man sputtered and looked helplessly about. "But I'm—."

Baron leveled his gun at him. "Don't say it."

"Do you have a horse for me?"

"No."

He peered at Donnelly, who was sipping whiskey with the major.

"Ye're not riding Jack," Donnelly said and passed the bottle to Baron.

"I order you to give me that horse." He turned to Baron. "Order him to give me that horse. He's your prisoner."

"So are you. I suggest y'all head out. Skeeter goes crazy after dark."

"Wh-what?"

"You never heard about Arkansas hill boys?"

Skeeter pulled a squirrel leg out of his hunting bag and bared his protuberant front teeth at the man before sucking the meat off the bone. "We turn into large rats after dark. And you know how rats eat anything." He snapped his teeth at the politician, who squeaked and darted behind Donnelly's horse.

Donnelly raised an eyebrow at Baron. "Irish are ye?"

"Yes, sir. Godspeed to you and Major Darling."

"It's Darley. Donnelly's just—drunk most of the time, or maybe he does it to aggravate me. Probably both."

Baron shrugged. "Eh, Shanks Evans has a barrelisto who carries a cask of the general's favorite whiskey wherever they go."

"Does he need another barrelist?" Donnelly asked.

"Skeeter, disarm the major before he shoots his sergeant, too."

Skeeter collected weapons and headed the trio down the road with the civilian whining about his feet and legs and bad heart. He'd be claiming vapors before they struck camp.

They went out again to gather prisoners and stopped when they'd had as many prisoners as they could handle. Wounded were everywhere, and they searched them looking for Rosen, giving them water when they could find canteens, but there was little more they could do and precious little water. Baron sent the remainder of his men and prisoners with a captain who was herding a sizable flock of prisoners himself and few men to hold them should they find the energy to pick up the abandoned weapons under their shuffling feet.

If spirits were high before, they should be soaring now, but the surge of victory was leaving, and the reality of war setting in. They'd chased Federals until darkness and exhaustion overtook them. Their mounts and prisoners shuffled back to Bull Run Creek and water. Wounded Federals and Confederates alike had the same idea. They walked and crawled to the creek. Some collapsed along the way, too weak to go on, and cried out for help.

"Water. Water." As long as he lived, he would never forget those cries.

Dark mounds inched along in the moonlight, still making their way. They were close. Maybe they'd make it. Friend or foe, there was nothing they could do to help the poor devils.

Water. Thank you, Lord Jesus.

Baron rode closer and noticed the rider in the dark. Rosen sat on his horse, still as a statue.

"We feared you were dead," Baron said.

"Wish I was. If I live to be a hundred, I won't ever forget this day."

"Don't imagine any of us will." Even in the moonlight, Baron saw the ominous dark streak down the side of Rosen's face. Blood, no doubt.

"I was behind you on the charge when a Zouave clubbed me with his gun. Surprised I wasn't trampled to death. It was dark when I woke up puking, and my head felt like it was going to bust open, but I tried to find a horse and get back to camp. Passed out again. Then I woke up with this guy tugging on my boot. My spurs was strapped on tight like you told me, so he couldn't get it off."

Rosen exhaled heavily. "I raised up and said, 'Ho, what are you doing there?'" He looked at Baron and shook his head. "The corpse robber didn't even say a word. Just grabbed his pig sticker and went at me like he was going to cut my throat. Fool shoulda stole my gun first. I jerked it out and blew the top of his head off. Brains, bone, blood went everywhere, and he collapsed on top of me. I finally rolled him off, cleaned out his pockets, grabbed up his sack of loot, caught his horse, and headed for the creek here. Tried to wash my face, but the water's so bloody all I did was smear it around. Knocked open the gash on the side of my head. It's bleeding again."

"Thank God you're alive. Wait a bit, and I'll ride back with you. Camp's not far."

"'Preciate it, sir, but I want to think this through. I'll see you in camp."

Baron had misgivings about letting him go on alone but respected Rosen's wish and watched him ride away. Nearing the creek, he understood why Rosen had backed away. Wounded men had dragged themselves with their last bit of fortitude to the water but were too exhausted to lift their heads. They lay there, heads submerged in the water they thought would save them. Dozens drowned for lack of a few more ounces of strength.

Bodies floated in the creek. Even in the moonlight, Baron could see the water ran red. The horse, exhausted and thirsty as he was, refused to drink. Baron slid down heavily, like a sack of rice, with no grace left in his bones, and scooped water in his hands, wetting the horse's muzzle. Cupping more bloody water in his hand, he brought it back to Charlie. The horse tried to turn his head, but Baron pressed his hand up. Charlie licked at the dripping water. After three attempts, he reluctantly drank from the sanguine creek.

It was Baron's turn. His tongue was so dry there was nothing to moisten his cracked lips. He knelt to drink but refused to foul his canteen with the polluted water. Charlie turned, anxious to be away. Shadows moved amongst the wounded. Baron hoped it was soldiers removing them to nearby hospitals and not ghouls robbing the helpless. Or worse. What could be worse? The goddess Hel reigned this day, but perhaps Lord Byron's creatures also walked the night. He dragged his sleeve across his mouth, trying to get rid of the taste of blood, and whispered a Byron verse.

> "There from thy daughter, sister, wife,
> At midnight drain the stream of life,
> Yet loathe the banquet which perforce
> Must feed thy livid living corse."

Baron shuddered and touched heels to the horse, who managed to lurch into a trot. Some distance down the road a hooded rider approached. The cloak fluttered about it wraith-like, for he couldn't tell if it was male or female or even human. The horse with its great feathered legs trotted steadily toward him, black as death.

The rider stopped.

Baron sucked in the night air and breathed out a quick prayer.

"Excuse me." The voice was high, female, Bostonian, and exhausted. "I need water for the wounded. A stream is nearby?"

"You're a long way from home, ma'am. Yes, it's ahead, but you should go upstream. It's…tainted."

She drew herself up straighter. "I'm a vivandiere. I became separated from my unit in the confusion and stayed to help."

Baron pulled out a cigar and lit it, studying her face briefly in the golden glow. She was too young to be out here alone. Hell, no woman had any business being here, nurse or not. "You've got more starch than most of your Federals."

"I go where I'm needed."

"You're needed here. Let me lead you up the creek."

"I can find it, but if you have a bit of food?"

"Yes, ma'am." He divided his spoils. The tins of mustard sardines he kept, reasoning a lady shouldn't have bad breath, though he doubted the poor souls she'd be tending would care if she breathed fire. "There'll be hospitals set up nearby to help you get home. Should you need vouchsafe, tell them you are under the protection of Colonel Stuart. I'll tell him you're about."

"Colonel Stuart! Our captain said Stuart himself killed my brother!"

"I imagine your brother was trying to kill us, ma'am."

He should have insisted she come with him, but they didn't need a Federal spy in their midst, and he was sure Stuart would be on the move as soon as everyone recuperated. Ahead, two boar hogs squealed at each other, trampling what was left of a body under them. The ferals had begun their grisly feast on the dead and dying. Why they felt the need to contest one corpse in this field of plenty, he had no idea. He'd stop to sleep if not for fear they'd mistake him for one of the dead.

Here lies Captain Callahan. Survived the war, but not the boar.

Chapter Fifty-Four

Doctor Boudreaux didn't gather me up to return home until after midnight, and yet the house was bustling at dawn. I lay awake, watching the sky lightening through the lace curtains. Another time I'd admire the spectacular Alexandria sunrise; now I closed my eyes and listened for the faintest roar of cannon fire. There was none. It had been replaced with rumbling wagons, shouting men, and screaming women in the street below. The aftermath was upon us.

Doctor Boudreaux looked up from his paper, surprised at my entrance. "I wanted to let you sleep after our long night."

I adjusted my nightcap and sat at the table, anxious for news. "I usually rise early, and the ruckus outside—"

"The wounded started arriving a few hours ago. I should have gone to the hospital immediately, but I will no doubt be there through the night. According to one paper, the Federals were soundly thrashed, but the Times says they routed the Rebels and have defeated them thoroughly. There are thousands of casualties on both sides, which is the only point of agreement. The best I can tell, gleaning from several papers. McDowell had the superior plan and troops, but someone forgot to tell the Southern troops they were beaten. Quite remarkable, really."

I sank into a chair at the table near him. The papers were tempting, but I didn't want to know the deadly details. Beula gathered fat slices of bread browning on top of the stove and set the toast caddy down along with oatmeal.

Mrs. Bastrom and J.B. were at the other end of the long butcher block table, making dinner rolls. She sliced off a chunk of dough, rolled it into a ball on the floured board, expertly tucking the edges under a few times, and set another perfect, white pillow of dough in the pan.

J.B. watched intently with large, tawny eyes, chewing on his tongue to aid his concentration. He patted, rolled, and tucked, not so expertly, his slightly gray, lumpy dough, set it aside, then started over. "We making rollth, Mith Lorena."

"I see that. Are you going to be a baker when you grow up?"

He shook his head. "I'm gonna be like Mithter Thilver and take care of hortheth. I'll take care of Gammy when she getth old and drive her around." He brightened up. "Maybe I'll bake if she wanth. She liketh thinnamon rollth."

"I do. We're baking pies today, but we'll make cinnamon rolls in a couple of days. We make good cinnamon rolls, don't we?"

He nodded his head vigorously. "We do." Looking back at his roll and determining it was sufficiently mauled into looking like a lumpy, bumpy albino toad, he carefully put it in the pan. Mrs. Bastrom cut a small "J" in the top of the roll. "You want me to make you one, Mith Lorena?"

"I'd love that."

Mrs. Bastrom pursed her lips. "Go wash your hands first. I don't know how you manage to get the dough so grimy, but at least start out clean."

"It's fine," I said, finishing breakfast and eyeing the newspapers again.

Doctor Boudreaux drained his coffee and pushed away from the table. "Do you want to go to the hospital? We could use help."

"Maybe later. I'm going to the newspaper office to see if they have a fresh casualty list."

I declined a carriage or horse, reasoning the walk would settle my mind, but I hadn't anticipated the wounded who had been dumped on the sidewalks, streets, and alleys, left in wagons and

carts without water, food, or care. I could no longer ignore the
pleas for help and began searching for water to ease the misery.
Many of the wounded died before help arrived. Like a ghoul, I
rifled their bodies looking for canteens or anything that might
hold water. A woman hurrying down the middle of the street
with a handkerchief crammed to her nose huffed at me as I lifted
another bloody body and relieved him of his empty canteen and
a small bottle of whiskey in his coat pocket. I closed his staring
eyes and laid two pennies over pallid lids. Slowly, I sank to the
sidewalk beside him and took a healthy swig of the whiskey.

Law, that was rough.

The rotgut burned all the way, but thus fortified, I hauled
myself up and looked for a horse trough to fill the five canteens
I'd liberated. After the first few stops to water the wounded,
the newspaper office vanished from my mind. "Do you know
anything of Stuart's men?" I asked each man I came across.

"No."

"Hit hard."

"Lost a few."

The noon sun beat down mercilessly on the wretches who
were slowly being taken away for treatment but mostly left to die
alone. With help, some walked to shade where we could find it.
Some who were able helped me drag others who couldn't walk. I
lined them up like cordwood in one alley and left a full canteen
with one of the least wounded and told him to flag anyone who
came by.

My legs trembled like a new foal's, but I forced myself to take
another step. *Thirteen. Fourteen. Jesus, help me. I am so tired.*

"Fancy meeting you here." The voice, little more than a
whisper, came from the stack of bodies piled on the sidewalk.
Clawing my way as carefully as I could through the gory mass,
I searched for the owner of the voice. Three of the men weren't
dead, but well on their way. How the one with shrapnel wounds
survived, I had no idea, but his moans when I turned him sent
my panicked apologies flying.

"Water," one man begged.

Water would pour out his perforated guts and kill him. Did he know that? "What's your name?"

"Abel Johanson, 3rd Rhode Island. Water, please."

"You've been gut shot; it will—"

He nodded weakly. "I know. Water, please."

I put the canteen to his lips. His fingers closed around my hand.

"The Lord is my shepherd—" *God! Where are you?* "I shall not want. He maketh me to lie down in green pastures; He leadeth me beside the still waters." I choked at the valley of death, but Abel squeezed my hand, urging me on.

He was gone before I finished. I looked through his pockets and found letters from a loved one. Stuffing them in my pocket, so I might write them later, I laid him aside and looked to the other wounded man.

"Nothing you can do for me, ma'am," he said. "A drink, please."

I didn't argue. His wounds were fatal. He might have survived with immediate attention, but it was past that, and he accepted his fate.

"Write my Ma later. Letter in my pocket. Tell her I died with my face to them."

I brushed the hair out of his eyes and put the canteen to his cracked lips. "Your name?"

He choked out a small laugh. "Worm meat, I fear." He peered at me wearily, but with a strange, haunting intensity as if he were fixing my face in his soul. The face, a solid square thing as if it had been molded in a box, was coated with dirt and blood and cannon powder. The eyes shone bright blue out of the blackened canvas. "Ezra Hodson of Wisconsin." He took a shuddering breath. "Write that letter, please."

"I will, Ezra. Do you have a sweetheart?"

He waved a fly away from his face weakly. "No, and I fear it might be a bit late, ma'am." His eyes closed, but a smile remained, fixed, serene. "I have some money in my boot. Send it to Ma. No sense letting the grave robbers get it."

"I will."

I retrieved the letter and money and scuttled away, looking for the voice. "Hello, where are you?"

"Here. Might have to bring a shovel. I 'pear to be buried in bodies."

The voice, weakened as it was, led me to the correct stack, where I found, to my shock, Colin Smith, the kissing sergeant I had met on my first trip to occupied Alexandria. His head was bound, but blood seeped through where the entire right side of his once beautiful face was bleeding with shreds of flesh poking out of the rough binding. His left arm and shoulder looked like he'd been mauled by a bear.

"I'm getting you out of the sun."

"I don't think I can walk."

"Then I'll drag you."

With the help of his few shuffling steps, I maneuvered him into a patch of shade where we collapsed. "What can I do?" I asked, holding the canteen to his parched lips.

"Hold me." His handsome mouth lifted into a slight, crooked smile. "If I might be so bold."

Leaning up against the building, I pulled him into my lap. He tried to lift his head up so as not to sully my dress, but I pushed it gently against my bosom and stroked his head, crooning to him as a mother might a child until all resistance melted.

"Colin, do you have family? A wife or girl you'd like me to write?" There was no subtle way to say, "You are dying."

"No wife. I dreamed of finding a nice Southern girl and settling here. I've fallen in love with Virginia. I left a fiancée behind, but she married a shopkeeper. The ring's in my watch pocket. Take it and my money. Keep the ring; use the money to bury me."

"Do you want me to write her?"

"Lord, no. I'll not have her weeping false tears over me. Bury me without note. I have been a stranger in a strange land." He shifted a bit and groaned. "Law, this hurts. Forgive my unmanliness."

Gently stroking his head with one hand, I fumbled in my pocket for the whiskey. "There is nothing to forgive. I have some whiskey. I use the term loosely."

Unable to work the cork out with one hand and not wanting to shift him lest I cause more pain, I pulled it out with my teeth. He choked on the vile concoction and looked up at me with a hint of his mischievous grin I first knew. "I've thought about sharing a meal and drinks with you often. I'd ask you to join me, but—holy Moses, that's terrible."

I spat the cork out. "I'd be pleased to drink with you," and took a blistering gulp of fortitude. It burned a fiery trail down my throat and into my gut. Coughing, I wheezed. "Oof."

"Uh-huh. Whiskey and grain alcohol. What a travesty."

He wasn't far wrong. I gave him another sip that didn't choke as much. Maybe his throat had been seared the first time. "No tombstone," he said.

I shouldn't be having this conversation with a striking young man in the prime of life, but he was slipping away drop by scarlet drop. "Your army friends might like to pay respects. Imogene and I will."

"Cipher something. My initials and unit. A bit of poetry perhaps."

I recited a bit of tomb poetry to him.

> "How loved how valued once avails thee not
> To whom related or by whom begot
> A heap of dust alone remains of thee
> Tis all thou art and all the proud shall be."

He smiled. "Yes, something like that."

"It's on the grave of the unknown female stranger here. Perhaps you can keep her company."

"I'd like that."

"Would you like to pray?"

"Yes, I would," he said wearily. "Mother used to pray with me each night by my bed."

We prayed and drank and talked, and I held him closer when the words began to slur. "You are loved, Colin," I whispered. His hand tightened ever so slightly on mine, and he slept. I laid my head on his and closed my eyes, wishing him peace and an easy passing.

Somewhere through the fog, men shouted. Heavy steps thundered across wooden planks. "Here. He's here."

"Good God. That's Miss McKenzie. I think she's dead."

I tried to rouse myself from exhausted and liquored sleep. My hand raised weakly from Colin's arm.

"No, not dead. She's drunk."

A crowd of men, Sergeant Smith's friends, surrounded us in the gloomy dusk made even darker by the shielding shade. "I'm not drunk. Sergeant Smith was in pain. I had some whiskey and gave it to him. He asked me to drink with him."

The men lifted Colin up and carried him to a waiting wagon.

"Careful of his shoulder," I called, struggling to my feet. My leg was asleep where he'd lain across it, and it buckled at my first step. One of the men caught me before I crashed and handed me up to Colin's friend Humboldt regardless of my protests.

"He's gone, ma'am."

Chapter Fifty-Five

"Have you ever been drunk before?" Doctor Boudreaux asked when I appeared for breakfast the next morning. "I have, but I wasn't last night." I poured some coffee and explained how I came to be drinking rotgut whiskey in public. "I like a tot of good whiskey occasionally, but I don't drink to excess—and didn't."

"Excellent! You can come to the hospital today."

"I thought I'd been dismissed."

He waved the idea away like so much cottonwood fluff.

Even with my soul-draining experience yesterday, it was Doctor Boudreaux who looked worn as a rented mule. "What time did you get home?"

He pulled out his pocket watch. "About forty-five minutes ago. I came home to bathe, change clothes, and eat. The girls filled me in on your adventure."

Beula brought a plate of ham and eggs to me with a large helping of grits with red-eye gravy. Her cheeks flared red when I cast an accusing look her way. "Adventure. That was the most horrific thing I've ever seen. They were piled in the streets, on sidewalks, and stacked up in wagons without a bit of care. I hope they've settled those poor men."

"I doubt it. Wounded are still coming in."

"I'll take but a moment to get ready. I suppose there is still not a train out of Alexandria for me."

The doctor shook his head. "No chance. All are bound with troops, wounded and otherwise."

Silver brought the doctor's small carriage around while I readied myself. Before we set off, Doctor Boudreaux warned me repeatedly to be prepared. I wasn't. At one building in town, surgeons were still working on patients outdoors with stacks of limbs piled high near their tables.

"Good Hannah." I clutched the seat with my hands and looked down.

"What? Here, watch out!" He jerked the horse to the side to avoid a cart laden with wounded men jouncing down the street around horses, other carts, and wagons, and sometimes pedestrians.

Following my gaze, he recognized what struck me. "Oh, Old Dominion. The army confiscated it for their commissary, and now it's a triage hospital. Sort out the fatally wounded and set them aside; treat the worst who can be saved; treat the others as you get to them. It's efficient, but soulless. As you can see from the pile of limbs, they've been busy."

"They leave men to die with no care whatsoever? They don't even try?"

"There's no time or personnel to waste on the dead. We must save who we can."

We traveled the rest of the way in silence, as I was too aghast for conversation. I had gone a different way to the newspaper office yesterday. I might not have returned had I known the grimness that awaited.

"Doctor Boudreaux, Mrs. Covington's waiting," A.J. called out to us before the carriage stopped. "Hello, Miss McKenzie. Hurry. I'll tend the horse."

The doctor sighed and grabbed his bag. "I don't know what she'd have done if I'd slept a few hours."

Mrs. Covington greeted us at the door, frowning. "You."

I motioned to the street. "There appear to be hundreds of men lying out here who would appreciate my help. I can leave if you like."

"You're desperately needed in surgery, Doctor. Doctor Craig collapsed." Pivoting back to me, she pointed toward the kitchen. "Help get breakfast out, please. After we take your...things, of course."

With considerable dread, I scanned the casualty list next to the door for Baron's name. I clutched my crucifix to send up a quick prayer of thanks when I didn't find his name, but oh, the heartache so many would find at this mournful roster.

Inside the ward, pallets lay on the floor for more wounded. They'd be stacking them soon. A.J. escorted me to the kitchen, where they loaded carts for the men. Toast and tea and bowls of mush. "Is there at least a bit of jam for the toast?" I asked, dismayed at the bland offering.

Mrs. Brodie looked at me as if I had asked for high tea and waved a wooden spoon toward a cupboard. "Jam's in there, but we're not having time to spread it."

"I'll do it."

"Sparingly."

"Yes, ma'am." I pulled out the jam and grabbed a jar of honey for some who had no appetite, hoping to coax them into eating, and hurried on to Ward B.

Constant Sorrel, who stole my heart the first day, now rested at the front of the room under a window. I was appalled at his deterioration since I'd last seen him. "Constant," I said as cheerfully as I could, though I wanted to sit and weep, "are you soaking up all the sunshine?"

The smile was weak but genuine. "I thought you'd left these hallowed, horrid halls forever." He waved at the window. "Yes, they think sunshine and fresh air will cure what the doctors can't. I expect they'll park me on the roof shortly." He started to laugh, but it turned into a wheezing cough.

"Here, drink this." I drizzled honey into a cup of tea and held it to his lips.

"Tea," his neighbor huffed. "Didn't we fight a war so we didn't have to drink tea? I thought we did." Nils Halldorson reminded me of the huge Swede who worked for Papa's lumber mill until he got the wanderlust and headed for virgin territory in Wisconsin. From the size of his remaining arm, he might have been a lumberjack himself. Maybe a bit of giant blood was inherent in all Scandinavians. I'd yet to meet a small one.

"Taxes on tea, I believe," I replied.

"There you go. We shouldn't be drinking it at all. It's un-American. What does a man have to do to get coffee around here and a biscuit? Do you make biscuits? I'd give my right arm for a biscuit like my ma makes." Nils waved his right stump, and his sonorous laugh echoed through the ward like a troop of tubas.

"Dammit, Nils." Constant's strangled laugh seized into another wracking cough.

I looked up from the toast I was spreading with jam. "I collect receipts, but I'm inept in the kitchen."

"Ma could teach you. I could teach you, but they won't let me in the kitchen. A biscuit would be heaven, but I'd settle for just a cup of coffee."

There was a chorus of amens from nearby patients. "You men stop harassing Miss McKenzie," A.J. said. "Doctor Craig's the one who ordered the tea and toast. It's better for you."

"Bullcorn," Nils huffed. "He's Scotch. It's revenge for dumping that tea in the harbor."

While a debate started about the Revolutionary War (a welcome change from worrying about the present one), Doctor Craig and his nefarious tea plot and favorite foods, I finished feeding Constant. He had little appetite, and it was hard for him to swallow. He ended the struggle with a frail but heartfelt thank you and let his eyes drift shut. "Come back and see me."

"I'll return." How he stayed so sweet I didn't know. His two brothers died in camp. He was the sole remaining son, and his mother refused to visit, deeming his fervor to go to war the reason for their loss. Now, he was dying. He might have survived the wound, but the pneumonia would harvest him. I was familiar with the journey. I kissed his forehead.

His eyes fluttered open. "Why did you do that?"

"That's how my mother used to check my temperature. I was seeing if you still have a fever."

"Do I?"

"Yes, I'll send someone with vinegar cloths." The raging fever gave his eyes a bright look as if shining with the vigor of youth and health, and his cheeks blushed rosy. I smoothed a stray lock of hair back from his brow and plastered on my Sally Sunshine smile. "I'll come back and brush your hair. You've already mussed it."

"Thank you." His chest rose haltingly, straining with the effort. "And thank you for checking my temperature. I needed a kindness."

"You're easy to be kind to."

The rest of my morning sped by helping men eat, writing letters, checking on Constant, and being elevated to changing the dressing on minor or nearly healed wounds. My promotion was due more to desperation than confidence, but I did the best I could and met the approval of the doctors and men, which was all I cared about. After dinner, the Texan Travis Williams allowed me to help him bathe as much as was decent.

"I'm surprised you unbowed your neck enough to allow help," I said.

"Not pride so much as self-preservation," he said and squeezed out the cloth with a powerful but scarred hand. "The first day one of the Ladies' Aide gals scrubbed my face with a soapy rag, making sure she got plenty in my eyes. I could stand that, but not her bragging about how she got that Reb good."

"The Ladies' Aide?"

He laughed. "You look so shocked. You've never heard of good Christian ladies being spiteful?"

"They can be the worst dregs of humanity, but I wouldn't think Mrs. Covington allowed such."

"They're her pets. Even so, I'm sure she'd oust Mrs. Goody Two Shoes if she caught her."

"You don't fear I'll soap your eyes?"

"No, I've been watching you. Aside from probably being a Secesh too, you have a kind heart and aren't letting politics govern your nursing. When we finish, I need you to write that letter for me."

"Of course, Mr. Williams."

"Let's not stand on formality. Call me Travis."

I lathered the cloth and washed his back.

He sighed in contentment like an old dog settling in front of a fire on a cold night. "Dear heavens, it's good to be clean, but what I wouldn't give for a proper bath."

While he finished with his private bath, I set out in search of Doctor Boudreaux. He was near collapse in the kitchen.

"Law, Doctor. You need rest."

"I'm going to the dormitory. I needed some tea first."

"Doctor, Travis Williams was talking about how much he'd like a proper bath. Could we set up a tub in the courtyard? We could heat water in the pots we do laundry in. It would be a bit of work, but they'd be cleaner, and it would save hauling wash water to them. Maybe string sheets up around the tub for privacy?"

"I'm sure most of the men are beyond worries of privacy with the degradations they've been through, but the ladies who come out to do laundry or smoke might appreciate not seeing the full show. I'll see what I can do, but now I need sleep before I drop."

Travis was stowing his razor when I returned, having given up trying to shave with one hand. His chestnut beard had been neatly trimmed once, but it was disappearing in new growth. There were a few clear cuts and gashes, but it remained mostly virgin territory. "I thought you got waylaid and was going to attempt this dross. I fear all I did was unintentional bloodletting."

"I'm sorry. I found Doctor B. and got permission to set up a bathing tub in the courtyard. With all the vacant houses, we'll liberate one somewhere." I pulled the chair next to his bed closer. "Let me help. I learned to shave my father when he broke his arm. He said I was marvelous, probably because I didn't cut his throat on the first attempt, but I did get proficient."

As reluctant as he was at first, he smiled approval at his restored bearded fashion when I finished. With the shaving kit stowed, I pulled out the lap desk I'd purloined and sat at the ready.

"Dear Uncle Ren," he began. "I'm still in the hospital in Alexandria. The one that used to be the girls' school known as St. Cat's. They took my arm, but I'm OK. I'm to be sent to DC to prison in a few days. I wish you could come see me.

"You'll be sad to know Jackson's sweet canary died. You should replace him as soon as you can to perk him up."

I dropped my pen at the mention of birds, paranoia no doubt, and glanced up at him.

"I thought I heard a flicker yesterday," he continued, "but never saw him. It would be strange to see one here, but I'll keep looking."

More birds. My hand hesitated, letting a drop of ink fall to the page. I blotted it quickly so as not to mar any words. He continued with inconsequential rambling about relatives, the battle, shoes, and a bit of poetry. I didn't know the key he was working from, but I deciphered some. They lost two spies, and he needed rescuing quickly. He told me to have the boy Jos take the letter to Mansion Hotel to send with their packet and gave me some money for him. It would get there quicker from there, he said. Then he drew a plunging Mississippi kite on the envelope and sealed it.

"This means more than you know," he said.

"Most likely not. I'm a bit of a birdwatcher myself."

He yawned and looked around. "Have you ever seen a kite hunting?"

"Yes, in Louisiana."

"They don't thrive in cages."

"I wouldn't think."

I left him to nap and returned to duty, working deep into the night. Doctor Boudreaux offered to let me use his carriage to go home, but I opted to stay and shuffled off to the dormitory.

The braid came down, and I ran my fingers through the untied strands. No hundred strokes. Not even a single one.

"Do you want to borrow my brush?" the girl in the bed opposite mine asked. "My name's Sardie. I work in the laundry usually."

"Thank you. I have a brush I'll fetch later." I tried unsuccessfully to stifle a yawn.

"Here, drink this," she ordered and handed me a small tumbler.

"What is it?"

"Covington's sherry. I also clean her room. A drop of it slips into my flask each time. I keep it for emergencies. You look like you could use it."

"I couldn't."

"Take it. It'll help you sleep."

I reluctantly swallowed the offering and drifted away nearly as soon as my eyes closed.

Summoned by the witching hour, I awoke shortly before the church bells chimed three. I lay awake, staring at the unfamiliar slat ceiling, and tried to get my bearings. Knowing I wouldn't be able to go back to sleep, I dressed quietly and slipped out of the room. Bedpans needed emptying and water pitchers refilled.

Given the hour, I shouldn't have been surprised to see the crow drifting wraith-like among the beds when I returned with a water bucket. "What are you doing here?" Covington asked.

"I stayed in the dormitory but couldn't sleep. I thought I'd make myself useful."

"You'll want to do something with your hair. Did you bring a brush? If not, I have combs for the men."

"I have a brush in my purse."

She tenderly tucked a blanket around a man and laid the back of her hand against his forehead.

"He has fever?" I asked when she returned to my side.

"It's broken finally. I poured willow bark tea in him by the gallon. Maybe it helped."

She jingled through the numerous keys on her chatelaine, searching for the one to unlock her office door. I waited outside, thinking she'd hand me my purse and continue her rounds.

"Come in," she said as if calling me in from the rain. She was unlocking an inner door to the office, but my purse already lay on the desk. "You look as frayed as a ragpicker's waif."

The second door opened, and she motioned me in, where I was enveloped with the scent of lavender soap cradled in a crystal dish. "Huh," I said, looking around. "I thought this was a storage closet."

"It was. I converted it into a hidey-hole since I spend most of my time here anyway. The girls can't relax when I'm in the dormitory."

I sat in the small chair near the door. Most of the space was taken up by a single brass rail bed and a small harpsichord. There were shelves of books on the walls, but when did she find time to read? Also on the walls, to my surprise, hung a guitar, banjo, and violin.

"Let me see about getting refreshment if Sardonia hasn't cleaned me out."

I looked at the glass with some guilt but accepted it. Her sudden attempt at friendliness puzzled me, but I wasn't going to question it.

"She steals a thimbleful each time she cleans. If she weren't such a good worker and not a drinker to speak of, we'd have words. It's probably for when she can't sleep for her backache."

Another glass was poured for herself, and the sherry went back into its not-so-secret hiding place. "Do you play? I saw you looking at my instruments. Did you think I took them from the soldiers?" She chuckled and stretched her legs out on the bed.

"I was surprised. It's like a fairy nook to find all this music here." I shrugged. "Yes, I play. Piano, guitar, and a little concertina. Not well on the last."

"I love concertinas! They are lively little musical bastards. Neither one thing nor the other. I'm going to get one when things calm down. My father was a doctor, as was my late husband. I was trained in music and being a proper wife. After my husband died, I gave music lessons to the poor and broken children. Now I tend to poor and broken men and sometimes play for them on Sundays."

Had she puffed the merest bit in my direction, I'd have fallen off my chair. Was this even the same woman I knew in the daytime?

She took my empty glass and stood. "And if you tell anyone I'm human, I'll deny it to one and all and demand your dismissal for hallucinations."

"Yes, ma'am."

I retrieved my brush and scurried away to the safety of bedpans and buckets. Blocks of blue moonlight created a keyboard effect of dark and light across the ward floor. The child in me wanted to take off my shoes and run a barefoot *glissando*. The McKenzie in me wanted to dance in the moonlight and see if the fae would join me. The nurse in me moved to a square of light, untied the braid, and hastened to brush out my hair so I could neaten it and return to work.

"Come here," a man's voice said gently.

I whirled around to see Travis propped up in bed watching me. "What are you doing awake?" I asked.

"The same as you, it appears. I couldn't sleep. Let me brush your hair."

"I, uh—"

"Please. I used to brush my wife's hair all the time. I can't braid, but I can brush."

If Mrs. Covington saw us, she'd have conniptions, but I relented and set a chair close to his bed. He scooped his arm under my hair and pooled it on the bed. I nearly went to sleep with the gentle brushing.

"That's one hundred strokes. Isn't that the requirement?" He handed the brush back to me.

"Yes," I replied quietly. "You know women well and how they like their hair brushed. Baron would be so jealous. He's always threatening to loose it. Baron. Captain Baron Patrick Callahan, my fiancée. Almost." I laughed.

"Fortunate man," he said and then smiled. "Almost. My wife had beautiful hair, too. Brushing it at night was always a sweet ending to the day. Like the sighing of a soul."

I hesitated my braiding. "Had?"

"Yellow fever last year. I rode away from my ranch and joined the army." His mind drifted somewhere far away and returned like a snapped rubber band. "What were you dancing to?"

"Pardon?"

"Before I spoke. You were dancing in the moonlight."

"Was I? I didn't realize." I had let my mind wander and get caught up like a child, dancing with fairies. How mortifying.

He dressed surreptitiously, declining any help, and held his hand out. "Tie your hair and come dance with me in the courtyard. It's been too long, and I need to stretch my legs."

The orderly making his way through the ward waved us on. "I'll cover for you if Mrs. Covington comes through early. Just don't go over the wall."

"I—"

"Come along," Travis said, holding his hand nearer. "I'm off to prison soon." We stopped in the center of the bricked courtyard, and he bowed most gallantly. "Schottische or waltz?"

"Your choice, sir."

"Waltz." He tucked his empty shirtsleeve in his belt. "Such a shame. I used to be so good at holding my hand elegantly behind my back."

"Hello, Travis." In the shadows by the gate a man sat, most likely a guard. "Miss."

"Hello, disembodied voice that must be Hugh," Travis answered. "Guard duty tonight?"

"Ayup. Gotta keep you Rebs from escaping." There was a faint rustling and a few tentative harmonica notes. "Waltz, you say?"

"If you don't mind."

We danced in the moonlight's glow to a waltz so sweetly played I wished it might never stop. A violin magically joined in, and the dance continued. The final strains quavered in the soft night breeze, delicate as a sundered spiderweb.

I continued to hold him, my head on his chest, reluctant to let him go.

He stroked my hair. "Are you all right?"

"Yes, just missing someone."

He sighed and laid his head on mine. "Me, too. Pray you'll see him soon. You must tell me about him."

Guilt coursed through me because I knew he'd never see the one he missed again. "We should return."

"Yes. I'd hate for you to lose your job emptying bedpans, vomit buckets, and washing worm-ridden bandages."

"Hmmm, yes. *Sic transit gloria mundi.*" Back inside, I lowered my voice. "Did you finish scouting?"

"Madam, I've no idea what you're talking about," he said with feigned surprise. "Might check Chester. By his breathing, he's coming undoped, and he's afraid of the dark."

Chester suffered from nostalgia, and they kept him mostly sedated except in the brightest part of the day when he sat in the courtyard near the flowers. He watched butterflies and birds in a small corner of the world safe from war. But I'd been warned, when panic seized him, his heart pounded so hard that at times they feared it might explode. His breath came chuffing now, rapid like a train going too fast down the mountain. There wasn't a doctor to be found, so I went back to Mrs. Covington's office. Her violin lay across the chair next to the desk. She didn't look up when I entered but kept glancing between the ledger and the list she was penning.

"What is it?" she snapped. The human Covington was safely stowed away, and Crow was back.

"That was beautiful playing."

"A waltz needs a violin, but I'm sure that's not why you're here."

"Mr. Chesterfield is getting restless. Mr. Williams says the medicine's wearing off."

"Yes, I'm sure he's a doctor. I'll send someone directly. Leave me alone so I can get this order done."

Maybe Chester would sleep until daylight when the demons depart. I pumped two buckets of fresh water and headed back to check on him. He tossed wildly, crying out warnings and urging others on. I reached out hesitantly.

Travis lay turned toward him. "Leave him," he said softly. "You don't know how he'll react if you disturb him."

He was right, so I returned to my buckets.

"Teddy! I told you to get down!" Chester screamed from behind me. There he stood in the aisle, staring at me and waving a crutch. He thumped toward me, faster than I believed possible. Dropping the buckets, I reached to catch him before he fell. His eyes were wide and horrified and unseeing all at once.

"Chester," I said, holding out my hand toward him cautiously. "It's all right."

"Get down! Get down!" He threw me down, shoving my face to the floor. I stared at the tiny black and white mosaic tiles, afraid to move. "Can't you see, Teddy? They'll blow your fool head off." With a practiced motion, he swung a crutch to his shoulder like a rifle and aimed.

I tried to get up, but he shoved me back down. Awakened patients streamed or hobbled toward us. Travis knelt by his side, trying to peel me away, but no amount of coaxing penetrated the battle. Chester fired his crutch at those closing in, rolled on his back, reloaded, swung back, covering me with his body again, and fired once more at the advancing patients.

"Halt," Travis ordered. "Let me handle him."

The water from my spilled buckets flowed toward us, soaking us both as we lay pinned on Chester's battlefield. He clutched his sopped nightshirt and looked at me miserably. "See what you did, Brother? Now they took your head off." He sat up, brushing at his shirt, and pulled me into his arms, crooning and rocking, tears flowing.

"Private Chesterfield," Travis said sternly. "Teddy must go to the hospital."

Still crying, he held me out gently.

An orderly and Doctor Craig helped Chester back to bed. "Are you all right?" the doctor asked me once they settled him.

"A bit rattled." In truth, my bones were jelly, and I feared to stand.

"Understandable. Thank you for not screaming like a banshee as most women would."

Travis took my hand and pulled me up. "Perhaps we should get you some tea. Let me get my britches on." I leaned on his bed, willing myself not to faint.

Dawn was barely breaking, but several loaves of fresh bread were already lined up like little brown soldiers on the table. I drifted in on the heady aroma of warm yeast and hot coffee. When Travis recounted the misadventure, kitchen maids pushed him away and clustered around like a bunch of mother hens, each jostling to comfort me until I feared I might suffocate.

"Give the girl air." Mrs. Brodie set two steaming cups of coffee down and flopped a hot loaf of bread on its side to slice. "I'll be for mixing up butter and sorghum for the bread. It'll put some grit back in ye."

"I'm fine."

She plopped down a bowl of marbled butter and sorghum molasses. "Aye? And ye've taken palsy recent?"

To my surprise, she was right. Even more surprising, I was powerless to stop quivering and clutched the cup with both hands lest I drop it. She buttered a slice of bread for me, dipping deeply into the sorghum veins.

"I heard what happened. Are you all right?" Doctor Boudreaux sat beside me and helped himself to the butter and sorghum mixture.

"I'm fine. Shook a bit. There's a missing cup under Mr. Williams' bed."

"Pardon?"

"A cup under the bed the housekeepers missed. It's odd the things you notice when you think you might die."

He sighed contentedly and handed me some bread slathered with the butter and sorghum. "We should see if our boys with no appetite might eat this. I'll talk to the housekeepers about the things under beds."

Not wanting to discuss my adventure further, I followed his thought about patients. "What if we mixed arrowroot with hot beef broth for those who have problems keeping things down?"

"I don't see why not, as long as we don't tell them we're feeding them baby food. Maybe boil root vegetables with the beef. Mrs. Brodie, can you do that?"

"Aye, I can make a soup and dip off broth. Mrs. C. can get the arrowroot."

"Excellent," he said, but his mind was already working on other problems as evidenced by the wrinkled brow and tapping fingers. "If only we could find a solution for poor Chester."

"Is there no cure?" I knew addled people, but they were mostly senile with old age.

"Not really. His father's taking him to a private institution with an excellent doctor next week. Otherwise, we'd be forced to put him in an asylum, I fear. We'll make sure he stays heavily sedated at night until then."

Since we were already in the kitchen, Mrs. Brodie fixed a proper breakfast and even permitted Travis to stay instead of banishing him back to the ward to await his tea and toast. She allowed we all deserved bacon and eggs.

"Do you want to go home?" Doctor Boudreaux asked.

"Maybe later. I'll help get breakfast out and do letters. I told Constant I'd check back with him. I promised the men I'd read *The Gold-Bug* today."

"We mustn't miss the exciting goldbug tale. Let me know when you're ready."

Constant was waiting patiently for me after breakfast with letter in hand. "You've returned. My heart gladdens."

"Do you want me to read that letter to you?"

"No, but do read it." He was so pallid I feared the news within.

The letter was from his mother. She looked forward to nursing him back to health as soon as her carriage could get her through muddy roads. "This is wonderful news. She's forgiven you."

"No. It's occurred to her I have a prosperous little farm, and she wants to make sure she gets it when I'm gone. My friend Efram should be here any minute. He sent a message from the hotel last night." Clearly exhausted, he sank back against his pillow.

"Do you want me to prop you up?"

"If you don't mind. We need to get through this. I have pen and paper for you to take notes."

Plumping the pillow, I drew him up and leaned him gently against the wall. It wasn't difficult. He was skin and bones.

"Never change, do you, Constant? Still stealing all the prettiest girls."

"Efram, glad you could make it." He was too weak to do more than barely raise a hand. The new arrival bent to clasp it in his large hands. "We have some things to do before—" Constant inhaled so raggedly I wanted to tell him to save himself, but he continued, halting to rest and catch his breath as needed. "Before it's too late. Captain drew up a will yesterday. He's a lawyer. I'm leaving everything to you. Bury me next to Judith. Ma will insist I be buried in the family plot, but I want to be with my wife and baby. She didn't want them when they were alive; she doesn't need me in death."

I stopped writing at this. "That's terrible."

Efram clasped his friend's hand tighter. "Mrs. Sorrel can be downright mean at times. Blamed me for getting Constant in trouble when we jumped off that creek bank. He got skinned up. I broke my leg, but I was the instigator of all evil, according to her."

"You ought to thank me. That bum leg will keep you out of the war."

"And the missus and young'uns are grateful. I act properly mournful about not being able to go, but thank God for broke legs."

Constant tried to laugh but ended with that terrible wracking cough. "Miss McKenzie, the will's in my Bible. If you'll get
it out, I'll sign it. I need you and Halldorson to witness it. Efram,
you take the will, and when the time comes, show it to her. Don't
back down. I already instructed the bank to transfer my account
to you. Hang on to the farm. It'll take care of you and those kids.
If you raise corn as generous as you raise kids, you'll be rich."

"You know I will." His eyes watered as he said this, and the
large Adam's apple bobbed. "Anything else?"

"Plant a lilac bush by our graves. Judith loved lilacs."

I signed the will after him and handed it to Halldorson. "You
gentlemen visit, but I'll check on you later." This wasn't the first
will I'd witnessed, but it wasn't getting easier with practice.

With Poe in hand, I headed to the courtyard where the group
called the book club awaited. I had read to them yesterday and
was amazed at my receptive audience.

Butterflies and bees drifted among the flowers, forming an
idyllic setting if not for the stained and tattered bandages fluttering like grim banners from the laundry lines. They reserved
a chair for me and clustered around it like eager children at a
magic show. Jos, the little colored orphan who had been adopted
by the hospital, took up his station by my side, eager for another
story. He wandered about the hospital trying to make himself
useful but had particularly attached himself to me like a stray
puppy since my arrival.

"Who's ready for a little ciphering and to see if we can solve
the mystery?" I asked.

"Me, me," they cried, mocking children until I laughed at
their antics.

I read, acting out the parts in various voices to add color. My
routine was a huge hit, and more men hobbled or wheeled their
way out to listen, drawn by the laughter. Even Chester came out,
smiling and greeting everyone as he ambled to the flowers near
the gate. The guard there pulled a chair closer and helped him sit.
Chester looked at me shyly with an apologetic grin. "Sorry for
interrupting, Miss McKenzie. Please continue."

I was thrilled to see him in such a good mood as if the night battle had never happened. Perhaps Gold-Bug would lift it further. Chester and the guard visited quietly, but I knew they were listening as they'd laugh from time to time along with the others. They must have been discussing the guard's new gun with its beautiful horn grip because he pulled it from his holster, showing Chester the piece and pointing to the details. The guard handed the gun to Chester, who looked at me with hollow, haunted eyes. I knew then he hadn't forgotten our battle scene. "Please don't—" I whispered.

Chester smiled at me in wan apology, lifted the muzzle to his head, and blew his brains out.

Doctor Boudreaux was the first medical officer to arrive, but there was nothing to be done. He pulled me up from the bricks where I'd collapsed with my face in my hands sobbing.

"I'm done." I felt like my soul had been sucked out of me and shredded. "I can't do this. I can't."

He patted me gently. "Let's go home."

Chapter Fifty-Six

Truth came to me in the night. She whispered in my dreams and took my hand to show me things I shrank from in the light of day. Chester was right to fear the dark. It was here she made all bare as a corpse laid out for bathing. I awoke with her whispers and warnings still in my mind. None would survive this terrible war. Not the dead. Not the living.

I vowed never to return. I had also promised Constant I would. And so, the next morning, I forced myself back to the hospital. Silver would check the train station after breakfast as he did each day. Today he would have good news, I told myself.

My first stop was to see Constant. Efram had stayed with him through the night, fearing he might go at any time. Constant was asleep, but his finger lifted slightly as if in response when he heard my voice.

"Is he drugged?" I asked.

"No. They said he'll pass into a twilight and move on."

Move on. What a delightful euphemism—as if he were padding from one room into another. "If he rouses or worsens, send someone for me."

I found busy work emptying bedpans, filling water jugs, writing a few letters, and I gladly accepted when A.J. asked me if I could change bandages as the doctors were backed up with surgery.

"Miss McKenzie, will you come with me, please?" Mrs. Covington stood at the foot of the bed watching me finish one patient with a critical eye. I scanned her face quickly for signs of disapproval but saw only the normal scowl.

"Yes, ma'am." With a gentle pat and quick farewell, I gathered my supplies and followed the matron. Was I in trouble? She said nothing, but that wasn't unusual. I slowed at her office, but she kept going, so I set my basket on the cart outside and hurried after her. Was I being dismissed? To the kitchen we went. She waved toward an aproned stranger. The woman was tall, nearly as tall as Baron, broad-shouldered with a ruddy complexion and graying strawberry blonde hair. A Valkyrie in skirts.

Nils Halldorson sat at the table with a cup of coffee. "Miss McKenzie, I want you to meet Ma. She came to help in the kitchen for a bit and fetch me home. She's going to teach you how to make biscuits."

Mrs. Covington rolled her eyes. "Good luck with the cooking lessons, but Miss McKenzie has patients, and I need her on the floor."

I raised a brow. *I've been accepted?*

"I'll be back soon," I said demurely to Mrs. Covington. "This shouldn't take long."

"I dare say it won't," she replied.

"Does she think you're a quick study or a hopeless case?" Mrs. Halldorson asked.

"Hopeless case. She doesn't hold a high opinion of ladies such as myself."

Mrs. Halldorson pulled ingredients from the pantry and set them on the table. "Why? Are you a doxy?"

Nils choked on his coffee. "Ma! Miss McKenzie's a property owner. A proper lady."

"No offense. Of course, the way some landed people marry off their daughters to the highest bidder, is there much difference?"

"Fortunately, my father believed in marrying for love. Mother believes you can love a rich man as well as a poor one."

She cut her eyes to her son knowingly. "Proper lady or not, you should know how to cook. You might not always have servants. I brought some of my favorite receipts." She pushed a small sheaf of papers toward me, which was a true treasure not only for the content but also for the paper.

"Thank you. I'll pay you for these." I pored over the pages written in small, careful letters to get as much on a page as possible.

She waved the idea away. "No need. Nils told me what you've been doing for these boys. Now pay attention. Butter or lard. Size of two hen eggs. Measure your dry ingredients. When you get used to making them, you can eyeball, but at first, measure. Two quarts of flour, two tablespoons cream of tartar, teaspoon of salt or so. Two teaspoons of soda dissolved in warm water. Mix up your dry ingredients and cut the lard in. Then add your buttermilk. Enough to make a soft dough. Don't overwork it. Roll it out on a floured board and cut out the biscuits. I use a glass."

I was paying close attention to her and following along on the receipt to fix it in my mind.

"Bake twenty minutes or so."

"Clear as mud," I said. "I'll practice when I get home."

"I'm sure you will," she said unconvincingly, "but I promised Nils I'd show you."

I should be insulted at the lack of faith, but there was just cause. "I tried to learn to cook when I was a girl. Mother threw a fit because it would ruin my skin."

"Yes, because perfect hands are so important." She looked at her son like, "What useless bit of fluff did you drag home this time?" and glanced at her own hands, which had seen a lifetime of labor.

"Mrs. Halldorson, thank you for taking the time to teach me. I promise I'll learn. I'll add your receipts to my collection. Who knows? Maybe someday we'll publish a cookbook."

She laughed. "Wouldn't that be something? Ingrid Halldorson's biscuit receipt in a book."

We continued making biscuits until A.J. dashed into the kitchen to fetch me. I flew to the next floor on Hermes' wings. Constant was so ashen I feared I'd missed him, but his eyes fluttered open when I spoke. "You're here." He attempted a smile. His breathing was shallow and labored, stopping and starting as if the spirit warred with the body about whether to stay or go. Efram sat praying with his friend's hand in his.

A.J. set a chair on the other side of the bed opposite Efram. I took Constant's hand. He had burned with fever since I first met him, but the hand was cold and clammy now as if he were dying by degrees. I kissed his forehead. The fever was broken, but too late to save him. "Yes, I told you I'd come. I didn't want to interrupt your time with Efram."

"Pah, he's no count."

Efram protested his ill treatment.

"What do you want me to do?" I asked.

"See to it my wishes are carried out. I've been with Judith. She's waiting." His chest rose and fell raggedly with the effort of talking.

"You'll see Judith soon." I prayed familiar psalms with him while Efram whispered along with me. Would I ever be able to open a psalm again without thinking of these men?

"It's so beautiful," Constant whispered. "Let us cross over." His hand tightened on mine, and he breathed out his spirit. His face relaxed into perfect peace, the most wondrous smile of contentment on his wan lips. I laid my head on his chest and sobbed, soaking his shirt with my useless tears. There was a muffled shuffling around me, but I stayed wrapped around him. Even through my wretched weeping, I recognized Nils's tread behind me. He laid his hand on my shoulder. "Miss McKenzie, it's not good to hold on to the dead too long. You should let go. His captain sent men for him." He squeezed my shoulder gently.

With great reluctance, I let go of the hand that still clasped mine. "I promised I'd see to his arrangements."

"I'll take care of it, Miss McKenzie," Efram said. "He's safe with me."

I allowed myself to be led away, not caring where I landed.

"Good grief, what happened?" Mrs. Brodie exclaimed when she saw me.

"Constant died," Nils said.

Boneless, I slumped onto a bench. Mrs. Brodie delivered a mug of tea. I thanked her, took a sip, and laid down my head, hoping maybe I could gather the fortitude to walk home. Mrs. Covington raced in a few minutes later. "Where's Jos? Has anyone seen him?"

There was a chorus of noes. The boy was usually underfoot and always joined me when I read either to the book club or individuals, but now seemed to be missing when needed.

"What happened to you?"

"Constant died," I replied, sitting up and drinking more tea to shore myself up for the berating I knew was coming.

"This is why I tell you all not to get attached. It ruins you."

"I'm sorry I'm not as strong as you. I don't know how you do it. I don't know how the doctors do it. I can't."

"We have to. Our hearts are benumbed of necessity, or we'd go mad, and these men need us." She sat beside me. "I'm sorry, I know you liked him, but praise God his suffering is ended." She surveyed the kitchen. "No one has seen Jos?"

"What do you need him for?"

"Mrs. Randall burned all the bandages instead of washing them yesterday, and this morning we're out."

"Reliable Randall?" I stifled a bitter laugh. Mrs. Covington crowed with delight yesterday when the older woman showed up. Reliable, steady, not given to fluff and foolery. If only she had ten more Mrs. Randalls!

"Old Reliable has been sent down the road to ruin someone else's life. I need Jos to go to Miss Josephine's and get bandages. Antony was supposed to bring them yesterday. What is it with these boys?"

"I'll go," I said and pushed myself away from the table. "I need to get away."

"Miss Josephine's is a—"

"I know, a bawdy house. We pass by it on the way here."

"Come to my office."

Her head swiveled back and forth, taking stock of her empire as we passed. There was no small Black boy to be seen anywhere. She was saddled with me.

An empty basket that usually held bandages sat on her desk. She unlocked the property drawer and fished out my purse. "Take your gun. Sometimes the men around there get liquored up."

Miss Josephine's wasn't far from the hospital, so I decided to walk. Regardless of the current trade, the house was in a nicer part of town. The residents who remained in the area complained about various businesses taking their neighbor's homes, but the Federals had other things to worry about, and truth be known, they probably felt a little salt in the wound for the uppity secessionists was good for them. I diverted my mind away from that with cares for Constant. With any luck, his body would be shipped before his mother arrived.

With my mind so engaged, I was at the house before I knew it and looked either way to see if anyone was watching me before turning into the alley to the back entrance. I certainly didn't want to be seen walking into the front door of a bawdy house. Most people were off the street and inside for supper. Someone cooked ham nearby. My mouth watered. A young colored boy promptly answered my knock and went wide-eyed when he saw me. "Yas'm? You lost?"

"Is this Miss Josephine's?"

"Who's there, Antony?" a woman called out.

"A lady calling, Miss."

The middle-aged woman who might grace any senator's arm at any Washington function appeared presently and smiled. "Hello, darling. How can I help? Please tell me you're looking for work."

"No, ma'am. I'm looking for bandages. Mrs. Covington sent me."

She wheeled around and frowned at the boy. "Did you not deliver those yesterday?"

"I plumb forgot with Miss Daisy and that soldier falling out the window and all." He shrugged his hands in the air.

She shooed the excuse away with her fan. "He can bring them."

I held up my basket. "I'm already here. One of the volunteers burned the dirty bandages instead of washing them, so they're in a dither."

"Oh, dear. I'll have the girls roll more, but several are ready now. Maybe that'll get you through."

Two girls in chemises stood in the background assessing me and whispering. An attractive woman in a blue silk wrapper walked into the room eating a cinnamon roll. She had a round baby doll face with large, tawny eyes like a great cat, and I couldn't help thinking I'd met her before. Surely, I'd remember.

"I was rolling bandages while I sat with Daisy last night," the woman said. "They're in my room." She broke off part of a cinnamon roll for the boy. He wolfed it down and sucked the remnants from his fingers.

"Antony," Miss Josephine said, "go fetch those bandages. Wash your hands first so you don't get sticky on them." She waited until the boy scampered out of the room. "Elly, you girls must stop feeding him treats. He's going to be round as a pumpkin."

Elly dipped her fingers in the wash basin near the stove. "What does it hurt to mother him a bit?"

The basket was loaded up with carefully packed bandages until we couldn't get another roll in, and Elly tucked a napkin over all. I thanked them and hurried away, anxious to get back as it was already getting late. Shadows were deepening, especially in the alley. A few steps away from Miss Josephine's, I heard someone following me. The steps were light, but unmistakably in my wake. I turned, prepared to confront whoever was behind me, and nearly dropped the basket. "J.B. What are you doing here?"

"I came to thee Mama. Thyee workth here. Don't tell Gammy. It'th a thecret. I brought Mama thinnamon rollth."

Of course. I should have recognized the resemblance. The tawny eyes were unmistakable. "I see. No, I won't tell her, but you should hurry home before it gets dark. Gammy will worry if you're late for supper."

"Yeth, ma'am." He scurried away in the opposite direction, and I resumed my trek. I'd ask him later about how he'd found his mother. Footsteps again. I whirled. "J.B.! You need—" Dear Lord. The last person I expected or needed. Fulkirk. The look of hatred sent a shiver to my core and set me to flight, but he raced ahead of me and blocked my way.

"I see you remember me."

"Major—" I tried to duck around him.

"Fulkirk, but not a major anymore." He grabbed my wrist before I could escape. "Lieutenant. Thanks to you. Your Rebs killed my brother," he growled. "You ruined my life, you little Secesh bitch. Now, I'm going to ruin yours." He slammed me against the building wall, pinning me with his body while he fumbled with his belt, his face corded with fury and breath reeking with liquor. "Scream; no one will care. Women scream here all the time. It'll give me a reason to cut your throat."

He was right. No one would come, and I was surprised to find I suddenly no longer cared. Too tired to fight. There was a cold stone where my soul used to be. The dragon fire that usually lived there was gone. This terrible war no one would survive had stolen it. "Do it. I don't care," I whispered. I turned my eyes and waited. When I did, I caught J.B.'s wide, golden eyes staring at me in fright at the end of the alley.

"Leave Mith Lorena alone. Thtop hurting her."

Fulkirk turned to look at the boy, his beard scraping across my face. His breath was hot, whiskeyed, rasping, "Go away, idiot, or I'll kill you, too."

"J.B., run, go away!"

"No!" He ran toward us, and I knew Fulkirk wouldn't hesitate to use the knife he was pulling out. He lurched toward J.B., towing me along even as I dug my heels in and pulled back. Fury rose, reviving the fire. I kicked at him and punched his arm, trying to hit his face, but he kept hold of my wrist, jerking me closer to him. My hip smashed into his holstered gun. I stomped on his foot, trying to distract him long enough to get his gun. He let go of my wrist and struck me in the face, sending me reeling into the wall. My breath whooshed out and struggled to return. He was nearly to J.B., who had stopped, unsure of what to do when I pulled my dragoon from my purse.

"I will blow your head off if you touch him!"

Fulkirk wheeled in a crouch, surprisingly fast, and threw the knife that glanced off my arm. The gun I had aimed at his chest fired and hit him in the knee instead. I wanted to empty it in him, to grab up the knife and stab him until my arm fell off and might have if not for J.B.

Clutching his knee, Fulkirk fell to the ground, blood gushing through his fingers, cursing and promising to kill me. I darted over and jerked his gun out of the holster and tossed it out of his reach.

"You may kill me, but not today, you pig." He tried to grab me, but I slipped away from him. "J.B." I said, clutching his trembling shoulders, "You run home as fast as you can and don't tell anyone what happened. This is our secret, like our secret about Mama, right?"

"Yeth, ma'am." His terrified eyes were owl-wide, but he turned and ran, arms flailing.

Gathering my basket, I hurried out the other end of the alley before someone found me with a shot Union officer. With any luck, Fulkirk would bleed out like the dog he was.

Mrs. Covington wasn't about when I arrived, so I slipped my gun behind some books on a shelf and collapsed. If only I could run like J.B., arms windmilling through the air, but I doubted I could make another step.

"There you are," Mrs. Covington boomed. She snatched up the basket, her face crinkling into concern. "What's wrong with you?"

"N-Nothing."

The office door thudded closed behind her. "What happened?"

"Nothing." I looked at my hands in my lap, refusing to meet her gaze.

"I don't have time for this. Tell me. You look like the blood's been drained from your body."

"It nearly was." Haltingly, I told her the entire ghastly story. "I'm a Secesh. With the Federals stinging from their whipping, do you believe I'd get a fair hearing for shooting an officer?"

"I'm as blue as they come, Pennsylvania born and bred, but you're right. Finish out the day normally to avoid questions. We'll figure out a way to get you out of town. Come eat even if you don't feel up to it. I'll get the doctor out early."

"Yes, ma'am."

"Where's your gun?"

I pointed to the bookcase.

She locked it up with the rest of my belongings, though I would have preferred it stayed hidden.

Supper was the biscuits we cooked earlier and potato soup. It was creamy and hearty, but I could barely swallow it past the lump in my throat.

Letter writing was something I could manage without effort, so I gathered up my lap desk as soon as I could escape. I was on my second letter; this one was a joy, as the man was a natural comedian. He explained his mother was a widow and worried constantly about him, so he tried to make her laugh.

"Have you told her about your wound?"

He looked at his missing arm. "I told her I was shot in the arm. Not that they took it. She'll know soon enough when she sees me. Back to the vedette adventure."

"Miss McKenzie?" Mrs. Covington stood in the doorway grim-faced with a Yankee lieutenant who even more sober-looking.

"May I finish the letter? We're almost done."

"Mrs. Hampton can finish for you," she said quietly. "We need you to come." Her face was drawn as if she was about to tell me my dog just died.

I steeled myself for arrest.

"Yes, ma'am." With a brief pat for my patient, I excused myself.

Mrs. Covington's shoulders, always taut as an inspecting general in the best of times, were even stiffer now. The lieutenant fell into step behind me as if he feared I might turn and make a mad dash for freedom.

We settled into chairs in Mrs. Covington's office, and another soldier took up position outside the door. I walked to the window and peered out.

"Are you looking for something, Miss?" the lieutenant asked.

"I'm looking to see if there's another guard outside the window."

"Do I need one?"

"You don't need one outside the door, but there he is."

"Lieutenant Fulkirk was found shot earlier and mentioned your name. Do you know him?"

I continued to stare out the window and prayed they couldn't see the blood draining from my face in the reflection. "I met a Major Fulkirk a few months ago. He was transferred to Washington due to an incident I was involved in."

"And what was the incident?"

"He was being an insufferable ass and insisted Doctor Boudreaux vacate his house while he was trying to save a woman. I pulled a gun on the major to make him leave the doctor alone. The woman died due to his interference, and the commander shipped Fulkirk to Washington."

"You admit you own a gun?"

"Yes, sir."

"It's right here," Mrs. Covington said.

Appalled, I turned, staring at her, mouth open as my stomach flipped like a fish on a riverbank. I knew she didn't respect me, but to so willingly betray me? She rummaged around in the drawer and pulled out my Deringer.

He smelled it. "This hasn't been fired recently."

I kept my poker face and my back straight. Inside, I was on the verge of crumbling. "Two days ago? You know Deringers."

"May I ask where you've been today?"

"She's been here since seven this morning," Mrs. Covington volunteered.

"Doing what?"

I sank into the nearest chair and shrugged my hands in my lap, trying to recall what all I'd done. "I emptied bedpans, filled water jugs, dressed wounds, made biscuits, wrote letters, read to the men, and sat with a dying man. The same as I do every day."

"I find it a bit difficult to believe a lady such as you dresses wounds, empties bedpans, and bakes biscuits."

"Come," Mrs. Covington said. We followed her to Ward A. "Did Miss McKenzie deal with any of you today?"

There was a chorus of replies naming what all I'd done. I expected someone to call out I had danced with them and sang with a heavenly host.

"Impressive," the lieutenant said. "I'm surprised you're not skin and bones. I still don't believe you dress wounds and bake."

"Hmph. All of my ladies work like field hands. Dr. Craig is the supervisor. You can ask him." Mrs. Covington scooted off toward the kitchen, motioning us to follow. There she addressed Mrs. Halldorson, "Did Miss McKenzie help bake biscuits today?"

"Yes. If not for her help, we wouldna got all them done."

His jaundiced look showed he still didn't believe me.

I started rattling off the receipt as best I could remember. "Two quarts of flour, two teaspoons of soda dissolved in warm water, a teaspoon of salt—"

"All right." He held up his hand to stop the baking lesson.

We trooped back out of the kitchen and past a small group of men with towels on their way to bathe in the courtyard. Travis Williams was among them and raised a brow at my escort. "Ah, Miss McKenzie. So, they've discovered your crime. Will you be tried or directly hanged?"

The lieutenant stopped. "What crime is this?"

"Why, sir, she danced the Charming waltz with me in the moonlight not a night before."

"I wonder how smart you'll be once you hit Washington?" the officer snapped and nudged me along.

Unbothered by the threat, Travis laughed, slapping his thigh.

We landed back in Mrs. Covington's office with only a smattering of half-hearted further questions along the way. "I don't know why he mentioned your name," the lieutenant said, "but you have plenty of alibis. It's a bit of a mystery, wouldn't you say?"

"It sounds to me like he was either confused or deliberately trying to lay revenge on Miss McKenzie," Mrs. Covington said. "Perhaps you can question him when he wakes."

"They took his leg, so who knows when that will be. He lost a lot of blood. Regardless, we have other things to do."

"Yes, I'm sure you do," Mrs. Covington replied.

There was a crash of metal on stone, shooting, and shouting as if a riot had broken out. "What the deuce?" The lieutenant said. "Is there a brawl in the street?"

Gunshots. More shouting.

"That's in the courtyard," Mrs. Covington said, racing toward the sound.

The wrought iron gate lay in the street. Patients, orderlies, guards, and kitchen staff milled around in the courtyard, talking and pointing.

"What happened?" demanded the lieutenant.

"Some masked riders came galloping in with ropes," said Hugh, who still stood with his gun in his hand. "They pulled down the gate and gathered up the three Rebs that were getting ready to take a bath. Said they were going to string the bastards up and rode off with them. They'll be dancing in the wind before you catch them."

"Damned if they are," he said, striding off.

I took a step, faltered, and felt myself going lifeless as lint.

Chapter Fifty-Seven

The last thing I remembered was the sound of shouting and feet pounding through the halls. When I came to, I was lying on Mrs. Covington's bed, the scent of lavender soap sharp and familiar. Her calm, steady voice broke through my haze.

"The lieutenant had the good grace to scoop you up and run back here, though he did dump you rather like a sack of potatoes. I called for Doctor Boudreaux and fetched smelling salts to bring you around."

Once the doctor arrived, she locked the door and explained what had happened with the shooting. She was remarkably calm as if this happened every day. It probably did, just not to one of her nurses.

"He tried to rape me," I said weakly but remained silent about him threatening to kill Boy, which had been my true reason.

"I didn't think you'd start murdering Federals for no excuse, but it's still a mess." He tugged at his beard like he did when he was thinking. "Mrs. Covington is right. We have to get you out of town."

"I'll handle that," she said. "I don't like calling in favors, but Dr. Covington saved the Springfield ticket master's daughter when they were near destitute. He vowed if I ever needed anything after Frank died, he would be there for me. We'll get a ticket, no questions asked." She hastily scribbled out a note and handed it to me. "If Dr. Boudreaux can get you there before seven-thirty, you'll get a ticket."

I nodded weakly, still in shock from the entire episode.

With methodical precision, Dr. Boudreaux left instructions for his most crucial patients and vowed he'd return as quickly as possible. Though he said nothing about the lynching, I could tell it was wearing on him. The three men were popular patients and especially favored by him for their uncomplaining, genial ways.

Mrs. Covington slipped a note into my quivering hand as I was leaving. "Mrs. Brodie's sourdough bread receipt. Heaven knows what you're going to do with it, but Godspeed, girl." She gave me a quick hug and hurried away before I could respond.

Once home, I packed necessities, the message bolero bound for Richmond, and a change of clothes, peering fretfully out the window at each noise near the house as I did so. Traveling without extra clothes made me nervous, but there was no other option. Doctor Boudreaux would forward the rest of my belongings. "You know you always have a place here," he said and hugged me tightly. "Do you have enough money?"

"Yes, sir."

"Take this, just in case. You never know." He handed me another sixty dollars over my protestations. "Put it someplace safe."

The rest of the household hugged me and cried until the doctor demanded they release me so I could go. "Women. I swear. She's going home, not to the gallows." He flinched and mouthed a wordless apology.

I clutched his hand. "Thank you for everything. Be safe."

Silver guided me out of town on the doctor's horse to Springfield Station. We spoke little on the two-hour ride, but I often heard muted whisperings of prayers. I passed the note from Mrs. Covington to the ticket master. He frowned but agreed to do what he could and got me a seat on the next train to Richmond.

"Be well, Miss Lorena," Silver said. He had refused to leave me until he knew I was at the station. "Angels wing you safely home."

The O&A wouldn't be here until 7:30 in the morning if it was on time, and trains seldom were these days with the military commandeering them at will. Even so, I didn't dare try to find a room and slept in the depot.

Not surprisingly, the car I shuffled into was filled to the gunnels, but I was so thankful to be out of Alexandria I would have ridden in a livestock car or on top of one. Making my way to an open seat, I scanned faces for anyone familiar or paying particular attention to me. There were only cursory glances of interest as I passed by men and women alike, and one fat, friendly baby who held his arms up to me. Nothing made me suspicious. At my seat, I slid my bag under it and scooted over near the window so I could watch for followers. No one seemed to be hurrying in my wake.

A soldier with his arm in a sling asked to sit next to me. He was so wan he looked about to collapse.

"Of course." I offered him a sandwich from the packet Mrs. Bastrom sent, which he gratefully accepted. He'd barely finished it and mumbled a heartfelt thanks again before he nodded off. I wished I could also, but I knew I would only dream.

I inhaled deeply. Somewhere near me, a woman had bathed in Florida Water to the point I felt immersed in a citrus orchard. Smoke (coal and cigar), bay rum, unwashed bodies, leather, vinegar—someone was eating pickled eggs. Overall, I was sure I could smell my own fear.

Opposite me, a young couple sat discussing some exciting travel plans. A conductor leaned down and whispered to the man and handed him a note. "Yes, of course," he said, and they followed the conductor off the train. Their places were promptly taken by a businessman, by the look of him, with an older lady who held a large carpet bag clutched protectively in her lap. They had claimed the last vacant seats. My poor soldier awakened only when someone thoughtlessly bumped into his arm as they passed by in the aisle.

"Do you want me to sit there?" I asked.

"Would you mind terribly," he replied, ashen-faced.

Though I normally enjoyed the scenery during train travel, and Virginia was particularly beautiful in this summer, there was nothing out the window to hold my attention today. It had to be pulled down to get a breath of air, which unfortunately meant it sucked the ash and cinders straight in. I wished for a bit of the soldier's laudanum so I could sleep too, but felt I should be drinking pots of coffee to stay on alert to see if anyone had followed me. How would I even know?

I looked around again as best I could, but no one seemed the least bit interested in me.

The man opposite me flipped his newspaper and continued to read. Presently, I noticed the woman's carpet bag starting to move of its own volition as if it were alive. Blinking rapidly to clear my eyes and imagination, I looked away and then back. It was still moving. Had a snake somehow slithered its way into the bag? With some difficulty, as the soldier had slumped over against me asleep, I slipped my hand into my pocket to the Deringer.

The woman opened the bag, and a tiny, fluffy orange head popped out. "Fifi," she crooned, "are you awake?"

"Mother," the man warned, lowering his paper, "don't let that pup loose. You'll never get her back in this crowd."

"Oh, how sweet. May I pet her?"

The woman pushed the pup out toward me, and I held her closely to my heart, hugging and kissing her. The tiny mite, thrilled to be out of the cocoon, licked my face until I thought her tongue might wear out. "I needed this so much."

My nerves, while not relaxed, at least eased. Reluctantly, I kissed the puppy and handed it back, whereupon she put it back in the bag. "I'm going to necessary," she said and departed, taking the bag with her.

The man shook his head and set his paper aside. "I bought her the little thing to try and calm her a bit over all this unpleasantness. She won't believe I'm too old to be called and weeps without ceasing. Hamilton Cantrell. Ham. That was my mother, Fern."

"It's unsettling, I'm sure." She shouldn't have worried. Although he looked quite fit, he was graying at the temples, matching his salt-and-pepper beard. The army wouldn't press him even if it went that far. I motioned toward the paper. "Are you finished with that?"

"No good news, I fear," he said, handing it to me.

If Baron's name hadn't appeared on a casualty list by now, it wouldn't, but I had to check anyway. I glanced at various headlines, making note of a few I would come back to. Casualty list. Page five. You'd think it would be of more import. The list was shrinking. Thank the Lord for that. I ran my finger down the alphabet. *A—B—C—Calhoun, Call, Callahan, Baron Patrick, Cpt. 5th Vg. Dec.*

My hands trembled so I could barely read the notice again. It couldn't be. The paper dropped from my lifeless fingers. My breath caught in my throat until I felt like I was choking.

A hundred images went through my mind. My beautiful Baron dead? I could see him looking down at me the last time we were together. That handsome face. Me laying my head on his chest, his arms wrapped around me. The mangled bodies in the hospital. How had he died? Images of battle. Charging into the fray. Cannon fire. Musket shot. Walls of sulfurous flame and lead dealing death. Did he die alone? Oh, dear God. His poor, crumpled body on the battlefield.

"Miss, are you all right?" He glanced at the fallen paper. "Someone you know?"

I nodded, sobbing now. Shoulders bobbing, I curled in on myself and tried to bury my face. My seatmate woke up and fumbled for a handkerchief. "Miss, what's wrong?"

"Casualty list," the older man replied.

"Oh, good God. I'm sorry." He handed me his handkerchief and awkwardly tried to comfort me.

I wanted to howl and scream and beat something, but instead collapsed into him. He twisted in his seat to hold me as best he could.

"Here now. What's going on?" Mrs. Cantrell demanded.

"Casualty list, Mother. Someone she knew."

"Oh, dear. Let me get my smelling salts. Young man, turn loose of her before you do something to that arm."

"I don't need—" I said.

I was shuffled out of my seat and into her arms despite my protestations, whereupon she fully revived me with her vile smelling salts. The soldier gratefully took his place beside the other man and held the bag and dog, instead of a distraught woman.

"It probably would have been a mercy had you allowed her to remain semi-senseless, Mother."

"Shush, Sam. I know what I'm doing."

"Yes, ma'am."

Through the fog of grief, I wondered if I had misheard her but could not hold on to the thought. My heart and soul and what was left of my mind flew only to Baron.

"It's God's will," Mrs. Cantrell said for the umpteenth time until I wanted to scream. "You'll see your loved one again in the by and by." I kept my head against the window Hamilton had mercifully closed and pretended to doze in hopes she would shut up before I murdered her. I didn't want Baron in the by and by; I wanted him now. When I wasn't weeping or feigning sleep, I did doze only to tour once again the nightmare battlefield of my mind searching for Baron. Had that nightmare in Alexandria been a warning? It was gray and hazy with the smoke of war still hanging low over it. I turned over one ravaged body after another looking for him, calling his name. Dead eyes stared up at me. Dead hands seemed to reach out for me. Dead bodies of every manner seeded the field of death, but not the one I searched for.

I arrived in Richmond exhausted and barely functioning. My soldier led me off the train and wished me well, plainly distressed at the inadequacy of words. "Thank you for your kindness. You're worn thin as a wasp wing yourself, thanks in no small part to my emotions, I'm sure. Please, go on to your family. I'll be fine. God bless you."

He smiled uncertainly but hurried away toward a group of waving people.

"You're not fine. Let me help you. Where do you need to go?"

I looked around, surprised to see Mr. Cantrell standing behind me with the pup. "No, I'm sure your mother needs you."

"Not at all. She's off to meet her sister while I babysit Fifi. Where to?"

"Oh, I need to go home. Winchester. Food might be nice." I tried to think. Did I need to do anything else besides leave the bolero?

"Let me check with the ticket master, but I doubt you'll get out of here at all." There was, not surprisingly, no train available to Strasburg. Check back tomorrow, I was told. With wounded men stumping down the street and the new capitol establishing itself, Richmond was more chaotic than Charleston on the brink of war.

I would have joyfully accepted him wounded... missing a limb.

"You'll need a hack and a room. Let's see what we can do."

"Yes, I need a room and a bath, but I can do it, really."

He waved off the hack I started toward. "He's expensive and will take advantage of you. Cyrus will be along directly, I'm sure. You can trust him. Here he comes now." He looked down at me with fatherly eyes and put his arm around my shoulders. "Come." Motioning to the older carriage he guided me toward. "Cyrus. This lady needs your help. A room with access to a bath. Someplace to eat. I need you to take care of her."

"Sure, Ham. Might be able to get you something at the Spottswood, but it won't be much. They're nigh stacking people up three high. Anything for a dollar."

The Spottswood was one of the newer hotels. As such, it was rather austere on the exterior, which I found depressing as I enjoyed grander architecture. It looked like a huge brick box with five rows of identical windows. There was no colonnade and no grand entry amongst the shop entrances on the ground floor. The interior, however, was quite elegant, and it boasted all the latest amenities: toilets, gas lighting and heating, running water. I'd be happy if they had anything.

"I don't care as long as I have a bit of privacy and a bed. I won't be here long."

"I'll check in on you later," Cantrell said as he shut the door.

Cyrus carried my bags into the hotel. "Hey, Jack. This lady needs a room."

"Full up."

He leaned across the desk. "You and I both know that's not right. You're holding on to those last rooms for desperate moneybags to come in and offer you a fat bribe. This lady has the money to pay for the room, and she needs it. Stop being greedy."

"That's not it at all," the clerk protested indignantly but scanned a register. "I might be able to put her on the top floor, but it's a tiny room. You'll have to hang your clothes on a hook."

"I just need a bed and a way to wash. How much?"

I was sure part of the wildly inflated price was going into Jack's pocket, but I tipped him anyway to let him know I might be worthwhile. With my bag stowed in the room, not much more than a closet, I set off for the tailor shop.

Cyrus had waited outside the hotel while I stowed my meager possessions, visiting with another hack driver. He thought I looked frail as a hand-me-down ragdoll and needed help more than some simpering fool who needed a good walk.

The woman in the tailor shop accepted the bolero with the message for Miss Hattaway without batting an eye. It sounded perfectly normal to anyone who might be listening, as I was not retrieving more information nor meeting anyone. She would pass the information along to the next link in the chain. Nothing more was needed. Thank God. I could not have done more had they held a gun to my head.

"I reckon you need food," Cyrus said when I reappeared.

"Yes, please." I had no real desire to eat, but, aside from that sandwich, it had been nearly twenty-four hours since my last meal, and I knew I needed something.

"There's good eating places nearby, but the hotel has a nice dining room."

"The hotel's fine. I'll let you get on with your business."

"I'll be around if you need me."

I paid him handsomely as I needed an advocate and appreciated him interceding for my room. The hotel was swarming with people waiting for the dining room, and I wondered if I should have found another place to eat. Upper crust, an abundance of politicians and military men milled about in the lobby. I recognized many of them but approached none, being in no mood for gay conversation.

"Miss McKenzie!"

An elderly woman waved frantically at me. She stood with an equally elderly lady who smiled and beckoned me over eagerly like a street vendor with sweets to a child. The woman knew me, so I wended my way through the crowd. As I neared, I realized it was Mrs. Milton from Fairfax Court-House, but my stars, what a shamble. Her immaculate little curls were gone, and instead the hair fluttered in sad wisps around her face and eyes like an overgrown horse's forelock.

"Mrs. Milton. It's good to see you."

"Oh, darling. I've worried so much about you. This is my sister, Alma Rommel." She pushed the hair out of her eyes, but it settled back like a sheepdog's. Her sister tucked the strands in her cap.

"You need to let me trim that hair," Alma chided.

"You're not cutting my hair. You've always been jealous of it. Just help me fix it."

"You know my fingers are too rheumatic to make those little curls. Be reasonable."

"Perhaps I can help with that later?" I offered.

Her face lit. "Oh, would you? I've been in such a dither." She held up a blanketed bundle in her arms.

"You have a baby?" I said incredulously.

She pulled the blanket free to reveal Thomas, the golden tabby cat with his wide, green eyes. The ears were singed and matted, as was his fur, burned to the skin in places.

The cat tried to meow at me but finished with a pitiable wheeze.

"What happened?" I asked in shock.

"Yankees! That's what happened." Mrs. Milton kissed Thomas on the head. "They burned my house and Thomas, too. Caesar tried to stop them, but they went wild. They broke everything they could. Stole anything of value. Sliced paintings as if they were assassinating us. Why they even hauled my beautiful piano out in the yard, and some fool reared his horse up on it and shouted, 'Lookee here, boys. My horse is playing piana." She shook her head. "Any fool knows a horse can't play piano."

"Mrs. Milton. Mrs. Rommel. Your table's ready." The waiter stood in the door to the dining room looking around, ready to give it away to any of the number of people crowding around him begging for a table. Nearby, Mrs. Chesnut stopped complaining and looked longingly at the waiter.

"Here," I shouted like a farm auctioneer.

"Will you join us?" Mrs. Rommel asked.

"Yes, thank you."

She patted her sister's arm. "Dear, why don't you put Thomas in the room? We don't want him getting frightened and flying over tables again."

Mrs. Rommel escorted me into the dining room before we lost our table. I smiled amiably at the people glaring that we had claimed our place.

"I'm surprised Letitia recognized you," Mrs. Rommel said. "Her mind comes and goes like the spring tide."

"Really?"

Mrs. Rommel ordered tea for them and looked to see if anyone was listening. "Yes, she's on the verge of madness, I fear. The Rebs started to torch supplies, but there was no need for the Yanks to pillage civilian houses and destroy them. They continued to Germantown, where I live. Lived. They burned my house straight to the ground like a bunch of barbarians."

"Dear heavens. No wonder she's confused."

"Caesar refused to leave her house. I suppose he thought they'd leave it unmolested if he stayed, but they didn't. Thomas stayed, Caesar stayed, and both would have burned to death if Nana hadn't gone screaming into the flames after them. She dragged them both out by the scruff of the neck with her skirts smoldering. Caesar sat down in a lawn chair and watched the house go up. When Nana looked around, he was having a brain storm, flames flickering in his dead eyes like some haint mirror. He never roused."

Mrs. Milton peered closely at me when she returned. "What's wrong with you? You look like you've been dragged down a corduroy road and back again."

Tears welled again, and I ducked my head. I wiped at my eye with the napkin and sighed. "I just found out my fiancé was killed at Manassas. It's been such a blow. He was my soul. I don't—I don't know how I'll go on."

She put her cup down and hugged me. "Oh, sweet girl. I'm so sorry. This damnable war. I took to my bed for a week after Ruff died. Alma had to come drag me from it and threaten me with all manner of vile punishments if I didn't shore up. You're stronger than that. You have to be. You have people who depend on you."

"When you feel yourself going, lock yourself away, cry for five minutes, and then get back to work," Alma offered. "It's the only way you'll survive."

We enjoyed dinner as best we could with Mrs. Milton in full presence of mind as if nothing had happened. She occasionally jumped at a loud noise, but nothing unusual other than fretting about Thomas incessantly. Had her sister exaggerated the situation?

I forced myself to at least eat some soup, leaving the salad staring at me unmolested. "I'll go to the apothecary to get a tea for Thomas. We can wash and curl your hair after that," I offered.

She clapped her hands like a small child. "Yes, please. Company's coming later."

Mrs. Rommel shrugged the tiniest bit at me in a who-knows way.

"We'll get you all prettied up then," I said.

Thomas was in such poor condition, I felt he needed something for pain and his poor scorched lungs more than anything, but I bought some salve anyway. As soon as Mrs. Milton's hair was washed and curled, I repaired to my room for a nap. I felt like an eight-day clock on day nine. Sleep would not come. Each time I closed my eyes, I saw Baron again and began to weep anew.

The next morning, the desk clerk looked up from the ledger he was working on before I said a word. "No, Miss McKenzie. I sent a boy to beg a ticket for you, but they have nothing. We'll check again in the morning."

"Thank you." I laid coins on the counter for him and the runner. He flipped the half dollar to the boy sitting in the corner and pocketed the rest. Not that I was the suspicious type, but I would go to the station later to ask, plead, beg, and bribe if I needed to. I would buy a horse, but there were none to be found from overheard conversations.

Mrs. Milton and her sister were seated in chairs outside the dining room, nearly hidden by a gaggle of officers and their ladies gathered in the lobby laughing and carrying on as if they were at a social club instead of in the middle of a war. I made my way through the throng of people toward my companions, who looked as weary as I felt. Mrs. Rommel spied me and waved. Mrs. Milton's hair was frothy perfection, giving her back some sense of normalcy. She teetered on the edge of emotional collapse, however. It was a precipice I recognized as I was standing right there with her.

"Lorena, there you are." Mrs. Milton said. "Alma has a table for us."

"Excellent, how's Thomas doing?" I asked, hoping the tea had eased his labored breathing.

Mrs. Milton threw her hands in the air. "That tea was perfect. He drank it and lay in my lap like he does, purring away. I woke up this morning, and that scamp was out mousing somewhere! I'm sure he'll be back soon to go to Fairfax with Ruff. He'll be happier at home."

Alma shook her head and mouthed no during all this. She drew her finger across her throat. How long would she be able to hide the cat's death?

"He's going to Fairfax?"

She nodded enthusiastically, her faithfully restored curls bobbing about. "Yes, Ruff and Billy are rebuilding the house. It was a shame to lose it, of course, but Ruff said he'll build one even better and just two stories since we're getting older. Caesar isn't a spring chicken either." She brightened like a child seeing a circus clown. "Ruff said Caesar has been so helpful. He's been climbing up and down the ladder bringing them nails and lemonade. He sat up on the roof with them and talked about how pretty the flowers are." She laughed. "Can you imagine three men sitting up on a roof like birds talking about flowers?"

"Yes, but first we're going to take you to live with Augusta for a while, right?" Alma said, patting her hand. "Your daughter's so anxious to show off that new grandbaby."

I stood dumbfounded. Mrs. Milton had stepped off the edge without me, and I doubted she was coming back. Maybe she was the fortunate one.

I was shaken out of shock by Mary Chesnut ranting about something. Again. "They should all be arrested, speedily tried, and shot for treason," Mrs. Chesnut declared loudly so everyone might hear her valued opinion. She was holding court as usual, and there was a round of laughter. I looked about to see who should be tried for treason and caught Colonel Chesnut's eye as he tried to distract his wife, but when she had an audience, naught but Jeff Davis himself could shut her down. James Chesnut certainly couldn't, even though he was trying now.

I moved closer, much to Chesnut's horror. His face reddened, and he tried to lead his wife away, but she brushed him off.

"Can you imagine these Yankee bawds riding into camp night and day to deliver valuable information?" Mrs. Chesnut continued.

Yankee bawds! How dare she! I had risked my life to deliver that information.

"General. Oh, general. I have a message of utmost importance for you. Secret dispatch. You must get through to General Beauregard at once!" She trilled all this and acted it out as if she were on stage. With exaggerated drama, she pulled imaginary combs from her hair and shook her head. "Let me take these tucking combs out. The message is hidden within my beautiful hair." She leaned forward conspiratorially, "And of course all these men starved for female companionship nigh swoon when this fabulous waterfall of hair comes tumbling down. Then our little damsel needs someone to cut the message loose, so he has to caress her chestnut locks. What a show that must be, and these men are foolish enough to be swayed by a pretty face and a hank of hair. One of them even rode into General Elzy's camp during the battle! Can you imagine?"

Her audience gasped.

"I have important information," she said in a falsetto voice, fanning her face furiously. "The Yankees are on your flank! You must meet them."

Then, taking the part of the general, she cast her arm out. "Out, out. Get out of my camp, madam, before you are shot to shreds." She looked around knowingly. "At least *he* had a bit of common sense."

An officer I didn't recognize, and one not impressed with her performance, spoke up. "The lady refused to go, saying she didn't care if she was shot; he must listen to her about where the enemy was. He did listen, thankfully, as she was correct. After she left, he said he wished he had a brigade of women such as her who feared neither shot nor bullet, but they would be stampeded by a snake or spider. If a large black snake came along, he'd lose his fearless brigade."

Mrs. Chesnut, refusing to budge, reclaimed the stage. "I don't care. We should take them out and hang them for treason. The next one of these doxies that rides into camp, hang her, and that will put an end to this nonsense."

The more she prattled, the more enflamed I became. Colonel Chesnut attempted to grab his wife's arm again, but she brushed him off like dandruff.

I stalked toward her. "Let me tell you who should be hanged for treason. The next officer who flaps his jaws about what goes on in camp to his gossipy wife so she can spread it like thin jam to anyone who will listen. No woman should know what transpires in an officer's headquarters. Especially a woman who doesn't have enough sense to keep her mouth shut in front of Yankees, reporters, and God knows who else is listening. No doubt every word of how information is being passed will be in Washington by nightfall thanks to your performance."

"Miss McKenzie, you have no right to speak to me—"

"No right? I've just left Alexandria, where I tended wounded from both sides. I've listened to your yipping for two days about what monsters the Yankees are and how noble our boys are. Let me tell you, when they're lying in a hospital with mangled bodies and broken minds, you can't tell the difference. They're men. They're boys who should be back on the farm dreaming about a pretty little girl, not whispering out their last breath calling for Mama. If you fine upstanding ladies are so concerned about the war, why not trot your dainty size threes to a hospital and care for these men you profess to hold so highly instead of fussing about what you'll wear to the next party?"

I pointed to Mrs. Milton, who was still lost in happy reverie. "Mrs. Milton lost her home in Fairfax Court-House, and Mrs. Rommel lost everything she owns in Germantown. These ladies lost everything, and what do they get to listen to? You prattling about how women who carried information that may have saved further destruction, let alone the loss of our armies, should be hanged for treason. The reason you're so upset is because they got notice, and you can't stand not being the center of attention. It's never once crossed your vain mind to cease your endless supper parties and balls and help others."

I surveyed the lobby caustically. All conversation had stopped. People were frozen in shock, mouths open, hands in the air. "I don't even know if my home still stands. Patterson was camped on my doorstep when I left. God help me get out of this detestable city. I swear I'll start walking today to escape this viper's den. If I found out tomorrow McDowell was descending on this place, I wouldn't open my mouth to a single traitorous officer so they could trade the information to their wives for a kind word or pat on the head. Beauregard, Lee, Jackson, or no one. None of the rest can be trusted."

Mrs. Chesnut raised her chin. "Aren't you the righteous little traitor?"

"Yes, I am, if you think I would trust anyone but them after you just proved someone has been revealing secret information to you." Casting a withering look on James, I swiveled back to my companions; Mary's circle swarmed angrily like a stoned hornet's nest, demanding I be taken care of. Instead, the waiter ushered us into the dining room immediately like conquering heroes.

I held out my arm to Mrs. Milton, who looked on the verge of breaking out into rapturous applause.

Chapter Fifty-Eight

My day was spent scrounging for some means out of town but no amount of asking, begging, bribing produced a ticket. I might as well have been tracking Pizarro's gold with equal results. I'd make the rounds again in the morning to find transport out of this asylum. If I had to, I'd buy a spavined mule and set off for Winchester.

With feet and nerves worn wafer thin, I returned to the hotel for a late supper with my ladies and confessed I would miss their company when they left. Even with Mrs. Milton's mind drifting in and out of reality, she was preferable to most who dwelt in the fantasy of how gay life was. Did they not take note of the grieving families arriving daily to collect flag-draped coffins? I wondered for the hundredth time where Baron lay. Had they buried him on the battlefield or sent him home to Georgia? My mind recoiled at the thought of him lying cold and dead any-where when he should be in my arms. I pressed the image out of my mind and swiped at the hot tear welling in my eye. I would have to visit his family.

I thought briefly about purchasing some sleeping powders to escape the nightmares but feared I would medicate to the point of death.

"Miss McKenzie! I have wonderful news."

I turned to see Hamilton Cantrell seated in the lobby, smiling as if he'd married an old maid millionaire with one foot in the grave and the other on marbles. "Oh, and what is that?"

"Are you ready to go home?"

I stared at him in disbelief. "Truly?"

"Truly." He smiled benevolently.

My heart skipped. "Oh, yes," I cried. "Like the girl with the cursed dancing slippers, I am ready for this dance to end." I clasped my hands to my breast. "Have you found a seat on the train?"

"Not quite." His smile broadened at my joy. "But Cyrus has agreed to get you to Atlees, where I've been assured you can get a connection to Strasburg. I'm going that way if you'd like to join me."

"Oh, that's marvelous news. Let me get my bag." Would I ever be able to repay Mr. Cantrell for his kindness? Never in a thousand years.

"Of course, but please hurry. We don't want to miss the train."

I raced up the stairs to my room, nearly knocking two people over, hurriedly apologized, and continued to my cubbyhole, where I threw my few belongings together. I'd sort them into some semblance of order later. Mrs. Rommel and Mrs. Milton were waiting for me when I returned to the lobby. I'd forgotten about my promise to fix Mrs. Milton's hair again after supper. "Oh, ladies! Mr. Cantrell has found a train that will get me on to Strasburg if I can get to Atlees. Cyrus is going to take us."

They looked at each other in surprise. "Really?" Mrs. Rommel said, "Augusta wired us yesterday she would be delayed because Union sympathizers had destroyed the tracks near Atlees."

The desk clerk leaning on the counter, reading a paper, looked up. "She's right. We got word our mail from Atlees was delayed."

"I don't know, but I have to get there. Maybe they repaired it. I have to get out of this town before I lose my mind."

"That's understandable," she replied. "Augusta can't get here soon enough. We should be well shed of this place." They followed us to the carriage and gave me another hug before Cyrus helped me in, and we rode away at a brisk trot. It was so good to be on the road I couldn't contain my silly smile or stop thanking Mr. Cantrell.

We were a few miles down the road when Cyrus turned westward at a fork in the road, leaving the main road, and I realized we were going the wrong way. I leaned out the window. "You've taken a wrong turn, Cyrus. Atlees is on the Turnpike."

He only laid the whip on.

"Mr. Cantrell, tell him. This is the wrong way."

"Quiet, Miss McKenzie." He'd lost that genial look and stared out the window now as if annoyed.

I'm being kidnapped! Grabbing my purse since it had the gun, I edged closer to the door furthest from him. As quickly as I could, I snatched the door open and threw my weight against it. He snagged my arm to pull me back into the carriage. Dangling half in and half out, I swung precariously from the open door, kicking at him like a mammoth jack. I connected with him a few times, but I couldn't get purchase to finish shoving myself out the door with him grabbing at my legs. He reeled me back in, sweating and cursing blue blazes. When he had me back, I pelted him with my fists, hoping to bludgeon him enough to make my escape. He answered by hitting me in my face with doubled fists and knocking my head back against the carriage so hard I saw stars and then punched me in the ribs and stomach, doubling me up. He slapped me for good measure when I bent over, knocking me sideways. "Now, don't give me any more trouble, damn it."

I curled up against the side of the coach, clutching my stomach, tears streaming from my eye that was already swelling, split lip quivering in anger and pain. A wave of black rippled before my eyes, and my stomach churned until I was sure I was about to vomit. I leaned toward the window in case I did. I didn't care if I puked on him—it would serve him right. Neither did I want to puke all over myself.

He knocked on the window. "Slow down, Cyrus. Don't kill the horses."

The horses dropped to an easy trot.

"I should have known something was suspicious about the helpful stranger," I rasped.

He snorted. "It's pathetic how easy it is to gain a woman's trust with a kitten or puppy. I've conned serial murderers into letting their guard down by asking if they know who a lost kitten belongs to. Add in a dear old gray-haired mother, and I'm a pig in clover."

"Your mother helps you?" I whispered, still out of breath and shocked that his mother would participate.

"Christ, no. I saw that old woman at the station and offered her $50 to carry that pup and act like my mother. You should have seen how fast she chunked drawers and hankies out of that carpetbag to make room for the pup."

I remembered then that she had called him Sam in the car and thought it odd then, but my mind was on Baron, and I had put it away quickly. "The pup?" I asked, remaining close to the window to get air and avoid fainting.

"Bought it from my neighbor, who had a new litter. Cyrus took a liking to it, so he'll keep her. The biggest problem was getting a seat near you to gain your confidence, but money cures all ills, and that young man leaped at the offer of $200 for his tickets."

I was astounded at the thought that went into his plan, but why? "Who are you?"

"Oh, forgive me. Hamilton Conway, Pinkerton Agency." He showed his identification. "You're under arrest for treason."

"What? What did I do? That flag?"

"You helped those Confederate prisoners escape from the hospital. That bastard Williams has been a genuine pain in the ass with his guerilla raids. We've been chasing his smoke for months, and it was by sheer luck he was wounded and his men unable to rescue him. That's why I was following you. Then, fortunate soul! I hear Mary Chesnut ranting about some harlot carrying information to General Beauregard."

"What on earth are you talking about? I had nothing to do with any escape. They were lynched."

"Please. Those prisoners weren't lynched. We never found any bodies swinging in the breeze or otherwise. No, that was a planned escape. My operative inside the hospital told me how close you two were, writing letters, him letting you shave him, the romantic dance in the moonlight. It was plain you two were working together, and you facilitated his escape."

Was it possible? Travis had been particular about sending his letter to The Mansion to be posted. Maybe. I didn't know how to answer this.

"You had an operative in the hospital?" It must have been Miss Adams who didn't seem cut out for hospital work at all.

"Of course. Gain the confidence of the Rebs so that they will reveal information."

It seemed underhanded, but what had my circle been doing? "Mrs. Chesnut has no idea what she's talking about."

Conway leaned forward as if he were about to tell the most fascinating tale ever. "I cornered her after that little speech and made over her. She's such a vain creature, isn't she? Get her to stand in just the right light so you can admire her complexion. Make over her. Assure her those young women have nothing on her classical beauty, and she will spill all. She confirmed you were the courier. Her husband told her so. He quite admires you. She was incensed, I tell you!"

He turned his head this way and that, imitating her, and made fluttering motions with his hand as if he were waving a fan about as he relayed the tale. I was never much of a Mrs. Chesnut admirer and had known her for years. Now, I positively wanted to strangle her.

"We wondered how Beauregard got information on the troop movements, and here it was laid right in my lap. No doubt there will be promotions for this, and poor Mr. Byles will be vindicated. Think how grateful he will be."

"No doubt," I replied glumly. "What are you going to do with me?"

"Cyrus and I are going back to Richmond. We're meeting someone up the road who will take you on to Washington, where you will spend a very long time in prison, I imagine. Or hang."

I eased my hand toward my purse. Conway shook his head. "I know you have a gun. I'll shoot you before you get it out. I'm under no orders to get you back in one piece. How about you hand it over to avoid problems?"

I reluctantly gave him my purse, and he withdrew my dragoon. "Nice weapon."

"Hmph." My fingers curled reflexively, imagining the pistol grip in my hand and pointing it at him. I still had my Deringer, but it was a single shot, and Deringers weren't always reliable, even though I was meticulous in the care of mine. He'd kill me if it misfired.

I slumped formlessly against the seat, drained of hope. It was nearing dusk when Cyrus stopped the cab. Conway helped me out and then tossed out my carpetbag. "Not sure if you'll need it where you're going, but I don't."

Presently, we heard hoofbeats, and someone called out, "Hullo, the cab. Moon's a-rising."

"Yellow and full," Conway called back.

Passwords.

I leaned against the cab, waiting for the next leg of my adventure and trying to figure out how I would escape. The rider came in, leading a horse. His hat was pulled down, but I recognized the cologne. *Please, Lord. Don't let it be him.*

"Hello, Miss McKenzie," he said, swinging off his horse. "Ready for the second act of the play? Or is it the third?"

He rolled the cinnamon stick toothpick in his mouth and grinned rakishly at me.

"Mr. Byles."

"In the flesh. What's happened to your poor face?" He frowned at Conway.

"She tried to escape. I had to change her mind. Just tapped her in the face and stomach a bit."

Byles gently but firmly held my chin and lifted my face to examine it. "It looks terrible. We'll get somewhere soon and put some ice on it. Would you like me to look at your stomach? Make sure you're not injured?"

"No!" I jerked away from him, horrified at the idea of him laying hands on me.

He smiled benignly. "Maybe later."

Conway handed him his report with full details of my many transgressions, I suppose, and departed. Byles looked at me, assessing his prize, his gaze traveling over me familiarly, impolitely, with no effort to disguise his thoughts. "My lady, Shall we? You'll need to remove your hoops, of course."

I was still in shock at his appearance. "What?"

"Your hoops. Remove them. Either you do it, or I will. If I have to get under your skirts, I will make it worth my time."

"Stay away from me," I snarled. Not surprisingly, he laughed. I turned away and hurriedly untied the hoops, letting them drop to the ground with a small swoosh.

"Would you care to leave some petticoats behind? We're going to be riding a while."

"No."

"As you wish. I regret I couldn't procure a sidesaddle for you, but I'm sure you'll manage."

"I'm sure I will."

He motioned me over to where the two horses stood. I was to take a sorrel mare who stood napping with one foot cocked. "Pretend you're praying, if you please."

I puzzled at the request but folded my hands before me, and he quickly bound them with a leather thong. "Is this necessary?"

"Yes, I believe so. You may decide you don't enjoy my company as much as I enjoy yours. While I would find you and then make you pay for inconveniencing me, I'd rather not play hide-and-seek tonight." He gallantly cupped his hands to help me mount, but I pushed them away. "As you wish, my lady. I see you still need a lesson in manners, but we have time."

It was more difficult with my hands bound and certainly not very ladylike, but I managed to mount unassisted. I shuffled around on the saddle, trying to adjust my skirts and petticoats under me to keep the wadding to a minimum.

"Do you require aid?" he asked as I straightened some of the bulk under me and then laughed at my answering glare. "Let me adjust these stirrup leathers for you." He shortened them to fit my legs, and I begrudgingly thanked him. I already wished I'd removed at least one of the petticoats, as there was no way to get comfortable.

He plopped my carpetbag in my lap, patted the mare on the butt, and adjusted my skirts behind me. "There. We look like we're going for a Sunday ride. If only we had a picnic." The mare had only a halter and lead, which he kept. He was in the saddle light as a sprite. By the way he mounted and sat a horse, he was an experienced horseman. He smooched his horse into an easy trot and towed my mare along. She thankfully had an easy gait as my stomach still ached.

He prattled on with nonsense conversation until I wearied of it. "Mr. Byles, why are you taking me back to Washington? You know I am innocent."

He guffawed so loudly that a bird on a nearby fence rail took flight. His features were in plain relief, backlit by the glow of the setting sun as if surrounded by a halo, when he looked over at me, smiling broadly and genuinely amused. "Oh, Miss McKenzie, you are many things, but innocent, I think, is not remotely in your repertoire. You're not being charged for the shooting of Fulkirk if that's what you fear. There are two witnesses who will testify that he was trying to assault you. It would be a public relations disaster for the army if it got out that one of Mrs. Covington's angels was attacked by a soldier. The populace would be in an uproar. No, he will be cashiered, I would think, and can go home, bragging about how he lost his leg in the war or some such." He waved a hand. "Small loss. Fools like him are easily replaced and not much missed."

I swallowed hard. So, he had survived, but with the loss of a leg. My head swam. Byles reached over and took my arm. "You look about ready to swoon. Did you think him dead?"

I nodded briefly.

"Ah, no. He's very much alive, though I daresay he carries a bit of a grudge towards you. Maybe we'll let him visit you once you're ensconced in prison."

I grunted when the mare stumbled into a hole.

Byles glanced over at me. "Ah, let's slow down. Conway worked you over a bit more than he let on. He can be such a beast. We'll get to town, and I'll see about some warm towels to put on your stomach. It will make you feel better."

His assessment of Conway was a bit ironic, considering his previous treatment of me. He slowed the horses to a walk and tried to converse, but I wasn't in the mood.

He whistled a bit of a jaunty tune. "Want to sing Dixie with me?"

"No," I replied miserably.

He started singing an old Scottish song I knew well. His voice was a remarkably clear and true tenor. He might have been a fallen choir boy. He stopped halfway through, "Do you know this song?"

"Yes."

"Sing with me."

I shook my head.

He shrugged. "My nanny was Scotch-Irish. She used to sing a lot of the old country songs to me. Maybe you'd like a different one."

I might have been listening to my father singing for the joy in his voice. He kept at me through several songs until I joined him in The Braes of Balquhither. Perhaps he would let his guard down.

> "Let us journey together,
> Where the blaeberries grow,
> 'Mang the braes o' Balquhidder.
> Will you go, lassie, go?"

He leaned closer, singing it with me, and smiled broadly when we finished. "That wasn't so difficult, was it?"

"No, it was a favorite song of my father's."

"Then let's find another he liked."

And he did. Oh, Papa, where are you? I wanted to start weeping again for missing him and Baron and for sheer fear of what would happen in Washington, but whether Byles had intended it or not, his singing had calmed me. I had been taut for so long that I felt as if I might break at any moment like a fiddle string too tightly wound. He'd been singing to me for the past hour or more, lulling me, drawing me out, soothing my heart.

"I've been thinking," he said. "Prison is really no place for a woman like you. I might get a promotion if they could prove you helped with that escape. Cyrus certainly hopes he will." He shrugged. "But again, how would they? There will be other opportunities, I'm sure. I'm a patient man. I've been to the prisons they would send you to. Nasty disease-ridden places. You would not survive."

"I agree." Was there a yet chance of freedom? Hope, a small, crushed thing in a dark corner, fluttered her sundered wings.

"What would you think about visiting my little farm outside Washington? I bought it from a young widow who decorated it quite nicely. I've added a few touches to make it my own, but it's very homey. I've entertained several ladies there who enjoyed it. It's private and peaceful. I'm sure you'd appreciate it much more than prison," he said brightly. "I have an old housekeeper who's very good at domestic affairs and minding her business. She could take care of you when I was away. In time, you'll look forward to my visits. Long for them, even."

"You really are mad," I said, ruined that one prison had been offered for another.

"I'm sad you think so. Would prison really be so much better?"

I'd been surveying the countryside for an opportunity to escape. The road lay before us like a ribbon in the moonlight. There were split rail fences on either side of us, and I doubted the fat mare could jump them even if I could get her away from

Byles. Down the road were some woods without fences on one side, though. I decided to make a dash for it and drummed my heels into the mare. The mare grunted and flicked an ear back at me.

"Oh, Miss McKenzie, please do stop kicking poor Isabelle. She's an old children's horse and will only go as fast or as slow as I lead her. You're just making her ribs sore. Besides, I did warn you about trying to escape. You will regret it even if you do. I won't, but you will."

He glanced over at me. "You're exhausted. Let's camp for the night. I wanted to push on to the next town, but we can't make it tonight. Let me get my little Southern belle tucked in."

I was sure I did look exhausted and crestfallen and hopeless.

We made camp in the clearing I had thought to escape to, and he helped me dismount. I didn't object this time as my stomach ached fiercely. I grunted and bent over in pain when I lit. He frowned. "You should let me look at that."

"No. There's nothing you can do."

"I'll fix some coffee. I have a few supplies with me."

I nodded and sat down on the blanket he spread on the ground. It was a small, flat clearing, but we would be sheltered by trees should weather arise. He returned from tending the horses with an armful of branches and a bucket of water, singing Annie Laurie. "Do you know this song, Miss McKenzie?"

"Yes."

"Sing with me."

I could hear Papa singing it plainly but shook my head.

> *"Which ne'er forgot will be,*
> *And for bonnie Annie Laurie*
> *I'd lay me down and dee."*

My eyes misted.

He looked up from preparing the fire. "Are you all right, Miss McKenzie?"

"Yes, it was the last song my father sang to me. I may not like you, but you have a lovely voice. You've been singing to me all night. Why?"

"Why, I'm courting you, of course." He smiled charmingly. "Is it working?"

I shook my head and huffed.

He laughed and continued the song. Then he repeated the last lines.

> *"And she's a' the world to me;*
> *And for bonnie Annie Laurie*
> *I'd lay me down and dee.*
> *I'd lay me down and dee."*

He unbound my hands and kissed one, then gently let it go. "I would, you know."

"You would what?"

"Lay me down and die for you."

"You're insane."

"So you've said."

A welcome fire was quickly blazing for coffee. "I regret I have nothing acceptable to serve in," he said as he handed me the tin cup and sat beside me. "I was pondering this earlier. I would have enjoyed serving tea and a lovely supper in my dining room tonight. I even plotted out the menu."

"Oh?" I said, looking over the brim of the cup and blowing softly on the steaming brew. I decided to divert him from the subject. Not only because the entire subject made me queasy but also because I was hungry and didn't want to discuss food. I'd eaten nearly nothing at breakfast nor really for the past two days. "Why do you hate Southern women?" I settled back against the tree stump behind me. It was rough, solid, somehow comforting.

I might have slapped him; he looked so surprised. "Why would you say that?" He reached over and patted my hand. "Hate them! I love them. My mother was from the south. Georgia. She objected to my father's harsh handling of her at times and escaped home. Father didn't realize she was pregnant at the time.

Mother never recovered from the birth, I think. Her health was quite frail, and she died when I was five, but I remember her glorious skin. She used to lay her silken cheek on mine and sing me to sleep or rock me. Such angelic beauty." He moved his hand up to gently stroke my cheek. "Very much like yours.

"My grandmother never forgave me nor Father for her death." He looked at me and shrugged, but I recognized the sadness and pain. Though I thoroughly despised the man, my heart went to the boy. "She made my life a living hell. Whipped me for not being able to play the piano well. Mother had long, lovely fingers exquisitely suited to the piano. I, alas, had my father's short, coarse hands.

"Finally, a servant took pity on me and got word to my father. He came immediately to fetch me. She swore he couldn't have me. He replied he would kill the old bat where she stood if she didn't turn me over. I was hiding behind a servant and watched all this. He was in a fury. I've no doubt he would have killed her without a moment's remorse.

"Then," he nudged me in the arm, "he waved a crop in her face after she gave me up. This one, as a matter of fact." He raised a riding crop with a braided shaft and lashed tip of the highest quality leather. Even in the firelight, I knew it had seen much use. "My father declared, 'If I had more time, I would tie you to a tree and flog you for what you've done to my boy.' I could see from the way her face blanched she had no doubt he would. I'm sure he would have shredded her pristine skin with the merest provocation. He strode out of there with me, handed me up to his manservant, and we rode away, never to see that plantation again.

"No, Miss McKenzie, I quite like Southern women. Most of them. I love their gentle ways."

He resumed stroking my hand. I clasped his wrist to move his hand away, but he deftly turned my hand in his and lowered his mouth to my open palm, kissing it softly and tracing his tongue along it. Then he kissed my wrist and nibbled it delicately, caressing it with his lower lip. The sensation went directly to my loins, and I shuddered. Quickly, I pulled away from him.

He smiled. "You try to deny me, but your body responds. I understand women."

"I don't know what you mean."

"You know quite well what I mean. You have a lover, but he's a gentleman, I think. A sweet walk in the park, chaste kisses stolen here and there. I could this very evening stir more passion in you than he ever has without being in the least indecent. I meant to have you tonight, but I have changed my mind. I want you to desire me, and you will."

I shook my head, tears springing to my eyes. "That will never happen, and I have no lover. He was killed at Manassas."

"Oh, my dear. I am sorry."

He pulled me to him, putting his arm around me. I tried to push him away, but he held me close, crooning to me and patting me. I started sobbing again. Longing for Baron.

He continued stroking my hair. "What will you do, wear weeds the remainder of your days?"

I nodded, still sobbing. "I will never love another man."

"I can give you a safe place at my farm. You will recover there. I wouldn't bother you, but one day I would come to you. Offer you solace. In time you will long for me. Hate it when I am not with you. Why would you waste your life mourning a dead man when I can offer you a life of love filled with happy children?"

I shook my head and wrenched away, wiping my eyes.

"Yes, I believe so. I intend to keep you there instead of turning you over to some dank, disease-ridden prison."

"You're insane."

"Do you think so? Perhaps it is our imperfections that make us so perfect for one another?"

"Assaulting me with Austen."

"What would you like me to assault you with?" The smile broadened into a lecherous grin, and he stretched out a leg. I shrank away from him. "Relax, Miss McKenzie. I'm not going to hurt you."

He broke off a piece of cheese and then held it to my lips. I tried to take it from his fingers, but he withdrew it, insisting I allow him to feed me. I received the offering as I was starving, nibbling it delicately from his fingers. He divided up some bread and cheese and a bit of dried beef and handed it to me on a handkerchief, which I gratefully accepted. "I would give anything if this were roast pheasant and rosemary new potatoes," he said. "If we were home, I would feed you sugared grapes and honeyed nuts and all manner of delicacies."

My stomach growled at the mention of the roast pheasant, but I did not miss the *if we were home* and quailed at the thought.

He smiled. "You really do have the most beautiful skin," he said. "In the glow of the campfire, it is even more enchanting. My fiery little angel." He reached up and stroked my cheek with his fingertips.

"I noticed the rose attar scent in your hair. I have lovely rose gardens I think you would enjoy puttering in." A faraway look took him. "Mary, Mary, quite contrary. How does your garden grow? With silver shells and Southern belles. Those pretty maids all in a row." He giggled in an unnerving way. "No, that isn't the way it goes, is it?"

I stared at him horror-struck.

"I was joking, of course. Be at ease."

I didn't think he was joking and wondered how many young ladies never left his farm. Now I knew where Mrs. Collins' sister had most likely disappeared. "I need to necessary," I croaked, reeling with horror at the thought.

"It's triggered by a stirring in the loins," he said knowingly with a half-smile.

"It's triggered by not pissing for hours," I replied bitingly, forgetting all decency.

He got up, rummaged around in his pack, and returned with a coil of light cord. A loop was securely tied around one wrist.

"You're uncommonly prepared."

"I knew my mission and my prize. Now, I would prefer you desire me. But do believe me, if you try to escape, I will find you—and when I do, I will take you. Hard. You must respect me." There was a predatory shift in his eyes. My breath sucked in. I had no doubt he would be on me like an animal should I try to flee.

"Good girl. You understand."

I nodded and tried to stand. He helped me up. "I'll deal with Conway over this beating, my dear."

He wavered between hunter and lover, but either way, there was no doubt he was quite mad. My hands were free, and I was out of sight. I had to get the Deringer and do something. I couldn't go back to Washington with him. In prison or on his farm, no one would ever find me. I stumbled over hidden roots and stones as I made my way through the nearby bushes, nearly going down twice. I wouldn't have gotten far even had I tried to escape.

"Not too far, Miss McKenzie." The cord tugged on my wrist to remind me.

Blessed relief. I didn't realize how full my bladder was until I squatted and burrowed around for the gun. His face lit when I returned as if I had been gone for days. With the gun held nervously in the folds of my skirt, I sidled around to get the best shot.

"Do you like Burns?" He patted the blanket. "Come sit beside me. We need to sleep soon, but I thought you might like a bit of Burns before." He started singing *Ae Fond Kiss*.

"Please don't," I said.

"You don't like that? It's one of my favorites."

I raised the Deringer. "I'm not going to Washington with you, Mr. Byles." With swiftness I was unprepared for, he whipped up a Colt and pointed it at me.

"It's a shame Conway didn't spend more time searching you instead of beating you," he growled and sprang to his feet, never taking the gun off me. "We seem to have a bit of an impasse."

"Not at all," I said and fired the gun. It struck him in the chest, knocking him down. He looked down at the wound in surprise where the blood bloomed. One hand clutched over it, but he forced himself to his feet, gun still trained on me. "You may have killed me, Lorena, I don't know, but you'll saddle the horses now, and we'll get to a doctor up the road."

"I think not. I have nothing to lose."

"I have no intentions of letting you go. I'll shoot you where you stand." He swayed wearily. "Don't test me. I'm not in the mood."

He was bleeding too badly to stay upright long, but I didn't doubt he might shoot me, so I picked up the blanket to begin gathering camp.

"Leave that," he said, waving the gun at me. "Saddle the horses."

"Yes, sir."

"Sir." He tilted his head to one side, watching me. "Could you not call me darling once, even in this late hour, my dear? Would it hurt you?"

Yes, it would. I care nothing for you. "The horses are saddled. Let me help you. Lower that gun so you don't shoot me accidentally."

He nodded and put his arm around my shoulder. Halfway to the horse, his arm slipped from my shoulder, and he slumped to the ground. I tried to pull him back up, but he pushed me away. "It's no use. I'm not going to make it."

I rolled up a blanket to make a pillow under his head. There was no sense in trying to stop the bleeding. The bullet had gone into the right side of his chest, clipping a lung judging from his labored breathing. He was mortally wounded. He took my hand with his free hand and let out a heavy sigh. "I always thought you might be the death of me, but I hoped I might be in bed and a very old man at the time." He smiled wanly.

"That was never going to happen."

"We would have had beautiful children, you know. I would have given you many."

I shuddered at the thought. "You're rambling, Mr. Byles. Do you want to confess or want me to pray with you? Will you take Christ as your savior?"

He tried to laugh, but it turned into a cough. "Oh, God, no. I am bound for hell. I earned my way. No deathbed confessions and conversions here."

With some difficulty, I pulled my hand free from his and started going through his pockets. "I'm going to make this look like a robbery. Forgive me."

His eyes fluttered, and he smiled. "Clever girl. That's what I would do. I wish I were feeling better. I like you in that pocket."

I was sure he did. His manhood was just below my fingers. With some difficulty, as he had turned on his side to ease his breathing, I leaned over him to get to the other one. He raised a hand to brush my breast. I wouldn't fight him now but rather kept clearing pockets in pants, jacket, and vest.

"I quite enjoyed being robbed," he sighed. "Thank you."

"Think nothing of it."

With that done, there was only one thing left. I reached for his gun, but he held tight to it and shook his head. "Let me keep it. Feral hogs."

I doubted he had the strength to fire the gun anyway, but I understood his fear. One of our field hands had fallen down a ravine when he was out checking snares and broken his leg. No one knew he was missing until the next morning. We started searching for him, but feral hogs found him before we did. The ground around what was left of him was churned into crimson mud. Bones and shreds of clothes were scattered about, but the snare lay twisted and broken nearby, its wire coiled like a serpent with its hapless victim still ensnared. The hogs were full, I suppose, and ignored the fat rabbit. Why hogs start in the middle, I had no idea, but it had to be an agonizing death.

I had nightmares for months afterward and refused to eat pork for a year.

"All right. Mr. Byles, I'm going to leave now and take your horse. I'm sorry it came to this, but I couldn't let you take me."

"Of course."

I fastened the bag of food and my carpet bag to the saddle. Byles wouldn't be needing it. I'd already turned the mare loose.

"Miss McKenzie?"

I turned toward him. "Remember I said to you I would lay me down and die for you?"

"Yes?"

"I also said I wasn't letting you go." He quirked a brow at me and raised his gun. Seventeen inches of flame belched from the muzzle. It felt like a fiery sledgehammer slamming into me and knocking me backward into the horse, who shied away.

I dropped to the ground.

Chapter Fifty-Nine

"Damn you to hell," I groaned and forced myself up. My right arm was severely wounded, with blood running freely and dripping from my fingertips. I wavered, hoping he hadn't the strength to shoot again, for I had only one bullet in my Deringer.

A small, satisfied smile lingered on his lips. His eyes stared lifelessly at me when I stumbled over to look at him. "Damn evil son-of-a-bitch." Still not trusting him, I tried to keep my distance while reaching over to peel his fingers from the gun. My breath shuddered out. He was dead. I stole his handkerchief and wadded it over the hole in my arm, but it quickly soaked, so I tossed it away. A chemise from the carpet bag would have to suffice. I folded it and wrapped it around my arm, then pressed my arm to my body gently to hold it in place. Even that made my breath catch. With some difficulty, I tugged his belt loose and wound it around my arm a few times. Pain so sharp I feared I might pass out shot through me when I tightened the belt, but I gritted my teeth and cinched the buckle. Then I vomited, the retching further jolting the arm I was sure was broken as I could barely move my numb fingers.

By the time I got his holster off and buckled around my hips, I was exhausted and leaking blood like a sieve, regardless of the swaddling. Earlier, I'd left his whiskey flask in his pocket for him to ease his pain, but now I liberated it with no regret except perhaps bothering to care that I had shot him to begin with. I gently wiped my bloody hand on him and shoved myself away with my good arm.

With any luck, I could find help before I collapsed. The horse, who thankfully was tied earlier, stood quietly while I positioned him next to the tree stump and pulled myself clumsily on. Had I the energy, I would have spit on Byles as I rode by, but in my mind, I could see him stirring one last time to reach out and grab the horse's leg to spook him and spill me. I gave him a wide berth.

Guided by moonlight and instinct, I rode on in the darkness as I couldn't remember this road. There would be a farm nearby, surely, if I didn't pass out or die from blood loss before I found it. Despair whispered in my ear, "I am with you." Hope was dead and moldering. Only McKenzie stubbornness kept me going.

The heavens opened in a chill, baptismal rain, drenching me. If luck were a road, I'd be in a far field. Why hadn't I thought to bring a blanket instead of his whiskey? My cloak would soon be soaked. I tilted back and drank like a grown man, letting it burn a trail like a torchlight down my throat and settle amicably in my stomach. It eased the pain and warmed my insides, so I had more. Even with the rain, I fought to stay awake. The whiskey wasn't helping. My eyelids drifted, trying to close. "Sing, Lorena. Stay awake."

Every song I could think of was one Byles had serenaded me with earlier, and I couldn't bring myself to repeat it.

Sing or die. If you pass out, you'll fall off this horse.

"And the only words to him did say. Young man, I think you're dying," I croaked out weakly and off-key.

Girl, I don't think he's the only one dying. Louder! Stay awake. Did I even care with Baron gone? No, I decided. Not really. Whiskey talking, but didn't Papa always say whiskey speaks the truth?

I kept singing and drinking, from habit now, until I saw a light bobbing in the darkness and began to laugh. Byles' spirit wandering, looking for me? Or the *baintsí* come to collect me. "I'm here," I cried. "I'm ready for you."

Lord, yes. Take me home.

The glow brightened. It was a lantern held by a man who raised it to peer up into my face. I sobbed with disappointment, relief, or perhaps madness.

"Ma'am. What are you doing out here in the dark like a drowned rat and drunk?"

I laughed. "Singing, sir. Singing."

Then he noticed my bloody arm and gasped. "Good God, what happened to you?" Grabbing the horse's bridle, he tugged me back down the road he'd come. "Hold on."

"Robbers," I whispered feebly, nearly gone and not knowing what else would explain the shot. I certainly didn't want to be associated with killing a Pinkerton man.

"Damn lawless country these days. Probably a bunch of them heathen Yankees marauding about pretending to be soldiers."

It wasn't long before he was shouting at a neat little white farmhouse that had been roused up, spilling womenfolk and children like a knocked beehive. Hands carefully lifted me from the saddle, but I cried out when the arm shifted. The rain had settled to a fine mist that eased my upturned face.

"Gunnar, take this horse and go get the doc," the man said. "Tell him to come quick. If the horse is spent, leave it in town at his place and ride back with him. We'll pick it up tomorrow."

"Yes, sir," the half-grown boy said, stuffing his shirt in his pants and slapping a hat on his head.

"Put your jacket on in case it pours again," a woman called out.

He dashed back indoors, running into the people who were dragging me in as unceremoniously as a sack of cheap rice.

The women laid me on a small corn shuck cot and shooed the men and children out like unwanted chickens.

"This is a lady," one said. "That's a fine dress, Elske."

"It was," she replied. "Blew a hole straight through her arm. Who would do something like that?"

The room I lay in was small, with whitewashed walls hung with embroidered samplers, a few photographs, and quilts. The women hovered over me like hens, but I couldn't focus on them any more than I could the room. I had general impressions of blue eyes in tanned faces and white nightcaps. Overall, concern and worry. Bless them.

"No way we can get this basque off with that arm so messed up, Miss," the older woman said. "I am Karoline, and these are my girls, Elske and Margarete. Going to have to cut it, but it's mangled anyway."

I nodded.

She unbuttoned the front and then snipped down the back seam, ever frugal, so something might be salvaged.

They gently peeled me out of my corset, cut my bloody chemise off, then cleaned and dressed the wound. The gentle bathing with warm water and crooning words soothed me near to sleep. The wound was mostly numb now, and my arm throbbed dully from my shoulder to my fingertips, but moving the arm was a different matter and sent pain so blindingly sharp up my arm and shoulder that I cried out piteously. Reluctantly, they left me naked from the waist up rather than try to get me in a gown or chemise. There was more clucking and excited whispering in German at the uncovered bruises. As my clothes in the carpet bag were soaked, one of the girls loaned me some fresh drawers and helped me put them on. Mrs. Vogt poured a hot toddy down me to help me rest as if I needed more liquor, but at least this was more soothing in warm milk with honey and ginger. I closed my eyes to visions of Byles' lifeless eyes staring at me, accusing me.

"Go to hell," I whispered.

I'm already there, waiting for you, my dear.

My eyes snapped open but quickly drifted shut again thanks to the liquor, exhaustion, and blood loss. I slept until the doctor arrived with great fanfare in the early hours of the morning. The house once again turned into a hive of activity, with everyone turning out, including children. Seeing a gunshot wound treated was a good reason to be up and underfoot. They had to be hounded out of the kitchen several times.

The doctor laid me on the dining table where he could get more light and proceeded to hmm and haw, as doctors do. "Robbers, you say?"

"Yes." The less said, the better.

"Damned sorry business beating and shooting a defenseless woman. Your arm's broke. Guess you know that. Don't think any ribs are broken or there's internal injury, but I imagine you're sore enough."

Pain washed over me in waves again. I replied faintly, "Figured it was."

"Should heal up all right. Looks like you lost a lot of blood. You're pale as Banquo's ghost. I'm sure you can stay with the Vogts for as long as you need, or we can move you to town to my infirmary."

"No, I need to go home as soon as I can. Winchester."

"That's not advisable," he replied gruffly.

"Have to," I said. "My girls."

"Ah, children. I understand. Still, it's not wise."

I didn't disavow the mistake. The deceit was justified if it got me out of here before someone came looking for Byles.

"Steady. Going to dose you with some chloroform so I can probe around in there and make sure the wound is clean, set the bone, then stitch you up. Too many flames nearby for ether."

The women continued to object about my state of undress, though I had a sheet draped across me, and insisted on trying to put a gown on me, to which the doctor threatened them one and all with bodily harm if they didn't get out of his way and let him get on with his work. I nodded wearily, and he put a folded cloth over my face, then a funnel-like device, and started dripping the sickening, sweet-smelling chloroform in through the spout. A feeling of suffocation immediately overwhelmed me, and I shook my head, "Stop! Stop!" I raised my good arm and tried to push it away.

The doctor fought to hold it on me. "Hold her down, damn it!"

Panic seized me until I felt I was dying. I struck out. Kicked. Thrashed violently.

"You men get in here and hold her before she shreds an artery," the doctor shouted.

"Let me cover her," Mrs. Vogt shrieked.

"To hell with that. I must get her under."

Mr. Vogt and Gunnar grabbed me, forcing me down. One of the other boys lay across my legs. Mrs. Vogt tried to squeeze under Gunnar to pull the sheet up over my exposed breasts. My last vision was Gunnar staring in amazement at my chest before my world faded to black.

When I awoke, the doctor was sitting by the table drinking coffee and eating raisin pie. I was still stretched out on the table, covered with a sheet and a quilt, but I shivered as if chilled.

"Morning, Miss." He glanced at his watch. "Yes, it's still morning." He took another bite of pie and washed it down with more coffee. "I predict you'll recover strongly if we can keep infection and pneumonia at bay. I packed the wound with onions. They should help. Sit up as much as you can to keep the lungs clear, but as stout as you are, I think you'll be fine."

"Figured as much about the onions." I wrinkled my nose. The overpowering onion smell further agitated my queasy stomach. "I can feel them burning."

"I noticed you have another scar on your other arm," he said. "Bullet wound?"

"Yes, a robber shot me."

He paused from forking another bite of pie in his mouth. "And robbers shot you last night?" An eyebrow cocked suspiciously at me. "What did you say you did? Jewel courier?"

I shook my head slightly. Someone had thoughtfully placed a feather pillow under my head that felt about to burst. "I have a boarding school, but I also raise horses."

"Ah, that would explain part of it. Your delicate looks are deceiving. You fight like a drunk Irishman. Took four people to finally get you down."

"My father would be proud," I whispered.

"And kick like a galled mule," one of the boys with a fresh black eye said.

"Oh, law! Did I do that?" I asked, mortified.

He nodded, touching it tenderly and grinning. "It's fine, ma'am. Can't wait to tell my friends I got it holding a naked lady down."

"Good Hannah, please don't." My cheeks flamed at the hazy memory of exposing myself to these innocent boys and colored deeper at the thought of me being spoken of so.

"Karl Werner," Mrs. Vogt gasped. "You'll say no such thing!"

"Be darned if I don't, Ma. I earned it."

"Out! The lot of you. Heathens." She wheeled on her husband. "This is your doing, Herman."

Dear heavens. I had hoped to keep my presence quiet, but there was small chance of that now. The doctor left instructions for changing the dressing and what to look for in case he needed to return. I thanked him and paid him with Byles' money. It seemed only fitting.

After the doctor left, they moved me back to the little, whitewashed room, where I slept most of the day thanks to the laudanum and exhaustion until Gunnar and Mr. Vogt rushed in. "Miss, hurry, wake up. Some men are coming up the lane. We're going to put you in the root cellar."

They half carried me, half dragged me to the cellar and sat me in a corner bundled up in a quilt. Elske sat with me, holding a small candle. "If they come down the stairs, I should have to put the candle out," she said. "Don't be afraid of the dark. Seldom snakes in here."

Though I loathed snakes, I much more feared the men storming the door. There was a tramping of heavy boots above and men's voices. The boots went throughout the house, one room after another. We looked up, following the footsteps. "Oh, no. I forgot my carpetbag," I whispered.

"Too late to worry now. Mother will explain it if they find it. More worried about the boys hiding that fine horse."

Our eyes stared at the kitchen floor above where the group stood now, floorboards creaking now and again. My breath held in my chest as if I was afraid they might hear my faint breathing, though I couldn't make out a word they said. Voices raised further in anger. Then boots stomped out of the house, and a gunshot. I jumped, knocking my arm against a shelf of canned goods so sharply I couldn't help the yelp of pain. Elske cried out and dropped the candle. "Oh, no." She scrambled after it before it went out. We waited, barely breathing, hearts racing like frightened mice, but no one came marching down the steps.

It seemed like an eternity later when Gunnar and Mr. Vogt came to get us. "They're gone."

They sat me in the kitchen and gave me some hot tea. "Union soldiers and a civilian," Mr. Vogt said. "The big man said he was looking for his fiancée, Lorena McKenzie."

The blood drained from my face. "They were after some items I left in Richmond." It was a lie, but I couldn't tell them I had killed a Pinkerton man. "My fiancé is dead. I feared they might come looking for me, but to use that ruse. Despicable." I shook my head. "I can't stay here."

"The boy with them, the little weasel, searched the house and was sure you had been here, or we would have denied it. He has a nose like a bloodhound and could smell your perfume on the pillow. We told them you were only winged and returned to Richmond to stay with friends and recover."

They had bought me time, but not much. Richmond was aswarm with Union spies, and they would soon know I wasn't there. I had maybe three days at most to recover my strength and leave. "What was the gunshot?"

"The big man was losing his patience and threatened to have a come-to-Jesus meeting with us if we didn't tell him the truth. The little weasel said shooting someone would put the fear of God in us. Then he took out his gun like he was going to, but the big man knocked it aside, and it fired wild. That's when we decided to tell them you'd been here and sent them to Richmond."

"Conway was the big man. He's the one who beat me. You were right to tell him I'd been here. He's ruthless. I cannot stay. I'm not sure how long he'll be thrown off track."

"We'll worry about that later," Mrs. Vogt said. "You can't leave now. Rest a few days at least. We'll alter your dresses and make some undersleeves to cover the dressing on your arm."

I had only two, the one I'd worn and another I'd stuffed in the carpetbag. "Do you think I'll be able to catch the train to Strasburg from town?"

"The stationmaster is my cousin," she replied. "We'll get you on that train. But for now, rest."

Gunnar brought me fresh wildflowers the next morning, and I broke out in tears thinking of the last time Baron picked flowers for me. He fell over himself with apologies, not knowing what he had done wrong. I tried to reassure him it wasn't his fault. In the evening, he sat beside my bed, holding my hand. To check for fever, he said, as one of the girls read poetry to me.

"Do you like this?" he asked.

"The poetry or the hand holding?" I asked, gently pulling my hand from his.

He blushed and ducked his head. "The poetry I expect."

Elske looked up from the book and smirked the tiniest bit.

"I love poetry, but it's nice that you keep watch for fever."

He would have fed me the chicken soup Mrs. Vogt insisted I needed to rebuild my bone; had I not insisted I could feed myself. Margarete took pity on him and allowed him to bring me my soup while she mended my dress unless he felt like taking up needle and thread. I feared he might try to be helpful, but he agreed to fetch the soup.

"Gunnar is quite kind," I said when he departed to the kitchen with the bowl one evening.

Margarete looked up from her mending. "He's madly in love with you."

I sighed. "Perhaps a bit of infatuation, but I shouldn't think love. He has a girl, surely."

"Of course, he is. Aside from being lovely, he saw your bosoms when you were flailing about on the table."

I flushed at the memory.

"Then you were speaking another language, and he thought it was incredibly romantic. Like you were speaking love words to him."

"What did it sound like? I speak a few languages."

"Really?"

"Latin, French, Italian, Irish."

She repeated a phrase that was definitely not romantic.

"Oh dear."

"What does it mean?"

"Nothing pleasant. I was cursing in Irish. Best forget you heard that."

She perked up like a chicken spying a June bug. That cherub-gone-outlaw look put me in mind of my two little miscreants at home. She even looked a bit like Persy with her fair hair and wide blue eyes. "I can teach you to cuss in German."

Yes, just like Persy. "All right. I'll teach you some milder Irish phrases if you'll promise to forget the one you just said."

A person can never know too many curses, so Margarete taught me some colorful German ones and a few useful phrases. Her father caught our language lessons and clucked at her. "Does she know *Sprich nicht mit mir, du verrückter Mann* yet? It means, "Do not talk to me, crazy man!" and handed me a mug of hearty ale that he thought was more useful than his wife's chicken soup for healing. "*Geh zum Teufel*—go to the devil is always handy." He grinned.

"I already taught her that, Papa."

"*Go raibh maith agat. Saol fada chugat,*" I replied after sipping the hearty ale, a welcome change from the chicken soup, which, albeit delicious, was getting tiring. "It means, 'Thank you. A long life to you,' in Irish."

Though the Vogts treated me like one of their own, I insisted they turn me loose on the third morning, and they took me to Hanover Junction to catch a train. I realized with some dismay that this was the same train Byles was headed for. I sent a telegram to Winchester so someone would be waiting in Strasburg for me. Gunnar wanted the horse, but if anyone recognized him, it would only cause them trouble. He sold easily, and I gave the money to Mr. Vogt.

A day I thought might never come was here, and I was on a train heading home. A young soldier took it upon himself to become my guardian. I was more than happy to share my bounty with him as I had little appetite anyway, and the Vogts had loaded me down with food. The laudanum lulled me to sleep, where I dreamed of Baron more and more in happier times. I was happy to be there and had to force myself not to take it, even when the pain ground on my nerves. It ever lured me with promises of rest and relief.

But relief from what? The pain or the grief? The grief would be there long after the arm healed.

As I requested, only Jacob and the carriage waited for me at Strasburg. I simply couldn't handle a large gathering in public. He hugged me carefully, tears rolling down his cheeks. "Good to see you, Miss Mac."

"You, too, Jacob. I've missed you so much."

He sniffed and spat a stream of tobacco. "We've all missed you something fierce. Maybe except Miss Boggs. Don't know why you keep that woman."

"Papa felt sorry for her after the children she was caring for died, and he thought the school was going to expand. I wouldn't have hired her myself."

He huffed his disdain. "That woman is Satan's handmaiden. Pretty sure I saw them dancing in the moonlight last night."

I smiled at the thought of spindly Miss Boggs and Beelzebub stepping out in the midnight hour.

With a steady hand, he helped me into the carriage. "Your luggage arrived a while back. Everyone thought you'd be along directly, but you never showed up. We was all worried sick."

"It's a long story. I'll tell you when I get home."

"You know they're doing up a big party for you."

"I figured they might. If they would give me a chance to nap first, that would be lovely."

The carriage was comfortable, and the roads were in good shape, so I slept most of the five-hour ride home. The girls mobbed the carriage as soon as it drove up, but Jacob cracked his whip. "Here now. Miss Mac got a broke arm. Don't be jostling her, or I'll give you all a hiding." They stood back in a respectful circle but then crowded back around as soon as he unloaded me, careful to avoid the slung arm, hugging and kissing me in turns, oldest to youngest, which Persy and Lucille decried as unfair and demanded two kisses.

"I understand y'all are planning a party?"

"It's a surprise party," Persy said. "Who told you?" She glared at Jacob.

"I'm a good guesser."

"Oh, yes, you are. I suppose you guessed that Lucille got in trouble then."

Lucille leveled a gimlet eye at her. "Only because you wanted to sneak out at night to ride."

Persy put her hands on her hips. "I was talking about when you took the blackberry pie off the windowsill while it was cooling."

"Who took the rest of the stuff for the picnic instead of going to class?" Lucille shot back. "And forgot to bring a knife to cut the ham, so we had to gnaw it like a couple of dogs?"

"Welcome home, Miss Mac," Annie said, shooing the girls away and hugging me softly. "Did you miss us?"

"Oh, yes. Very much, but it's all coming back. I do need a nap, though."

"No doubt. You look gray as last week's wash water."

I looked up at the house that was draped in crepe. "Has someone died?"

"We read the news about Marse Baron," Della said. "The whole house in mourning. I...we—" tears flooded her eyes. "We sorry, Miss Mac. Everyone loved him."

"I know, Della. Didn't realize you got the news. Don't cry." I swallowed the lump in my throat. "You'll get me started again."

She nodded and ducked her head. Beth, Imogene, and Annie hustled me up to my room, where a bath quickly appeared. Undressed and bathed, I slumped into my bed, which I sometimes wondered if I would ever lie in again. Annie redressed my arm, carefully rebound the splint on it, then propped it on a pillow. "You sleep as long as you like, girl."

A quiet supper would have been preferable, but the girls had been planning this party since they got the telegram. I couldn't deny them. They even put on a play and music. Despite my weariness—heart, soul, and body—I enjoyed myself, though the gaiety was strained at times when something or another reminded me of Baron or recent events. Even so, I thanked them sincerely at the end of the night.

I stayed in bed the next day and thought I might never stir from there. I was home, and Rosemount was in good hands with Beth. What if I just quietly faded away? My mind cast about for Papa. He was gone. The Pines was gone. I tried to avoid the biggest hole in my heart but couldn't. Baron was gone and would never hold me again. I rolled over and pulled a pillow to me, wishing it was him, and started crying anew until I fell asleep.

My only escape from blessed slumber was when I sorted through the mail without much interest until I came to a letter from Major Clinton Geary. Inside was a receipt for one yellow mare named Lorrie and five hundred dollars with the note, "I am not a thief. Kindest regards, Maj Clinton L Geary, USA"

"The hell you aren't," I whispered. "Luri. Her name is Luri."

Beth came in the next morning with breakfast. "How are you feeling?"

"Better, thank you. I was exhausted and in so much pain from jostling my arm around. I think I overmedicated on laudanum."

She looked at me with her head cocked to the side as if thinking about how or what to say next. "Charlotte's parents collected her last week."

"I wondered when this would start. Any others?"

"Not so far, but Lucille's uncle has been making noises about coming for her."

"Not unless her parents say so. She stays here." They were still in Europe and, with Lincoln's blockade, might be stranded there for the foreseeable future.

I mauled the eggs on my plate, not wanting to ask the question hanging over me like a cloud. "Did the McKenzie Men make it to Manassas?"

"Ah, your McKenzie Men," she said with a sigh.

My heart iced over. "What happened?"

"They got held up in a small town on the way to Manassas and started drinking. As things are prone to do when they drink, a fight broke out. With each other. With other soldiers. With civilians." She waved her hands helplessly. "The sheriff came with men to break it up. Dooley took another swig, stood there swaying back and forth, and shuddered. 'Aye, that's good then.' Lifted the bottle to the sheriff. '*Sláinte*, sir.' Took another big drink. 'Ah, there she is. Makes me want to kiss your mother.'"

"Oh, dear. Please tell me he didn't say that."

Beth nodded. "Then, with the sheriff fuming, Padraig said, 'What? Again?'"

"I'm sure that went well."

"Another fight erupted, and he arrested a full two dozen of them before the town was in full riot, saying they could cool their heels for a while. When the train finally pulled in, he refused to release them even on the commander's orders, proclaiming he was the one in charge there, not the colonel. The free McKenzie men refused to move without their friends. The colonel threatened to shoot them all."

Sipping my coffee, I for once wished Della had dosed it with brandy, as she had been prone to do lately. "I assume he didn't."

"Only by the grace of God. Connall Brennan lined them up and said, 'Fire away, sir. We're not leaving without our brothers, then.' The colonel demanded the sheriff turn his men loose. The sheriff stood his ground on his authority and refused. The two bulls circled each other and blew snot for a little while until the colonel gave up and loaded the rest of his men."

"How did you hear all this? Did someone send a letter?"

"Oh, it gets better, and no. I heard it firsthand. Little Joe tried to break his father and the others out of jail by tying a rope to the bars and riding off. The bars held. His cinch snapped, and he fell off his horse and broke his arm. He was sent home to recover.

"Since they couldn't break them out, they went after others who weren't arrested because they'd been in taverns or otherwise occupied." She blushed when she said this, so I guessed where they had been occupied. "When they found out about their jailed companions, off they went for more liquor and passed it to them through the bars. Everyone got drunk all over again. The sheriff had all he wanted of them and turned them loose the next day."

I could envision the whole debacle in my mind. "Dear heavens. Is Little Joe all right?"

"Yes. The local doctor plastered it. He went on to Manassas, but the doctor there sent him home. He related the whole story. Letters have been pouring in, complaining about how they have yet to see the elephant as they had missed the battle, and the war may be over before they do."

I knew the aftereffects of "seeing the elephant," as they called it, and it wouldn't be nearly as glorious as they thought once they were in real battle. "I'm sure they'll have plenty of opportunities, alas."

I picked at the eggs on my plate with little interest, worried about the men, sick about Baron. Always and forever sick about Baron. "I assume they finally arrived in one piece?"

"Yes. The soldiers there said, 'Well, look. Here come our Fighting Irish.' The commander grumbled, 'Yes, if I can keep them from killing each other long enough to turn them loose on the Yankees, the war will be over in a week.'"

I laughed despite myself. "He might be right about that."

She pushed me back when I started to get up. "You need to finish eating and regain your strength."

"I'm not hungry."

"Eat. You look like a gutted snowbird. Even Annie is railing about how thin you are."

I could only finish a small amount of the food Della sent, but I promised to eat more later if Beth sent Annie to help me dress. Jacob brought the dog cart buggy, and we went down to the cottages to visit Little Joe and tour the fields.

Jacob looked over at me in alarm. "Are you all right, Miss Mac?"

I pulled my gaze away from the man on the big bay horse in the distance. My heart tripped when I saw him, thinking it was Baron riding in until I realized it was only Jacob's son. Irrational hope withered away, and I teetered on the verge of tears again. "No, let's go back."

Chapter Sixty

I walked the halls and grounds of Rosemount at night like a specter. Afraid to sleep. Afraid to dream. During the day, I tried to pretend to be normal, but I was never good at it and often caught the worried looks of both servants and girls.

I wept again, but only for five minutes, and then wiped my face and shambled back to the house. The Lace Guild had agreed to teach the girls to make Irish lace and were inside now with them. I settled on the porch with Dierdre Monahan's sweet baby girl, who had been nursed and was ready for her nap. She lay in my good arm, sucking on her sugar tit, bright blue eyes staring into mine, blinking sleep away, but it was coming. I crooned softly and sang to her, intoxicated by pure love and baby smell. Scented powder. Baby breath. Baron would have given me beautiful blue-eyed babies like this.

Content yourself with being an auntie to these children, girl.

Annie rocked next to me in case I needed something, knitting quietly. I rocked and sang the baby to sleep, half dozing myself until I jerked, suddenly awake, aware something was amiss. Another dream.

There he was, down the road. I cocked my head. Was I still asleep?

"Annie, take the baby," I said quietly, afraid I might drop her at any moment.

"Miss Mac?"

Her gaze followed mine, and then she looked into my face, which I'm sure was white as a grave angel. "Take the baby." She snatched up the baby and hurried inside.

There it was. I had finally gone insane. Travis *had* died. Here he came with Papa and Baron, who brought Luri home to me, too. Ah, poor Luri. But who was the fourth wraith? Had they come to collect me? Pray God they had. I was ready. I closed my eyes, willing my heart to stop so I might be with him.

"Lorena?"

That was Baron's voice. I opened my eyes. He sat before me on Charlie, staring at me, puzzled. He looked real. I could smell them and the horses. The leather squeaked as he dismounted.

Only one faint step toward him and I fell out at his feet. I awoke in his arms, surrounded by the men and my people staring down at me. "You're alive," I said, still not believing it and reaching up to touch his beard, which covered his entire face now. "The papers said you were dead."

"Yes," he huffed, "as soon as I read that, I knew it was a lie."

I stroked his beard, hugged him, and kissed him shamelessly. "You look like a wild man with all this scruff."

"Cause the Cap'n barely let us stop to eat, let alone shave," said a boy who had scarcely sprouted some golden peach fuzz of his own.

"Let's get you inside, and we'll talk," Baron said, scooping me up as if I were nothing more than a feather.

"Dinner is ready in case anyone's interested," said Della, who stood with hands on hips surveying the scene, happy I was sure for the resurrected dead but not so enthused about her food cooling on the table. Had Jesus interfered with dinner by his second coming, she would have talked with him about his ill manners and poor timing.

Once introductions were made and we settled around the dining table, I tried to put my mind in order. "How did they claim you dead? Colonel Stuart gave you furlough to see me? How did you find Luri?"

Baron laughed and held up his hand. "Whoa. To the reports I was dead, I gave some letters to one of Jackson's couriers who was helping with surgery during Manassas and asked him to mail them. He got sent back out and was killed. They identified him through the letters and never corrected the mistake."

"Blew his head clean off with a cannon shot," Skeeter said, making a whistling noise and motioning toward his face with his hand.

"We're in polite company," Baron said, glaring at him. "I left out the details of the mistaken identity on purpose."

"Yassuh."

"To the leave." He thumbed toward Travis. "You may thank Major Williams for that. His men sent word to him about you being stranded in Richmond, and he contacted General Beauregard. Beauregard sent word to Jackson to grant me leave and rail passes to get you out of town."

"My birdwatchers headquarter in Richmond when we aren't out birding," Travis said by way of explanation. "I had passed the word to keep an eye out for you and help if you ever needed it. They were trying to get you transportation when you disappeared. You had already told me about Baron when you were helping me once, so I knew who he was when he started asking around Richmond for you."

Baron nodded and continued. "One of Travis's men caught your speech to Mrs. Chesnut and saw you with Mrs. Milton and Mrs. Rommel. They told us you left with Conway, but he returned without you and too soon to have made Atlees, so we found the hack driver they pointed out, and he said he was hired to drop you off down the road. He didn't bother to mention he'd turned off the turnpike, so we rode all the way to Atlees looking for you."

I snorted. "He was in on the kidnapping."

"We found that out on our second trip to Richmond after we lost your trail and didn't find you in Atlees," Baron said. "We about wore out horseshoes tracking you down. We tracked down

Conway and Cyrus and proceeded to get some information out of them."

"Cyrus weren't no problem," Skeeter said. "He kept saying, 'Don't hurt my Fifi!'"

"You were going to beat a woman?" Beth gasped.

"I wasn't touching a woman or Fifi," Baron replied with an exasperated huff. "Fifi was his pup. He'd have sold out the lot of them for her. Not that I blame him; she was cute. He admitted Conway worked Lorena over, so I took a pound of flesh from Conway in return, who admitted he met Byles on the road to Hanover Station."

I wish I'd been there for the thrashing I knew Baron gave him and felt a bit of guilt, but not much. If ever a man deserved a beating, it was Conway.

Travis nodded. "You might say a pound of flesh. He had to be poured onto the train like molasses when Baron was done with him. Cyrus decided he wanted to return to Washington, too."

I was astounded at the lengths they'd gone to in order to find me. "I love you all so much for trying to find me, but how did you find my trail?"

"Largely thanks to Skeeter," Baron said in between shoveling more fried potatoes onto his plate.

Have these men eaten in a week?

Skeeter looked up from the new helping of food Della had brought him. I wondered where he was putting all this food, but no one else seemed surprised at his appetite. He had fallen in love with her cooking, and she had taken him under her wing it seemed, as she fussed over him constantly. "The mare you rode threw her right front foot out to the side a bit when she traveled and had odd shoes with a longer toe on them," Skeeter said. "She wasn't that hard to track, except for the rain and being sent down the wrong road."

Imogene sat next to Travis and, unbidden, cut up his steak for him. She usually cast a spell on any man who came into her realm, but I watched with some amazement as she visited demurely with him, offering shy smiles. It was she who was completely captivated.

Della filled up Baron's plate with more ham steak, which he did not decline. "I hadn't planned on bringing Skeeter along, even though he's my best scout and sharpshooter, but he's in trouble with London again." Baron glanced at the boy with the hint of peach-fuzz beard.

Curious, I stopped worrying at my creamed English peas and asked why.

"Brother London asked what we thought was the most attractive thing about a woman," Skeeter said. "I was smart enough not to mention his wife's mouth again and said I reckoned she had the purtiest, dainty hands I ever seen on a woman. He groused about me thinking about his wife all the time and added some very unchristian comments. I said I could see why she used her delicate little hand to clobber him upside the head with a frying pan. He took exception to my observation."

Baron glowered at him. "Yes, and we had to save your life yet again."

"Not my fault!" Skeeter protested. "If he didn't ask stupid questions, he wouldn't get ranklin' answers."

"Yes," Baron said, "and if a frog had wings, he wouldn't bump his butt when he jumped, but you being sensible and not aggravating Brother London is about as likely as a frog growing wings, isn't it."

Baron left off railing at Skeeter and returned to praising him. "At any rate, thankfully, I had him along because he was good at tracking you for a while." Everyone at the table, including Persy and Lucille, who were normally like fleas on a griddle and couldn't keep still, was enthralled by the story now and quietly ate and listened. "We thought we were right behind you at times," Baron said.

"We heard singing," Skeeter said. "Then Cap'n heard your voice and said that was your voice and why were you singing along with that man?"

Skeeter beamed a smile at Della and grabbed more hot rolls from the plate she offered him. "I commented about him having a purty voice. Cap'n growled and spurred up, but we wasn't close to you. Wind was carrying the voices, I reckon, like it does at times. Sometimes it muffles sound, and sometimes carries sounds for miles."

"Yes," I replied, "we heard the battle in Alexandria as if the cannons were in our yards."

"Heard the gunshots," Baron said quietly. "I thought I was going to lose my mind." He swiped an unsteady hand across his brow. "We finally found the camp. Then Skeeter looks down at the body and remarks about how the fella looked like me and that at least he could sing."

I gasped and had to drink some water before I could even respond. "Good Hannah. I can see why Brother London is always after you."

Baron lifted his head and glanced uneasily at me. "He did have a beautiful voice."

I stared at him dumbfounded. "And? You thought I liked him?"

"Don't reckon you did that much," Skeeter said. "You done kilt him."

"He was a madman," I snapped. "He kidnapped me and meant to keep me prisoner. Then he kept trying to get me to sing along with him, and I finally did to get him to relax so I could try to escape. What is wrong with y'all?"

We settled back to finish dinner and enjoy some fresh blueberry cobbler with cream. I was surprised that my appetite had returned, but after so long of not eating, I still ate like a sparrow, and according to Baron, I was so thin that I looked like a thrush's ankle. I was, admittedly, racked bones, but now that he was back, the flesh would return.

"What happened after you found him?" I asked.

"We fed the hogs," Skeeter said.

Several of the girls looked around, confused.

"If you will please be quiet," Baron said, thumping him on the head. "We dragged him into the brush."

"We thought we were right on top of you, but we were miles away, so you were long gone," Travis said. "Skeeter found blood on the tree where you'd leaned and the bloody handkerchief. We knew you were hurt. Then with the rain, we'd already lost your trail and had to divine where you might have gone. You passed two farms before you stopped at the Vogts'."

I frowned. "Did I? I had my head down in that downpour, and I must have missed seeing the roads."

"The Vogts' place was the third farm we found," Baron said. "You had to stop somewhere for help, we reckoned, so we were going to turn the countryside over, looking for you. Dadgum, those people anyway. They denied you were there, but we searched the house. It was plain something had happened. There were still bloodstains on the table and floor. Then Skeeter smelled your perfume on that pillow."

"Wait. You were the ones searching the house?" I looked around at the men, and now it all made sense. "I was hiding in the root cellar with one of the girls. They thought you were robbers who beat and shot me."

"Robbers?"

"I told them robbers had accosted me." I looked around the table. "I couldn't explain I'd been kidnapped."

"True." Baron screwed up his mouth in disgust. "The root cellar. Why didn't we think of looking for a root cellar?"

"Cause you was hellfire for getting back to Richmond after I threatened to shoot one of them to scare the truth out of them, and they said Miss Lorena was back in Richmond," Skeeter replied, scooping another bite of cobbler into his mouth.

For the first time, I noticed Lucille and Persy watching him moon-eyed and wondered if the attraction to boys had kicked in or if they thought they had found the perfect partner in crime. Whichever it was, they devoured his every word and watched him like a cat after a canary. I almost felt sorry for him. Skeeter seemed unperturbed about the whole affair, but even I could see Baron's rising temper at reliving the debacle. He rubbed his thumb over his crooked forefinger as he did when he was angry. Under his jacket, his bicep flexed each time he clenched his fingers into a ball. I would not have been surprised to hear someone say he charged through their house and started tearing it apart in his thwarted search. I started to lay my hand on his to calm him, but that's when he threw both hands into the air.

"Off to Richmond we go, but there's no Lorena," Baron said, almost growling. "Travis turns out every operative he can find, but they swear you haven't been back. Not that it did much good," he said, finally pushing his plate away and refusing more food. "No one in Richmond had seen you. Conway didn't have you. That meant the Vogts had lied to us, so back we go to our good farmers to negotiate the truth, and now I was hot."

"He thought they were keeping you prisoner," Skeeter said. He made a motion with his hands, pushing out from his ears. "Smoke was boilin' out his ears. We about wore our horses out hightailin' it back there."

"Prisoner!" I gaped at all of them. "For what?"

Travis waved a hand through the air. "Ransom, forced labor, wife for one of the boys, spare wife for the husband."

Gasps went around the table.

"Miss Mac, were you going to marry someone else?" Persy asked.

"Moses, Mary, and Joseph, no! That's ridiculous."

"Who knows what goes on with some of these people? They were lying to us like horse thieves," Baron said. He was beginning to sweat, as if he were reliving the chase. "The family poured out of the house and in from the fields when we pounded down the road. Mr. Vogt waited at the head of his clan, musket in hand, but I was in no mood for more games when we stopped in front of them. I told them flat out I was tired, I was angry, and I was in no mood for more of their lies. If they didn't cough you up or tell me where you were, we were going to tear their house apart board-by-board until we got the truth."

"'I told you—' the farmer began.

"Mr. Vogt thought he was going to bow up to me, but I was having none of it and shut him down before he even got started with more lies." Baron sipped his coffee irritably at the thought of having to deal with the farmer again. "'You told me she was in Richmond,' I said, and told him we'd been to Richmond and beat the tar out of two men who swore you hadn't set foot back in Richmond. We stopped in town and talked to Doctor Jonas, who treated you at the farm for the gunshot wound that broke your arm. Then, I demanded to know where you went after that, or were you still there?

"'You think we'd give her up to you after the way you beat her!' the boy named Gunnar shouted." Baron glowered. "I demanded to know what he was talking about."

There was a pause as he poured some whiskey into his coffee. His jaw clenched in anger, recalling the conversation and emotion, I was sure. I could only imagine how livid he'd been after being accused of the beating. "'She'd been beaten badly before she was shot,' Mrs. Vogt said. 'Her face, ribs, and stomach were all bruised. You're saying you didn't do that?'

"'Hell no, I didn't do that,' I said. 'Conway did that.'"

"'You're not Conway?' Mr. Vogt asked. 'She thought you were Conway.'

"'I'm her fiancé,' I said. 'Captain Baron Callahan, Confederate States of America. This is Major Travis Williams, CSA, and Private Skeeter Flynn, CSA.'

"'Her fiancé is dead,' Gunnar said. 'She told us that. Stop lying.'

"I dug out my pocket watch and reached back into my saddlebags to pull out a packet of letters and tossed both to Mr. Vogt. 'Who are those letters from and addressed to?' I asked him. 'Whose portrait is inside that watch? I'd prefer you didn't read the letters. They're personal.'"

With anger spent, Baron slumped back in his chair, worn from the emotion of recounting the story, the fear, and anxiety wearing him thin.

"Mr. Vogt looked at the items and walked back to hand them to Baron," Travis said, tearing his gaze away from Imogene, who was adjusting his napkin. "He returned to his family, still holding his musket but not as firmly now, unsure of what to do.

"Gunnar grabbed the musket away from his father and pointed it at Baron. We drew our guns and pointed them at the boy. The boy said they weren't giving you up, and that we could have stolen that stuff. Besides," Travis said, looking at me with some apology, "he saw you naked. He raised his pointy chin up, all defiant, and demanded to know who had a better right to you than him."

All eyes swiveled between Travis and Baron now. You could have heard a moth sigh. Travis continued. "Baron narrowed his eyes, fury rising. 'You what?' he demanded.

"That boy didn't have brains enough to recognize death when it was upon him and plowed right on like he had good sense. In righteous fury, he insisted he had seen you naked and wanted to know if the captain had."

There was an assortment of gasps and giggles around the table, but every eye was locked on Travis. I couldn't believe Gunnar had blurted that out to Baron. I wouldn't have blamed him if he'd hit the little fool.

"'I have, too,' the one named Karl blurted out. 'That's how I got this black eye. Laying on her naked form.'"

Oh, dear heavens. Not Karl, too.

"Miss Lorena," Persy said, wide-eyed. "You were letting boys lay on you naked?"

My cheeks were flaming now, but all I could do was shake my head, aghast.

"Mrs. Vogt gasped as I started to dismount, fully intent on murder," Baron grumbled.

"I can imagine both counts," I muttered, still mortified at the shocked stares turned at me, let alone the images I knew to be going through everyone's heads.

Travis picked up the story again. Baron was too busy gritting his teeth to talk. "'For God's sake, Gunnar! Karl! Herman, get control of these boys before the captain kills them, or I do,' Mrs. Vogt screamed." Unable to control himself, regardless of Baron's murderous glares, Travis laughed at this. "I thought she might knock all their heads together before the day was done. Mr. Vogt jerked the gun away from his oldest son. 'My boys mean no harm, Captain. Miss McKenzie reacted violently to the chloroform Doctor Jonas gave her and had to be restrained. Unfortunately, the sheet slipped from her top, and they may have seen more than was decent.'

"Bereft of the musket," Travis continued, "Gunnar stepped forward, fists raised. 'I ain't afraid of you.'"

Travis raised his fist and thrust out his chest defiantly, imitating the boy. "His voice broke pubescently at the worst time. 'I'll fight you for her.'"

"Oh, dear heavens. Surely not," I said, quite imagining the entire fiasco.

Della looked to Baron when Skeeter reached for the bottle of whiskey that had appeared on the table. "Do you allow this boy to drink?"

"Yes, ma'am." Baron replied. "He's twenty, though he acts twelve."

Lucille smiled winsomely at him. "I drink whiskey at home."

"You're not at home," I said. "Skeeter, don't share your whiskey with her."

"Baron sank back in the saddle," Travis went on, "relieved that you hadn't been assaulted by the two boys. 'Young man,' Baron responded to him. 'Miss Lorena McKenzie and I have been handfast for years. I would go through hell and half of Texas for her, but only half because it's a gawd-awful big state, and it is Texas. One day you're going to find some pretty young lady who will adore you for wanting to fight for her, but Miss McKenzie is mine. Besides, if you ever met her mother, you would give up your stake to her in a heartbeat. Her mother is the queen of the harpies, and even Satan flees in terror when she's flying.'"

I glared at Baron, who ignored me, but there were nods of assent around the table.

"'She'd be worth it,' Gunnar replied glumly.'" Travis scowled like a very unhappy young boy as he recited this.

"'We'll discuss these words of wisdom about in-laws later,' Mr. Vogt said, glancing uneasily at his wife. Then they admitted they put you on a train to Strasburg so you could go home to Winchester." Travis shifted his focus back to Imogene, forgetting about me and the Vogts completely.

"I offered to pay them for taking care of you," Baron said, "but they said you'd already paid them handsomely. Then Mrs. Vogt persuaded her cousin, the stationmaster, to get us and our horses on the next train even though we had generous passes. She even sent a big basket of food with us."

"And a lot of good that did us," Skeeter grumbled.

"Yes, with the best luck known to man, a train broke down in front of us, and we were stuck on the tracks for two days. I shared the food with the rest of the soldiers who didn't have any."

Baron smoothed his mustache with a napkin. "And that's how we left the Vogts and found our way to you."

I shook my head. "What an adventure. It's a wonder someone didn't get shot. Besides me and—that fellow." I wasn't sure I should mention his name, dead or not. Brightening, I thought of them riding up the lane again. "Was that Luri I saw with you?"

Baron lit like a full moon. "Yes! Darndest thing. We were going over the battlefield after Manassas looking for our wounded, and there she was, ambling around like she had good sense. I told Skeeter I knew that horse and I whistled at her. She came trotting right over. She had a Union rig on her, which I didn't think you'd want, so I gave that away except for the halter. Someone with the initials CLG had her, it appears."

"Hmph. Yes, I locked horns with him over her, and he decided to liberate her. I wonder if he got killed."

That he did not. Only hammered, though he needed more for stealin' poor Luri.

My heart leapt to hear Papa's voice again. *There you are. Where have you been?*

With me men, o' course, an Luri. I knew ye'd be fine. Yer a McKenzie.

I appreciate the confidence, but I needed you.

An' I'm here now, am I not, then?

Yes, you are. I love you.

An' I love ye too, girl. Always have.

"Let's go look at Luri," Baron said and took my hand. Though I would have preferred to go alone, everyone followed us to see Luri.

She was tied to the rails in front of the veranda. She nickered, burying her head in my chest. I held her and stroked her shimmering golden neck, and the girls swarmed around, hugging and petting her. "I missed you, girl."

Baron snorted. "I hope you missed me as well."

"Silly man," I replied, sniffling. "You drive me to madness with pining and worrying. Always have."

"All right, now come here," Baron said, leading me away. He dropped down on one knee and pulled a glittering ring out of a ring box, extending it toward me. "This was my grandmother's ring. She had it remade and haloed by sapphires because they are my birthstone. Your birthstone is diamonds, as is hers. She thought the sapphires around the diamond would signify my protection of you always, though I have done a piss-poor job of it so far, but you know I would lay down my life for you. *An bposfaidh tu me?*"

I had wished for this from the first time I met him. I dreamed of this and longed for it with all my heart, but I was still deeply in debt and had no idea if I would even have a crop market this fall. Smiling wanly, I placed the ring in his palm and covered his hand with mine (though I didn't spit in it as I had years ago with Annie when I made that fond wish). "This is all I have ever wanted," I said, "but the time is not right. You will know when it is."

He nodded and stood up slowly as if unfolding in a sad, gentle breeze. "I will, and when I come to collect you, I will not take no for an answer."

Lucille crossed her arms over her chest and looked up at him with those wide, but not so innocent, brilliant blue eyes. "Will there be kissing?"

Baron took me in his arms, and there was kissing.

Acknowledgments

If I thanked everyone who helped make *The Rain Crow* a reality, this section would be another chapter of its own. However, I must try to express my gratitude.

First, to the wonderful writers, readers, and citizens of TheLitForum.com. Through its many iterations, the people there have always been supportive, informative, and the greatest of mentors and friends. It is, by far, the greatest master class on writing. If there's a question, someone is there with an answer. There are so many generous people there that I cannot name them all, but know that you are loved and appreciated.

To my posse: Beth Shope, Donna Rubino, Laura Weller, and Tara Parker. Tara, rest in peace. You are missed, my friend, and I mourn that the world will never enjoy your wonderful stories. I could never have finished this book without these talented writers and beta readers. I am constantly in awe of their talent and insight.

To Diana Gabaldon, who has been one of my staunchest advocates and mentors. She is full of grace and always willing to offer advice or encouragement. I cannot count the times that conversations on the LitForum have turned into valuable lessons, which, in turn, sparked an idea, a phrase, or a way of examining a problem that transformed a weedy dilemma into a flower garden.

To Jack Whyte, my dear, departed Jack. He was always encouraging of my stories but brutally honest, and every writer needs that. At the last conference where I saw him, we holed up in a corner, drank, and talked the night away. We discussed every kind of ancient military warfare a person could think of—military medicine, King Arthur and how he pulled the sword from the stone (and how Jack discovered it), Celtic burial mounds, the American Civil War, and everything else that two fertile, writerly, and historically bent minds could conjure.

When I left the party, he called out after me, "Write the damned book!" Then he called it out again and made me promise I would. That book is not *The Rain Crow*, but it is in the works.

To Chris Humphries, who encouraged the story and believed in it. It was a joy to discuss ways to handle aspects of historical writing with such a talented writer.

To Joanna Bourne, who is a master at writing dialogue and description and doesn't mind sharing how to do it. As Diana says, "Every writer's secrets are all right there on the page." At our last writers' retreat, she sat curled up on a couch, tapping her chin with a pencil, and said, "I have my MC trapped in a brothel, and I'm contemplating bad things happening to her." She thought some more and added, "And I wonder why I'm never invited to polite dinner parties." She taught me that it's okay not to be invited to polite society. Just write the story.

To Amanda Long and Jamie Warner, who were so gracious to give me medical advice when the morgue refused and my previous doctor feared I was plotting mayhem.

To Kiki, one of my fans and friends, and the creator of my dragon shawl.

To Deleyna and Heart Ally Books, LLC. I put *The Rain Crow* away and didn't plan to try publishing again. It was a practice book, I decided. Deleyna refused to leave it alone. She was familiar with my writing and bits of the story. "It's a story that needs to be told," she kept telling me. Thank you for all your hard work and for believing in me. It is strictly due to her prodding that *The Rain Crow* is not in the bin.

Sabine Sloley shines as a meticulous editor with an incredible eye for detail. She is a true professional.

To my lovely editor, Lori Brown. I was told at the beginning that she might not take *The Rain Crow*, and I feared she wouldn't. Then, when she did, I was afraid of what might come, but the edits were all needed and perfection. I cannot recommend her highly enough.

To Margie Lawson. I still have the sewing kit you gave me in Denver and the fond memories that go with it. I've taken so many of your classes and learned so much from each one. I am deeply indebted.

A very large thank you to the American Civil War Forums, not only for being an invaluable fount of knowledge but also for their help with research questions. I can't recommend them more highly for any Civil War buff.

Posthumously, to agent Janet Reid, who always signed her correspondence with "Your number one fan." She probably told many people that, but she was a dear friend and fed me encouragement through many dark times. You are missed and gone too soon.

To Hetty Cary. Thank you for sharing your story with me and letting it inspire *The Rain Crow*. I am not ashamed to admit that I have shed tears for you and your handsome General Pegram.

Lastly, to my valued readers, thank you. Although I have tried to remain true to history and the story, *The Rain Crow* is, at the end of the day, historical fiction.

I have strived for accuracy, but sometimes details must be rearranged or adjusted for the sake of the story. I hope you will not fault me too deeply for straying from the path from time to time.

About the author

Julie Weathers, like most writers, has always loved creating stories. When she couldn't get to the library, she started writing her own. However, it wasn't until she was grown with children that she considered writing again—and that happened purely by accident after she won a $10,000 horse that turned out to be worth $500. The editor of a magazine she wrote to about the contest offered her a job, which lasted twenty-three years, writing race and human interest stories.

Julie has been a horse wrangler in Arizona and a babysitter (for horses, not people) on a premier racing Quarter Horse farm in Texas. Training young horses was her favorite job, though she's also been a lady bronc rider, an award-winning real estate agent, a reach forklift driver, and—at times—someone who scrubbed floors and took in ironing. She's experienced life in all its ups and downs, including feeding cattle with a team of horses in forty-below weather.

Her greatest accomplishment is being a mother, but finishing *The Rain Crow* feels pretty darn good, too. Of all the challenges she's faced, feeding cows in subzero temperatures was among the toughest—fingers frozen to the reins is no fun—but completing this book ranks right near the top. She hopes readers enjoy *The Rain Crow* as much as she loved bringing it to life.

www.ingramcontent.com/pod-product-compliance
Lightning Source LLC
Chambersburg PA
CBHW060209030726
47499CB00004B/976